To Be Loved

They lived, and he existed, just for her.

To "Mouse", I will always love you.

~Prologue ~

In the back of every humans mind, lies a fear. A fear so deep, and ever present, that it stops the heart from beating in its chest. It causes the body to react in a way that makes it tremble. It causes pain and then the blood pressure rises, the mouth starts to water. The brain tries to send signals to alleviate this reaction, but it's the eyes, the mind, that takes pictures faster than the speed of any camera ever made, and replays them over and over like a video feed. The brain shuts down, tired of trying to fix the body, and the heart takes over, beating wildly. Telling the mind to scream, run, and hide.

In the life of a firefighter, even though their body and mind are facing their worst fears, they stay. They tell their hearts and mind and souls to be still in the face of danger. The aftermath of such a raging storm echoes throughout his or her mind for the rest of their lives. The pictures, the video feeds, they never cease to exist for them.

These men, these gentle giants, mighty men of galore, these heroes; they will never be forgotten. They will never be in our minds as nothing short of amazing. Their lives will never be talked about through the ages, but their faces will be remembered in every life they touch. Their bravery in the sight of terror will always be the backbone that brave men stand on.

Never again will superheroes be so entertaining. Never again will the gods be thought of as idols. Children of the 9/11 generation will know what they want to be when they grow up because of these men.

To their families and friends, they are not only great men; they are fathers, brothers, sons, best men. But in the moment of their own fears, they are just men. Praying to their God for help.

They will be honored. They will be respected. They will live in the hearts and mind of every man, woman and child around the world as hero's. God's walking among men. Angels that are with us…

~One~

"Monroe County Dispatch on the air for Luna Pier Fire, you have a structure fire at 10420 S. Harold Drive. The Luna Pier boat marina is at that location. Your time out is 2039."

Following every radioed dispatch for the fire department is the sound of a blaring siren that echoes all around the little city of Luna Pier, Michigan. It can be heard for miles around, night or day, seven days a week. Citizens of the city know when they hear the sirens there will be firemen racing to a scene in which someone or something is in need of help. Most citizens don't mind the sound of the sirens, but some do. Those are the ones that have not yet been affected by the tragedy of a fire, or the death of a family loved one. Once they are, they will forever be grateful for the sound of help on its way.

Curtis Stone was woken from his slumber on June 12th 2015 by the loud beeping of his pager lying next to his alarm clock at home, announcing a fire call over the air. He was not on duty yet, but he was on call. Everyone on the department was. There was never enough man power on the department these days. The life of a firefighter was a hard life. It was trying for the family man; it was physically rough on the weak, and demanding on even the most dedicated of men. For women, it was harder.

Even though he dreamt of ignoring the beeping sound of his pager, he knew the sirens were loud enough to wake the dead, and plus, his alarm would be going off in ten minutes anyways, his shift started at 9, so he rolled out of bed and got dressed. He walked into his dark living room where his keys and black, zip up boots always were on nights like these. Right on his desk where he could find them in the dark, and as close to the door as possible.

A structure fire meant a lot of work would need to be done after the call. Hoses would need to be drained, trucks would need to be cleaned and fueled, gear would also need to be washed and aired out. After fighting a fire, no man or woman on the department wanted to do overhaul. Curtis sighed at the long night ahead of him and walked out the front door of his house. He was ready to responded lights and sirens to the scene of a raging, burning boat marina.

"Luna Pier Chief 2 to Monroe County Dispatch?" he called from his radio.

Once in his truck still parked in his driveway, Curtis could see the smoke rolling and billowing over the rooftops of the city, the last billow of smoke was caused from an explosion he could hear and feel from his house blocks away. He reached for his radio again on the dashboard of his truck and called central dispatch again.

"Luna Pier Chief 2 to Monroe County Dispatch!?!" he beckoned over the radio, as he backed out his driveway switching on his lights and siren. The fire at the boat marina was out of control already he noticed as he raced down Harold drive. Central dispatch needed to answer him quickly so they could send him some back up.

"Luna Pier, to Luna Pier Chief 2. Go ahead Curtis."

Asher. Curtis thought. He had never been happier to hear his brother's voice. Asher wasn't central dispatch, but Curtis' brother at the fire department could get the job done.

"Asher, we have a working structure fire down here. Flames are showing and there has been at least one explosion. Call Eire now for more man power and send for back up. Get engine one and two rolling now! I want task and rescue on scene. Empty the station Asher."

Curtis knew he could trust his brother. Knew his father, the Chief, would be on his way to the scene as well after hearing that transmission. Other departments would be standing by also in case they needed more man power or assistance. Sometimes medical calls would happen right in the thick of things and another department would have to cover their calls.

Once Curtis arrived on scene at the marina, Curtis got out of his truck, his jacket opened in the blowing wind, his arm shielding his eyes from the burning fire and smoke billowing out of the marina windows.

The marina was a place Curtis knew all too well. He had lived in this city his whole life. The boat marina, which held many of the cities resident's boats and yachts, including his and his father's, and many of his closest friends, was going to burn down to the ground tonight if they couldn't contain the raging inferno in front of him.

He prayed that no one was in the building.

It wasn't until Jerry, the chief of police pulled up; kicking gravel all around Curtis as he stopped the police cruiser, that Curtis learned there were three teenagers in the upper floors. Jerry was pointing them out to Curtis just as another explosion rocked the ground they were standing on. Both men hunched over and covered their heads. Gas tanks were scattered all around them. Paint, fuel and oil tanks; everything around them was flammable and at risk of exploding.

"Time to play." Curtis smiled at Jerry just as the engine one pulled up the dirt gravel drive of the marina. He bumped fists with

Asher who had jumped off the truck before it had stopped to greet him, as the rest of the firemen in trucks came to his rescue up the drive.

Curtis wouldn't be fighting this fire alone. His brothers and sisters on the department would follow him into the hell of flames that were licking up the windows and crawling out the roof over the ledges and up into the evening sky.

Each firefighter had a duty, a calling. Some operated pumps, others manned the hoses. Most ran into the smoke, axes in hands ready to bust down doors and windows, tear up roof tops for ventilation, and to save the lives of those who were lost and dying in the smoke filled rooms.

Tonight, every man had a job to do. They all knew their places like actors on a stage. They knew their parts and followed their roles. Any mistakes could be life threatening. There was never room for mistakes during a fire. People died on nights like tonight. But not on Curtis's watch. He wasn't about to lose anyone tonight.

When Curtis and Asher finally reached the top of the metal stairs leading to the top floor of the marina, Asher pointed Curtis in the direction of the teenagers. It was Asher's job to find the way, following behind Curtis while he worked the hose and made them a path through the flames. Knocking on his helmet, Asher told Curtis, with a thumbs up, that they were almost there.

Curtis could see the room they needed and turned to Asher with a fist bump. They would get these stupid kids out and be back to the fire hall in time for the end of the fight on TV tonight.

Once inside the room that held the trapped teenagers, Curtis stopped mid way in and was bumped by Asher in his tracks. There was a gaping hole in the center of the room and the kids were trapped in the corner on the other side holding onto the broken out window for their lives.

They needed the ladder truck that was at the fire hall broke down. Curtis hung his head and cussed allowed.

Curtis knew their ladders on the other trucks outside wouldn't reach up this far, and the only other department who had ladder trucks was Monroe Town, and they were not only twenty minutes away but they hadn't even been toned out yet. This building would be a pile of ash by the time they got here.

Curtis turned to Asher with only one request. He grabbed his helmet and through their masks he hollered to Asher. "Go get the ladders Asher."

Curtis never had to explain himself to Asher. That was why they worked so well together. Curtis told him what to do, and Asher did it. Things just flowed better that way. Curtis turned back to the teens and motioned for them to stay where they were, while he hosed down the room and floor around him.

By the time his ladders came up, Asher was nowhere to be found. Curtis knew Asher was still tired from the twenty four hours he had just worked. Curtis laughed out loud at his younger brother.

"Pup." Curtis said aloud to no one at all, as he laid the ladders across the gaping hole in the floor and turned over his hose to one of the rookies who had been eager for some action.

Curtis made the decision to climb across the ladders to the kids and tried to usher them back across the ladders. Pleading with them to hurry and to not look down, because if they did, all they would see were climbing red hot flames that were floating on the floor under them like the waves crashing against the pier walls just down the road.

Asher had chosen to walk back up the stairs just as Curtis was crawling back across with the girl and one of the boys crawling in front of him. When the explosion of a can hit the ladder and knocked it off balance, the back edge of the ladder where Curtis was, fell into the hole.

Every man dropped what they were doing and reached for the ladder before it could fall the three floors down into the burning flames below them. Asher was at the top of the ladder reaching for the kids, but the weight of the three of them was dragging the fire men off their feet.

The floor was slippery from all the water and Curtis feared they would all end up at the bottom. Curtis looked down for the first time that night. He looked the fire right in the eye and denied that it would win. Not tonight, he told it.

Curtis looked back up at Asher; he took off his mask when he felt his boots melting under him and sighed aloud visibly. The girl was sliding towards him screaming, and the boy was clinging to the ladder like a scared child. Neither one was reaching for Asher's hand.

Why they had been up here tonight Curtis didn't know, but his forgiving heart knew they were paying for their sins now. He looked up at the men who were trying to save them, and knew it was his own weight they were fighting against, not the kids.

Curtis's feet were on fire now, and his legs were next. Curtis, was a tall man. Almost 6'6 last time he checked. His weight was well over 250 pounds now. There was no way Asher and the two new rookies could pull up the ladder with him hanging on the end, and the girl who was thrashing about like a fish on a hook. He had to hold still or they all would fall, including Asher and the rookies.

Curtis locked eyes with Asher.

Asher started pleading with the guys to pull harder as he looked his brother in the eyes. He knew his brother would let go if he had too. Asher stood up and tried to pull with all his might, but the two guys lost their balance and started to slip into the hole. One fell over the edge but held onto the splitting wood of the floor.

Asher was now holding onto everyone; one rookie who kept losing his footing, the ladder that held his brother and two stupid teenagers, and the other rookie who had fell and was now reaching for his leg like Asher had the strength of five men to pull him up too.

Asher's heart was tearing in all different directions. He knew he couldn't reach for his radio and call for help; he needed both hands to hold onto the ladder. He squatted down and tried to lift the ladder gripping both sides of it, but he wasn't strong enough, all he could do was hang on and plead with all of them to hang on too. The floor was wet and flooding under him as the hose that had been forgotten behind him was left to thrash about wildly threatening to knock him over with the force of its pressure.

Curtis looked up at Asher one last time. They'd never said goodbye before. But now he had too. He knew his legs would break on the way down, knew his gear was no match for the chemical flames of the fire below him. Knew his lungs and burning legs would never recover even if someone got to him right away.

Curtis whispered to Asher just before he let go "I'll see ya soon brother." He had to let go so Asher could save them all. He didn't have a choice anymore.

Asher's screaming voice was the last thing he heard before the sounds of fire and his breaking bones filled his ears.

~ Two ~

Later that night...

  Asher Stone had known the gut wrenching fear of death. He had saved the lives of men who were being faced with death, held the hands of those who were dying, breathed air back into the lungs of those who he wouldn't let lose the fight with death. But tonight, fear and death were winning.

  At 3 in the morning in his brother's hospital room, Asher was finally thinking about heading home. After working more than his usual twenty four hour shift, he had just fought the worst fire of his career. He had also almost lost his brother on this hellish night. His was physically, and emotionally, done.

  Asher had woken up at the foot of his brother's hospital bed from a nightmare just minutes ago. He had been trying to save his brother again from falling, and couldn't. Over and over in his sleepless dreams Curtis would fall.

  There was nothing else he or any one could do for his brother tonight.

  Finally Asher gave up trying to sleep in the hospital. Even though his body hurt, even though looking at his brothers black burnt body and the smell of burnt flesh mixed with rubbing alcohol filled his nostrils, Asher's eyes were just too heavy to stay open. His body was too heavy to stay upright any longer. He needed to go home to his bed.

  Asher stood to his feet and sighed. He stuck one hand in his pocket and reached out the other hand to Curtis and gently bumped his fist with his. "I'll see ya soon Curtis."

  Asher rubbed his bad shoulder that was now throbbing from all the nights' events.

  It was time for Asher to go home, check on his dog, make himself a stiff drink, have a smoke and make his way into the comfort and warmth of his bed. On some nights like this, he never made it past the chair in his living room, but tonight, he had every intention of making it up to his room to hide under his covers.

  Looking at his brother, Asher knew it would be a miracle if Curtis made it. Asher said a prayer before he left his room, and hoped against all odds that his big brother would make it. He needed him to make it. But in Asher's heart, he knew his brother was too far gone. Curtis was only days if not moments away from leaving them all behind.

Asher also knew if Curtis ever did wake up he would never be the same. Hell, even if Curtis woke up now, he wouldn't want to live like this. His broken burnt body would never heal. He would never be the same man he was before tonight.

Asher turned and walked out of his brothers room hanging his head, trying not to let anyone in the hall see the tears that were now running down his cheeks. His life would never be the same, not after tonight.

There were a dozen doctors and nurses crowding the nurse's station and more emergency personnel from around Monroe County gathered in one place then Asher had ever seen together before.

Everyone was here tonight standing vigil over Curtis. Damn if his brother didn't know everyone on this floor, Asher thought as he walked past the crowd.

Headed towards the elevator on the fifth floor of Mercy Hospital, holding his and Curtis' firemen jackets in his arms that smelled of smoke and fire, Asher felt defeated. Black ash soot streaked his face and arms and neck.

They had put out the fire tonight, but the fire had won. Curtis was dying behind him. He was still burning alive from the outside in even though he was sleeping in a drug induced coma.

Asher reached up for his shoulder again and gave it a squeeze. It hurt more on nights like this then it ever did.

"ASHER!!"

Their father Frank, the chief of the Luna Pier Fire Department, caught sight of Asher in the hall. He started lecturing and cursing at Asher from down the hall in his wheelchair.

Hopefully for the last time tonight, Asher thought offhandedly as he pushed the button to call the elevator to his floor.

"Damn it! Get back here!" his father called after him, pushing his wheelchair closer to Asher. "You should have done something! How could you just let him go Asher?"

His father yelled again, rasping out his demands as he coughed from smoke filled lungs, before Asher could get in the elevator.

"You understand he's going to die don't you! They won't do anything else for him. You killed him Asher! You let him go!" Again the old man started coughing.

Frank's assumptions were wrong tonight, and Asher knew his father should be in a room of his own hooked up to an IV and oxygen, but the old man was a pain in everyone's ass and had refused any care. He wouldn't even listen to his own family.

When the doctors had explained to the family that even if they did all they could for Curtis, he wouldn't survive. Frank had given up hope for himself along with his son. He didn't care how badly damaged his lungs were. His oldest son was dying.

"All was lost." He had whispered aloud to no one.

But Asher had heard him. Asher sighed deeply and groaned aloud. He was tired, worn down, and he felt helpless. He knew deep down his father wished it was Asher lying there in the hospital, not Curtis.

Asher had seen Frank passed out at the marina, choking in the smoke as Asher carried Curtis' broken body out of the burning marina to the waiting ambulance. Asher ran back in to save his father only to hear him rant and rave all the way to the hospital about what Asher should have done.

The elevator opened next to Asher and he prayed his father would leave him alone so he wouldn't have to call for another one.

Asher angrily turned and faced his father. He looked around the crowd to see the faces of those who knew the story was different and hadn't happened like his father thought and the ones who were shocked by the news and wondered in amazement. Asher wasn't unused to this feeling. He'd been the brunt of his lunatic fathers ravings before and through clenched teeth he quietly told his father what he wanted, not wanting to make a scene in front everyone who was watching to see what Asher would say, "Dad, I'm not doing this again! Not now..." He breathed in a tired whisper.

"I'm going home!" Asher told him, backing into the waiting elevator.

Asher's brother was not going to make it much longer, and all the older man could think of to do was tell Asher that this was all somehow his fault. It was just like his father to start something like this.

His father never did have a filter when it came to cussing out his own sons in front of everyone for not doing what he told them too. Asher still hated his father for this. The man was great and known for what he did, but in his son's eyes the man was a tyrant. They feared their father like no other man. But tonight, Asher had enough of fear.

All wasn't lost.

Asher flipped the old man off when he entered the elevator and watched as the doors closed on his father's stunned face. Curtis was their fathers prodigy, not Asher. His father would never understand what had happened tonight. No matter how many times he told him. Frank had already assumed it was Asher's fault.

Asher knew tonight wasn't any different then any other night and his father was bound to find something to complain about or blame Asher for, but for some reason-tonight was different, he thought to himself. It wasn't just the fire, or that his brother was dying, there was something else different about tonight. He'd felt it all night. It had haunted him before the fire, and had returned now that everything had settled down.

Asher felt his whole being change in a split second as he took his first steps into the elevator. Like his destiny had just altered upon entering the elevator. With his father outside the closing elevator doors forgotten, a rush of fear and adrenaline hit Asher like a ton of bricks. He'd felt this feeling before of course. But that had been years ago... He'd felt something close to it when Curtis let go of the ladder, but this, this was very different.

When the doors of the elevator closed, the moment felt like his last. His instinct was to hold on to whatever he could find. Was he falling? Was there a thief waiting to kill him? He almost dropped the burden of the coats he was holding.

Fate hadn't killed him in the fire, had it come now to rip the life right out of him?

Asher could face the fears most men faint in. The scene of a raging, burning building; when others are running away, he runs straight in, with just a hose and some water to put it out with. Late night car accident; family of four trapped in a burning vehicle, parents and children screaming while he fights against time to save their lives.

Tonight, none of those things compared to what was waiting for him in the corner.

Waiting in the silence of the employee elevator, holding a basket of blood packets, which should have scared any normal person further, was a small woman. Just a dark haired beauty. A woman, just an ordinary nurse judging by her attire, was making his heart pound in real fear, like he was facing death or something much worse.

Asher rested his head on the outer wall, white knuckled holding the rail behind him for support; he dragged air into his needy lungs, and just looked at her.

Mine. His heart whispered.

An odd feeling for sure to have mingled in the grips of fear, but there it was.

She reached up for the floor buttons with elegant tiny fingers, nails painted a deep red color. She politely asked him what floor he was going too with a grin he couldn't help but love. When she gazed up from smoky shadowed eyes into his, he lost all feeling in his legs.

This wasn't just any women... But yet she was. Her beauty was astounding. Unreal even.

Who was she? He wondered. He had to know.

Mine. His heart echoed again.

He could see that she was just an ordinary woman. So why had she just scared the hell out of him? And why couldn't he speak? He couldn't find his voice to save his life. His heart was still racing and his mouth felt dry like it was full of hot flames, robbing him of speech and coherent thought.

Asher looked at the women in front of him. Really looked at her. She was small in stature, her real ruby red lips were still grinning, he'd never seen real red lips like hers before. She had deep dark chocolate hair that curled down her body in long swirls that was at least waist length. She had her bangs pinned to the side with a red and gold butterfly clip. Her eyes were the same perfect matching color as her hair. With just a hint of red, if that were possible. Must be a trick from her lips, he thought to himself.

She was dressed in black scrubs that accentuated her creamy white complexion. She had one foot propped up on the other leaning against the wall like she had been riding this elevator a dozen times before and was waiting as patiently as she could to reach her floor. A simple gold necklace hung around her neck and fell hidden beneath her white top under her scrubs. He wondered what the charm was that held the chain so heavy between her two beautifully shaped mounds.

Asher had to shake his next thoughts out of his mind.

Asher was tall, 6'4 in height. At 32 years of age he had finally reached his peak in growing taller, and wider he'd hoped. The last he checked he weighed 235 lbs, mostly made of muscle, but by some men's standards he was just towering and strong build. He made time to work out at the department unlike the others; he was always busy responding to the never ending calls of the city in distress, and a mountain of paperwork that never ceased to exist in his office, but he made time. He had too. Working out to music was the only relief of stress for him. That, and walking on the pier.

Between working out, carrying hoses, ladders, lifeless bodies and air tanks up and down stairs on a daily basis since he was old enough to carry at least one of those, had given him the body others had dreamed of, and because of that he knew he needed to work out regularly. Whether at home or at the fire hall, he always made time to strengthen himself. He needed to be strong. He needed to be able. It was a code he followed along with everything else he did to prepare himself for all the dangers he faced.

He always felt the need to be shorter though, smaller even. With children and pets he found himself crouching down, with adults he always tried the sitting position. Chairs, sofas, they seemed to take the edge off his towering.

With this young lady, she was tiny, but she seemed the right height for him…

What was he saying? He brushed his shaggy blonde hair with his hand and tried to remember the floor he was going to.

But she had already pushed the button "L" for the lobby…

She must think me a huge dork, he thought wryly. He gave her a smile, and then he said "Sorry, I got a lot on my mind tonight. I wasn't expecting anyone to be in the elevators this late at night." He tried explaining to her hopping she wouldn't take offense to his frightened silence.

She nodded back at him with a charming smile, and then the great feeling of dread returned. He tried his damndest to shake it off when she looked down at her blood packets giving him a reprieve of his overwhelming moment, tucking her hair sweetly behind her ear.

Then he realized he was blushing. How was this possible? He never felt this way around women. How had one simple little gesture like that make him blush? Make his blood rush to places it shouldn't. She was adorably cute though, he told himself, letting the blush slowly return as he realized he wanted to flirt with this woman.

Better yet, who was this woman? How had he never met her before? He'd been in this little city all his life, been in and out of this damned hospital thousands of time. How had he never met her before?

She obviously worked in the hospital, her badge said as much. Her gorgeous hair was covering up her name though and he couldn't quite make it out. He wondered at the possibilities of what her name might be, but nothing fit. It must be the fact that he didn't know her that was causing these feelings of dread, he wondered.

Who was he kidding? He rested his head back against the wall closing his eyes and he reminded himself he had just fought the worst fire of his life. His brother was dying, and his father was the biggest ass he'd ever met. That's all this was…

He just needed to go home drink a cold beer, smoke a few cigarettes, shower and get away from everything, and sleep. He couldn't remember the last time he'd slept.

He tried to remember his dog Cookie as the old elevator crept one floor to the next. He could see her excitedly wagging her tail in anticipation and doing circles in the middle of his kitchen waiting for him to pick her up and show her attention. She would sleep with him tonight, get lost somewhere in his blankets and keep him company in the morning. He might even take her out to do some errands with him tomorrow.

Love at first site?
Emie never believed in it…
But seeing Asher Stone for the second time tonight, the brother of her patient she had worked on earlier, Asher standing so tall and sure of himself in front of her, feeling the same thing she had felt earlier when she had first seen him; that shocking blow to the gut, like fate had just slapped them upside the head and showed them the person who might just be or might not be the others soul mate.

She was slowly beginning to believe in it…
There was no way on this day, one hundred or so years after Emilie Whitby's life had ended and she had been reborn into this world

a new being, that this, she thought wishing she could wave her hand at him for effect, he was even possible. She told herself this trying to make her self believe it. Looking down at all the blood in her hands, because that alone, the blood in and on her hands, metaphorically speaking, should have told her everything she needed to know about her love life.

But it wasn't working. She couldn't stop looking back up at him. Couldn't take her eyes off the gorgeous, walking god that was Asher Stone. Couldn't stop wanting him, in a very un-vampireish way…

Something always went wrong on this day, she told herself shaking her head. But this, this feeling, the one feeling she had been waiting both life times to experience, why had it come today? Why did it have to be him?

She couldn't take her eyes off him even as the elevator descended and echoed each floor they were passing like a clock thronging the passing of a forgotten hour. She was drinking him all in, she thought almost licking her lips. But not really, she corrected herself grinning like a love sick fool.

So what did this mean? This human, Ash, or so said the back of his huge bunker coat; was trouble. For her at least.

Love? Yeah right!

One, he was a human. Two, he was twice her size. Not that she couldn't take him, she reminded herself, it just seemed odd. The man she had always imagined and dreamed about was not of this size, and definitely not a man.

Three, he smelled delicious. Not just his fleshy scent, like most vampires were so attracted too. No, this was a mixture of something altogether different. A cologned mixed earthy, manly, sweaty smell. With a hint of smoke and fire.

She hated fire! What was she thinking? She was a vampire! There was no way a firemen could be her souls mate.

Where was Asher going anyways, she wondered. Why was he leaving his brother and family? His brother was on the fifth floor, dying, from third degree burns throughout most of his body. Even Curtis knew his own time was up. His mind was delirious, his dreams and subconscious were losing their hold on reality.

She knew this, because unlike the human in front of her, she was a vampire. She was a real, live, walking nightmare. Asher had sensed it when he had first stepped foot into the elevator. His body temperature rose, hairs stood up on his arms and neck, then his heart started to race and his mind panicked. Every human reacted to her presence in the same way. If they knew she could read them; their thoughts, their feelings even their emotions, they would probably hit the ground running.

Asher had been trying to sleep by Curtis when she had come into his room to draw blood work ordered by his doctor, when she had felt the knocking blow Asher had. Mine. Her heart had felt the same thing. He hadn't even known she was there the first time she had seen him. She could feel their dreams; both Asher and Curtis's, see the scenes of the disastrous fire that had almost claimed all their lives. Asher had feared for everyone's lives but his own, and still did. Even in his dreams, he was still trying to find the way out for them.

Did he always have nightmares? She wondered. He would if he ever found out who she really was! That was for sure. It wasn't just that she could read minds, or that she was a freak of human strength and embodiment. No, it was what humans feared most. She was death walking. She could tear a human to shreds with her bare hands. She could drink a person dry of every last drop of blood, without leaving more than two pinpricks on their skin, and without them even knowing what had happened to them before they lost all consciousness. This knowledge alone gave most humans nightmares.

Asher would never sleep if he knew who she was. He feared death more than even he knew of.

When he had walked into the elevator with her, she could see those fears. He feared being trapped. He had thought her a threat to his life. She wanted to laugh at that, but it was heart wrenching now. If he only knew...

Human instinct was to fear her. Everyone did. But he not only feared her, he feared being trapped alone with a beautiful girl. She smirked at that thought.

He hadn't talked to any one outside the department in a long time, except family, and she was definitely not family.

She was beautiful; she could read inside of him. A curse that was, she told herself. She knew the thoughts of men and how they seen her. They had seen her only for what they liked on the outside. They knew nothing of who she really was.

Usually she had time to use her abilities to change her appearance, but she hadn't had the chance to use her abilities to make him not see her, and then when reading his thoughts, she couldn't do it. Asher was seeing something different about her, which caught her off guard. He'd seen her hair and thought it beautiful instead of unnaturally long, he found her curls sexy and an odd highlighted color of brown perfection. He'd compared it to creamy chocolate. He must be hungry; his mind had lingering on the food.

Her skinny tiny stature had attracted him, and her pale white complexion had warmed him. The only thing she had time to change was her eyes. If he'd seen the blood in her eyes, he might have lost it. She'd changed them slowly when he caught sight of her. Easy to do while he adjusted from frightened to relaxed, or slightly so.

Asher was still very nervous. When he hadn't responded to which floor he was headed for, she just assumed he was going home; it wasn't likely he was visiting anyone in this lonely hospital at 3 in the morning, he probably needed the lobby.

She was headed for the basement. A place she was sure he didn't ever want to be in.

When he smiled in a simple 'thank you', not only had she known she was right, she felt her cold, dead heart thud, just once. Then he spoke aloud to her and she felt his voice speak through her heart.

He was lonely, he was tired, and he was hungry. He just wanted to go home, like she had desperately wanted to do all night. She couldn't help smiling also at the little dog he was picturing, even though she seemed oddly small for a guy of his size. But he adored her, Cookie, and it was so endearing the way he loved her that Emie almost melted at his heartfelt thoughts. What she would give to have someone love her like that.

He felt something for Emie too. She looked up at his thoughts. Something of the same thing she was feeling for him. All she could do was rub her foot on top of the other and try to look bored, when inside they were both dying to stop the elevator from going any further.

If she could cry, her tears would have made her look like a fool standing in front of him, bleeding drops of blood, but they would have eased this pain, this deceiving feeling of hope.

Being cold and dead, or undead as her brothers always called themselves, meant she couldn't really cry. But she would forever feel lonely. Empty inside. No one would ever love her. No one would ever want her.

Until tonight… she fervently hoped.

Asher was standing across from her, holding onto the rail behind him for dear life. Time passing for him slower then it was for her. Maybe seconds for him, but minutes were flying by for her. They were just passing the third floor when she had decided to offer him her condolences for his brother.

But then she remembered his brother wasn't quite dead yet, and maybe condolences weren't in order.

She should tell him that his brother was going to die, and possibly his father, but that last wasn't for sure yet either, she could smell something off in his father's blood she was carrying, or at least she hoped it was his fathers and not his, which could and usually did mean cancer, it had a distinct smell. She was tempted to make sure whose was whose by smelling the packets herself, but she knew that would definitely scare him.

How did one tell another that? She was too unsure of the humans and their feelings and the way they communicated. Cristina had been helping her with this. The more time she spent with her human friend, the more she learned from her.

If she said anything to him about it, he would ask her how she knew this, and then she wouldn't know what to say. Like many times in the past, she just didn't say anything at all.

One of the curses of being a vampire. Never, ever, tell. Never.

She was tired of it all, she thought as she rested her head against the wall behind her and sighed. She was tired of hiding. Tired of changing locations, and friends, and jobs. Tired of building dreams and leaving them behind to start new ones, as the humans aged and she remained the same.

She just wanted to live. To be loved. She hated this mundane boring life of hers. No matter how much her and her brothers tried to fit in with the humans, tried to have "fun", it never worked.

And finally, finally after years of being alone, a man walks into her life she can not have. A man who reeks perfection, and oddly still of smoke. A hero even! A woman couldn't ask for more than that. Could she?

She looked over at him again. She couldn't help herself. He was in an old, sweat soaked, blue and orange Detroit baseball t-shirt, his dark tan bunker trouser were hanging off his waist held up by only two red straps. A faded pair of blue jeans was under his bunkers. His boots looked like they were made for fishing, not walking through fires with.

He was a very cute guy in his firemen gear. What was it about a man in uniform, she wondered.

He was a handsome man, with shaggy blonde hair. Late twenties maybe, early thirties she wondered. His eyes were the color of the sea on a cloudless sunny day, that kind of blue that just takes you by surprise when you first see them. He was broad shouldered; the kind her best friend Cristina would faint over if he took off his shirt.

She wondered if he was all muscle under that sexy tight t-shirt he was wearing. His arms were huge, bulging under his shirt sleeves. Could she fit her hand around them she wondered while trying not to eye him too curiously by putting her hand up to measure. She could just make out the designs of tattoos on his arms poking under his sleeves and curling down his inner arm, but she wasn't sure what the designs were. It was tempting not to lift his sleeves up so she could see them better. He was tan, but she'd bet her left arm he had a farmers tan, at least below his pant line anyway, she thought wryly.

Oh, Cristina would be having a field day with her thoughts, she almost giggled to herself.

He was a hero by trade, he had the body of a god, but still he was just a man. A very good man. One whose fears haunted his nights.

He needs me... The thought hit her like the elevator had stopped abruptly. Her abilities would ease his fears, give him the strength and the will to do his job, to save lives, or at least sleep better at night after doing it.

But how? How was she supposed to love a human without taking away the one thing that made him who he was?

Would he fear her too? Would the knowledge of her true identity be too much for him? She would lose him and kill herself from the loss if she fell for him too hard. She'd seen it before.

But could he love her? The way she was longing to love him. Could he love a vampire, and could she love a human? The thought made her weak with hope.

Emie was about to find out. She might as well take that leap, she thought. That leap into the unknown where the body says No! Don't do it. But the heart and mind are so curious, the body fills with butterflies when you lean over the edge and take a peek; and then you just can't help yourself... you leap.

She had to find out. She had to know more about him. She, was doomed.

Three

"You're the brother of the fire fighter who was brought in tonight, right?" She asked. Just a simple question. Nothing too complicated for him. Would he respond, she wondered, trying to act human.

His heart was racing and his eyes were not looking at hers. They were rolled back in his head that was leaning against the wall. He was tired. He wanted to go home. Maybe she should leave him alone, she wondered.

The old decrepit elevator was moving so slow, noisily announcing its protest of the long day's use. He'd have time to answer her, but he'd have to hurry…

Asher took a deep breath; this was it, he thought. This is what happens between men and women in normal conversations outside the fire department. They talk about things other than fires, and trucks, and meetings. They talk about family, and their lives. Cars. Food even! He loved food.

Did she know how to cook; he wondered as he lifted his head and looked at her. He caught a glimpse of his smile in the shinny wall behind her and hoped to God his smile made up for his disheveled appearance.

Her smile lit up her whole face when he looked over at her. What had he done to deserve that smile? She was so beautiful.

He was going to find a way to keep this beautiful women talking to him. Find a way to take his mind away from all the things he feared, all the things that haunted him, and just be with her.

Mine. He remembered what his heart had whispered to him.

His father would just have to deal it. He was done with all the long boring years of training and school. His degree exceeded anyone else's on the fire department. He was done with living at the fire hall.

One day the department could be his if he wanted it. But he didn't. Any more responsibility was the last thing he wanted. He was just an officer, and a damn good one.

Thoughts of his brother dying entered his mind and he heard his father yelling at him about responsibility and all the reasons why he shouldn't be talking to her, but he shook them off. Curtis would want him to do this, he told himself looking at the woman he was about to make his.

"Yes. I'm Asher." He said proudly, even politely held out his hand in greeting. But he realized too late her arms were full of blood packets that belonged to his brothers, his father, even his own blood he had donated for them both, and that of many other firemen on the department.

Emie smiled politely as he slowly took back his hand. Nodding at his sweet gesture in greeting, she said "I am Emilie. My friends call me Emie."

"It's nice to meet you Emie. Are you from around here? I don't believe we've ever met." He let the question hang in the air for her.

Her accent was different. British maybe? He was curious even more now. It was sexy as hell, he thought.

He never would have guessed her name, Emie, could be so damn cute either. He absolutely loved it from the moment it crossed her sweet lips.

In this small little city it was impossible not to know everyone. Well, it was impossible not to know the sons of the fire chief of Luna Pier. Everyone knew who Asher was. But he didn't know her. He'd never run across her before in public. He had to know who she was. He had to find out more.

Of course she knew who he was, how could she not! She thought excitedly as she read his thoughts. Everyone knew his family. Every single women around here secretly dreamed of the Stone men. She had seen Asher's face more then once in their thoughts.

And, he did know of her, she knew.

"Actually, I'm still kind of new here." Would he buy the lie, she wondered curiously. How would she ever explain to him that she remembered the day he was born? She would have to go with the lie she had told everyone else and made them believe it.

Did she live here alone, or with family? Or was she married? He could work around a boyfriend and family, but not a husband, Asher knew.

Another sharp pang entered his chest. The elevator stopped on his floor. He noticed the 'B' button was still lite up for the basement floor. She wasn't getting off with him. Another sharp, ripping pain to his chest.

The old, slow, decrepit, noisy elevator had finally made it to his destination, but he wasn't finished talking to her though damn it! Funny how it seems like he'd been in this elevator for hours with her now. Everything that had happened tonight seemed like days ago.

They both looked at each other urgently, they knew the short ride was over; this was his last chance to say something, anything. Get her number, email, address! He thought quickly.

He held the door before it could shut, tried to be just the right amount of gentleman, and yet a little flirtatiously lean towards her without seeming too over confident. He hated guys that fell all over women and invaded their space.

He wanted to do this just right. Say the right thing. He needed her… and he could sense she felt the same thing by the look on her face. She was hoping too he wouldn't go.

"Are you hungry Emie? Want to grab a bite to eat?"

Oh, the irony, she thought, she had to be careful when she bit her lip when she smiled now not to show a fang, or worse, both fangs.

If this guy only knew how very, very hungry she was for him. How her fangs were dripping venom this very moment just smelling his scent. She could see the pulsating beat of his artery beating in that rhythm of old and it was making her lips visibly tremble at the thought of them succulently drinking from his neck.

He's been sweating recently. Most likely when he was out saving his family, she thought off handedly. Her mind was beginning to cloud. Both their thoughts racing through her mind. She could see all the images of his family throughout his mind. His brothers, his sisters, his parents. His dog.

Who he was, what he was, was the only thing keeping her from the thoughts of killing him, or taking one quick sip.

He was thinking quickly of any restaurants in the area that was still open this late. Luna Cafe was the only one open this late, he thought wondering if she was off work soon. He was so hungry…

Emie had never been to a restaurant. Not even before her life changed. She'd always wanted too; the smells coming from them always seemed sweet and pleasing to her senses. She could still remember walking past them with her family, holding on to her daddy's hand, savoring the sweet smells of the one in Whitby.

Should she take a chance? Her shift was over once she dropped off the blood to the lab.

She looked over at Asher and wanted too. Just looking at him made her want him in ways she knew she couldn't.

She could do this. Take her life to a new level. Pretend to be the human girl by his side. She really could. She wanted too. The thought excited her thoroughly. She'd pretended to be many things in this life, why not this?

But what should her response be? She was nervous and wished she knew how to fidget. Had she waited too long to answer him, she wondered.

He was still finishing his thoughts on where to go when she figured out what to say.

She tried to seem awkward, like Cristina, her best friend, when she was nervous. "I, umm… Yeah, but I have to get these to the lab first."

Before she could look down at them he was ready to respond. His mind worked out things faster then the others she knew. She liked that too.

Emie was headed for the basement, and Asher wasn't about to follow her there. He had brought in many victims that were still down there he was sure. People who had had lives days prior to a fire or car accident. People who now didn't have a life, or a home, or even a family anymore. Their loved ones would be moving on without them. It seemed horrifying to think about it.

Asher would not be following her down there. Not tonight. Even though he wanted to.

"Right, right. Of course. I still need to head back to the fire hall, take the fire truck back, shower, get the smoke off me." He grinned. "I just don't like eating alone, and since everyone I know is still here…" racking his hands nervously through his hair, he thought to himself how bad of idea this was and sounded and he used to be so good at this when he was younger. Smoother even. But the night's events were starting to take a toll on him. He was shaken in ways he never thought possible tonight around her. But when he looked at her and seen the excitement in her eyes that he was feeling, he knew she didn't care what he was saying, just that he was saying it.

"So, would you like to meet me at Luna Cafe in thirty minutes?"

He had been staring at her, trying not to look into the eyes of this out of his league, beautiful woman. Finally he did, and he could have sworn the whole elevator had just dropped off its hinges and was falling into the basement, taking him with it. She looked so damn cute and sweet to him just then, like he had just offered her the moon. And he didn't deserve to be the one to give it to her.

"I would love to."

That was all she had said. Four little words. He had heard her of course, but for just that moment he wanted to just look at her, wanted to believe he could give her the moon and the stars to go with it. He was memorized by her beauty. By her unmistakable attraction to him as well. She had just brought his whole world to a stop with those four little words.

She didn't seem to mind that some stranger she had just met, not only asked her out on a date in an elevator in the middle of night, but was also staring at her. Did she feel the same heart wrenching feelings as him? The same soul mate, love at first sight drama he hated to hear about from every friend and sibling he had. Did she feel the same way he did about losing her? Like if he didn't follow her, or ask her to meet him somewhere, that he would lose her forever. Did she feel that tugging at her heart like he did?

"Yes." She whispered. So softly, so stunned as he, that he didn't even notice.

But why had he met her tonight? Of all nights, why couldn't anything in his life be easy, simple, he sighed to himself. Why on the worst night of his life had he met her? Was fate giving him a gift for saving his brother and father's life? If she was his soul mate, or whatever, what was he supposed to do now? Besides kissing her like a fool.

Emie didn't know either, but she didn't care anymore. She felt this deep in her old bones and wanted so much more.

That's when his stomach growled and they both looked at his belly. Asher knew then watching her smile shyly at his stomach that this was the woman for him. She seemed understanding and compassionate. All very good characters in a woman. He disliked rude and inconsiderate women.

Blushing from ear to ear, Asher said "Ok. I'll see you soon."

Asher smiled and Emie knew from that moment on she was going to be lost without him. She already missed him, and he hadn't even stepped away from her.

I'll see you soon. Who said that now a days? It was so endearing. It wasn't a good bye, it was a promise.

She couldn't help herself, she had to smile back again. He was so infectious. She was beginning to think she was going to need him more then he needed her.

"I'll see you soon." She promised back.

When he turned around, letting go of the doors, he turned and looked back at her, his head slightly cocked to the side sheepishly with his hand in his pocket, like a kid in a toy store he was beaming. He even leaned forward a little, with a grin that stole her heart and a wink that took her breath away. Not that she needed to breathe; she just noticed how it caught in her throat. How everything this man did made her stop and stare.

Asher had very nice strong broad shoulders she noticed as he walked away and the doors closed. The back of his neck muscles were huge! She even caught herself stretching her neck to watch him leave through the last little crack in the doors, trying not to drop the blood all over the floor. Had he been lifting weights since the day he was born?

As the doors opened on the basement floor she was finally able to think. She shook her head and walked out of the elevator.

Asher Stone had winked at her. He'd flirted with her… He asked her out on a date!

Did one call a late night snack at 3 in the morning a date? She hadn't a clue! She laughed to herself out loud and didn't care. She walked out into the sterile smelling hall, lighted with bright fluorescent lights and headed down the white corridors for her lab.

If her heart was still beating, it would be racing. If she could feel flushed, her cheeks would be pinker than they'd ever been. If she could stumble, which she was sure that she was about to do, she'd fall straight into his arms.

She'd never, ever been this happy. Never.

Her future was so unclear now, but somehow brighter then she ever imagined. Could he be the one she'd been waiting for?

She needed Cristina! So she headed straight for her office instead.

"Asher? Asher Stone! In the elevator? At three in the morning?"

Emie knew when Cristina was excited. Her cheeks flushed, and her eyes bulged. Her body temperature rose to a very tempting degree and her thoughts were always scattered. She was typing away at her computer, but Emie could see the smile on her face and that look in her eyes as she exclaimed aloud.

It was an amazing sight.

Emie could only smile and watch. And listen. Her ears would be filled with all kinds of ideas, and what she should do next, and what she should wear even though she knew she'd be wearing her scrubs to the cafe since she hadn't brought in a change of clothes to work tonight. She could already see her best friends mind working.

"He asked you if you were hungry? Such a guy. If he only knew, right? He must have seen you before, or has heard about you."

That last Emie was doubtful of. Asher really had no clue who Emie was. And that was a good thing, for now.

Emie had taken a seat on the step stool beside Cristina's desk that was used for finding medical charts and heaps of papers in the file rooms down here in the basement. Cristina's office was darker than the rest of the floor. Country music was playing softly on her computer. Emie still had some time to kill before she needed to be at the cafe, so Emie settled in her seat on the floor and smiled waiting for Cristina to turn around.

Emie knew she could rely on Cristina. She had never had to come to her before for anything. She had always been the one who had listened to Cristina. Her life was so much more interesting. Her son, her crazy ex-husband. All the countless men in her life now that Cristina was starting a new life here in Luna Pier.

Often times Emie had dreamed of doing just this with her. Telling her a secret part of her life she couldn't share with anyone else. She was glad to see that Cristina was just as excited as she was.

Cristina worked in the basement with all the medical charts. She was the new Electronic Medical Records Specialist for the hospital. Cristina was in charge of seeing all the hospitals old paper charts and records; from patient's medical records to billing records, and also all the administrations records, safely into the new computer systems, and also creating new software for different departments to use.

Their small city was still trying to keep up with the times, along with adding new additions to the hospital and remodeling the old building, adding a clinic to help with all the new residents. They were also making all the updated requirements to their patient and billing and administration.

"I've never, I mean… yeah. I've never really been on a 'date' before." Emie thought, wrapping one of her fingers through her curls that were hanging down in front of her. "What do I say?" Emie questioned herself. "I'm not going to be eating." and by that she meant she would be drinking a whole wine bottle full of blood on her way over there just to make sure he wasn't tempting to her anymore, Emie thought as she absentmindedly played with the creases in her scrubs. "How do I act? I've never even been to a restaurant before. I really want this to work Cristina! What do I do?"

This Emie had said with a sigh that surprised her how much it was true. "Have you ever met him?" she added.

Cristina finally scooted away from her computer and leaned in towards her. Her straight long brown hair falling down over her shoulders.

Emie loved her hair. Cristina was finally letting it grow long, and it was really looking very pretty. Emie took some time while Cristina was going over in her head what all she needed to tell Emie, to look more intently at her eyes. Cristina had the same color eyes as Asher. That beautiful blue that was almost indescribable. Nothing really compared to it now a days. The lakes and oceans and even the sky didn't have that brilliant blue tone to it anymore.

"You need to just be yourself. You are so pretty, and funny, you're gonna have a great time Emie. Honest.

"He seems like a nice guy. And no," she added as she scooted back to her computer, "I've never met him, but I knew a friend who dated him once. Or was it Curtis?" she did that thing she did where she scratched her head and stared off collecting her thoughts.

Sometimes it frustrated Emie when humans would do this, she would have to be patient and listen to them retell their thoughts out loud. Sometimes she understood it better in their minds. It was even harder to pretend she hadn't heard what they were thinking, or when she liked something else they thought about better. Emie was happy she didn't have to pretend with Cristina anymore.

They had been fast friends a few years ago. Cristina had seen through Emie's secrets. She was an avid book reader and her latest topic had been vampires, like everyone else now a days. Emie hadn't cared when Cristina found out. It just felt so good to have a friend again.

"Anyways," Cristina said, surprising Emie out of her thoughts. "Go have fun. Be yourself. Everything will work out just fine. I promise."

Emie froze. It was Asher her friend had dated. Her friend had called off a whole five year relationship with him eight years ago, but Cristina didn't think that was important. She had felt he was worth a second chance.

The woman in question had thought Asher couldn't commit. They had been together for five years and Asher couldn't tell her he loved her.

It seemed odd, Asher seemed the type to be very loving indeed. Why then did he have a problem telling her? Emie not only wanted to know why, she wanted to find out for herself. She wanted to be the one he loved, not that other girl.

Emie slowly smiled back at Cristina. "Thank you. I knew I could come to you."

Four

Emie left her office still thinking about Asher; his tall, well muscled body, his gorgeous shaggy hair, his beautiful breathtaking eyes. She'd never been attracted to that before, but seeing him so close, smelling him, knowing maybe one day she would be able to reach out and…

She had to stop those thoughts. She was headed for the incinerator where she would log in the yesterdays blood, but the bags would never make it into the burning fire. She did this every night. Hide the blood bags under her roller cart from the camera's above her. Then she would switch them in her office and pour them into wine bottles. No one would ever know what she did on these last few hours of her shift.

Emie loved this part, but hated it. Her body would tense; her fangs would drip with venom at the smell of blood, but also at the heightened fear of being caught. She must look a wreck on the cameras. She always felt so dishonest with her work. Like she was stealing from the hospital, even though technically she wasn't. And like Cristina had said, if they knew what the alternative was, they would be just fine with what Emie was choosing to do instead of feeding on humans.

How her brothers survived on only what she brought home was something she never asked about or wanted to know.

Turning her cart around she turned off the lights and closed the door behind her, she rolled her cart back into the long lonely hallway and headed for the morgue. There were two bodies being embalmed by the coroner, she would retrieve their blood as well; log it, put it under her cart, make her last trip to her office to fix her bottles, turn off her computer and lights, then head up stairs to clock out for the night.

She couldn't wait to see Asher again. She was in a hurry and didn't stop to talk with Angie, the coroner. When she was all done for the night, she made her way back to the elevators and smiled when she got in. This is where her life had changed for the better. This is where she had fallen in love.

Emie was walking out the back doors of the hospital after her shift, with six bottles of blood in her bag to take home for breakfast for her, and a wooden case full of more bottles in her arms for her brothers; she felt at ease that the long night was finally over.

This ending to one of her worst days hadn't been as bad as she thought it would. It had turned out to be just another day at work, minus the fire chief and his oldest son's life hanging by a thread, and that she was going on a date with one of his other sons. Frank, the fire chief, was going to be so mad when he found out her and Asher was dating, and so would Joseph, her older brother who was the mayor of this city, and so much more than that to Emie. The two men had never gotten along in the past. Political matters or something like that and for some odd reason, she didn't really care tonight. She, was going on a date. Even if it was with the enemies' son, she jokingly thought.

She opened her car with her remote and set her case and bags in the back seat of her new car she had just bought a few weeks ago. She rubbed her fingers lightly on the edge of her new car as she stood back to admire it shutting the door. She had picked this particular car for a reason. One, it was red. Two, she had seen on a commercial on the internet that it had touch navigation system in it. After doing a review on the company she fell in love with the fact that at the touch of a button they would give her directions to anywhere she wanted to go. Shopping was her favorite thing to do, and even though she knew Michigan like the back of her hand, they were constantly changing everything. New towns and shopping malls were going up everywhere. Just like here in Luna Pier. She had used the navigation more often in the last few weeks then she liked to admit.

And three, did she mention it was red? Her and every vampires favorite color.

She didn't need anything big or expensive like her brothers. Joseph drove a new black, sport car. They all liked to tease him that he now drove the bat mobile. Jordy and Jeremy, her two younger brothers, both drove 4x4 pickup trucks, decked out to the max. If it was new, her brothers had to have it. They all had something or other tucked away in the garage. Mostly old, fast cars and more motorcycles than she could count.

She didn't want anything flashy this time around, just something little for herself; she only drove a few miles a day to work and back. All she needed was a radio and a car that could go for miles on a tank of gas. They had pulled this car right off the showroom floor for her, and she loved it!

Emie inhaled the night air around her and closed her eyes holding open her door before she climbed in. Her senses were alive tonight. She could see, hear, smell and taste everything around her.

There were two nurses behind her chatting about the new doctor on the fifth floor over by the front doors; she had to admit they were right. He was quite a sight. Across the street an old man had fallen asleep on his porch. He smelled slightly of rum and cigars, and something…old. She would be seeing him soon in the basement of the hospital.

Down the road at the gas station cars were still stopping into the city off the expressway for fuel and a snack. Almost every one that stopped into this little city had the same thoughts as they looked down towards the water, they wanted to stay and have a look around. They wanted to know what laid behind the huge lighthouse at the water's edge. They always made a note of the name of the city so they could come back one day. This latter never seemed to cease here during the day. The gas station was open twenty four-seven to travelers in and out of the city.

And the lake. Emie inhaled again at the shift in the breeze. The lake was still ever softly moving. She could hear the waves on the shore even though she was almost a mile away from it. She could smell the sand and the rocks. The crisp warm summer night came alive around her when she stopped to notice it.

She wished she were out on the rocks that surrounded the pier. She absolutely loved being out on the pier at night when no one else was around. The shine of the dancing moon on a cloudless night like this on the lake followed you whichever way you went. It would sparkle like diamonds on the blackness of the waves.

But tonight, she had a date. Much better, she thought to herself as she climbed into her new car and cranked up the radio volume. Tonight her life was about to change.

Again.

Pulling in to Luna Cafe for the first time ever she felt a little out of her element. But she wanted to see Asher again. She wanted to read his thoughts and know what he thought about her.

She wanted to know more about him. Who were the faces in his mind? What did Curtis really look like? Why was his father yelling at him when he had walked into the elevator? What had went wrong tonight? Why had he walked away from his family and walked straight into her life?

Emie walked in the two front double doors and was greeted by the waitress she knew. She was checking out a patron of the restaurant at her drawer at the greeters counter.

"I'll be right with you Emie." She beamed from behind the counter.

Luna Cafe restaurant was as old as the city itself. Emie knew the young lady at the counter. She had seen her at the post office on more than one occasion. Pregnant and always looking tired. But she never complained, even though she felt like she lived in this restaurant. She always greeted Emie with a smile and invited her to her family's restaurant.

Emie liked her.

"Well, well." She greeted Emie, wiping her tiny hands on her apron in front of her.

Emie greeted her with a smile. "You look… not so pregnant anymore."

Because of Emie's abilities she could no longer hear the child's thoughts and knew she was no longer carrying the child.

"No, not anymore." She beamed proudly. "The little one is with his daddy tonight.

"What brings you here this time of night?" she asked in her deep, ever present Greek accent, as she absently rubbed the womb where her newborn no longer was.

Her accent reminded Emie of Greece, Emie had been there once, a very long time ago. A time when she had been abandoned by her parents when she had been turned into a vampire. Emie had been running for her life then. Landing in Greece, so far away from home, had been a comfort. She'd never wanted to leave there.

The family restaurant was an American type greasy spoon restaurant. The young woman's family had come from a little town in Greece Emie remembered well, but the waitress had been born right here in Luna Pier.

It was the most popular restaurant around. Unless you wanted seafood, then you wanted The Louise, a little fisherman's restaurant next to the fire hall. Catfish, perch, pike, walleye, anything that could be caught off the pier, you could be served at The Louise. Where Luna Cafe was known for its burger and fries, The Louise was known for its wine and seafood. People from all over the Detroit metro area came to Luan Pier for both restaurants and a nice long walk on the beautiful, breathtaking pier afterwards.

"I'm meeting a friend here actually." Emie craned her neck as she said this, expecting to see Asher waiting patiently at one of the tables.

The restaurant, being in a community by Lake Erie, was filled with fisherman type d cor. Ceramic ducks, or ganders as they were known around here, peeped their heads out of the blinds looking out into the world. Ones with long necks were looking down on to the people sitting in the booths. Flower vases full of pink and white irises lined the tops of the booths next to them. Light tan and pale green colors highlighted the walls, along with real wood floors and trim that outlined the walls, windows and booths. Fishing nets draped the walls and some of the windows as curtains along with picture scenes of the lake, and Luna Piers past.

Emie looked around out of curiosity and took in her surroundings. Three gentlemen who looked like truckers were sitting at the counter drinking coffee and eating pie while watching the television, highlights of the earlier ball game; she smiled at that. A few other travelers were sitting here and there, and a cute young couple was sitting in the booth section next to each other huddled over a cell phone. Two male cooks were in a little window behind the counter discussing a new movie she knew, retelling their favorite quotes.

She could smell fresh muffins and pies, bagels and biscuits; the scent lingered in her mind and brought back memories of home, of England.

"Oh! Who are you meeting? Maybe I can help you find him."

Emie noticed the excitement and how she had assumed her friend was a he. Her smile reached her cheeks and she grinned like Asher and Cristina, minus their dimples of course.

"Asher. Asher Stone."

"Asher..."

Emie was a little worried when she started looking around. She wasn't sure if he was here or not, and she was sure if he was here she would have known it, for some reason that seemed odd to Emie.

"I know Asher. But I don't... I don't think he's been in here tonight." She was still looking around, so Emie did too.

Emie used another sense of looking. She was looking for his thoughts.

He wasn't here. She couldn't hear him, and she couldn't see him.

"Well, let me seat you and get things started for you. If I know Asher, and I know Asher," Her mind was suddenly filled with endless moments of Asher eating at this restaurant, while she was reaching for two menus and two sets of silverware out of a basket next to the greeters counter. "He'll be here soon, he never misses a meal." This last she said with a shake of her head and a smile.

Emie felt from her that she knew he would be here and her fears were eased a little. Was this the dating anxiety she had seen and read about in movies and books? Emie thought about that. These last twenty years or so she had finally taken up reading again. And with the way the television industry was going you couldn't help but be interested in watching the television.

Emie was excited, and nervous. It was nice to be able to experience all these emotions and feelings, but scary at the same time.

Emie took her seat, ordered water, and waited. The menu held her interest for awhile. She was trying to remember what certain foods tasted like. She had truly forgotten. The smells from the kitchen helped. They left a teasing taste on her tongue. It melted there as well. Turned to ash.

She had just looked up at the clock when she heard the waitress on the phone with Asher.

"I am not breaking off an engagement for you Asher Stone!"

"No. No. No. I just need you to send her down to the station. I have some reports I have to finish. They are investigating the warehouse fire we had tonight."

Emie could hear his distinct voice through the phone. He sounded desperate.

When she started with the what's and when's of the fire, Asher rushed her to find Emie and send her his way, with a burger and fries of course

When she walked up to Emie, it also dawned on her that she didn't know the waitress's name. She wondered when would be a good time to ask her. But her intent look on her face told her that something was amiss.

Her thoughts were of doing bodily harm to Asher…

Emie started to wonder if she really had time for this. She really wanted to see Asher again, but when she glanced out the windows before the waitress could begin, the sun was soon to rise, and Emie would have to make a mad dash for home before the rays could seek her out. She still had some time, but not much.

Emie had listened to the waitress's thoughts as she retold some of them to Emie.

Emie sighed. She had to smile, not just at the waitress who was now wringing her hands and shuffling on her feet; the girl really did like the idea of Asher and Emie together. Emie enjoyed that little bit of foresight from her. But, no, she was smiling also at Asher. She could see him on the phone, desperate to save the end of this night. Desperate to save them. Why did he need her tonight? What else was he thinking?

Asher had been at the fire hall for less then ten minutes when both the Chief of police and the Fire Investigator were drilling him at his locker about the fire.

Asher hadn't yet discussed what had happened tonight with anyone. He was putting his gear back together and hanging up his helmet, praying he wouldn't need to put it back on for at least the next twenty four hours.

"My brother is lying in a hospital bed breathing his last breaths. I'm not about to talk about it any time soon!" Slamming his locker door shut he'd hoped he'd never have to talk about it. Ever.

Curtis had to make a choice between his life and life of the teenagers that were trapped on that floor, and the lives of the other firemen who were going to have to search for his body once he let go of the ladder.

"Those kids shouldn't have been there." Asher was now pointing his cold dirty finger at the two men. "Sure as hell shouldn't have been pleading for help after their own stupidity burned down the whole building with all of us in it!"

Asher hadn't meant to holler at the chief of police, but his and Jerry's friendship went back to when they were kids, and Jerry was just going to have to understand.

Jerry had that look on his face that said he wouldn't be denied these reports and Asher wasn't about to tell him where he could shove his papers. But he wanted too.

"We can't find them! No one has seen them since you guys brought them out. This isn't just about them Asher. We think its arson."

Asher looked at Jerry more curious now. He had his attention now. "Arson?" He questioned quietly aloud.

"There have been a lot of these fires started around Monroe. The call comes in and it's always a big building like the senior citizen complex the last week. You guys find teens trapped and then no one see or hears from them again.

"I need to know more about them and I want these on my desk sometime tomorrow Ash! That's an order." Jerry told him this in a very authoritative voice, pushing papers into Asher's chest.

Asher knew he couldn't break this order when he seen what papers had been handed to him. Fire reports, not police reports. Jerry was tricking him into both.

Fire reports were to be filled out the day of the incident, by either the person in charge or any firemen that was on scene. They all hated writing reports. Usually the rookie's did it.

Tonight, they all were at the hospital with his brother and father. Some were there being treated for smoke inhalation, most of the rookies anyways, others were already home safe and sound. He was the first one back to the station tonight, so he was stuck with the duty. Most of those guys might not even come back tonight he thought to himself.

He shook hands with both men, took their condolences, then cleared the call with central dispatch in the radio room and headed for the showers. The reports could wait for that. He needed hot water on his shoulders.

It wasn't until he had his head and shoulder under the hot water with his sore callused hands on the steamy tile wall that he remembered the elevator ride and he had that sinking feeling again.

He'd forgotten about her already.

How could he possibly forget about her! She'd changed his life so quickly. Moments in an elevator with her, and he already felt his heart sinking at the thought of not seeing her again.

He stopped mid shower, making sure briefly that his hand was dry, then walked out of the shower to check his phone for the time.

He was late. She had been there, if she had went at all, at least fifteen minutes, alone. No women would wait that long for him.

"Think Asher, think!" he rested his head back against the now cold tile. When his stomach growled, he knew. The girls at Luna Cafe would give him anything he asked for. He loved living in a small city some days.

Ten minutes later, after he had called the restaurant and finished changing and trying to make his body smell halfway human again, instead of like an ashtray, his stomach fell through the floor.

Someone had shut the big red door and was walking in. Emie was walking in, to his fire hall. He couldn't see her around the big fire trucks yet, but he knew she was there, headed straight for him.

His first reaction to her again was the same as before. That scared feeling. The need to run.

But he knew he was just having cold feet. He never got cold feet. He never ran away.

As Emie looked around the department, finding her way through between two long green fire trucks, she was mesmerized by the smells of smoke in the dim lighted sights around her and the sound of a dispatcher echoing over the radios throughout the department.

This place smelled just like Asher.

Ladders hung from the sides of both trucks. One of the trucks, which must be out of commission because the hood to the engine compartment was open, was equipped with a huge ladder with a bucket on its upper deck, and huge lights were atop the truck ready to light up the night skies. In the midsection were step rails that led to the upper decks, a cab behind the truck would hold at least four men. All kinds of gadgets and hose ports and levers and gauges were lining the walls of the upper and lower deck. She couldn't help but wonder what they all did. The trucks were plugged into the ceilings by some sort of air cleaner system hooked up to their mufflers. Maybe to keep the exhaust out when they were started, she wondered, tucking her hair behind her ear as she looked around. Her shoes were making that squeaky sound on the freshly clean floor announcing her arrival.

She found it all so interesting at first, until she heard a heart beating. Listening for another, and hearing none, she relaxed to the sound. Then she felt his warmth, her tongue melted and her venom dripped. All these things she could suppress, but the pain in her dead heart was wrenching at his thoughts. He was scared of her again, and then he was excited to see her.

No one, absolutely no one had ever felt like that around her, without her abilities. She hadn't even had time to change his mind, yet again; his mind was too busy wandering around with thoughts of her.

He wasn't close enough to see her eye's, but somehow he remembered them. He could still smell her, and she hadn't even known what she smelled like, until tonight. Did vampires really have a smell?

Then it was her hair, she could see in his mind that he was looking at her and dreaming of running his hands in the softness of her hair. That made her smile and turn towards him.

She looked at him and saw his genuine smile. He was so gentle and kind and caring the way he thought of her. Her heart waltzed around in her chest trying to beat. Or was it butterflies?

He was standing at the back of the trucks leaning on a door frame by a little room with a desk light on, one hand tucked in his pocket, the other running through his hair. He was wearing blue jeans again with a skin tight dark blue shirt. She'd never met a man so, so... what was the word she was looking?

Sexy.

That was it. That made her smile widen. He was the sexiest man she'd ever met.

He must have been waiting for her. She could smell as she drew closer to him he had just showered like he had told her he would.

Well, so far he was honest and handsome.

She didn't want to think about the other women he had in his life before tonight. The one in Cristina's mind was very pretty. Unlike Emie, she had short bobbed blonde hair, a tanner complexion. She was also taller. And just- pretty, Emie thought with a gentle sigh.

Emie couldn't help but wonder if she could be enough for him.

Emie always felt her skinny shortness was a huge flaw. Like her long curly hair was starting to drag the floor, like a character in a horror movie she had watched once, even though her hair was only just past her hips.

Asher was grinning as she got closer to him. He couldn't believe this woman was really here. She had not only waited for him at the restaurant but now she was walking into his work. Looking around like she was genuinely interested.

Well, who wouldn't be? Everyone liked fire trucks. And firemen, he smiled hopefully.

"Well, hello there."

Emie handed him his bag and with a cheekish smile, staring straight into his lovely eyes she said proudly "That'll be $8 please."

Emie had always wanted to be a delivery person. The thought of going to all the different houses around and meeting all the different people, see into their minds and read their lives, it was just so appealing to her.

Asher's smile widened too. He really liked a girl who could hackle with the best of them. And in this department she would definitely need those skills.

"Do you take debit?"

"No, sorry. Only American Platinum. " Emie shook her head enjoying herself immensely.

"Well, I wasn't approved for that one." He said shyly, leaning closer to her and wrinkling his face in a smirk. "Hero's salaries suck these days. Will this do?" He reached for her hand and lifted it to his lips.

Never! Ever! had any human touched her since she was turned. Not even Cristina. Emie knew it would burn and set off a frenzy inside her to feed on them, so she had always averted being touched by a human. Just being too close to someone would send shivers down her spine.

Asher's lips and hand felt warm, and soft on her cold hand. Like the hot water rippling over her body in her baths at night after work. Like a dip in the hot ocean on a summers warm night. His lips were soothing, a gentle caress. The stubble from his unshaven beard looked only a few days old, and very roguish indeed. It softly tickled the back of her hand. She hadn't felt a tickle on her body in years. It sent shivers all over her cold skin.

If she had been a human she would have been shaking.

Thoughts were racing in both their minds; she wished she could share them with him.

She took in a soothing deep breath mixed with his scent and exhaled. "I hope you tip as well as you pay." She hadn't a clue where that had come from, but she could tell from the expression on his face it had the right effect.

His eyes! Oh his eyes, she thought to herself as he looked down into hers. She knew she was frozen in place and didn't have time to worry about it looking up into his eyes. She was memorized.

Now Asher's heart was pounding. It had stopped beating when he reached for her hand, and then it skipped a beat when he touched the back of her cold tiny hand with his lips, now it was drumming in his head so loudly he couldn't think straight. She was looking at him like she was feeling exactly the same way. He loved that she was feeling it too.

He felt like a school kid again. He felt giddy inside around her, and he hadn't even known her for very long.

He was so unsteady at the moment he was afraid to speak in fear of stuttering. "I sure hope you'll stick around long enough to find out sweetheart." This he said with a wink as he took the bag from her other hand and turned to walk into the radio room, still holding the hand he had just kissed moments ago.

"This is our radio room, I hope you don't mind but after I eat I have to finish these reports here."

She sat in the chair he held out for her, and looked up to tell him she couldn't stay long anyways.

"...I bought breakfast for my brothers too and need to get it home to them before it gets cold." That was something humans would do for their family, right? She had always done that for her little brothers. Always provided for them. It was something she would do if she were human, she thought. And they were the type of boys when they were boys that could eat someone out of house and home. She needed the excuse so she could escape before daylight.

When he started feeling saddened by her absences that wasn't even present yet, she had to hide a smile. This was so unfair for him. She would bet all the girls wished they could get into the minds of their dates the way she was.

He sat next to her, in a very squeaky chair, and started opening his bag. While he ate his meal she asked him frequent questions about the department. It seemed to ease him talking about the familiar. He showed her pictures on the computer of different scenes, different firemen, and stories of his past.

She was curious about why all the fireman had nicknames, so he told her those stories too.

"…and just incase someone walks in and calls me by my nickname," he said to her as he wiped ketchup off his cheek, "I should tell you that it has nothing to do with my size." He grinned at her when she caught on to the joke.

"So what's your story then?" she was longing to know so much more about him she hated that she had to calculate the time on the computer. Had she really been here over an hour already? She had exactly ten minutes to make it to her car before the sun rose over the lake or she would be in need of a miracle.

"The guys around here call me Mouse." He didn't even look at her for her response, just rubbed his hands together under the desk and shyly bent his head away from her down towards the desk and kept on retelling the story, but even he chuckled at the name. "A week after I joined the department we got a late night call at one in the morning. I came in dragging my butt to the station. I was tired and hadn't slept much, but I was determined to make the truck.

"Rule one on the department is, first rookie to the station takes the radio. I was the first guy here. I walked in here kicking myself for rushing and grabbed the radio." He motioned to the room around them.

She could picture it all because he was.

"I called into central dispatch, 'Luna Pier Fire to central dispatch.'. I get no response, so I try again. 'Luna Pier Fire to central dispatch.' Still, no response. The assistant Chief at the time walks in on me, pulling up his bunker gear, pointed his finger at my hand and announced: 'Hey, why don't you try using the mic for the radio instead of the mouse for the computer!'." Then he looked at her and waited for his nickname to make sense to her.

"They call you Mouse?" She asked sweetly when she got it.

Asher nodded his head blushing.

She couldn't stop the smile, and tried to stifle a giggle. It was cute. A big guy like him with nick name like that, it must affect his ego just a little. But it was still very cute. Especially when he told it while blushing. He liked the name. She could read it in his heart. It was his mark.

While she listened to him, she took the time to look at his arm. His muscles alone should have been enough to captivate her attention, but his tattoos were so intense, she couldn't help memorizing them. She followed the flames down his arms as they licked around his muscles, highlighting his vein. The bottom of a stone design peeked out from beneath his shirt sleeve. The letters 'LPFD' were engraved in the stone.

"We pick on each other a lot like that around here. They still find ways of giving me hell about it. Like the day I pulled out of the station with one of the trucks still plugged into the electric on the wall." He told her this, now stretched out leaning back in the squeaky chair, more relaxed now that she too had accepted him and his silly name. He could tell she was looking at his tattoos and it worried him a little. Some women didn't like men with tattoos. "They all said Mouse looked like he was dragging his tail down the expressway."

"Expressway!" she blurted out unexpectedly. His words triggered her mind. She needed to be on the expressway already. She moved too quickly and her hand bumped his leg, wondering when they had moved closer to each other while they had been talking.

"I lost track of time. I'm sorry." And how could she?

Well, there were no windows in this room they were in she reminded herself.

"No, no. Of course, here I'll walk you out." Asher was stunned by her surprised look.

"That's ok," she tried to stop him as they both stood and she ended up rubbing her hand down his hard chest and lower in the process as he stood. He was so tall! And there was so much muscle there! She almost couldn't believe what her hands were feeling.

Asher reached out both hands to steady her and also him, trying not to knock her over. He had a good grip on her hips when her hands ran down his chest as he stood. His body shook and trembled when her face bumped into his cheek and shoulder then his chest. She was a good deal smaller then he was. He could feel her breathe in his scent and he was stunned by her reaction. Again the fear returned as she took another breath, and then a wonderful sensation overtook him. He wanted this woman.

Asher smelled so wonderful. That same lingering mixture of ash and smoke, cologne and his irony blood. It was so intoxicating. Emie felt dizzy with a strange new desire.

Emie really shouldn't like the smell of fire. Fire could kill her if she got too close to it. There was no stopping the consuming power of it. No putting out the fire. She would burn quickly, and turn to ash.

Emie shook her head as she repeated in her mind his name on his bunker coat she had read earlier. Ash. It was so ironic that the one person in this world she wanted to love had name like that. The one word that could be used to describe her death.

Daylight. She could see it through the windows in the bay by the trucks. She had to hurry.

"I really must go Asher. I've had a won-" Emie was looking up at him now. His eye stopped her speech mid sentence. She couldn't help that her hands were now running slowly up his big, bare arms that were too close to her. He was too close to her. Closer than anyone had ever dared to stand.

And then he looked at her lips. Which caused her to look at his lips.

She didn't know whether to smile or breathe. Either one would send him mixed signals. Either one could be her saving grace.

Asher was looking down at her. He stopped breathing. His thoughts were empty, then he moved closer to her looking at her lips and his thoughts started racing. He wanted, no, he needed to kiss her. He'd never needed anyone. But he needed to kiss her right now.

Why did he feel like all eternity was destined upon it? She was moving in closer too, and when he looked back to her eyes it drove it him crazy that she was looking at his lips the way she was and wanted him as much as he wanted her.

Emie could see in his mind his intentions. He was about to run his hands up in her hair and cup her face so he could kiss her. She had to close her mind to all his thoughts, and her own, before he did this. She could feel and wanted everything he was feeling in that moment but she just didn't have time to find out. She started counting the seconds and pushed him away.

"I have to go, I'm so sorry."

Five

Emie headed west out of town, away from the sun. Away from him. She reached into her glove box and grabbed her scarf she kept in here for just this reason, to keep her skin from burning in the sun. Put on a pair of sunglasses to help keep her eye's from blinding and a pair of gloves all before she reached the top of the overpass going over the expressway.

She could feel her dead heart breaking, cracking, shattering even. He was just a normal everyday guy. She wanted to cry.

She could feel her mouth watering with venom. Blood seeped out into tears that were longing to be shed but couldn't.

She couldn't be with this guy. She couldn't.

Her body wanted him. Her hands, her lips, her tongue, her teeth. She wanted to feel his whisper on her skin like the wind, she wanted to run her fingers along his body and learn his curves and textures. She wanted to feel his warmth, his touch, his embrace. She wanted to know him. But she couldn't. She couldn't.

She took the turn on to the ramp of the expressway on two wheels and floored her car as fast as the little six cylinder engine could go on the on ramp.

She wanted to keep going past her exit. The music blaring on her stereo wasn't helping her. It tunes and rhythms and deep basses along with lyrics of two lovers in love made her want to take her brand new car on the longest ride of its life. Until she ran out of gas.

He had shaken her to her core when he'd almost kissed her. She wanted to move in closer and abandon herself to him and him alone. He'd barely touched her and she was trembling still. Where he'd held her hips had left imprints. She hadn't even known the touch of a man's hands on her hips could feel so sensual.

She drove right past her exit. Drove until she had filled her car twice and it was night again.

Florida was a place she knew during the day she would have to hide, but at night it could be her playground. Tonight she intended to see an old friend.

Shelley and Emie had been friends since 1930. Shelley had been publishing her first book in those days and Emie had wanted to meet the author of the first women air pilot, first women vampire pilot. She was so intrigued by her journeys and discoveries. They had talked for days on end.

When Shelley had made her disappearance into to the Atlantic Ocean, never to be found or heard from again, one of her many exploits, she took on a new identity. She wanted to work with Emie and her family. So she became a nurse. She had worked in Ann Arbor Michigan at the main hospital in the cardiac unit until the late 70's then she told Emie how much she missed the ocean and took a trip she hadn't yet returned from.

Shelley was one of the oldest vampires Emie knew. Her name came from the Mayans. It meant 'Out of the sea'.

The wisest too. Shelley was blunt, to the point, and very opinionated. Emie knew she could rely on Shelley for all the answers she needed.

"Wait, wait. He runs into burning buildings for a living? Because he wants too?" Shelley was typing away on her laptop while taking this all in. The evening sunset over the ocean on this side of Florida was just as breathtaking as she had described in all her endless emails, Emie thought, lounging in one of Shelley's soft wood lounge chairs right on the edge of the water. The waves were almost touching her bare feet in the sand. The rushing sound was like music.

Emie put her head back and waited. She watched as the last pink rays fell under the water and took a deep breath. This time of year she would have a good 8 hours to sit out here in silence and think. Maybe go for a swim with the manatees.

She hoped Shelley didn't want to go out tonight. Emie wasn't good at going out to clubs and bars. She never knew how to act. She wasn't looking for a date, especially now. And there really wasn't anything else to do there when you didn't know anyone there to converse with. Shelley was the complete opposite.

Shy, that's what her brothers called Emie. She hated being shy. She didn't know what to talk about with humans. She was always to busy reading others thoughts and wondering about their lives. Wishing she still had one.

Shelley was getting frustrated with her laptop. Vampires usually did. "All the commercials say high speed, faster internet, but they still take forever!" Shelley shut it with a humph. " Now, why are you here?"

Emie closed her eyes. So much for sympathy.

"I mean seriously, you're one hundred and some odd years old, this was bound to happen some time. Why fate waited so long, I can't say. But it has. Take the gift Emie, or I will. He sounds absolutely delicious." She leaned forward and let her red, golden curly hair fall down with a light shake.

"But, he's a man." Emie almost exclaimed.

"Yeah! Unless you're batting for the other team now I don't see a problem with that."

Emie smiled. How could she not? "You're missing my point. How do I tell him who I really am? What if he doesn't like me then?"

Shelley didn't care much of Emie talking about Asher not liking her. She knew Asher would love Emie any way he could get her judging by what Emie had already told her. "Just change him." She shrugged to Emie.

"He has a family, work, and friends. A life Shelley! How do I just take that away from him?" She looked at her then, "You know what all of us would do to get that back."

Shelley didn't answer. She knew there wasn't an answer to those questions. She also knew Emie's abilities to see her decisions. She told Emie in her mind what words couldn't say.

This was something only time would tell, and fate was obviously on Emie's side this time.

"You're just going to have to wing it." Shelley looked at her, made eye contact and nodded towards the water.

Emie turned, and for the first time that night seen Shelley's plane waiting on the docks. Emie knew then what she would be doing all night, and she couldn't wait. It was just the distraction she needed.

They both raced for the pilot's seat.

Asher was sitting on the front of Engine 2. It was Saturday night and he had just finished washing all the trucks. He was sitting there in front of the fire department on the apron, staring off over the expressway watching the golden rays of the setting sun disappear under the bridge of the overpass, the west side of the city, smoking a cigarette.

Today was day 2 for Curtis, he thought quietly to himself. He had made it two nights longer then they had all hoped for.

It was also day 2 of not seeing Emie. He sighed at that last thought. She had literally disappeared into thin air. By the time he had walked outside the fire hall that first morning she was already pulling out of the department driveway. He had watched her drive over the expressway and she had just disappeared.

Asher had been kicking himself ever since then for many reasons. One, he knew her first name was Emilie, which he loved, but he didn't know her last name, which meant asking anyone who she was, was next to impossible, but her nickname was Emie and he liked that. Two, he didn't get a number, an email, nothing. And three, he felt like an ass for talking about himself all night and not asking her any questions about herself! And four, he had tried to kiss her right there in the back room, like some big over barring ogre. They weren't technically even on a date. What had he been thinking that night?

He rubbed his head again just thinking about it. He wanted to know so much more about her. He could only hope he hadn't scared her off.

What did she like to do in her spare time? What were her hobbies? Where did she live? Could she cook? What did she think of him? Was she as turned on around him as he was with her?

Everything about her was everything he didn't think he wanted in a woman. She was tiny, she worked in the medical field like him, probably long hours like him, which is hard on any relationship. She had gorgeous brown hair, a sexy smile, big brown eyes... Wait. He liked those, he thought as he shook his head catching himself smiling again. What was it about her? He wondered as he took another hit of smoke.

He realized his mind was scattered. It made his stomach hurt. All he knew was in light of this horrible week she was a phenomenon that was haunting his days and nights.

He lifted up his head, breathed out his smoke and finished watching the sun go down.

Then out of nowhere, he saw her car. Was it her car, he wondered as he squinted at the little red car driving too fast down the overpass. As if thinking about her brought her back out of thin air. Like a butterfly she was fluttering right into his heart.

When she passed him she waved sweetly. Her head turning towards him taking him all in, smiling like an ancient goddess.

He sighed. Then he dashed for the front of the fire truck, tossing his cigarette over his shoulder. His dad was going to hang him, Jerry was going to pull him over on his way back into the station, but he didn't care. He had to follow her.

Horn blaring, lights flashing, a sweet little southern country song playing quietly on the radio he was now turning off about Jesus taking the wheel, he pulled off the apron and turned right onto Lakewood Drive, following her heading south through the city, hoping he was headed for her house.

He felt like such a fool as he followed her. The road was named after the trees lining the street. Lake on one side, trees on the other. How did he not know her! He knew the name of damn road!

Emie seen him behind her, watched in the rear view mirror as he pulled the big fire truck off the apron and headed straight for her. Her body responded like the lights on the truck. She even slowed down for him.

He had turned his lights off and was just behind her now on Lake Wood following her at the 15 mile an hour speed limit. In a fire truck! She wondered who was the bigger fool; him for following her like a stalker, or her for falling for it.

She pulled over. It's not like she could drive home and let him on their property. He couldn't go in. He couldn't. Not yet.

Asher parked behind her, air brakes hissing, his hands shaking. The smell of the summer night hitting him for the first time, but his mind was counting all the ways she would reject him. But still he walked over to her. The light from the street light his only guide to her car. The black trees and the darkness of the void from the lake was enough to envelope anything not standing in the light now that the sun was down.

His scent hit Emie like a ton of bricks. She had missed it, his scent. He still smelled of sweat and smoke. Today it was mixed with a soapy dirt road, oily garage smell. She also recognized his cologne. She loved it. The product was old. It was older then he was.

She had taken off her scarf and gloves when she got off the expressway, but she'd kept on the glasses.

In her mirror she could see him walking towards her in a pair of jeans and his long fire boots, a dark blue t-shirt with a white Maltese cross on the left side of it. When he leaned in her window and knelt down the Maltese cross on his shirt read the name and number of the department. 18-L. His ball hat was turned backwards and read LPFD.

His smile warmed her whole body like fire that scared the hell out of her. He was a curse. A drug. The devil in disguise?

Her steering wheel was in danger of being bent to the dashboard.

"Good evening Ma'am, would you be interested in giving a donation?" He proceeded to take off his big firemen boot and held it up to her window.

She breathed him in again. His scent tasted so good, and he was ever so cute.

"I would, but I'm… um, about $8 short." She winked, while tapping her little fingers sexily on her lips.

Two could play at this game, he thought. "Oh that's right. I owe you dinner." He grinned and added just as a police car drove past them. He did a double take at the officer in the patrol car, Jerry was shaking his head at him, "Could I interest you in a second chance? I promise to not molest you this time." This last he said as he turned his head back towards her. But he said it with such regret he confused her.

"'Molest' me?" she asked in all sincerity. What had he meant by that, she wondered.

"The other night, I um, I leaned in for a… I mean, I never should have…" he trailed off scratching and cursing himself out in his head, looking down and moving dirt with his foot.

This wasn't like him, she was sure. He was just as nervous as she was.

It was the thoughts of his ex that made him think like that. She had never liked when Asher had gotten too close to her when they were younger. She had complained about every aspect of his life. His love for the fire department, his tattoos, every time he tried to kiss her or be physical with her. She always told him he was too clingy, and then would tell him he was too big. She had confused the hell out him.

Emie listened and wondered how could anyone deny him any of those things? She loved all those things about him already.

She reached up and put her glasses on top of her head as she reached inside his mind. She could do that so easily with him. Make him see her as she really was, instead who she should be. He liked who she was. She made him forget about her deep blood red eyes, and let him see inside her heart so quietly he wouldn't even know she had done it, and brushed his hair out of his eyes so she could see him. She loved his shaggy hair.

Smiling Emie told him "Asher. That wasn't why I left." He looked so deeply into her eyes she felt like he looked right into her empty soul.

Then he dropped his boot, as she heard a vibrating sound coming from outside the car. There was a loud beeping noise coming from his hip. She had to admit, it caught her off guard too.

He cussed aloud, silently to himself. Central dispatch was announcing, loudly she might add, a medical call on his fire radio speakers. The sirens would follow throughout the city in seconds. He stared off behind them at the truck and listened to his radio, and then he rested his head on her window while he replaced his boot. His mind was grateful it wasn't another fire, but his heart was heavy and tired. She wanted to stroke his hair, hold him while he slept and protect him. Secretly turn off his pager so it wouldn't wake him.

She shook her head. Where these his dreams or hers? The thought made her smile. She could get lost inside of him for hours, if only she could spend more time with him.

He raised his head. "You're going to have to promise me dinner tonight again before I walk away or this guy's not gonna make it."

The guy in question was a 55 year old male having chest pains and shortness of breath, so said the lady dispatcher. Emie had been in the medical field long enough to know he was having a possible heart attack or stroke. Time was of the essences.

She almost had to laugh, his mind was pleading with her to say yes, shout out her number that he had no clue how to remember, he was hopeless this hero of hers. He was about to save some poor man's life with his years of knowledge and training which lead him seamlessly through his job, but for the life of him he couldn't figure out how to keep her around.

"I'll be waiting for you when you get back to the station." She promised and wondered how long a medical call would take him to finish and if she could call Cristina and get dressed for a date in time, unload her car of all the gifts she had bought for herself and everyone else in Florida… all while grinning at him knowingly.

Asher leaned back and looked towards the truck. Good thing he left it running. He looked at her one last time. Took a deep breath and sent up a prayer to who ever had sent her to him to send her back after this call.

"Just don't run over my heart when you pull in, you left it there the other day and I haven't picked it up yet." He said tapping his hand out on her window as he stood up.

She had to bite her lip after it betrayed her and formed an 'o', giving away how much he had affected her. She hoped her fangs didn't show, and tried not to giggle like an idiot. This guy, she thought shaking her head, was good.

He winked at her, and she waved him ado. She watched her hero climb into his fire truck through her side mirror and back into the street behind them and raced off lights and siren to do what the average human was too shaken to do.

She sighed as she put her car in drive and headed home. Her brothers were going to torture her over all this and her disappearance, and she couldn't wait to retell it all. As she opened the gate with her remote she could hear them discussing it.

It was time to face Joseph.

Joseph watched as his little sister pulled over the bridge onto their land and up the wooded drive lined with stones. Trees older than her. Stones older than them both.

He was a few years older than her, but he was way beyond her in wisdom. Proving his point for him, she drove up the way smiling like a school girl over a boy she had just met. He knew this decision was harder on her then most she had made in both their lives. Making the decision to keep them all alive had been harder, but wanting to love a human? That was going to take more courage then he had.

And, whatever her decision, even if she decided to turn Asher too, they would honor it. They wouldn't interfere with her decision. Making this kid apart of the family, that was another matter altogether. Something that had to be discussed. Sooner rather than later.

Joseph had worked to hard for this family and all they had, he wasn't about to let some kid come and ruin it all for them. He wanted to know more about Asher, who he was, what kind of person he was.

Joseph knew Asher's father and he didn't like the man. He could only hope and pray Asher was nothing like the man. The last thing Emie needed in her life was a brutal, domineering man.

When Emie reached the steps, he started painting again pretending like he had nothing better to do, he was contemplating how much time he had till sun rise, before he would have no choice but to abandon all the things that needed to be done outside, and try to make a dent on the inside. He still had to feed and tend to the horses. There was so much work to be done; he wished she wasn't so distracted; he missed and could use her help around here again, he thought with a sigh.

Emie set down her bag of wine bottles on the front steps. "These are a little stale."

Joseph smiled and noted the labels. Two nights ago. The night she didn't come home. The night he had had to drill Jordy and put up with all his teasing remarks about her and where she was.

They all loved Shelley, but knew for Emie to drive all the way there alone, on the spur of the moment she must be in need of some girl time, alone and they wouldn't be following her.

"How's the human? Stoner is it?" Joseph had to smile, and grin at her as he dipped his paint brush back in the can. She was always telling him he needed to not be so serious all the time. So he was proud of his remark.

"Asher." She stated, as she too hid a smile. "Jordy told you?" she asked shyly.

"Yes."

One thing she loved about Joseph, he knew just the right thing to say at just the right times. "How are the boys?"

"Restless. You forgot to feed them before you up and left." He stated simply. He wouldn't tell her what they all had done to feed that hunger. Emie looked happier tonight and that pleased him. He suddenly realized that she might need this guy. She had needed something for a long time now. Cristina had been a welcome distraction for Emie and this life, and a nice distraction for him as well. But he knew he would have to find another way to check Asher all out, her heart sounded as clueless about Asher as he was. She was his little sister after all. It was his job to protect her.

Emie grimaced and contemplated not feeding the boys at all. She had stopped by the blood bank in Monroe on her way home tonight and stole some extra blood before they cremated it. The boys would have enough to get them through the weekend until her shift on Monday night.

"How are the horses?" she asked just out of conversation. She was glad to be home. Glad to be out of the human world and back into reality. Then she remembered she needed to call Cristina before she had to meet Asher again.

"Triton misses you. You're going to have to walk him tonight if you want him to let you ride him anywhere anytime soon."

"I know. I'll take him treats later." First she had to coax her brothers into unloading her car so she could change. She was running out of time. "Are the wolves out tonight?" she asked this only because she couldn't see what was going to happen with Asher tonight. She hoped him discovering what she was could wait a few more days, but they never knew these things. A humans will could change as quickly as the turning of a page, leaving them as lost from one chapter of their lives to another.

Unless you were Jordy of course. But he was useless, or she should say, mean! He never liked to share her future with her. Always stating she would find out soon enough, then disappearing into thin air, as if to tease her further.

If Joseph could remember how to sigh he would have then. She was unsure, and that scared him. "I'll call them inside when you leave." It was unlike her to be so spontaneous, and careless. They had a family, a past and future to protect.

He began painting again like they hadn't said a word to each other.

And with that Emie started to go inside. She always knew when Joseph was done talking.

Why did Emie feel the need to hug him all of a sudden? She thought as she walked up the stairs. This was an odd feeling. It had been years since she felt like this.

So Joseph knew her plans too. So much for privacy tonight. But he wasn't against her going through with this. Why was she the only one who thought this was a bad idea? Why wasn't anyone stopping her?

She walked inside and faced her chiding brothers.

Jeremy and Jordy were twins at birth. They had this twin intuition that she abhorred. It had followed them when she had turned them from humans. It was more irritating now then it had been before when they were kids. They could read each other and also her and Joseph. Follow their thoughts and speak to their minds like she could, but from greater distances. They, meaning her whole family not just the twins, were all linked in ways she couldn't explain. Their abilities far exceeded anyone else's she knew of.

The boys were already unloading her car for her, she could see them out the front door she had just entered behind her while she kicked off her new flip flops she had just bought in Florida under the vestibule in the front hall. They were keeping their distance. Good, she thought to herself as she headed for her rooms.

"Girl stuff." Jordy had said to Jeremy, behind her.

Fine, she thought, as she climbed the stairs to her room. For the first time in a long time, she felt mentally drained. She needed a moment alone.

Both boys had an ability unlike any other vampire. They could move through time and space. Jeremy couldn't see too far ahead of time, unlike Jordy, just a few moments, enough for a good peek, but mostly because he really didn't care. But Jordy, he could see as far as he wanted, but never talked about it. They hardly ever did, only when it was convenient for them.

Manipulating matter was something they enjoyed. Walking through doors, peeking through walls. Not like doors or walls could stop a vampire, but it was nice when they stopped breaking them and learned to do this instead.

Emie had waited till they were twenty two before she had turned them. She had wanted them older, a little wiser, not to live the rest of their lives as children. But they never grew out of their childlike ways. They had been the biggest pranksters she'd ever known. Together they made quiet the team. Talking in the same kid-dish, manly voice, finishing each other's sentences. It was so creepy. Even for her.

In the early 1900's, the plague in London that had taken their parents, had threatened to take the boys as well. Emie wasn't about to lose them too, so she took what she had and used it to save them both. Joseph too, he had been the first she remembered.

1903 felt like eons ago to her. So much in her life had changed since that night. She still didn't know who her maker was, or why he had chosen on that night to do it. For the longest time she thought she had just been attacked by some rogue vampire wondering their property while she had been sitting in their barn reading one night alone. But now she knew differently. Their lives had affected so many others. Changed so many lives, for the better.

The only thought that plagued her mind now was Asher. How in the world was she going to explain all of this to him? How was she to face the night alone with him, if fate allowed such a thing for her.

Emie's phone vibrated in the back pocket of her jean skirt. She set down her bags as one of the boys flew past her and set down more bags on her bed. "It's Cristina." Jordy told her as he flew through her door and headed back down to her car again.

She could see Cristina's picture on the face of her smartphone. She smiled at her phone, remembering when she and Cristina had bought the phones together. Cristina's was white. She knew Cristina was going to give her a tirade of questions and answer herself a dozen times before she would let Emie speak.

Emie smiled again and pressed answer.

"How could you go to Florida without me! Florida! Really! You know I need a vacation Emie. Just because I never take a day off work doesn't mean I wouldn't do it for a rendezvous with you in the middle of the night.

"I love Shelley and all don't get me wrong, and I know we haven't been friends as long as you and her, but still. Really?

"I can't stand it here. The weather is miserable, it's rained every single day, and you left me here! Do you know how lonely that basement is? I only work down there because I know you're down there with me..." and so on she went, while Emie dug through her closet for something to wear.

"Cristina, I needed some time to get away. I needed some time to think about what I was doing. If I'm right or wrong... I needed answers."

"And," She smiled to herself, all this she said to try and stop the tirade. She had every intention of making it up to her because she loved her so much, and she was absolutely right, but she needed her to focus. She needed an outfit. Quickly. "I made a decision. When I got back tonight, he followed me in the fire truck and asked me out again." Emie was still smiling about that. What guy does that?

"Well?" Cristina breathed stumbling for words.

Surprising since the girl could throw out words faster than Emie could throw a fastball.

"I said yes." Emie waited for Cristina to respond. Then she waited a moment longer. She really hated talking on phones and not being able to read her mind.

"I could use your help picking out an outfit for tonight?" Emie asked sweetly.

"If you'd been descent enough to tell me how the first date went, which I'm assuming wasn't all that great since you RAN away! I'd be able to help you with the second! But right now... I'm not feeling it!"

If that had come from a text message Emie could just picture all the exclamation points and the mean smiley faces with the tongue hanging out Cristina would have sent her.

This was unfair to Cristina. Emie had confided in her just before she had left for the weekend about Asher, and then left Cristina hanging. She wished now her phone wouldn't have died before she had left for Florida. It wouldn't really have mattered, the islands her and Shelley had went to had absolutely no service, and some places didn't even know what cell phones were. On the way back home Emie had charged her phone, but didn't turn it back on till she reached Toledo.

"I'm sorry. I really am. I know that's not enough, but he's on a call and should be back to the station in like five minutes and I don't know what to wear." This last, Emie whined like Cristina usually did, hoping it would have the right affect.

Cristina paused and Emie wished she could hear her thoughts. She wasn't close enough.

"That white silk dress with the spaghetti straps that ties down the front. You know the one I'm talking about? The one that goes down to your thighs in the front but flows open in ruffles longer in the back. The one with black roses on it! Wear your chain and that bracelet I gave you. You'll look great. Don't forget an anklet and wear that short dark jean jacket you like."

Emie was dressed before Cristina said how she would look, picturing in her own mind where Cristina was going with the dress.

Emie wasn't the type of girl who knew how to dress. Cristina was the kind of girl who had class and style and knew just how to dress Emie. They did great shopping together.

Emie owed her a new wardrobe for all she had done for her. "Ok, gotta run. Shopping tomorrow? I heard it's supposed to rai-"

"Don't say it! I hate rain! I hate Michigan! What ever, yes, go. Have fun. Call me tomorrow." That last Cristina said begrudgingly.

"You're the best. Love yah!" Emie threw on her jacket as she ended the call, tucked her phone in her pocket of her jean jacket and darted down the stairs.

Joseph felt the peck on his cheek as he seen her coming, and waved goodbye as she peeled out down the drive. He wondered if she knew the dress shoes in her hand were supposed to be on her feet...

Emie pulled into the dimly lit fire departments driveway. There was a blinking red light just above the bay doors where the rescue squad usually parked inside the red brick building. It had been twenty minutes since Asher had left on the medical call.

She parked in front of a chain link fence that divided the departments drive from the restaurant next door, next to a big, and black, 4x4 pick up truck. The back window read LPFD in big bold red letters. The sides of the truck had silver and black checkered racing flags going down it from its truck doors to its tail gate, a long red light bar attached to its roof for fire calls, roll bars in the back of the bed with four big round lights that sat on top of the bars. If he wanted to be noticed on scene, this truck could light up the night she thought.

When she stepped out of her car and peeked in the trucks window, she could see a mess. Shaking her head, she had a feeling this was definitely Asher's truck. It said a lot about who he was, and what little time he had to himself.

He had big Fire Rescue books scattered on the seat and floor and a huge black winter coat that read Luna Pier Fire on the back. It hung over the passenger seat. It also looked new. The side front pocket had his name written in bold white letters.

Ash. Just the thought of his name made her shiver.

Two black and green cans of energy drinks were sitting in the cup holders, probably still full, and more cans littered the floor. Two packs of cigarettes lay on his seat with a blue lighter sitting next to them. Now she understood why he smelled of smoke and ash all the time. How had she missed that, she wondered.

She stood back and bit her lip as she placed her hand on his truck window. This guy really needed a woman's touch. A nice truck like this, she wondered what his house looked like. She could just picture it littered with his stuff from his long days away from home. He was probably so tired when he got home he just went straight to bed, not waking up till it was time to leave again. If he had time to sleep at all between shifts and calls.

Stroking the edge of his truck as she walked to the back tail gate he had down with his gear sitting on the back, she couldn't help but jump up and swing her feet while she waited for him to return.

She noticed that the inside of his bunker coat was all taken apart. She took a whiff of it and smelled fresh laundry soap. He must have had it cleaned after the fire the other night, but the scent of smoke still lingered. She reached for the insides of the coat lying on his boots and started putting it back together for him, one snap at a time the best she could figure out, just as she heard the trucks rolling down Harold drive headed back to the station.

~Six~

Asher was headed back to the station with his arm hanging out the window of his fire truck, the cool night breeze blowing in through all the windows cooling his overheated sweat soaked body. He closed his eyes briefly and hoped to God she was waiting for him. He couldn't make a fool of himself twice.

When he turned the corner and pulled up the apron so he could turn the truck around and back into the station he saw her. Swinging her feet on the back of his truck, all dressed up.

With a sigh of relief, he flashed his lights at her and pulled down on the air horn cord, and then he proceeded to try and back up the truck. All the guys in the back seats teasing gestures made it hard for him to keep the tires on the yellow lines. When he finally got it in park, he couldn't wait to strip out of his work clothes and run far away from this city with her.

Where ever the night would take them.

Emie saw him come out the bay doors ten minutes later. He was slinging on a black leather coat over around his back and up his broad shoulders, he laid the collar flat. He was dressed in a black cotton dress shirt with silver buttons, untucked, and a pair of designer dark blue, boot cut jeans. Emie sighed heavily at how tight and snug those jeans were. His black work boots matched his shirt and coat. He topped it all off with sexy black leather cowboy hat. She could smell his cologne and his musky soap as the wind trailed his sent around her. He must have showered while she was waiting.

She contemplated running for her life. Or maybe his? He had a look on her of intent and hunger, and for a moment she feared him. He looked great. And he wanted her. It was written on his face. And in his proud, sure of himself walk, he was telling her tonight was going to be the best night of her life.

Emie counted the steps it would take him to reach her and wished he would hurry. She felt the urge to touch him, be near him. He was all hers tonight.

"Hey there sweetheart." He grinned his little sexy grin and winked at her while sliding his hands in his tight jean pockets. He cocked his head to the side and leaned forward a little.

Was it his height that caused him to lean forward like that, she wondered.

Emie raised her brows and almost winked back. She was so captivated by his walk. It was like a trance. She bit her lip and smiled back. "Hey there sexy."

When he reached her he blushed, the blood flooding his facial features had almost made her faint with hunger. She licked her lips and swallowed back the venom filling her mouth. His temperature rose slightly and his scent filled the air around her.

Asher reached for her hand and bent over it. "Hungry?" he asked nervously looking up into her eyes and then he kissed the back of her hand softly.

Did he really just say that, she thought laughing on the inside. For you? All the time. She thought secretly. He would look back on his words one day and laugh she told herself.

Emie nodded her head to him in acceptance. She truly was hungry now.

"I know this great place," he told her, leaning towards her like he was telling her a great secret only she could know, while rubbing his thumb across the knuckles of her tiny hand in his. "It's a drive, but I thought it would give us some time to chit chat for awhile. And get me the hell outta here."

His mind was filled with his brother, and not wanting their time to be interrupted again by another call.

Good, she thought, Curtis was still alive. He must be a fighter. Getting Asher away from the city seemed like a good idea.

"Sounds like a good idea to me too."

He helped her down off his gate and closed it up. She noticed how his hands lingered on her hips, then how he reached for her hand as he walked her around to her side of the truck and opened the door. She eyed the distance up to her seat while he threw all his books in the back seat, and before she could climb up he swooped her up in his arms and seated her in her seat.

She loved it as she giggled. No one had ever treated her like that before. Like the lady she wasn't anymore. Like she needed to be treated like one. Even though she didn't.

"By the way," he said leaning in to her seat, handing her the belt behind her. "What the hell is your last name?" this he said looking cheekily at her, chuckling a little when she did too. He just had to be closer to her. To take in that sweet scent of hers. And he was determined tonight to know who she was so he wouldn't lose her again.

Asher had to raise his leg up on the step bar then, he needed to hide his excitement of being so close to her. She would notice if she looked down.

Emie had noticed. Oddly it touched her in places that had never been turned on before. Emie had also known what he meant by his question. It was just the beginning of the questions she could see in his mind. He didn't want to lose her after tonight. He wouldn't be able to make a fool of himself a second time for her.

Emie took in a deep breath then. "Whitby. Emilie Whitby." She breathed sweetly to him. She even extended her hand out to him in a sweet greeting.

Asher knew her name then. Everyone did. He just hadn't expected her name to be Whitby. Her father was the owner of this city.

Great. His father hated her father.

Damn!

"Well Miss Whitby, it's a pleasure to finally meet you, officially." Asher planned on doing this right tonight. Taking her hand and folding it around his so he could slowly kiss the back of it softly again, then he backed away slowly closing her door. This gorgeous women, dressed in white and a cute little jean jacket was his kind of women. He was excited just thinking about the rest of the night. Everyone and everything else was just going to have to wait.

Walking around the truck he saluted the fire hall and said goodbye to it for the night. He climbed in his truck, revved up his V-8 engine and headed north to Ann Arbor. It was a good forty five minute drive to the Saloon and he planned on using that time wisely. He wanted to know everything about her. Everything.

Resting easy once on the expressway, he informed her of where they were headed, a club with great food and dancing. Then he started with his questions.

"So your father is Joseph Whitby? Right?" He asked, turning to look at her.

Emie swallowed hard. No. Her brother was Joseph. They owned all of Luna Pier and then some. What Asher thought was his city belonged to her brothers.

"Yes, but the man you know isn't my father. Our father passed away some time ago." She hoped he would leave it alone so she didn't have to lie more to him. "My oldest brother is also Joseph Whitby, the third. He sits on city council now as mayor." Joseph had to leave every twenty years or so. Wait for a new council so he could take his seat back and run the city the way he saw fit. Always taking on a new role of another Whitby.

Luna Pier had changed so much these last ten years, with the new Ferry service that ran from the Pier to Putt in Bay in Ohio. It had brought so much business to the city. Hotels had went in, stores and restaurants, schools and the hospital. It was a new and improved city. She loved it. They had even expanded past the expressway and into Eire Township. There were three exits into the city now instead of one.

"Oh. I'm sorry for your loss Emie, I didn't know."

Emie took a moment to let that in. His character and gentlemanly ways were stunning to say the least. "Thank you. Like I said, it was some time ago, I was young. But thank you."

"How many brothers do you have, if you don't mind me asking?" he asked, genuinely curious now.

"Just two twin brothers. Jeremiah, who we call Jeremy. And Jordan. I call him Jordy." She smiled when Asher thought of her favorite show on tv that Jordy's name reminded her of. "And, of course Joseph."

"So what do your brothers do?" he asked, sifting in his seat uncomfortable after she took a moment to say more about them. He regretted asking her when she started talking, feeling like an ogre when she had to start talking about her parents again.

Boy he was going to make this hard on her. She tried not to lie when she could, but she knew this was bound to happen at some point tonight. "We all inherited our parents businesses, rentals, and the family stocks when they passed. My mother passed when the boys were very, very young and my father not too long after her. Joseph put us through school and pretty much raised us. He is the smartest, wisest man I know." She was looking out the window now, watching the night pass them by. She missed the parents she knew before she had been bitten. Not the ones who had rejected her. Or the father who had chased her with a shotgun off his land in Whitby, England so long ago.

Her father and every gentleman with a pitch fork or an ax had hunted her. They had not a clue what vampires were, or that she could have been given a chance. She had survived alone for years, but she had missed her family desperately. She had longed to show them what she had become, she wasn't what they believed her to be. Only her brothers had believed her.

"Well, you know what Joseph does, but you probably don't know that Joseph has a medical degree he never got a chance to use it after they died, so I followed in his footsteps. Jeremy on the other hand loves animals. Horses mainly. He raises and breeds all different kinds of horses. Draft horses like Clydesdales and Belgians; Arabians and thoroughbreds for racing. Some of the fastest horses in the Toledo Horse Race's are his." She looked at Asher then, beaming with pride at her brother's accomplishments.

"I did not know that." Asher said rubbing his chin astonished.

He was genuinely interested and she was pleased. She seen in his mind how he remembered horses he used to ride as a child at some family members home. He must like to ride, she thought wonderingly.

She loved their horses. But, wow was he in for a surprise.

"Jordy, well now he's a little different." Very, very different, she thought offhandedly. "He has this fascination with castles and the like.

He spent most of his child hood drawing and building castles out of whatever he could find. In school he found his enact in architecture. On a trip to London one year, he started working for the Duke of Broughton in search of hidden rooms in England, Scotland, and Ireland's most famous castles and battlements. He found treasures and dungeons; the queen even called him to Buckingham Palace once and he found secret passages there he still is not aloud to talk about this day."

"Seriously?" he questioned her.

"Oh yes. He can go on for hours talking about his journeys too. It's a passion for him you see. And he loves it. He's become quite the business man with his explorations."

Now he was dying to meet them. Great, she thought as she turned away from his thoughts. She should have lied and said something all together different. Why did she feel the need to tell him everything? She threw a look out the window and could hear her brothers in the back of her mind saying "Way to go sis."

Oh well. She wanted him to like her. Now she had him. He hadn't a clue how fascinating her life really was.

Would he find it interesting to know she'd been on the titanic when it sunk on her way over to America? Or that Jordy and Jeremy had stolen all the jewels from its sunken ship a few years after, and almost every treasure hidden in the Caribbean, from all the maps Jordy had found?

No... Not yet she reminded herself.

Asher was fascinated. Finally, real people. They wouldn't ask him endless questions about the department or the city. He could just sit back and learn about their lives. New adventures. This excited him.

"And you, you work in the hospital?"

Emie smiled over to him. She loved his inquisition. "Yes, I work in the lab down stairs. I am the head phlebotomist of the department in the hospital. I also work at the blood bank in Monroe."

This news baffled Asher. "You seem awfully young to be head of anything." He inquired slyly. How old was she, he wondered. She looked old enough to be out with him, but not old enough to be what she was already.

She knew he was hinting at her age. She turned a little towards him, bending her knee on the seat.

"Thank you." She left him hanging. Why not pretend, she wondered. She was tired of lying to him anyways, and this was funner.

"Why did you choose that field?" Asher had noticed she had turned, and it had turned him on quickly. Her dress was shorter in the front then he had realized and her legs looked amazing in the dim light of his truck. He needed to talk to her, distract himself.

This went on the full forty five minutes. He asked her more about her job, and what she liked to do in her spare time. She told him about their land on the outside of Luna Pier. He didn't know that on the other side of the canal where she had been headed too tonight was their private drive. A bridge that lead past three stables and up the beach to their house, the Whitby mansion he had seen through the trees in the winter was hidden every other season to the rest of the world by those same trees.

All of it was hidden from the world she told him. Between the break walls and rocks on the beach, the fence that surrounded their land on all sides and the forest of trees their land was in. Six miles of pure, untouched Michigan. She told him of the ponds and the small lakes throughout where the fishing was better then the lake some days. "The catfish grow huge some years." With Joseph's help that is. The wolves loved the fish.

"I never knew all that was back there. It just looks like woods from the expressway, and barren land from the water." His mind was dreaming of it.

In his mind he could see the pastures of horses, the wildlife running free. The four of them four wheeling and dirt biking, riding horses, just living.

He almost had it right, Emie thought.

Emie's life was more exciting then he had expected these last few days. He couldn't wait to find out more. He even wondered if her brothers liked to play golf… not that he had ever had time to learn, but he'd like too.

They pulled into the Saloon right at ten pm. He helped her out of the truck and held her hand as he opened the doors for her and walked her in. He was hungry she noted.

The saloon was packed tonight. Country music blared over the sound system; dancers were out on the dance floor enjoying themselves immensely. It was dark with disco type lighting dancing to the country music. Neon frames lit up the walls and lined the trim.

She had to suck in the venom of her monstrous emotions and planned on being a human for just one night with him.

The d cor around the place was a mix of rich Nashville life mixed with back wood country. There were ranch style ropes and cattle skull hangings and rebel flags draping the walls. Pictures of horses and mustangs everywhere you looked. Record labels and the newest country music artist posters were plastered all around.

The sights and smells of saw wood mixed with leather were overtaking her senses more than the need to feed on every beating heart on the dance floor.

Asher led her to a table that lined the blackened windows. He had never been more excited about having a girl on his arm. Emie had caught the attention of every young man in the bar tonight. Asher couldn't help but to covet her.

A young waitress took their order. He ordered enough for an army she thought. A big burger and fries, soup and salad to start, then chips and dip with a side of mozzarella sticks for an appetizer.

Emie stuck to water and a medium rare steak over a salad. The bloody meat always hit the spot, but the veggies would turn to ash in the pit of her stomach, giving her what she could only describe as heartburn as venom flamed inside her. She usually just pushed the veggies around her plate anyhow. They were more for a womanly show.

He talked about a variety of things while they waited for their food, and then all through their meal. She learned he wrestled in school. Caught glimpses of Curtis when they played football together in junior and varsity teams. They were only a year apart she learned.

His younger brothers, Jesse and James, were twins also like her brothers were. James was a firefighter and Jesse was police officer. He had two older sisters. Aqua and Aquilla. They had a younger sister, Isabella, who was obsessed with the new vampire stories.

"Apparently her name was in one of them, and she feels she is destined to become one too." Asher smirked as he pushed his French fries through his bloody ketchup.

This line of conversation made Emie very uncomfortable. She hadn't expected it. She couldn't help the thought that crossed her mind as he swiped another French fry through his ketchup. It reminded her of… She almost got up and excused herself to the ladies room, but she was rooted to the seat under her and her venom was dripping again.

Jordy whispered to her mind, Easy there killer…

Emie rolled her eyes when Asher wasn't looking. Leave it to her brothers to be monitoring her every move tonight.

"We call her dizzy Izzy." Asher said chuckling at his sisters nick name. "She's only nineteen. Still so young…"

Asher was worried about his little sister. Like Joseph had worried about her all these years. It was touching to see him feel like this. He looked so rough and tough on the outside.

"She needs a job like we all had when we were her age."

But none of them wanted her on the department, Emie noticed.

"She's attending the community college this summer. She wants to get into the medical field too. You two might have a lot in common."

She smiled at this. She and Joseph might be able to help her along. That is… if this all worked out…

When he had eaten everything the waitress had brought him, he set down his napkin. He wanted to dance. Emie had never been unsure of her dancing skills till tonight. In that moment she had never been more thankful for Shelley's endless bar hopping and clubbing. She took his hand as he led her to the dance floor.

Asher was suburb at dancing, Emie thought. He knew all the right moves with all the right songs and could keep up with her unlike anyone she had ever met. She loved dancing, and could tell he did as well.

Asher felt like the luckiest man on the floor. He didn't know how to go slow and had no idea how to cool down. He was over heated with a burning passion for her. Dancing with her was just igniting the flames stirring inside of him. Emie followed his every move, her anticipation of his next moves exceeded anyone he had ever danced with. They moved with such a fluidness they seemed to be reading each other's minds.

After three songs, the DJ caught site of Asher and announced that he was "In da house!" to the crowd.

"Oh great." Asher said aloud, whispering in her ear as he twisted her neatly in front of him and slid his arms around her body as he turned her towards the stage. He told her that he was sorry. "When it gets this late, they all get a little rowdy."

The DJ, Doug, was calling Asher up. Asher kissed her cheek and begged her to stay put at the foot of the stage.

"Come on Asher, sing us a couple rounds!"

Emie's jaw dropped. He could sing too? She searched the minds of everyone around her. They all remembered him singing in the past and suddenly Emie was astonished.

Asher, now with a mic in his hand winked down at Emie when a familiar song played on the speakers. It was a new popular upbeat song that twisted her heart all around every time she heard it. Every women she knew was in love with the cowboy who had climbed the charts of country music over night with this one song. And the guy she was with was singing it better then he did. She couldn't believe it!

Asher was good. He was very good. She listened and cheered him on like every other woman in the building, clapping along with the beat of the drums.

He reached down for her hand and pulled her on stage when the last strings of the guitar ended. She helped him out a little with that, and reached herself into his arms. As the music faded, the Dj got the hint of their entwined bodies and staring glances, he played a slower song.

Asher knew this song by heart, but he'd never had a woman who he could sing the part with. Even in the truck with Emie tonight he had blushed when he heard it.

He knew he could sing it to Emie. He felt every word in the song was true with her now that the words were flooding through his mind again. He led the duet in the beginning for her, not wanting her to feel pressure to have to sing on stage. When the sensual song spoke of kissing, Asher watched as her eyes closed in a silent prayer. He walked around behind her, reaching for her hand and kissing it. But when her part to sing along with him came, she floored him. Her sweet angelic voice echoed throughout the mic, he leaned it over to her as she started to sing. When she placed her hand on his she sent a shock through his body he couldn't control.

Emie knew this song by heart. She had bought the cd when it first came out because of this song. At the time, she was alone and the song was just that, a sweet melody. Now, the words were bringing on a whole new meaning to her. He handed her the mic at her part in the song. She sang it to Asher like this song was exactly what she had been meaning to tell him about that first night at the fire hall, but had never gotten the chance.

They sang it perfectly together.

At the end of the song, he kissed her. Just like in the song. He couldn't sing a song like that with her and not. He had been holding her hand, stroking her face, so close to her singing about a kiss, he couldn't resist.

For the first time in her lifetime, Emie was being kissed. She knew she could handle the light brush of his lips on hers. It was tempting, oh so tempting... She reacted just fine to his touch though, to his hold around her waist, to the cheering crowd around them. She knew she could do this.

She wanted to do this ever since she had left him a few days ago. And he had wanted it just as much as she had that night.

Then she heard the strings of her favorite song and wondered if the DJ knew she could do this one just as well. The DJ was wondering in his own mind how Asher, the best country karaoke singer in all metro Detroit, had found the best female singer and not told him about her. Little did he know, Asher had no plans of sharing her tonight with anyone. She sent the guy a quick wink when she had the mic and started to sing; she knew the words of this song too were going to seal her fate with Asher.

Asher's heart started to race as he felt Emie's smile on his lips. He hadn't expected her to grab his mic and start singing like she was singing now. She had every woman in the crowd's attention with her party song. The Dj threw him a mic, not like she needed his help, and he stood there as her back ground music made him blush singing with the woman who was stealing his heart.

He was taken back by this woman so far he felt himself falling for her. Was it possible, he wondered, that she was it? She was finally the one he had been looking for. The one he knew was out there somewhere, but just couldn't find. Had he been waiting for her all along?

She had to be. Because no one else could ever measure up now.

~Seven~

When he pulled into the fire hall at 4 am, Asher felt the night had flown by. They had ate dinner, danced, sang a few songs together, and danced some more.

He had been going to that bar for years. Singing country music was something his mother had encouraged him to do. She had been born and raised in the south, and Asher who had spent so much time with his mom, had picked up her accent and her love for the music. Tonight the crowd had left him alone when they had seen him on a date. It was the first time ever he had brought a date to the Saloon. The guys there had told him it wasn't a good idea, the date would either leave jealous of all his attention, or the girls in crowd wouldn't take so well to him seeing he was taken.

They were all so wrong.

Asher felt the whole Saloon and everyone in it disappear tonight when he was up on stage with her, and while dancing with her. Did she know how well she could sing? He loved her voice; he loved how her voice leveled and echoed with his. How she lifted her face up to him and put her whole heart in her voice. How she danced around the stage like she owned the place. She looked on fire at times with the emotions he knew she was feeling too. She heard in the music the story it had to tell and played the part of its character so well. He'd never had such fun on the stage.

Asher had been smiling the whole way home. Emie had been listening in to his thoughts. His mind was all abuzz. He had plans for their next date, he made plans to talk with his family and introduce them, he even had plans of kissing her thoroughly when they made it back to the station.

Which was all probably her fault, the song she had sang was about her being there for the party, going to get her some... What was she thinking? She thought as she shook her head nervously, pretending to bite her nails. But she had thoroughly enjoyed herself. Dancing with Asher was not only sexy as hell, but the way they moved together and timed everything they did just right had her wondering if that would be the way things would always be with him.

Emie was scared.

Yes, she'd said it. Scared. Nothing had scared her so much in one hundred and thirty two years until this really sexy, adorable, cute and handsome, good smelling, amazingly good singer, and did she mention a hero, walked into her life! Literally! A hero. Of all people, she thought nervously.

This couldn't be love. People didn't get scared when they were in love. Did they?

Emie had this sudden urge to actually bite her nails she was pretending to chew on. She was sitting cross legged in her seat and tapping her foot to the music he had playing softly on the radio. She was glad he didn't think she was ignoring him. They were getting close to town now. She was even more nervous now...

How was she supposed to kiss him again? Did she just let it happen? Would he be a gentleman enough and break it off like he had on stage so she wouldn't have too? What if she liked it just as much and kept on kissing him? What if she couldn't resist and bit him?

Sometimes the frenzy was just too much. She had heard so much about vampires and humans and accidents. She didn't want Asher to be an accident.

She had to shake it off. She wasn't that irresponsible.

They pulled off the exit and he headed over the expressway back into town.

"I had a great time tonight Emie." Asher said as he reached for her hand and held it in his on top of the arm rest.

"I had a great time too Asher."

She smiled and tried to seem honest. She traced her finger around the knuckles of his hand and knew she was; she was just nervous.

Vampires did not get nervous, she sighed when he pulled into the station next to her car.

"City is quiet tonight, all is well." He turned to her and smiled as he turned off the truck.

She smiled at his thoughts. He really meant it. He put his heart back into hero mode and was ready to fight fires and save lives at a moments notice, but for now he was happy to have some alone time with her. She felt his steady heart beat and his body relax. It seeped into her body and felt great.

"Wait for me, I'll help you down."

He walked around the truck and opened the door for her. He was unsure how to do this, she thought it was so cute, his reaction to her. He was afraid to slide his hands up her legs and lift her out now, even though he had done it earlier without thinking. Now, for some reason he was afraid to touch her again.

She reached around his neck and slid into his arms anyways. It felt like falling. This rush of feelings. She loved it. She felt like giggling. And Emie, never giggled.

And so she did as he twirled her around just once and laughed out loud too.

"I was going to get side rails for this thing, but I'm thinking I might wait a little while longer now."

Grinning down at her when he set her down, Emie noticed his voice was deep when he told her this, deeper than before. She found his eyes then and seen the sincerity in them. It took her breath away.

When he noticed she didn't release her hold on his neck he smiled at her. She was looking at his lips again, and he loved that. He couldn't stop himself, he leaned in for a kiss. And then he had to kiss her again. He wouldn't let this moment slip away for nothing. It was too perfect. She was just too much. He felt the whole world just go away.

It was amazing how for her, she had wanted to kiss him again; more then she craved biting him, when just moments ago she was afraid of his kiss. Parts of her brain were racing at once. She wanted to hold him closer, be closer to him. Inside him, all around him, all at the same time.

Looking at his lips, she felt as though butterflies were rushing through her, tickling her soul and dancing in her heart. She watched as he ever so slowly brought his lips down to hers. And when his lips touched her, she couldn't help but to reach up on her toes and press her lips into his. She wanted him to know she wanted his kiss. She never wanted his kiss to end. He was a great kisser, she thought to herself smiling.

Kiss me Asher. She whispered to his soul. Just kiss me.

Asher couldn't believe this. Couldn't believe he was kissing Emie. Couldn't believe he was holding her in his arms like this, alone. No one was out here tonight. He didn't want to let her go. Didn't want to stop kissing her. Thought briefly that if he could throw his fire radio on his hip far enough, he'd throw it straight into the lake. If it went off right now, he would try.

Asher recklessly kissed Emie. Unlike anytime before with anyone, he just lost himself in kissing her. The passion, the emotion, the feelings; they were overwhelming. His body reacted to hers. The way she reacted to him. She tasted and felt like everything he had dreamed about.

Better.

Her hands were slowly curling up the right side of his hairline to the back of his neck, entwining them and playing with his hair at the back of his neck absentmindedly as he parted her lips with each kiss. Her lips were meeting his as he pulled her deeper into his. She followed his lead like no one ever had.

His hands were holding their bodies close. He bent her slightly so he could press himself into her. Her body was just the right height for kissing. His body had known all along. He stepped one leg inside of hers and brought her closer to him in between her legs, lifting her slightly off the ground down his leg.

Emie's mouth opened unwillingly when she felt his body pressed so neatly against hers. She felt him in her core, and it drove her body to an uncontrollable desire. Stronger than the needs that had been threatening her all these years. He was unraveling her piece by piece tonight.

When he brushed her hair with one of his big hands and reached behind it to her bare neck, then down, down past her hips and the small of her back where her curls ended and then back up the length of her hips and up through her jacket to her ribs through her dress, she became completely undone. She'd never felt so alive then when she was with him. And this, this was wonderful.

Asher took advantage of her mouth when she moaned aloud. He needed her closer. He wanted this woman. Everything about her he wanted. He held her face in hands and reached for her tongue with his, when she met him there, willingly, and collided with his tongue, he reached down her body and found his way down her dress where it stopped at her thighs. He followed it up her thighs with his hands to her hips and lifted her body on his, pressing her back on the side of his truck, trying to hold her and hoped he wasn't crushing her. She was feeling it too, he could feel her intensity, and she wanted him too. She was holding his face now, kissing him, wrapping her arms and legs around him and kissing him harder than before.

She was wearing a damn thin dress. He wanted it up higher, but hated ravishing her on a first date. So he just held her, held her bottom close to his fullness. It would be enough, he told himself. She was enough. He couldn't believe it.

She really did. She heard his thoughts and wanted to scream her acceptance. This was enough, but it wasn't. She felt higher. Like she was floating but wasn't. The world was crashing down around her like the distance waves unendingly crashing on the shore behind them, and she didn't care.

Asher had to stop himself. He had to pull her closer. He buried his face in her neck when her moan broke their kiss when he pressed his fullness up into her once more. If he didn't stop this he was going to do more then he wanted with her.

She cried out to him as he rubbed himself harder against her. He wanted her to know he wanted her. She cried his name silently, while he kissed her neck and lower.

Asher pulled his body away. He had to. She slid down the truck and he held her while he returned to her lips. Kissing her again and again. Both moaning and breathing heavily.

He whispered her name. Whispered up and down her neck as he licked her sweetly tasting her. Her skin was cold, but he couldn't think straight enough to offer her more warmth. He wanted to kiss her lower, trail kisses between her lovely breasts, pull that sexy string that held her dress closed and find his way to her nipples and suckle her. His mind shouted at him to stop. She seemed too innocent for this. He still hadn't a clue how old she was. She looked and felt so damn young.

Emie was clutching him again. She wanted him, no needed him back where he was, pressed against her. Kissing her lower in all the places she was aching for him to kiss but wouldn't. She was wet, and left cold. For the first time her body felt cold, truly empty. His hot breath and hands were her only warmth.

Asher pulled her into a tight embrace then; close to himself. But this time, he just held her. Kissed the top of her head. Deep breathing calmed his body down. He put one hand out on the truck for support, the other was wrapped around her body. He wouldn't take her out here like some, some- he couldn't even think of it. She wasn't that kind of woman. Not that he had ever done that either, but still, he wasn't about to with her.

Emie heard him. She hadn't known what she was doing. Didn't know she was tempting him while she was taking advantage of not being tempted to kill him. She laid her head on his chest and just breathed. Relaxed. Wrapped her arms around his waist under his coat and took in the scent of his chest and his shirt, letting the time just pass like this.

She wanted it just as badly as he did, but she agreed too with him, now wasn't the time or place.

"I'm sorry." He placed his head on her neck after a moment and hugged her tightly, and even though she knew what he meant, she asked him anyways.

"For what?"

"For taking that so.. so far. I promised you I wouldn't-"

She wouldn't let him say the word. She didn't like that word. He was whispering down her neck and driving her crazy. "You didn't." She ran her hand up his neck and lifted him so she could look up at him. "Look at me. That was very... mutual, Asher." She winked.

Asher sighed, long and hard. This beautiful woman was giving herself to him. Accepting him, just the way he was. Someone or something was handing her to him on a golden platter, and he didn't deserve her. He was so worried he would lose her any second if he didn't hold on tight to her.

"You're a very good kisser Mr. Stone." And she emphasized the word 'very' as she slide her hands down his chest, enjoying the way his warm chest felt rock hard under her hands. Looking up at Asher she could see clearly the future she could have with him. And she wanted it more than anything else.

"Well you little lady, you are a breath of fresh air." He stuck his hands in his pocket as he said it. He had to step away from her, or he wouldn't be able to let her go home. He was so glad he had walked into her life that night, and she had rolled into his tonight.

"When can I see you again Emie?" he questioned her. Hoping, believing that after tonight she would want to see him again too. And soon.

Emie knew she had to spend some time with Cristina in the morning. And that her afternoon was booked too. But her evening was free. "Tomorrow night?" she asked shyly.

Asher had no plans tomorrow other then paperwork at the department. So his evening would be free for her. He exchanged numbers with her and told her he would text her some time tomorrow.

He walked her to her car and said his goodbye. He tugged on her fingers as her hand started to slip away from his to open her door. He opened it for her and twirled her in his arms and he gave her one last kiss good night, that Emie couldn't help but lean into. When he broke the spell after five very heated kisses, with a groan and a chuckle, Emie said in a deep breath "I should go…"

As he watched her drive away all of the feelings; the rushing inside his blood, unmistakable fear of something he didn't know, and the feeling of falling, all flooded his mind and body and left him empty. Unsure of himself.

He couldn't wait to see her again already. The excitement returned. He wondered how he was going to make it until then.

Emie spent her morning floating.

The weather was miserable in Michigan this time of year. Everyday was rainy. If the sun shined and your hopes got to high, the skies would darken and the rain would fall.

Emie didn't care today. The sky could fall for all she cared. She was just glad that after a night like last night she wouldn't be stuck in the house on a sunny day. It was cloudy and rainy and she was going shopping.

She woke Cristina up too early at nine, and yes nine was early for someone who worked nights, Cristina reminded Emie when she entered her house unannounced.

When Emie couldn't wait any longer at the front door, she let herself in waking Cristina up the rest of the way and walked into her bed room, pouncing on her bed.

"Just because you can doesn't mean you should." Cristina had hollered over her shoulder and rubbed the sleep out of her eyes while yawning and rolling over.

"I mean, it's not fair. Vampires should at least have the courtesy to wait for us 'slow' humans to get out of bed and answer the damn door!"

"No." Emie told her, trying to be patient before she started her tirade on all the nights events. "This is just easier all around." She laid down next to her on her side, and did the girly thing, resting her head on her hand.

Sitting up and trying to tell Cristina everything just seemed odd. Kind of like how Asher felt when he towered over people. So Emie laid down next to Cristina instead.

"Ok, are you awake now?"

Was she really going to think of him every moment of forever now, she wondered happily. Every thought this morning had been about him, from what she would wear today, because she just might happen to run across him; to how her brothers should clean up their own appearances just incase too, to how the house should look, how the dogs should act. Should she wear her hair up or down? She had been giddy for hours like this. Cristina would be her only savior from herself today.

"Almost." Cristina said, yawing more deeply this time. "Can't we do this over coffee in the kitchen?" And with that Emie was gone. Cristina rolled her eyes as she tapped her fingers together and straightened her covers neatly.

Emie returned with a piping hot cup of leftover coffee, heated up in the microwave.

"Fresh coffee?" Cristina chided, trying not to spill the cup Emie had hurriedly handed her.

Emie was already under the covers again, without the slightest of movement of the bed.

"It takes to long!" Emie whined. "I hate that coffee pot, there's no rushing it."

"That's why it tastes soooo good." Cristina reminded her as she rolled her head towards her. She could tell Emie was just playing. She looked so happy in that moment.

Cristina rolled her eyes out of spite when inside she was beaming for her friend. Asher had given her friend something in all her one hundred years that no one else could, and she couldn't wait to hear about it.

Cristina took a sip, "Ok. I'm ready."

"Are you sure? You don't want a bagel, or a donut-?"

"Just tell me already!" Cristina said impatiently aloud, smiling after she took a sip of her coffee. "I'm ready now."

Emie was beaming. She went on and on for at least an hour. Every detail, every smell. Every thought.

Cristina was jealous. She not only was single, but she was human. And some days she longed to be a vampire like Emie. But she had a son. Neely, who was sleeping in the other room. Neely who was her life, her reason for still breathing.

Emie had teased once about turning Cristina, and all the things they could go and do together. But some days Emie was adamant. Emie wouldn't change Cristina unless she had no choice. Cristina always wondered why, but never questioned. Emie was her best friend now. She wanted to keep it that way.

"I'm scared Cristina."

"Of what? What could you possibly be afraid of?"

They were laying face down now, holding unto the pillows under them and facing each other. Emie started drawing pictures on the sheets with her finger.

"I've got butterflies. I can't stop them. I can't stop thinking about him, picturing him in mind. Talking to him!" This she said with a dubious look at Cristina. "I have been carrying on a conversation with him all morning and I haven't seen or heard from him in hours."

Cristina had to laugh at that last. Emie had fallen hard for Asher. It was cute. "Emie love," she said to her rolling over on her back, " you my dear are in what we mere humans like to call the thrills of passion." Cristina looked over at Emie when she didn't respond to her jest. Emie had gone silent. Which was never a good thing.

Emie wanted Asher now. She couldn't believe these feelings. There was no one else she wanted more right now. Not even Cristina who she couldn't wait to see this morning. But like the coffee pot she abhorred, and many other human things like it, love between a human and a vampire couldn't be rushed.

Asher had a life, a family, a job. She couldn't expect him to give all that up for her. And moving into his life as the vampire she was… It wouldn't be all butterflies and roses forever.

Emie looked up when she noticed Cristina was looking at her. "Everything went so perfectly last night. What if something goes wrong? What if he finds out about me?" Emie had to gulp down her venom, the thought brought out anger in her and her inner monster had to be leashed. "What if he, what if he… what if he hates me Cristina?" She looked at Cristina for help.

Cristina looked at Emie in awe. She must really love this guy. The scary thing was Emie didn't know while she had been saying all this, she had forgotten to turn her eyes brown. Cristina had to wonder more about that before she responded to Emie. It was alright if Emie slipped a time or two if front of her, but what if she did this in front of him?

"Emie, listen." She had to roll over and face her again for this next part. "When I look at you, I see something so special, so precious.

You are a gift to everyone who knows you and has the pleasure of calling you a friend. You are my best friend. Asher will feel the same, if he hasn't already fallin for you. How did you two meet up again anyhow?"

Emie had to laugh at the memory. "He followed me home in a fire truck." Emie giggled.

Cristina laughed out loud. Emie never giggled, and she had never heard such a thing before. "He followed you in his fire truck?"

"Lights and all." Emie looked up at Cristina and loved how this made Cristina feel. It meant Asher really did feel something for her, now that she thought more about it she could see it too.

"So do you love him?"

"It's been less than a week. How can I possibly know that already?"

They were at the mall now. Emie was in her favorite spot in one of the stores. Checking out necklaces, bracelets, and sunglasses that matched the outfits she had already tried on. Cristina was measuring a pair of jeans up to her waist in the mirrors.

Emie knew her feelings about Asher. Knew how she needed him like she needed the one source of life to her, blood. She craved him right now like she craved taking down the closest human and sucking him dry. Her mind kept thinking of his hands, and his kiss, his body and how she felt when he made her shiver and tremble. He had shaken her to the core last night. She wanted him again, she sighed.

"Stop thinking ahead of me." Cristina knew her mind could wander faster then her own. She seen her sigh out of the corner of her eye and knew she already was seconds ahead of her. "Yes. I think you can. If he knows it or not, I'm not sure. But he will." She smiled brightly at Emie and told her with her mind that he would be a fool not too. Emie was a good catch, and he would be lucky to have her.

Emie had that feeling again. She wanted to hug Cristina. It was a new feeling, but she was beginning to like it. This need to hold, and be held by others in a warm embrace. She just smiled back. Wishing Cristina could read her thoughts.

Asher had slept most of the next morning. He surprised himself by falling asleep as soon as head had hit the pillow last night. When he woke, he had to look for Emie. His dreams of her were so vivid. He could have sworn she was there in the bed with him.

Emie. He couldn't stop saying her name as he rolled around in bed and tried to bring the dream back. As he showered and dressed for the day it was the same.

He called his mom and talked to her about his father and brother, and this beautiful new girl he had met.

"Her name is Emie mom. She has big brown eyes and an amazing smile. She's always smiling mom." The thought made him smile. He caught a glimpse of himself in his sliding glass doors in the morning light, smiling like a fool as he drug his fingers through his hair.

His mom loved hearing this from him. "Well it's about time honey."

They were sitting together now, at her house over coffee on her swing out by the water overlooking the pier that stretched out into the lake. The day had been misty and rainy, cloudy, but it was warm enough now to sit outside.

All moms loved it when their kids were falling in love. He loved telling it just as much. It was the first time he'd ever talked about another woman to anyone like this, including his mother.

She just smiled and patted his hand as she sipped her coffee.

"You know, I love grandkids." She hinted hopefully.

Asher smiled back. He sat back and noted her statement required no response. His mind wandered to a little brown haired girl whose curls bounced around as she ran around his parent's yard. Was it wrong that he knew her name already? And the little shaggy blonde hair boy with his fathers eyes, whose name would definitely not be junior, and the little guy would never see the inside of a burning building if Asher had any say in the matter.

"I'm working on it mom." He said as he smiled into his cup. He'd never seen himself as a father, but with a loving woman like Emie, he could see his life changing.

He made a trip by the fire hall after visiting with his mom. He had to check on things. Pay some bills, check his email, and write up some reports, sign paychecks. He kept checking his phone for a text message though. Every time his phone vibrated, it almost bothered him when it wasn't her, he thought with a smile. Wondering still if this was love he was feeling. He put on his head phones and finished with the days reports. He needed to go for a run around the city and try to run out these feelings he was having.

It didn't work...

The evening had finally let some light pass through the clouds, Asher noticed as he walked out of his parent's house after dinner that night. He got in his truck remembering what his mother told him about his brother Curtis after dinner. His brother wasn't going to make it. There was nothing left the doctors could do for him, but make him comfortable, and give the family these last few days to make the right decisions.

Asher looked down at his phone. He promised Emie he would text her tonight. He wondered if it was the right thing to do. His brother was dying and all he could think about was how much he wanted to see Emie. Curtis would understand, he told himself. Going back up to that hospital room was not something Asher wanted to do again. One, his father was there. Two, seeing his brother lying there like that… Asher just couldn't do it again tonight. He had seen him earlier in the day. Curtis was still lifeless.

He reminded himself if Curtis was in his shoes, he would be all over Emie too. One thing the Stone men were known for, their love of women. And Emie wasn't just any woman. She was becoming to mean more to Asher then anything in his life ever had.

He looked through his phone for her name and texted Emie.

"Emie?" he texted her.

"Asher."

She texted him back with a smiley face almost immediately. Seeing her name pop up in his message did funny things to him. He'd never thought it possible.

"Busy?" he responded with a smile.

"I was just getting ready to take a walk out on the pier. You?"

Asher smiled at this. He loved going for walks around Luna Pier. "That sounds wonderful, care if I join you?"

"I would love that!" She said with another smiley face.

"I live right on the pier on Fourth Street. Meet me there?"

"I'll meet you there."

Asher's heart started pounding. He couldn't wait to see her. "See you soon Sweetheart." He said back with a wink face. Then he started his truck and headed home. He would need to let his dog out and smoke before she got there.

Emie tucked her phone in her shorts and put on a small sweat hooded jacket over her tank top. She slipped into her flip flops before she raced out the door and headed for Lake Wood drive. She couldn't wait to see Asher again and texting him had only heightened the feelings she had been feeling for him all day.

She headed out jumping over the canal for the pier off of Fourteenth Street that would lead her all the way down to his street. When she got close she could see him out sitting on the ledge that lined the pier, smoking. He looked so sexy sitting in the dark under the cloudy moonlight. His mind was wrapped around thoughts of his brother Curtis, and he was ready for the distraction of being with her tonight. Emie couldn't help but smile at the thought of being alone with him again tonight, and wondered where things would lead too.

Would he kiss her again she wondered.

She walked slowly up to him, waiting for him to throw out his smoke.

Asher heard her light foot fall as she approached him. He looked over at her just as he finished his smoke and tossed it unto the rocks below him. She was sure a sight in her shorts. Her unzipped hoodie was falling lightly off her tank top shoulders baring her breasts to the chill in the night air. Her long hair was curled down her shoulder hanging low at her waist and he had this longing to move it away and cup her face so he could kiss her again.

"Hello there." She smiled sweetly to him in greeting as he hopped down off the pier. He was wearing long gym shorts and a white cut off sleeveless t-shirt. She was surprised to see his other arm was covered in a half tattoo sleeve when he turned towards her. She hadn't remembered that from the previous night and the thought bothered her. Had she been that distracted by him?

"Hello." He said, breathing out all his nervousness. Standing to his full height, he worried again about the difference in their height, but thoughts of how perfect they fit together stirred emotions in him he wasn't prepared for. He had to shake off his growing hardness he always felt for her whenever she was near and tried to smile at her. "Shall we?" he motioned down the pier turning to the side.

Emie felt the chill of the night as she passed the warmth of his body. She pulled her jacket a little tighter and was taken by surprise when he reached for her hand and pulled it to his lips to place a sweet kiss on the back of her hand. Then he held it in his hand as they walked down the pier. She absolutely loved it when he did that. His need to touch her floored her.

"How was your day?" he asked nervously, not knowing what to say at all.

"It was good." She said, looking up at him honestly, remembering her shopping trip with Cristina and how her whole day had been about memories of him. She had talked to him all day in her mind, thinking of things she wanted to talk to him about, things she longed to tell him, but had no idea how to brooch the subject of her immortality. "How was your day?"

"Good too. I was busy. Had a lot of things to take care of at the station. Spent some time with my mom." He said with a smile. Remembering the conversations he had with her. Grandkids. He'd liked to get started on that right now.

Emie almost tripped when she heard his thoughts. Her mind raced and she forgot they were trying to keep up a conversation. She could never give him kids... She tried her best not to sigh at all the reasons they were wrong for each other.

Asher was looking out over the lake as he walked hand in hand with Emie. It felt so natural being with her. Everything felt so right, and at the same time so wrong. His family had so many decisions to make over the next few days, and all he could think about was this lovely woman next to him.

"Emie, can I ask you a question?"

Emie looked up at him quickly. His mind worked so fast, she hadn't expected the question, and his mind wasn't telling her what he wanted to ask. "Yes, of course. Anything."

Asher smiled down at her. He wanted to know so much about her. What was her favorite color? What did she like to do in spare time? But he settled for the one question he just had to know.

"Where do you see yourself in the future? I mean," he chuckled at his own thoughts, "What are you doing with a guy like me?"

Emie's heart almost broke in half. Of course he wanted, needed to know a question like that. She knew so much about him already, he really didn't know anything about her. What plagued his mind the most was the difference in their statuses. She was the wealthy daughter and sister of possible millionaires. He was just the son of a fire chief.

She smiled as she watched herself walking on the pier in the pale moonlight shadow on the lake. How did one talk about themselves? She always hated this part of friendships.

"Well, I work a lot." She jested over at him playfully. "I'm in a desperate need of a distraction, so I guess that's where you fit in." she winked at him playfully. "I don't have things figured out like a lot of people assume I do." She told him while looking back down at their feet swinging their hands together. She snuggled up closer to him and rubbed his arm with other hand. "There is so much more I want to do in this life Asher, I guess I just need someone to share that part of my life with. You know?"

Asher knew exactly what she was talking about. There was so much he too wanted to do. Places he wanted go, things he wanted to try. The Fire Department was holding him back from all of that, and unlike his brother, Asher had no desire of living his life just to die in a fire. He wanted out of this place. He wanted to live. Looking over at Emie, he hoped she was the woman who would live with him.

"I know exactly what you mean." He lifted her hand above her head and twirled her around like he had on the dance floor.

"Can you see yourself living like that with a guy like me sweetheart?" He questioned her, as he bent her forward wrapping his arms around her from behind her to look at their reflection in the lake together that she had been staring at.

Emie looked in their reflection. She not only could she herself wrapped up in his arms, but she could see the future he was seeing. She wanted all the things he seen. But that wasn't his question. He had asked her if she could see him in her future with her. And she could. Would it be so wrong if she said yes, knowing what their future holds together. Pain, and possibly a lot of pain.

Emie held unto Asher tighter in her arms and sighed, a bloody tear welled in her eye she had to brush away. She couldn't say no anymore. He felt to good by her side to ever let him go.

"Everything I know about you already confirms that. Every new thing I learn about you just drives me crazy and makes me fall harder for you." she told him honestly, laughing a little as she said it. "All I know now is that I have never felt like this with anyone else Asher. And apart of me hopes this will last forever." She said as she fell back into his arms and turned her head into his arms, brushing her cheek softly against his arm. She closed her eyes and prayed to God he heard her prayers. She wanted this man and no one else.

Asher was still holding her arms across her like a dance move he hadn't finished yet. He twisted her back around and lifted his hands in her hair up to her face. "You and me both sweetheart." He said as he kissed her nose and listened to the way she giggled.

They were winding around the lighthouse where the pier led out into the lake and circled around to the north side of the city. Railings on both sides of the pier kept the onlookers on a path that would hug them in a close walk down a dimly lit walkway out onto the water.

Emie and Asher stopped at the first bend. Emie was looking out over the lake taking in the sight of the moon dancing on the water, and the light breeze. Asher was behind her.

He was trying to stand close enough behind her to catch her sent in the breeze. His body reacted in a way that moved him closer up behind her. He reached out and put a hand on either side of her on the railings, trying not to crowd her with his closeness, and also, trying to hide his bodies reaction to being so close to her, so Asher propped his foot up on the railing next to her. Her hair blew up against his chest and down his middle; he watched it as it teased and heightening his body more.

Emie turned her head and smiled up at him. "I absolutely love it out here." She had to resist the urge to lift up her arms in the wind and lean up against the rails. The waves beneath her were crashing into the rocks. She felt herself moving with the rhythm of his heart beat and the waves.

"Yeah." He breathed in silently as he looked out over the night. Asher loved that he had found someone to share this place with. He loved it out here too. He looked down lovingly at her. Looked at her bare shoulders and lifted her jacket back on her.

"So, what are those tattoos of on your arms?" she asked. Seeing his arms around her she could see where the ones high up on his arms wrapped around his shoulders to his back. Flames licked up and down his arm in ways she hoped they never would. She still wondered about them, what they were and what they meant to him.

Asher was worried about this question. He always wore sleeveless shirts when he walked on nights like these, and had wondered how she would feel about the old tattoos he had gotten foolishly when he was younger. They were still in style now, but some people, people like her and her family and his for that matter, didn't care much for them. He was tired of defending them sometimes, but now was the first time he wished he could just erase them and hide them.

"I got them when I was a kid... They're re just a mix of Fire department, Medic, and some New York 'We will Never forget' ones. Graphic designs of fire and barbed wire around the crosses that I thought at the time was cool." He looked over at his arms then, and then looked over at her in a sexy grin. "They wrap around my chest, back and shoulders. The blue flames on my left shoulder that wrap around the medic cross meet together on my back and chest in the middle and mix with the red flames, stretch out and go back down over my right shoulder to meet with the fire maltese cross. "

Emie ran her finger down the edge of the ones on his right arm and noticed how Asher closed his eyes in excitement at her touch. "And now." she questioned lightly.

"Well, some women find them very appealing." He hinted for her to tell him how she felt by bumping her shoulder.

Emie giggled at that, when was he ever going to learn that she was falling harder every day for him. "Well, I was never one for tattoos myself, but on you," she shook her head laughing a little out loud when she noticed him craning his neck looking at her sheepishly as she followed the outline on his right arm and was dying to know how she really felt. She looked out over the lake again and sighed away a rush of feelings that was threatening to over take her again. "On you they look very, very sexy."

Asher breathed her in. She was such a sweet mix of the night around them and her floral sent he was beginning to love. When Emie moved back a little and giggled again, he had to know what else was on her mind.

"What?" he whispered into her ear.

"It's just you. Us." Emie breathed in a big gulp of air. She was breathing in air she didn't need just to sustain the feelings welling inside of her.

"What?" he questioned inquisitively as he nuzzled her neck breathing in more of her scent.

"We've spent our whole lives in this place Asher. Walking down the same roads. Probably even passing each other. And now..." she said closing her eyes and letting the answer linger for him and wasn't surprised when his mind knew exactly what she was trying to tell him. She closed her eyes tighter then and breathed in his scent too.

"I know." He whispered. And he did. He felt the same as she did.

He leaned his head against hers and he moved her hoody down on her shoulder to give him better access to place a kiss and lingered there for some time. "I know it sounds odd so soon, but I honestly can't picture being without you now. I already want you in my daily life. I find myself thinking about you all damn day Emie. I'm so afraid of doing something, or saying something wrong."

Emie leaned her head into him. She could feel his hesitation in finishing his thoughts aloud. Men were like that. Never wanted to give away too much. But she knew what he was thinking. He was afraid of losing her.

She could feel his growing hardness behind her. When he enveloped her in an embrace she smiled to herself and couldn't imagine her life without him now either.

"So what do we do now?" she questioned. Looking back at him.

Asher knew of only one thing he could think of. Kissing her. He turned her around slowly and stepped down from the railing. He cupped her face in one of his hands and cupped on her curls in his other hand and ran it down her curl, savoring the feel of her hair on his hand.

"I know what I want to do." He said to her looking down into her eyes. He had shivers running all up and down his body. He needed to kiss her. He needed to show her what his heart couldn't say in words. But for the first time in forever his heart was racing and his lips felt tight. He was hanging on her next words like he was asking if he could breathe.

"Can I kiss you again Emie?" She was staring at his lips again and it made him smile. It was like she was reading his mind sometimes and he loved it.

Emie was shaken to her core by him. Lost in this one moment in time. It was so perfect. She was almost trembling with the need to kiss him too. "Please." She begged him looking up into each of his eyes, standing up on her toes reaching for his lips with hers.

That was all Asher needed to hear. He bent down and kissed her like his whole life depended on it.

And when he kissed her this time, he wasn't slow, he wasn't careful, he kissed her with all the bent up passion he had been feeling since he had last seen her.

Why it felt like days had gone by since he had last touched her, he didn't know. He only knew she felt like heaven in his arms.

Emie couldn't help herself. She almost cried out when his lips touched hers. She almost lost all control when he parted her lips and she felt his tongue slid around hers. Her hands found their way up the front of his shirt to the back of his neck and she reached up into his hair and pulled him gently closer to her.

Asher reacted to this by lifting her body up on the rail and neatly fitting his body into her. He wrapped one arm around her body and the other up into her hair like she was doing to him. He molded himself into her so she could feel his hardness where he knew her body wanted him. And he kissed her over and over again.

Emie was coming undone. She was shattering and falling to pieces all around them. Her body wanted so much more than this. She wanted to drink him. She wanted to taste him. She wanted to feel his body inside of hers. She had never craved someone in so many different ways before. Her mind, her hidden monster, her body, they were all battling for pieces of this man.

Her heart wanted to burst into flames with the desire that was overwhelming her. She wanted to scream it to him because she knew he couldn't hear her needs like she could hear his. His thoughts and hers were mingling in her mind. And in the end, they both wanted the same thing.

Asher started kissing down her neck and Emie had to hold back the growl that was rippling in the back of her throat. She was jealous of where his lips were. She wanted hers on his neck...

"Asher." She called out his name in a half whisper.

"Emie." He breathed. He followed a path down her neck to her shoulders, trying to steady his heart from beating out of his chest. His hands were shaking too bad to trust them to touch her anywhere. He followed his path back to her neck and couldn't decide which way to kiss her. Back up to her mouth or lower...

Emie wanted to control his mind. Tell him which way to go, but she too didn't know which way her body wanted. She wanted him all over her. She could feel every inch of his length between her legs and it was driving her wild. He felt larger then she remembered and had ever thought possible.

"Asher, please." She begged again, pushing herself up against his hardness.

Asher pulled her closer to his hardness and went back to her lips. He kissed her harder now. Sucking in each of her lips, biting down. He moaned her name when he felt her pushing into him again. Then he lost his battle of being a gentleman. He nipped and sucked and kissed his way down her chest, leaning her body dangerously back over the railing, but holding her like he would never let her fall, moving the top of her shirt down just a little with his tongue so he could find the tip of her nipple and suck it into his mouth, but he couldn't reach it.

His shaking hand came around and he had to reach for her, pushing her breast up just enough so he could do just that. This had been the pain of his desire for many nights not doing this to her yet.

His hand had barely had time to hold her in position for his mouth to suck in her harden nipple he had just flicked with his tongue, when his pager on his side started to vibrate and beep.

"No! No! NO! Damn it all!" he cursed letting go of her breast with his hand and growled into her neck, and groaned as he moved her top back in place over her breast. He had to grip the rail behind her so he didn't take his pager off his shorts and throw it into the lake. He was breathless and hard, and totally out of control, but he waited for central dispatch to announce the call over his radio, pulling her closer into his embrace.

He knew he wasn't leaving Emie out here if it was just a medical someone else could handle. There were enough people at the station for that. His heart started skipping when the sirens started blaring. Adrenalin was raging through his veins in anticipation. He hated the moments in between the beeping and the announcement. He held her closely to his body and buried his face in her hair and neck.

Emie held him tightly as she too waited. She couldn't help but chuckle too. He was such a guy. Pouting over losing his prize. She was just as breathless as he was in that moment and desperately wanted him to return to what he had been doing. She felt his breath let out of his body as he listened to the dispatcher.

"Central dispatch on the air for Luna Pier Fire, you have a structure fire at 4343 First Street. That's 4343 First Street. Caller there says the fire is in the upper floor and spreading."

Both Asher and Emie turned around. Just south of the pier they could see the house in question. It was right on the water like Asher's house was. There was fire rolling out of the upstairs window.

Asher cursed at the house. Almost flipped it off before he realized who he was with. Normally he would be excited about a house fire. It was a time when the guys got to put on their gear and play with the hoses and fire trucks. But right now all he wanted was to stay here with Emie.

Emie smiled at Asher as she watched him look at the house on fire and cuss at it. She knew he had to go. This is what he did. The smell of fire and smoke was filling the air around them already.

"Go." She told him softly. When he looked at her, she added "Just be careful."

Asher rested his head on her shoulder again and stepped his legs out from under her growling. "Emie I'm sorry." He squeezed her tightly in his embrace and wouldn't let her go. He hated that he had to leave her like this. For the first time he understood what one of his best friends, Ken, meant when he said he hated leaving his wife in the middle of the night. Ken would rush with all haste to get out of the fire hall some nights to go back home.

Emie pulled him tightly too. "It's ok super man. I understand.

"Go. I'll walk home." She told him.

"Super man?" he questioned her stunned as he helped her down off the rail. No one had ever called him that before.

"Yeah." Emie hopped down and winked back up at him. She reached up on her toes and kissed him on the cheek and added "If I say your name again you'll never make the truck."

Asher had to start walking backwards, shaking his head playfully at her, away from her, or he knew he wasn't going to be going on the call at all. "I'll text you afterwards?"

"Yes. Please. I'll be waiting for it." She promised.

Asher took one last look at her, she had her hands tucked neatly in her short pockets and she was smiling again. He shook his head in amazement at her. No other woman had ever understood this part of his life. But she had. He turned and ran back the few streets from the pier to the fire hall.

The fire on First Street was raging by the time Asher got the truck out of the station. He told the rookie in the driver's seat to follow the main road back to Lakewood and turn down First Street. "It's at the end of the road by the water."

It would be the first fire he would have to battle as acting Chief. With his father and brother out of service, this left Asher in charge.

He had never wanted this, and had a hard time grasping the responsibility that was facing him. But all his training kicked in as soon as his boots hit the ground.

He called to surrounding departments for back up and barked orders at his men. Everyone knew their places and the fire was out before it had a chance to engulf the entire house, or worse the adjacent houses.

Once he had the trucks back in the station, the call cleared and his gear put away, his shoulder started hurting with an ache he couldn't handle. He stood there by his gear and looked at his phone torn between texting Emie or going home to a hot shower.

One of his brothers, Jessie, answered that dilemma for him. "Asher, there's no other officer in charge at the station. Which means you're needed here to stay the night with the men until the next shift in the morning when Bob can come in to cover for you."

Bob was one of his Lieutenants. Another guy who didn't want any more responsibilities on the department, Asher thought offhandedly.

Asher stood in the bay with the trucks. The lights were turned down low and the men were headed up to bed. He started shaking his head with his hands on his hips. He didn't want this. He didn't. Tonight would have been Curtis' night to stay the night. Asher wondered how he had forgotten to change the schedule?

Rage was building inside him. He felt like throwing something. If he were alone, he would have, he thought.

He lowered his head and hated how mad he felt. It wasn't Curtis's fault. It was his for staying on the department as long as he had knowing this wasn't really what he wanted in life. What he really wanted lived at the other end of town and was sleeping alone without him.

He just wanted his brother back. Curtis wasn't even gone yet and Asher missed him so much it hurt.

He rubbed his shoulder and walked back to the showers. He was going to have to text Emie after his shower when he crawled into one of the recliners and tried to get a good night's sleep. He kicked a bucket over on his way around the back of the truck and threw the door open in the bathroom so hard it hit the wall with a loud bang.

~*Eight*~

Emie had spent the first part of her night watching Asher at the house fire. She had never witnessed firefighters fighting a fire before. It was really something to behold. Each one moved with the speed of a man on a mission. They knew their places and where they needed to be at all times.

It was really something to watch as a man climbed a ladder and fell into a black smoke billowing window. It had to be impossible to see inside there. How did they see inside a room filled with black smoke, she wondered as she watched. Two other men stood on the roof, cutting holes, venting the heat and smoke out. She watched as flashlights shone out the holes and windows on the upper floors, but the men inside couldn't be seen through the smoke.

When Emie seen Asher standing behind one of the trucks after the fire was out, she watched as he tried to reach for his shoulder under his bunker coat. What was hurting him, she wondered. She watched as he poured a whole bottle of water down his jacket in the back and adjusted his shoulder again. Then he sat down on the truck and talked up to one of his men. His thoughts were so scattered. He heard what the other guy was talking about, but pain clouded his mind.

She watched as they loaded the trucks and left the scene. She knew it would be some time before he texted her that night and she wanted to be home when he did. So she ran the rest of the way home.

When she reached the front doors, she wasn't expecting Joseph to be waiting for her inside.

"We need to talk Emie." Joseph told her when she closed the doors behind her in the main hall.

"I would appreciate a little privacy when I'm with Asher-"

"That's not what I need to talk to you about." He headed down the hall and Emie knew she was to follow him. She wondered what it was that was going on. Joseph never kept anything from her. Was she so distracted tonight that she missed something important at home.

When they reached his den and Joseph sat behind his desk, Emie took a seat in front of him.

"Joseph, what is it?" she inquired.

"You're putting us all at risk here Emie. Everything we are, everything we do here. You're going to have to come to terms with this sooner rather than later and stop playing with him." He was looking straight at her now. His arms lying on his desk, his hands folded together. With his messed up blonde spiky hair and red eyes, he looked very much like a determined vampire one was never to cross. His deep angelic voice filled not only her mind but spoke in a way to her that only his abilities could do. Joseph could not only make you see what you should do, he could make you do it too.

"Because none of you have ever done anything like this?" She questioned him, ashamed that he might have been out there watching her tonight. "How many times have the boys brought women home?"

"Never humans Emie! This has nothing to do with sex or dating. You can do whatever the Hell you please when it comes to that. I'm not father. This is about Asher." Joseph made her see what he was saying. He hated talking to her like this, but they all hated being compared to their father, and Emie knew better then to act like he was playing a parental role right now.

Emie knew what he was talking about. She needed to find a way to tell Asher. She was feeling more than just sex and dating with Asher, and Joseph knew it.

Hiding this from Joseph was not a good idea. Leading Asher on when she knew what all could go wrong, was very wrong. But she still hadn't a clue what she was to do about it. "I know, I'm sorry. I just don't know what to do Joseph." She told him absolutely helpless.

Joseph leaned back in his chair and took Emie's thoughts and emotions into his heart. Ran them through his mind, tried to find a way out for her. He knew how she felt about Asher, but this was too dangerous if she was toying with him. He had to make her understand that if she felt this strongly about Asher that she needed to inform him of who she really was. What she was. And that would have to be handled gently, and she was going to need their help, whether she wanted it or not.

"When you decide, if you decide, I want to know about it before you do so. This could end badly for all of us Emie. I understand your need for privacy, and we will respect that. But you need to understand that this has gone far enough. It's time to move to the next step Emie. For his sake."

Emie sighed. She knew this already. Asking Joseph for help was not something she wanted right now. She needed to think about this.

"That's fine." He said, reading her mind. "But I want to talk more about this in the morning."

Emie hung her head and reminded him she had to work tomorrow night. He knew that already, but she told him anyways. Last thing she wanted to do before she went to work was argue with him. It always made for a bad night at work.

"We will have the whole day to discuss this further. You won't be able to leave the house tomorrow anyways. It's supposed to be a sunny day. And I need you to look over some of the renovations plans before the workers get here at 10am. You've been neglecting a lot of things around here Emie."

Emie looked over at the mantel where Joseph always kept a warm raging fire going. This house, this place, just being a vampire was too cold. She knew what he said meant she would spend her day cooped up with her nagging brothers instead of out with Asher like a normal girl would be doing with him. She could never spend the day out in the warm sun with him, on the beach or just walking around town.

Emie agreed with him and headed out of his den. She started to walk up to her room slowly, thoughts of Asher and worry over what could happen if he discovered the truth overwhelming her.

Jordy appeared out of nowhere on the stairs in front of her. One minute the stairs were empty in front of her, the next, he was there sitting on the stairs hanging his head like he had been there waiting for her all night.

Emie remembered when he was young. How he used to do just this on the stairs when he should have been in bed sleeping. Instead he was waiting up for her. Their relationship had been so different from her other brothers. Jordy used to worship the ground Emie walked on. She couldn't help but smile at him when she stopped walking and he looked up at her.

"I was young, and thought you were an angel." He said to her jokingly.

"Well I am now. So you better behave!" She said poking him in the arm as she took a seat next to him on the wood stairs.

Jordy knew he still loved his sister like he did the day he was born. He couldn't remember her holding him that first night, but he could see himself in her mind and could feel the adoration coming from him at his first glimpse of her. He'd loved her every day of his life, and had always worried about her. His visions, even as a child had plagued his mind. As a child he thought they were just nightmares like she kept telling him they were, but as the reality of what happened to her came true, he learned his visions were more then just dreams.

"I need to talk to you Emie. About what I've seen." He hoped she wouldn't chide him like she had done when he was a child. Ever since that night when all their lives had changed, he'd never spoken to her again about his visions like he needed to now.

Emie hadn't wanted to know anymore since that night either. She knew after it happened that somehow Jordy had known. Somehow he had a power to see the future. It had been fun and games for her brothers now, but for her, it was haunting. She wanted to protect her brothers from whatever she could. And this she knew she couldn't protect him from.

"Do I need to know Jordy? I worry if I know too much it will change things." The way things were going with Asher she didn't want to change a single moment.

Jordy thought long and hard about what he needed to tell her without giving anything away to her. The more he knew about their future, the more he longed for her to know. He needed her to tell him what to do. What to stop and what to let happen.

When it came to Asher, and all that was about to happen around the world only he knew about, he just wanted to save her from the hurt that was coming. But she was right, he couldn't change it. What worse could happen if he did?

"If I tell you that you need to go to him tonight," and he emphasized the word tonight, "and tell him something, would you?"

Emie froze in place at that. "Asher? What should I tell him?"

Jordy smiled. He knew Asher was dying to know if Emie felt the same way he did, and he would need to know it in the days to come. Emie was cheating in the worst way by knowing how Asher felt about her. What she didn't know, what was about to come, what was going to tear her world in two, was that Asher needed to know that beyond a shadow of doubt Emie loved him.

"Something great and terrible is coming. You need to tell him you love him Emie. Or you won't get the chance too."

Jordy smiled then, the future changed in a instance, like the turning on of a light.

Asher was standing outside leaning up against the red front door smoking one last cigarette before he texted Emie and headed for his chair. He ran his hand through his hair and tried to think of what he'd say to her. Tonight would have been the perfect night to ask her to come over to his place. Try his best to figure out how to get her to spend the night and never leave him again. If it wasn't for the fire tonight, he was sure he would have. He could only hope she would have.

He was still so unsure of Emie. He really didn't know her very well. What little time he spent with her, he couldn't imagine his life without her. But when she wasn't with him, his mind would tell him things his heart didn't believe. He felt so torn.

Sometimes the fear would enter his mind and he would question it. He hated his fear. It never left him for very long. Little things would ignite it inside of him. His pager, the sirens, central dispatch calling out his department. A patient he knew was going to die. Being in a closed room too long. Not seeing Emie.

Not seeing her plagued him like no other. Like she wasn't real. If he didn't find her he never would. If he didn't tell her how he felt she'd never know.

Asher looked down at his phone he pulled out of his pocket and was about to text her when he seen her shoes on the ground in front of him.

A gut wrenching blow hit him. Like something had attacked him. He choked on his smoke and tried to regain control. His fear was filling his whole body and he couldn't contain it.

Emie felt like the worst kind monster when she scared Asher. She was so lost in his thoughts she had just walked right up to him. She really thought he would have heard her. Sometimes she forgot what she was and who he was. How had he not heard her footsteps?

He had been thinking about her spending the night with him. That couldn't happen yet. Emie was in such a hurry to tell him that she almost forgot to tell him she was right there in front of him.

"Asher? Are you ok?" She reached out for him and tried to pat his back as he coughed.

Asher, still trying to get a grip on what had happened, kept telling himself it was just Emie. He really needed to relax when she was around and try to figure out why she sparked this up inside of him.

Emie wished she could tell him. She felt like she was stringing him along by not telling him. But, after what she had heard outside she needed to tell him something altogether different tonight.

"Yeah, I'm fine." He coughed, trying to straighten up. "I just didn't see you there." When he finally looked at her, all of it, the fear, the scared shitless feeling, it all left. There she was. His Emie. Standing close enough for him to touch. For him to kiss.

Emie smiled at that. Not again. They always seemed to end up kissing instead of talking.

"I thought you were gonna walk back home?" He thought out loud. But he was glad she hadn't.

"I started too. But I ended up watching you guys fight that fire. Nice job, by the way." She winked at him. Putting her hands inside her jacket pockets so she wouldn't be tempted to touch him again. "It's the curse of working midnights, I guess. I tend to be up at night when I should be sleeping." She shrugged at him. She looked down at the road in front of her. This was going to be harder then she planned. Another lie. She never slept.

"I know how you feel. So you watched us?" he questioned her excitedly. He hoped she was impressed. It wasn't every day a girl like her came along and would accept what he did on short notice. Especially when he had stopped doing what he had with her.

"I did. Very impressed." Emie hung her head quickly. She didn't want him to see her flinch at what she had said from what she had heard in his head. Carrying on a conversation with a human was so much easier with Cristina then it would ever be with him. If she could only tell him…

When Asher caught it in his head, he shook it off as being overly worried.

She was thankful for it, but it left her worrying more. She needed to take control of the conversation tonight. She needed to tell him what Jordy had told her too. For whatever reason, he needed to know this.

"Can you go for a walk with me, there's kind of something I wanted to talk to you about."

Dread. Those dreaded words, worse sometimes then fear of death, it filled Asher. He hated those words. His dad always said them when he was mad at him. A girlfriend had said those same words too right before she walked away from their five years together.

Worse still, he couldn't leave the department right now. Even though he would go anywhere with her right now, he couldn't. What did she need to tell him? It worried him so much he was ready to go anywhere with her.

"I can't, there's no other officer in charge tonight. I missed it when I did the schedule today and left the guys with no one to run the place." He was trying to find the words to say he was sorry, when she added

"Oh, no, it's ok then. I'm sorry. You're working, Should I be here? " She asked worriedly.

Opps. She'd done it again. She was so worried about talking to him; she kept making a muck of their conversation. She had no idea he was working tonight. How had Jordy missed that?

"No, it's fine. Everyone's sleeping." Asher racked his brain trying to think of where he could take her so they could talk. He smiled at her when he thought of the perfect spot. "Ever sat in fire truck before?"

Emie's eyes lit up with excitement. Even though she was undead, there were still some things that excited her. Sitting alone in a fire truck with Asher was one of them. "No, but I would love too."

Asher quietly led Emie into the fire hall. He loved how she looked around his department like it was the most interesting place in the world to her. He pointed out the trucks to her and told her what each one was. He laughed when she asked the obvious question that everyone did, why did they name the trucks.

"We don't name them Tanker and Pumper. That's what they do. The pumper truck pumps water out when hooked up to a hydrant, and the tanker holds water in a reservoir."

Emie was tempted to check her cheeks to see if she was indeed blushing. She had never felt silly. Turning to Asher she just nodded. He would have to just think she was silly.

Asher thought she was adorable.

He pointed to the Pumper- engine 2, he corrected himself mentally, and told her to climb in. He helped Emie in the best he could without grabbing her delicate bottom that he was dying to hold in his hands again. Once she was in he shut the door quietly and climbed in the officer's seat on the passenger side. He watched her as she looked around inside the cab and read everything.

When she caught him looking at her, she shyly asked him "What?"

"Nothing. You're just so cute sitting there."

Shyness. She never would have thought she could be this shy around anyone. Emie looked down at her hands and a seriousness took over her. She felt when Asher felt it. She knew when the moment was right and started talking. "There's something I need to tell you Asher." She looked up at him. He sighed and settled in for a talk he had no idea of what was to come.

"What is it sweetheart?" He wondered quickly, worriedly, did she have a boyfriend? Was there someone else? Did she have a kid? Did she not like him? She sure as hell kissed him like she had, he reminded himself. He tried to calm down, but old fears prevented it. He really liked Emie. He really wanted Emie.

Jordy was right, Emie thought. It really was unfair of her to know how he felt and not tell him how she felt. "I've never had someone in my life." Emie choose each word carefully. Even though she had said this over and over in her head on her way here, she wanted to say just the right thing. "I've been so busy with school and work, and growing up. No one's ever come along that has just… captivated me the way you have Asher." She let that linger for a while in him. Which she was glad she had. His fears of her with someone else were finally starting to dwindle away.

But she pause for moment. She stole a second out of time to think about it all again. Was it too soon in their relationship to just blurt out she loved him?

She honestly didn't know if she could do it.

"We just seem to be moving so fast." She stopped when his breath caught and he started worrying about how young she was. She would have to leave that thought alone. Even though she longed to tell him more.

"I know. I know. 'I'm' moving to fast. And every time I'm around you I just can't keep my hands off you." Embarrassed he stopped talking too.

Opps. Emie didn't mean that.

"No! Honest. That's not what I meant." She turned in her seat more and looked over at him. "Asher. Believe me. I feel the same way as you. I love every moment we have spent and shared." she smiled to him reassuringly. And she really did feel the same as him. In every way. "It's just... you don't know me, and there are a lot of things we need to talk about. There's so much Asher, that I want to talk to you about, and share with you."

Emie was finally able to relax. It was the first time she was able to be herself around him. She wanted to tell him more. Tell him who she really was.

Asher knew that, he told himself. Of course he did. He should have been spending more time with her and keeping his hands off her. But his days were spent here or at the hospital. Thinking about the hospital only brought on thoughts of his brother. Asher put his head down torn again.

Emie worried about his thoughts. She stopped what she was thinking. She couldn't finish what she was going to tell him. Now she understood what Jordy was trying to say. If something happened in a few days, Asher needed to know she'd wait for him.

"I need you to know Asher, I totally and completely understand what all you are going through right now. With your family, the department...". She looked around at the department then and sighed. She waited for him to look at her again before she finished.

"I know right now you are going through so much, and the time we need to spend together..." She took a deep breath she didn't need, it only fueled the need. She really didn't know how to ask a guy whose brother was dying, who was trying to run a whole fire department by himself that he needed to spend more time with his girl friend. When that said girlfriend was someone he was probably going to break up with when he found out she was a monster. There really was no good way to say this... "I just don't want you to think you need to stop and be with me when you need to be with your family, or here, right now. Do not feel pressured to have to call me, or text me, or make time you can't keep. I'll wait for you Asher. Take all the time you need right now, and don't worry about trying to rush us, or make us work. I'm not going anywhere. Honestly."

Emie could hear all three of her brothers inside of her head. They were all going to ring her neck when she got home. There wasn't any more time. They were all running out of time. But what else was there to say when the man she wanted to be with was sitting next to her, begging her that this wasn't the break up talk he was dreading. He wanted her just as much as she wanted him. But... Why did she feel the need to scoop him up and take him to her home and make him see the truth?

What the hell was she supposed to do?

He couldn't deal with monsters and fairy tails right now. His brother was dyeing for Pete's sake!

You have to tell him Emie. This from Jordy. And then Joseph pushed his will like life and death depended on it. That, worried Emie.

Asher looked at Emie in amazement. She was exactly the kind of woman he had been looking for. There was no doubt now. Someone who understood family, his demanding work, his exhausting schedule. Damn, but he was falling in love with this woman. He sighed greatly and thanked her.

Emie almost gasped at what Asher thought. He loved her. From just his thoughts, knowing how he truly felt about her, she wondered if she could tell him now. Emie felt the intensity from what Jordy wanted and worried she wouldn't get the chance if something happened to Asher. "I just wanted you to know that I-"

What?

When she stopped to think what she wanted to say, they both looked at each other. Time stood still and hung on her coming words. One of those moments where there was perfect silence, but the sound of it was deafening.

He needs to know you love him Emie. Jordy's words rang true in her head. But her own heart, her breaking, dead, cold heart didn't know how to give away the one thing she had kept closed up for so long. She knew one day she might regret this if she didn't. Asher would hate her one day and she would be left with this one moment in time when she had given away the one thing that could save her from the worst kind of heartbreak.

Looking at Asher though, hanging on her next words. Almost begging her to say it aloud. She didn't know what else to do.

"Asher, I-" Emie stopped herself from looking at Asher. Damn it, why couldn't she say it. Why couldn't she tell him she loved him? Her heart felt like it was in her throat. She'd made a point of getting him here alone to tell him this and she couldn't. She didn't know how to say it. She looked down and rung her hands. She did love him. She did. She just didn't know if he could love her, forever.

"Just wait." Asher had to stop her. She looked on the brink of tears and he knew how she felt. He felt it too. He felt like an ass now for feeling everything else he had and confusing the hell out her.

He opened his door, jumped out of the truck and rushed around over to her door. Opening it he reached out for her.

When she let go and fell into his arms, it was in that moment, in that fall, the way she fell knowing he'd be there to catch her that he knew how she felt. Knew she secretly loved him and just couldn't say it.

Emie reached up and held unto him around his neck in his hair pulling him closer to her. "Asher." She whispered in a breath that was more pain then it was love.

Thoughts of Jordy came to her mind, she tried to close her eyes and will it away, but she kept seeing her little brother sitting there on the steps, hanging his head, wanting her to listen to him, but not knowing how to get her to do it. It plagued her.

Asher took in a deep breath of Emie. Holding her seemed so right. He lifted her up and held her tighter. When he finally let her down he looked down at her into her eyes. What he seen was a torn apart Emie. She was right. He didn't know anything about her. Just what he had seen. She needed his assurance that he felt the same before she could give herself completely over to him anymore. What woman wouldn't? He brushed her hair to the side that was falling in front of her eyes and kissed her forehead.

"You're absolutely right. We need more time spent together like this." He smiled down at her knowing that it didn't matter what he was doing with her, he loved spending any time with her. "If I am moving too fast for you, all you gotta do is let me know sweetheart. Right now," He looked more intently at her willing her to understand. "You're right about my life, it is a little out of control right now. And I'm just as lost as you trying my best to figure out why fate brought us together now." He willed her to understand what now meant.

He knew she would, so he finished. "But I can tell you this Emie." He reached for her face and placed it in the palm of his hand. "I have never met anyone like you before. Hell, I've never needed anyone like I need you. And I sure as Hell don't deserve you." He chuckled. Looking at how serenely she was looking at him, he almost forgot what he wanted to say. "I'm a wreck, and a mess. But I know what we have started is the best thing that's ever happened to me. Right here with you, right now, it's the only place I want to be. Every time I'm with you, I never want to leave you. If -"

Emie couldn't take anymore. She was about to cry at all his words and she couldn't. He was able to say everything she was supposed too but yet he felt like a fool. No, she was the fool. She reached up on her tippy toes and kissed him.

Asher couldn't and wouldn't let the passion he was dying to let go of unleash itself on her. He wanted to kiss her back. He wanted to push her up against the truck, lift her up on him and take her right then and there. But he couldn't. He slowed his kiss; he gave in and took what he could but he tried his hardest to stop the rushing feelings inside him. He let go of her lips and leaned his head against hers. Breathing in and out he felt her doing the same and knew she felt it too.

"We have all the time in the world right now. I swear it to you, I'll make more time for you." It meant more to him then he could ever explain that she understood this about him. That she too wanted him as much he wanted her. That she made a point of coming out here tonight and tried to tell him this. He reached around behind her pulled her tight up against him.

Emie read his thoughts. Finally, he got it. He understood what she couldn't say. She knew he would leave this and everything he held dear behind to make this happen.

Slowly she wrapped her arms around him as tight as she could and hugged him. And there it was, she told herself. That feeling she had been looking for. That feeling of being held, loved, protected and cared about all in one embrace. She let it linger inside of her, loving Asher more for it.

She looked up at him. "And I promise; I'll always wait for you. Just know that, ok? No matter what happens, I'm waiting for you." She had been waiting forever for him already. What was a few more days? What they had said tonight, what they had felt, it would just have to be enough.

Jordy sighed in the darkness out on the road. His little sister had almost changed the future again. But with those last little words, she had fixed everything.

Nine

"Good morning Sweetheart. I hope you slept well."

Asher had waited as long as he could to text Emie. He hadn't slept well, dreams of getting tangled up in Emie had haunted his night. Not having enough of her, wanting more of her. When he had finally given up trying to sleep, he reached for his phone and texted her.

After she had left last night, he felt a like a heal for trying to start a relationship with her when he knew his life wasn't ready for it. He needed her; he wanted to be with her. But right now wasn't the time. He had family to take care, a department to run. He vowed himself to sleep that he would make things right with her and slow things down.

After he got his life under control, well, that might not ever happen, but he was sure he would know when the time was right, he would start spending more time with her. Date her like he should be dating her. Not taking from her what wasn't his to take.

But, after he texted her, there was just something there… nagging at him. Something, some kind of force was trying to tell him something. And didn't know what it was.

"Good Morning Asher." She replied with a smiley face. Emie was still lying in bed day dreaming of the life to come with Asher. What could be, and what might be. She tried to think of ways to tell him what he needed to know most about her.

"I was wondering if you wanted to get breakfast this morning?" he asked.

Leave it to Asher to be thinking of food already, she thought. But it hurt to think that she couldn't leave the house this morning with him. Her thick drapes in her room were pulled tight to block the morning sun from coming in her windows off the lake.

"I would love too, but my brothers have this whole house renovation day planned out for us, and I have to work later tonight at the hospital…" And with that she knew it was starting. The lying, this being lie number three, the days she would long to be with him and couldn't. She hated this part and wondered why she had bothered with this at all with him. But thinking about that only brought on thoughts of not being with him at all. And that she knew she couldn't do. Not anymore. She was as destined to be with Asher, as she was to being a vampire.

" I understand family and work. Do you mind if I text or call you today?"

"No. Not at all." She added, " Please. It will give us a chance to talk." She smirked.

"Yeah. Something we haven't done much of..." He winked backed.

"I'll talk to you soon." She sent him another kiss and waited for his reply. Laying back on her pillow she sighed. He stirred up so many emotions inside her that she thought were long gone and dead.

He sent back a kiss to her and she closed her eyes and let the memories flood her mind of just how wonderful his lips really were.

Asher left the fire hall that morning in a wonderful mood. He wished he could have spent the day with Emie. It was a beautiful June morning, the sun was shining brightly and there wasn't a cloud in the sky. There was so much they could have done today outside in Luna Pier, but there was a lot Asher needed to do today. He needed to hold on as long as he could before he seen Emie again. He tended to lose a grasp on everything when she was around.

Not that he was complaining. He loved how he felt when he was around her, he thought with a smile on his face. Thoughts of her lately always had him smiling.

He pulled into the parking lot of the Luna Cafe restaurant and parked his truck next to the Chief of police's cruiser. Jerry, Ken Kruse and a few other men on department were also at the restaurant he noticed. Their cars and trucks were the only ones in the parking lot with huge red light bars on their vehicles. Asher walked in the doors feeling like a man lost in the clouds. But his friends were here to help spend his morning getting back into the reality of his life.

His men were seated at a round table in the back of the restaurant. When they seen Asher walk in they called him over to sit with them. Asher took a seat next to Ken and Jerry when one his favorite waitress handed him a menu. He didn't need it, the specials on the board he knew by heart. He smiled sweetly at her and thanked her for sending Emie to him the other night and then told her he would have his usual.

When she brought him coffee, and Asher waited for his breakfast to arrive while he laughed at one of Jerry's jokes.

"So, Asher. What do think of the arsons?" Jerry questioned him after a round of jokes had died down.

"Arsons?" He looked at Jerry questioningly. He knew the boat marina had been labeled as such, but what other fires had been also?

"Yeah man. These last few fires. They've all been set with boat fuel and fireworks and the owners were never home." He looked at

Asher like he should have known this, but Asher was still sitting there looking dumbfounded.

Asher knew there had been one other fire other then the first street fire last night. He hadn't been on that call. He remembered the owner being there last night when he got on scene, but he hadn't been in charge of talking to the guy.

"Those kids at the marina that night haven't been seen or heard from since. The caller from last night wasn't the owner, he split as soon as we showed up. The actual owner got there after the fire and wanted to know what in hell happened to his house. The one on sixth street the other day, the owners hadn't been home all day. That fire was ignited also with fireworks and boat fuel. Whoever is doing this, they're leaving a signature behind. But it's clear, it is arson."

Asher took that in, remembering one of the men talking about a smell at that fire last night. It hadn't looked or worked like a normal house fire they had said.

"It sounds like kids are doing this. Their sloppy and know our response time. I think it's time we have a meeting." Jerry continued on, leaning in and telling Asher about the smells inside the fire and how they needed to warn the men. Those fires had burned hot, and living in Luna Pier all those fires needed was an east wind to ignite more than one house. "Haven't you been watching the news? There's a lot more going on around us we should be worrying about."

Asher stopped breathing. He hadn't watched any tv in awhile. He used his hot cup to warm his hands from the chill running through his body. If there was an arsonist starting fires in Luna Pier, they could have more trouble than they needed. His mind had been so distracted with…

Ken, next to Asher heard the conversation the two men were having and knew this was more than Asher needed to handle right now. Jerry was always acting like a cop instead of a friend to Asher. Ken was the young Fire Chaplin on the department and one of Asher's best friends. He knew Asher's mood when he had walked in was gone now, and could think of only one thing that would lighten him back up again.

Ken leaned towards Asher's younger brother and looked over at Asher as soon as the waitress set down Asher's food. Ken hadn't seen Asher eat in days and knew he couldn't afford to miss this meal, and with the conversation Jerry was having with Asher was only spoiling his appetite. Anyone who knew Asher knew he looked like he had been missing more then one meal a day since the marina fire. "So, Asher. Who was that beauty you were running away with the other day? I don't believe we've ever seen her around the department before."

And that was all it took for the other men to join in the banter towards Asher, Jerry's conversation forgotten. Everyone at the table wanted to know who the woman with Asher was.

Asher sat back in his chair and stared at his food. He wanted to know more about what Jerry was talking about, but he really didn't have the mind or the stomach to process it right now. He smiled over at his friend Ken who he could always be count on to lighten up the mood around the fire hall, even after some of the worst calls, Ken never liked to linger on the bad for too long. He had a wife and two little girls at home that Asher adored like his own family. Ken never liked to bring that home to them, and this was how he did that. Getting everyone's mind off the bad, if even for just a moment.

"Her name is Emie. Emilie Whitby."

"Joseph Whitby's sister?" This from James, his younger brother.

Asher knew what James was thinking. Their father and the Whitby family went back for generations.

Asher's father Frank had been fighting with the city and Joseph for years over what the fire department needed when it came to gear, new trucks, or supplies. Asher and his siblings had been raising money for the fire department since they were kids because the city always made financial cuts starting first with the police and fire department. Frank was not going to like the idea of his son dating Joseph's sister. Not at all.

Looking at his brother James, who was a lot like Asher's father and hated the Whitby family, wondered what James was thinking now. James had been married once to a girl with the same last name as Emie. He wondered if they were related.

Asher didn't care. Maybe their relationship, if he even got that far with Emie, maybe it could be the tie that bonded everything together with his family and the city. Hell, maybe even Asher could learn something from the Whitby's and run for city council himself. Something his father should have thought about years ago instead of just fighting the city.

"Yes." Asher told his brother pointedly, as he leaned over his breakfast and started dipping his toast in his yokie eggs. He was still reeling from what Jerry had said, memories of the fires tried to rear their ugly head just as he was about to take his first bite. Asher looked over at Ken and seen the way he was looking at Asher. Asher knew from his look that he too knew that Asher needed a distraction. And Emie was not just a distraction. She was becoming what Asher could only hope was the love of his life and his Angel he needed so desperately. So Asher continued the conversation that he knew the men wanted. He told them about Emie. How they met, their first date, and about how damn beautiful he thought she was.

Talking about Emie seemed to spark other conversations. Ken talked about his wife and kids. Jerry talked about his daughter who was in basketball at the high school. Bob talked about his daughter also.

Asher had time to finish his whole meal, which he hadn't realized had filled a void inside of him he hadn't known was there. Asher felt a hundred times better.

When they cleared out of the little restaurant three hours later Ken stood next to Asher's truck and talked to him more privately.

"So, Emillie Whitby? Really?" Ken asked with a huge smile on his face for his friend.

Asher put a leg up on his truck wheel as they leaned over the bed of his truck in casual conversation. He lit a cigarette and blew out the smoke before he answered. He was smiling just as much as Ken. "Yeah. Ken, let me ask you something, I remember you and Miranda, you guy's hit it off quick, but how did you know? When did you know?"

Ken had to chuckle at that. He'd been with Miranda since right after high school. It had been 15 years for them, and it had been an ever changing relationship for them. He loved her more and more every moment she was with him. But he knew this question. He had felt same way Asher did right now when he had fallen in love with Miranda.

"It all happened so quick Ash. One minute we were just talking, and I couldn't stop looking at her. The next minute we were planning out the next time we could see each other. And it just got to this point where we never wanted to say goodbye anymore. It's been that way ever since.

"There was this one moment though, we had just starting dating and I knew it was all happening but I wasn't trying to rush it or anything. I had come to church with an old girlfriend who was wanting to join the church, we sat together in the front. Nothing going on, just two friends sitting together, and as we were walking out after the services, Miranda who had been working in the back in Sunday school, she seen us walking out together, and the look I seen in Miranda eyes Asher, man it killed me. She was crushed, and so unsure of what was happening. I had hurt her, and I hadn't even done anything wrong. But that look, it haunted me. It still haunts me. I knew then that I loved Miranda and I never ever wanted to hurt her. I thought I had lost her in that one moment. But she just smiled at us and carried on like nothing had happened, but to me, man," he said shaking his head, the thoughts clearly still weighing on his mind, "so much happened in that one moment.

"So I guess you could say it was then. You don't realize it until they're no longer there. When you miss them so bad you can't stand it. That's when you know."

Asher looked up and knew exactly what he meant.

"It's weird Ken, I mean, I never really ever wanted anyone before, you know what I mean?" He questioned him, not really looking at him, just talking to him. "She's all I think about, all I want. There is no where else I want to be man, no one else I want to be with. I just want to see her, and spend time with her. It's never been like that before with anyone."

"It's serious then?"

"I think it is for me. And she seems just as taken by it Ken. She's always right there ready to spend time with me. Ready to… well, you know." Asher took another hit of his smoke to hide his bashfulness. He wondered why he felt that, he had never had a problem talking about women and things they had done before. But with Emie, it just seemed rude to talk about her like that with anyone.

"Wow, it is serious." Ken liked to know this. Asher had never had anyone to speak of in his life after his ex. Girls had come and gone, but they had always hated Asher's fascination with the department and never understood why he spent more time there then with them.

"How does she feel about you and Fire Department?"

They both knew what this question meant. There was honor and pride in these men. A dedication none of them could describe when it came to the department. When someone's life was in danger, or when the department itself needed them, they would always answer the call. No matter what. People on the outside just didn't see that or understand it. They too would have to feel it, or the friendships never lasted.

"You know, she totally gets it. She knows what I'm doing, where I'm going, and she's ok with it. She has a demanding job and family. Trying to make time for each other is going to be hard, but it will be what we need and want. I really think this just might work Ken. I really do."

Asher finished and flicked his cigarette away and continued after he adjusted his shoulder. No matter what position he was in lately, the damn thing bothered him. "I need this to work Ken. I need her like I need a vacation away from all this. There's so much going on right now, I find myself just wanting to run away with her sometimes."

"That might be what you need man. Do you know how long it's been since you've taken time off?"

Asher had to think about that. He was too sick with the flu last summer to go up north to his cabin. The guys usually went up there once a year on a trip. They would hunt, fish, four wheel all around East Lake in the upper peninsula. "Yeah it's been it awhile."

Thoughts of Curtis came rushing back to him. Up north at the cabin was Curtis's favorite place in the world. And so it had been Asher's too. They lived for those trips up north. They would prepare for it all year long. Buy the things they would need to fill the cabin, make short trips up there to make repairs, make preparations and just goof off. To get away from everything and everyone. To just be themselves.

Now, with Curtis dying, he knew a lot of things were going to be different now.

What Jerry said about the news started to creep in the back of his mind. "Hey, what did Jerry mean about the news? What else is going on?"

Ken looked away. Asher knew that was bad. Ken looked like he had seen a ghost off in the distance. Asher almost followed his gaze to see.

"You know how it is. Wars and rumors of wars. Some people go missing and all of a sudden it's all over the news that the enemy is here. It's nothing. Just a lot of hype and speculation and what if's."

Asher knew the United States was at war. He also knew the reasons why. He and Ken hadn't joined the military after school like a lot his cousin and class had at graduation. They were needed here in the states to watch and care for the home front. That was their calling. This is where they belonged. When and if war ever came home, they would be here to keep watch. To help.

Ken slapped Asher on the shoulder, it was that male comrade showing of affection. Ken's way of saying everything was ok. And with that Asher knew it was time for Ken to head home. His wife was going to kill him for taking so long at breakfast with the guys. But she would forgive him like she always did. Ken and Miranda had one of those unusual relationships. They had been married for fifteen years and still held hands, still cuddled on the couch together. They never did or went anywhere without each other. They even texted each other all day long. Asher admired their relationship. One Asher hoped he could have with Emie.

"Tell Miranda I said hi." Asher told his friend as he walked to his car. Ken waved behind him and raced home to his wife.

Asher opened his door to his truck and climbed in. When he started it, he looked out the window behind Luna Cafe. A chill ran up his spin as he looked past the restaurant and past the burnt down Marina. Behind the Marina, behind the canals that divided Luna Pier from the Whitby land was a mansion of a house that was lost in the forest around it. Only the tops of its peaks could be seen from the city. He knew now that he knew Emie that the land and house was just that. A home for the Whitby's. But when he was younger, the stories of old of what was back there still haunted him.

Asher shook it off. His sister Izzy last night had her nose buried in one those vampire books she liked and it drove Asher crazy. Why she liked those new novels he would never understand.

It was all the talk now a days. Vampires and Werewolves. It was no wonder he couldn't shake that fear from the old stories whenever he looked over at the Whitby land.

He cranked up the radio to the country song and sang aloud with the windows down and headed home. "People are crazy!"

Emie was walking around the house behind her brothers, going from room to room, looking at blueprints and discussing what all would needed to be repaired and done around the mansion. Joseph had one of the servants taking notes and carrying the papers as they went along. His mind was filled with more than Emie had ever seen before. He was worried about the renovations. He was worried about how distracted Jordy had become lately with his visions, and he was worried about Emie and Asher.

Jordy had even made a comment about stocking the kitchen with human food and upgrading the main floor bathroom. "Just incase." He had winked at Emie, knowingly letting her in on a secret only he knew about.

Emie sighed as she glanced at her phone again. She couldn't help but be distracted by the fact Asher hadn't yet texted her. She was worried about him too. What was he doing? Was he alone with all his thoughts and fears? How was his brother doing?

Emie couldn't wait to get to work tonight so she could check on Curtis. She knew his condition was headed in the wrong direction. She knew he wasn't going to make it much longer, but she hoped for Asher's sake his death would come quickly so his family could let go of him and grieve.

Moments later, when Joseph and the boys were discussing plans for his den that wouldn't include her, her phone vibrated in her pocket. Joseph noticed when it happened and let her know it was ok for her to take a moment by herself to respond.

Emie walked over to the fire and sat in one of the circle of chairs. It was Asher.

"How is your day going sweetheart?" his text asked.

Emie took a deep breath. She was so overwhelmed by the emotions of the day and the way she felt for him. She texted back right away so he would know she had been waiting for him.

"Boring. Following my brothers around the house is not something I wanted to do today. How is you day?"

"Good. Had breakfast with some friends. Went home, got some much needed stuff done around my house. Stopped by the hospital and spent some time with my brother. I'm at the store now getting some things and realized something I needed to ask you."

Emie smiled at that. She could just picture herself there with him, walking around the store enjoying herself. She wished she was there with him.

"Anything, just ask."

Wanting to ask her questions, getting to know her better, 'talking', like he promised her he would do, as he came around a corner in the store he realized he didn't know very much about her. Like her favorite food. So he asked.

"Just incase I ever need to know, what is your favorite kind food?"

Oh! If he only knew about these questions he always seemed to ask her, she thought as she watched her brothers argue about a picture none of them liked hanging in this room. Quickly she thought of a cheeky reply.

"I love a good raw piece of meat. Something dripping with juices and pink."

Asher stood in the middle of the grocery store stunned by her reply. He had to lift one leg up on his cart to hide any evidence her reply had done to him. "My kind of woman." He replied back with a winky face.

"And you?" she asked, enjoying this conversation tremendously. "Just in case I ever need to know?"

Asher loved southern cooking. But for the life of him, in the middle of a store, he couldn't think of anything sensual to reply with southern foods. So he said, "I love dessert. Lathered in cream or bathed in fruit."

"I'll keep that in mind." She told him.

Asher's mind swam with all the possibilities of Emie's body lathered in cream and bathed in anything. His shopping trip needed to come to an end soon. Every food he seen brought him closer and closer to insanity thinking about her.

"When can I see you again Emie?" he asked her sweetly, honestly.

"I will be at the hospital all night tonight." she hated that she had to work tonight.

"I was going there tonight with my family. Mind if I stop by and say hi?"

"Please do." She sent him an encouraging smiley face and hoped he would. It thrilled her beyond words that she could see him at work.

"I'll text you when I can from there. Maybe we can meet up in our elevator?" He winked.

Emie's smile almost brought tears to her eyes. She had never shared anything with anyone before. To hear him say 'ours' about something they shared filled her with a joy she had never expected.

"I'll meet you there." But her moment of joy was spoiled by Joseph's intrusion.

You really need to stop playing Emie.

Emie growled over at her brother. He wasn't even looking her way and yet he had intruded like he promised he wouldn't.

It's time to talk. He reminded her.

Emie waited as her brothers approached her and sat down. Joseph walked over to the mantle by the fire and faced them.

"He has to know about us. Before you and him can go any farther in this relationship." He told her.

"Why? Why now. He's about to lose his brother and you all know that!"

Jordy answered her question. "I've seen it Emie." And more.

He wouldn't tell her what the more part was about, he knew she didn't want to know, but he did show her what would happen with Asher. Asher would become one of them soon. But before that, there was a storm coming, and that he could show her.

Life here on earth was ever changing. People and societies were constantly building and dying off. This last century had lasted longer than any of them had predicted. The world had grown stronger in technology and war was eminent. But this would not be a war between the humans or the one they planned for; it was going to be a war between them. The vampires. A war that would destroy the world as the humans knew it. A war that was already in the making. And the Whitby's had no idea how to stop it.

Telling Emie, saving Emie; her brothers didn't know how too.

There were vampires like them who co-existed with the humans peacefully. Enjoying their freedom and living like they were both human and vampire. But there were also vampires in the world who wanted control. Who wanted to rule this world instead of the humans, and take over as kings. Some centuries, those vampires outnumbered them. This century was one of them. Stopping them in this day in age would surely mean the humans would find out their secret. And that would cause a war no one could predict the outcome. Not even Jordy.

Emie sighed at her brothers thoughts. They had been hiding all this from her.

Joseph told Emie about the fires around Luna Pier. "They weren't kids Emie, like Asher thinks. They were rouge vampires. They know we are here and they are testing our boundaries. They can not breech our walls, but Luna Pier is an open playing field for them. You putting yourself out there with Asher means they see you too."

Jordy spoke up then. "Last night, while you were out there watching the fire Asher was at, I had followed a group of vamps. They were watching Asher. Then they watched you."

"So what do we do?" Emie questioned him worriedly. She was worried now about Cristina, about Asher and his family. All the people in the city she knew and loved were vulnerable if these rouge vamps were in Luna Pier.

"There's time. They are just testing us now, like they are doing all around the world." Jordy went into details about different countries and the alliances he had in those places. "What their intentions are none of us know about. Rager, my friend in Ireland, has seen one of these groups. He says the military knows about them and are fighting against them keeping everything a secret in our intelligence agencies.

"Our friends the Weavers in Paris said the same about a cell there in France. This war the Americans are fighting in the Middle East very well might be a war with vampires they are fighting." Which everyone in the room knew was going to end worse then when it started. Because if the government knows about vampires, then the whole world would know soon also.

Joseph stopped Jordy from going on further. "We will take it on day at time from here. We have time, and we have much to do." This last he directed towards Emie.

Emie knew Joseph was talking about her and Asher. Emie had a mess to clean up. She could see that now.

Thoughts of Asher flooded her mind. She looked at Joseph before she left the room without them and told Joseph how she really felt. I love him Joseph. I love him.

Nothing else mattered to her right now then loving him and protecting him. How to go about doing that, without losing him was an entirely different question. She needed time away from her brothers. She needed to think. And she couldn't think when all they wanted to talk about was war, and decorating their den. She shouted back at them "Let me know when you're ready to start talking about my room!"

~ *Ten* ~

Driving to the hospital that night Asher found himself speeding through the little city at a pace he was sure was going to get him pulled over for. But he couldn't help himself. He was in a hurry to see Emie again.

Asher had spent his day getting things done. He ate three meals, cleaned his house, and spent time with his dog. He went and seen his brother, which he knew would probably be for the last time, a trip he knew he would never regret. The doctor there told him it was time to let Curtis go. He would be telling Asher's family soon.

Asher took this as a sign that it was time. Holding out for his brother to one day wake up was just cruel. Curtis wouldn't want to wake up from this. His body was too badly burnt and broken. He would need extensive surgery and much more. The doctor had assured Asher that his brain had been crushed in the fall. There had been no brain activity in days. Curtis, if he ever did wake up, would never be the same.

Then Asher made a shopping trip to stock up on things he knew he was going to need at home and around the department. He knew people would be spending time at the fire hall in the coming days and food was always a good thing to have around the department.

He thought of good times with his brother, and tried to spend time thinking about his family. He even went over to Curtis's house to check on things. The little house on third street looked abandon. Curtis had always kept up on his yard work. Asher made a mental note to have someone come over and tend to it. They would have to sell everything after Curtis passed.

Asher looked over his brother's truck while he was there. It was a new red pick up truck. He thought to himself it was newer then his old one. It'd be a pity to let someone else have it. Asher would have to talk to his parents about letting him have it. It would be a nice memento of his brother.

He had tried to watch the news, he really had, but he couldn't pay attention to it. Nothing the media were talking about made any since. Hadn't the US been at war since 9-11? What was different now? Who were they looking for?

Everything he had done today made him think about Emie though. He'd seen things that reminded him of her and he had missed her. Wanting her in his life had become a constant thought today and drove him wild when he thought of seeing her again. There was so much more he wanted to know about her and learn about her. He knew spending time with her was the only way to find out those things.

Asher had found himself thinking about Emie every minute of the day. No one had ever had that effect on him. No one had ever consumed his thoughts, overwhelmed his emotions, high jacked his heart like Emie had. It was humbling to say the least, but also endearing.

Ignorance in love had worried him all day, and the fool he was when it came to women scared him to death. Losing Emie now would certainly impact his life in a way he wasn't prepared for yet. He had to get to her to stay in his life and his heart for as long as he could. He needed this woman like he needed to breathe.

He texted her as soon as he parked his truck and was walking through the revolving doors of the main entrance of the hospital. She had agreed to meet him in their elevator they first met in. To Asher, the slow decent into the basement felt like the longest ride of his life.

When the doors opened on the basement floor and Asher seen Emie waiting in the hall for him, Asher couldn't believe what he was seeing. She looked the same as she had the day he had first met her. It was like deja vu. The same black scrubs and white shirt, the same shoes, everything was the same. Everything but her smile.

Emie's smile now was so loving. She was smiling for him. Because she too felt what Asher felt.

Emie took one look at Asher and knew he was ok. He looked good, and healthy. Happy even. She had never needed to know those things about anyone before. The need to know them about Asher was different, and yet so relieving. Her brothers had scared her today and she found herself worrying about Asher.

She felt like flying into his arms, but steadied herself. Joseph and Jordy's words were still haunting her. But she knew she had time for that later. Right now Asher needed her. He needed her to be everything she had been. Not some demon vampire that would scare the hell out him. Not yet.

"Hello there." She greeted him with a smile.

"Hello sweetheart." He greeted her back stepping out of the elevator and into the hallway with her.

Asher enveloped her in a hug as soon as he reached her and sighed away a part of him that had been breaking all day. She was like a healing high to him that filled him with joy and pleasure. She was better than any drink or nicotine. He fell to pieces when her arms wrapped around his neck and she held him just as close like she had needed to touch him too. Like her day wasn't complete until she had this direct contact that he had been longing for all day. Knowing that they had forever to spend like this if they choose too was all it took to settle him down, calm his fears of losing her. It was the best feeling he had ever felt in his entire life.

Emie had to close her eyes when Asher's mind wrapped around his every emotion. Her abilities to help people feel the emotions they needed was a power she never had time to help Asher with. Just her presence in his life was enough for him. It humbled Emie. She too needed him. Needed his stability, his strength to live, laugh and love life together with her. She didn't understand it yet, but she believed in it.

Emie nuzzled closer to Asher's neck and warmth. He picked her up in his arms and held her closer letting her slide down his body and when her feet touched the ground he nuzzled his face in her hair and breathed in her scent.

Asher had finally found the peace he had been searching for all his life. He had been a guarded book all his life, and now he felt like the pages of his life finally had meaning. Finally had a purpose. He was holding on to it with all he had, just to see what the next chapter in his life was going to be. There was so much healing he needed, and was going to need. And Emie was all of that and more.

"Emie, I have to meet my family in about an half hour upstairs." This he said as he pulled back and looked down on her. "Do you have time to get away for awhile to meet them?"

Emie knew this was important to him. Important in any relationship. The meeting of the families, getting to know the others in their lives. She worried about it. She knew his family might not approve of his choice. With all the strife that had been there for years between their families. And there was the whole she was a vampire thing... But somehow she knew she had to do this. Joseph's words still wrung in her head. It was time to move to the next steps in their relationship. She breathed him in and looked up at him.

"I would love to meet your family Asher." She smiled up at him.

He smiled back, placing a simple kiss on her lips, he lingered there just long enough to feel the passion rise in him that he had missed all day long.

At the sound of a woman's voice clearing they both turned and looked towards the sound of Cristina standing in the hall next to them. She smiled brightly at Emie and pushed the button to call the elevator.

Emie looked lovingly at Cristina. They had just spent half an hour in Emie's office discussing Asher. Cristina had agreed with Emie with her choice to not tell Asher who she really was. It wasn't time yet.

"Cristina, this is Asher Stone. Asher, this is my very best friend, Cristina."

Cristina chuckled at Emie and winked at her. She held out her hand to Asher in greeting. "It's nice to meet you. Emie has told me so much about you."

Asher was blushing three shades of red now. Cristina looked like she knew every last detail about how Emie felt about him. "I hope it was good things," he took her hand in his and shook it gently. "It's nice to meet you too."

When the elevator arrived again, Cristina, Emie and Asher walked in. Asher held Emie's hand as Cristina stood in the back. He pushed the button for the lobby and decided they would go to the cafeteria till it was time for his family to arrive. Cristina was headed for the third floor and winked sheepishly at Emie when they stepped off the elevator into the lobby of the hospital.

Emie was so glad to see Cristina, even if it had been for just a moment. Her approval of the two of them was written all over her face and it warmed Emie to the core.

Emie held Asher's hand as they walked to the little caf on the main floor. The hospital was changing rapidly over the last year. The only time she ever stopped in the caf was when Cristina was famished and didn't want to eat alone on their lunch breaks. Normally she would sit with a tray full of food for Cristina and pick at things so no one would guess she wasn't eating. Emie had hated the façade. A charade they all had to play in order to keep the secrets of her life. But she always played along.

Now with Asher, she would have to do the same. It sadden her to think about it, but the alternative was even worse. She walked with him through throngs of people there; nurses and doctors, hospital workers, guest in the hospital that were visiting family. She could see in the minds of those who knew her and some of those who knew of Asher, small town that this city was, she wasn't surprised he knew a lot of people here. He nodded at another couple who were waiting in line holding their trays also. They smiled warmly at them when they seen Asher and Emie holding hands.

"So, have you had dinner yet?" Asher asked.

"Yes, actually I did, before I left home. Are you hungry?" she was so relieved for the out he had given her. She hated lying to him.

"I did too, I had fast food. I could eat dessert though, you?"

Emie smiled up at him, he was so cute when he thought about food. He was so shy about it. His shoulders hunched and his stomach made noises like it was begging him for food. "Yes. That sounds good. They just put in a new bar over there. It's full of fresh desserts." She pointed it out and watched as his eyes lit up at the bar full of his favorite food.

Asher moved her through the crowd and decided on what he wanted. They walked over to the drink coolers next and he grabbed a soda for him and held the door open so she could grab herself something too. He looked her up and down as she reached in the cooler for her water bottle. She was unlike anything he had ever believed he would find in a woman. Her figure, her hair, her smile. The way she looked at him like she was just as taken with him stirred things inside of him that was very inappropriate for him to be feeling in a crowded room.

He paid for their small meal and led her into the dinning area. She chose a booth seat and he slid in next to her.

"So when will everyone get here?" she asked him.

Asher looked out the main hall to where the front entrance was. "They should be here soon. Izzy promised to text me when they get here."

"Your sister?" Emie asked.

"Yeah. My sister, my parents, and hopefully my two brothers." Asher rubbed his eyes after he opened his drink. Everyone was coming up here together to say goodbye to Curtis. He hopped they wouldn't mind meeting Emie first. She just might be the ice that breaks every one's mood tonight.

Emie listened in to his thoughts and grabbed hold of her abilities tight. She was going to need them tonight she could see. If need be, she would just pretend she needed to get back to work. She inquired of their names, and some small talk to get his mind off things. She learned that his grandparents would be up here later too.

"You're sure your ok with this."

"Oh, yes. Honest. I'm just a little nervous that's all." She adjusted her hair like Cristina would do, and wished she had brought her phone with her so she could take a quick glance at herself. She hadn't felt this nervous in so long, she had almost forgotten what this felt like. It wasn't like she had changed much from the last time she had looked in a mirror. Her image was frozen in place and had been for some time now.

"Emie, you're beautiful." Asher said setting down his fork, realizing he had just eaten almost the whole piece of the red velvet cake they had picked out. She had told him it was her favorite too and he had hogged the whole thing. "My family is going to love you. They all already know about you." He said adjusting in his seat and leaning in towards her more. He could feel the chill coming off her body and he wanted her to relax and be herself. Not the bundle of nerves she appeared to be now.

"They do?" she looked sheepishly at him, lowering her head and looking down at the table she thought, wow, when was the last time she had felt like this? Around anyone!

"Well, yeah. Izzy says it's written all over my face that I'm-"

He paused. Why had he paused? Emie stopped breathing so she could listen into his mind, but it was his heart rate that was deafening hers.

Asher's smile lit up his face. She could tell it was a smile bigger than she'd ever seen. It reached his eye and a very small, microscopic tear had formed at the corner of his eye. His cheeks, how she adored his rosy cheeks when he felt bashful; were filling with heat and rushing blood. She was dying to place her palm on his cheek so she could feel it. The presence of his blood so present in his body made her mouth water.

Asher laughed a little aloud, knowing it was true now what Izzy had said about him the other night. "Izzy says I look like I'm in love." He looked at Emie, looked straight into her eyes. He wanted her to know that not only did his family see it, but he did too.

Emie couldn't help it. She smiled too. His happiness over that statement was so contagious. She wished she could pinch her pale cheeks so he could see the blush she knew she was feeling, but would never outwardly show like the one he was sporting now. She had to contain her excitement over his statement of love.

"Well." And that was all the words she could form at the moment. She looked down and her smile never faded.

"And my mom, she can't wait to meet you." Asher added, cause really, what else could he say. He had just confessed to loving her, and all she had said was "Well." But her feelings were clearly there in her smile. He'd be a fool not to know what that proud smile meant.

Emie knew she should say something back, but just as she was about to tell him she felt the same, his phone whistled.

"Speak of the devil." He grunted aloud, looking at his phone "It's Izzy. They're here." He texted Izzy back and told her he would meet them in the front entrance.

Looking over at Emie he realized she was ready for this. He only hopped that she would share her feelings for him. She hadn't said otherwise, but there hadn't been time. Stupid as he was, he had surprised her with it. He should have waited he thought as they slid out of the booth and he reached for her hand again.

Holding Emie's hand had become something he had never seen himself doing with someone. But he liked doing it with her. It was contact. Contact he couldn't seem to live without now. He smiled down at her when they reached the main hall and liked that she snuggled up next to him and held onto his arm with her other hand. He smirked to himself knowing she needed it too.

Asher felt his hair raise on the back of his neck as his family walked through the main doors. It didn't matter what they thought about her, he thought. His father could go to hell in hand bag for all he cared. This woman meant the world to him, and if he couldn't see that then the old man was blind.

Emie held onto Asher. His feelings for his father were worse then Joseph's feeling for his father. She calmed him as gently as she could, felt as he took a deep breath and physically relaxed. Which relaxed her in return. They would get through this together she knew.

Izzy was the first to greet Emie. She was so excited to meet her that her blonde curls bobbed when she walked up to them. "Hi! I'm Asher's sister Izzy." Izzy said holding out her hand to Emie.

Emie returned her greeting, "Hi Izzy, It's nice to finally meet you." shaking the small, young woman's warm hand. Something in the back of Emie's mind hesitated at the feel of Izzy's hand. She felt Jordy's presence and almost turned her head to look for him. But she steadied herself and shook it off. Her pestering brothers needed to give her some space, she said in her mind just in case they were listening.

Asher's mother was right behind Izzy smiling brightly at Emie. But behind her eyes, in her heart, Emie could feel the pain that no mother should ever know. She was dying inside. Slowly. Emie willed her the strength she was going to need tonight. This woman was very strong, Emie was sure Joseph would like her immediately. But tonight, if she made it through tonight, she was thoroughly broken. No mother should ever have to bury a child.

"Emie. It's nice to meet you." His mother smiled.

"Emie, this is my mother, Cyndy Stone." He said quietly in a voice of reverence towards his mother. "My father, Frank." He stated simply. "And my younger brothers; Jesse and James." And then he added, as if waiting a blow to the gut, "Everyone, this is Emie. Whitby." He hadn't meant to say her name like that. Like her last name was an after statement. But to his family, he wanted them to know it didn't matter what her last name was. At least to him.

Jesse smiled approvingly at Asher she noticed. He liked Emie too. But Frank, he was casting daggers at Asher. When he finally looked at Emie, she had to try not to cringe. His anger towards them was very evident.

Emie reminded him of Joseph. And Joseph reminded him of why Curtis was dying.

Blood sucking-

Emie heard his thoughts and had to cut him off.

"Well," Emie hurriedly stated. As happily as she could fake, she looked at each of them in overwhelming greeting.

Frank knew something he shouldn't. Emie was instantly scared. A feeling no vampire should ever feel, but for Emie, who loved Asher, yes, she said it, loved him like life itself, she was scared. This new information meant more then she knew how to handle in front of his family. She could already hear Joseph screaming in her head, and knew he was right. It was time to bail.

"It is such a pleasure meeting you all. I hate to cut this short, but I've already been away from work too long."

She turned to Asher as she finished and reached up to place a kiss on his cheek. He was still holding her hand and didn't look like he was about to let her go just yet. "I'll call you later?" she asked sweetly.

"Ok. I'll, see soon." Asher relented, but still wondered worriedly why she was bolting. If his father had caused this by his unwelcoming stair, Asher would surely put him in his place later.

Emie was surprised when he finally let her go. He had held her hand a moment too long, noticeable to everyone, confusion written on his wondering face. She wanted to stay. She wanted to go up stairs with him and be there while he said good bye to his brother. She wanted to hold his hand and be everything he needed her to be in those moments. But she couldn't. And he didn't understand why. It was all now because of Frank.

It hurt her like a knife cuts through the heart. How was it possible Frank knew her family were vampires?

She was hurrying towards the elevator doors, their elevator, when she heard Joseph tell her he was on his way. She would have to cut him off before he got up here. Her brothers were on edge already, this would just fuel them to no end. No harm had come to her, and no harm would come to her tonight. She couldn't say the same for the Stone family.

When the double doors opened wide, she walked in not looking back.

Joseph was going to be livid. She knew Frank had his reasons for hating them. Frank and Joseph had been fighting over money and politics for many years. But she had never thought he would blame Joseph for his son's death. She had never ever thought that he knew they were vampires. Never, she thought shaking her head as the elevator descended to the basement. She hugged her arms and for the first time in a long time she prayed. It was the only true comfort she had felt other then being in Asher's arms.

Her life was spiraling out of control. Down into a pit. She could only hope she was able to save herself and Asher.

She could see them all walking into Curtis's room, as she rested her head against the back wall of the elevator. They would all hurt, and break. All those wonderful people were about to face the worst human pain possible. And there was nothing she could do to help them. She would never be able to either, not now. She really had been a fool thinking she could secretly act like a human and no one would notice. Frank could ruin all of this for her. Make Asher see her for the monster she was, and wasn't. It hurt to think it, but it was so true. She wasn't the monster Frank and the whole world thought she was. She'd spent her life trying not to be…

When the doors opened and Joseph was standing on the other side, she ran into his arms. It was an awkward hug, seeing she never hugged him, and he had no idea how to hold her, but it was a hug nonetheless.

"I'm sorry. I'm so sorry." Tears of blood flowed from her eyes, her heart cracked. All the tears she had kept bottled up before with Asher when she couldn't cry and needed too, finally broke free. "Joseph, it hurts so bad. I love him. I love him so much." She wept into his chest.

Joseph groaned and sighed. He wrapped Emie in a strong, awkward hug and told her it was all going to be alright. All his anger, all his frustrations, none of them mattered now. Damn all of them, he told himself. Emie was crying in his chest she barley measured up too. His little sister had taken the weight of the world on her shoulders, and all she had ever wanted was to be loved. She wanted to love Asher so badly she was willing to risk so much.

"How does he know Joseph?"

Joseph sighed and stood up a little straighter. He didn't know how or why Frank knew. He squeezed Emie tighter. "I don't know. But I'll find out soon. I promise."

When Emie started to look up at him in protest, he calmed her and told her softly Not tonight.

There was a storm coming, and he had to deal with Frank soon, but Asher was about to lose his brother and best friend. And to Emie, nothing else, not the world and all the damn humans, not the threat of an impending war they might lose, and not even the fact that Frank had almost given her away in front of a crowd full of people, nothing else mattered to her then the pain Asher was about to feel.

Joseph wanted to take it all off her shoulders. He wanted to tell her a secret he too had been hiding from her, but he couldn't. She would have to go through this. She would have to understand Asher's pain and feel it so she could him. But she wouldn't be alone in it. He would be there for her tonight, whatever she needed. Joseph held her until her tears stopped. Until she had used his shirt as a rag that was all stained with her shed blood. Until she could walk away on her own and handle the night's events on her own.

It was almost too much to watch her do it. As proud of her as he was, she would forever be his little sister. She was stable and sturdy, but when she was hurting she could crumble under the weight. And he loved her for how wonderful she truly was. Emie was the most caring, compassionate woman Joseph had ever met. She cared deeply, and loved honestly. She wore her heart and feelings on her sleeves sometimes, and her mind was always worrying about everyone and everything. She really needed to learn she couldn't change the world or fix everything. It would be the death of her one day.

When she left his side and returned to her job, he knew she could handle things. He also knew the nights events were about to change her fate. But that also was something he couldn't take from her. Joseph left the hospital in search of his brothers. They would have to decide again what needed to be done. Frank would just have to wait till after the funeral to be dealt with.

When Asher and his family got up to Curtis's room, the fight Asher had been dreading started between him and his father.

"Where have you been?" his father barked, outside the room. The rest of the family had went into Curtis's room, and Frank had stepped in front of Asher blocking his path. The aging man, the same height as Asher and his brothers, was barely holding onto life these days. His graying hair was all most covering his dark blonde hair, and his rumbled clothes made him look like a man who was falling to pieces.

Asher had known he had taken to long at the department and getting things done around his house, utterly ignoring his father for days. He knew his scattered thoughts of the fire and Emie where slowing his progress. "Dad, I had to help with all the investigations. Some one has to clean up, someone had to pay everyone this week. Someone had to run the department because you foolishly ran into a burning building without even a squirt gun that night!"

"That's what I do! That's what we all do! That's what you should have been doing that night instead of sitting on the truck! Saving your brother! And you sure as hell shouldn't be -" and with that, his last words meant to be about Emie and her family, his father started hacking. Coughing up what sounded like his lungs.

This was all Asher could take. His father was well into his fifties, too soon for him to have Alzheimer's, but with every passing day Asher believed he had it. And tonight his father had pushed him too damn far. Damn it all, he knew he had taken some time out during the marina fire to sit on the back of the truck and dump a bottle of ice cold water down the back of his neck into his gear, but he was right up there with Curtis when the floor gave way and the ladder fell. He watched as his brother fall three floors down to his death in the hell blinding, burning first floor of the boat marina warehouse, he also ran like hell down three flights of stairs, skipping as many as he could to save his brothers life. With an air bottle strapped to his back, a mask he could no longer see out of, and an ax. He was everything that night his father swore he wasn't.

When he had found his brother, he didn't even stop to save his own father who had passed out in the smoke. He had carried his screaming, burning brother's body straight to the arms of Corey Young, the paramedic on scene, and then headed back for his father.

Asher brushed his hair out of his face, pointed his finger at his father, was ready to defend himself and Emie, who he knew his father had been about to start in on him about, and prayed to God someone stopped him before he hit the old man. His brother was dying. And it wasn't his fault.

It was the gentle clear of a woman's voice that stopped him dead in his tracks. That fear, his fear returned full force. The fear of death tapping him on the shoulder. His father had even gasped at her.

"I'm here for Curtis."

Asher turned; he had expected to see the grim reaper or the angel of death. The rush of fear, the flood of emotions, it had hit him so unexpectedly. Ironically he had expected to see Emie, a thought that threatened to plague his mind for the rest of the night, but the woman standing before him wasn't neither. Her hair was the color of orange flames. Stunning really. She had it neatly up in a bun, with tight spiral curls hanging here and there. She was dressed in a simple white lab coat and a little white skirt. She was holding a chart in her hands. Curtis' chart.

"My name is Shelley." She greeted the family and turned to his father. "It's time sir. You need to say your goodbyes now." She solemnly walked into the room and stood in the corner and waited as the family took turns.

Asher waited. He hated his father for not calling him. For not trying to come and see him. No matter their differences, he should have called him. Someone should have told him how his father had felt these last few days. He shouldn't have waited until now to tell him.

Asher forgot about his father's words, he wanted to be alone with Curtis one last time, so he waited just inside the room. He watched as they all took their time. Holding hands and weeping around Curtis. Telling stories of when they were young. Making jokes about Curtis and all things he would be saying now, if he could.

It was finally time to let him go and pull the plug.

"It's your turn honey." Asher's mother told him quietly, sliding her hand inside of his for comfort, and pulling Asher over to his brothers bedside.

Asher hoped his brother could still hear him, and not feel the pain at the same time.

"The worst is over now." she reminded him in a whisper.

His mother was good at that. Keeping the faith, holding everyone together, all while dying inside herself. Her son was dying, and she was comforting everyone else. He loved her so much. A mother shouldn't have to bury her children.

The tears hadn't come till Asher was alone with Curtis. The woman named Shelley had even stepped out for the moment.

He held his brothers hand and let the tears finally fall. Curtis had been his best friend. He had always been there for Asher, through good times and bad. He was always able to count on his brother no matter what happened in his life. Curtis had been the big brother every brother should be.

"I tried Curtis. I tried like hell. I couldn't pull you up man." Asher wept. "Why did you have to save them? Why did you have to let go? Why was it you, and not me? Damn it! Why?" Asher hated that now he finally felt what he should have been feeling all this week. He would never see his brother again after tonight. Even though seeing his brother like this, his body badly burnt, broken, bleeding through the gauze that was holding his skin together, he still didn't want his brother to leave him. It was so final what they were about to do.

Asher laid his head on his brother's bed and wished it wasn't his brother laying here. He waited for answers he would never get.

He knew some of the answers, they had come slowly. He knew now why it wasn't him. Thoughts of Emie crossed his mind. Fresh tears ran down unto the bed unbidden. He knew if his brother had known about Emie, he would have done what he had to save Asher.

Finally Asher cleared his head. He told his brother he would see him on the other side, told him he would see him soon like they always said, grabbed his lifeless foot, gave it a little bump with his fist like they always did, and looked over his burnt lifeless body, just as Shelley walked back in with the family.

Everyone circled around Asher holding his hand as Shelley pulled the plugs.

When the heart stopped, she silenced the machines and blackened the screens; silently she gave him a quick injection of venom in his IV no one seen. His heart would start beating again and he would breathe on his own, but not for long. He was going to need a lot more.

Emie was walking down the hall of the fifth floor wondering if she should go check on Asher and his family. Frank may know something he shouldn't, but right now he was grieving. His family was too. She wondered if she could use her abilities on him, maybe change his mind about her, then remembered she couldn't. Men had free will. When they knew what or who she was, she could no longer be of any use to them. Especially if they feared her, and Frank feared her in the worst way. She could feel it dripping from the man down stairs.

Just as she was about to stop at the nurses desk to ask about the Stone family, she sensed and heard the mind of her friend Shelley. Emie looked around everywhere trying to find her. What was Shelley doing here, she wondered, just as she seen Asher and his family all filing out of Curtis's room.

Emie's eyes found Asher then. He was crying.

Men didn't cry. There was some unwritten rule about it somewhere, she had learned that along time ago. Growing up in family full of men, Emie knew this all too well. This man, her hero, he had showed so much emotion in the last few days, it hurt her to see him hurting like this.

Asher seen Emie running up to him from the nurse's desk. Fear and hate, anger of the worst kind was raging inside of him just a moment ago. It was amazing how just one look at Emie and all of it just washed away into hurt. He took her in his arms and just held her. He wept harder then he had in years. Letting it all out, the hurt and anger, his fear of death that crept around every corner, all these years of working for the department where he hated being, but made himself because of his family. He didn't mean to do it to her. But his heart, and body, and soul, needed her in that moment. Needed her to hold him while he wept and let it all go. He held unto her, tight enough so his body could feel her there, tight enough so his heart and soul could release years of hurt and pain, until every inch of his existence was washed clean.

He hated letting go of his brother. They had vowed as brothers to protect each other. This wasn't supposed to happen to any of them. All of his feelings rolled out of him and he held onto the one thing he knew would save him.

His family walked side by side out, nodding at her like they knew he needed her more then them in that moment. Emie felt so lost. She had never held a man who was in this kind of pain. She struggled with it. She only knew if this was her brother, she would do this too. So she held him. Almost falling to the ground with the strength of him, with the weight of everything he was letting go of, but she held him strong. She held him firm. She would be his rock, whatever he needed. Everything he was feeling, she took from him, left him with a sweet release and the peace he had been searching for. The only gift she could give him in his grieving moments of grief.

Asher squeezed her, lifting her up onto his chest off the floor. Probably harder then he should have, but he needed to feel her. He thought about how Curtis had never met Emie in that moment. He never would. He would never meet his kids, or meet a woman of his own who would give him a family to raise like Asher was planning with Emie. He made a promise to his brother, and to God. He would love this woman with everything he had, till his last dying day.

He had to come down from this, he knew he did. He wanted this woman, and crying was no way to keep her around. His pride got the better of his fall.

Coughing quietly and catching his breath, he whispered to her softly, "I'm sorry. I didn't mean to do that to you." he said while straightening to his full height and setting her back down on the ground.

"You have nothing to apologize for sweetie." She held his big hands in both of hers and tried to smile at him. He was breaking her heart.

She couldn't take all of this pain from him. She had to leave this pain; he had to mourn his brother. But what she could leave him with, she did. What he needed was peace.

Asher looked back at his family, trying to hide the tears he couldn't stop from falling. All he wanted to do was look at Emie, get lost somewhere with her. But he knew he needed to follow them home. "I gotta go. I need to be with them." He said to her as he looked over at his family, wiping big tears away from his face. They were standing waiting for an elevator together, weeping like he had. His little sister was distraught. She had never been through the loss of any family member before.

 Emie knew this. She knew how important family was. There was time for all the things that needed to happen between them. He needed this time to be with them and grieve.

When he looked at her, she reached up and touched his face with her hand lovingly. "I know. Go. It's ok. You're going to be ok." She assured him, cupping both hands around his face. She gave him the ability to walk away as she looked up into his eyes. Not just from her, but from his brother who he was leaving behind.

He needed at least that.

Asher wrapped her hand sweetly around his and kissed the back of her hand, lingering sweetly and promising her he would see her again. With a wink, he walked away.

Emie had to wipe a blood stained tear from her eye when he did that. She loved how he kissed her hand in such a sweet gesture but his eye had been filled with an unshed tear when he had winked at her and it had ran unbidingly down his cheek.

She looked after him, watching him wipe away more tears as he waited for the elevator, trying to look brave and stand tall with his family, but just looking at the way he stuffed his hands in his pockets she could tell he wasn't feeling at all brave or strong in that moment. She had never seen such a heart wrenching thing before in her whole life.

Her heart wept for the loss of his brother in his life. Curtis had been his best friend. She wondered if this was why God had brought the two of together. If she was meant for him, or if he was meant for her.

The Stone family was all waiting for the same elevator she had met Asher in. Both of their minds thought at the same time. Asher looked back, looked right at her, like he had heard her, and then walked out of sight into the elevator inside with his family.

"Emie!"

Emie turned quickly at the sound of Shelley's voice. Shelley was standing in Curtis's room. Emie ran in the room behind the curtain. Shelley was wiping Curtis's blood from her mouth.

Emie's jaw dropped to the floor. If Shelley hadn't been her friend, and a stronger vampire then her, she would have killed her right then and there.

"What? You said he was dying, so I came to rescue him." Shelley said with a shrug. "I always had a thing for men in uniform, you know that." Shelley winked at Emie sheepishly.

Emie looked at Curtis who she knew would wake soon. Screaming. He would be lost and raving mad for days. The transition between human and vampire was painful. It would be more painful then when he fell three floors and broke every bone in his legs and arms. More painful then when his body started and finished burning. Shelley would have to take him far away from here. Hold him prisoner, and help him through his transition.

"Shelley! What have you done?"

"I'm rescuing him, duh! It will be fine. Trust me. The nurse was coming to do this herself anyways; well, not this... I just took over." Shelley was looking down at Curtis as she said this. Taking in the body of the man she deemed as hers with great pleasure. "She will wake up in the morning and not remember a thing in the closet over there. The doctor will sign off thinking the girl finally did her job, and we will stroll out of here with his body and replace it with the dead guy I brought in from Florida who died in a fire the other night. Look here."

She showed Emie the chart where Curtis's family had signed the no autopsy line and Curtis was to be sent straight over to the funeral home to be cremated in the morning.

"It's perfect. No one will ever know. I get a hero of my own, and you get to tell yours later that his brother is still alive. It's a win win situation.

"Stop looking at me like you're about to expire Emie! The sprinklers will go off and you ruin his chart!" Shelley held his chart close to her and glared at Emie.

Emie was torn. Shocked. Pleased? "Does Joseph know about this?"

"Of course, who do you think helped me with all this? It's a grand plan if you ask me. We will need Curtis' help soon with the-"

"Stop. Stop. I don't want to hear anymore about this silly war, storm, or whatever it is my brother's are planning for." Emie was tired of all that talk. "Come on, let's get him down stairs."

Emie shook it all off and helped Shelley with her plan. They had to get Curtis off this floor and down stairs quick. The screaming would start soon, and they wouldn't be able to keep him quiet. With his size, he was sure to look like a monster.

Curtis was the same size as Asher, this should be fun she told herself wishing she could kick Shelley. She let her know it too through all the process of exchanging Curtis's body for the other guy Shelley had brought up. It was indeed a grand plan. Shelley had figured out every last detail. She even had Joseph working on the minds of the security guards watching the cameras. They would never see her or Shelley making the exchange or Shelley carrying a man twice her size out the back doors to Joseph's waiting vehicle.

Asher was going to be angry. So angry. Asher was never going to speak to her again. And if she didn't expire on her own, she'd die years from now of a very lonely heart.

She watched as Shelley drove away. Shaking her head she walked back inside and wondered if life could get any crazier.

Eleven

Two days later…..

It had been raining all day. Asher was sitting on his front porch just staring out over the lake, sipping on a cold glass of whiskey. Cottonwood was flying all around like snow in the wind. The sun behind him was setting and the last storm had passed over Luna Pier but was still looming and dark out over the lake. Darkness was encroaching upon him.

He had wasted the whole day just sitting in his house trying not to think about his brother or his family. He just wanted to be alone. There was only one person he wanted to see right now, but he didn't know if he was strong enough to see her again.

The last time he had seen Emie he had cried on her shoulder. It still bothered him, but it softened his heart to know that he could share something so strong with her.

His phone buzzed then in his jean pocket. He pulled his phone out and looked at the screen. It was Emie. She had sent him a smiley face.

He went through all the little faces on his phone until he found an image of a rose and sent it to her. It was cheesy, he hoped it was cute.

"Just wondering if you were missing me?" she asked him.

Asher sighed, if she only knew.

"Look up." Was the next text message he got from her.

Stunned, Asher looked up. Emie was leaning against the pier wall in front of him. She was dressed in holy jeans shorts and a lacy white silky tank top, flip flops, and her hair was pulled to one side hanging over her shoulder, her curls hung down her side.

She stole his breath away.

Asher got up and tucked his phone away. He walked down his porch steps in a hurry and jogged over to her.

Emie watched as the only guy in the world she wanted to be with hurried over to her side. He looked to her like the hero he was, dressed in jeans and boots, he wore a black firefighter t-shirt that covered the front in flames surrounding a Maltese cross. He had his hat on backwards and she could read the red bold unmistakable abbreviations of the Luna Pier Fire Department on it.

He did that thing. That thing that gave her butterflies. He shoved his hands in his pockets and his face turned red when he stood in front of her. He wasn't a shy man at all. But whenever he first seen her, his pulse would race, his breath would quicken, and all thought would escape him.

It was the cutest thing she'd ever seen.

All he could see or think of was her. Like a child he would forget the world existed, and she would become the center of him.

Asher's aching soul had been searching all day for something, anything to bring him out of this storm he had been facing the last few days. And like the storm fleeing over the darkening lake, leaving the night filled with a starry sky and a bright moon shining down on him, Emie had walked into his life once again filling his heart with a joy he could only feel when he was with her.

Asher took a long deep breath and smelled her freshness in the misty air. He smiled at Emie and felt her sweetness enter into his body. He knew for the rest of the night he would be ok now, and maybe even some of tomorrow.

"How are you holding up Super Man?" She asked shyly.

Again, she took his breath away with her sweet, honest smile. Asher could see there behind her eyes how real it was, that smile of hers. Damn, he thought. He wondered if anyone had ever smiled at him like that before.

He looked down and shook his head running his hand through his hair messing it all up. "Like I'm falling out of the sky, breaking up into pieces."

He wondered how much she knew of his comic book hero he had treasured as a boy. He needed someone to rescue him, and she was just his kind of hero.

Emie walked up to him and placed her hands on his heart. "Sounds like you could use a dose of kryptonite." Emie could see his troubled heart. She could see the chains wrapped around him weakening him. He needed something and Emie was ready to freely give it to him.

She wasn't good for him, just like kryptonite wasn't good for Super Man, but for whatever reason, every little bit of her she gave to him just seemed to strengthen him.

Asher didn't have a chance to ask her what she meant. Couldn't kryptonite kill super man?

It was in her kiss she sweetly placed on his lips that he found his answer. Like a peace that passed all understanding, like amazing grace falling around him at his feet, she gave him the one thing he needed.

Love.

He didn't need to look at her to see it anymore. She didn't need to say it. It was there in the way she tenderly kissed him. It was in her hands that gently wrapped around his arms. It was there in her toes as she bent them up to lift her lips up to his. Her body radiated it.

Asher placed his hands on either side of her hips and let her lips take each of his in a lovers embrace. He could only imagine the songs he could write now. Finding someone like her that had stole his heart and gave it back it to him just when he needed it was a joy unlike any other. It did things to a man that made him want to get down on bended knee and confess his unworthiness but his whole hearted devoted soul to a woman. Asher wanted to forget about anything else that had ever made him happy in the past. Nothing compared to Emie.

He was falling harder for her as she didn't hold back and was the strength he needed standing there giving him the reasons he needed to keep on living life. Lifting her hand up into the back of his neck; he didn't know how much he could take. He ran his hand up between them and held unto her cheek pulling her deeper in his own kiss. He placed his hand on the back of her hip and pushed her towards him giving him a better access to her sweet mouth that he craved.

She was giving him back the one precious thing in life he had lost. She was putting his life back to the way it used to be.

He held her face in the palm of his hand and held her to him. Kissing her was like breathing. He needed to kiss her. He wanted to kiss her. Hell, he wanted so much more, but kissing her was something he had to have.

Emie could feel his broken heart mending. She could feel her love stitching as it threaded through his heart and put the pieces back together that had been falling apart.

Like the strings on a violin making beautiful music, so did his heart beat just for her now. Stronger, beating and rushing for her. His blood was pouring through his veins now carrying a source of life it had lost just moments ago. She could smell Asher's blood in ways no one else could. Fire, mixed with smoke in his blood. His heated body was overpowering her senses.

Asher could feel the moment he had to stop. He needed a release he couldn't ask of her tonight. But he needed to spend every moment distracting his thoughts of all that had wounded him, and fill it with little moments of her. Moments he would sell his soul just to have with her.

He placed his head on her forehead and sighed in almost a growl. "You do things to me when you kiss me like that Emie."

Emie laughed out loud as she wound her fingers through his hair at the base of his neck. "Never knew I was such temptress."

Asher stepped back and took her hand in his. He lifted it up to his lips and said "You have no idea sweetheart."

Emie wondered how he didn't know what he did to her yet. His tight jeans and tight shirt, his teasing tattoos that were begging to be traced by her fingers, like her touch could cool the flames that crawled and stretched up his arms and around the hidden places under his shirt she was dying to see. She wondered curiously if she could talk him into a swim out in the lake just so she could get him to take his shirt off.

"What are you doing out here anyways?" he asked.

"Oh, I worked a day shift today and filled in for one of the girls. She's working my midnight." Emie said sweetly up at him, so memorized by his blue eyes she almost forgot the question she was going to ask. "I was thinking about going for a swim tonight and just wondered if you wanted to come and play outside with me?"

Asher had to puff out his cheeks and blow out a laugh. Emie was so cute and adorable to him. There was an innuendo in her request that made the man in him want the woman in her.

"Swim?" Asher questioned. He hadn't swam in the lake since he was a kid. Swimming with her though would be like a dream come true.

"Yeah." She nodded to him when he asked. "You now how to swim right?" she asked daringly.

Asher stood up a little taller. Of course he knew how to swim, but he always forgot how to do things when he was around her.

He looked at her clothes a little skirmish. He wondered what she was wearing under her clothes. "Of course, did you bring a suit?" he questioned, looking like he was peeking under in her shirt. He looked back at her and placed his hands on his hips so he wouldn't start taking her clothes off.

Emie giggled inside at his boyish thoughts. "I did." She winked back at him biting her lip and wondering if he would say yes.

Asher smiled widely and looked over the lake. The waves were steady and calm. He could smell the heat in the misty air and knew the lake was warm enough for swimming. He looked back at his house and wished he didn't have to leave her while he ran in and changed.

"Sounds like fun." He nodded over at her. "I'll be right back."

Emie watched as Asher stepped off the pier and headed for his house. He was fun to mess with. One of the things she loved about him.

Asher climbed over the wall of the pier and looked out to the water where Emie was after he had changed. She wasn't facing him, letting her hands skim the warm the water under her. She didn't hear him as he kicked off his shoes in the sand, or when he slowly walked up behind her into the water. He could hear her laughter as he gathered her legs under her and pulled her under the water with him.

He twirled and spun her in the water in his arms, holding her above the water with him.

"What I would give for some dancing music right about now." he said to her. He was swaying to music he could hear in his mind like they were dancing. Her legs and arms were wrapped around him now.

"You can't hear it?" She asked him.

"Hear what?' he questioned smiling at her playful mood.

"I can always hear music." She was letting him hear it now from her mind. He was swaying to it like it was playing out loud for the both of them.

Breathless, he wanted to know more. "Do you play Emie?"

Her smile widened. "Yes I do. I play a lot of instruments."

"What is you favorite?"

"I love to play the piano. I don't know what it is, but it's just…" she looked up into the night feeling free. She'd never felt like this before. She was able to share things with him no one had ever asked about before. "Magical.

"What about you? I know you like to sing. What do you like to play?"

"The guitar mostly." He told her, loving the magical look in her eyes. She was honestly happy. He wondered if she was always like this. "But I love the sound of the drums when I'm playing. It's that connection, you know? The way someone can play along with you, and follow your lead." As he said it, he knew that feeling with her now.

It was just like she had said. It was magical.

Emie knew that feeling also. But only with him.

"Are you ready?" He questioned her suddenly.

"For what?"

Asher could feel the pulse between her legs. The heat that was there surrounded his growing cock in the tepid water. He had the urge to just plunge into her.

Without notice he let go and fell into the water with her. When she held on tighter to him he pulled her tighter into him. Closing the awkward distance between their bodies. Her slim white bikini did nothing to hinder the feel of him neatly pressed up into her.

Under the water he held her as he twirled her around. When he finally stood up he pressed closer up against her and stirred a desire in him that he couldn't control.

He held her face in his hands kissing her with an urge to feel more of her. He slipped one hand after the other under her bottom pressing her body onto his, pushing into her and pulling her up and down his length to a sway that he could feel was driving her crazy.

Her moans broke free of her lips and Asher had to bury his head in her neck. He was shaking with passion so out of control he couldn't stand in the water. They were deep enough now that there bodies were covered, and he was sure she could no longer touch bottom.

Emie couldn't control the desire she felt for him. She wanted him. More of him. She knew what it would mean if she let him take her. She welcomed it. But she wasn't sure if he was ready.

Asher sighed and tried to control himself. He wanted Emie, there was no doubt now. But he still wasn't in a place he wanted to be with her when it happened. And certainly not after the day he had had.

He wasn't ready for this to end though. He wanted to spend all night out here with her like this.

"I can't contain it when I'm with you. I always wanna be this close with you." he pulled her tighter to show her his meaning.

Emie whispered to him then. "I know."

Asher held her in his arms for as long as he could. Try as he might, he tried to wait for the feelings to die. But they wouldn't. Every breath, with every movement of the water, it brought their bodies lovingly closer together.

"We should probably keep on talking." He whispered to her jokingly.

Emie giggled out loud. "Yes. We should."

He started to kiss her neck then; he could feel the swell of her desire as she heated more. He reached for her lips and kissed her powerfully. Then back down her face to her neck and lower. As his muffled groans followed his every kiss, his body reacting deafeningly stiff knowing the path his mouth was taking.

His heart raced the closer his lips got to her chest.

The sirens ringing all throughout town startled them.

Every cuss word he had ever uttered filled his mind. She let go and her legs fell between them but he pulled her back against him and waited. He had to think.

Emie was almost giggling and asked him softly "Do you have to go?"

Asher's mouth started dripping with anger. He didn't want to let her go. He didn't have his radio though to tell him what the call was. He was off tonight, but he needed to know how bad it was and if he would be needed tonight.

Things were getting hectic around the city. They had fought more fires this week then ever before.

Asher looked back at his house, it felt so far away from where he was. He looked back at her and said "I need to see what it is sweetheart." He looked down at her body as her breast bobbed in the water up and down.

He had to shake his head and close his eyes. He didn't want to go.

The sirens ended and she had to lift up his face. He wasn't opening his eyes.

"Asher, it's ok. Go if you have to." He was trying to shut off the world again.

When he looked at her, she could have sworn she seen tears in his eyes. He really didn't want to go.

Fear. A fear so strong took over his body. But it was only for a second. It wasn't that he was weak, no, not that. It wasn't that he was afraid either, he just worried. Emie knew she could give him what he needed, but Asher always found it before she could give it to him. It's what set him apart from others she had known. He was strong. He had courage. He was everything that a hero was made of.

Emie would have given anything to take away the pain she saw there in his eyes.

Asher finally let her go. He looked at his house and put his hands on his hips. "My radio is on the porch. Follow me back?" he breathed looking back at her.

"I'm right behind you." She reassured him.

When Asher laughed, Emie wondered why.

He moved back in the water in front of her and reached for her behind him and pulled her on his back. Once she was neatly behind him he stood and ran playfully out of the water back to the beach.

Emie laughed the whole way back to the beach.

Asher had brought two towels with him earlier and had left them on one of the rocks by his shoes. He could see from the porch as he looked back at the beach that Emie was carrying them both as she climbed over the wall of the pier. She had her hair over one shoulder again, trying to shake it dry with a towel. He pushed his repeater button on his radio that would replay central dispatches message for him and watched as her toes sank into the grass in front of his house. His desire for her would never end.

He downed his glass of whiskey and lit a cigarette before he headed back down the stairs. Blowing out the smoke he had to make a decision. It was just a smoke alarm over at the apartments. He wanted to wait to see if it was just a false alarm that the guys could handle without him.

Emie watched as Asher came down the steps and back towards her. She waited for him and tried to listen in on the call. She hoped it wasn't a fire. He didn't want a fire tonight.

Asher reached for his towel she was handing him and wrapped her in it, picking her up he carried her back to the pier wall. He loved her laugh and the way she squealed in delight.

"So, anything interesting?" she asked after he set her down and she snuggled up in the warmth of the towel as she watched him dry off on the wall.

He hopped over the wall before he answered and gathered their things. He was listening in on radio transmissions and could tell he was going to have to leave her soon. He threw out his smoke and said "I think they can handle it, but I will have to go when they clear the call and make sure they run the overhaul." He told her from down in the sand shaking it out her clothes.

Emie watched as his muscles rippled when he put on his shirt. She had forgotten the entire time she was out in the water to look at his tattoos. She tucked her nose into the towel and took a deep smell, it smelled of his laundry soap. Clean and fresh. She suddenly missed his smell.

Asher hopped back on the wall next to her and stood on the ground. He placed her things next to her on the wall and shook off the sand on his feet stepping into his jeans one foot at a time then he put on his shoes. He messed up his wet hair and looked at her playfully.

"You have no idea how much I needed this tonight. Thank you Emie."

Emie looked at him lovingly. She shrugged her shoulders at him and said "Even super man needs to have fun once in awhile."

Asher's eyes danced in the moonlight. Emie could read it in his heart. He felt and looked mended.

"One of these days you're going to have to let me return the favor."

Emie eyed him curiously. There was a double meaning in there. She could see it in his cheeky smile and hear it in his mind. She had made him feel on top of the world tonight. She had been the hero tonight and rescued him.

Asher looked over the lake. "I missed swimming."

Emie laughed at Asher then. He had his hands on his hips and looked every bit the boy in the man's body.

He looked at her then and asked her what she was going to do tonight.

"I'll probably stay out here a while." She told him looking longingly back out over the water. She too had missed swimming and wanted to get back in as soon as he was gone.

"I'll look for you when I get back. If you're still out here I'll join you."

Emie smiled at that. She couldn't wait.

When Asher left she gathered her things and stayed wrapped up in his towel out on the rocks enjoying the smell of him. She watched as the storm passed beyond site. She breathed in the night air and found herself walking back out into the water. She stayed out there for hours swimming under the water.

Emie enjoyed being out here in the warm lake at night. She would walk the beach and find things the humans would leave behind on the beach and in the water. Farther out in the lake were hidden treasures humans didn't even know were out there laid. The lighthouse out in the midst of Lake Erie was a place she loved to visit.

Swimming closer to shore, she listened for signs that Asher was back. It wasn't until she sat on one of the large flat cylinders on the shore that led back up to the pier where she could still have her feet dangling in the water, that she heard his truck pull back into his drive.

She listened as he walked through out his house. She listened as he let his dog outside and every drawn in breath he took as he smoked. As he let his dog back inside, she listened again as he unzipped his pants and stripped off his clothes. She smiled at his thoughts. He didn't know if she was still out here, but he had to find out.

Asher walked off his porch with another towel in his arms. He had to know if Emie was still out there. He'd only been gone an hour and a half. He hoped she was still.

When he walked up onto the pier wall he leaned forward and looked over the wall. Sure enough, she was sitting on the cylinder in front of his house wrapped up in his towel.

He searched his brain for something witty to say to her, but all his speech was gone. She'd taken not only his breath away but all thoughts also. His heart was pounding.

Emie looked back then and just stared at him. She tried to smile, but she was taken by his thoughts. She too was speechless by the sight of him.

Asher hopped over the wall then. He landed in the sand and walked up onto the cylinder behind her. He sat down behind her and took a deep breath as he wrapped his arms around her.

Emie was looking out over the water again, her nose buried in the towel she was holding up to her face. No one could see them out here tonight. The wall would shield them from everyone.

Asher sighed as he rested his chin on her shoulder. He took in the scent of her warm body mixed with the night air. "I thought you would have gone home by now."

She shrugged her shoulders. "I wouldn't be able to sleep anyways. Curse of working midnights. Can't sleep at night when I should be."

Asher knew that feeling all to well. He hated tossing and turning in bed when he couldn't sleep. He'd end up cleaning his house when he should have sleeping.

He nodded his head in understanding to her. "No point in being lonely tonight when we could be together."

Emie leaned back into Asher then. She nudged her nose on his arm and felt as he stirred behind her and held her close to him.

When she reached her hand to trace his vein, her right nipple rubbed against his right arm and made him flinch moving his hand away. "There just nipples Asher's. No reason to be afraid of them." She jested at him pulling his hand back for her to examine.

She looked at the vein then that had caught her silent interest as she listened to his mind and what had caught his interest. She had bared the top of her breast to his eyes and what the sight of it did to him made her smile deeply as his mind traced and memorized them like she was doing to his hand.

With a deep sigh, Asher drug his wandering eyes away from her breast and tried not to think about the nipples he knew where under that towel waiting to be touched.

"How's the department doing?" She questioned him.

"All is well at the moment. Hopefully the guys can get some sleep tonight. They are tired." He told her lovingly.

Emie looked back at him then and looked into his eyes. He was tired…

"How's your family doing Asher?"

Asher admired her for caring about his life the way she did. "Everyone's holding on." He smiled at her reassuringly.

Emie smiled back and looked away. He wanted her to know they could handle it. She was glad for it. They were a strong family.

"Did you swim?" he asked her.

"Yeah. I had to stop before my skin turned scaly." She laughed, remembering the way her skin used to feel after swimming long hours at home.

Asher examined her fingers then. They were so skinny and tiny compared to his. He rubbed the tip of her fingers with his. He hoped it was turning her on. When she nudged him with her right breast as she sat up a little, he could feel her harden nipple and knew she was.

Emie moved her fingers off his hand and went back to his arm. He was bare now to her, if she turned around she could look at his tattoos. When she did, the moon light was hitting his left arm just right. She traced her fingers up his flames to the cross on his arm.

Asher closed his eyes at her touch. No one had ever done this to him the way she did. He savored every second of it. She traced the outline of the flames and the cross and followed the lines around them. It was stirring him higher and higher.

Emie turned then and looked at his bare chest. She followed his flames that ran up his arm across his shoulder with her fingers and traced them across his chest and neck muscles to where the red flames met the blue flames on his chest and intertwined.

Emie looked at his face then and stopped. She leaned in and placed a kiss on his lips.

Asher felt her lean in. Felt her kiss his lips and tried so hard not to break her spell by moving.

When she stopped Asher opened his eyes and looked down at her. "You're driving me crazy, you know that right?"

Emie grinned at him then. "Yep." She stated simply and turned around. She pulled his arms around her over her shoulders.

Asher lifted his left hand then and moved it off her shoulder. He whispered in her right ear what he was doing. "I just want to feast on these for awhile."

Emie leaned back and closed her eyes. She watched inside his mind what he was doing. He was stirring his need for her just by looking at her.

"We should play a game." He announced.

Twelve

Emie opened her eyes then. "A game?" She listened to his heart then, and followed his meaning.

Asher moved her forward and she turned around to face him. "Like truth or dare. The games we played as kids."

Emie smirked at him. She'd never played those games as a child. But secretly she wished she had.

He drug a finger over the top of her bare breast watching everywhere it went. He was trying to coax her into his game. He had no idea what he was doing, but he had to do something with her or he was going to pick her up and carry her off to his bed and make slow love to her all night long. All he knew, from what he could tell of her breathing and the way her breast responded to his caress, was that she wanted this too. She wanted to play and tease him just as much as he wanted to with her.

"What are the rules?"

Asher knew he had her attention then. "We will pick categories, and ask one question each for each category. We will have five tries to answer the question correctly about each other. If we get it right, we get to choose something to do to the other. If we get it wrong, the other gets to choose se.

The thoughts that were going through his mind were stirring her heart. She wanted him to do all those things. "There should be a limited amount of time aloud to do those things in. Just to keep the game going." She told him. Looking at him curiously.

"10 seconds." He told her.

"Who goes first?"

"Ladies first, of course."

Emie smiled to herself then. "First category." She said as she returned to leaning her body up against his looking out over the lake.

Asher waited patiently, loving that she wanted to play.

Emie tried to think of one she could win. She did her best to stay out of his mind so not to tip the scales of fairness. "Food. What is your favorite food Asher?"

Asher thought of it. "You have five guesses, sweetheart." He whispered in her ear. "Choose them wisely."

Emie knew what it was before he even thought of it. But for the fairness of the game, she gave it a winning shot. "Cheese burger?"

Asher held up one finger. "Nope."

"Pizza." This she knew was his favorite. Everything he ate had to have cheese in it. A pizza covered in cheese seemed like something he would love.

Asher stilled behind her and Emie knew she had won the first battle. She turned around then.

Asher hung his head and smiled. He got excited as she turned her body around and sat on her knees. He didn't have a clue what she wanted but he couldn't wait to find out. He looked up and was captivated by her smile.

"There's this thing I've wanted to try." She told him. "But I've always been too shy to try it."

Asher had to steady himself. This had to be the most hellish idea he had ever had. But he was ready for it.

Emie was ready and willing to play. She was so excited. "So I need you to close your eyes." When he did, she added, "And stick out your tongue."

Asher tried to open his eyes, but her sweet little hand was right there ready to cover them up as she squealed a protest. "Ok. Ok. Here." He told her as he closed his eyes, laughed and stuck out his tongue.

Emie shyly but ever so sweetly leaned forward. She let his tongue slide ever so slowly in between her lips. When her lips bumped against his and she had him temptingly inside her mouth she started to move her body back and forth sucking on his tongue.

Asher didn't know how much he could take. He was swollen and hard and so overheated he was dizzy. He counted squinting his eyes tighter trying not to embarrass himself and explode all over her. With every stroke of her lips on his tongue he thought he would lose all control. She was so shy she was trembling. He almost steadied her as he got to eight, but she finished before he did and announced "10." proudly.

Emie sat back and glanced quickly at her handy work. He had tempted her so bad these last few times they'd been together, finally, she felt like she had paid him back.

Asher caught himself sitting like a fool looking at her with his tongue sticking out. He shook it all off the best he could and said "My turn. Food, right?" he groaned.

Emie nodded her head yes while biting her lower lip. She turned quickly in his arms and leaned back up against him. She held up five fingers with her elbow on his knee and waited for him to start.

Asher dug through his mind. He could remember having this conversation with her over text message, but for life of him he couldn't remember her answer.

He tried to remember the night they went to the bar together. When he had it, he announced it triumphantly. "A pink, juicy piece of meat."

Emie lowered her whole hand then. She leaned her head back and looked up at him smiling and nodded her head reassuringly to him.

Asher placed a kiss on her cute smile and felt like a fool for winning. He hadn't a clue what to ask for as a reward. Well, he did, but he didn't know where to start.

He decided on the two things that drove him mad with desire. He could start there. What guy wouldn't? Emie's breasts were divine.

He took a deep breath and he said "Turn around sweetheart."

Emie turned around again and held the towel up around her shoulders. She looked at him then but she didn't look inside his mind. She had an idea she knew what he wanted already. Even though it was killing her not knowing what would happen next, she loved the feelings welling up inside of her.

Asher lifted his hand and felt the tremble in it as he reached for the bow tie that was holding her breast together in her suit. He looked at her for reassurance, and with her nod he untied the bow.

Emie waited while he 'feasted'. In his words. He hadn't yet looked at them fully even though he'd tried earlier. She watched and loved how his mind all but worshiped them. He was in love with her. Every inch of her.

Emie breathed the word "10." More than she had said it. It broke her to say it, watching Asher's mind had been heavenly.

Asher shook his head then and closed his eyes like he was snapping a picture. Emie smirked at him as he opened his eyes and she replaced her breast the way they were.

She turned around quickly and took up her spot in front of him. "Next category." She said a little more out of breath then she had thought she had been.

"Animals. What is your favorite animal?"

When he thought of it he was more then ready for this category. He had a favorite animal no one knew of. He held up his hand for her ready to countdown.

"Dog?" Emie wondered aloud.

"Nope." Asher said proudly.

Confused, Emie had thought that was it. She tried another, then another, after four she was getting worried. She had named all the domestic animals. None were it.

"Want a hint?" he asked whispering in her ear. "It lives in the desert."

Stumped beyond everything, and not wanting to cheat she blurted out an answer. "Snakes?"

"Nope. That was five sweetheart."

Emie leaned her head back, looking up at him. "What is it then?"

"A camel."

Emie looked at him quizzically then and he gave her the answer.

"What do I smoke Emie?"

He laughed out loud when she gave him her best angry face and pouted. She knew the answer.

Emie had an idea then. "But I bet I can guess what you want now though."

Asher took pity on her then, but had a feeling she would never guess it. "Double or nothing, you can't." he said kissing the top of her head.

Emie winked at him as she said "You've been dying to slip your hand inside and touch my boob."

Asher drew his brows together and choked on his next words. "Damn!" he said aloud.

Emie smiled proudly. She didn't even have to cheat to know that one. She turned back around proud of herself. "Ok, your turn. What's my favorite animal?"

Asher knew this one without even thinking. He remembered the animals she had at home and knew they had to be her favorite. He looked right down at her and said "Horses." He almost died laughing when her mouth formed an 'o'. He'd won again. And he was damn proud of it.

Emie smiled then and had to give it to him. He deserved it. She knelt in front of him again. "Your wish is my command sir." Then she looked up at him so seductively she worried he would faint.

Asher shivered inside. He pulled her closer to him on her knees and said "There is this one thing; I've been dying to do. But every time," He shook his head and looked back at her as he said, "Every damn time I try, I get interrupted."

Emie smiled knowingly. He had tried it out in the water, but the call had hindered him.

She wasn't sure she could handle a full 10 seconds of it…

Asher reached up, took advantage of his chance, and undid her bow tie again. He cupped her left breast in his hand and brought it to his mouth shakily.

Emie counted the seconds and lost track after four. Because of what he was doing, because he was sucking on her so sensually, she had to hold on to his shoulders for support. When she lost feeling in her legs she ran her fingers up into his hair and pressed him farther into her.

Asher let go when he had counted to twenty. He was sure she had lost track of time somewhere around 5 and 10 because she never stopped him. "I'll have to wait till my next turn for the other one." he winked.

Emie eyed him not wanting him to wait at all. But then she remembered this was a game, and she loved it just as much as he did. She turned around, putting herself back together again. "Alright lucky, next category."

Asher thought about that one. He loved winning. "Vehicles. What's your favorite vehicle Emie?" He asked in her ear, licking her lobe seductively.

Emie's hand popped up right away. She had this one.

Asher laughed and started guessing. He tried cars, but she shook her head no. He thought maybe a truck, thinking she might have liked his. Then he tried a SUV and started to get worried. When he asked about a sports cars, she shook her head again and looked back up at him.

"One left."

"Monster trucks?" he asked with a wink. Knowing he was going to lose now.

Emie turned around then and smiled wildly.

"Motorcycles." She grinned at him.

Asher was stunned. This was something he didn't know about her.

"Really?"

"Yeah, my brothers have them." She told him honestly. "I don't drive them, per say, I just like riding on them. They're very sexy." She winked at him playfully.

Asher knew he had lost, but he was happy now to let her have it. He loved her answer. It hadn't surprised him when she said it. "Alright sweetheart, what I can do for you?" He let his legs fall over the side of the cylinder with her in between them.

Emie looked at his chest and wondered curiously about something. She crept forward towards him till she was close enough. "Ten seconds right?"

Asher nodded worriedly.

Emie reached her fingers up his chest and found what her fingers were itching to touch. She had wondered if she did to him what he had done to her, if she would get the same reaction. She was surprised when he closed his eyes and tried to breath. It was working she seen inside his mind. She flicked her fingers on his nipples and watched as his mind went blank.

When she got to ten, she stopped and squeezed at little. He opened his eyes and mouthed the word "Wow".

"That was a first." He said aloud.

Emie smiled wickedly.

"Next category."

"Color." She blurted out. She wanted something easy.

Emie took a deep breath and thought of his truck. It was black. "Black?"

Asher held up his finger to signal one down.

"Blue?" she scrunched up her face in wonder.

Asher put down another finger.

Emie sat back then and really had to think. Then she had it. "Red. Fire engine red?"

Asher hung his head in answer. She had killed him last time with his nipples. He could only imagine what she wanted next as she turned around again.

Emie leaned forward then. "Count aloud for me?" and then she leaned forward more.

Asher threw his head back then and started counting. He couldn't hold onto reality as she flicked his nipples with her tongue. But he counted, and thanked God when she stopped. She had done both nipples now and he was still dying to do her other one.

"My turn." He shivered.

Emie grinned wildly. She turned back around and sat in her new favorite position.

"Pink?" He watched as she signaled no with one finger. "Orange?" Nope, there went her other finger. "Yellow?" Nope. Damn it!

He thought more carefully this time. She had guessed his by the color of his favorite thing. Red.

All of sudden he thought of her car. It was red. Woman always picked out their favorite color in cars, so he tried that. "Red." He said more than asking.

Emie slumped in his arms, and let her hand go down. She was loving this game. It was showing a lot about how much they knew about each other already. When she started to turn around, he told her no, and laid her back over his left leg.

Asher moved her top off her other breast and took it in his mouth. He was hungry for her now. He could only hope she was counting, because there was no way he was keeping track. He could taste the saltiness of the lake on her and it made him lick just as much as he was sucking. He wanted her to feel it this time, and to never forget the way he made her feel.

Emie moaned. She tried her best not to scream. She held his head and almost begged for what he was doing to her. She knew when ten seconds had past and she didn't care.

"Asher." She breathed.

"I know." He said with a last kiss on her nipple. "Next category."

When he lifted her up she lifted up her top. It was her turn now. She needed a win again. He had awakened something in her and she planned on showing him.

"Body parts."

Asher couldn't believe it. "You're cheating!" he whined.

Emie knew she was, but she couldn't resist. "Just following the rules." She winked. "Breasts."

Asher sat back then and leaned on his hands smiling. He shook his head at her as she smiled knowingly back. "Alright, what can I do for you sweetheart."

Emie leaned in then and looked around them just incase. No one was around, she knew this without looking, but she did it anyways. She loved when reality hit him and he looked too. When he looked back, she looked at him playfully and said, "Stand up."

Asher gulped then. He had to cough in his hand to cover up his grin. He opened his mouth and all he could do was smile. He breathed out and did as she wished. He knew what she was going to ask for. So he stood up anyways.

Emie smiled up at him playfully and undid his swim trunks in front of her. She could feel his hardness by her hands and she couldn't wait to see what lies inside.

She bent her head to peek inside, and reached a finger inside to run along the skin she seen there. When it bucked up, she gasped aloud and giggled. He wiggled more for her fun and placed his hands on his hips.

"Well, take it out if you want it. You got four seconds left."

Emie looked up in a hurry then.

"Three." He winked down at her.

Emie reached in, lifting up on her knees and took him in her hand. She lifted him up then as he slid easily out of his shorts. She sat back on her heels then and took in an eye full.

Asher let her look a few seconds more and then tucked himself away. He couldn't help but be turned on by the situation and kept looking around even though no one could see them out here.

He sat down in front of her again. "My turn. Even though I'm pretty sure I already know."

Emie grinned at him and knew she should be blushing, she felt it all over her body.

"I can not tell a lie." She laughed.

Asher bent forward and whispered in her ear. "My shoulders."

Emie shivered, she couldn't deny it even if she wanted too. She knew they were. They stirred a desire in her she couldn't explain.

When Asher felt her lower her head, he knew he had won again. He drug his nose along her cheek as she lifted her head up to him and reached for her lips and kissed them softly.

He'd only kissed her once.

Surprised she looked at him questioningly.

"I want to place ten kisses anywhere on your body I want."

Emie shivered again. The thought of his lips all over her body made her do it. She couldn't help it.

Asher counted aloud as he placed number one on her neck. Two were on her shoulders. One between her breasts then one on each nipple, after he bared them to his lips.

Number seven he had her stand up for so he could kiss her belly button. Then he untied one side of her bikini bottom and placed a kiss on her hip there.

He drug her bottom lower and got up on his knees to place kiss number eight right at the top of bare mound. He took a deep breath to steady himself seeing that her lips below her suit were naked and bare.

Kiss number nine he placed in the entrance of her lips he had spread where he sucked softly and whispered "Ten."

There inside her lips he placed number ten and licked inside of her to find her button she loved to rub on him when he held her. He sucked her in to his mouth and let her go. He felt as she went weak and caught her in his arms as she fell into.

He had a feeling she was a virgin when she had shyly looked at him and softly touched him. He knew now by the way she melted that she was very untouched by any man. His hunger for her grew then. She would be his. But he wanted her slowly.

Emie rested her head on his shoulder as he took her in his arms. She moaned his name as he picked her up.

"I know sweetheart." He picked her up and set her down around him. He lifted her face and kissed her. He didn't want to play their game anymore. It was going to undo him. And he wasn't ready for it yet.

Asher lowered himself on the cylinder and sat flat. He let Emie scoot to her favorite spot on his body and nuzzled up into her when she found him. He held her face in one hand and cupped her bottom in the other. He growled aloud grinding her unto him. He kissed his way down her neck when she lifted it up.

"Asher." She breathed aloud, trying not to scream as she lifted herself up him. Going back down was enough to make her tremble.

He held her there and attacked her mouth again. He had to keep her still for a moment longer. He bucked wildly for her. Drove her mad till she was begging for more.

Asher couldn't take much more then. He knew what they both needed, but neither would say it aloud.

He picked her up and carried her out to the water where they could have a little more freedom, never breaking his kiss. When he was deep enough in the water he placed his head on her shoulder. He was breathing erratically. He pulled himself out of his shorts and pulled her in closer to him. She wrapped her legs tighter around him then.

He placed his head on her forehead then. "Trust me?" he asked.

"Yes." She breathed back at him.

Asher reached in between them again into her suit and moved it away and pulled her back to him, letting the back of his cock slide up and down in between her lips freely.

Emie grabbed Asher around his neck and held tighter onto him. She had wanted this so bad but had no idea to get it. She let him place his hands on her hips and work her body up and down him and moaned louder now that they were out in the water and far enough from anyone in hearing.

Asher lifted her and kissed her neck and shoulder. He begged her in her ear to let go and fall to pieces. To trust him. When she did, he couldn't hold back anymore. He had waited for this moment for too long. Even though he wasn't inside her, he didn't care. He wanted her to trust him. Trust he wouldn't take something that wasn't his to take yet. But this, this he could give her. This he knew she wanted.

He held her head through it as he held her hips too. He ground into her until his body shook. He held off long enough until she came. Then he followed her.

He kissed her everywhere he could till she fell off him into the water. Her legs were too weak to stay around him. He kissed her more until he was sure she could hold herself up on her own.

He held her in the water until it was time for both of them to come back down to reality.

Emie had her head on his chest. His well muscled peck that most men would be jealous of. She placed her hands on it and lifted herself up and looked at him. She bit her lip forgetting altogether why she had done it. Was she going to say something to him?

Asher grinned down at her. He moved her hair that had tumbled over her shoulder back over it. "Feel better?" When she nodded playfully and turned around backing into him. He held her again tightly.

"Thank you Asher."

He kissed her shoulder and said, "We keep this up, and we can watch the sunrise together."

Emie stiffened. She had no clue what time it was. "What time is it?' She asked turning around quickly.

Asher looked at her awkwardly. "Have somewhere to be?"

"I have a meeting at 6." Emie looked at him worriedly. What time was it?

She was lying, and she hated it, but the sun would kill her if it rose and she wasn't paying attention.

Asher lifted his hand to her face. She must be tired. He felt bad now. She needed at least a little bit of sleep.

Asher looked at the horizon, then back at his house. "Come on, let's go check."

Emie let him lead her to the beach and she wrapped herself in his towel as he hopped the pier wall and ran inside to go check the time.

She dressed quickly, and hopped the wall before he could see her. By the time he returned she was drying her hair stepping off the wall and onto the grass of his yard.

"It's only three, just now." He told her comfortingly.

"Oh good." She breathed a sigh of relief. She didn't know why it felt later, but it had.

Asher looked up at the horizon and wished he could turn back time. "You still have to go though, right?" he asked putting his hands on her hips.

Emie looked at him sweetly tucking his towel around her lips. She nodded her head yes. She did have a meeting, but not at 6. She had to let him believe it so she could escape the sunrise.

Asher lifted his finger and pushed down on the towel and kissed the lips she had been hiding. "Want me to drive you home?"

It was gentlemanly. She knew it was, and her heart broke over all the reasons he couldn't. "No, I'll walk." She took off his towel and handed it to him. She reached back on the pier wall and put her tank top back on. When she faced him again, he had put the towel around his neck and was holding it on either side.

"Thank you again."

"For what?" she asked honestly.

Asher sighed aloud and wondered when the last time was he had this much fun. "For asking me to come outside and play."

Emie smiled and winked at him as she stepped past him and started to walk home. She turned when she was just out of reach. "You can come outside and play with me anytime."

Asher growled and watched as she walked off into the darkness.

Thirteen

The next day...

Asher felt like he hadn't seen Emie in days. Every time he thought of her he needed her. He had wanted her sometimes in ways that he couldn't explain today.

Life and death had gotten in the way. He wasn't about to let anything get in the way anymore. He wanted this woman so bad he couldn't stand to be away from her anymore.

His family had stayed together that first night, sleeping in the family room huddled around each other for comfort. They next day was spent in preparations for Curtis's funeral and his final arrangements. Asher was in charge of what was left of Curtis's life. His house, His vehicles, the cabin up north. Everything Curtis had left behind would be sold, or given to family and friends. Curtis had left no will, so Asher would have to decide what to do with everything.

Asher had wanted to text Emie or call her after the night they had spent swimming last night, but it never felt right in the moments of grieving and being busy today. He wanted to see her again so bad it hurt. She was so much fun to be with, and that was the one thing he missed most about Curtis.

Some days he wondered if Emie was an angel sent to him from Curtis. Like he knew just what Asher would be missing in his life, and somehow God was giving him a gift.

Asher was in need of a break from it all. A break from his family who were in constant grief over Curtis, and from all the countless people who seemed to be flooding his parent's house with their sympathies. He was so tired of hearing the endless apologies of everyone around them. Sometimes when people didn't know what to say they thought a simple "I'm so sorry for your loss." Or "Is there anything we can do?" was enough. But it wasn't. Apologies weren't needed, and there was nothing anyone could do to do to make any of this any better. He needed something else to fill the empty void he was feeling. The loss of his brother was so great at times. There was only one other thing he wanted besides his brother.

Emie.

Asher was headed into the hospital, for the same elevator he had met her in, the same one he got in three days ago when he said good bye to her and felt like he'd left his whole world standing there on the fifth floor with his dead brother.

He wasn't ever going to do it again.

Asher was tired of saying goodbye to Emie. He was tired of having to leave her, and was tired of losing her in his thoughts and dreams wondering if she was going to leave him.

Ken had told him the moment it had happened with him. And last night it had happened to Asher.

He wanted to text her every moment of every day. Wanted to tell her his thoughts. His plans for them. He wanted to share his past, his present, even his future with her. There was so much more he wanted to learn about her. He would never be able to get enough of her.

He wanted to know how to get to her house so he could visit with her. Show her his house so she could come visit him.

He wanted so much more of her, and tonight he planned on getting her. With her permission of course. First he had to ask her to attend the funeral with him tonight. He wasn't sure if it was a good idea either. But he needed her to be there. They needed to say goodbye to Curtis so they could move on. So he could move on. And tonight he was going to do just that.

Once he got to the hospital he stopped and picked her up some flowers at the little store in the lobby. He had some sent to his mother and sister as well, with all his love.

Stepping into the old elevator, he could see his image in the reflection of the steel walls. He was dressed in jeans and a white button up, sleeves rolled up dress shirt that made the muscles in his arm look as if they would split the sleeves apart where he had them rolled up too. He knew if he kept growing like this he'd have to buy new clothes again come winter. Would she take him shopping, he wondered with a shy smile. Would she stick around long enough for him to find out, he wondered again worriedly?

He rested his shoulders on the wall as the elevator started it's descent into the basement. The fear of where he was headed threatened his plans for the night. He was ashamed of how it bothered him. How seeing dead bodies down here was ten times worse then seeing them in the real world. He hated seeing the dead. He shook it off when thoughts of Emie's smile came back into his mind. He couldn't wait to see her.

He stepped off the elevator into the bright fluorescent hallway; the smell of alcohol filled his nostrils. Reading the signs in front of him, he was still unsure of which way he wanted to go. To his left was a waiting area and a corner that lead to another hall with a big plaque sign that read "Personal only past this point."

He agreed with the sign. Tonight he wasn't breaking any rules here.

To his right, he saw different offices lining the hall. Surgery waiting room, Surgery post op, double doors that led to the operating rooms. Further down the hall, some lights were on, some were off. The hospital must be saving on energy at night. It made the hall seem scarier.

He shook off the chills when he reached another hallway. He scratched his head trying to decide which way to go. One hall was darker then the other. The hall he was headed for had a sign that read "Records department", and down the other hall he saw a sign he couldn't quite make out because it was near the end. He picked that hall since he needed to read the sign. Just as he was about to step into it, the darker hall, he heard a woman's gasp.

He turned slowly and hoped it wasn't that nurse he had met the other night. He never wanted to see her again as long as he lived.

Good, he thought. It was just Cristina.

"Hi there, I'm looking for-"

"Emie, yeah I know. She's, um.." Cristina's cheeks heated. Damn this guy was hot, she thought. Emie was so lucky, she thought. And look at the flowers? She grinned to herself. Cristina was instantly jealous of her best friend. "She is upstairs in a meeting." Cristina told him.

He stepped back a little from Cristina. He hated crowding people with his height.

Figures, he thought. He had braved one of his worst fears coming down here for nothing. Well at least he knew he could do it again if he had too.

"Ok then." He lowered the flowers. "Do you know how much longer-"

"I'm not sure, she's technically not working tonight, I think she was planning on going to your brother's funeral though. She might not even come back down here after the meeting."

"Do you know what room she's in?" Asher said cutting her off. This friend of Emie's was a talker. A good looking woman too he could tell. She was tall and sure of herself. She talked so fast he wasn't sure he completely understood her, but he had a feeling he should listen to her. She knew Emie better than he did, and he was sure she would help him with whatever he needed.

"If you take those elevators back up to the second floor and wait there in the main lobby just off the elevators, she will have to walk past you when the meeting is over, you can't miss her."

Asher thanked her and she watched as he walked back down the hall. How romantic, she thought as she turned back into her office.

Asher was back in the elevator again. Their elevator. He should have texted or called before he got here, but he was looking to surprise her tonight. He was headed for a floor and a waiting room he didn't know if he could find. But he was determined, damn it.

When the elevator doors opened on the second floor he was against the back wall with one hand in his pocket the other holding the flowers he hoped would save him from feeling like he should have called on her sooner.

He felt his stomach fall back down to the basement. Emie was standing right in front of him, and for a second, he didn't recognize her. He could have sworn… No. He just needed more sleep that was all. There was no way he had seen what he thought he had.

"Emie." He breathed with a smile after he blinked his vision clearer and seen her beauty.

Emie was exasperated to say the least after walking out of the meeting room. Those board members where all buffoons! She told herself shaking her head as she walked down the hall, adjusting her bag and all the books of reports she was carrying.

She had just finished arguing with the board members of the hospital all the reasons why her department couldn't handle any more 'Economic' cuts. She needed more supplies. She needed a few more staff. She needed to be in charge of her own money!

She had been arguing for almost an hour with them, swearing these big dummies were going to drive this hospital straight into her basement if they weren't careful. Even the doctor's were all on her side for once.

She had every intention of calling Joseph when she got down to the lobby, until the elevator doors opened and Asher stood in its depths.

Was this the same scared shitless feeling she had given him that first night, she wondered. Had he seen her anger? Her fangs? Her eye's? She could only hope he hadn't. She hadn't expected anyone to be in the elevators this time of night.

"Asher." Emie's whole being lightened up. She stood in place almost stunned. There he was, right in front of her again. Her whole body felt warm, she hadn't felt like that in over a hundred years.

But what was he doing here? Why wasn't he at the funeral home with his family?

"I was looking for you down stairs, and ran into Cristina. She said I could find you up here."

He was walking closer as he talked to her. His voice deep and rough. His scent, his body, his clothes, she took him all in and just watched. She slowly remembered her thoughts. Who was controlling who, she wondered. Had he heard her thoughts, or just read the confused look on her face?

"I was gonna wait, but since you're done…" he trailed off; he was standing over her now, the same rush of emotions pulsing through him. For once in his life he was enjoying his height.

And to think of how close he was to missing her, he thought. It only made his smile that much bigger. He would surely have to thank whoever was in charge of his fate for this.

He couldn't believe she was standing in front of him again. Close enough to touch. Last night had not been enough for him. He needed to touch her again. Her hair, her eye's, her lips, her scent, they were everything he remembered, and yet better somehow.

He wanted this woman with a passion so great it threatened to over take him. Turn him into some savage beast. He took a deep breath and steadied his raging feelings. Breathing in her scent and taking in her beautiful body he truly didn't deserve.

Emie got lost in all their emotions. She felt he needed her acceptance for something. Emie would freely give him anything in this moment. Unconditionally.

"These are for you." He held the long stem red roses out for her. He knew now what her favorite color was. The girls at the store had asked him more then once if he truly wanted such a big bunch of roses, twenty four must have been overdoing it.

It wasn't until he filled out the card that they figured out why he wanted so many. Asher told Emie sweetly in the card "I miss you sweetheart." What she had wanted to know last night.

Emie smiled up at him now. "No one's ever brought me flowers before." His card was so sweet she couldn't believe he had written that, but then again, he was so good with his words like that. She bent forward and took a deep smell of them. They tasted delicious but the scent and sweet taste melted inside her mouth into ash. It was his scent that lingered in her. His blood mixed with an ashy, smoky, heavenly-hellish scent that drove her insane.

Would his name be symbolic of everything she could never have? She closed her eyes and inhaled deeply again.

She would have taken them from him, but she was laden with books and folders and a big black bag that read "Monroe County Blood Bank" hung over her shoulder.

Asher stood there for a second, just looking at her smile at him. He had to smile at her too when he realized he wasn't. He was lost for words. He couldn't even remember why he was here.

Oh this is stupid, Emie thought! She was a vampire! Vampires didn't act like some love sick human girl who swooned at the sight of a handsome man. She shook off the feeling and his and then she was taken back by his own thoughts. He was looking at her lips and he wanted her again. Wanted to kiss her again.

She felt like blushing. So much for being a vampire. She felt that same heat rise in her body as he reacted to hers. Felt herself melting from the inside out.

Goodness, she thought, he hadn't even touched her yet!

Who was she kidding? Asher could melt her just by touching her.

When she looked down shyly, breaking his spell over her once again, she seen the bulge in his pants and had to close her eyes before she did something like laugh out loud at him. His jeans and his shirt were so tight. His excitement for her was very, very evident. She couldn't help but measure his size and think Well, maybe size does matter. She almost had a moment to herself to remember just how wonderful his size felt last night, until he spoke again.

"Emie," He reached out and held her hand in his. He had to touch her again. "I swear sweetheart, you're gonna have to start wearing your hair differently or somethin." He had to say something to get her eyes off his crotch. It was embarrassing how she had affected him and how he was reacting to her, but he couldn't help himself. She was so damn beautiful!

She instantly reached for her pins in her hair and wondered if it was a mess, and smiled cheekily at him knowing where his thoughts were headed.

"Or throw on some god awful makeup, and real bad smelling perfume, and for all our sakes start dressing in baggy jeans and an old t-shirts, cause... damn girl..." He sighed aloud. "I'm a fool Emie. And I'm falling, I'm fallin real hard for that body of yours."

This last threatened to turn her to stone. The way he raised his voice high, then stumbled over his words, and paused, and finished his sentence with that deep rough voice she was learning to love so much.

What in the Hell was a girl supposed to say to that!? Seriously? She hadn't a clue.

Her hair was tied in a loose braid down her side, not hanging in curls like he liked. Her outfit was a tight black business dress. She had a pencil in her ear and felt like a real nerd, or at least that was the look she was going for this afternoon before the meeting. But he saw her differently.

He seen her hair as something he wanted to let loose and run his fingers through bringing out the curls, her black stockings as something he wanted to run his palms up and down and learn its textures and her curves as he slid them down her legs, and he wanted to undo every last button down the front of her dress and slide it off her shoulders...

Such a guy, she thought, disapprovingly shaking her head ever so slightly.

She could play this game too. She rubbed her hand up the side of his arm, leaving goosebumps the higher she went and leaned closer to the flowers again. Looked up into his eyes and watched his gaze follow her breast.

"Well, seeing how you look in them tight jeans and old t-shirts I think that might even be a problem for you too. Then what would there be left for me to wear? Hmm?" She questioned this last with a wink.

That might have hit him below the belt, she thought. He was trying to be all sweet and here she was turning him on higher. Good thing the board had chose that moment to walk out, or he might have told her what he would or wouldn't like to see her wearing.

"Stairs?" They both questioned each other it at the same time, as they watched the men walking towards them, neither wanting to be crammed in an elevator with a bunch of old, over cologned, snobbish men. Even if it was their elevator. They glanced at each other sideways from over there shoulders as they greeted the gentlemen with easy careless smiles.

She ran ahead of him, giggling, like an idiot she told herself, down the stairs after they passed a few floors in silence, jokingly telling him she'd race him. Neither had known what to say during the silence, so this felt like a great way to break the ice.

He tried to catch up until he realized how many more stairs they had to go. He took his time then and knew she was just running the heat out of him like a cold shower.

She waited for him at the bottom. Leaned on the door and acted tired as he rounded the last set. He wouldn't have a chance beating her ever, whether she was wearing high heels or stilts. The frown that threatened to over take her smile, knowing just what being a vampire meant when you're trying to love a human, she overpowered. She wouldn't think about those things tonight. Not tonight she told herself.

Grinning at his huff and puffing, he asked her where the closest bathroom was as they opened the doors and headed for the lobby. Emie told him where the closest one was and told him that she would be waiting out at her car for him.

She knew what question he had for her now that he was thinking about it, it was eating him up inside, and she couldn't wait to say yes to him. He had to take a moment away from her to think about it again before he asked and she wanted to give him some space.

Once outside, the sun was finally setting behind the clouds coming and Emie knew she had the rest of the night to enjoy being out of the house. It was only five o'clock. The funeral started at seven.

When she turned around and closed her car door, she watched as Asher walked out the hospital doors.

Asher was trying to fix his shirt and adjust himself in his jeans and was thinking hard about how to ask Emie to go with him tonight to the funeral home. He also wanted to spend more time after that with her. He didn't want to say goodbye to her tonight. He hated saying goodbye. He knew what was coming; his paper he had written for his brother's eulogy was burning a hole in his pocket. He was going to need more of her tonight then he deserved to ask for.

He contemplated asking her to drive up north with him this weekend, but he thought that might be rude of him. She didn't seem like the type of girl who slept with guys in the first weeks of dating. She came across as an old time girl who liked to take things slow and know that she was being cherished. And he liked that about her. He liked making love last.

No, he told himself. He wouldn't ask that of her.

Emie's heart sank when Asher changed his mind. She had been waiting all this time to say yes to him. She could just picture being alone with him for days. Pretending she was scared out of her mind as she held onto him while they four wheeled around those dirt muddy roads he was picturing. Bathing in a hot tub on his porch and staying warm by a fire out by the lake in an old swing. It was going to rain the whole weekend. It would have been perfect. But he wasn't going to ask her now. And there was no way for her to tell him she wanted to go.

But at the same time she feared what it would do to him now if he found out her secret. She also wondered if it would be to late now. He had fallen pretty hard for her already. She really, really didn't want to hurt him, or lose him. She never wanted him to find out who she was. For the first time in a long time she wished she wasn't who she was. And leaving the protection of her home and going away with him, she knew there was a good chance he would figure it out on his own.

"Cristina said you were planning on going to the funeral tonight?" Asher asked when he reached her.

She wondered if this was ok, as he placed his hand on her car next to her.

"I came here tonight, to ask you if you would go with me." He felt like a kid as he said it. "Damn it! That sounded so much better in my head. Why do I feel like I'm in high school again." He looked away as he took his hand off her car and leaned his back against it tilting her car slightly, but then pretending shyly like he hadn't moved it at all setting it back down right.

His size really bothered him, she had to wonder why. She seen him differently. Like a big teddy bear she wanted to hug and squeeze. Not like the ogre he was imagining he was. Especially when he was holding two dozen roses.

When Asher turned his head back to her she was smiling. Did she always smile, or was it just him?

Emie couldn't relate to high school, but she could relate to not knowing how to feel when she was around him.

"I would be honored to be by your side tonight Asher." She told him honestly as she leaned next to him on her car and reached for his hand, entwining her fingers through his.

They looked towards the dark red sky of the setting sun.

"What time?"

"Oh, I need to be there in about an hour and a half." He looked at his watch and laughed.

"Well get in then! A girl can not be expected to get ready in that-" Emie started to say as she turned towards the front of her car to get in when she felt his arm around her stopping her, his body pressed neatly up behind her in an embrace, before she even heard him think about it.

He whispered in her ear, "Not your car sweetheart. My bike." He pointed over to his black and orange Motorcycle, parked alone facing Luna Pier Road and watched as her head turned towards it. When he felt her still at the sight of his bike he knew she would go with him. She had just told last night she loved motorcycles.

She considered this for just a moment. "My purse?"

"I have saddlebags." This he said while pressing himself against her, holding her hip against him begging her with his hand.

"My flowers?" she breathed recklessly.

"I'll buy you more." He promised. Kissing her neck on the side that was bare, loving her reaction to his touch, and with his kisses he promised her a good time.

She opened her car door and threw her purse in along with his roses he left on her seat, locked her door with her keys and headed over to his bike. Hell with her stuff! It was tucked safely inside her car.

Emie loved his bike instantly. She ran her fingers down the leather seat while he attached his helmet. He handed her one like his. She chuckled at first at the thought of it, but had to play along she knew. Most motorcyclists wouldn't ride with a partner who didn't wear a helmet. With him being a firemen and all she knew he was one of those.

If he only knew, she told herself secretly and sighed.

She was glad her hair was braided when she placed her head in the helmet and watched as his body rocked on top of the big cycle. He revved up his engine while she climbed on the back of him and smoothed her dress under her. It wasn't too long a ride home, and she was happy for it.

Asher reached back and patted her legs, she gave him a thumbs up like she did her brothers, he took the hint and they rolled smoothly away.

He took off down the expressway at full speed. She absolutely loved it. She lived only one exit down; one mile was all she was going to get at the moment on the bike with him. She raised her hands in the air, played with the wind in her fingers.

Asher watched Emie closely. Her bare legs wrapped around him. Her arms felt cold, but still she raised them and absentmindedly played with the wind. She looked beautiful in his mirrors. Watching her made it hard to concentrate on driving. He had to smile shyly at her when she caught sight of him looking at her.

Heading up the overpass on the Erie Road exit, her exit, Asher had mixed feelings about what he was doing. He'd never been to the Whitby's home. No one had. It was locked up tight with gates and fences. Signs were posted all around. "No trespassing." "Beware of guard dogs."

No one knew what was on the other side was more dangerous than any guard dog, or a crazy man with a shotgun.

Emie had already told Jeremy she was coming. They were supposed to be rounding up the dogs and making sure nothing would be in Asher's sight from the drive to her house. She needed to change into different clothes for the funeral. She hoped too that she would have a little time to show him around.

Nothing was supposed to be in his way. Nothing, except for three very hungry vampires. Three very tall, very scary, intimidating brothers.

Asher was impressed when the black, old rot iron, ten foot high gates opened for him. He drove right into the heavily deep wooded entrance; she pointed his way down the overgrown paved path, that was cracked with deep holes here and there that he had to dodge. Even though the sun had set, there was no daylight shining through the woods, just his head light. She reminded him over his shoulder that they were still remolding the place.

Driveway must be last on Joseph's list, Asher wondered.

When he rounded the next turn, he noticed the beach laid up just ahead in the clearing. He stopped his bike and looked back at her. "Mind if we make a detour?" He had never seen the beach from this end of the city and he was hoping he could spend just a little more time with her alone tonight before he had to face the inevitable.

Emie heard his heart racing over the rumble of his bike. He truly did want to see the beach, but his body was aching to feel more of her. She looked in his mirror and eyed him seductively holding him closer to her. He was literally begging her in his mind now, and he didn't even know he could do that.

With a nod of her head in agreement Asher took off down the road to the end of the tree line where the beach lied. He pulled his bike through the sand close to the water's edge and turned off his bike. He was parked sideways along side the lake facing the lights of Toledo. Looking out over the water he took in a deep breath of anticipation and placed his shaky hands on his thighs.

Emie took off her helmet and shook out her hair. She too looked out over the evening sky on the lake and sighed. This part of the beach was her favorite. An old tree, in the shape of a glove that she could snuggle up in and read a book all night long, sat just to their left.

"Want to see my tree?" she asked in a somewhat giddy voice.

"Tree?" he questioned, leaning back into her as she held onto him. Her breath was on his ear and neck as she spoke to him and the feelings of desire he felt for her when she was near returned to him in waves. He looked back and seen the peculiar tree she could have been talking about.

"I found it when I was little out here. Whenever I just wanted to escape, or run away, I'd come here. I love to read." This last she to him as he looked back at her. She knew he needed a place just like this and was more than happy to share it with him. "So I come down here a lot and sit for hours reading. I lose track of time sometimes. Between the waves and trees, it's the perfect peaceful serenity for someone looking to escape life. "

Emie slid off his bike and walked backwards holding out her hand sweetly to him. Asher got off his bike and followed her. Kicking off her dress shoes towards his bike, Emie walked him over to a tree that was shaped like what he thought was a ball glove too, through the sand. He had to shake his head at her as she let go of his hand and hopped up into it effortlessly, like she had been doing it since she was a little girl.

Her tree was lying on the outside of the tree line that lined the sandy waters edge. Tall grass lay all around it like sea grass. Seashells and rocks were strewn everywhere. She was kicking her toes out and smiling at him invitingly. She knew they didn't have much time, but her body wanted his just as much as he wanted hers.

Asher was trying to find his voice. All thoughts of well mannered conversation he couldn't find in his brain anywhere. Emie's body and lips were all his eyes could see. Were all his body could concentrate on.

He hated when he shoved his hands in his pockets, but honestly, if he didn't, he was going to fall to his knees and run his hands up her stocking legs, and God forgive him, but he wanted her so badly in that moment that falling to his knees and worshipping her was the only thing he could think of to do.

"You are so adorable when you do that Asher." She told him, cocking her head to the side sweetly looking up at him.

"When I do what?" he asked her nervously, worried she had read his thoughts.

Oh, when he found out she could... she thought to herself. He was going to definitely be irate with her.

But in that moment, he was standing before her, with his hands stuffed in his pockets shyly. She knew his thoughts were anything but pure, but his actions were so gentlemanly they were adorable.

"When you try to act like you're not dying to kiss me." She whispered just loud enough for him to hear. She wondered what it was he was waiting for.

Asher took a deep breath and walked over to her. He pulled his hands out of his pockets and vowed to never do it again. She had just told him he never had to hold back with her, and he promised himself he never would from now on.

She wanted him to be reckless. He could feel it running off her like a sweet demand.

Asher closed the distance between them quickly. He ran one hand down the braid that was hanging down her side and stared into her eyes. When he reached the end he pulled off the little band holding onto her braid. Throwing it over his shoulder he eyed her curiously as he slowly unraveled her hair with his hands. He let it fall sweetly behind her letting his fingers linger in the curls.

"Just so you know sweetheart, every time you put your hair up, I'm gonna wanna take it down." He informed her seductively.

The swell of emotions that raced through him was evident in his jeans. He leaned down and placed his hands on the tree to support him so he didn't crush her. He knew the moment he found her lips would be the moment that the world would melt away and he welcomed it.

Her mouth met his in the darkness and he kissed her. Damn it, he kissed her like he was starving. He could hear his own moans as he felt her hands crawling up his chest to that spot behind his neck where his hair met his shoulders and her fingers ran up into his hair and she softly pulled at it. It was like a jolt right to his cock.

He reached his hands up behind her into her hair like she was doing to him. He couldn't resist the feel of her body in his hands one moment longer. He ran a hand up the back of her, and he placed the other neatly under her pulling her towards him. He pushed her body lower into him, neatly wrapping her legs around him, kissing her and pushing his tongue inside her mouth like he wanted to do with other parts of her body.

Emie held Asher in a lovers embrace. Her arms were solidly wrapped around his neck, holding him close. Her legs were pulling his body neatly up against her. Kissing Asher, letting Asher kiss her, Emie couldn't seem to get enough of the little heaven they were in. The crashing of the waves behind him up onto the shore mixed with the pure smell of the fresh warm water was enough to serenade them.

Time though, always seemed to be their enemy. They both knew where they should be in that moment. Getting ready to attend his brother's funeral. But neither wanted to move away from each other. Neither one wanted to let this moment slip away from them.

Asher ran his hand down the side of Emie's body. He molded his hand around one of Emie's breast and gently squeezed. When she moaned and her body arched up for more of his touch, he braced himself against her and slid his fingers inside her first two buttons on her dress, pulling them softly down. He pulled down her bra next and felt her nipple slide between his knuckles and squeezed again.

Emie felt the world slipping away again. The feel of her breast in Asher's hand again, the sound of the waves falling upon the shore behind him in the rhythm of her falling emotions, the knowing of all the wonderful possibilities that could be happening next fluttering around in both their minds was enough to cast out any fear of anything stopping them from living in this moment.

Asher moaned and pulled away from Emie's kiss. He looked into her heated eyes and saw only beckoning. Slowly he lowered his head, finding her nipple wanting and waiting as she leaned back, hard and accepting to the touch of his tongue, he suckled on her breast, holding her body through the waves of moans and aching she was feeling for him.

Asher called out her name as he moved to her other breast in a moan of pure desire. He wanted so much more of her in that moment. He wanted to curse himself and fate for bringing this perfect woman into his life at the worst, possibly busiest time of his life. He wanted to take this beautiful woman right here and now and show her a side of himself no other woman had ever seen in him before. He wanted to love her slowly. Find and make the sweet passion that was unfolding in them that they were both feeling and let it take them higher then he believed either of them had ever been before.

He could feel it rising inside him. He was heated to the depths of his core with it. His cock was all but busting out of his jeans dying to impale himself deep within the depths of her soul.

Asher returned to Emie's mouth then. He lifted her up into his arms, turning he fell into the sand below them bracing his back against the tree.

Emie crawled closer to Asher. She had to hike up her dress to get closer. His bulging cock was bucking with excitement when she pressed against him. His hands roamed inside her hair and down her back as he kissed her neck and shoulders. Her body was screaming now for more of his touch. Asher was pushing her over an edge she was afraid of falling over, but his embrace felt like a promise of security she had been searching her whole life for.

He ran his hands down her back past her hips and found her bare bottom with his hands. She was wearing a thin thong and a garter belt he could feel that was holding up her stockings. He groaned in his kiss. He couldn't get enough of her body, and everything she wore just drove his wild side crazy.

"Emie." Asher found Emie's ear and moaned into the column of her neck. He could feel her pushing against his hardness and knew what she wanted, knew what her body was reaching for. He had longed to give it to her again today. His breathing had accelerated. His need for her right now was overwhelming him, but knew he still couldn't take her yet. This place, even with all the romantic surroundings of the beach and the waves, this still wasn't the time for them. He wanted to make love to her in a bed, not on a sandy beach.

Asher ran his nose up and down her neck, kissing and licking her everywhere he could. Her smell was intoxicating and driving him mad. The taste of her cool skin was making his mouth water for more. His hands were roaming her body and try as he might he couldn't linger on just one spot. He wanted so much of her.

Emie heard his thoughts and wanted to do nothing more then to claw at him and beg him for things they both wanted. She took a deep breath and smiled up into the night that surrounded them. As Asher placed a long hard kiss between her breasts, she reached into his hair with both hands and pulled his face up to hers to kiss him softly.

She let a wave of calm pass through them both and listened as his heart rate slowed. It saddened her to feel the pleasure drain from her own body. The heights she had found last night and today from the feel of his kiss, the warmth of his touch, the way her core desired the rough feel of his manhood against her; she prayed that whatever fate was taking this away would soon bring it back to her again.

Asher sighed into her kiss. He hated this, hated when he had to stop kissing her, or worse, say goodbye. He reminded himself he at least didn't have to say goodbye. Not as long as he could help it. The happy thought over took him and he picked Emie up into his arms again and laid her down in the sand.

Giggling, Emie asked him what he was doing.

"Promise me something, Emie?" Asher said, playfully looking down into her eyes.

"Anything, Asher." And she meant it. She would stop time for them right now if he asked for it.

It was in those moments, that Asher knew his world would never be the same without her. It wasn't the times when they shared passion or the times when he was so happy he couldn't imagine life getting any better. It was times when she looked at him like that. Like she lived and breathed to be with him. Like she would give him anything he asked her for. He didn't deserve her, he knew this, but he couldn't live without her either.

"Promise me, no matter what happens tonight, you won't leave my side. Stay with me, and be there for me when this is all over." He asked in a breathless sort of way. He'd never needed to beg anyone for anything, but right now he felt like he was begging her for something even he didn't know what it was.

Emie sighed up at Asher. She hated the loneliness he was feeling. The depths of it were heart breaking. This wonderful man, who knew everyone and needed nothing, was lonely still. He had found in her something he also had been searching for. She would never deny him this. How could she? She needed the same thing of him, and wondered secretly if who she really was, would be enough to push them apart.

Emie smiled and said "I promise Asher."

Fourteen

They turned onto an old cracked cement road that steered them away from the beach towards the old Whitby mansion.

Asher knew he would see it soon, that huge mansion he always tried to find in these woods as he past them on the expressway. When he finally did, he was in awe. It was much bigger then he had imagined. The house stood inside of huge oak trees that shaded its lower levels from the sun and moon, but through them you could see an empty void behind the house; a moon lit lake.

Asher pulled around the gravel circle drive, lined on one side with old hedges and more trees, a pond on the inside, making the perfect circle maze, with openings on all sides, paths that lead in all directions. Lamp post taller than him self lined the walk up to the massive house, they were dimly lit with just enough light to see up the path to the house, without casting light on the dark gloomy mansion.

The Whitby mansion, in its entire dark splendor, looked gothic this time of night. Green, English ivy lined the north side of the house they had pulled around, up and over the front and door way, giving the mansion dark gloomy shadows.

Huge winged horse statues jutted out from the corners of the massive stone stairs. Black goblin knockers where hanging from the thick old wooden doors. Asher could see them from where he had parked his bike.

The windows on the first and second floors were made of stained glass and probably older then the building itself. The morning and evening sun would look amazing shining through them. He wondered what rooms the windows where in and was curious to see them from the inside.

He could have sworn he could see bats looming in the window sills as he glanced at them. This house was everything he had heard about as a child, and then some. He could feel the rush of fear again creeping up his spine and tried to hide the goose bumps and the raising hair on his neck.

Asher parked his bike in the middle of the driveway and Emie climbed down.

"Would you like to come in Asher? It might take me a minute." Emie told him as she shook out her hair that had been trapped in her silly helmet she didn't need.

He was still looking around in wonder. "Yeah."

Emie wondered if he was going to trip on his way in, he kept turning his head this way and that. His thoughts were filled with his own haunting images of her home. She had to laugh quietly at his thoughts. If he only knew.

Emie didn't hear anyone on the inside, which should have been her first warning. The hall was empty as she opened one of the front doors. The first thing he noticed was the ladders and paint buckets. There was scaffolding reaching up two floors in front of the huge front windows and doors, also around the staircase. She hoped he would understand.

"I'm sorry; you're going to have to excuse all the mess Asher. Joseph has started a lot of projects around here. We are still in the process of repairing Whitby to what it should be."

Asher nodded in her direction, but he was captivated by the glass diamond chandelier hanging in the open ceiling of the front room. He wondered in amazement at how brightly it shined and lit the entire room with radiant light.

It wasn't until they had walked further into the front hall, and she set down her keys that her brothers walked out from the dining hall doors to their adjacent left. As they walked further into the hall that Asher was awed by, between the limestone floors, and the other dimly lit crystal chandeliers, to the hard wood beams that arched the ceilings and lined the marble staircase, Asher couldn't stop looking around. The walnut walls of the hall seemed to make its depths seem darker and deeper then the room really appeared.

Asher stared at the two double doors as they thundered open and three very large, men of tall height and stature, walked out from a cigar smoky darkness. Asher had spent most of his adult life worried about his height and build. Emie's brothers were the same size as he was. It was no wonder she felt at ease with his size and bulkiness.

The way they carried themselves though... Asher didn't know what it was about them; all he knew was he suddenly admired these men he had hadn't even met yet.

Emie had to smile at their entrance when she heard Asher's thoughts. They had that 'rising from the crypt' creepy look to their entrance. She wasn't impressed at all by them.

They were dressed handsomely in new black evening attire, she felt like she had gone back a few centuries to a time she didn't miss. Although they did look stunning in their suits, the only thing missing were there top hats. The women at the men's dress store in town must have had a blast with these boys, Emie thought to herself.

"Well, well. Hello there." Joseph greeted them both, closing the doors behind him.

Emie noticed he was dressed in a tall black suit, buttoned in front, with a dark black, no collar shirt. His spiky brownish-blonde hair looked like real spikes atop his head. His white creamy complexion and blonde streaked hair was the only color to his attire.

Jeremy and Jordy were dressed similarly. Dark black suits, black shirts, unbuttoned at the top of course, like they were aloud to wear them that way because it looked good on them. She had to admit, they did. But they were adorned with more accessories then needed really. Red jeweled gold cufflinks, red handkerchiefs, black sunglasses, gold watches and red signet rings. They reminded her strangely of men you didn't want to meet alone down a dark alley, or a gambling parlor.

They were removing their dark rimmed sunglasses, just as Emie remembered their eyes. Asher was so impressed with their dress he hadn't looked at their eyes yet. Emie had changed his mind just as they walked over to shake his hand.

Asher felt very underdressed. If they were planning on attending the funeral tonight, they would be severely over dressed for this small community. And he would feel severely under dressed in his firemen uniform standing next to them.

"Asher is it?" Joseph winked at Emie so quickly she wondered if Asher had time to notice the jester. In the past few days they had called him everything but his right name, she was glad to see that secretly they knew it all along.

Emie took a deep breath, her brothers smelled fresh and clean, instead of like the outdoors and horses. She found herself missing the absence of it at the same time. They looked and smelled totally unlike themselves tonight. But beneath the façade, they were there, trying to give her a gift of some kind. Were they planning on attending the funeral also she wondered?

Asher looked scared out of his mind as he reached forward and shook each brother's hand. She wanted to help him, but she knew he needed to do this too, on his own.

"Yes, Asher Stone. It's a pleasure to meet you all." He said in a pleasant, not so scared voice. She steadied him just a little, just a little bit as he said his next sentence. "You must be Joseph. And Jeremy? Jordy?"

Asher surprised her when his mind figured them all out. Joseph carried himself like he was the oldest, Jeremy had that good ol boy smile, like all cowboys should have, and Jordy had an air of sophistication about him, like he had walked with kings and dukes and could spar with the best of them. She was very impressed indeed, he had been listening to her that night and had remembered.

After last night though, nothing should surprise her anymore when it came to Asher's attention to detail.

And even though the two younger brothers were identical twins and most people had a hard time telling the difference between them, she was still amazed he had found the little subtle differences that she knew to be their separate identities. Not many people could do that. She assumed that because his younger brothers were twins also that it just made sense to him.

"I will be attending Curtis's funeral tonight with Asher." She informed them aloud, wishing they would finally spit out why they were dressed the way they were. She had much more to say to them, but they looked as if they were totally ignoring her and she didn't like the way they were looking at Asher. She had to admit, he really was something to look at, and his scent was still something of a mystery to her. " If you'll excuse me gentlemen, I-"

She was neatly interrupted by Jordy who looked straight at her with a direct look so suddenly she almost gasped, and in a deep solid voice that scared even she, he said, "Yes lil sister, do hurry back."

And then by Jeremy who did that twin thing she hated, speaking on the heels of Jordy, finishing his sentence in that same exact voice, same bone chilling, English tone "We will see to Asher and make him more comfortable while he waits for you. Do hurry though; we don't want to be late."

She looked at Joseph then for help. Did they plan to attend? She wondered.

When Joseph nodded at her he looked at Asher then. "We plan on attending also. Your brother was well known in this city, I'd like to my respects to your family."

Then Jeremy said to Asher, "Do you like brandy?"

Then Jordy asked, "Cigars?"

Emie looked at them all in awe. Not only did they plan on attending, they planned on drinking with him also.

Asher had noticed the exchange, smirked and nodded towards her brothers as he rubbed the back of his neck to try and knock off the hair raising feeling he was having. He had sisters too, and knew what the looks and silent gestures meant.

Emie had a murderous look on her face for her brothers who were smiling sweetly back at her. All but Joseph, who honestly, looked quite bored by the whole thing. He almost looked like he needed to check the time, like he had somewhere else more important to be.

Had they been planning to go to his brother's funeral? Did they want too, or was it just a formality in politics she wondered.

Emie look towards Joseph with a pleading smile that Asher at first thought was a look for help, then he thought she was silently telling the man he needed to reel in the dogs before she embarrassed herself and strangled them all in front of her date. Or worse, stomp her foot in protest like his sisters did.

This was even better than his family fights. It was a nice little tit-for-tat that finally took the edge off his fear of meeting them. But the thought of her leaving him here returned his fears. He had hoped to go to her room, or apartments she had called them once before. But he knew with her brothers here, that was not something he was about to do. He himself would strangle any man who tried to follow his sisters upstairs to their rooms.

Although, brandy sounded nice. It wasn't a cold beer, but the thought of the hot liquid and the burn of the cigar mixed with the rush of nicotine, would warm his thoughts and heart. It was just what he needed before heading to Curtis's funeral. He looked down at his feet and shuffled just a little at the thought of his brother, trying to hide his emotions in front of her family while she scrambled with them over their choice of drinks.

"Must you really-" Emie stopped when she heard his thoughts then. They whispered loudly in her mind as if he was whispering in her ear again. She stumbled on her own words aloud to her brothers.

Emie, this from Joseph, he needs this Emie. Let us take him to the den. He will be fine. You have my word.

Joseph knew how to communicate with humans. He knew what they needed physically, mentally. Where her abilities lied in being able to read them and comfort them, he had the ability to see them, truly see them. To heal them, bring them comfort in his talk, his walk. He could also scare the hell out of them if necessary. This last, she feared most; Jeremy and Jordy only teased and played with their food, but Joseph on the other hand could kill a man with just a haunting look, a look that could invoke heart failure even in the strongest of men.

She shook her head then and said "Well then, if you must, give me just a moment then. I won't be long." This she smiled at Asher, assuring him she would be back.

Fear.

Real, unadulterated fear.

The kind that takes your breath away, and makes you want to hide in the darkest corner, trying not to breathe, fearing that just the sounds of your breath would give away your location and you would die. You curse your own heart for beating so loudly because you can't hear your own thoughts, let alone the movements and sounds around you.

Asher could say he now knew this fear unlike anytime before. He tried to understand it, tried his damndest to make it go away. Knew in his heart, if Emie were only here with him, he wouldn't be feeling like this at all.

These men that he honestly did not know, this large, dark, manly smelling den that quite drastically displayed a wealth untold he had never seen before, the roaring fire on the south wall from the huge stone hearth with bright popping embers from logs that had been burning for some time threatening to burst out of the hearth and catch the entire room on fire, even the dogs, if they were even in the same category as the average dog, they looked more like wolves, were large, well mannered sleeping by the fire; all this added to the room the surreal feeling of powerful men in their own right.

The 'dogs', just happened to be laying too close to him for comfort. Joseph had introduced Asher to them when he took his seat. Even their names, Lycan, Thorp, and Willow; all hinted towards mythical wolves. Werewolves at that.

Asher was sitting in one of the many richly clothed wing back chairs that circled the fireplace. It not only felt ancient, but also looked and smelled older then all the men in the room.

He had been tricked by the brothers to sit. As he did, they stayed standing; Joseph by the mantel with one of his black leather booted foots resting up on the edge close to the raging fire, his elbow leaning on the ledge that held large statues of wolves and eagles and oddly placed evergreen branches. Jordy stood over by a near window, eerily staring out into the darkness with a cheeky smile on his face that shone in his reflection. Jeremy was somewhere behind Asher, making his comfort zone dissipate further in the depths of his surroundings. Maybe he was over by the desk somewhere, Asher wondered. The wings on the chair made it impossible to see behind him.

The giant desk that looked more like a tree opened up and cut in half, laid down on two massive stones pillars was striped and sanded to smooth perfection, then stained a black cherry color to match the chair. The chair that sat behind it, large enough he could have sworn it was a throne, could only hold a man of Joseph's size without making the person sitting in it look like a troll.

Asher noticed everything about the room was strategically placed. Nothing was here without purpose. It was a powerful mans room, where he worked during the day comfortably and content, and then entertained only the closest of friends at night. There was even a pool table set up in the dark east corner, surrounded by long wall hangings that held many different wood carved pool sticks. There were enough balls to change for every set game. He had even noticed a dart board on the west end, and a long shuffleboard that went the length of the two windows on the north side of the room. It was definitely a gentleman's den.

Brandy and whiskey decanters were set inside a large round globe of the world. The globe was cradled in wood and stone. Glasses set around the ledge of it that made spheres, making the earth look more like Saturn. This was placed in the circle of chairs as a coffee table of sorts.

The cigars were offered him by Jeremy who had seemed to appear out of nowhere. Then the brandy.

Asher pulled out his own lighter, for some reason fearing that if Jeremy lit it for him something might happen that Asher couldn't put his finger on. Jeremy even left Asher's side like he had missed out on a prank gone wrong.

These guys were doing a great job of acting like the champions of Emie. All that was missing were the shotgun cases of loaded weapons. That might have been overdoing it though. But still, they had gone to great lengths to make him feel uncomfortable in here, so he just expected it all to happen. Someone might pull out a gun, or an old aged pistol that would fit the d cor to a 'T'.

Joseph had enough. He had heard his brothers, read the scared mind of Asher; Jordy by the window trying not to laugh aloud, and Jeremy who had planned on lighting Asher's cigar with a log.

They had their fun. Now it was time for business.

Joseph had plans of taking the whole family in his SUV that was being brought around by Herman, the front footman, to the funeral in town. But when Asher and Emie had pulled around the front drive, Emie had seemed so happy riding on Asher's impressive bike. And Asher still wasn't dressed, which meant he needed to stop by his house first to change. Which also meant, Emie was going to go with Asher and not with them.

This last he wasn't sure how to handle. He had never had to play the father-meets-boyfriend-with a shotgun on the front steps with Emie before, so he was a little out of his league and had recruited their brothers for help. Mistake one on his part.

He wanted to tell the little pip-squeak to head home, change on his own, and bring back the proper vehicle to be driving his little sister around in. Not that Emie needed the protection of a vehicle, but still. It seemed like something a fatherly figure would say.

At the same time, he wanted to meet Asher. The son of his long time rival in the city. His father, Frank Stone, and Joseph were going to have words soon. Joseph just needed to give the old man some time to grieve first. It still bothered Joseph that Frank knew they were vampires and this knowledge had slipped past Joseph. He needed to know if Asher knew what his father did. He hoped by being in a room full of vampires, and not being blinded by their sister's beauty, would prove him right or not.

As a teenager, Frank, who was still growing into the straps of his bunker trousers, would attend the council meetings with his father before him, pleading for more money for the department like Joseph had something against the department and wouldn't give them anything. Frank's anger would rage inappropriately at the meetings.

All Joseph wanted from the department was written proof of what they wanted and why. His knowledge of fighting fires and medical response was very limited. He had been focusing on building a city back then, not running a fire department. That, he had left to the departments head in charge. Not that the uneducated volunteers knew what they were doing at that time.

Joseph was glad when the times and standards had changed in the fire services. The men now running the department, like Asher and his brother Curtis were well trained and skilled in all aspects of the business. These were men Joseph was looking forward to dealing with. These men he could work hard for. Deliver the best that this world had to offer to them.

Now that he knew where Frank's anger had stemmed from, and probably the night that it had happened, that he somehow knew what they were; Joseph wanted to corner Frank in the worst way and have it out with him. If only to help Emie.

Looking at the young pup sitting in Joseph's father's old business chairs, Joseph wanted to invoke fear in him. He wanted Asher to see and respect him for the man he had worked all his life time to become.

Jordy and Jeremy took note of Joseph's determination and immediately followed suit. They knew when the fun had ended and business was about to start. Jeremy handed Jordy his drink and lit cigar as he turned from the window and they both walked to stand on either side of Joseph.

Joseph took his time reading Asher. Asher was still taking in his surroundings; he wouldn't notice Joseph who was intently looking into his soul. Or at least he shouldn't have.

But Asher did.

Asher looked up at Joseph over his drink, then to the two others who held a domineering stance next to Joseph.

Fear. Asher was learning to hate fear. He wondered what it was they were staring at.

His childhood fears of vampires entered his mind. He had previously thought that these men very well could be drug dealers, or gamblers, or anything other then what his mind had been picturing before he had met them. He really hadn't known Emie that long, they very well could be the kind of men Asher didn't want to associate himself with and he was just beginning to accept that fact when he had looked up at Joseph and seen a very frightening sight indeed.

His mind wrapped around what every child he knew growing up had said lived here, whispered the one word that scared every vampire. The one word that drew out their fangs and made them hiss.

Their own name.

"Vampire." Asher said under his breath in acknowledgement and took a quick sip of brandy. He hadn't meant it at first, it was just an old memory that had crept up out of nowhere, but what he saw when he did made his heart skip too many beats. He started to choke on his drink, and dropped his cigar.

Jordy was there beside him in lightening speed to catch the burning cigar before it hit the carpet. Asher still continued to choke on the burning liquid he had inhaled while looking at Jordy curiously. How was that possible? How had he moved so quickly?

Had he really just seen three men hiss and fangs? Had he really just seen fangs protrude from their teeth?

Damn it all! Joseph whispered in their minds to the boys. Did he see us? He questioned them, referring to their fangs and hiss.

Both men were too stunned at their own reactions to Asher's words that neither one could answer him. It had been years since someone had said those words aloud to any of them. Their acting had been played so strategically, Asher was the first in many years to see through them.

"Well then, I think we've killed- ...enough time." Joseph closed his eyes at his choice in words. "Emie should be back down any second. Why don't you wait for her in the hall Asher, me and the boys will make our way over to the funeral home now. We will meet up with you two there." Joseph said, excusing them all, while Asher stood and choked all three men ushered him out of the den.

Asher hadn't known that they were all vampires. He wasn't secretly plotting to ruin them all like Joseph had thought. Asher was really in love with Emie, and now because of them, he believed they were all vampires.

Asher was thinking about his father now, and how he had overheard him as a child saying something much like what his friends had about vampires living behind this fortress. Joseph felt like such a fool now. He prayed he could fix this.

Joseph knew that he should have patted Asher on the back to help relieve him of choking, but because of what Asher had said, and what he had seen, Joseph was glad he was still choking and couldn't say more on the subject as they headed out the doors of his den, but he did want to kill himself before Emie could find out what all had transpired in here. He threw his cigar into the fire as he shut the doors, sucked back his venom and anger at Asher, and followed out all the men, guiding a frightened Asher out in front of him.

There was nothing he could do now. They would have to leave and let the two lovers work this out. She would kill him when she found him, and he knew he would just have to let her.

Emie had changed into a simple, long, black, silk dress. Dark red and orange flowers were strewn about its length like paint thrown on a canvas. It had a simple, yet exotic appeal to it. She would adorn it with a simple black sweater to cover her bare shoulders, but she would wait till later to put it on, hoping her cleavage wouldn't be to revealing or inappropriate in the tight noodle strap dress.

She shook her hair and watched as the curls coiled and tugged down her body. She remembered how Asher's mind would wrap his fingers around and in her hair, and how he had done just that out by the beach.

She took one last glance in the mirror and impressed herself with her choice of dress tonight. Cristina would be proud.

She headed out of her apartments in the north wing and headed back for the main staircase. She was so excited about seeing Asher tonight that as she flew down each step, she had forgotten to listen for him. She had just assumed he was still in Joseph's den. She stopped at the edge of the last landing, stunned to find Asher standing at the bottom of the staircase in shocked silence, looking up at her in disbelief.

Vampires…

No, that's not possible! Asher tried to think quietly as he heard the door at the top of the landing open and close. Her brothers had just neatly exited out the front doors in such a rush he hadn't had time to question what had just happened in the den.

He was still choking on the burning feeling in his lungs from the hot liquid of the brandy. He couldn't believe what he had seen. What he had seen, what scared the hell out of him, was the possibility of it all.

He had to see Emie, he had to know if it was just his imagi-

Asher couldn't finish his thoughts as he watched a blur like the one Jordy had caused in the den, descended one set of steps onto the set lower, heading straight for him.

She looked like a ghost.

If his suspicions weren't fulfilled with her brothers, then they were now as he watched her stop so suddenly from floating, or flying, whatever it was she was doing.

Asher's world came crashing down around him in one swift blow. Like someone had shot him through the heart with an arrow. He felt pain like he had never felt before. The shock that replaced it left him in disbelief. If she to was a vampire, then what the hell did she want with him?

Emie took in his presence at the bottom of the stairs and realized too late her mistake. She had worried this would happen. Worried she would get to comfortable around him and something like this would happen. But what Asher had seen, she wasn't the only reason he was looking at her like that. Something had happened in the den.

Emie stood as still as she could when she seen him there. She hadn't known if he had noticed her running like a bat out of hell or not until he replayed it in his mind. Then he replayed her brother's fangs and how he knew what they all were.

Then he seen her eyes all red she had forgotten to hide, and had to close his own. The realization of her, the woman he loved, being one of his worst fears, was just too much to take in.

Emie put on her best face, changing her eyes and her frown. She smiled at him and pretended nothing had happened in the space of his heart beats. "Oh, hello there. Did my brothers-" she started to say as she stepped down one step at a time. Then, there in his mind she could see everything. Everything her brothers had done. She was going to slaughter her brothers, piece by piece. Leave their body parts hanging outside in the trees for the dogs to find and let their heads watch eerie as the dogs ate their pieces from the porch. Horrible as that sounded, for the first time in her life she hated them enough to find them and do just that.

"Leave? Yes." Quick short answers were all he could say at the moment. Her brothers had left; they had left him all alone to figure out all he needed to know. But Emie looked so stunning in that dress, he was confused by his feelings for her. Her hair looked just as he had remembered it down. Silky, curly and shiny. Damn but he loved her hair.

Just a moment ago her eyes had been a different color. They had been as red as blood. Another confirming blow to his gut. Now they were the deep brown he remembered, and now they would never be what they once were to him. Her eye's had been memorizing to him. Real. Now he knew they were just as much a scheme as everything else about her was. A lie.

And somehow she knew. It was written all over her face right now. She knew he knew. She couldn't pretend anymore. The question was, did he have enough time to find out what to do about it?

They were running late now, he thought as he dragged his eyes away from her body and looked at his watch, removing his foot off the bottom step and trying his hardest to breathe, but that only brought her scent inside of him and made him dizzy. He only had forty-five minutes to get home, get dressed, and get back to the funeral home where he should of stayed at tonight instead of doing all this. Damn, but he wished now he would have stayed there.

Shaking his head he looked down at the floor and stuffed his hands in his pocket, not knowing what to do. He didn't have time for this.

Again, his mind moved faster than what she could read. His mind was cursing himself for trusting her so deeply already without getting to know her better first, and Emie felt like she was dying inside all over again. All she wanted to do was tell him that she couldn't help falling in love with him. But she had to keep up the façade until she knew for sure where this was going to go. It was still possible he had just seen something he shouldn't have and would forget about it soon. Like her running...

What was she thinking? Of course he had seen something. Normal people didn't run like that. Normal people didn't have eyes the color of blood. Normal brothers didn't bare their fangs at the word vampire! Or tease the hell out of someone till they caused them to be frightened!

He knew she was a vampire now.

She was going to kill her brothers slowly soon, she reminded herself fuming. She tried to finish each step down towards him slowly, looking at him, not knowing how to apologize, and not knowing what to say next.

After the longest stretch of silence they had ever experienced, he said calmly "Shall we?" as he reached for her hand.

She could not only feel his heart racing but realized why it was hard to hear. It was skipping. This wasn't healthy for him she thought. She took his hand in hers and walked down the last step. His hand was ice cold instead of its usual warmth.

Emie was just as surprised as he was when he had decided he was still going to the funeral with her. She really thought he was going to tell her to go to hell and walk out without her. He hadn't really made a decision; he just went with what he knew to do. The gentleman inside of himself he was battling with had won out. She took his hand and told his heart, just incase his heart was still listening to her, that she would follow him anywhere.

Asher let go of her hand as soon as he reached for the door. He couldn't touch her anymore. He finally understood why her hand was always so cold. He recognized it now. It was the chill of death. He felt this chill before, and only now did it make sense. He was so shaken when he realized this, he had to let go of her. It just confirmed what his brain was trying to scream at him.

He opened the door for her and let her beautiful body pass by his as he took in her scent again. He closed his eyes for just a heartbeat. Let it sit inside of him. But it only clouded his mind, it took away the thought of what she was, only made him wish she wasn't, even though he knew what she was now. And then he started down the stairs ahead of her and didn't turn back to her until they had reached his bike.

Thoughts of being late for his brother's funeral were now racing through his mind as he reached for his helmet. He couldn't be late. Not with her brothers there with his friends and family. Now that he knew what they were… He couldn't be late.

Asher tried to shake the thoughts from his mind. Just hours ago he was madly and irrevocably in love with this woman. But he was torn between thoughts of what any other human would and should do with this knowledge of who she was, and the pounding echo in his heart that was trying to remind his mind that he was in love with this woman.

This knowledge left Emie on the brink of tears. He'd said it again and again. So many times. He loved her… He'd all but said it aloud, and might have said it to her tonight before all this tragedy.

This was her fear. Falling in love with a man; loving him enough to lose him. Like a mountain she had to climb, she had to figure out how to face her fears and not lose him. Hold unto him with both hands, show him who she really is, and show him she loved him just as much. But in the end, facing her worst fear, losing him, letting him go, she didn't know if she could do that. She wasn't ready for that yet.

His touch had always been so predictable and welcome. When he took it away she didn't know what it would be like to live life again without it.

As for the rest of his thoughts, he wouldn't have to worry about her brothers, they would be lucky to make it through the first part of the services. But she knew in the back of her mind somewhere, that her brothers were not the murders he was thinking they were. They just needed more time to show him who they really were.

She ran her sweater up her arms and covered herself with it snugly; the cool night would feel colder in the wind as they rode back to the pier.

Asher turned to Emie, really looked at her while she was looking away from him putting on her sweater, ready to hand her a helmet wondering if she even needed it now, and was trying not to think about the how's and why's he knew of her family.

All he knew was he loved her with a passion that almost caused him not to care what she was. He had to concentrate on where they were headed and the fact that his family needed him right now to be of a sound strong mind. Not this divided broken mess. All of this could wait. Couldn't it?

But Emie was behind him now; she had climbed up behind him without a word, a vampire was behind him, holding him! And all he could think about was he wanted to stop his bike and kiss her. Kiss her like it didn't matter as he revved up his bike.

Her hands started doing that little thing where she lifted them up and down in the wind as he sped off, not like before, he could tell it was different for her now, but he still loved it watching her in his mirror. Her face was more solemn in his mirror then before too, her beauty was still ever present though. The way she held him this time, he could feel it. She was holding him like she didn't want to let him go, as he made his way around her land and back to the expressway. She hadn't told him yet that she loved him. Had she? He wondered. Or was that all a farce too?

They were headed back to Luna Pier faster then they had left. He couldn't help himself. He was driving as fast as his heart was racing. Emie's dress was neatly tucked under her, her legs exposed to the night air around them. This he knew because he was just a man, and when he had watched her climb onto his bike and prepare herself for the ride, he had reacted instantly to seeing up her dress in the mirror.

He had to close his eyes at the stop sign at the end of his exit. Close his mind to all his racing thoughts as he slowed his bike. Rocking it a little, not sure which way he was going, he found the strength to fight it all and return home with her.

He sped through the city like he was flying. He knew these roads like the back of his hand.

His mind remembered the nights when he was a child playing in the fall out by the canals with his friends. They had teased each other with old ghost stories and talks of vampires the closer it got to Halloween. Someone had said they knew of vampires on the south side of town. No one had believed the kid then though.

Except Asher.

Asher had known then that there was an old mansion on the other side of Luna Pier. He also knew there were wolves over there like the ones he seen tonight in Joseph's den, even though no one had believed him about that when he told of their howling at nights during the full moons. Vampires had been a stretch on his childhood imaginations, but the chilling thought that they really did exist, combined with his younger sister's endless chatter about them; had caused a reaction her brothers hadn't expected tonight. They had been looking at him over their own glasses and cigars. Joseph had that intent look of him that said he was looking deep into Asher's soul, but it was the other two, with their hungry smirks. They looked like vampires to Asher.

Asher pounded his fist against his bike as he drove down Lakewood Drive, just before his street. Why now? Why tonight? Why had she done this to him?

Emie seen in his mind her brother's reaction to his own thoughts. How could they do this to her? What had they thought would happen when they played with Asher like this? How had Jordy not seen this? Or had he? That last question in her mind was going to haunt her until she had the answers. Had they done this to her on purpose? Was this what Jordy had been trying to tell her the other night.

Jeremy and Jordan, in the space of a millisecond, which shouldn't have been long enough to be noticed by Asher, but somehow was, had flashed their fangs at Asher and hissed when they heard him say vampire.

Joseph had scolded them openly but he too had reacted, and Asher, poor Asher had spit his drink and choked on it.

All three men had followed him out of the den and informed him they weren't going to wait for their little sister since she had a ride with him on his bike back. They stupidly told him they would see him at the funeral, and left him, alone there in the hall, with his thoughts his only comfort.

When Asher reached Fourth Street, his street, he turned down and headed for his house, revving his engine a little too loudly down the little road that was lined closely with houses. He was thinking of all the reasons he should have left her standing on the steps in the hall. She was and would always be a vampire. No matter how much he loved her, he couldn't fix her. He couldn't bring her back.

Emie's thoughts sadden her to her bones.

She's Dead, damn it! Dead! Damn it all! Sometimes he could fix dying, but he couldn't fix dead he told himself.

Emie couldn't take much more of this. Every word he thought of in reference to her, was like spikes inside of her.

She had kept back the tears. Somehow. She was keeping her cool and listened to his every thought. She had no idea how she was going to look at him when he got off the bike. But she would be brave. She would even if it killed her.

Jordy's words entered her mind. She hadn't told Asher she loved him. She hadn't taken that step and told him, showed him how much she loved him. Instead she had taken the easy road and not done Jordy's warning that Asher needed to know she loved him. Was it too late now?

Asher pulled up behind his truck in his drive. He looked at Curtis's truck that was now parked next to his. He thought about driving Curtis's truck to the funeral, but thought it might be odd.

"Did you want to take my truck now that it's getting late?" he asked her as he took off his helmet and shut off the bike.

Emie knew he would be wearing either a suit or his dress uniform, so she was certain he would want to drive his truck.

"Yeah. We should take-".

He was already off the bike thinking of how he could get her to stay outside while he changed. He didn't want her in the house. This crushed her and caused her to forget what she was thinking. He was already letting go of his feelings for her.

"your truck." Finished saying after their thoughts interrupted her.

Emie smiled at him like he hadn't just slapped her in the face. Smiled like he was still acting like the sweet guy she had been dating for the last week. All while she was reading his mind, how he was picturing her eating his dog, and couldn't get the grueling image out of his mind.

He was being mean now. He didn't even know anything about Vampires. How could he think so badly of her when just hours ago he had loved her so deeply?

Her pause caused him to turn around. Like she had said it in reference to his thoughts. Could they hear him, he wondered. Her brothers must have earlier, but could she also do that?

She simply sighed and looked over at the water. "Do you mind if I take a walk on the pier while you get dressed? I promise not to wander too far; I know we are running short on time."

Asher had to swallow the lump in his throat, he tucked his hands in his pocket as she stepped off his bike without his help. Maybe she could hear him, and he had just made an ass out of himself picturing this sweet woman eating his dog. He wanted this woman still he thought as she stepped too close to him. He wanted to take her hand and walk up his front steps and show her his home, where he had lived and dreamed of her for days since he'd met her.

Yes it was messy, and yes it was definitely a bachelor's pad that every guy dreamed of having, but it was still the place he had dreamed of her coming over to enjoy with him one day. Maybe even cook with him in his kitchen while they sang their favorite songs and danced in the kitchen. It wasn't very romantic dreams, he knew of course, but they were his dreams. And he wanted them even now that he knew he couldn't be with her anymore like he had dreamed.

"I'll meet you out there in a few minutes." was all he could say as he turned to walk up the steps.

Fifteen

Emie waited there on the pier in front of Asher's house. Her most favorite place in the whole world.

Lake Erie, this far south, was a very busy place to be indeed.

Ships from all around were pulling into the Toledo Harbor that was lit up like New York City, welcoming its travelers. Luna Pier was also ferrying small ships in and out of its bay to and from the Islands in Ohio.

This time of night, when the sun was setting in the west casting a dark blackness on the lake, it made the ships look like they were gliding on nothing at all.

The lighthouse, guarding the entrance to the Maumee bay, east of Luna Pier, north of Toledo, was brightly shining its light off into the night sky to alert those ships of the rocks and the islands.

Emie had visited the lighthouse before. She had heard stories of a ghost who dwelled in its keep and she had wandered out to see who was really out there. Vampire that she was, she was able to not only swim all the way out to it, but she was also able to walk under the water all the way to it.

The things she had found, not only in this lake, but out in the sea also, she had stored in her favorite treasures in her rooms.

Vampire or not, she had been afraid of the light house. Many ship captains had told stories of how they had felt beckoned by the spirit and how it had led them to the rocks, tearing there ships to pieces. Could this same spirit lead her, a vampire to her own death?

But alas, it had just been a mannequin in the upper windows, dressed in a "I love Toledo" t-shirt. He had been signed by many passer bys, and what looked like a dozen or so coast guards. So she too had signed it.

Emie was trying so very hard to distract herself at the moment, trying to stop herself from breaking inside. She lowered her head and rested her hands on the pier in front of her, trying to tell herself that leaving would be the best thing for the both of them.

But she just couldn't. She had promised Asher tonight no matter what, she would stay. There was also a war that was coming, dooming them all to an unknown fate. She couldn't high tale and run now, hadn't she been expecting this?

Sooner or later he was going to figure it all out.

Even now, as the cool, June moon lit night sent shivers through her cold body through her sweater, when she could simply disappear and let her stupid brothers clean up the mess they had made, she couldn't. She couldn't leave Asher. She loved him to much already. She had to find a way to tell him.

She looked out over the water where they had swam last night. She looked at the rocks and the cylinder where they had played that silly game together and he had held her in his arms all night long. She had felt so safe there in his arms. She looked back at the water then letting her mind remember what all he had done to her out in the water. Her body could still feel his.

Emie had started to love Asher somewhere between an elevator ride and a dance floor. She hated that she finally knew what love and loss felt like all in the same night. She hated that he was still upstairs, alone, sitting on his bed contemplating what he was going to do.

She couldn't leave yet. She had to stay and pray he made the right decision. The decision to love her. To let her love him. To Be Loved.

Asher was still not dressed. He'd managed to lose his brother, fall head over heels in love with a vampire, and lose his soul mate all in a few weeks time. Hours ago he was on his way over to the hospital thinking of the ways he wanted her in his life, and now he was trying to figure out how to get her out of it.

But did he really want too?

Who was he kidding, how did a vampire love a human? How was a human supposed to love a vampire? What had she been thinking when she had agreed to see him? It was written in every other book in the stores now, but he hadn't read any of them. He hadn't given them a second thought.

Until tonight.

He still remembered what she had looked like that first night. He still remembered her scent the night of their first real date out in Ann Arbor. She had smelled so heavenly as he held her close to him, while he kissed her so passionately. He could still feel her in his arms. Even now he wanted her like that again.

Asher stood and dressed, telling himself this all would have to wait till tomorrow. Or at least until the funeral was over. Last thing he needed was another thing his father could hate him for. Arriving late for his own brother's funeral with a beautiful girl on his arm would be one of them.

He reached into the pocket of his jeans and pulled out his notes, his brothers eulogy. Asher sighed and tucked it into his dress pants. He tied his tie in his bathroom mirror and tried not to look himself in the eye. Coward that he was, he couldn't stop himself from loving Emie.

Hell was going to have to take her from him first.

Coming down the stairs he had to hold on to the rails tighter then normal. That rush of fear he always got when she was around had returned. He understood it now. His body had always responded to what his mind couldn't see. Emie was waiting for him outside.

Asher grabbed Cookie, his little Chihuahua, who had been growling out the front windows at Emie; let her out the back door, smoked a cigarette while she finished her business and tried to keep her from running out front where Emie was waiting for him on the pier. The nicotine rushed through his head, made his hands shake for the first time ever, the heat filled his lungs and he felt the sweet release of relief. Then he downed his triple shot glass of whiskey he had poured himself on his way out the back kitchen door.

He took one more puff as he carried Cookie sweetly back up the steps, he remembered his dreams of Emie and Cookie playing together on the living room floor, he opened the back door and let her back in then walked down the back steps, tossing his smoke over the porch. It would never happen now. All of his dreams were all going up in the smoke around him. Like a fire he couldn't put out. Like a pain he couldn't stop from hurting.

He stopped at his truck. Emie was leaning on the side of his truck, the same side he had kissed her on their first date. He hadn't even paid attention to the dent on that side until tonight. His porch light illuminated it. He could still feel her pressed against him when she had made that dent.

Vampire. He said it again in his mind as he walked towards Emie.

Emie had to turn her head and look away from him when he said it.

He knew he was killing her now or something worse as she turned her head from his thoughts. It was written on her face. Slowly. Very slowly she was dying inside, she almost whispered to him.

He was also lying to himself. And she loved it. Odd that she was enjoying his battle in his mind to much to give him the privacy he needed to figure things out. The more she followed his mind around his house, the more she fell in love with him. He was trying to convince himself she was evil or something out of a horror movie, all while missing her, even though she was standing right here waiting for him.

Asher stopped briefly in front of her, he hadn't meant to ask her how he looked, he had never needed anyone's opinion before, but he had needed something to say to her so he wouldn't be tempted to be enraged with her, or worse, start kissing her again.

A picture of what he would have done right now with her had all this not happened tonight entered his mind. He probably would have smiled shyly at her and done a little dance twist like a singer would do on stage to show off himself and then he would have asked her how he looked.

He hated he couldn't even smile at her; it was tugging at his lips, she was so damn cute standing there looking like she didn't have a clue that his world had just came crashing down around him. He could only hope she would think he was acting this way because of his brother and where they were headed too. Odd how he had thought more of her these last few days then his own family.

"How do I look, Emie?" Saying her name, slowly letting his tongue move around her name, he didn't think about what she was. Just that she was standing here with him now.

Emie. The Emie he knew. He wanted to touch her, he wanted so damn bad to kiss her and get lost in her hair as he let go of everything that was causing him pain.

Emie noticed his tie was a little crooked after he asked her that question. She slowly walked up to him, letting him know what she was doing, keeping eye contact when he looked at her wide eyed, and then she reached out at a very slow human pace to straighten his tie.

She listened inside at his thoughts, and thought the hell with it, she smiled up at him at his little dance move he was imagining, if he could pretend nothing had happened, so could she.

She let her hands linger on his chest. She knew this very well could be the last time she got to touch him. He was dressed in a light blue dress uniform shirt, with a dark blue tie and dark blue dress uniform pants and shoes. His upper chest and arms were threatening to bust the shirt wide open.

His shirt had a white Paramedic patch on his left arm that was embroidered in red and blue with the Medic star of life in the middle. It matched the tattoo on his arm she had seen there the last night. On his right arm, he had a white Firefighter first responder patch with a Maltese cross in its middle. It too matched his other tattoo on his arm. His name was on his left front pocket, on a name plate that said 'Fifteen years of service'. On his right side was a fireman's badge, which held a black stripe on it in memory of his fallen brother tonight. She let her fingers trace it, knowing she was sending chills up his spine and loving it.

His collar was decorated with officer bars. His flat officer hat had a gold braid on it. His dress coat was slung over his arm, he must be feeling too warm to wear it at the moment she thought to herself. He was very nervous, she sensed. But he was holding up just fine.

"There, you look very handsome tonight Asher." She would have added that his cologne smells delicious, but that might have been pushing it just a little too far.

She couldn't believe how much she was going to miss this man if he decided to leave her.

Asher kept his eyes diverted from hers. He couldn't look at her. He couldn't let these feelings that where drumming in his head to touch her, kiss her, take over and lose himself in her. He had a funeral to go to.

"Thank you." Was all he said as he opened her door.

Emie was looking at the truck judging how to climb in with a dress and high heels when he took her by surprise and wrapped his arms around under her and lifted her up to her seat, nice and slow and gentle, just like he had before. She took the seconds she had and used them to smell him, to touch his shoulder gently; she ran her fingers through the hair on his neck and down the base with her palms.

Asher couldn't take much more; he stepped away once she was in and started to shut the door. She still smelled heavenly, still looked amazingly stunning. Why had she chosen to wear that dress tonight? Her breast mounds looked amazing in that dress and he knew he would be looking at them all night like a bad habit.

There was still so much about her he wanted to know, but couldn't allow himself to find out. Not tonight, he kept telling himself. He was running late already.

Things about her that he wanted to know now would be different then the answers he had thought he would get. Like her childhood. Had she had one? Had she went to school? He knew she had friends, but were they vampires too? Had she killed her own parents? Her brothers?

"Asher?" she asked him gently before he could step to far out of her reach. When he stopped short and looked into her eyes she almost forgot to finish. His eyes looked so lost in his thoughts. "If there is anything I can do tonight, if you need anything from me, don't hesitate to ask, ok?" She had to ask. Had to stop his mind from wandering. His heart was already racing with his fears of her and the funeral. Could he handle all this tonight, in one night?

She knew she could do this. Knew she could stay by his side, listen to his rampage of emotions, knew even if this gentle man who hated her at this very moment broke down again and started crying over his loss of his brother, she would be there for him. Be there to hold him, comfort him, will him back to a place that would strengthen him and help him move on.

Even though she could do all this, her abilities wouldn't give her the power to take away his hate for her. Once he knew who and what she was, there was no taking it away. A humans will could not be broken. Bended, yes, but not broken.

Asher looked at her this time. She had a heart this vampire of his. And she wanted him too, just as much as he wanted her. He could tell by the way she was looking at him. He wondered if her need to touch him was as strong as his. His fingers were itching now to run through her hair, down her curl that was lying neatly on her arm. Tears were threatening to drip down his cheeks.

He thanked her and shut the door instead.

The Funeral Home in Eire was packed tonight. Curtis Stone had not been just a hero around the city, but also in the county. In the state.

Joseph had walked around looking at all the awards that Curtis had achieved in his lifetime. He had taught CPR all around Monroe County for its residents. He had taught a few classes in the community college for EMT and paramedic, and also assisted in clinics for teaching at firefighter school programs all around the state and even in Ohio. He'd even taught a few dispatcher classes there. This meant that almost everyone in the emergency management departments all around the state of Michigan knew him. Or knew of him. And were here tonight.

The Stone family was a large family. Seven children, two son-in-laws, one daughter-in-law, eight grandchildren, two where married, two great grandchildren with one more on the way.

Frank had ten brothers and sisters, and his wife Cyndy had five brothers, both of their parents were still alive to enjoy the fruits of their labors and the many, many grand and great grandchildren. Happy marriages on both sides of their families meant there was enough family members to pack out every holiday and birthday, every graduation and wedding. Every funeral.

Joseph, while waiting, stood in awe of this family. They truly had the American dream. They had left their mark on this old city he had created. Made enough memories to fill the pages of history with.

Emie would feel the same awe as well, he would have bet his life on it. His little sister had always wanted family. She had sacrificed their lives just to keep them with her forever in her immortality. She couldn't imagine a life without them. But if ever asked, she did it to save their lives, to give them a chance to live. He'd never tell her vain secrets though.

Joseph loved his sister. Loved her enough to hate what had happened tonight. Hated that he was to blame. Hated that right now he was more worried about her then he'd ever been. Asher could very well destroy her with just his hatred for her.

Emie didn't put a lot of stock in what others thought of her. She'd never been one to dress in the newest styles, or care about the latest trends. She always got stuck in ruts and was happy with them. Pants and shirts had always been Emie's trend.

But lately, lately she had wanted more out of this life. She had started shopping more. Acting more like the human she had forgotten how to be. Dressing in clothes that he thought she looked amazing in, buying enough accessories to fill up her closets and then some. He'd had to redo her closets just to help her organize it all.

Her favorite store was in the mall. A new trend that blended designer and rustic in a comfortable mix of worn and torn; expensive but worth every dollar.

Joseph waited. He really tried.

Where were they at? Had Asher drove the bike and wrecked? Why couldn't he hear her thoughts? Why couldn't he feel for Asher's?

His mind was a horrible thing to get lost in. All his thoughts scrambled together with possibilities and scenario's... Some day's Joseph hated his ability. Some days it haunted him. Knowledge and wisdom had been a terrible thing to waste on him.

Jordy was standing close by, close enough that Joseph could see him and watch his reactions just incase he seen Emie first.

Looking out the windows he saw Cristina pulling up the long dirt road drive. She had been a sight for sore worried eyes. That and she was just a sight, as pretty as she was. She was the reason Emie had taken this new turn in her life. Cristina was the reason Emie was now enjoying living. She was the reason Emie was now happy. And he was the reason she was now dying inside.

He watched as Cristina walked up the front steps of the home.

Cristina found Joseph when she walked in the parlor. She didn't know why she was here; she just knew she should be. She'd spent years in this city alone with her son. Trying to start a new life over again had been hard until she'd met Emie. Emie had been her saving grace. Cristina knew tonight she wanted to be here. Be with her friend, and her family, and Emie's new boyfriend. Seeing Joseph sent chills up here spin. He was a tall domineering man, who stood tall and proud of himself. He was so handsome Cristina couldn't help the rush that overtook her. But she instantly felt that something was wrong. The way he was looking at her now was unlike any other time.

"What is it Joseph?" she questioned him.

Joseph breathed out slowly. "It's Emie."

"What's wrong?" Cristina asked as she placed her hand on Joseph's arm.

Joseph looked at her. Looked at her hand on his. She wasn't afraid of him and he had never understood that.

He knew she knew they were vampires, knew Emie trusted her with their secret, but standing here in front of all these people, he worried about how much to reveal. "Asher knows."

Cristina gasped. "Does she know he knows? Well of course she does..." looking in Joseph's eyes was all the answer she needed. Cristina knew as she took a step back gathering her thoughts. Of course Emie knew he knew. "But where are they?" she said looking around. "Are they ok? What happened?"

Joseph reached out and took her hand. He knew she was strong enough to handle his abilities. He was the only one in the family who could do it. He used it on her now, pretending like he was just holding her hand, which he did because he had always wanted to, only because there was too many people in the room to hear what he needed to tell her. He let all that had transpired in the den fill her mind like she was standing in the room with them when it happened.

Cristina had to put her other hand on his arm to steady herself. She knew he could do this, just like she what all Emie could do. Emie had never kept any secrets from her. But she hadn't expected it, and it was making her dizzy. She looked up at him and tried to hold on to him.

Asher had been so afraid. "I see." She said to him.

Joseph took a deep breath. "Now you know." This he told her, knowing she had seen more tonight then she really had. He released her hand before he could show her anymore.

She didn't let go of his arm, he noticed.

"I promise Joseph, I know her. She will be ok. She will know what to do. We just have to let her. She's braver than you think. And stronger than even she knows how to be."

Joseph looked at Cristina. He knew she was right. But he hated to admit it.

"Where are they Joseph?" she begged of him looking around.

"They are coming. They should be here any minute." He told her. He was proud of her in that moment. She felt the same as he did for Emie. He was glad he had someone to trust her with. "Could you go and sit with the boys? Try to loosen them up a little?" He knew Cristina was good at that. He smiled at her sweetly and pleaded with her to do it.

"Yes. Of course." Cristina looked out the window he was standing next too. "Will you tell me when she gets here, like you just did?" this she asked of him looking at him more intently. "And bring her to me?"

Joseph nodded to her. He knew their friendship would change now. He could hear what she was thinking. Everything he had ever felt for her he could hear in her own heart. He had to stop himself though. He didn't want to show her what his heart was begging him to show her. It wasn't time yet.

He watched as she walked away from him reassured. Watched as she walked over to the boys and greeted them. Watched as she did just what she does best.

Joseph sighed as he turned back to look out the window and heard Asher's truck pull in the drive. He looked out the window reading all of Emie's thoughts. Every ounce of blood he had left inside of his thirsty body boiled up and vanished inside of him.

Asher was late. Just a few minutes.

He parked his truck next to all the other fire department trucks. It wasn't hard to tell which trucks belonged to fire men. The light bars on top of their trucks were a dead give away for a fireman. That and the bold red Maltese stickers on the back of them all. Every firemen in the county must be here tonight, Asher thought, a little pleased so many of them had come here.

Had they waited for him in wondered? Or just started without him. Was his father waiting for him at the doors cursing him, instead of being with his grieving family?

Were they all still alive? He thought off handedly.

Asher stopped thinking at the site of Joseph standing in front of his truck.

Joseph hadn't been there a moment ago, Asher thought to himself. He hadn't even been outside.

Asher put the truck in park instead of running over the monster in front of him.

Joseph was looking at Asher like he was going to rip his head clean off his shoulders. Asher had to concentrate on breathing, swallowing the saliva that was rising in his mouth, threatening to drown him. His heart was racing again.

Despite it all, he held his ground, and stared Joseph down. He may be just a human, and Joseph may be able to rip his heart out of his body, but damn it, Asher was not going to let him take the best thing that had ever happened to him right out of his truck without a fight.

"Emie, could you ask your brother to go back inside." Asher closed his eyes then. He remembered he hadn't told her that he knew anything yet. Well, they were eventually going to have to talk about it at some point tonight, right? Why not tonight, everything else about this night was messed up anyhow. He thought to himself as he reached for Emie's hand.

Emie was just glad Asher still hadn't looked at her. She had to glance in the passenger side mirror to make sure the bloodstains of her tears were gone, so he couldn't see. He had been so mean in his mind on the way here. So hateful. His loving feelings for her couldn't compare to his hate.

"At some point tonight, Asher, we are going to have to face what we've both been hiding from each other."

She opened her own door and slid her hand out of his grasp before he could hold her hand and hold it the way he always had before. She didn't want it now. She knew it wouldn't mean the same as it had before or feel the same either.

Asher climbed out of his truck and slammed his door shut as Joseph walked over to Emie. He could see the love between them like he had for his siblings. They were a family. A family of-

Asher shook his head. He had to stop thinking of it. He couldn't say it anymore. They were a loving family just like his family was. And Joseph had worried about his little sister just like he would have.

He knew now she had heard his thoughts by what she had said. He hated himself for everything he had thought. Her words echoed in his heart telling him he had hid things from her too. But he couldn't face those things now.

Asher tucked his hands in his pocket as he waited for Emie leaning on the front of his truck. She must know that he knew. She wouldn't be hugging Joseph now like she was. Holding unto him for dear life, like the ride here had been a trying experience for her. He wanted kick himself for all his stupid thoughts.

Asher looked to the doors of the funeral home. Her actions wouldn't look out of place here. He let her have her moment with her brother.

When had he started caring what others thought of him anyways? Everyone was just going to have to wait on him tonight. He didn't care anymore. He was here and Curtis was already gone, it wasn't like either one of them was going anywhere.

Joseph hadn't a clue what to do with Emie. He didn't know how to hold her again like this. How to stop her from crying. Or soaking his coat in blood. She was going to run out soon, and then he was going to have to carry her body out of this place kicking and screaming when she attacked someone.

That made Emie giggle. Leave it Joseph to start being funny now, she thought. Thank you. She told him. I needed that.

"He doesn't deserve you if he doesn't love you baby girl." This he told her aloud. It didn't need to be hidden.

His nickname for her brought down one last tear. Her father had always called her that growing up. She reached up, stood tall, and knew he was right. She could do this tonight. What she did tomorrow would have to wait till tomorrow. She just needed to turn her mind off from Asher for a while. She looked up into the eyes of her big brother and willed herself to be ok.

Only seconds had passed for Asher. She hadn't caused too much of a scene, so she took a deep breath of the fresh night air, and walked over to him. She started to reach out for his hand and she had to steady her resolve. She loved holding his hand, but Asher had stuffed his hands deep in his pockets. He only did this when he was nervous; she knew this now that she was getting to know him. Little things like this she would always remember about him. She knew this might be the last time so she held out hope that he too would reach for her hand.

Emie breathed hard. This was the bravest thing she had ever done before. She could do this. She could. As long as he stopped hating her she could do this, she thought as she held her hand out to him.

Asher looked at Emie as she walked up to him. At first glance, she looked like the same girl he had met. The same woman he had fallen in love with. But there was something so real about who he knew she was now.

He watched from the corner of his eye as Joseph walked past them back into the funeral home. Asher had to try hard and not look away from her. Not watch the monster as he walked towards Asher's family and every one Asher knew.

She was reaching out in a gesture to take his hand and be the same loving caring person he knew she had pretended to be. He waited for what seemed like forever before he could take her hand in his. It wasn't until she tucked herself neatly next to him and held onto his arm so tenderly that he realized she was still the same sweet, too cute and adorable woman that had changed his life forever. He realized also as he stood to walk with her next to him that all she had ever wanted from him was to be loved by him. It was going to make all the difference for him tonight. He slid his arm down and reached for her tiny hand in his. He picked it up and kissed the back of her hand. Let it linger there as they walked together through an open door.

A funeral for a firefighter is unlike any other funeral. The death of a firefighter who had been burned alive was the worst kind of death imaginable. When a human body burned; the flesh, the mind, it felt everything. It was a torturous death.

For the family of a firefighter, this kind of death was a haunting nightmare. The heart ache would never stop hurting; the tears would never stop falling. There was no comfort in knowing how he died. Only that he was now no longer in pain.

Joseph knew this now as he watched from his seat towards the back. But Joseph couldn't think about that now. Now all he could do was watch Asher and Emie as they walked in together.

As Asher walked in with Emie by his side, he was greeted by throngs of friends. Everyone was offering their condolences. Then, by his grandmother who took him in a tight embrace. Asher seen the hurt in her eye's and felt her need in her embrace to hold her family close. He also felt Emie's hands slip away from him, and it worried him. She had promised not to leave him tonight, no matter what. He was going to hold her to that promise even though all the circumstances had changed.

"Oh Asher." His grandmother said to him in a heart wrenching voice. "How are you doing sweeting?" She asked him as she held him at her arms length, unbidden tears falling down her face.

"I'm ok, grandma. There's someone I'd like you to meet." Asher turned, and sure enough; Emie was standing next to him. She was so somber, it was breaking him.

She was shyly looking away from him, rubbing her arm like she was cold.

He smiled at her, took her hand in his again and shook it a little getting her attention. She was looking at the ground looking out of sorts like she didn't belong. He wanted her to know she did. When she looked up at him trying to understand, the realization and change that took over her smile, made tears fell down his cheeks. It wasn't just the mood in the room, or the coming events of the night that did it. It was her.

He really did love her. He loved how she responded to him, like her whole world depended on him now. She was so sensitive and attentive to him. The way she responded to him just then took his breath away. He didn't deserve her, and he knew it.

If she only knew, he thought to himself.

He turned back to his grandma, wiping tears from his eyes. "Grandma, I'd like you to meet..." He paused, only because he had never said it. "My girlfriend, Emilie Whitby." When he said it, for the first time he actually glowed. He could feel the heat of it warming his cheeks and his heart. It was like a slow fire burning inside of him turning him on.

"Oh!" His grandma exclaimed out loud looking at Emie. "Cyndy has told me so much about you. And you're just as pretty as Izzy said you were." She added with a tearful wink.

Emie found it so endearing. Here was this grieving grandmother, who had lost one of her own, and yet she'd taken out the time to greet her and compliment her. Emie took her aging outstretched hand in greeting in her own and thanked her. "It's a pleasure to meet you as well. I hate that I am meeting you all under these circumstance, but it's very nice to meet you all the same." She said, trying her best not to look back at Asher. His heart felt tears were too much for her in that moment.

"Well, I hope Asher has been just as kind in the telling of his family. It so nice to know that he's found someone. We'd been worried he never would." She jested at Asher.

Asher hated that he hadn't even mentioned his grandmother to Emie. She was a very important part of his life. Another realization that hit him hard.

So much he had left unsaid. He hoped he'd get another chance. He stole a glance at Emie. She was so pretty he still couldn't believe it. He didn't think he deserved another chance.

Emie tried to listen to his mind. It was like listening to static. He had pushed her so far away, now, well now she couldn't tell the difference anymore.

Just then Asher's father walked up.

Emie reached for Asher's arm. This was a problem she hadn't planned for. She willed her brothers to be still. Willed them not to come to her rescue no matter what. They didn't need to make scene. Not here.

Joseph answered her by coming up next to her and standing by her side. There was no way he'd leave her alone now.

Emie closed her eyes and held tight to Asher's arm.

Asher felt Emie tense and he tensed in the same manner. He nodded at his father.

There was something unspoken between them all. Asher knew one day he and his father were going to have to talk about it, but he hoped and prayed, tonight wouldn't be the night.

Frank stood up tall and acknowledged his son. "You're late." He said this while spurning a glance at Emie and her brother.

"Where's mom?" Asher asked, not wanting to fight with his father. There was no reason to introduce him to either Joseph or Emie. He'd already tried once and his father had scared her right off, like he was doing again now. Asher felt a surge of need to protect Emie from his father. He'd never felt like this with anyone else. But he knew there was no in hell he would ever allow his father to treat Emie like he had his family. Ever.

"She's where she should be. Where you should be." Frank was staring his son down now. He glanced at Emie again trying to make her feel as unwelcome as she should feel. He didn't want any of them near his family tonight. Especially Asher.

Emie took a quick breath, she hoped Asher would understand what she was about to do, but it really needed to be done.

"Asher, why don't you go see to her." She turned and looked at him then as he did too. "I have something to ask my brothers." This she told him knowing he would accept as she excused herself from his father's heated glances.

Asher looked down at Emie. He looked over at Joseph who answered his thoughts with a nod of his head. He didn't want to let her go and feared losing more than just her presence if he did, but he knew they were right. He needed to go and see his family alone.

He reached down and kissed her lips, pulled her in an embrace and whispered in her ear "Wait for me sweetheart. You promised.".

"I know." Emie whispered into his. But she couldn't promise it again. She clutched him instead. Holding him for what felt like the last time.

Tell him you love him Emie. This from Jordy who was sitting behind her.

But she couldn't.

She breathed him in deeply, let his scent fill the voids she was feeling. She let her lips linger on a place on his neck, she felt his pulse there quicken and his body tighten at her touch. The monster inside her never even surfaced this time. It let her have this one precious moment with him. She turned and walked past Joseph. She couldn't even take his offered arm. She was so lost she just wanted to run.

As she walked over to where her brothers were sitting she felt so apologetic for everything she had done. This night shouldn't be for him the night he discovered the evil things in this world. He shouldn't be feeling what he was about her. He was torn between love and losing her. He was fighting a battle he couldn't win. He should just be grieving, she told herself. He should be spending all his time with his family. Not with her.

She knew what she was. She was a monster. His worst nightmare. She had been so unfair to him and she was just now realizing it.

Emie looked out of sorts, like she didn't know where to be, where her place was. With the man she loved or with her family who loved her, who she didn't really love any more at the moment. They had taken their seats together in the back anyways, solemn and uneasy. They looked every bit the vampires they were, and hadn't meant to be.

Her brothers felt the same loss feeling she did. They loved her, and they had hurt her. They were all paying for it now in her silence and crumbling spirits.

Joseph noticed when Emie couldn't handle Asher's thoughts as he stared at her. He watched as her and Cristina got up and walked to the ladies room. Emie would need a minute to contain herself. He watched as Asher noticed as well. He watched as Asher sighed and finally realized that Emie knew his thoughts. It frightened him. He had just been picturing a slaughter in his mind if one of them got hungry.

Joseph made Asher look at him with his will. When Asher did, Joseph glared at him.

Asher excused himself from his family and headed out one of the backdoors. Joseph listened to his thoughts and followed his every move.

Sixteen

"Cristina, I don't know if I can do this anymore." Emie said from behind a bathroom stall.

Cristina was leaning up against the stall door the same way Emie was from the opposite side. Their backs against the thin door. She knew Emie's head was in her hands and there was tears, blood, dripping down her cheeks that no one else but her was allowed to see. Knew also that Emie didn't cry.

Cristina sighed and wondered what she was supposed to say to Emie. She really didn't know what to say. Emie had made this decision to love Asher. She leapt into his arms and had fallen so in love with him. Cristina wasn't sure how to fix this for her friend. She knew she would do anything for her, that Emie more than anyone else she knew, deserved to be happy, but Emie didn't deserve this.

Asher was a fool.

Joseph had explained it all to her when she entered the funeral home. She had watched him run out to Emie through the open door and watched as her best friend cried in the arms of the man she had secretly admired for many years.

Cristina sighed. Her feelings for Joseph stirred at all the wrong times. Like tonight.

Cristina realized too late that Emie could hear her thoughts. She shook her head trying to focus on her friend.

"You know, you are my best friend Emie. I would do anything for you." Cristina looked up at the crisp white ceiling and felt her tears fall down her cheeks. "I know you think you can't do this. But I know you can." And she really meant it. She knew her friend was a strong and an amazing person. Asher just didn't know her well enough yet. "He will come around, honey, I promise." She smiled at the thought of Joseph coming around one day also. Maybe they could all be one big happy family together. Cristina would like that very much, she thought to herself.

Emie opened up the door then. She looked at her friend trying to smile. "Really?"

Cristina knew what she meant without being told. She smiled back at her and rolled her eyes.

Emies felt her spirits lift just a little. Wouldn't it be something if what she had said was true. Or could be true.

Cristina was right. She'd done all she could do to show Asher who she really was. She wasn't just a vampire. She would just have to wait for him. Like she had promised him she would. Asher was trying very hard. She had to give him a little credit and try to trust him.

"You can do this." Cristina told Emie. Taking her hands and placing them on Emie's shoulder.

"But what if he can't?" Emie questioned. It was a valid question. There was still the possibility. That, and there was also Frank. He was still a threat. If he told Asher what he knew, this could all go wrong.

"Then he doesn't deserve you. You are amazing Emie. You are kind, and compassionate. You are beautiful, and sweet. You're smart and intelligent. You may be a... whatever it is that you are," she paused only cause she remembered belatedly that she wasn't supposed to say Vampire allowed. "But that doesn't mean you don't deserve this honey. Fate is trying to do something here. I don't know what it is and I don't know anyone else that deserves to find love the way you do. And it will happen. I promise."

Emie looked at Cristina. She could see in her mind everything she was trying to say out loud. Everything she felt Emie deserved. Emie could only hope she was right.

With a deep breath, a hug, and a quick glance in the mirror, Emie and Cristina returned to the crowded funeral parlor where more people had gathered to pay their respects to the Stone family.

Emie looked around intently to find Asher. Her eyes needed to see him. Needed to know he was ok. Wherever he was. But she couldn't find him. She searched the crowd worriedly and found herself standing next to her brothers.

"Where is he Jordy?" She questioned him.

"He's outside Emie. He's ok."

Jeremy and Joseph exchanged a look of acknowledgement with him at her.

She returned a look at all of them of skepticism. She didn't trust them tonight. She walked towards the door Jordy had showed her he went out of and headed outside.

Emie found Asher with his back resting on a pillar. He was smoking. She read his mind as she slowly walked up to him. She didn't know what to say to him if he looked her way, and she felt uneasy about approaching him.

Asher felt Emie when she walked up by his side and gently touched his hand; slowly he put his knuckles in the palm of her hand and turned it in a sensual caress. She looked up at him when he looked down at her.

"I won't leave until you tell me too." Emie's eyes uncontrollably turned red with tears she had to wipe quickly away. She knew he seen it. But she nodded at him in a steady promise. Even though she didn't think she could physically leave him.

He heard the promise he had asked of her tonight. And the words she had said to him the other night, when he had made promises at the fire hall he no longer knew how to keep. When this was all over tonight, he didn't know how he was ever going to be able to see her again. He also knew she was giving him the sign that she knew what he knew. She was sweetly letting him know it was ok to tell her he was done with her.

But deep in his heart he knew he couldn't do it. Trying to reach for her hand before she pulled away, he was taken by surprise by another firefighter, his best friend Ken, telling him it was time to start the services.

Asher nodded at Ken who was hanging out the door to tell him what he had. When Ken retreated back inside the parlor Asher firmly gripped Emie's hand and squeezed it getting her attention back to him.

"I asked too much of you tonight. I shouldn't have asked you to come here." He leaned back against the pillar and looked up into the night sky. "I'm not strong enough right now to see the future or be able to tell you what I'm feeling, cause Emie I'm a mess." He laughed out loud and said "Hell, I don't think I can even go back in there right now." He sighed and closed his eyes.

Emie understood. They hadn't discussed anything yet. He couldn't, and she knew that. The timing had been all wrong. She only wished she could fix it. But she knew she couldn't.

Asher finally looked down at Emie who was looking at the ground. He knew he had to leave her side. He knew where he should be, where she should be. So why did he feel like running from this place, stealing her and never looking back. For a split heartbeat, he almost did. He didn't care what happened.

No one would fault him for it.

When she looked at him hurriedly, her face revealing she had heard his thoughts, he almost laughed out loud.

He reached his hand slowly up her cheek past her ear and into her hair. He watched as she closed her eyes at his touch. She wouldn't look up at him, but he needed her too. He kissed her forehead and lingered there. When she choked on a sob he reached up his other hand and tipped her chin up and held her face in his hands. He softly bent down and kissed her lips. Then he kissed her again.

When her lips trembled under his lips he smiled. "Can you forgive me Emie?" he asked. He kept his eyes closed as he rested his head on hers.

"For what Asher?" She asked astonished.

"For being human." He stated with a smirk.

Emie didn't know what to say. She didn't know what he meant. And she never would. They were out of time.

Asher walked in with Emie almost bumping into Joseph who took Emie from him. Asher solemnly walked away vowing he would fix everything with them tonight. He didn't know what to do or how to do it, but he was going too.

Asher looked back at Emie and watched her walk back to her brothers, as he found his family. He smiled as he watched her face go from heart broken to pure anger at her brothers. They deserved it tonight. Asher looked at her brothers one last time. He shook off the feelings of fear and knew he had to finish off tonight and get this over with. She would just have to keep her promise and wait for him.

The Chaplin on the department, Ken Kruse, led the services. He spoke of Curtis in better times. He told everyone how good of a man Curtis had been, the lives he had touched, and changed, and saved.

There wasn't a dry eye in the whole building.

Each firefighter took their turn at the podium. They all spoke kindly of Curtis, shared stories, read a fireman's prayer, held each other when one would falter, like all firemen do.

In the end, it was Asher who had the most impact on the crowd.

Emie wanted to give him strength. She wanted to help him. She wanted to tell him the truth. She wanted to tell him she loved him, and always would. What did it matter now that he knew who she was? She could take away his pain so easy right now and give him back his brother. Curtis had lost his life, but he was still alive.

Joseph's staying hand on her leg stopped her rushing emotions that were all tangled up and threatening to undo her.

No Emie. It's not that easy.

And with that she knew he was right…

Asher's tears had made Joseph stagger also. Joseph never cried, never. But tonight he wanted to.

"My brother wasn't just a man. He wasn't just a firefighter. He was my …brother." His tears were falling like rain drops now. All over his notes he had set in front of him. Asher couldn't stop them. No matter how hard he tried. So he just kept talking. Finding the strength in the words he knew were true.

"He was the brother of every man and women here. These men standing around you all, sitting in the seats next to you, walking next to you in a supermarket or on a crowded street, they are my brothers too. They are also yours. Like Curtis was. Ready to fight for you. Protect you. Die for you."

Asher had to shake his head. This was so hard. He had so much more to say. But he couldn't finish. He couldn't. Curtis had given his life for others. Not just the night he died, but every night. But Asher wanted his brother back. He wanted to feel his arms around him now, encouraging him to go on. He needed his brother right now in his life, in so many ways he would always need him. Not the life of a few teenagers who were God only knew where, living their lives like no one had just given up theirs for them. Who would never see the life they had taken or chose even to live a better life. They would never know what they had taken away from his brother. What they had done to him.

He was standing there, tears falling, dripping down his lips. He covered his mouth, it was aching and watering like the tears were too much for his eyes so they were pooling inside his mouth. He knew in his heart if he finished what he was up here to say; when he finished, this would finally be the end of Curtis's life.

All the firemen got up, every last one of them, walked up to Asher and held him. Let him weep and cry, mourn his brother in their arms.

Emie almost fled up to him. She almost gave up everything she had lived to protect to run at a superhuman speed to hold this man. She wanted to take away his pain so bad that she almost died with the effort to give it to him. Asher didn't deserve to feel this pain. He needed her.

It took both of her brothers who were sitting on either side of her, and Cristina who had dropped to her knees in front of Emie, to hold Emie, to keep her in her seat.

Asher stood tall after a moment and walked over and picked up the urn of Curtis's body that was surrounded by flowers and pictures of him, and brought it back to where he had been. Set it down on the podium and looked out over the crowd. "We know what dangers lay ahead of us when we leave the safety of our department. We also know, what would happen if we don't go." Asher wiped away his tears one last time. He refused to cry anymore. "Curtis knew the night he died he had to do what he did. It was what he was trained to do." This he said to his father. "What he felt in his heart, as man, to do. He gave his life for another.

"This man…" Asher looked down at the urn, and placed his hand on top of it, then looked back up at the crowd. "My brother, was a real… hero." Asher looked back down at his brother, tears falling anew. "I'll see ya soon brother." He whispered. It was their parting saying, on every call, at every goodbye. They always added a hug, or a fist bump. It ripped at Asher that he could never do that to his brother again.

Asher had finally said goodbye. Everyone in the room knew it too. Every ear in the room heard him, and every heart ached for him.

But it was Emie who Joseph ached for. Asher was a good man, that's what he had come here to find out tonight. And even though he would give his sister anything in this world, he couldn't fix what he had broken. He couldn't give her back the life he had taken from her. Asher would never turn from his hatred of vampires. Especially when he found out the truth of the secrets they were keeping from him now. He would forever see them as murderers, people who took the lives of others. Lives he was sworn to protect. He wouldn't stop hating her to see that she wasn't what he thought she was. He would never understand what they had done with his brother.

Emie had made her decision. Joseph was right.

She had to leave.

As soon as the service was over, Emie looked to Cristina; her eyes filled with blood. "Will you take me home please?"

It was clear to her brothers she didn't want to go home with them. None of them argued with her. They all knew the damaged they had done tonight, and didn't fault her for her murderous feelings towards them.

Cristina looked at her friend and said "Sure honey. Let's go." As she ushered Emie out.

Emie looked through the crowd for Asher asking Cristina to wait. She made sure she blinded every last person in the parlor. They would no longer see her tonight because she couldn't hide her tears from them. When she found him, she looked at him and whispered aloud to him "I love you." and then walked out of the funeral home with her best friend by her side.

Asher had been talking to Ken when he felt Emie get up from her seat. He wanted to get away from everyone. To get out of here and leave with her. He didn't care where they went or for how long. He didn't even care what they talked about. He just wanted to start over with her.

When he found her, he watched her get ready to leave. As Ken's words slowly died away, he watched her mouth the words he'd been dying for her to say. "I Love You."

Asher couldn't breathe anymore. He couldn't feel his feet, or his legs. He'd lost all feelings. His heart, for a moment in time, stopped beating. When it restarted backup it pounded so loud he couldn't hear anything else.

She loved him. But why was she walking away?

"Ken, excuse me for a minute." Asher told his friend as he tried to follow her.

The throng of people prevented him. He kept excusing himself as he pushed past them all and wanted to scream at everyone to please move!

When he finally reached the doors and opened them wide, he watched as Josephs SUV pulled onto the main road following another car.

She was leaving him. She was breaking her promise to him, one she had been making to him since that night in the fire hall next to the trucks. That night she said she'd told him she would always wait for him.

    And for the life of him, he didn't know why.

Seventeen

Letting go. Falling. Never knowing when it would end. Being completely and utterly defenseless, feeling so recklessly free, you don't even care that you're falling. Not feeling one bit of insecurity. Not feeling anything at all, but butterflies.

Emie had felt that way. Felt like she was falling. She would never feel that again.

Emie had went back home the night of Curtis's funeral. She'd broken her promise to Asher and snuck out the front doors with her brothers and Cristina when no one was looking. She'd felt heavy and cold, as dead as she truly was.

She had slept. Well, sleep didn't come to vampires, but to Emie, she had lain lifeless in her bed for days. She remembered Asher's thoughts and doubts. She wanted to erase them all for him, but she couldn't. Like a tv show, they replayed in her mind over and over again.

Emie felt like she had been sleeping for hundreds of years. Like she was dead, and just couldn't wake up. She needed someone to wake her up. Shake her. Put her back on solid ground.

She had locked away the world in her room. No one would disturb her, no one that mattered anyway.

She rolled over and wept again days later. There was no one who could take her pain away. No one.

She wanted to go and find him. Try again. She was so confused about her feelings. Something was telling her she couldn't and at the same time was telling her she could. But in the reality of her mind, she had been a fool. She couldn't be with him. There was no way. He wasn't strong enough to handle who she was, and he wouldn't want to anyways, she thought.

No one could give her back what had been taken away from her. Not the life that had been sucked from her broken body hundreds of years ago, and certainly not the love of a great man. She didn't want or need anything else. Just those two things. Life and love. What else was there to live for?

Asher had turned out to be more than she had ever dreamed of in a man. He was playfully, he was fun to be around, he was honest and compassionate. He had courage and pride, the kind most men didn't know the first thing about.

His love would have lasted a lifetime.

He loved so deeply. His love would have been true. His love would have been great.

She would have loved him back. She did love him still. She knew now she always would.

Emie was left with nothing. Just an empty space inside of her soul. Nothing else mattered now.

She was coming undone. She was disappearing. She only wanted to be loved by him.

Months later...

Joseph had been standing in the rain for hours, just standing out in the driveway. Rain had soaked his cold hard body through his clothes.

His whole world around him had stopped months ago. Everything he had worked for, everything he had dreamed of had just stopped. Nothing around the house or in the city had been touched by him in months. He just didn't care anymore.

Emie had disappeared. Just fallen off the edge of the earth.

In this day in age, times had changed. He couldn't jump on his horse and ride out from dusk till dawn to search for her. Couldn't pound on the neighbor's doors and ask them if they'd seen her. Life was so different now then it had been a century ago.

He had searched all of his land. All of Luna Pier. All of Michigan, Florida, and England. Everywhere he had known she had ever been.

He had help in his searches; his brothers, the police, he'd even hired a vampire investigator a month ago. He'd called in some favors to some of their kind to help find Emie also, but, no one could find her.

He still couldn't find her, couldn't even hear her anymore.

Joseph had never hated a man. He had never wanted to passionately take his time and kill a man. He had never premeditated murder.

Asher Stone was going to die one day. If not by his fangs, then by fate's. And Joseph would cherish the day.

Asher didn't have a clue what he had thrown away. What he had given up on. Joseph looked down at the mud his boots were sinking into in the pouring rain. Asher didn't understand what his little sister really was. She wasn't evil. By God, Emie was the very essence of what heaven was all about. Joseph just hadn't a chance to tell Asher that. To show him. He knew now he should have. He should have helped Emie when she had needed him most instead of worrying about everything else.

Nothing else mattered to him now. They could take away everything he had worked so hard for. He didn't care anymore. Only his family mattered to him.

Out there in the rain, standing alone, Joseph gave in.

Emie would either come home when she was ready, or she never would at all. He couldn't wait anymore. They had to move on with their own lives. They needed to prepare for the war that had already begun. Thousands of humans were dying faster than ever before. Vampires were taking over the world without the humans even knowing. Soon it would become the talk of the media. They would need to be ready when it happened.

The Stone family was still a possibility of a threat to his family.

Joseph walked to the stables. He had things that needed to be taken care of. A lot of things. Starting with Emie's horse.

Emie hadn't died. She was still walking around somewhere. At least he hoped. As he was feeding the horses and sloshing through the mud he remembered how Asher's everyday thoughts had just been too much for her. She had made that connection with him, like she had everyone else she knew on a deep personal level, and could hear his thoughts, even though he lived on the other side of town, she could still hear him. She could still feel him hurting. She must have had to get as far away from him as she could to relieve the pain that was too much for her.

Joseph was now in Triton's stall. Emie's horse.

Triton had been so restless these last few months. Joseph had just left him inside today since it was raining again. September was always rainy in Michigan.

Who was he kidding; this thought made him sigh as he looked in Triton's stall who was still lying in a cloud of his own glossy white feathers. Michigan was always rainy. Made no difference what month it was. Triton wasn't lying down because of the weather, he was distraught. He too missed Emie deeply.

Why was Triton so sleepy, Joseph wondered? He wished Jeremy would hurry back home from Florida. Animals could sense when something was wrong. Or when their masters had-

Joseph couldn't think it. Couldn't think that Emie could be gone from his world. He couldn't.

Joseph started rubbing Triton down with his large hands. He started with his long snout and worked his way down to his shoulders, all the while trying not to think of Emie.

He worked his way to Triton's sides and back, the calming strokes through his feathers were working. Triton had gone from digging his feet to just nodding his head.

Joseph knew if Emie didn't come back soon he was either going to have to put Triton down, or take over Emie's care completely. Scylla, his horse, was already very jealous.

He made his way to Triton's back and up with calming voices and rubbed his palms gently on Triton's wing arm, then caressed his fingers through his feathers.

Triton allowed this for some time. Then he reared up and spread his wings to their full length. When Joseph backed up towards the door, Triton came down and huffed out his nostrils at Joseph. Triton was now a very angry Pegasus.

Joseph could hear the animal's thoughts. Triton wanted Emie. Joseph wasn't Emie.

Days prior, Jordy had tried the same things. It wasn't until they asked for Jeremy's help that they decided he would have to be put down sooner rather than later. Triton's misery was leading him into hysteria. He would become a danger to them all soon. If Triton left the confines of their land, they would all be ruined.

No one wanted to do it. So they waited.

Joseph left Triton some fresh hay and meat in his pale. He shut the doors to his stall and walked out into the dark hallways.

Joseph turned at the sound of a familiar beating heart. It was Asher's standing in the open door leading out into the pasture by the beach. Joseph's fangs dripped with venom and his claws threatened to find Asher's throat.

Asher had walked the beach from his house until he came up to Emie's tree. He had climbed walls and rocks and fences to get there and when he found it, he couldn't help but remember that night there with her.

He missed her. He had stood there forever in the rain, until he was drenched through. His jeans and boots were covered in sand. Thoughts of Emie flooded his mind. They ripped at his heart.

Emie had left him the night of the funeral in wonder. He hadn't expected her to leave when she had. She had broken her promise to him. It still chilled him to think that she did it.

He had never really known her. Not knowing her was what was killing him though. Not being able to find her was worse.

He should have spent more time with her.

He couldn't help wondering who she was, even though he already knew. He couldn't call or text her anymore. She never answered him.

He ran his hands through his wet hair and looked up into the rain. Damn, he missed her. He had missed her every day.

Tonight he wanted answers. He wanted to know why.

Asher headed for the stables where he hoped he would find either Emie or her brothers. He wished against all odds she would be there in one of the stalls. He was ready to talk to her now.

No, he needed to talk to her.

No, he shook his head at his thoughts as he started running, he needed to hold her and kiss her. He needed her more than anything else in this whole damn world.

The reality of what, who she was, was too much for anyone to grasp. The thought of what all was happening in the world around him, it was all too much for him. Knowing now the possibility that his brother's death was caused by something or someone much like her, left him feeling hopeless and drained.

Everyone was trying to tell him what was going on, but he wasn't listening. He didn't care about the world or the people in it.

He longed for the feelings he had when she was near. Her love for him had been the best damn distraction. He wanted her back. He just wanted to hold her again.

Asher knew the time he had needed to think about things had turned not only into days but months. He knew he needed to make up for it in ways he didn't know how. But he was determined now to start figuring that out.

Seeing Joseph standing in the hallways like a shadow in the midst of what little light was in the stable returned a fear Asher hadn't felt in months. Returned all the feelings he had been having and reasons why this wasn't a good idea.

"I can hear your thoughts Asher. I can see your fears. Now is not a good time to be regretting your decisions or running away from the damage you've already caused this family. Just say what you came here to say and get the hell out of here." Joseph growled that last bit as he set down a rake and a pale. Stretching up to his full height, he could see himself in Asher's mind standing in the darkness of the hallway just a shadow. He turned away from Asher and hoped the boy would take the hint and leave whatever reason he was there behind them both.

"I want to see Emie." He gulped down his fear and begged it to leave. "I need to talk to her." Asher knew he didn't have to holler over the distance between them. He knew Joseph could hear his whispers and even his thoughts now.

Joseph had to stop himself from running down the hall and killing Asher when he had said her name. Joseph didn't think Asher was worthy enough to even speak her name let alone be in her presences again.

"She's gone." He simply stated.

"What do you mean she's gone?" Asher took a step into the hall, hoped Joseph just meant she was gone from the house. Not the gone that was haunting him now.

Death had been knocking at Asher's doors too many times in his life. He'd tried not to let it win. He'd done his best to fight with it and save as many as he could. But sometimes it would steal even the closest of Asher's friends and family, leaving Asher with gaping holes. If death had taken Emie from him...

Joseph greedily read Asher's thoughts. He smiled at the pain he knew it would cause Asher if Joseph lied. He contemplated lying to Asher, something Joseph had never done before, but he honestly couldn't do it to Emie. If she ever did find her way back home, she already had enough to hate him for; he wasn't about to cause her more pain.

Joseph whispered into Asher's mind, She left.

He left Asher standing there in the hallway, stunned. There were some things Asher would just have learn on his own, or never learn at all in his case.

~Eighteen~

Jeremy was heading home from Florida. Emie had disappeared months ago. Leaving behind her brothers to wonder where in this big ol world she was.

Jeremy had to admit he was taking his time going back home, he had his seat laid back in his pick up truck, smoke rolling out in the breeze, one hand on the wheel and his other arm out the window, his radio blaring to whatever he could get in without any static.

He'd made it into Kentucky and had been driving in the mountains for some time now. There was something about having his arm resting out his window in the wind as he rolled up and down the hills. He wondered now why he wasn't living down south. He loved being down south, he loved the different seasons, he knew his way around here like the back of his hand.

Jeremy hadn't found Emie in Florida. Her best friend Shelley and Asher's brother Curtis had helped him search for her. When Jeremy had walked with Curtis on the midnight shore of the beach they discussed Emie and Asher.

Curtis hadn't seen his family since the night of the fire. He knew they missed him, and were still mourning his death, but they couldn't see him until he learned the difference between his instincts. He wasn't adjusting to this life like Shelley had hoped. Humans were so tempting to him now. With every passing day it got worse.

Jordy had shown up that night long enough to fill in Curtis of the latest events that were happening around the world.

Curtis's mind now was filled with decisions and planning.

Curtis wanted to know how Asher was doing. He couldn't believe Asher had fallin in love with Emie and then had let her go. Emie was breathtaking and beautiful, and a perfect match for Asher. Curtis wondered if Asher just needed some time.

Jeremy knew he would have to tell Joseph soon that he hadn't found Emie. Joseph would have to continue the search for her. .

Jeremy was working his way up I-75, he had a lot on his mind tonight, about his family and his horses. But he didn't really want to think about any of those things. He just wanted to enjoy the ride home with music and the nice warm breeze.

He looked down at his gas gage. He was going to need to stop at the next exit.

Jeremy was different from the rest of his family. His abilities were somewhat the same, but his mannerisms where as different as night and day. Jeremy spent more time in the southern states with his friends and horses, away from the family. He had a business of his own to take care of; horses and gambling.

Jeremy had an unusual love for horses. Animals of any kind really, but it was the horses he loved so much. They responded to him like he was their savior. In some emergency situations, he was. He was able to bring them back to life, stop them from dying. He felt sometimes like his mission from God was to save them, not the humans. And he was happy for it. He liked horses better.

He raced them, he bred them, he practically lived with them. So his southern slang that dripped from his voice was understandable to most people even though his heritage was the complete opposite. He was born and raised in Whitby England. Emie and Joseph had moved him and Jordan to the United States in 1912. They took a voyage on the Titanic on a cold April day and sailed across the ocean. They didn't make it across the cold ocean that night of course, but that's another story.

He was thinking about another time, another place in history, when he drove right by his exit. Which was odd to him. He never did that. He let it go with a sigh and continued on to the next exit.

Even though Jeremy was a vampire, he liked to drink, he liked to smoke like Asher. The nicotine didn't do much for his stone body, but the heat, that was what he felt.

Jeremy ate his steaks as raw as they would cook them for him. Flipped just once on the grill to give it a crispy taste. Tomato's were nice too, but they always turned to ash in his belly, but the gooey liquid tasted as close to human flesh as he could get sometimes. Whiskey was his choice of drink; again, it was the heat he liked. He liked the feel of the warmth. He ate at bars, restaurants; any where he could mingle and meet new people. If you could sing country music, cuss like a sailor or rope a horse, Jeremy liked you.

His favorite music was country, but he liked a mix sometimes. Rock and roll, r and b, but never classical. He hated listening to Emie play on the piano all those countless hours before there was television. Classical music was never his thing.

Jeremy was lost in his thoughts again as he came up to his exit. He couldn't shake the feeling that he was going to be the last one in his family to find that someone. He really didn't believe in love, but then his whole family had fallen in the depths of it, and now he was starting to see that there was something missing in his own life. But he often wondered how there could be something missing if there wasn't something there to begin with?

Jeremy took the next exit getting off the expressway and drove into the now dark mountains, hoping there was a gas stations down the road just a lil bit before he ran out of gas.

Juliet had missed her exit miles down the expressway. She'd gotten off at this exit hoping there was one down the road, but her SUV had stalled out before she got the chance to make it over the second hill.

Her cell phone battery had died earlier during the day. So when she got out to walk, she had two choices. One, walk back up the hill behind her and down, then over the expressway to see if there was a gas station on the other side, or two, walk straight ahead into the mountains and pray she had to only go up one more giant hill…

Juliet chose option number three she had completely made up on her own. She opened up herself her hood so someone might stop and offer assistance, and then sat under her back lift gate and waited. She had a story to write, so she waited. And waited.

Two hours later she saw headlights. Juliet had never been more scared in her life. She thought of all the people that could be behind those headlights. Drug dealer, rapist, murderer, vampire…

She knew little about vampires. Everyone was writing about them now days though. But she had chosen, as an author, to stick with historical romances instead. She loved letting her heart and mind live in another era, if just for a few chapters in a book.

So when the headlights turned into a big ol red four wheel drive pickup truck, with four big dual back tires, pass her, pull in front of her, her mind was wandering around all the possibilities of who could be in it.

The man who got out of the truck was a tall man, she noticed as she jumped out of the back and headed towards the front. He had short, blonde hair under his ball cap that was turned backwards. He had on a pair of black sunglasses and the sexiest smile she'd ever seen. He was wearing light blue jeans and a grey t-shirt covered up with a black leather jacket and a black zip up hoodie that matched his black leather boots.

She read his license plate. Michigan. He was headed north, what a coincidence she thought.

"Good evening, ma'am." Jeremy said kindly as he walked up to her. This pretty little thing was sure a sight for a guy like him, well, for a vampire like him that is. She had long blonde hair that tumbled down her shoulders in swirling curls around her arms.

She was dressed in a double layered little white silk top with half sleeves that elegantly revealed her wrist; a low cut neck that revealed more than just her delicious neck, the shirt clung to her breast and revealed nipples that looked more than just cold. She was wearing tight white washed jeans he noticed as she watched him walk up to her.

She seemed just as turned on as he was, with just a hint of fear trembling through her.

"Car troubles?" Jeremy couldn't wait for her to speak aloud. Her thoughts were all scrambled and he loved that she was flattered by his accent. She wondered if it was a southern accent, or a British one. She was in for a surprise if she ever found out, he thought.

"The car is running just fine, till I missed my exit and ran out of gas." She smiled sweetly to him, trying to turn on a sweet, could you help me out kind of charm, without sounding like some little lost kitten who didn't have clue what she was about.

She nervously inhaled deeply and Jeremy listened as her mind wrapped around all the things she tried to compare his scent to.

Jeremy smiled. "I did too. Some redneck must have taken down the exit sign a ways back on the expressway I reckon."

That did it. She was counting now, trying not to faint. She almost had to reach out for her car to keep her balance. He laid on the accent a little thick that time. That and his musky scent was driving her wild. Why did leather and horses do this to women?

Juliet nodded and agreed with him. She knew if she didn't say something soon he would think her a fool and not help her out. Men hated foolish women. Why did she care, she wondered belatedly.

She had a book signing to make it too now and she didn't have time for a hot young cowboy coming to her rescue. He could just drive off and come back with a few gallons after he was done with his own fill up for all she cared.

Or you could take a ride in his truck and get to know him better?

Where in hell had that thought come from she wondered, her eyes widened in shock. It scared her even though it was her own voice that had said it, but it didn't quite reach her will. But then again... now that she had thought it... just may be she could.

Jeremy had to smile at this little lady. She was nervous. She was every bit of what the word sexy meant, and she was smarter than the average women. She could feel who he was, sort of, and sensed the goodness in him; he could feel her probing him even though she probably didn't know she could. She'd taken his bate he'd offered her mind and wanted it just as bad as he had.

"I guess so." Juliet took another deep breath and braved the moment by asking him for help. "Could you.. I mean, I'm not a thief or anything, I just need to get some gas so I can make it back on the road. If you could just take me with you, I can buy my gas and be out of your hair in no time." She ask as she tucked her hands in the pockets of her jeans and smiled sweetly.

She was hungry too he noted, but she hadn't mentioned that. He was in such luck today. "Where you headed too?" he inquired.

"Michigan." She said shyly.

"Michigan? Really, where at in Michigan?"

"Jackson. A little town called Hanover." Well, she was headed to Jackson were her book signing was, but then she was headed home to Hanover.

"Ah, a country girl." Jeremy winked.

"No. My mom, yes. Me, not so much. I was born and raised in Jersey before my parents got a… anyways, I'm sorry, that's not important; I live in New York." Juliet was definitely nervous now. She pushed around some dirt and tried not to look at him so much. She felt very insecure around him.

He looked too good in those tight jeans she told herself. What she could see in the moonlight anyhow. But he also had a rough look to him. He could do some damage to her heart if she let him. He could be trouble, but she needed him to be the hero tonight. Her mother was going to kill her if he didn't.

Jeremy had to wonder at all of that. She was still picturing going home and dealing with her parents who had told her not to do something. Probably not driving out on her own alone. She could just hear them saying "We told you so!" when she got home. If he didn't turn out to be a rapist or a murderer she had no intention of telling them what happened tonight.

Jeremy almost rolled his eyes at her thoughts, if she only knew. Then her mind stretched farther, seen them laughing together and enjoying Christmas together. Quickly she erased that from her mind, but he wanted it back.

"And you?" She asked politely. Pointing towards his Michigan plates.

"Luna Pier." He could tell by the look on her face she hadn't a clue where that was. No one really did. His little city was a lot like hers. Back in the woods, a drive by kind of city. Blink on the expressway and miss your exit. "It's a small little town just off 75, about 6 miles or so into Michigan."

"Oh. Ok."

It was sweet, her gesture. She smiled even though she hadn't a clue. She lived over by the westside of Michigan. She'd never really traveled east. She didn't know what she was missing, he thought to himself. If she didn't like the country, maybe she would like his little city on the lake instead of New York.

When she started looking around in the dark, he knew that was his clue to lead her up to his truck, they needed to get her gas so they could both be on their way. "Well, shall we then?" He lifted his hand and stepped back so she could head toward his truck.

"Uh, yeah. Just a minute." She told him excitedly.

He watched as she closed her liftgate, grabbed her purse out and walked in front of him to his truck. And he watched as she walked right back into his heart.

She had the body men dreamed of. Her heartbeat was hypnotic. And she smelled fresh. Warm.

Jeremy shook his head. He needed a distraction. Fast. His venom was dripping from his fangs and his mouth was watering for her blood.

He picked up his steps walking a little too close to her. "Um, listen," he said as he smoothed his hat on his hair a little, "you're gonna have to excuse my truck, It's um… not used to a pretty little thing like you sitting in it."

Juliet had to smile at his shyness all of sudden. "That's alright. My car, it's not used to…" she looked at his boots as she leaned in a little, and then winked at him when she said, "Guys like you either."

Jeremy grinned back at her and stuffed his hands in his pockets. She was playful this one. "Ah, I see. So that could also mean if I was to flirt with you a little tonight, I wouldn't have to worry about a big city buck looking to hunt me down, now would I?" he questioned, with a deep rough male voice. He also leaned in a little closer and winked back as he reached for his truck door to open for her.

Juliet liked this guy. Probably a little too much. It was too soon she kept telling herself. "No. There's not." She was shaking her head stunned by his blunt question, and liking that he wanted to flirt, so she took a chance and asked when he opened the truck door for her and took a peek inside at the mess, "So, does that mess mean that there's not a pretty little country girl somewhere ready to chop my head off if I flirt with you tonight?

Jeremy had stepped to look back at her after moving his horse bridles and leaders to the back seat, throwing a few hoodies back there as well, and pushing a few bottles of whiskey under the seat. His smokes were sitting in the ashtray out of his reach, so she'd have to deal with that. The truck was dusty from him having the windows down. He sure hoped she wouldn't mind that pretty little white shirt getting a little bit of dirt on it.

"Nope." He smiled back at her and loved how well she could jest with him. He held his hand out to help her step up. Her cute, blue flannel, striped dress shoes might slip on his rails if he didn't. When they did, he caught her in his arms, holding her there probably one or two seconds longer then he should. But damn, she sure smelled good. "I, um…" he couldn't think or help himself, he smelled her again. "I'm sorry." He said, kicking himself for scaring her, as he placed her in the truck.

Juliet was in shock. Total shock. Here was a scruffy, redneck, real cowboy with all his horse stuff thrown in the back of his truck; everything she hated in guys like him, and she was swooning in his arms. He smelled like fresh wild grass, leather, horses, smoke and whiskey. She hated all of those things! But on him... oh my, she thought.

Jeremy had heard her thoughts. Shut the door and walked to the back of his truck where he had to take a moment. What was he thinking? Women like her never did this to him. Especially ones with beating hearts. She was a human girl for Pete's sake! He could not, absolutely could not do this to her. He'd never thought about doing that with a human.

So why did he feel like he didn't have a choice anymore? Why was he harder then he'd ever been before just from holding her in his arms for minute too long.

Why hadn't he wanted to let her go, he had to wonder. Letting go of her felt like losing something.

Jeremy coughed as he got in the truck, revved it up to a purr, and felt his dead heart thump when he heard her mind say she loved the sound of his pick up truck.

Flashes, Jordy's thoughts, played throughout his mind and he had to shut them off. He wasn't about to do what he saw with her.

Vampires didn't do that to humans! He thought, more then said to Jordy.

You will. Was the last thing he heard Jordy say as he pulled away off the side of the road, and headed into the darkness. Praying he too, didn't run out of gas.

Jeremy drove into the small town of Williamsburg and found a gas station off the main road. There was a restaurant attached to it. He walked in with Juliet by his side. At the cash register where they went to pay for gas, there was a tv on playing the news. The events on the news were gruesome. All around the world were riots that were now hitting the United States. Cities were being destroyed by fire.

In the back of his mind he heard a familiar sound.

Emie.

He turned and looked at a little booth in the back corner of the restaurant. Emie was sitting there alone reading a book.

"Well, I'll be damned." He stated simply.

"What is it?" Juliet questioned.

Jeremy turned to her. "It's my sister."

Juliet followed his gaze to a small stature woman who looked just like him.

"Excuse me for minute."

Jeremy walked to the little booth and slid in the seat in front of his sister.

Emie acknowledged Jeremy with a gasp.

"Hey." Jeremy said to her reaching across the table for her hand.

"Let me guess, Jordy found me?" She questioned him pulling her hand away from his.

"Nope." He said to her honestly. "I was headed home from Florida and stopped in here for gas."

Emie followed his gaze to the woman at the register. "Playing with your food again?"

Emie always hated when her brothers did this. They would find a human that needed to be taken out of this world, and would toy with them until they were ready to take them.

"No. Not her. I found her on the side of the road. She ran out of gas, so I offered my help."

Emie listened to his heart. She found there the same emotions she herself had for Asher the first time she had met him. She wondered if Jeremy had finally found his mate. She looked down at her book again. "I didn't want to be found Jeremy. Are you going to tell Joseph?"

Jeremy thought about this for a moment. He'd done the same thing as her many times. Driven off not telling his siblings where he was going. Escaping the mundane life in Luna Pier for adventures of his own. "How are you doing? Are you ok?"

Emie knew what he was asking. He was asking if she was taking care of herself. Eating. "Yes." She closed her book then and looked up at her little brother.

"I took off emptying my account. Took just enough to take care of me. I drove till I ran out of gas. When I stopped in this little town, I filled up and drove around. I found an old back road that headed up into the mountains not far from town. As I was driving around this sharp curve I saw an old dilapidated house for sale. It sits up off the road. I went back into town and stayed at a hotel till I found the real estate agent. I paid cash for it and I've been working on fixing it up. It's a nice place Jeremy. It's got forty acres on the river."

"And you've been eating?" he questioned looking around, making sure no one was listening. Juliet was busying herself getting snacks and something to drink.

Emie knew her new diet of animals would disgust Jeremy. She nodded her head at him and left him to wonder what she had been doing to survive. It wasn't like he could boldly ask her in front of the other customers in the restaurant.

"Alright, I understand."

"I'm building barns on my land. I want to come back home and get Triton and bring him back here with me." She told him.

"All you gotta do is call Emie. I'll help."

"I know." She wasn't ready to go back home just yet.

Jeremy sat up straight in seat. "Just call ok? Tell Joseph so I don't have too." He all but begged her.

"I will." She thanked him with her smile and reassured him she was ok. "Go. She's waiting."

Jeremy winked at his sister and slid back out of the booth. He headed back over to Juliet and paid for their things and Emie's. He knew Emie would come home when she was ready.

Nineteen

June 2016

It had been a year since Curtis had died. Asher found himself sitting right where he had one year ago, sitting on the front end of engine two after washing it, watching the sun go down.

Asher had just returned from New York, a vacation of sorts that he thought would help clear his mind. But it hadn't. The buzz all around New York had fueled his fears about Emie and who she was. It had also brought back memories of his past and how he wanted to tell her about so many things. He found himself walking around New York talking to her in his head. Sometimes even wondering if she could hear him. He would tell her over and over how much he missed her. How much he wished ever since he had talked to Joseph and found out she had left, that he could go back in time and undo all the hurt he had caused her. He missed Emie with a fierceness that just got worse as the days went on.

This year had been a bad year for storms. Ice and snow storms in the winter gave way to a cold drenching spring rain.

On days like today, when the clouds were chasing each other and there was a heightened chance for a tornado, the weather service would put all the fire departments on weather watch and send them out to spot tornadoes.

Asher missed his brother most on days like today. They used to love to sit up on the overpass or out on the pier and catch up on old times. There was no fires to put out, no lives to be saved. They would just sit and wait and watch.

Asher had been thinking all day of his brother, and of the woman he had met that night a year ago.

Emie.

Not Emilie, not Miss Whitby, not the nurse that worked over at the hospital. Not the vampire he feared in his nightmares. The women he longed for in his daydreams.

Just Emie.

He hadn't time to get to know her then, and some days he wondered what it was he missed most about her.

Was it her sweet scent that lingered on his uniform for days? Or just seeing her? Seeing her hair tumble down her body, her curls bounce when she walked? Seeing her kissable lips, or the feel of her hips that drove him crazy? Or was it her voice. How it sang to him even when she was just talking to him?

She was so playful and cute. She was adorable...

Or how she had brought life to his music, and then he'd never had that magic again like that night at The Saloon. He'd lost all interest in singing altogether.

Damn! What he would give to kiss her again right now, he thought rubbing his bad shoulder.

He hated looking in his mirrors on his bike all that summer after she'd left him. She wasn't behind him, holding him, putting her face in the wind, or running her hands up and down in the wind. It had been an amazing site to see. He wondered all the time if he would ever see that again.

She wasn't in his truck, sitting crossed legged leaning towards him to smile like whatever he had just said was interesting and had lit up her soul, singing with him to every song that played on the radio. He hardly ever had it on anymore. He'd sold his truck for the same reason. It just wasn't the same anymore without her sitting in it with him. He drove Curtis's truck instead.

Emie had crossed his mind so many times over the last year. All the dreams he had started having of them having a life together haunted him now. There was no one else he wanted to share his life with now. No one else measured up to her beauty, or her happiness. No one looked at life like Emie did. Like it was an adventure to be lived instead of endured. She shared the same out look he did, and he had longed to discover it with her.

No one else matched him so perfectly.

He had wanted her to stay with him. He had wanted to love her. He didn't know how to do it though. He didn't know then how to get past who and what she was. Now... well now he just didn't care about who she was anymore.

There was so much he longed to know about her. Her life. Who was Emie? When had it happened to her? How had it happened to her?

He hadn't known she could hear his thoughts that night. When he had been so unsure, and had cast bullets at her unknowingly. Emie had heard everything. She'd endured his torture so she could provide him with the one thing he needed that night. A shoulder to cry on, a woman's love, a friends devotion. There she had been, waiting and wanting to be anything he needed, and he had just left her sitting in the back row like he didn't even know her. Like he'd never needed her. He'd used everyone else but her to cry on. Instead of going to her, he worried senselessly about her family attacking them all. He knew now they never would have done that. There'd been many murders in Luna

Pier over the years. None of them were linked to the Whitby's. He'd even checked.

For the first time in a year, Asher started to remember his thoughts when he had been with her. How cruel he had been to her. He had even thought foolishly she would eat his dog. How had she not slapped him across the face for that?

So much had happened since that night. Life had happened. Finding out she had left and that it was all his fault from Joseph, had been like a knife to Asher's already grieving heart.

Asher looked down at his swinging feet and threw a towel over his shoulder. He was ready to stand when more thoughts entered his mind.

She had known all along, from the moment on the stairs when he had seen her running towards him like she had been floating. She looked so damn hot that night dressed like she was. Just for him. She heard him curse her. Heard him want to know how she could ruin his life, when all she'd done was save him from his self.

No, he thought foolishly, she had heard him long before that night. She'd known all along how he had felt about her. How much he had loved her, and then he had thrown it all away.

Asher remembered that night she had taken his hand and led him out to the water. How she had played that game with him and had fun with him. How she had turned around constantly and let him hold her like she never wanted to leave his arms.

She had given him more than love that night.

And still she'd loved him. Wanted him. Waited for him to grieve with his family. She had promised she would wait, but he couldn't hold her to it. No one could hold her to such a promise like that after what he had put her through.

Which also meant she had heard him that first night in the elevator too, his fears. Then his attraction to her. Even though she knew his fears, knew his faults, knew how eagerly he had wanted her, still, she had loved him. So sweetly and softly, but he had just thrown her away like dirty laundry.

Asher hung his head and swung his feet again. He could feel the pain of losing her crashing into him again. She hadn't left him. He'd left her. Left her alone. He should have left everyone that night and followed her.

When she had cried on Joseph's shoulder, it had been for comfort from him. Asher had hurt her, and Asher knew that now.

He was such a fool. Such a fool for losing her. Such a fool for letting her go home that night without him. He should have run after her, followed her home instead of watching her leave. He was the coward for letting her leave so he wouldn't have to decide what to do.

It had been so nice with her by his side. It felt great to finally have someone in his life. So nice to introduce her that day to all his family and then again to all his extended family and friends. Everyone he knew, knew he had been with Emie and was seeing her.

Asher had spent the next year telling everyone in the city that they weren't together anymore when they would ask where she was. People he knew, that had known her, that he hadn't known knew her, were still asking him what had happened and why weren't they together anymore. He had nothing to say to them. He didn't know where she was.

Emie was all over the news. She was one of the ones who had disappeared. One of the thousands that were missing.

Why had he thought she had only existed for him? Everyone in Luna Pier would proceed to tell him everything he didn't know about her. Everything he needed to know, and everything he didn't want to know anymore. Emie and her family was a god send to this city, in more ways than he could ever have imagined. How had he not known of her before he had met her?

The girl at Luna Cafe told him how comforting she was to talk to, one day while he was sitting at the restaurant alone. Told him "She really listens when you talk to her. Like she really cares." And Emie had. The waitress was telling him something he already knew; Asher could remember all the times Emie just sat and looked at him, listening so intently to him.

Emie and the waitress had become fast friends. Enough to ask the young girl every time she seen her how the baby was doing, and inquired about the girls health. Emie had pointed her in the right direction when it came to a doctor, and in the end, he had saved her life during childbirth.

Even the old guy at the post office, Charlie, who had been hanging up a missing poster with Emie's face on it when Asher walked in one day, knew who Emie was. Asher hadn't known the guys name until he had asked Asher if he knew the girl poster. Asher had been in the post office almost every day of his life, sending mail and getting his mail, and the old man had never talked to Asher other then in greeting. Charlie proceeded to introduce himself that day and tell him how beautiful Emie was, and how he had missed her smiling face around the office. He told Asher about how Emie had helped him decide on the d cor around the office that was a calm and pleasing blue, like the water, and had even went shopping for the frame on the wall that held a beautiful old black and white picture of the light house out in lake. Emie had taken the picture for Charlie. She had signed the bottom of it. To Charlie. From Emie. Asher had to choke back tears and flee the post office that day. How many times had he seen that picture before and not seen Emie's name at the bottom.

He remembered that day clearly now. It was the day he had stood at the scene of a fire afterwards remembering the night he had met her. He remembered over and over again her telling him her name. "Hi, my name is Emilie. My friends call me Emie." He remembered the way her name felt, like butterflies.

The guy's at the gas station had asked Asher more then once if she was back in the city yet. He was starting to get the feeling that they were thinking he was a fool too for losing her, and that they would jump at the chance when Emie got back to ask her out.

Every single time he went to the hospital someone there would ask him where she was, and how nice she had been to work with. They had all seen them holding hands walking around the hospital the night his brother had died.

Then they all would ask him the one question he hated. "When do you think she'll be coming back home?" all their voices rang together in his head now. It would rip his heart open when they asked. He didn't know. He didn't even know where she was. He'd only seen Joseph once, and he knew better then to try to ask Cristina. She may be sweet and adorable like Emie, but she also looked like a women you didn't mess with. Emie had told him before she had a temper, and he wasn't about to find out how intense her temper was. Asher had enough sisters to know not to mess with women and their friends. You could lose an ear if you tried.

Even his own dog would look outside for Emie after she left. When ever Cookie would bark out the window, which was rare enough that it stopped his heart when she did, Asher couldn't help but take her outside and smoke a cigarette. Hoping, praying, Emie was out there somewhere.

He'd find himself sitting in his recliner on sleepless night after tossing and turning for too long, just sitting there staring out his open sliding glass door in the living room, listening to the waves rolling up on the beach, wondering where she was.

Where did a vampire run to when she wanted to be alone?

Emie hadn't been at all what his worst imaginations had made her out to be. His childhood fears of vampires and wolves had been just that, childhood fears. Everyone around him had confirmed what he so selfishly couldn't believe himself.

Ken and his wife Miranda would watch him sit and stare at their television, they both knew he was heart broken. They could never understand his pain. They were too in love. They told him many times to go look for her. Ask her brothers where she was, or if they'd found her.

Miranda who was watching endless shows about zombies, was saving up and stocking the garage with supplies. She too had heard on the news what a lot of people feared. Asher knew something was coming. But he didn't know what. He was afraid to blame it on vampires like some people were. It would mean everything he was trying to believe in Emie, might not be true. Sometimes he wondered if they would need her help. Would she be strong enough to help them? Would she even want too after what he had done to her.

Emie was known to have been so much more the a monster. She wasn't at all like the stories told. She didn't run the city seeking to devour all the inhabitants. Joseph wasn't a monster either, Asher told himself as he swung his feet. His father all these years had led him to believe the Whitby family was just that. Money hungry monsters, bleeding the city dry, and keeping it all for themselves in that big ol mansion. But Asher knew better now. Emie was a servant in the city, working in the hospital and giving all she could to help those in need. And Joseph was an overseer of the city who helped the city by lending and funding it where ever it needed to improve it for the better, keeping it safe by updating its administration, leading it into the future instead of holding it back in the past. Creating a little piece of heaven for them all.

His mind wandered back to when he was little. He could remember playing ball too close to the canal fence's with his friends when he was young, in the fall, when the wind rushed through the autumn trees and the leaves would fall in the chilly weather, it would bring out the seasonal fears in everyone. The mansion could be seen in all its glory through the bare trees in the fall. He could remember his friends teasing voices as they coaxed him into jumping the fence to retrieve a baseball or a football, telling him the vampires were going to get him, or the wolves would attack him. He remembered how the rustle of the leaves would spook him so that he would jump at the tiniest of movements.

They had been right of course, his friends, about the wolves. Not about her.

How old was Emie? Had she known who he was then? Had she seen him then, playing with his friends. Had she known then they would be together? So many questions he had left unanswered about her.

Asher knew he still didn't know enough about vampires. Didn't know anything really. Talking to his sister, Izzy, or watching it on tv would only distort the truth about Emie more. Like the new sexy movie on Tv he had watched the other night. They had turned vampire blood sucking into this sexy exotic experience. He had even excited himself one lonely night thinking about her doing that to him. Even though the thought of her having fangs like her brothers scared the hell out of him.

For once, he was honestly curious about vampires. But who could he ask? Who would tell him what he needed to know about Emie? What would he do with the information once he found out? He had not talked to anyone about her since he found out who and what she was.

A vampire.

Asher looked up into the darkness; he wondered when it had gotten so dark on him. He was taking his towel off his shoulder and preparing to stand up and put the trucks away when he seen a cars headlights come flying down the overpass. He shook his head at their recklessness and watched as they slowed to the speed limit. When the little red car passed by him, his heart fell to the ground in front of him.

It was Emie.

He watched her look at him, watched her turn her head back to the road and drive away.

Asher's mind went back to a night a year ago, when she made a promise to him next to this very truck he was sitting on.

"I promise; I'll always wait for you. Just know that, ok? No matter what happens, I'm waiting for you."

That's what she had told him. Asher wondered for just a moment. He let his heart go back to that night, her serenity, her honesty. She'd meant it. He'd fucked everything up, not her. She might still be waiting for him. And he knew he had to find out.

Asher threw the towel he had back over his shoulder and headed for his truck without even thinking about it. There was no way in hell he was going to lose her again. Not because he needed answers. Not because he thought he needed her protection from everything that was going on in the world on the news. No, not for any of those reasons. He drove off after her, hitting the hydrant that he backed into for the first time ever, because he loved her. He could die the happiest man in the world if only he could lay eyes on her again.

He had to catch her. He had to wrap his big arms around her and kiss her. She had said she loved him when she left. It was his turn now.

Emie was coming home to Luna Pier for one thing and one thing only.

A war was coming. And it was headed straight for Michigan.

Jeremy had found her months ago in Kentucky. She had called Joseph then and told him she was safe. Jordy had showed up and stayed with her for weeks. Talking to her about everything that was happening.

When Jeremy had showed up talking about Triton and Asher, Emie knew she couldn't stay there much longer. Cristina also was begging her to come home. The neat little life Emie had created for herself there would never amount to the life she had left in Michigan.

No matter how busy she was, no matter how she tried to entertain herself, she couldn't stop thinking about Asher. He was where her home was.

Jordy had been telling her about what had been happening in the world around her she had closed herself away from. He told her if she didn't come home soon she was going to lose everything she held dear.

What they all didn't know about Asher was his fears. And Emie knew his fears. No one knew he carried the fears he did. He was a fireman. He fought and battled against those things that were the human's worst nightmares. House fires. Car accidents. Death. And there were many other things there too inside of him, she just hadn't had the time to find them all out. He didn't want her to come home the way everyone kept telling her. He needed space from her. He might never be able to recover from what he had learned.

She was worse then all of his fears. She was a monster. She and she alone could take away the one thing from him he was afraid of losing.

His life.

He needed to live. He had brothers and sisters on the department that needed him. Friends, real friends, he had called them his brothers and sisters too. He couldn't abandon them. Or the city he was sworn to protect. The city her brother had been working all his life to create was where Asher lived.

Taking Asher for herself was wrong. He belonged there. Not with her. Not in the dream she was dreaming for them. Or the life she was longing to live with him.

Emie loved him, yes. Loved him truly and deeply. She wanted him more then she had ever wanted anything in this world.

She had come back so she could help her brothers protect what they all wanted in this life. Keeping her distance from Asher was something she was going to have to deal with. He was going to have to deal with it too. She would watch him and love him from a distance. Protect him. But she wouldn't interfere in his life anymore.

Asher's careless whispers in his mind that night at the funeral had been more than she could take. Then she had listened to him for days afterwards. His heart had been breaking right along with hers.

Asher wanted a life. He wanted to love someone. He wanted to spend all his free time together. But Emie could never be with him in the daylight. She could never eat with him; she could never sleep with him. She worried even about being alone with him every time she was with him. There were things she craved from him he couldn't give her.

Asher wasn't just a man, he was a good man. Asher had a family. A big family. She wouldn't fit in his life like he wanted her to, like she wanted too. They would see right through her; they would hate her as he did. She would keep him from them, and she didn't want that. Family was important. And he wanted a family of his own someday. She couldn't give him that either. Just more troublesome brothers.

Speaking of family…

She was almost to her exit. Her music was turned up loud. The sun was setting and she could finally take off her scarf and glasses. The clouds rolling into Luna Pier made the city look darker then the night that was coming. Night time was when rogue vampires where running wild. Luna Pier needed the protection that only her and her brothers could give. There was only the four of them, but they could handle it.

Vampires only loved once she thought as she got to her exit in Luna Pier. She had found her love, but she had lost it. She would morn Asher until he died. Then she would wander this world alone. She didn't want to be a stumbling block to her brother's lives. She would need to move on and start over then.

Emie couldn't wait to get back to the her house, she thought as she turned onto Luna Pier road, the main road going into the city. Just being this close to home, to her Cristina, and Asher, made her want to cry. She had promised herself she wouldn't. Not tonight.

Cristina was making plans to move back down with Emie. Her son, Neely, who loved Emie, was excited too. Cristina had a life she planned on disappearing from, and she would often have to move to start over again. There were some things in life that needed running away from. Cristina knew her and Neely would be safe with Emie. And Emie couldn't wait to have them with her. But those things were going to have to wait now. Wait till it was safe for them to leave. She needed to make sure Asher was safe too before she left.

The sun had just set, she thought she could drive past the fire department without being noticed, but as she reached the bottom of the hill she saw him. Saw the man she had ached for every day of the last 365 days, give or take a few. He was sitting on the front of one of the fire trucks, just watching her go by, just like before.

Emie could do this, she told herself. She could drive right past him and not even look. He wouldn't notice her this time of night.

But his thoughts entered her mind. She could hear them as if he had spoken them right to her. Her resolve shattered to pieces.

Emie. Asher's voice whispered her name in her heart and mind.

Emie closed her eyes and drove right passed him. But she had looked.

It wasn't until half way down Lakewood that she realized there was a huge truck coming up behind her. No lights were on, just the unmistakable grill of a pick up truck in her rear view mirror. Her little car could probably fit right under it.

Emie closed her eyes again and wished she still had the remote for the gate in front of her in her car so she could fly right through it.

Asher's mind was racing. Would she stop? Would she talk to him?

Why was he following her, she wondered? He was the one who had wanted nothing to do with her... or so Emie had thought.

Emie. Asher begged from behind Emie. He knew she could hear him now, so he tried calling out to her over and over.

Asher hadn't just thought it this time. He was calling out to her. His beg sounded like a cry. But why? She could hear it in his mind as if he was clearly standing in front of her speaking to her.

Her first thought was which brother she was going to kill first for telling him he could do this; her second thought was would she scare him if she responded to him. She had longed to talk to him for so long.

Would it ruin her chances with him if she did? What chances did she really have? She couldn't be with Asher. She couldn't, she thought helplessly shaking her head gripping the steering wheel tighter.

If she'd known then a year ago what she knew now, she never would have gotten in that elevator with him.

Emie had reached the gate to her property on the old dirt road bridge that went over the canal. She didn't know what to do now. All she wanted was to get through that gate and to get away without hurting him, or herself. But she'd have to get out of the car and open the stupid gate first.

Asher revved his engine behind her. The loud roar of a V8 engine roared all around them into the silent night.

I will run right over that gate if you leave me here behind it.

This he stated as a fact, Emie saw. She knew he couldn't, the front of his truck would get smashed, the gates were impassable, for a reason. But it was the fact that he would that hurt her the most. She looked in her rear view mirror at him and looked into the eyes of a very determined Asher.

God, how much she missed him, she said to herself in a prayer. Asher wasn't thinking about anything else, she could read his mind, her own emotions where running wild in her mind. Did he just want to talk, or did he just want her out of the City.

Asher had decided to get out of his truck just as the clouds opened up and let go of enough rain to blind him. He could see over his arm he was using as a shield that her lights where still on in front of him, saw her lights flash as she put her car in park, but he couldn't see if she was getting out. He wished he had her ability now. He wanted to hear her thoughts. He wanted to hear her. See her.

Would she get out, he wondered as he tried to walk between their vehicles.

Now in front of his truck he hollered "Emie!" into the night around them. Into the darkness that had enveloped him. Into the rain that was drowning him. There were no street lights down this far, nothing to help him see but the lighting flashes that were scaring him. The graveled drive was turning to mud, he couldn't walk up next to her car, she was parked too close to the edge so she could go through the gate; he would slide off into the canal if he tried. The trees were swaying eerily in the wind. He was feeling eerily insecure and vulnerable like them. But he didn't care. He was here. He was finally close to her again.

Lightning would follow the thunder he had just heard with a loud crack. And with it, she was standing in front of him.

~*Twenty*~

Asher forgot how to breathe. Totally forgot.

She looked every bit the vampire he had feared in this drenching rain. Her long brown hair looked black and was getting wetter by the seconds, hanging down her shoulders straight passed her hips, past the length he remembered. She was getting soaked along with her cute little jean jacket and thin white dress. When he looked down he saw her toes sinking in the mud.

Was she wearing flip flops?

Emie's eyes had a deep dark red glow. Red blood his mind registered. He was glad she hadn't chosen to show her fangs in that moment, his composure might have wavered.

Emie thought about smirking, and showing off at least one fang. She could do just that. He liked to play. She missed playing with him. But she didn't want to be a monster to him anymore. She just wanted to be his. She let her eyes take back the shape he knew, and looked at him.

When she finally looked at him, she couldn't believe it was him. He had lost weight. He seemed... she couldn't explain it. All she could do was stand there unbelievably in awe of him.

It was Asher. He was right there in front of her.

Emie sucked back in the venom that was beginning to overflow in her watering mouth, leaking from her fangs. Asher smelled so good. His blood was racing through his veins and it was heated by a smoke scent that was so intoxicating to her even after all this time.

It was her love for him that stopped the monster inside of her.

Emie, talk to me. He pleaded with her, even though the rain was pelting him, he pleaded with her even though now his heart was sinking with his shoulders and booted feet were drowning in the graveled mud. She wasn't speaking to him, she was just eerily standing there in front of him.

Emie gave in then, more like her heart did; he was going to have to learn one way or another.

Asher-

To say she had scared him was an understatement; her voice he hadn't heard in so, so long, this time inside his head, an ability he wouldn't have guessed she had; it visibly shook him and sealed his fate. Reading thoughts was one thing, entering others minds was all together different. He knew Joseph could do this, he had learned the hard way with Joseph. Learning Emie could do the same, it bothered him more than knowing she had read all his thoughts a year ago. But he stayed himself. Hadn't he just wanted this?

"I'm just here to fix something, and then I'm leaving here Asher. You don't have to worry about all that anymore. You can-"

"What? Why?" His voice shook with fear and anger when he interrupted her, and he could tell he stopped her thoughts in her tracks. He had to shout it at her; she wasn't standing close enough to talk in the rain. The rain that was clouding his vision making it hard to see her, dripping off his hair and running off his nose and lips, making his body tremble and shiver with real cold chills now. Whether it was fear, or anger, or just the cold, he didn't know anymore.

Was she really worried about him being worried about her? Shouldn't she be mad at him?

Emie was shocked by his questions. "Because you don't want me-"

"You can't possibly know what I want, you left me, Emie. You left me, and didn't even tell me why."

Lightning crashed around them then, followed again by raging thunder. He tried not to jump, and knew if that had been in a movie that would have been awesome timing. The storm was officially here.

"I heard you that night Asher, I heard you, loud, and clear." Emie chimed in while the thunder was still pounding around them. "And I can still hear you now." She said to him quieter now.

She turned her head away and said "You wouldn't even talk to me then. There was no talking to you then." Emie had stood as tall as she could next to him. He was a towering man for sure, but she was stronger then he would ever be. She wouldn't let him win this battle without a fight. She had been hurting for far too long to let him off the hook that easily.

She looked up into his full height, standing as close to him as the rain and mud would allow.

"You didn't give me a chance Emie. You didn't talk either. You knew what was going on. You knew what had happened and you didn't say anything." He jumped in before she could say more; he wanted her to understand why he thought all that then. "My brother had just died" he said slowly but demandingly, licking the rain off his lips, trying to control the emotions that one sentence held.

He reached up his hand in defeat and shoved his other hand through his hair. I didn't know what I wanted then. He knew when he thought it she could hear him, so he added I just knew that I wanted you. He didn't think he could say it aloud. But he did it anyways looking right at her. "I just wanted you, Emie. Just you."

He put up his arms, ready to take her arms in his hands and beg her to come back to him, but he lowered them in defeat. Realization hit him dead on. He knew she couldn't have talked to him then. She was right, he wouldn't have listened. And it could have ended worse then what it had.

"You said you wished I hadn't been there that night. It was the last thing you-"

She couldn't finish. Emie tried to hide the tears. Tried to wipe them away, but blood was easy to see. She was choking on the words she didn't get to say, the words she wanted to say were overpowering her.

She didn't want to argue anything more. She just wanted to go back and forget the memories they couldn't erase.

"Are you ok?" Asher's whole demeanor had change in an instant.

She could feel him go from angry and scared like he was flipping a switch and immediately he started worrying about her eyes. He really didn't know anything about vampires.

Emie wasn't looking at him when he asked, so she didn't know if he had said it aloud or in his mind. She couldn't respond anyways, she just fell to the ground with her face in her hands. Weeping.

She would choke on the words she needed to say if she said them. She could feel for the first time in this new life, her life, expiring. What she had been fighting for so long not to happen to her, it was happening. The pain and anguish, it was finally killing her. Vampires couldn't feel what humans did. Pain was something they no longer felt. When it overpowered them, it could kill them.

Asher knelt down next to her. Emie was crying. Did vampires do this? Break down? He wouldn't have thought it possible moments ago. His hands were out stretched towards her, ready to hold her, but she wasn't looking at him and he didn't know what to do. She was just sobbing, and it was breaking his heart. And there was blood. Lots of blood, flowing down her cheeks like tears. Was this how vampires cried?

But she wasn't just a vampire, she was Emie. The Emie Joseph had held because Asher had hurt her. The Emie everyone in this God forsaken city had missed, including him. The Emie he loved.

He suddenly wanted to hold her. The Emie he had loved and lost. The Emie whose smile had lit up his days, and then she had turned his world into darkness. Like the darkness he knew now she must be living in too. Had she missed him, he wondered, like he had so desperately missed her. He wanted to hold her and rock her. Kiss her and softly and tell her it was all going to be ok. They could love each other. Well he could love her, but the question still was if she could still love him.

Emie looked up at him then. Had he really just said he loved her? Had he loved her then? Had she been wrong all along? Could she have stayed with him? Had he changed his mind?

Jordy's words came back to her mind. You need to tell him you love him Emie.

Asher didn't know much about why her tears were blood, but he knew in his heart he needed to stop them. He cupped her face in his hands, scooting closer to her in the gravel mud.

Damn but she was cold. Colder then he felt. He was all kinds of pissed off now. Pissed at himself for letting this happen to them both.

"I didn't know then what I know now sweetheart. But I do know now." then he added, looking down in her eyes, her tears, in his mind he told her what the pouring rain wouldn't let him say aloud.

Teach me how to love you. I need to love you Emie. I need you to love me. He pleaded.

"I have never loved anyone as much as I love you Emie." He said it aloud, said it to her eyes, because… because he just had too. He had to say it to her. She had to hear it. She had to believe it.

Emie could see his tears welling in his eyes. She could feel his emotions overflowing in his heart. He was torn between his fears of the unknown, and not knowing what to do, not even knowing what it was he was asking for. Just that he couldn't live anymore without her.

She looked at his chest and could hear his heart pounding out his feelings. And in the rain, she could feel his warm hands on her cheeks and smell his warmth more then before. She missed his smell. She missed Asher.

Emie looked down at his chest where his heart was beating. She placed both her hands there over his heart. His blood was warm and fresh, tainted with nicotine and that sweet mixture of smoke and ash filled her nostrils. He was human, yes. He wasn't made for the love of a vampire. He was made for a woman.

Emie reached for his hands and pulled them away from her face, but he wouldn't let of go of her hands. "You can't Asher. You don't understand what I can't give you. I can't give you…" she had put her head back down to bite back her words. She couldn't say them, because it meant she really couldn't have him.

"Give me what?" he asked shaking her hands in his, and even though he could see one fang biting into her lips, even though it was adorably cute, even though that scared him like a reality slap in the face, he didn't care. He didn't want anything else in this life but her.

Damn but he needed her to talk to him. He hated himself for not listening to her more. "Sweet heart, tell me." He asked trying like hell to lift her face so he could see her, but she kept tucking it away.

He was losing his mind being this close to her and not being able to see her.

I can't give you the life you need. You don't know me Asher. You don't know what this would be like. What it felt like to be this close, and not be able too...

She showed him in his mind all of the things she couldn't give him bowing her head. Family, children, days outside being a family with his family, and even his friends.

Asher still wasn't sure if he liked the whole mind thing now. It was dizzying to say the least. Like he was being drugged with her moving through his mind. He was just glad he could finally hear her. He knew there was more, so much more to her thoughts; he just hoped the important words would flow through her to him unbidden. He didn't want any more secrets between them.

He was so sorry for the things he never got to say to her. He wasn't about to waste this chance he had been given.

He didn't care about his life anymore more. The life he had been leading before her. It didn't matter to him anymore. He hated it before he met her, and had cherished the idea of a new life with her. When she had left him, she had left him alone with the life he hadn't wanted, and he didn't know how to get back the life he wanted with her.

Now she was right here in front of him, she could take away his whole life right now, it wouldn't matter. The whole world could stop right now, it felt like it was now anyways with the rain and thunder. The wind felt like it was driving away everything he's ever known, leaving just her, sitting here in front of him, weeping over all the reasons why she couldn't love him, why she shouldn't be with him.

"Damn all those reason Emie! I don't care about them anymore." He just wanted her to stay. Nothing else matter.

She was humbling him, sitting there shaking her head no at him. He didn't know where to go from here. He loved her more in this moment then he had before. She was giving up something she wanted badly to save him from herself. Because she thought he was worth something in this life, even though he didn't think so.

Until now. Now he realized what his purpose was in this life. He lived; he existed, just for her.

"Give us a chance Emie. That's all I'm asking sweetheart." And it was. So he added "I'm not strong like you, I can't fight for you. I can't break through walls and gates to find you." he looked up behind them at the gates for emphasis. "I can't search to the end of the earth to find you." he said lowering his head back down to hers trying to get her to look at him. "I can't take on all your brothers to prove that I am good enough for you. You have to come to me, and you have to let me try sweetheart." He lifted her chin then and made her look at him. Or make me like you are so I can be with you forever.

He hadn't a clue where that had come from, but now that he'd said it he knew it was from his heart. His will was getting stronger. Just seeing this woman in front of him, breaking down for him, wanting him, trembling even; was making him come undone. He wasn't gonna lose her again.

Asher. She cried into his mind. His words even now were breaking her. "I can't." she whispered through her tears and the pouring rain with trembling lips. She could barely look at him now. She couldn't take away this wonderful man's life.

Asher sat back on his heels. She was flat out denying him. She was ripping his heart out.

She'd even quit talking to him. The only sound left in their presences was the passing of the storm. The soft pelting of the rain. Asher didn't know what else she was thinking. She wouldn't invite him inside of her.

So Asher kissed her. If she wouldn't listen to him, then she would have to feel his need for her. That's exactly how they had done it before. And it felt just as real to him now as it did then.

He was weak in the knees and his hands were trembling as he grabbed her and pulled her up to him, kissing her slowly. He let his lips just linger on hers. He pushed against her roughly, begging her to love him. He held her close, knew how tightly he could hold her now. Knew, now that she had sank into his body that she had reacted to him and now he could recklessly kiss her with all abandonment.

Her hands were back at the nape of his neck and it made him cry. He hadn't even known he had missed that too, but he had.

He kissed her lips, sucked them into his. Weeped like a child with her as he tasted blood on his tongue mixed with his own salty tears.

Emie, his Emie was in his arms. He was holding her. After all this time all he could think was he could finally now feel her again. Finally he could kiss her again.

He said and thought her name over and over as he pulled her as close as he could onto his body, into her favorite spot on top of him. She would hear him. She would know with his kiss that he wanted her. All of her, and only her.

He reached for her and touched her everywhere. He cupped her face, her cheeks, He smoothed her hair down her back with his hands and pulled her hips closer to him and then on top of him, rocking her in his lap as he ravishly kissed her.

Emie had dreamed about this for so long. Well, not the rain, not him on his knees begging her in the mud. But she'd dreamed of his arms, his kiss, his warm body. His hands on her face, in her hair, pressing her hips into his body. The sound of his heart beating. His heart. The heart of a hero, the heart of the man that had loved her at first sight.

Love. Emie had never believed in it before. But here it was. Holding her, kissing her. Breathing life back into her worn and weary heart. Begging her to love him back. Keeping her alive when moments ago she had been dying.

Emie reached up to him and wrapped her arms around his neck. She pushed down on his body as he pushed up into her.

Asher's radio started beeping loudly through the rain to his pounding heart.

Damn it! They both thought out loud together. Their lips parted but never left each others as they listened for his radio.

"Monroe County dispatch on the air for all Monroe county fire departments. The weather service has now issued a tornado warning for our area. I repeat, a tornado warning has been issued for our area by the National Weather Service. Roll call will follow." Then the beeping was long and loud. Every fire departments tones were being set off. The long blasting sirens throughout the city followed.

Asher wouldn't stop kissing Emie, he had bitten her lip to keep her from breaking their kiss during the call, now that it was over he went back to kissing her even though his mind was screaming at him to stop. He ran his hands up her bare thighs threw her dress and squeezed her bottom closer on him. He wasn't letting her go.

His heart stopped when the rain stopped. The wind took on a new howling. Bending trees instead of moving through them. When the rain picked eerily back up the wind blew it sideways.

That was a bad sign, Asher knew. He was trained for this.

Asher's lips were open, begging her, pleading, his temple was pressed against Emie's, all while trying to think how much time he could spare here on his knees for her. They were still embracing. The thunder and lightning crashed and boomed all around them. He knew it was a sure sign of worse weather to come.

But still, she didn't say anything to him.

"I have to go." He whispered, gulping down rain and blood. His heart was breaking. He didn't have her promise yet. She could leave him while he was gone, and he couldn't do a damn thing to stop her.

"I know super man." Emie sighed aloud looking up at him. She was beginning to feel an awful lot like the girl always waiting on super man.

Asher squeezed his eyes shut tight and hung his head. She had always called him that. Always thought of him as super man. But tonight he wished he didn't have to be that man. He wanted to be just a normal guy that got to sit out here with her and not leave her.

She could see Asher. She could see his thoughts, the work that needed to be done. Quickly.

She placed her hand on his heart and squeezed his shirt, she didn't want him to go. She wanted to beg him to stay.

Neither moved, for a moment they just took time to sit there quietly, even though the worst storm in Luna Pier's history was raging around them. Even though his radio was telling him he needed to hurry.

Emie moved her hair off her face and couldn't look at Asher. She held onto his shirt like it was a lifeline to her heart. She wiped away tears that were sure to be freighting to him. She wanted to run away with him. Pick him up and carry him far away from here. But she couldn't.

Asher stood up and picked her up letting her slide down his body at the loudest crash of lighting he had heard all night.

"Don't go." She begged in a broken whisper, holding his shirt tighter.

Asher placed his forehead on hers. "Emie…". He took a huge breath and struggled to breathe. He kissed her forehead and let go of her. He had too, and walked over to his truck.

His fire radio was filled with roll call from all the surrounding departments, his would be next, and he wasn't there anymore. Dundee and Ida, which were towns directly north and west of him were getting pounded by the storm and reporting funnel clouds in their area, headed straight for Luna Pier.

He stopped at the door of his truck, looked back at Emie. She was still standing there watching him. He reached in his window and answered the radio just as the dispatcher toned out his department again. He looked back at Emie one more time as the sirens blared all around them. She still hadn't said she loved him.

You have to follow me Emie.

With that he jumped in his truck and backed down the drive. Turning on his light and siren in his truck, he left her there. Left her and prayed she'd follow him this time.

Emie needed Joseph. She needed him to tell her what to do.

When she pulled up around to the side of the house he was leaning against one of the pillars on the side porch. Waiting for her in the rain. He tossed her a bag of fresh clothes when she reached the steps.

Emie stood in the rain. Drenched like a drowned rat. How did he know? She hadn't seen him in a year. She hadn't even told him she'd left and didn't plan to come back. And yet here he was. Giving her the one thing he knew she wanted more then anything.

"What do I do Joseph?" She pleaded with him to answer her as she looked down at her bag.

Joseph knew she knew the answer. She'd known it all along tonight. So he reminded her of her earlier thoughts.

If you'd known then what you know now, you wouldn't have gotten in the elevator. If you hadn't gotten in the elevator, you wouldn't have him at all Emie. He knew she wanted Asher in her life. Even if it meant just being friends and loving him from afar, she would do anything for Asher. Anything that kept him alive and in her life. But he also knew the deep desire she felt in side her foolish soul now was stronger then anything he or anyone he had ever known had felt. And he wished her well. She loved Asher.

"Go tell him you love him Emie."

That was all Emie needed to know. She couldn't live in this world without Asher. Joseph was right. Even if she could go back in time, she would still get on that elevator. She would still do everything in her power to get him to stay with her. Whatever it took to keep them together. She would do it.

Standing there looking at Joseph looking at her drowning in the rain, she knew she had to find Asher. She had to tell him. She couldn't let him spend this whole night out there fighting alone without knowing she would wait for him.

No. She had to tell him she loved him. That's all that needed to be said anymore.

Emie got back in her car, changed out of her jacket and dress and headed for the station. She could see through the rain, but she couldn't see through her tears.

~ *Twenty One* ~

Jordy had been standing out in the rain with them tonight. He watched and looked after Emie. Made sure she was ok. Made sure Asher didn't hurt her again, even though Jordy had a feeling Asher wouldn't. He was the one who told Asher that Emie could change him to be like her. He had hid the thought in Asher's mind like bait, and Asher had taken it.

Joseph and Jeremy would protect him tonight out here in the storms. No harm would come to Asher or his men tonight. They owed Emie that much.

Jordy had seen all their futures early in life. Just before Emie had turned. He had been just nineteen then. Still more a boy than a man.

The night Emie had been turned, he was the first one out to the stables that night when they all, including his parents, had heard Emie's screams. She was being sucked dry by a huge vampire he couldn't defeat. The monster had bared his fangs at them all that night, stopped Jordy dead in his tracks as he tried to run out to save his sister, until his father had waved his torch in front of them, making the vampire run for his life leaving Emie to die. The vampire had left her lifeless on the cold ground. But what the monster hadn't known was he had changed her.

Joseph had told Jordy later, it might have been them that had scared the man into injecting his venom in her by accident. Jordy knew how that felt, being scared. His venom would drip from his fangs at just the thought. It was just a reaction of their body. If they'd not come running in to save her, she might have died. If she hadn't been changed, they all would have died. She saved them all, his brothers and him, not their parents though, they thought Emie was dead to them when she turned and wanted nothing more to do with her. They died from a disease that spread through England like wildfire.

That night was much like tonight, the night Emie was turned. Cold, raining, thunder and lightning scaring the hell out of all of them. He had seen it many nights before hand. A monster killing Emie, but she had told him that the nightmare he was dreaming was just a dream, she had comforted him and told him that nothing would ever happen to her or them.

She had been wrong of course.

Jordy was now sinking in the mud behind a tree, listening into the night for screams he knew would come. Again.

Rain pelting him in the arms and shoulders. Lightning crashing all around him, wind plastering his shirt to his chest. Still, he waited. It would be any second now.

Emie had been his first love in life. She was his sister, yes, but she had held him as if he were her child, and he had loved her. He would play with her hair as a baby while she rocked him. No one had hair like Emie's. He had loved her hair so much that when his father or Joseph had held him he would cry. When his mother held him, it just wasn't the same. He had wanted Emie. His big sister, with the amazingly soothing voice, and beautiful long silky hair. She had hated that of course, hated him pulling on it as a baby, hated him brushing it as a child, but she had let him nonetheless.

Now she was in love with a man. A human of all things. Loving him, like she had loved them, strongly and deeply. With everything in her power to give Asher. A gift the man didn't deserve.

Jordy knew what it was like to be a man. Emie had waited till they were 22 to turn them. He had wanted this life back then, thinking it was a cool lifestyle. Who wouldn't want everlasting life, superhuman strength, a body the women would dream about at night.

He had been so wrong.

Two days ago he realized why his life had been changed. Why his sister had been bitten, why he had to make this long journey through life alone. He'd seen Asher's sister Izzy at the bookstore in Toledo. He seen his soul mate. Watched as his whole future, not just a few seconds, passed before his eyes.

It had only happened a few times in this life, like with Emie and Jeremy. Seeing Izzy's long spiral springy curly hair had shaken him as he followed her around the store. His mind seen her dying and blood soaking that pretty blonde hair. She was on a beach, lying in the sand, screaming into a storm, but no one would hear her.

He wished he could find her now. He wished he could see where she was, and where she would be when she would be attacked, but he couldn't.

She had been right in front of him, looking for books in the book store. He watched as his future rolled out in front of him. She would be lying naked, dying in the grass by his house of all places, all while she was standing at the checkout counter of the coffee shop in the book store getting a cup of hot steamy coffee.

He could feel her lips kissing him in some of his visions of her, while she sipped her coffee and she quietly peeked inside a book on the other side of the book shelf where he was standing behind. And when she started to walk out the door, dropping her bag of vampire books at his feet, he reached down and helped her and smelled her scent like he was taking a deep breath of the night air that would be surrounding them in a few nights.

In an instant, she had felt it to when she seen him. When she touched his hand thoughts of all she dreamed of, started to come true. She knew he was a vampire, and didn't care. He on the other hand had carelessly told her his name and that he was Emie's brother. He read there in her mind that she had known all along that Emie was a vampire too. And when Izzy noticed what he was doing, reading her mind, he had given away his own secret. But she hadn't cared.

And now, on this hellish night, she would be on the beach not knowing the fate that waited for her, she had just wanted a quiet place to read her books and dream about Jordy. Not knowing he would be there, waiting for her, to rescue her. He would save her life and take her to shelter in the barns. She would love him. Forever.

Jordy listened in on Emie and Asher. Smiled as he watched Asher kiss his big sister and make her see how much he really did love her. Then Jordy apologized to him over the distance as Asher drove away, for what he was about to do to Asher's little sister because he loved her already.

Asher would just have to forgive him later. Hopefully without the lighter that he always had hidden in his jean pocket...

Asher had made it just in time for roll call. Every fire fighter in the city had showed up. It wasn't everyday that they got a tornado warning. There would be wind and possibly lightning damage. Trees and wires would be down all around the city even if there wasn't a tornado. A good storm like this could destroy a city. There could be a fire or fires with the way this city was built. Houses so close together. Lives were on the line tonight. And he had to be here.

Emie was gonna have to come back to him if she wanted him. He couldn't play the lonely hearted fool anymore.

Asher grabbed his gear and jumped in the closest truck and drove off to save the city.

Asher didn't notice Emie's car as it pulled into the station behind the truck. Emie was too late. She pulled up next to his personal truck and watched him drive off in his other one.

Someone was tapping on her window. Frantically. She rolled it down and immediately shielded her eyes from the pouring rain.

"Come on! Get inside. Hurry!"

It was Jesse. Asher's brother, one of the police officers who was on the department. He was shielding the rain too, and motioning her up to the fire hall, while dodging the rain and holding his coat up to block the rain. The howling thundering sounds of the storm sounded like a freight train rushing through the city.

Emie turned off her car and ran in. She might as well start here.

It was chaotic in the fire hall. The fire radios were loud and she could hear other fire departments on them calling for help. Stepping on the toes of central dispatch "Send help to Dundee!"

Dundee was a small little town north west of Luna Pier. She knew the town and wondered what all the commotion was about. So she listened in to the minds around her.

Tornado.

Everyone was thinking it. Everyone was afraid of it. One was headed right for Dundee and all of Monroe, including them, was in its path.

The sounds of scared firemen sounded like something out of a horror movie. Men who were trained in disaster and emergency situations were in need. Pleading for it on the radios.

Every man on this department wanted to help. They listened in awe at the sounds of their distress on the radio's and on the tv. But did they leave their own city that was being pounded by the storm helpless and defenseless? The worst of it wasn't even here yet. It would all be over soon.

Emie was at a loss. What could she do? Vampires weren't afraid of tornados. They could be swept away in them, and fall right back down to earth, dirty and little light headed from riding in a storm. Their bodies were unbreakable.

Joseph was going to be so upset about this storm. It was sure to do damage around the house and yards he had been working so hard on.

Jesse ushered Emie into the kitchens. A small room just off the truck bays. There was a fridge and a stove and lots of tables and chairs. All scooted out of place, the men had all abandon an evening meal she noticed.

Jesse had to shout at her, the noises around them were so loud. Firemen were bumping into her on their way to the other trucks and some equipment. He informed her their were people coming here for shelter. He asked her if she could handle seating them in the back meeting rooms, and in here. "Tell them to sit tight and bunker down. This one's gonna take off some roofs." He shouted with a smile.

She couldn't believe it. Jesse was smiling at her. Did he even know who she was? They'd met once or twice before. She had just assumed his whole family would have hated her for leaving Asher. She had wondered often what Asher had told them.

Emie shook her head in wonder and was hoping Jesse wasn't talking about a tornado and was just referencing the storms. But either way, he had left her there alone.

Two families, fire men's families and a few dogs were there with her too. All huddled around and scared. The full force of what was happening hit her harder then she had expected. Lives, not just property was at stake here.

Emie knew if she ever wanted Asher to know she wanted to do this with him, be apart of his life, then she needed to stay and prove it.

She worried also about Jordy's premonitions. Was this storm related to anything going on in the world. She could only hope not.

She made popcorn, watched the news on the storms as they ripped through towns and then passed, made coffee and hot chocolate, and then tried not to bend her ear into the radio room every time she heard Asher's voice on the radio. His voice was so distinct. That rough deep manly voice, that held just a little southern accent like Jeremy's, she had to wonder where it came from. He wasn't from the south, was he? From what she knew of him, he'd been here all his life.

When the injured came in with no fire fighter's or medic's to help her, she made a call over to the hospital for a makeshift triage center to show up. Some doctors and nurses she knew came over to help.

She learned her way around the kitchen in the hours she spent there. Found very old silverware and cups and very outdated dishes in the cupboards. The old microwave sitting on top of the stove didn't work and neither did the stove. She wondered how they made out without the first. Cristina had gone through two since she had met her.

Why was all the important things they needed here so outdated, she wondered. From the popcorn machine that was too big for the room, down to the coffee pot that had to be too small for all of them. She tried to clean up their dinner mess for them, cover up their food and keep it warm for when they returned.

The meeting room was older than the rest of the building. It had an old bar that stretched the length of the front wall to the doors of the Chief's office. Years of use on the bar stools shown in the leather upholstery.

Old pictures of the department hung on the walls along with a small dart board that hung next to a huge 52 inch flat screen tv, making it all look out of place. A trophy case wall was set up with awards and flags and trophies they had won in the past. One award she hadn't had time to read was sitting in the glass case all by itself. It had something to do with September 11th and New York City, but she had had to help someone find the bathroom, and she forgot all about it.

There was a pool table for the guys, but it had equipment on it. The pool sticks where a little dusty and some were broken she noticed. She wondered if they would play if they had a new table.

Long rectangular tables were set up in the middle to form a square U shape. Equipment and papers were on each one. She could see where they had been training today, but she was still confused by the huge yellow ball with cords and wires on it. What could they possibly be doing with that?

She met various firemen as they came back to the station. They all introduced themselves to her politely. They all instantly accepted her when they learned who she was.

She loved the nicknames. Junior, who looked too old to be called such, was a bald, short, well mannered, easy going guy. His genuine friendship with them was endearing.

Po, who she later learned was Derrick, was a tall younger guy, recently engaged. He was a sweetheart. Kept asking her if she needed anything.

Giggles, also known by his last name as Peterson, depending on who was talking to him, was tall and very skinny. He held and carried himself like a man on a mission, until he talked to her. Then she could see the man who she liked better. He had an easy smile, one that lit up his face and everyone around him. People would actually stop what they were doing just to talk to him when he smiled.

Half, whose real name or why he had the nickname Half she didn't know. His mind was full of getting home to his family. He had worried about them a lot tonight. She admired him for that.

Ken's wife Miranda sat down and talked to Emie for at least an hour. Her and the girls couldn't sleep tonight not knowing if Ken was ok or not, so they stayed at the fire hall and waited out the storm till he returned. She talked of memories of Asher and Ken and how they met. How they used to sit in the recliners at her house studying all night long sometimes when they were in training. She talked of how much Asher loved food, and loved when Miranda would cook for him. Emie had to laugh at loud at that. She already knew this about Asher.

Emie watched as Miranda stroked the hair of her youngest daughter Katie who was lying in her lap awkwardly at the table. Miranda looked over at Emie and wondered how she should tell Emie of the many nights Asher had spent at their house just staring off in space. How she would watch Asher outside smoking one smoke after another. He had been so lost without Emie. So heartbroken. No matter how much they had pleaded with him to start dating again, Asher wouldn't listen. He wanted Emie. He was bound and determined to wait for her.

"Emie?"

"Yes? Is there something you need Miranda?" Emie knew where Miranda's thoughts were and prepared herself to act surprised by whatever Miranda confided in her.

She tried not to be jealous of the child laying in Miranda's arms. She had thought about not being able to give Asher children, and here was one family he looked up too and wanted for himself. He would love them and protect them for the rest of his life. Would they ever be able to handle who she was? Would she have to lie to them too just to protect them.

"I just wanted to tell you how much Asher cares about you. I know we've never met before, and I'm no one to be giving advice, but Asher… he's a good honest man. He doesn't love easily. But when he does, he loves with everything he has to give. And I really think he loves you." see added with a heartwarming smile.

Emie knew all this already. She didn't know how to respond to this woman she'd just met. But she could read inside her mind how much she cared for Asher, another thing Emie hadn't known about Asher, and to Emie, Miranda's advice was important to her.

"Asher and I talked just before the storm hit." She told Miranda. She wanted her to know they would work on things.

"Well good. You make sure Asher brings you by sometime. The girls and I would love to spend some time with you." Miranda said to her encouragingly.

Emie smiled back at her honestly. She could just picture it all in her mind the way Miranda was. But Emie was still so unsure about it all.

Emie spent the last few hours learning about how Dundee was hit the hardest. An f3 tornado had gone through the heart of the town, taking out houses and trees. At one point she heard that a hotels roof was on the expressway US-23 in Dundee.

Emie heard calls come across the radio all night for fires and medicals all around the county. It was really something to listen in on. She didn't know what half the calls meant, but she had enough medical background to figure it all out.

So this is what it was like for Asher, she thought. Hearing a need and answering the call. She also found herself wanting to help.

She noticed when the bay doors were opened that the howling wind and pouring down rain had died down considerably. Walking out the bay doors to get some fresh air, she couldn't believe what she seen around the department. Tree limbs and leaves scattered the road. Along with garbage can lids and house siding. No street lights were on, or lights in the houses. The church across the street had no lights but she could see the pastor on the inside with family and friends, looking out the windows at the night like they were also in awe. Had they sought shelter there? She wondered how much of the city had lost power.

She realized around three in the morning that this was going to be a long night for the firemen. Clean up around the city alone was going to take some time. She had to wonder if Asher would be back before the sunrise.

Would she be able to leave this place when it did? Or could she stick around all day into the evening until it was safe to leave.

Walking back into the fire hall she could smell the old familiar smells of the department. There was still an ever present smell of ash and smoke. It reminded her of Asher.

Around six in the morning, on a cloudless, cold and foggy sunrise; the firemen came back home. Three fire trucks pulled onto the apron of the fire department drive.

Firemen in all three trucks jumped out and started to remove their dirty gear, helmets, and water soaked boots. The large tanker was being hooked up to the hydrant to be refilled before it was parked in the station.

One of the rookies in the radio room called over the radio to central dispatch, echoing throughout the department that the horses had returned to the barns, an old firefighter saying in years past, clearing the call.

Emie had to stand in awe of it all. She never thought she'd be standing here. Never thought she'd be so close to Asher again.

Emie peeked through the bay doors and spotted Asher. He was hooking up hoses to tanker. His bunker trousers were hanging off his jeans. He stood tall and removed his shirt to wring it out. Three guys followed suit, and Emie had to turn her head. But she looked back at Asher.

They were all laughing together. He was their leader now that Curtis was gone, their friend. He was their Chief.

Brothers... she remembered. They were brothers.

Asher's body was tan and muscled, his tattoos shined colorfully in the morning light. When he turned around, Emie seen how scared his back was deeply down his left shoulder to his hip. She covered her gasp with her fingers as she looked at it closely.

Asher hid it well; she couldn't help but wondered what had happened. It must have been terrible whatever it was, she thought feeling sorry for him.

That's what had been hurting him all those nights, she thought off handedly. How had she not noticed it before, she wondered.

She watched as they cleaned the hoses and drained them of water, hanging them in the tower to dry. She watched as compartments were opened on all sides of the trucks as they cleaned and put away their equipment. Axes, flashlights, generators, chain saws, gloves, hoses. How did they fit it all in those trucks?

And then, oddly, she watched as one woman carried bagged toys from a supply closet and set them in the compartments along with rubber gloves. They looked very out of place in there Emie thought with all the equipment. Where these for children who they would see on a scene? No one would ever have guessed teddy bears were in those compartments.

Emie read the fire women's mind and could see the children they had given toys to on this horrible night, and others like it. House fires and car accidents mainly. This clutched at Emie's heart deeply. She had to wipe a tear away at the thought of all this department had gone without, updates and repairs that needed to be done, and these men and women, heros in Emie's mind, made sure they spent money on toys for children.

Emie moved out of the way of the sunlight that was entering the fire hall and headed back for the kitchen, she would have to hide from the sunlight until everyone was gone. Asher might be able to sneak her out a back door if need be. She knew she could call her brothers if she had to. They were waiting in the silence of her mind for just one word from her.

She wouldn't need them today.

Asher was tired. He was sitting on the back of Engine 2 exhausted waiting for the truck to be topped off with water. Yesterday he had worked a twelve hour shift. They had checked the trucks during the day, made some repairs, played water ball with the hoses and the big yellow ball they had attached to wires for drill. The new guys had a lot of fun pushing that big ball around with the hoses, he remembered with excitement about the drill and doing it again soon.

He'd washed every last truck before the sun had set yesterday just to get his mind off the things he couldn't have in his life. His brother, Emie, a vacation… Vacations would never be the same anymore without someone to enjoy them with.

The night's events had been horrifying. Half of the city was without power. He looked around at the church across the street and the street itself, the debris was scattered all around.

They'd had to assist with evacuations of the hotels and help the hospital with diesel fuel for the generators. The transportation of some of the patients had to wait until it was safe for flights out of Toledo to land the helicopters. The guy whose leg had been crushed by his own truck outside his house, almost didn't make it tonight because a helicopter was late. Asher hated amputees, he thought as rubbed his bad shoulder, as much as he hated giving cpr, he always felt so helpless.

Trees had to be removed off the roads, debris had to be hauled away. Wires had to be guarded until it was safe for the electric company to come out. Gas leaks had to be monitored. And someone had to watch the stormy skies for a tornado.

Dundee had been hit harder, but he couldn't spare any of his men to send to them.

Asher had to keep track of all his men and the team he had assigned himself too. Two fire departments from the south who weren't affected by the storm, Morin Point and a department out of Toledo had been called to assist with a another house fire on fourth street. His street. Asher was so thankful it hadn't been his house. That was the last thing he could deal with tonight.

Asher bowed his head and ran his hands through his hair. He was going to need a cigarette and a shower soon. Both shoulders were now starting to ache from all the nights built up tension.

He looked up into the cold, foggy morning and watched as the sun came up over the lake. His thoughts returned to Emie. He had thought of her name a hundred times tonight. Felt the stir of emotions as he thought about kissing her. Then he had to shake her from his mind. He hated nights like these that took him away from the only thing he wanted to think about.

When tanker had been filled, all the trucks were parked and equipment was cleaned and put away, he joined everyone in the meeting room for a quick meeting. No one was going home till he had a talk with his men. His father had gathered everyone but then headed to his office to call the Red Cross; there were families in need of them tonight.

Asher stood by the television and waited for them all to settle down while he put his shirt back on. He leaned against the pool table for support. His hair was a mess and his trousers were threatening to fall off him. He couldn't remember the last time he had lost this much weight. His shirt was soaked through giving him chills. Even his nipples were standing at attention.

Then he saw her. Emie. She had kept her unspoken promise to him. She'd followed for him. To the one and only place where she knew she could.

She was standing over by the kitchen. She looked amazing in her dark designer jeans and shirt. Asher couldn't breathe looking at her. He couldn't believe she was real. It felt like forever since he had seen her last.

Asher noticed when Ken was saying goodbye to his family. He noticed the way Ken kissed Miranda and Asher was hopeful that he would get the chance to have that back with Emie.

Emie was standing in the kitchen doorway watching the men closely when she had finished cleaning up. She had wondered what they all were doing sitting around the tables. They were all drenched and tired. Somewhere stretching and working out leg cramps, gulping down two and three water bottles, throwing them at each other playfully.

She watched as Asher ran his hands through his hair and rubbed his shoulder, and then he looked up and saw her. The moment he thought of her name all she could do was stare at him. When he smiled, her smile crept up her cheeks. He truly did still love her, she could feel it inside of him.

She watched as he noticed Ken and Miranda. Even though Emie's heart hurt at not being able to give Asher a family of his own, she watched as his mind showed her what he really wanted. What all he really needed, as Ken and Miranda embraced. All Asher wanted was for someone to love him.

Asher's attention was taken by one of the fire fighters comments. He started the meeting and needed to get it over with. Quickly. The men and women wanted to go home, see to their own families and property, and he wanted to get lost in Emie's world again.

"You all did great tonight. I don't have anything to say other then what a good job you all did, and we need volunteers for the rest of day. There's a lot of work left to be done."

Asher went on for ten minutes. He took down names and organized some teams for clean up. Scheduled some men for over time to stay at the department. He couldn't help but glance over at Emie standing in the doorway listening intently. He had to make sure she was still there. That she was real and not dream.

His father Frank stood in his midst, told the men they had done well also and listened to the rants and raves from the previous night. Asher's brother James read from the reports and his other brother Jesse met with him after they were finished to discuss one of the trucks.

"One of the floodlights on Task got ripped off when Ken backed in the bay doors."

Asher rubbed his forehead and closed his eyes. Ken had been known for backing into everything and anything lately. He remembered the hydrant he had hit earlier with his own truck and wondered if Ken had been thinking of Miranda the way he had been thinking about Emie. He'd have to share that one with Ken when they were alone and ask him.

He sighed looking over at Emie. He still didn't know what she had been doing here until Jesse informed him.

"Emie is an amazing woman Asher. She took over here and helped with the loads of people that were coming in. She fed them, cared for them, listened to them. She even set up a triage center for the wounded." Jesse followed Asher's gaze over to Emie and hoped this little bit of information would help in getting the two of them back together.

Asher was amazed. He felt sick at the fact that he ever had thought she was anything less than what Jesse had said she was. Amazing.

When the room had cleared, most of the men had went home to their families. His father was off for the day so he left too. Just three men remained; Ken, Derrick, and Jesse, but they were out of sight up stairs sleeping off the nights work.

Emie hadn't moved from the doorway. She was leaning of course, to look more casual. But when he caught her attention from the pool table she straightened up. He sweetly winked at her and made a 'come here' motion with his finger.

Asher couldn't wait for her slow pace. He ran up and caught her in his arms. Lifted her and twirled her around. Letting her fall down his body into his kiss, grabbing the back of her hair and holding her to him. He repeated her name over and over in his mind, knowing she could hear him. She was in his world now, and he wasn't letting her go.

In that moment, Emie wasn't a vampire or a human. She was just Emie. His Emie.

It was a deep kiss, this kiss of his. He was taking her lips inside of his again, sliding them back and forth. Pulling in her upper lip in between his, and then her bottom. Kissing her so thoroughly she thought she was melting in his arms.

His hands were roaming her hair, playing with her curls and barely holding onto her but then pulling her so close to him she had to lift on to her toes and hold his neck just to stay connected with his lips.

Emie really was the one holding onto him. Holding on for dear life. He was so happy for that. Asher took his hands and ran them around her hips and held her behind her back so tightly that he grabbed his wrists to lock her in. He wasn't letting go either. Then when she moaned he deepened the kiss and held her head again while he invaded her mouth with his tongue and bent her body backwards and then back upright again.

His body temperature rose with each stir of his body, his brow started to heat. The fire hall was no longer cool from the evening storms. The sun outside was heating the rooms one by one. The smoky fire smells stirred around them in the light breeze blowing through the fire hall.

He tried not to breathe so he didn't have to stop kissing her. His poor heart was going to pound out of his chest. He just couldn't believe she was in his arms again. He'd never felt passion like this. Never.

In just a kiss.

The radio on his hip made them both jump. He sighed when the call wasn't for him. Another fire department had cleared a call with central. He rested his head on her head when she wrapped her arms around his waist and hugged him, a little too tightly. Yet another sign she wasn't like him, but yet another reason why he loved her more.

Emie wasn't going to let go of him just yet. It was so nice to hug him. She had no idea why. She'd never held someone before, let alone a human who's bloody beating heart was thumping in her ear, a steady reminder of who he was. Trouble, she giggled silently.

Asher had a hard on he knew Emie could feel. He wanted things with her that he'd only dreamt about. Now she was here holding him, his body was responding to her like no other. He needed to calm down.

"Emie, I stink sweetheart." He said to her when she savored his smell. He shook his head at her in wonder while he stroked her hair.

Her smile took his breath away when she looked up at him.

Emie associated his mixture of scents of ash and smoke with him, and didn't think he smelled bad at all.

"Which reminds me, I forgot to tell you something. Well, two things actually." She told him trying to pull back to look at him better.

Asher waited as he was longing to kiss her again. If she only knew how much he needed and wanted her right now. "You can tell me anything sweetheart."

"I forgive you." She announced sweetly.

Stunned he moved her from his chest and looked down at her. "For what?" he did have a lot to be sorry for though...

"For being human." This she told him reminding him of the night of the funeral.   And with a sigh of relief she was glad she had finally said it to him.

Asher grinned. He was proud of her for standing up to him last night. He was even more proud of all that she had done here. And now here she was, in his world, accepting him for who he was.

Asher bent low and kissed her again. He couldn't believe it. So this is what love feels like, he thought. The kiss heated immediately because she responded in a way he hadn't expected, she'd called out his name in his mind and he came undone again at the sensuality in her voice.

Asher took a chance on Emie. He kissed her deeply and let images of them in the shower fill his mind.

Emie began to moan. Asher smiled in her lips. When she opened her eyes she was smiling too.

"No one will know?" she wondered aloud.

That was all she needed to say to answer his unspoken question. He led her to the shower and changing room in such a hurry he thought he might trip over something on his way.

Shutting the shower room door behind them he pushed her up against it and kissed her again. Pulling each of her lips in one by one.

Emie felt brave enough this time around to let her kisses wander as he fumbled for the lock on the door. She lifted her leg up his he had pressed between her, placing his thigh right at the ache between her legs. There was the rush she was looking for again. That feeling low in her belly that started in her lips and ached down her chest. The one that moistened her woman hood, and left her aching for more. She wanted the feel of his bulging hard on pressed against her making her frantic and moaning like he had done before so long ago.

When his thoughts drifted there too, her mind went blank, she watched as he kissed her neck, how he pictured their naked bodies together and she started pulling down on his pants. She had to get closer to what she wanted.

All their clothes were scattered on the floor now. Asher had Emie pinned against the door again, lifting her high on his hard on as he rubbed between her lip folds. She almost screamed his name, but bit her lip instead.

Something in the back of her mind stopped her though. "Asher. Wait. Wait, stop."

~Twenty Two~

Reluctantly, he stopped. He lowered her back down to the floor and rested his head on her shoulder trying to contain his breathing. His breathing was uncontrollable, he didn't think he had it in him to stop, but he did.

"I have to tell you something Asher. It can't wait any longer." Jordy's words filled her head again. She ran her fingers through his sweaty hair and held him against her forehead like he had done to her so many times in the past.

You have to tell him Emie.

Emie lifted his head off hers and made Asher look at her.

"Asher, I love you." she choked on the words, her eyes filled with tears, but she said it. She said it out loud what her heart had been dying to say all along. She loved him.

"I've loved you for so long." This she told him stroking his face tenderly, wishing now she had told him sooner.

Asher's smile filled his whole face. His heart overflowed with the joy of hearing her words. Without a thought he picked her back up and carried her over to the shower room, away from the door just in case anyone passed by, and turned on the radio, loud enough to block their voices, then pushed the button that turned on the shower against the wall.

He had her pinned now against the steamy wall of the shower, letting the cool water fall down between their bodies as he held her face in his hands and bent down kissing her face all over. Telling her over and over that he loved her too.

Emie let her hands wander up and down his shoulders along his tattoos, kissing him there, tracing them with her tongue revealing more of her neck for him to kiss. Her body melted as he dragged his nose up her shoulder bones to the back side of her neck where he sucked and licked up to her ear lobes. She reached in between their bodies and chased her hands up his abdomen to his chest. She wandered their, throwing her head back as he kissed her lips. Found his hard nipples and knew he was more than ready to give her everything she had ever dreamed of. She played with them too making him groan. She knew he loved it.

She let her hands wander lower down his body, feeling his tight abdomen. Lower still, she found the source her body was aching for. He was long and hard and throbbing. Everything her body needed and then some. She stroked him, and ran both her hands around his wet slippery member.

He was hers. She could feel it. He wanted her.

Asher had handled all he could of her sweet caresses around him, he reached for her hands and pushed them against the wall behind her, where he whispered to her to keep them there. He lowered his head while she was lost in the waves of passion and lifted her breast to his mouth where he sucked in her nipple between his lips and sucked on her there like he had done so long ago, and had done almost every night in his dreams of her. He played with her nipple with his tongue and drove her mad.

Asher's desires over the last year had been heated and stirred every time he thought about doing this to her. The way her body reacted to this pleasure had sent him spiraling in a frenzy he couldn't contain last year. Now he could take her higher then he ever had, and not stop. Nothing could stop him now. And he couldn't wait.

He took his time with her first breast, letting her enjoy more then he was. Then he did the same thing with her other breast. He let her ride the waves until he felt when she started reaching for him again. He knew then it was time, she needed him. And he needed her.

But before he could take her, there was one more pleasure he wanted to give her. He pressed her body up against the wall and braced both her hands above her head with one his. He used his other hand to grasp his cock and slide it between her folds. There he slid in and out of her folds where he could feel the button of her woman hood waiting to be caressed. He could feel her on his tip with each stroke, but he had to hold her body still against the wall. She was melting with the pleasure of it and it turned him on.

He waited as long as he could, he stroked her over and over again till she trembled and begged him for more.

Twice, not once, but twice, Emie felt her body climax to heights it had never been before. Asher was amazing at whatever he was doing.

"Asher, please! Please…"

Asher smiled in her neck where he was sweetly kissing. He whispered in her ear, "Tell me Emie. Tell me what you want."

Emie shivered as the last tremble racked her body. More. Deeper. I need to feel you there… She whispered in his mind as she lifted her leg around his thigh. She made him let go of her hands and reached her hands up in his hair and pulled his lips down to hers. She sucked in one of his lips and bit down it. I need more Asher. Please. She begged him.

"Not enough Emie. You have to use your words. Tell me what to do to you." He told her as he sucked on her lips and then her neck.

He lifted her then, wrapping her legs around him, he held her sweet cheeks in his hands. "Tell me!" he growled at her kissing her.

"Make love to me Asher!" she begged him. He was so close to her there now she couldn't stand it let alone think straight.

Silently he asked her permission, knowing he was changing everything in that moment. Changing his world as he knew it to be. Once he joined his body with hers, making her his, he knew he would never be the same again. For better or worse he had to do this though. He didn't care about the consequences anymore, his heart be damned. He had to have her, he had to have all of her. Right now. But first he had to ask.

Emie?

Yes! "Yes Asher, damn it, please!" Emie whispered in his mind and out loud. Her head was now pressed against his forehead, her fingers gently digging into his skull. She repeated herself over and over until he did.

She really hadn't wanted this to move so fast, only yesterday she thought she was lost to him, but her body was so heightened she couldn't wait anymore for him. She knew what was coming and welcomed it.

Asher smiled at her words, he couldn't wait either. He wasn't in his bed where he had always dreamed of making love to her, but he didn't care anymore. He put one hand on the wall behind her, one hand under her and held her up by pressing and thrusting his body into her sweet body.

She felt like heaven in his hands. Like an angel's face was pressed up against his good shoulder kissing his neck and begging him for more. He could hear her begging for more in his ears, in his mind, he could see her tears dripping between their bodies. He felt the same way about her and showed her with every thrust into her heavenly body.

He'd known she was still a virgin when he'd entered her. Now, she was his. No one else's. Ever.

Emie was pushing and squeezing all around him, milking him of every last ounce of pleasure. He gave and he took from her, and then gave all that he had to give her. Her body took his and together they were lost to the world in their own pleasures.

They climaxed not long afterwards. Together. His thrusting lasted as long as he could, but her body felt like satin and he couldn't stop himself once he started coming. She had already came in the first minutes of him evading her. His name had echoed through the walls when she came and he'd loved it. He knew she was beyond satisfied, so he took his own pleasure in her pleasing body and held her tightly away from the wall on top of him as he exploded inside of her over and over until every last ounce of his pleasure had left his body.

Asher held her there kissing her, pulling in and out of her only because he didn't want to stop, until his strength gave out and she slid down his wet body. He laid his head on her neck and pressed her against the wall as he tried to catch his breath. His massive arms he rose over her head and rested them on the shower wall so he couldn't touch her anymore. He could feel her in his bones. In his soul. His release inside of her had opened up a hole inside of himself that had taken all his strength away and left him filled with only love for her.

She stood there with his length still inside her, bucking wildly excited from his release, her hand steadying his raging heart that was overflowing with many different emotions. Leftover tremors from his orgasm.

Emie stared shoulders. He was totally bare and naked to her now. His lovely, soft, well muscled arm and shoulder that was damaged by some unknown fate was still beautiful to her. He was hers now. She could say that now. He, was, hers. Forever. The thought made her soul dance, made her heart flutter with butterflies. The smile she felt now was one of overwhelming possession.

She felt shaken to her core. She was really here with him. Loving him. Touching, running her hands up and down his lovely body, and holding him. She wasn't dreaming, and this merciless love they were making wasn't over. It would never be over.

She laid her head back against the wall of the steamy tile. Looking sweetly up at him, she told him "I have never felt this weak before.".

He was grinning now. "Welcome to the club sweetheart." He joked of her virginity. Then he stepped away from her into the water and started wiping down his body.

Emie stayed right there under him. Watched as he showered in wonder. She wanted to ask him about his shoulder, but she thought maybe now wasn't a good time. She herself was still coming down from all her emotions. But it wasn't just her virginity that had her weak in the knees. It was the overpowering intensity of both of their emotions that she could feel. She had been filled to the brim and had tipped over when she felt everything he did. Never before had someone else's emotions mixed with her own, brought her to such a soul stirring moment.

Asher watched as Emie watched him shower. He knew when he turned around she would be able to see his scars. He wasn't ashamed of them, he just wasn't ready to talk about them. Plus, he wanted to talk about her. He had promised himself earlier he would make her talk. Make her tell him everything. He was tired of not knowing anything about her life.

Emie listened to him and knew he would want that. He was still so clueless when it came to vampires. She watched as he visibly relaxed thinking about her again instead of himself.

"Just ask. I promise to tell you everything Asher."

Asher turned around then. Water dripping off his head and lips. He looked at her lovingly. His smile was brighter then she had ever seen it then. But then, he looked sternly at her. He placed his hands over her again on the wall towering over her. "Even the things you don't want me to know? Even the things you think will scare me, or I'm not ready for? You promise to tell me everything?" he begged. Raising her hands on either side of his bad shoulder making her look and touch his scars when she promised him this.

"We both have a lot to talk about Emie."

Emie looked up into his eyes. She had never witnessed a man so severely dominate in his own right that he could shake her from inside her core. She almost smirked at the thought, but then thought better of it. He was being serious. So should she. Even if she was a vampire and he was just a mere man.

She inhaled deeply and told him "Whatever you want, Asher. I promise. I don't want to lose you again Asher." She reached up then and cupped his face, "I don't want there to be anything between us. Ever again. I love you Asher. I have always loved you." this last she said breathlessly.

Joseph interrupted her thoughts then and she wanted to kill him.

We need to talk Emie. Bring Asher.

Something had changed in Emie. Asher noticed it right away. He turned off the water and asked "What is it?"

Emie couldn't believe again how quickly he noticed things. It was going to be hard to hide anything from him if she ever had too. First, she needed to kill her melding brothers.

Emie sighed, looked down and placed her hand on his heart. She didn't want her time with Asher interrupted or to be over so quickly.

"Joseph wants me home." She whispered to him looking up at him. "Something's wrong. He wants to see you too..." she offered, hoping this was going to be ok with him and worried about it, biting her bottom lip, accidentally letting her fang show.

Asher visible shook and sighed. He reached down a hand to rub her bottom lip she was biting. He let his finger brush her fang and it sent a chill down his spine. "I swear, you are the sexiest thing I've ever seen."

Emie grinned and took a deep breath again. She inhaled his scent. His soap was a mix of leather and sandalwood. An old smell she had missed. She looked over his chest and shoulders. She had always found well muscled shoulders incredibly sexy. His tattoos that ran down his arms and his chest were well drawn. She wanted to run her fingers around the details of the flames that encircled each symbol.

"Let's go meet the big bad terminator, and see what he wants." Asher said jokingly standing to his full height then.

"He heard that." Emie wrinkled her nose in frustration at him.

"Good." Asher said as he dried off his body and hers, then he walked Emie back into the locker room. He hoped the man had heard all the screams coming from Emie too. He may be just a weak human compared to her brothers, but he was hell bent on loving Emie and there was no one on the face of this earth that was going to change his mind.

When Emie finished dressing he watched as her hair hung down her body beautifully.

"Emie?"

Emie looked up at Asher and smiled at his thoughts. He shyly wanted to ask her for a picture of her on his phone for the next time they were apart so he could see her whenever he wanted. He hated missing her.

"Before we go, can I take a picture of us?"

He sounded so shy about it standing there behind her in nothing but a pair of jeans that she had to agree. Normally she wouldn't do this, but with him, everything was possible.

He hadn't had anything this past year to look at. Just his memories of her. His thoughts went back to a movie he had watched about vampires. He wondered if it was true what they said about vampires and mirrors and pictures.

Emie shook her head as she walked up to Asher. He had so much to learn this hero of hers. "You are so cute when you are shy Asher." She smirked, when she stood next to his half naked body and smiled sexy into his camera on his phone. At the last second she kissed his cheek.

Asher grinned at what she had done. He hoped the picture was there when he looked at the picture and knew he was going to enjoy it when they were apart. He was smiling and laughing in the picture the way Izzy had told him about a year ago. He looked amazingly happy in that moment. Because she was kissing him. Because she was here with him. It would be the first of many pictures of their life together.

Emie looked over his arms at the picture. "Will you send it to me?" she asked.

Asher smiled and hit send, then he finished dressing. He was ashamed of the holes and rips in his jeans and the shirt, he really needed to go shopping for new clothes. He stretched on an old, black EMT t-shirt and slid on his shoes.

Emie watched as he dressed next to his locker and heard his thoughts about shopping. She was more excited about the idea of walking hand in hand with Asher around the mall then she had been about shopping for anyone else. His clothing choices were not at all what was in style now. She had to admit though, he did look good in old tight ripped up jeans and t-shirts.

Asher shut the door to his locker and turned to Emie. She was tapping away on her phone and she looked determined. "Ready Emie?"

"Yes, but I can't leave with you." She sighed and looked up at his stunned expression. "There is a car waiting for me out back. There is something I need to tell you, Asher."

Asher took a deep breath. "Ok." He prepared himself for the worst. He didn't want her to leave him just yet. Was there something that bad wrong that Joseph was taking her from him? Had Joseph told her they couldn't see each other? Asher knew he couldn't fight him if he had...

Asher's thoughts stole her breath. She watched as he tucked his hands in his jeans after he threw down his towel. "No, it's nothing like that. Honest.

"I can't go out in the sun light Asher. Ever." Her shoulders slumped at her words and she had to look away from him. Those words meant more to her then she could handle right now. She could never be out in the sun with him.

Never ever, she thought quietly.

"One of the servants is here to pick me up in one of our cars we use for days like today."

Asher took that in. He didn't know she couldn't be out in the sunlight. Had he ever seen her in the sunlight?

No, no he hadn't, he thought to himself as he ran his hands through his hair. He thumped and packed a smoke against his palm that he really needed to smoke. She looked defeated hanging her head, turned away from him, and he wondered how he could tell her it didn't matter to him anymore. He stuck his smoke on his ear and walked over to her.

Yes, he had dreamed of days walking on the beach holding hands, taking her up north to his property and four wheeling around the lake. But those were just dreams now.

"It will kill me Asher." She told him as she placed her hand on his heart when he reached her. She needed him to know this.

Asher had to sigh at the way she looked up to him He grabbed her hand that was on his chest and squeezed it reassuringly. He raised it to his lips and kissed the back of her hand.

He remembered that night out on the pier he'd spent with her a year ago and he knew it didn't matter to him. He loved her. He would just have to adapt to the moon light hours instead with her.

"I get it. No tanning for you." He winked at her. "I can handle that Emie." He told her lifting up her chin.

Emie wondered if he really did…

He placed a hand on one of the lockers behind her and asked. He could tell she didn't believe him. "Emie." He knew she could hear what he was thinking. He didn't want there to be any doubt anymore.

Emie couldn't believe he had this power. Her venom dripped. "Ok." She reassured him

" So how do we get you out of here then?" he wondered, pulling away from her. Tucking a hand in his pocket he fiddled with his lighter, he needed to smoke as soon as possible. He could feel the with draws setting in and that was never a good thing.

Emie knew when he did that thing with his hands, tucking them in his pocket that he was feeling vulnerable and shy and she found it utterly adorable. She also realized now it was also tied to his addiction. She would have to remember that. "Do you have a back door?"

Asher lead Emie back out into the main bay where the trucks were. There was a laundry room that he led her through that had a back door.

Asher walked out into the sunlight and met one the servants like Emie told him to do. He was a tall man. His skin was dark and he was wearing dark sunglasses. Asher had to wonder if this guy was human or something else. He looked more like a robot than a human. It bothered Asher that he had to rely on this guy to take care of Emie, and he had no intention of letting him do more then he had too.

The man handed Asher a heavy foil blanket and waited in the alleyway next to the door of a black car he had held open. The windows all around the car were tinted to the point Asher could see his reflection in them.

Asher walked back in the door and seen Emie standing in the corner. She was hiding from the light that was let in by the open door and the windows above the washing machine they used to wash their turn out gear.

"Wrap me in the blanket and make sure it covers me completely." She told him hurriedly.

Asher looked at her worried. His mind told him this was too important to mess up. What she said earlier repeated in his mind over and over. The sunlight can kill me Asher. He didn't know why this was yet, he just knew it scared him.

Emie smiled up at Asher. "I'll be fine. Trust me; we do this all the time." She encouraged and trusted him and waited as he wrapped her up tightly in the blanket. Years of training kicked in for him and she didn't expect him to pick her up when he did, she was taken off guard.

She loved knowing that he cared so much about her now when only yesterday she thought she would never see him again. She was still surprised he was able to carry her though. It must take all his strength to do it, she thought.

When he reached the car, Asher felt a helplessness that overtook him. He walked her over to his truck instead and he set her down on his passenger seat. He covered her up with his big fire department jacket also, just to make sure, and then he closed the door. He instructed the driver that they no longer needed his assistance and watched as the guy gasped openly at Asher, removing his dark sunglasses. Asher noticed his eyes were black. There was no white, no pupil. Only a black void.

Walking over to his side of the truck Asher took a moment to himself. Thoughts of him and Emie still filled his mind. He was trying to grasp the facts that were haunting his mind. This new world of hers was so unknown to him. There was still so much he needed to know about Emie so he could keep her safe. So he could stay with her. All he knew now was he needed to get her out of here and back home where she would be safe.

He looked up at the fire hall and wished he could just take some time off work to spend with her. He hoped all his questions could be answered today about her. He was so confused. He wasn't leaving her until everything was clear.

He saluted the fire hall goodbye for now and nodded at the dumb founded driver as he climbed up into his truck.

She was his damn it all! And he wasn't about to give her up to anyone. Not even Joseph. Not again. Not like he had that night of his brother's funeral. He wouldn't lose her again. He knew, also, his brother Curtis would be telling him to do the same thing. And that meant everything to Asher.

Emie had waited until Asher returned and climbed in the truck with her to uncover her face just a little. She smiled at Asher as he lit his smoke and took off through town. She hid back under the covers telling him to take the back entrance onto their land. He told her he wanted to drive around first before going to the house. He needed to see down Lakewood if everything was being taken care of.

"Will you be ok?"

"Yes." She peeked over the blanket at him again and watched as he drove, blowing smoke out the window.

Once they were under the cover of the trees on Lakewood, Asher peeked under the blankets and told her it was ok for her to uncover a little. He hoped there wasn't enough sunlight in the truck now to do any damage. When he looked over at her again, she looked too cute hiding under the blankets smiling at him.

He rubbed his face remembering how just yesterday he had missed her in his truck, and now here she was.

Emie knew there were still some things she needed to talk to Asher about before he met with her brothers. Joseph wasn't telling her why he needed to talk to her and Asher, but she was sure she knew what he wanted. That stupid war they all kept talking about. She really didn't care about it anymore. She had Asher safe and sound and she'd never leave his side again.

Emie looked over at Asher. He was looking out the windows watching the city go by, hanging his arm out his window. He was holding onto his fire radio in between them on the arm rest with the other hand. She longed to reach out and stroke his arm. He looked every bit the hero that he was. His thoughts on the other hand weren't as strong.

To look at him you wouldn't think he was afraid of anything, she thought to herself. He was tall, and handsome. He walked and carried himself like he was proud and sure. But in his mind, he was haunted by thoughts of failure and rejection. He worried about everyone, and everything. He longed for an out from it all. He was constantly thinking about the next call, and strategizing in his mind what he would do planning out scenarios. He was unlike any other human she had ever known. She loved getting lost in his mind.

He stopped by his house to check on things and let Cookie out. Emie gave him a look when he got back in truck.

"What?" He questioned her.

Emie looked back out at his home. She wondered if he still worried about her meeting his dog. "It just seems odd. You're such a big guy, and she's such a cute, tiny, little dog."

Asher had to grin at her when she looked back at him using her hands in a 'tiny dog' gesture. He backed his truck up out of the drive and headed back for Lakewood drive. He thought about the day he had met Cookie.

"I bought this house about two years ago. When I first came to look at it she was out walking around in the yard. She was all dirty and looked like she was starving."

Emie listened intently to him. She loved when he told her stories. She loved how he started them and how he finished them with meaning. She loved seeing everything he pictured in her mind. It was like she was there.

"I knelt down, trying to get her to come to me, but she wouldn't and ran away.

"When I bought the house and the previous owners gave me the keys, I walked in alone and she was just sitting in the living room wagging her tail at me." Asher smiled out the window thinking about her just sitting there looking at him. "It was like she was welcoming me to her home. She even came up to me and let me pick her up. She kept kissing me like she was so happy I was there. I never found out

how she got in there. She just… came with the house I guessed."
Asher shrugged his shoulder and laughed a little.

Emie couldn't believe his heart and how much he loved her.
What other guy would just take in a dog like that. As dirty as Cookie
had been, most people would have just booted her out. But Asher had
kept her and loved her. He gave her a home and took care of her like
she was his own. He never asked questions. She was just his. It was
as simple as that.

They drove further down Lakewood drive. The flowers and
trees around the city had been budding before the storm, but now
throughout the city branches and tree limbs were scattered
everywhere. Trash cans, siding off houses, and debris lined the road
and various yards. If it wasn't for the sun and the birds chirping, the
squirrels darting across tree limbs and power wires, Luna Pier would
look like a disaster area.

Asher's friends and neighbors were working in the streets to
remove debris. A few firemen were chain sawing a broken down tree
that had been struck by lighting and blown over in the road. They
waved as he passed by. He knew if this had been any other day he
would have either been out there helping with clean up or at home
sleeping off the nights work alone.

Alone. Asher thought about how that word affected him now.
He reached over for Emie's hand and held it in his under the blanket.
She had turned in her seat to face him like she had a year ago on their
first date. It took his breath away when she did it. She used her other
hand to stroke up and down the contours of his arms. She found her
way up to the edge of his tattoo and traced the outline of the medic star
and the flames that licked up the staff. No one had ever touched his
tattoos before. It felt amazing. It was almost a dizzying experience.

He knew she was going to say something even before she said
it. He could see her thinking seriously now. Reading his mind was
something else he knew he was going to have to get used to. He could
see her doing it now and hoped she would do more of it.

"I haven't been home in almost a year Asher. Would you mind
staying with me for a few days?"

Asher smirked. It was like answering a given question. She
already knew the answer, but she asked it anyways. "I would love
too." Asher said over to her. And he meant it. Someone else could take
over at the department. He needed time off. He needed to be with
Emie.

"So what should I be expecting from Joseph?" he asked.

"Oh, big brother stuff I guess." Emie eyed him and listened to
his thoughts hoping he would take the bait of her lie. "Don't worry, I
won't let him bite." She winked at him when he caught on to her joke
and looked over at her.

Asher laughed out loud at this. " Ah… yeah, that was a good one."

Emie watched him closely. She still couldn't believe she was sitting here next to him. His hair was a mess blowing lightly in the breeze. His face was lit up with his laughter. His blue, blue eyes that she loved were dark and pure in the sunlight. He was infectious. And he was hers. Again.

Emie knew Joseph already knew everything he needed to know about her and Asher, she had spent all night arguing with him in her head about the way things were going to go even though this war was raging all around them. She wouldn't go back home alone no matter how much he begged. She was never going to let anything come between her and Asher again. Starting with all the things Asher needed to know about her and her world. He was strong enough now to handle things.

"Can I ask you something?"

She gave him a smile in encouragement to go on. It was like he had read her mind. She wanted him to ask her anything.

"I know a vampire's diet consists of blood." That made him gulp. Then he gulped again. "Human blood. So how do you… I mean, what do you… I know you would never-" and with this he half heartedly chuckled and choked. It was the knowledge of what he really didn't know about her, but the love he felt for her… he really didn't care how she ate. He just… He just needed to know. He looked at her then for help with what he couldn't ask.

Emie stopped him when his thoughts turned to that of her taking down humans for blood. She squeezed his hand and reminded him "Think about where I worked Asher. What did I do for a living?"

Asher thought about that. He almost laughed when he figured it out. She worked in the blood lab, and at the donor clinic. "How did you get it out of the lab?"

They were headed over the bridge now onto Whitby land. Emie hid under the blankets again as they went over. There was no more shade up here without the trees.

She knew Joseph would open up the gates for them. She peeked out again when she felt the tires hit the paved drive. They would be under the shade of the Whitby forest for awhile now.

"I was in charge of taking all the used and left over blood to the incinerator at night. We burn it at night when it's done being tested. Anyone who is brought into the morgue at the hospital to be embalmed, their blood was also given to me. Instead of burning it I put it in old wine bottles.

"Everyone at work thought I was an alcoholic." She laughed to herself. "I also worked for the blood bank, so they brought over their extra blood too once a week to be incinerated.

"Everyone in the city who takes in blood, all the different labs around Monroe County, doctors offices, the funeral homes, outpatient surgery; the hospital requires they report it and bring it in with their hazards material boxes like sharps and needles. So my only source of blood came from there. I have been doing that for many, many years Asher." With the exception of what she had to do this last year. But that really didn't count she told herself. She had done only what she had been created to do, and had only chosen the humans she was supposed too.

Asher hadn't asked her what she'd done this last year, and she hoped he never would. She'd broken into the hospital once or twice, but Kentucky had a whole different system then Michigan did. There was never enough blood there for her to survive on. She had to find other ways.

Asher's next question came from her last comment. "How old are you Emie?"

Twenty Three

She squeezed his hand at that, and sat up straighter. He had relaxed immensely after she had told him she didn't kill people. Now she wanted to joke with him and say "A woman never reveals her age." See if she could get him caught up in the moment, but then she thought better of it. He was and needed to be serious, so should she.

She took a deep breath for good measure. She wasn't as old as some vampires she knew, like Shelley, but she was older than he thought. She looked down at his arm and drug a finger up one of his veins in his arm. She couldn't look at him when she revealed this. "I was born August 20th 1879 in Whitby, England."

Well, that explained her sweet British accent, Asher thought. He ran his hand through his hair and thought about that. He did the math quickly and realized she was 137 years old. He was only 33. He wondered if she minded just being 24 for all intensive purposes. She didn't look 24 though. She looked a whole hell of a lot younger.

He watched as she smiled at his thoughts and looked down absentmindedly playing with the hair on the back of his hand.

"How old were you when this happened Emie? What happened?"

Emie sighed at that question too and looked out the window ahead of them. She hated retelling this story to anyone. She told him to take the road before the house and wind through the back roads by the beach. They would have ten or more minutes to talk while they drove around.

She inhaled deeply and let it all out. "It was exactly a hundred and twelve years ago the night Curtis. I was twenty four then." She didn't know why that bothered her now, she hadn't cared that she was labeled a spinster back then, but now... Now it did. She knew a time would come when he would ask why she never married. She still didn't know the answer to that. Just that no one had ever come along like he had. She looked back at his arm that was holding her hand and went on. "I was young, but I was old by some standards. I had spent all my time with my mother and Joseph at the hospitals working on the sick that were plagued by the illnesses over taking England for many years. She never left the hospital sometimes, my mum. When I wasn't with them at the hospitals, I was at home raising Jeremy and Jordy. They were young when it happened. They were men by my father's standards, but someone had to keep an eye on them, so it had been left up to me to raise them.

"Father was a Lord Viscount in Whitby. He had lands and a shipping business. The boys were helping him with both, but we still never saw much of our father." Emie left that subject alone. She had never liked her father very much. He worked too much, and drank half of her life away when he had been home. It was no wonder her mother was never home either.

"I never had a lot of spare time to read. When ever I found the time, I would get so lost in my books. I would lose track of time and place, like the world just disappeared... I was an avid romance novel reader." She smiled proudly back over at him then. "For my birthday, Joseph had bought me a book that had been published here in America the previous year. I had wanted 'Dorothy Vernon of the Haddon Hall' so badly I remember hugging Joseph and jumping up and down squealing when he gave it to me."

She knew he hadn't a clue what book she was talking about when he looked at her to go on, so she continued on. "I couldn't wait to sit down and read it. So on that night, while everyone was asleep, I headed out to the barns.

"A storm was coming, so I hunkered up there for the night in the lofts with blankets. That's where I spent most of time when I read. Reading to myself or to the horses." She laughed remembering. "I used to love being in the barns when it rained. The smell, the sound, it was so intoxicating."

Ironically, they were passing the barns right then. Emie looked out at the barns that Joseph had built to match their father's barns exactly. They were painted white and red with the Whitby crest hanging over the main double doors. Sun light was breaking through the trees that surrounded the barns and blanketed their lands.

"I climbed up in the loft, opened the double doors looking out into the moon lit pastures, spread out a blanket, covered myself up and read till I could barely keep my eyes open any longer."

What happened next, haunted Emie every day. She hoped Asher could handle the depths of it. Her brothers till this day never could. She looked over at Asher who was watching her intently. He was whispering to her heart now that it was ok to go on, he was here now and she would be ok. She loved him for it and squeezed his hand back that she was holding.

"I didn't hear anyone in the barns with me that night. If I had... my mind must have thought it was just the horses below me."

Asher noticed when she wasn't really looking at him anymore. She was going back to that time he was trying to picture.

"I was to chapter nine I think, and there was this butterfly," Emie smiled and looked down at her necklace and pulled it out of her shirt, it was a small golden, broken butterfly wing. It was the same butterfly. She had saved his remains in the book and later had him dipped in gold. She noticed Asher had eyed it curiously once before, so she showed it to him.

"He kept landing on my book, distracting me. Just as I was about to shoo him away, someone closed my book on him." Emie bit down on her lip then. Just remembering what the rouge had done to her brought tears to her eyes. She wiped away the single blood drop that fell from her eyes. "I looked up and seen the face of this… lovely man." There was no other way to say it, Emie thought. He truly was lovely.

"He was about my age, but his eyes, they were blood red. I whispered vampire aloud. When he smiled his fangs were there on his lips like a hiss. I screamed so loudly I thought my own ear drums were going to burst."

Asher tensed when he felt Emie's hand tense. He could just picture the frightened girl she had been. He knew what his own heart had felt like when he had seen her brothers that night. He could only imagine what it had been like for her, alone.

"I have never been so afraid… He grabbed my head and forced my neck into his mouth. We fell to the ground out the double doors. It felt like we fell forever… He held my body over his legs and his teeth dug into my neck and he bit down again. His venom paralyzed me immediately, so I heard and felt him slurping all my blood from my body, and there wasn't anything I could do; till I passed out. The next thing I remember is Joseph holding me, and my father chasing the man with a torch. Vampires are afraid of fire, you see." She said in an afterthought. She had been lingering on every detail as she told him the things that had haunted her. They haunted her still after all these years.

When she turned back towards Asher she saw the haunted look in his eyes. His mind was there with her. He was picturing it all wrong of course; his imagination couldn't wrap itself around the pain. He was blinded by hatred and anger. She decided to leave out the part about fire for now. He didn't need to know about killing vampires just yet.

"Hours would go by. I would get stronger and heal myself. Joseph would hold me down in my bed and plead with me to stop screaming, but I couldn't. I wanted things. Bad things." She shook her head and looked down remembering and folded her hands in his.

"They realized what I had become. What I was becoming. My father knew I had been attacked by a vampire. Stories had been going around about vampires like crazy, but father hadn't believed them till that night. He told me to leave. Literally grabbed my arm and lead me out of the house." He had been afraid of men coming to the house to kill them. But she was still haunted by the fact that he didn't want to save her. Protect her. How did a father do that to his daughter?

Emie shook off a chill that was shaking her. "I remember standing there in front of the mansion, wondering what in the hell I was going to do after father had shut the doors. Where was I supposed to go? I had nothing, absolutely nothing. He hadn't even let me change my bloodstained clothes." Emie's mouth watered at the pain she felt just remembering. Instead of wiping away the blood tear she sucked it in and savored it.

"I knew what I was. But I was still me! That part hadn't changed. It never has." Emie said looking over at Asher. She surprised herself in revealing this to him. She had never told anyone this before.

Asher had never heard her talk so much before, he was happy she had finally found her voice. He was finally glad to be learning about her past. He just hadn't expected this... But he needed to hear more. He needed her to go on for as long as she could.

So Emie went on. "I had read enough books and novels to know what evil things awaited me in the world should I ever choose to leave home. But I had no clue what it was like to be what I was, let alone being all by myself. I was hungry for something, and I knew it was blood. So I stayed away from the town and instead made my way to the hospital. I walked in the back doors and found my way to the morgue. I drank every dead body I could find. And I waited there many days, waiting for them to bring in more.

"I would only leave to venture out to see how I would do amongst the humans. When I learned as long as my hunger was stated that I could walk amongst them, I started walking through town. That's also when I learned about my abilities." She bent her head and closed her eyes. She could still hear the very first thoughts of the men and women she had known all her life. People she had thought were lovely and respectful were instead vulgar and shameful. "They would look at me in disgust. I could read their minds, my eye's, my hair, I was a mess. I felt this overwhelming desire to throw something at them all, but I learned that was also just my abilities. My mind started throwing out my powers at them and I could change their minds to see what I wanted them to see. Make them see me as the woman I was. Not the monster I had become.

"I also knew I was going to need things. Things I would need to survive on. Clothes, jewels..." she smiled as she said this. "So charged on all of his accounts everything I would and I adorned myself so that looked like my father's daughter. The daughter of a very rich and powerful man." She had done it out defiance for her father knowing he would get all of the bills of sale and have heart palpitations.

"Then I left the country. I traveled to France and Spain, Greece. I even gave my new voice a try on stage in the opera for a while."

Asher winked at her at this. He could tell she was enjoying talking about it now the way she was looking at him. Now he understood why her voice had sounded so perfect that night.

"I just couldn't leave my family for very long. I was shy and quiet. I didn't fit in anywhere. I missed my brothers, and my mother. So I returned home. Only to find the plague had taken my mother, and left my father bedridden.

"Joseph found me out by the barns crying. I had just seen mum's grave where they had been digging one for father. It was so foggy out that night I hadn't even seen Joseph walking towards me. I'm not sure why he trusted me, he's never told me that. But he stood there, just waiting for me to talk to him.

"So I told him it was ok, that I was ok. I knew when I was face to face with him, that I could never... never ever hurt them.

"I wasn't going to hurt him or eat him, like father had said I would." She said to him as she thought it disgustedly.

Asher silently hated himself. He too had thought that about her. He wanted to dig himself a grave next to her father and bury himself inside it. No wonder she had left him. She wasn't only running from him, she had run from her father too last year.

He knew what hating a father felt like.

Emie sighed again looking down at her fingers as they idly played with Asher's hand. She gulped down her venom at Asher's thought. Her father had done that to her and she hated him now more so for it.

"Joseph, he trusted me. He told me about the boys being sick. We came up with a plan to save them, and him of course. We waited as long as we could; they had just turned twenty two when Joseph said there was nothing else he could do for them medically. They just weren't getting over it, and no medicines where working."

She stopped talking then, remembering. Remembering how she turned Joseph. How scared she had been for him, not knowing what would happen to him.

"So you... changed them?" Asher asked slowly.

Emie turned and held his hand in both of hers, pleading with him to understand. She had no other choice but to help her brothers. "I had to. It was either lose them forever to the same fate we had lost our parents too, or give them the gift of life I had been given."

Looking at Asher she could see the confusion about it all in his eyes, but his heart knew she had to do what she had done. He would have done the same thing for his family. For her.

Asher stopped the truck in the middle of the road, he turned towards her and moved Emie's hair off the side of her face and tucked it behind her ear, and then he let his fingers drag down the side of her face and neck to the curl lying down her shoulder. He let his hand curve around the curl and slid his hand down the curl. It tickled his palm all the way down. He took a deep breath and inhaled her scent. The heavenly mixture of flowers and an earthy stone smell of her body. He'd been doing just this in his dreams for months, to finally do it, it felt so damn good.

She was really here with him. She was his. Finally.

Her words echoed in his head. They were why he had stopped the truck. She had to know he didn't fault her for doing what she had done. "Emie, I would never judge you, or tell you what you've done with the life you were dealt was anything short of perfection. What I know about you," he corrected himself knowing he had done just those things before, just known her, but never would again, "what I have come to love and desire about you Emie is your passion for life. You gave them life Emie. You choose to save them. You'll find no judgment here from me sweetheart. Only an immeasurable amount of love for you." His lip quivered when he said that last. It was so hard to say it out loud. Like he was tearing out his heart and handing it to her. But he did it. And he meant it. He only hated not saying it before now.

"I love you Emie. Ride or die, I love you." It was a fire men's oath and he hoped she understood it.

Emie's eyes dripped with unshed tears as she looked into his eyes. She hated them, her tears, because she knew what they must look like. She wiped them away ashamed. She loved this man so much. Knowing he felt the same for her and believed her just made her love him that much more. No one had ever said anything like that to her. No one had ever made her feel like this, or showed her her true self like he did. It was so comforting to know he loved her.

Joseph was calling to her now. She knew she needed to get inside the house, but she needed to kiss Asher first. So she did. She reached her fingers up to his face and kissed his lips ever so tenderly and passionately. She climbed in his lap and threw off the blanket. There was no sunlight in here for her to worry about.

Asher could hear the pounding in his ears from his pulse. He wanted Emie to finish talking to him. He loved hearing about her past. Who she was, and who she had become. But she was kissing him now so wildly, and he couldn't deny her. His hands ran under the bottom of her jeans and up her back inside her shirt.

Asher heard a growl rise up in Emie and he slowly let go of her.

"Joseph is getting impatient." She told him angrily, placing her head on his forehead.

Asher raised a brow and let a growl out too. He wasn't sure how to react to her, she'd scared the hell out of him again, but his silly half hearted growl made her throw her head back and laugh so loud he couldn't help but laugh too bashfully. He held onto her tighter, he wasn't ready to let go just yet, but he wasn't about to have the big brother come out and drag them off impatiently into the house either.

Emie and Asher drove the short distance back to her house and went inside the house through the back doors and she led him through the back hall entrances. Asher was still amazed when he looked around this old home. The mahogany paneling was dark and the checkered tile flooring was cold. The house reminded him of an old movie made in the fifties.

Emie led Asher into the back family room behind the large staircase. The huge tinted windows displayed a view of the sunny sparkling lake. Asher noticed there was a seating area next to a fireplace. It had been a warm sunny day outside so there wasn't a fire, he had a feeling though that this fireplace could heat the whole down stairs.

Her hand felt cold inside of his, he wondered if the need for the fireplaces where more for their own comfort. When she nodded up in agreement to him, he knew it must be true.

"I like hot baths too." She winked at him. Just so he knew.

He walked around the room with her as she pointed out different things about the room. Jordy had a collection of very old cameras, to the latest models on shelves. On the tables all around the room, where knick knacks they had collected on their journey's that Asher found very fascinating. Photographs lined the massive walls of pictures from around the world they had taken.

Emie liked the back family room. They called it the family room because it was just that, a place they all made together and only shared their time together during good times. It was a place where she could feel like she was outside even though she was stuck inside. Their large grand piano was displayed against the windows where she could read or play music all day long when she was alone. Or just plain bored. The windows were inlaid with sunscreens and tinted so the sunlight could not penetrate or hurt them in this room.

Just as they sat on the comfy red and brown loveseat with the overstuffed pillows that Emie loved, Joseph and Jordy and Jeremy walked in through the main hall behind the stairs. Emie watched as they took their places. It was good to finally see them all again, together. She had missed them. She got up off the couch and hugged them all slowly. Then she went back to Asher's side.

Asher noticed they weren't overly adorned like the last time he had seen them. Joseph and Jordy were still dressed elegantly in black dress pants and crisp, starched dress shirts. Jeremy was dressed more like him in jeans and a skin tight black polo shirt with boots.

Joseph stood by the fire place like he always did when he was addressing the family. Jordy was over by the windows. Jeremy sat in the big comfy oversized red chair next to them. His smile, Emie noticed, wasn't there. His good ol boy cheekiness that she loved about him wasn't present either. This was a bad sign.

"Asher. It's nice to see you again." Joseph addressed him.

Emie gave him a look when all their thoughts turned to why it was nice to see him again. Asher did smell good to her, she hadn't realized how he smelt to other vampires until they explained it to her.

Asher nodded in agreement to Joseph's greeting, clueless to the joke.

"I know things between you and Emie are different now. I understand, and I'm happy for the two of you. I'm not in a position as her brother to give any type of blessings, but you have them if you wish them. Emie has chosen you, to share her life with you, and none of us here will try to interfere with that. We are all very, very sorry about the way things happened last time you were here. We want to welcome you to our home, our family and our life."

Asher was more stunned then pleased. He hadn't expected that, but he welcomed it. "Wow. Thank you Joseph. That means a lot to me." He stood up and even though it scared him to walk up to the vampire he knew Joseph was, he shook his hand like a man would do. " I promise to take care of that trust and honor it." He nodded at Joseph who nodded his agreement in return.

"We know you will." Joseph stated as a fact to Asher as he looked at Jordy knowingly.

Asher went back to his seat and sat as close to Emie as he could get. He reached for her hand and held it in his. It was hard for him, as a man, to cling to her. He knew he was supposed to be protecting her, but her brothers sure were intimidating.

"I know Emie has told you our past. But in order for this to work, I need to tell you about our present, and about our future. Including yours."

Emie sighed at this. She hoped they wouldn't go into that right now. Asher didn't need to be worrying over whether to become a vampire or not because of their love. She didn't want him worrying over it. When the time would come, it would be his decision, not theirs.

Asher waited expectantly. He wanted to know this. He needed to know all that Joseph was going to tell him. He felt it in soul.

"We live in seclusion here. In the privacy of our lands and our home. We have each worked hard to provide for each other. To build a life here. Emie is the first of us who has wandered outside of this and brought someone in. You.

"If you want to be with her, you have to protect her. Her life, her home, her family, her secret. The world can never know we exist. It would mean ruin or even death to her and all of us. Do you understand? Your secrecy means life or death for her."

Asher understood this better now. He hadn't before, and that could have meant everything Joseph was saying now. "I do. I understand." He looked at Emie and promised her. He knew this much he could keep for her.

Emie smiled knowingly at Asher. She knew Joseph was over doing it. Asher really did know this already. She looked at Joseph and told him to get on with it. Joseph was making eye contact with Asher through his whole speech which meant he was instructing Asher, and Emie didn't like it one bit.

"Now. I have some bad news."

Emie stood up then. No! she screamed in his mind, pointing her finger at him.

Asher watched as Emie and Joseph stood in front of each other. Emie was making gestures that he was sure Joseph must have found freighting. Joseph was staring Emie down like he was trying to put his foot down and wouldn't be denied something. Asher knew there was a discussion going on he couldn't hear.

He looked over at Jeremy who was sitting on the overstuffed chair next to him inspecting his hands. He wondered if he could talk to Jeremy in his head the way he did Emie. Could he hear him too he wondered.

Yeah, it's all in their heads now. Jeremy whispered into Asher's mind without even looking at him.

Can you hear what their saying? Asher questioned Jeremy.

Emie turned around then and dropped a look on Jeremy that made Asher chuckle.

Nope. Jeremy lied. He smirked, winked and shrugged his shoulders over at Asher looking back down at his hands.

Asher sat back and sighed. This was a tight net family like his own. He couldn't help but wonder what was going on. What bad news did Joseph have for him?

Would he have to become like them? Is that why Emie was so upset?

Could he do it? He wondered more seriously.

Thoughts of old stories, and vampire movies crossed his mind. Everything Emie had just told him. Asher felt his resolve breaking. He needed a cigarette.

Jeremy's head shot up at Asher's thoughts. Smoke?

Yes! Asher replied back to him. As odd as it was to talk to him like this, he felt he was starting to like it.

Emie turned on her heels and stared down Jeremy. When Asher and Jeremy had started talking, everyone in the room had listened intently. Even Jordy was surprised at how Asher had responded to them all. He really didn't mind at all that he was in a house of vampires, when a year earlier he had all but bolted from the house running to protect his family and friends. Now he was joking with them and wanting to go off alone with Jeremy.

Emie was still worried about Jeremy though. Jeremy had taken longer adjusting to this life then any of them had. He had not only turned several horses and dogs into creatures they didn't yet have names for, but he had also turned some of their own servants. He was a loner now, sometimes leaving the house and traveling for years on end. He kept in touch of course, and Jordy always knew where he was.

Jeremy had started his own empire. Gambling hells, horse tracks, and many exploits around the southern areas that Emie never wanted to know about. She loved her brothers each in their own way, but what they did outside of their house was none of her business as long they weren't getting into trouble.

Emie didn't like the idea of Asher being alone with Jeremy. She didn't want Jeremy doing Joseph's bidding now and turning Asher before she was ready. Asher wasn't ready. And there was a secret they were all hiding. Something Asher needed to know that she was sure she didn't want them telling him.

"Seriously? You really think I'd do that to you?" Jeremy promised her that wasn't his intention. He would smoke with Asher and try to relax him. There was a lot of information that they were all about to tell Asher, and as a human, he was going to need this break so he could handle it all.

Plus, he told her, Asher's just the kind of guy I like to get along with. I would never do that to you Emie.

Emie looked more contrite at Jeremy this time. She believed him, but she still didn't like the idea. "Fine, but not in the den." That was a place she was sure Asher wasn't ready to see again.

Asher nodded at her then. He didn't need to read her mind to know what she was thinking.

She turned back to Joseph then. They had more to discuss about Asher.

"Come on Ash." Jeremy said aloud to Asher standing.

Asher stood happily, hoping he was going to smoke and not be led to his impending death. Glad he wasn't going to the den...

As they walked out, Emie turned her sights on Joseph. She listened as they walked into the garage. She listened to their conversations. She would listen with everything she had in her to make sure Jeremy didn't divulge anything that would cause Asher any unnecessary distress. He was about to learn that the world as he knew it, wasn't at all what he had believed it to be. If that was even possible.

Emie finished her conversation with Joseph. He bended to her will and would allow her to talk to Asher instead of himself, and not to tell him about his brother Curtis. Emie was adamant about it. Now wasn't the time.

Emie didn't like that her brothers were so worried about the attacks from the rogue vampires, but she understood now that it would affect Asher unlike she had thought.

Emie headed up to her room to change, and she would wait for Asher's return alone in the living room.

Jordy was sitting on the landing waiting for Emie to come out of her apartment. He knew what he needed to tell Emie. He listened to her mind softly as she danced around her rooms happily. More happy then he had ever seen her before. He wanted so badly to take this last year away from her.

Now, he couldn't help but feel the edges of a vision coming to him again. He had explained it to Joseph who had come up with a plan, but for an unknown reason, Jordy knew he needed Emie in on this. It was more then he alone could handle. He had done something very wrong last night, and he had no idea how to tell her about it.

When he felt her presence getting closer, he moved to the edge of the step he was on and waited for her to take her seat next to him like she had done before.

Emie looked down at her little brother who was waiting for her on the steps. He had done this so often when he was younger. She was still haunted by the last time he had done this.

"You know it's kind of creepy when you do this, right?" She jested to him.

Jordy smiled, and looked down at her when she sat on the step below him. "I get it, I'm a freak. Don't remind me."

Emie smiled knowingly at him. She liked that she could joke with her brother more now. Ever since she had met Asher it had been that way with her.

"I need to talk to you Em."

Emie knew what they were about to talk about had been a long time coming. She wanted to sit here as long as she could and listen to her little brother.

"There are things about to happen, things that none of us can stop. Not even me." He said to her looking down at his hands as he wrung them. "I know you don't want to know the future, and you don't want me to change it, but I wish I had last year."

Emie reached up and touched his hands. "I don't want you to think you should have Jordy. What happened happened, and it happened for a reason." She willed him to understand this. "Asher needed that time to be able to understand how he truly felt inside. He needed to know that this, us, was what he wanted and couldn't live without. And I," she took her time as she said this last. "I needed to know if I was ready for it as well."

Jordy looked at Emie as she told him this. He knew she was right. But still, he felt like there was something he could of done. And there was that thing he had done last night. He needed to tell her.

"You both know now the love you have for each other is real. I can see that. But what's about to happen isn't going to question that. It's going to tear us all apart Em. Everything we know now, and everything we have is about to change."

Emie sighed at his serenity. She didn't know how to handle this. But she believed in fate, and destiny. She needed to restore his faith in that.

Asher and Jeremy were getting ready to make their way back into the family room. She looked at Jordy and said "You're going to have to trust us Jordy. You're going to have to trust in what will happen is supposed to happen. No matter how bad it might be. Trust that this gift you have been given isn't about fixing the things that may seem wrong, but preparing for them. Trust that who and what we are as a family is enough to get us through this."

Jordy thought about what she said as she patted his leg and walked away from him assuredly. He knew her happiness now, and her belief in love was what was clouding her from seeing what he needed her to see. He shook his head as he walked down stairs and headed for the dungeon to the one person who understood what he felt right now. The person who could be his doom in the future.

Asher looked around the garage as they descended the back steps. This garage was different then the one he had parked in earlier. The main doors were open letting in the morning sun off the lake. It was breathtaking from this far south of the pier. Untouched, unlike the rest of the city.

All the way down there, Jeremy had chatted with Asher about sports. Asher loved baseball. He'd never had time to watch it or even go to a game. Jeremy knew a few of the owners and told Asher he'd get him good seats. Asher knew it was just the sort of talk a hunter would use on his prey to get him to trust him. He thought about shaking the thought from his mind when Jeremy slapped him on the shoulder and joked around about the tasty ribs he liked to eat at the game. Asher shook his head but the eerie chill never left his back.

The guys had a collection of many different sorts of vehicles out here. Asher noted that they were from various years dating back to early nineteen hundreds. An assortment of bikes by the doors caught his eye.

Jeremy was sitting on the bench beside the doors in the shadows next to Asher, hiding from the daylight. Their smoke was rolling out the doors into the daylight.

Jeremy had handed Asher a cold beer out the fridge.

"Beer?" Asher questioned. Just to make sure. He could tell from the tint of Jeremy's lips and drink that he wasn't drinking the same thing he had handed to Asher.

"Yeah. I dump them out when I leave the house and fill them with… well, you know. It's my cover. Keeps me from taking down the good guys like you." Jeremy winked as he pulled in another hit of his smoke.

Asher sipped and looked at his beer in amazement. He remembered what Emie had told him about her wine bottles. It still shook him visibly to think about what would be in this bottle later.

"So, you can't tell me anything?" Asher asked, one hand holding his beer, the other he used to light another smoke with. It felt nice to finally be able to take a break and relax smoking and drinking a cold beer.

He had worked all night keeping an eye on the city during the storm. He was tired all the way deep down in his bones, he thought as he blew out his smoke.

"Don't ask man. I'd like to keep my man card today, if it's all the same to you."

Emie would have his head if he told Asher anything, so Jeremy started talking about things Asher would like. "Do you ride?" Jeremy asked. He noticed Asher was eyeing his orange, custom built motorcycle.

"I do. I have a soft tail too."

Jeremy knew that motorcycle well. Asher was thinking now about the night he rode with Emie behind him smiling as he admired Jeremy's bike. Jeremy too smiled at Asher's memories. Asher had a nice black and chrome bike. Sure to make all the girls in Luna Pier jealous. "2001?" he asked.

"Yeah." Asher's mind remembered the year. The year he had bought the bike back from New York. Trying to escape his father's plans for his life. He rubbed his shoulder absentmindedly thinking about New York.

Jeremy listened in on Asher's thoughts. He shook his head remembering that year to well. It was time to get him back to Emie who was waiting for him. Jeremy could hear the music coming from her piano in the main living room. He hated taking Asher back in the house, but he knew this was something this man had to face sooner or later.

"We should take them out for ride one day." Jeremy told him hopefully as he hopped off the bench.

"Yeah we should." Asher flicked what was left of his smoke out and finished his bottle. It was time to return the others. He was dying to see Emie again and get her alone away from her brothers.

Asher eyed Jeremy knowingly with the beer bottle he set down on the bench as Jeremy gulped down the remaining contents of his. He left it there for Jeremy. Hoping he was doing the right thing.

Emie heard Asher walking into the room. She had been thinking about him before he walked in. Asking herself why she had done this to him. Everything Jordy had tried to tell her was running circles around in her mind.

She was playing a newer song now, one that was on the radio all the time while she had been in Kentucky.

Asher knew the song she was playing and it brought a smile to his face. He remembered how much she loved singing with him on their first date. When Jeremy excused himself from the room and left them alone, Asher walked up behind Emie and leaned against the piano.

God, he loved her voice when she sang. It was magical.

When the second part came into the song where the male singer joined in, Asher took over the song.

Emie followed his voice; with his highs and lows she anticipated his every move. She joined him in all the right places. They acted the part because they knew them by heart. They had both known the song from the last year. They had sung it to each other over and over in their heads, but never face to face.

Asher looked at Emie and knew she had seen his thoughts. She sang with him so well she was giving him chills. He had never experienced this before in his whole life. He had dreamed of it, yes many times. But to sing a song to a woman he loved, to have her sing it with him like she was, like they were playing the roles of the lovers in the song, while she pounded on the keys and followed him every step of the way; Asher found himself in a heaven he had never knew existed.

He sat down with her on the bench as they sang the choruses. He placed his hands on her hips holding her as he gave the song everything he had.

Emie finished her song and watched as Asher sang to her. Everything about who he was; his name, his career, the song he knew and sang to her, it was like the one thing that could destroy her was consuming her with him. Fire. It was so ever present in their relationship.

She had missed him and all the desires that were stirring in her now. His scent filled her mind warmed her body. Her inner monster was craving him.

"Emie," Asher said as he came closer to her. "I know there is a lot for me to learn here. Please know I still want this. There is no where in this world I would rather be right now then here with you.

"We can learn to love again, just like in the song."

Emie lifted her fingers off the piano and placed them in her lap. She looked out over the lake as she thought about how to respond to him. She could only hope once she told him everything that he would stay with her. She had to learn the hard way how humans reacted to knowing what she was. What kind of life she led.

She was ashamed of her life. Who she was. But she was more afraid of losing Asher again, it would kill her. It was weakness on her part, and she knew that, but she couldn't take anymore heartbreak. She vowed to protect this man and his family no matter what happened. Their love, her love for him; that was something that would never die.

"If you'd told me yesterday, we would be here sitting like this, talking, I would have laughed at you. I just can't wrap my mind around what you're doing here, why you want to be here with me." Emie looked up at him, wide eyed in amazement. "You're like an addiction Asher." Emie looked up at him sucking back on tears. "Ever since I first saw you, I was memorized. You've overpowered me. I feel like I'm so drunk on you I'm staggering."

She turned into his legs that were on either side of her. "I wandered around lost for months, like I was lost in this world without you. I can't even think sometimes." She said as she shook her head and looked back down at her lap. "I'm so addicted to you. I'm hooked on thinking and dreaming about you. I get so frustrated when anything interrupts our time together. " She shook her head again thinking about it. It felt so silly. But she smiled up at him anyways, not caring if she sounded like a fool.

Asher knew what that felt like. Knew his own addictions in his life where nothing compared to this addiction, this high of being with Emie. Just being in her presence was better then any thrill he'd ever experienced.

He tucked her hair behind her ear again and rested his arm on the piano. "There is this rush of adrenalin we get, as firemen running into a burning building. It's like no other adrenalin rush I'd ever experienced. Coming down off that high is easy after a call. But I used to long for it day after day; I couldn't wait for the next call to come in."

He looked down at her hands and took them in his and looked back at her face. "But Emie, ever since I met you, I feel like you have knocked me on my knees sweetheart and have me begging for whatever this is between us."

Emie turned her head a little bashful at what he'd said. She still couldn't understand why he loved her.

He waited till she looked back over at him and then continued, she looked so adorable when she did. "This rush, this high I feel when I'm with you; I don't ever want that to end sweetheart."

Asher reached his hands up into her hair, lifted her face up to his. Made her really look at him. "When you left that night Emie, I felt like I had lost part of myself. I couldn't find you to save my life!" he laughed, looking down he dropped his hands down to her hands in his, remembering how hard it had been for him. He traced her fingers with his thumbs.

She picked up her hands and ran her hands through his hair lovingly as he continued, looking sweetly at him. She wanted him to talk like this forever to her.

"Just tell me everything. I'm not going anywhere Emie."

He stood then, pulled her up to him and walked her back over to the couch where they had been sitting. He needed her to start where they had left off.

Emie sat on the couch and sat Indian style facing him. She tucked her hair behind her and then wrapped it over one shoulder. She looked at him and asked "You're sure you're ready for this?"

Asher smirked at her and jokingly said, "No." And it made Emie smile, wide. She loved him so much.

She steadied herself and started right where Joseph told her to start. "In the beginning of time, the angels walked with God and man. They were created to help God. To walk around this earth and be His eyes and ears.

"When man fell, and got away from God, they started to think of themselves as gods. Man continued to fail God continually. They built a tower so high they thought they could reach the heavens. This of course angered God. He destroyed their tower and confounded them, spreading them throughout the earth."

Asher knew this story. His mother had raised him in Sunday school. He listened more intently to her then he had at church when he was younger, wondering if the beauty before him was indeed an angel.

"The angels were instructed then to keep closer to the humans. The humans no longer wanted God in their lives. Generations would die off not knowing who He was.

"He allowed some of us to be seen by the humans. But in order to protect the humans from the angels who were also falling away from him, he set boundaries for us. The humans could use fire to destroy us if they had too. Also, we were to stay out of the sun light. Leave the humans alone during the day to see to his will. We were to see to his will at night."

Emie sighed and looked down at her hands again. This was the part she didn't want Asher to know about. The part that made her a killer.

"When we are faced with a human he requires Asher, we are to take their life. His chosen ones can never be taken by us. We have to leave those alone he has plans for. But the rest, are fair game."

Asher took a gulp at that. He remembered Jeremy's earlier comment. The good guys like you.

"We are called Vampires." Emie knew Asher knew that already. But she wanted to let it sink in again, if only for one more moment in time. She wanted to give him one more chance to run. Surprisingly, he didn't want too. He was still waiting for her to finish in awe of everything she was telling him.

"The old vampires couldn't procreate other chosen vampires. We were dying off in the old centuries and God aloud it. Humans were slaughtering us, hunting us. They called us spawn of Satan, and witches. They burned many of us at the stake along with innocent humans they assumed were like us. Many times they would decapitate us or the innocent ones and bury us with our heads in our hands. For us, this didn't work, but for the humans that paid our debt, it was terrifying.

"The fallen demons were helping them. Making humans believe they were doing God's work.

"That night I was changed," Emie cringed at this, and looked down again. She really didn't know why she had been chosen for this life. "I don't know if I was chosen or if I was just some random meal. An accident. The vampire never returned for me or sought me out. Most of us stay with the ones we choose. We teach them and train them, show them how to live. Some humans can't adjust to the change; their mind develops this crazy frenzy for blood. They enjoy the hunt and killing." Like Asher's brother Curtis was. He was having a hard time with this life. They all worried for him.

"Joseph learned after I had changed him, of our ways. He had met others like us who taught us the way. We've lived our lives in secret, doing the bidding of our calling, but staying away from the ones who are chosen and led to do the will of our creator.

"Joseph chose to be the leader of our family. He chose to build this city and grow our inheritance into what it is today. Jordy, he's sought out to find the mysteries of this world. Hidden treasures in the human world. Jeremy, well, he is his own person really. He never has found his place in this world. He loves horses and gambling. He stays close with us as a family, but he likes to be alone."

Family reminded Emie of the talk she was supposed to have with Asher.

Asher was stunned by all this information. He could read in Emie's eyes that there was more. But he had a question for her first. "You're an angel?"

Emie laughed at that looking up at him.

"Do you have wings?" he wondered aloud.

Emie sighed and closed her eyes. Even though they were spread out behind her glistening in the sunlight, even though she longed for him to touch her feathers the way he caressed her hair, she knew he'd never be able to see them. It was God's way of protecting her from humans.

Emie didn't answer his question. She wasn't supposed to ever tell anyone. But one day, she would show him, she told herself silently. One day...

"There's a storm coming Asher. That's what we need to tell you about. It's a war. Between the vampires and men. The vampires want to take over; they want to control the humans. They are turning humans and killing humans by the thousands, everyday. We, meaning a small majority of us, are not sure what to do about this .

"Jordy says the war is between God and the fallen. The fallen are trying to take over this world. Destroy God's chosen ones, humans and vampires." When Asher's mind thought of the fires around the city, the unexplained disappearances on the news, then Emie continued. "It's already starting Asher."

Asher was thinking of his family and friends when Joseph walked in the room.

"This isn't the first time this war has happened. Many societies throughout history have been wiped out by the fallen. It's the reason for our secrecy. The humans have always had the capabilities to destroy us. The fallen attack back like they are doing now. The temptation to rule, to own this world is a fight between all of us.

"The humans have grown in strength and power in this age to a point where they are indestructible. The fallen are trying to take that power from them. The weapons of this world in the wrong hands could destroy everything you know and then some."

"Why can't you stop them?" Asher asked helplessly.

"It's a big world Asher. We can't interfere with the will or the decision of God. My responsibilities are here. My family, the city, you." Joseph let that last sit with Asher.

Asher was worrying now like Joseph knew he would. He needed to know that they would be here for them all. They would be the help they were destined to be.

Joseph looked over at Emie. He needs to know about his brother.

Twenty Four

Standing in the Whitby's old dusty barn loft at mid-night, Emie had never felt more human than she did today. She was tripping on the mats that lined the hallways in the barns, she was dropping tools on her feet, and the bats up here had scared her when she started dreaming of Asher for the hundredth time tonight.

Asher was home at sleeping, finally, she thought as she was looking for am old feed bag for Triton. She'd left Asher sometime after noon, sleeping soundly in his bed. He had been in a hurry to get away from her world for awhile and back into his. He had been hungry and needed to check on his dog. He had asked her and Joseph so many questions that she worried for him after she had left.

She hadn't expected him to sleep so long though. He had told her he just wanted to shut his eyes for a little while after he had shown her around his house. Seeing his bed had been too much for him. He lost the battle of trying to stay coherent after being awake for over twenty four hours.

She'd snuck into his room around eight o'clock tonight and was surprised to find him still sleeping. He was so tired, she had thought to herself. She chased away his nightmares one last time, and left him dreaming of a baseball game instead. She'd seen that his house was decorated in sport memorabilia, so she hoped dreams of sports were better for him then the nightmares he was having.

Emie remembered Cookie as she kicked around some hay barrels looking for Triton's old favorite bags. Emie shook her head at all the mess her horse had made in his stall; years worth of chores around here were starting to overwhelm her.

Cookie was Asher's little dog. Emie didn't know enough about dogs to know what kind she was, just that she was small enough to fit inside of Asher's hand and forearms. Asher had called her a bell dog, but the joke had been lost on her. Fast food and restaurants had never been her thing. Cookie was black and white, her fur was soft from the years of Asher's love and attention, and she had the cutest little bat ears that flopped when she ran and pranced around.

Emie had left them both earlier; Cookie was sleeping soundly nuzzled up next to Asher, and that left her with only one thing to do, she finally made her way out to the barns to see Triton.

Triton, she had heard, had missed her so much he had refused to let anyone of her brothers near him unless it was to feed him or let him out for the night.

But no matter what Emie did, she couldn't stop thinking about Asher. Couldn't stop thinking about their grim future. So much so that she hadn't heard the old wood floor cracking right under her feet when she had went back up into the loft.

Emie fell through the old floor boards when they gave way under her weight. She didn't worry about it though as she was falling. She knew she'd hit the ground and land on her feet.

But she didn't. She landed on her stomach on top of something. Something that had caught her fall felt squishy. Something...

"Asher!" Emie exclaimed looking down at him, trying to shake off the dust and wood so she could see him better.

"I'm fine, I'm fine." Asher called out from under her in a huff.

Asher had woken up alone at home. He didn't know why he expected Emie to be there when he woke up in his bed, but he had and she wasn't. When he couldn't find her anywhere, he started to panic thinking he had dreamed it all. He'd left his house in a hurry to find her.

What scared the hell out of him now was when he seen her falling through the opening in the floor. Not thinking that she would be fine on her own to fall like that, he had tried to catch her and failed miserably when she fell on him instead. She scared him again when he opened his eyes and seen a monster on top of him. He knew right away it was just her, but he hadn't expected to see her eyes and fangs all at the same time.

Asher instinctively grabbed her face.

Emie.

It wasn't until he blinked a few times, getting the dust out of his eye that he seen her eye's and mouth go back to her beauty.

Emie sat over him giving him a mean stare. Like she had her brothers earlier. One that was just as scary as her fangs.

"You're going to be a lot fun at Halloween, you know that right?" He grinned.

"You, really need to stop scaring me." She said each word one by one, letting him know he had been endanger of her hurting him and not wanting that to happen.

Asher wanted to chuckle at that. How did he scare her?

"You, really need to stop freaking out so much." He told her honestly, enjoying the banter. Grabbing her nose and pulling on it.

He lifted up a little, his shoulder and hip was killing him tonight and this wasn't helping him. Then he sighed deeply up at her. He brushed her hair out of her face and smiled at her.

Her hair was falling all around them. He absolutely loved her hair. He took one long curl and ran his hand all the way down its silky length. She was smiling at him now and Asher had to sigh at her. She truly was breathtaking.

"Why didn't you tell me you were coming? I could have let you-" Emie heard something then. She bared her fangs at the stable doors and listened.

Asher shook his head. She really was a sight. More now that she could be herself around him.

Emie was worried about the wolves. Where were they? "How did you get in Asher? The dogs?" she asked him this still looking at the doors, then, turned quickly to hear him.

Asher wondered why they still called them things dogs. They weren't dogs. "Joseph. He seen me at the gates and let me in."

"Joseph?" Emie smiled slowly. So, all that big talk earlier tonight about humans and Asher and how this was a bad idea, meant he secretly was still ok with it? She wondered to herself.

"Yeah." Asher knew that her smile meant something, but she wasn't going to clue him in on it. Joseph had told him as he closed the gates back that the dogs were put up for the night; he was free to visit with Emie. Asher guessed that meant Joseph was adjusting to him being around.

Emie smiled at his thoughts, and moved to a more comfortable position for him, she had to be crushing him.

"Why do you call them things dogs anyways? They're not dogs, they're wolves." He drawled out the word 'wolves'.

"Kind of. You just have to know they are dangerous for you Asher, they are Josephs, and even I can't control them. Believe me; I've lost a few hands trying." That last she wanted to kick herself for. Asher didn't need to know that.

Asher took note of that and nodded. He didn't like it, especially about her being harmed, and then wondered if she was just joking, or had she really lost a hand. And if she did, how... well maybe he didn't want to know.

Asher stood when Emie got up off him. She helped him out by patting the splintered wood off his back and front.

Emie took note of Asher's attire. He was in jeans again. Raised by brothers who wore only the best of what companies from all over the world had to offer, it was his jeans that stirred something inside of her. That and his scent. Nothing compared to how Asher smelled. Nothing.

"What were you doing up there anyways?"

"I was-" looking up, she paused when she wondered how she was supposed to tell him what she had been looking for. "I can't tell you… yet."

Emie was looking cutely at him biting her lip shyly. Her hands were in her back pockets. He figured there was something up there he wasn't supposed to know about.

"You're right, I don't wanna know." He stood his full height, stretched and thrusted his hands in his pockets.

"There's still a lot I need to show you Asher. Things that I think we should take one step at a time. Ok?"

Asher was sure he could handle it all. He had learned so much today about her and her world. He was away from his world again and was just starting to pass through hers. As long as she was with him, he knew he could handle anything.

The city would be fine without him for a few days. He'd even left his fire radio and phone in his truck so they wouldn't be interrupted tonight.

"I'm not going anywhere sweetheart." He winked at her.

"How many fairytales did you read as a kid?" she asked sweetly.

"Fairytales?" that one he had to think about. He thought wolves and vampires were from scary nightmares and were stretching the realm of his reality, what else from the story books could there be that was real? "You mean like dragons and princesses?"

And with that, Triton announced he was still hungry and wanted out. He was banging against the door next to them.

Asher turned around and hoped there wasn't a dragon behind door number one. He had to gulp down his fear. "Do I want to know what that is?" he questioned Emie, who was standing behind him now.

Emie smiled, measured his racing heart beat, and then placed her hands on his chest when he turned around. "Only if you're ready." She eyed him questioningly. "That, is my horse."

Asher looked at the door. He hadn't meant to grab her hips when the banging started again, but he felt safer when he did.

"Ho-orse?" he stuttered looking at her sideways. "That doesn't sound like a horse."

Emie closed her eyes and used her abilities to calm him. His humanness would never allow him to do this. He didn't need his humanness when he had her, she smiled.

Asher felt something seep through his whole body like a painkiller racing through his veins. "Yeah, I think I'm going to like that a lot." He smiled down at her when he felt her calm. He knew immediately it had been her that had caused him calm. He had felt it in his dreams today also.

Triton would not be ignored. His hoof came through the wood. Joseph wasn't going to like that at all, Emie thought.

Emie tisked at him aloud and reached for the upper half-a-door all while trying to keep Asher calm. He had thrust his hands back in his pockets again when she stepped away from him.

Triton didn't give her much time to back away before he thrusted his head out the opening and shoved the half a door wide open.

Triton wouldn't be denied. His creamy white glossy wing span filled his stall and lifted his front feet off the ground a little. Emie stepped inside and reached for him calming him too.

"Asher, this is Triton.

"Triton, this is Asher." She said to her horse as she patted Triton and calmed him with soft gentle strokes. She used her ability to emphasis that Asher was her mate. Like it or not.

Triton's tan head and creamy white mane bobbed up and down in acknowledgement.

Asher on the other hand looked dumbfounded. Thoroughly stunned still standing out in the hallway.

"You said horse. That's… that, is not a horse." Asher said as he shook his head.

"Like I said, one step at a time. Ok? For all intensive purposes, he's just a horse." She grinned at him sweetly. Petting Triton's soft furry neck soothingly.

Emie used her abilities again to calm Asher's heart. "He doesn't bite. Honest." Encouraging Asher to come closer into the stall.

Why had Asher honestly thought he did, he wondered? "Can I pet him?" Asher whispered his thoughts aloud walking into the stall behind Emie.

Emie smiled deeply, "Yes of course. Triton is a big baby." She said looking up at Triton.

Triton puffed out his mouth and snout at that comment.

Asher took the few steps up to Triton slowly, eyeing the gigantic 'horse'. Standing next to Emie who was so small, Triton looked like monster of a horse in comparison. Then he reached a shaky hand up his snout to pet him. He knew a little of horses. Knew enough to approach him slowly and reach out his hand flat, to work his way from the horse's nose so he could smell him, and then up his head to his mane, before he could rub his neck, where Asher found two, long, scared over fang marks. That explained a lot …

"That is Jeremy's fault. All of this is really…" she started, lost in thought. "After Jeremy turned, he was always so hungry. It was hard to state him sometimes.

"Triton was my horse. Jeremy went to the barns one night, he was going to leave in search of food, and couldn't resist trying horse first."

Again Asher noticed she was lost in her own mind. Probably centuries away. He waited and let her remember.

"Joseph walked in just as Jeremy had started feeding. Triton had fallen to the ground and was trying to shake off Jeremy. Joseph intervened, but it was too late. Jeremy had already released enough venom inside of Triton to change him. We watched for days as Triton changed. Wings, fangs, that deathly horn on his head! None of us could make sense of it." She smiled up at Asher then. "But he was family, he was mine, and none of us could bare to shoot him or finish him off. So we kept him."

Asher's mind went back to the dogs. Joseph must have wanted guard dogs... When Emie sighed, he knew the answer.

He couldn't believe it. A real Pegasus. He looked back into the rest of the stall at Tritons wings. They stretched out behind his back. Tritons feathers were the largest feathers he'd ever seen. His hands itched to touch them.

Emie walked under Triton and back up against Asher, she placed his hand under hers and reached out to Triton's feathers. She closed her eyes when Asher's mind described what he was feeling to her. He placed his hand on her right hip and moved his body closer to hers.

"Do you have wings Emie?" he questioned her softly in her ear. She hadn't answered his question earlier.

A whisper that ran through her soul and frightened her all the more. She loved him so much already, so quickly.

"I do." She whispered back to him.

Asher closed his eyes moving his hand through triton's feathers back to her side. "Can I see?" he asked.

Emie closed her eyes also. She wanted to feel him touch her so intimately, but she didn't have the power to allow it. She reached in his mind though and showed him what she really looked like with her mind.

Asher wrapped his arms around Emie, his angel. Held her close and breathed her in. He could see her wings, her eyes, all of her beauty that was her. That was his. He ran his ran hand down her shoulder, down her spin and across her back where he thought her wings should be. He could see in his mind where she was showing his mind what he was touching, what she was feeling, and that was enough for him.

Emie wondered how long it would take for Asher to be able to ride Triton. Fly with him.

"I was just getting ready to ride him." She hinted, looking up at Asher sweetly.

It hadn't taken as long as she thought. A few times around the pasture, making Triton gallop at an unruly pace, and Asher was wondering too what it would be like to fly.

Ready? She silently asked.

Asher steadied himself. Took in a deep breath. Even though he knew he wasn't, he told her yes.

She liked that he could do that now on his own without her abilities.

"Just don't let me fall, ok sweetheart?" He whispered in her ear.

Emie smiled into the moonlight. "Never." She told him as she ushered Triton at full gallop onto the beach.

Asher watched her body instead of the trees flying past him. Her hair, curls and all, bobbed up and down with each gallop. Her body moved Triton like they were connected. He had his hands on her legs and could feel her thighs squeezing Triton, holding onto him. Her hands were wrapped in his mane.

Asher seen the lake in front of them getting closer and wondered if they were going to walk on water, not like that would surprise him now. But when he seen Triton's wings spread out like an eagles, he wrapped his arms around Emie and scooted himself up close to her.

Emie steadied him just as Triton lifted off the ground, his back hoofs jumping off the sand into full flight. His wings smoothly rocked them up through the air, took them high above the city and up into the midnight clouds.

Asher was stunned at first, he couldn't breath, and then he couldn't help but look everywhere. He wanted to take it all in. Everything. The disappearing lake, the stars, the floating clouds all around them. He couldn't believe this.

Emie was thinking of something altogether different. Asher's breath in her hair, his mouth kissing her neck, his wandering loving thoughts, mixed with Triton's rise and fall of his wings; she was quickly addicted to this.

Emie could feel his body trembling behind her after hours of flying. But she wasn't sure why.

"Asher?" she questioned.

Cold. He shivered.

She hadn't realized it was cold this far up. The clouds always looked so warm.

Triton galloped down the clouds and back to the warmth of the lower sky at her request.

They were back over the lake again so not to be seen. She followed the light from the lighthouse back to Luna Pier.

Landing had been easier then Asher had thought. Triton had been gifted at this, and Asher was still in awe over him. But as he pranced excitedly splashing around the beach close to waters edge, Asher too needed to get his feet back on solid ground.

Emie slid off and reached up to catch Asher. He told her what he thought of that in his mind as he stumbled off Triton laughing. He landed in the sand face down.

Triton pranced around as if to say 'Stupid Human'. Emie patted him, leaned up against him and they watched as Asher rolled over in the sand.

Asher put his hands behind his head and stared at her.

They stayed like that for some time. Words, thoughts, nothing needed to be said. Their bodies knew what their hearts wanted.

Asher woke in a hazy, sleepy state. His muscles and shoulder ached and were stiff from the nights sleep. Rubbing his face deeper in his pillow-

Emie.

Asher was wide awake now, confused. He didn't have red, silk pillows. He adjusted his eyes to the darkness and blinked away the stupid crusty things in his eyes that were blurring his vision.

That wasn't his head board either. There were red curtains instead.

He couldn't see much around him, the curtains were closed all around the bed. He could see the woman lying next to him though. She looked like an angel.

She was.

Emie's curly, rich chocolate brown hair was lying all around and down her naked body and under her. Her lower leg was peeking out of her sheets that were teasingly coiled around her body. She was resting her head up on her elbow and was looking intently at Asher.

Asher laid his head back down and closed his eyes. All was well he thought sleepily.

Emie had felt him stir. Watched as his dreams faded away beyond his grasp. Asher had slept for over twelve hours. She wasn't sure why, but she assumed between the storms, the clean up, and her fairytale land, then their love making on the beach; it had just all been too much for him.

"You don't sleep either, do you?" he questioned from his pillow.

Emie giggled. Asher thought of old wives tales when it came to vampires, and they always made her laugh when he thought about them. Humans still had it all wrong.

His eyes opened wide with the realization of something. "Please tell me this house of vampires has a toilet?"

"No sorry, but I'm sure we can find something for you."

Asher buried his head in the pillow and sighed. "Just point me to the nearest tree or fire hydrant." He mumbled into the pillow. "How did I get up here anyways?" he asked looking over at her again.

Emie let his mind wander back to the night before. He remembered Triton, remembered their flight. She couldn't believe his vision was so impaired compared to hers. He'd missed so much. Then he remembered the beach and rolled over blissfully. His pleasure of the night's events visible from his morning erection.

Asher grabbed the sheet to cover his embarrassment.

"You fell asleep around six this morning. I was worried the dogs were out, so I carried you up here."

Asher looked at her dumbfounded again. "You, carried me?"

Emie flashed a grin at him reminding him of her fangs.

Vampire. Right. Asher rubbed his face and his eye's. "Any chance you have food here?" he asked as his stomach growled.

Emie shook her head 'no', laid her chin on his chest and stared up at him sweetly.

"Luna Cafe it is."

Asher started to rise when Emie stayed him.

"Wait." The sun was still up. "I need a few more hours before I can go out. Ok?"

Asher sighed. He was desperately hungry.

Emie was too but she didn't mention that. She was going to need to visit Cristina at the hospital, but she wasn't sure if she could get all she needed. They were going to have to make a trip to the blood bank later.

Asher's curiosity got the better of him. "Emie?" He rolled on his side making her do the same and look at him.

Emie had been waiting for this question. She didn't interrupt him.

"Are you hungry?" cheekily he raised his eyebrow.

Oh how she loved this man!

She smiled at the memories that flooded her mind. He had asked her that twice before, but he didn't remember them now. "You used to ask me that when we first met." She reminded him.

He thought about it and chuckled.

Emie laughed when he thought about the movie he had watched about vampires. Her voice echoed and shook the room. Asher kept saying over and over in his head That's not scary. That's not scary at all. First sarcastically, then more to tell himself he meant it.

"Cristina LOVES that movie." She pointed out to him, just a little embarrassed by her outburst, and yet she felt so much better being herself around him. He was taking it all very well. "But, unlike them, I am not a 'vegetarian' and can not survive on animals alone. I don't like to eat animals. I need human blood, and as tempting as yours is, I'll stick with my wine bottles, thank-you."

Asher cocked a smile at her while he played absentmindedly with the sheets, his face looking down.

"I really have to pee now, Emie."

He said this a little shyly and a little more embarrassed then he had wanted. He knew his cheeks were heated and he must be blushing. But damn it all, how often did a erotic female vampire, who was totally naked under the sheets with him, laugh like that showing her fangs, all while looking so damn sexy he wanted to take her right there and then, and could if he wanted too. If he didn't have to pee...

Emie threw off the covers, knelt beside him and whispered in his ear that she better be his last erotic vampire.

Hours later, at the Luna Cafe a little restaurant in Luna Pier, Asher and Emie were enjoying a meal together. Well, Asher was enjoying the meal and Emie was enjoying watching him eat.

She had ordered water out of pure habit. He told her what else to order for herself so she could take it home and he could eat it later. Even though he had ordered an appetizer of cheese sticks, a salad with a roll, a burger that only his big hands could hold onto, a basket of fries they were pretending to share and a dessert that hadn't arrived yet. She smiled and shook her head. Where did he put it all, she wondered.

She thought it sad that he always wondered when and if he would get the chance to eat again. He always worried about that. Always felt too busy to sit down and eat like this. His radio was standing on the table next to his drink, turned down low. A reminder to all of who he was. That he was ready to answer the call to save a life.

There was a single thought on Emie's mind tonight. She wanted to know about the scar that ran down his shoulder to the other side of his waist. The scar was deep, jagged. The pain he must have endured when the injury happened must have been crippling. What happened to him? And when? She would get her answer tonight if she could only find the courage to ask him. She hoped by asking him in his world instead of hers it would encourage him enough to tell her.

"Asher?" she waited for him to finish chewing for him to answer, even though he had looked up at her already.

"What is it sweetheart?"

Emie was actually nervous. She knew he could read it in her eyes now. She wondered why for the first time in her life, all that she had went through and endured, why was this so hard. Maybe because she knew what the answer held. His pain, his fears. He had so many unknown fears. No one knew about him what she did. No one knew how this brave fireman feared being trapped, feared dying. No one knew where his thoughts went to when the sirens rang. No one knew how much he cared for the people in this city. He was so much like Curtis that it scared her. One day would she lose him to his bravery?

"Asher, I noticed your shoulder the other day..." she left her question wide open. She knew he would know what she couldn't ask.

And he did. Sadly enough.

Asher wiped his mouth. He wasn't done eating yet, but suddenly he was done.

"Here I thought you would be kind enough not to ask."

Shyly, ever so sweetly he eyed her, and she almost rescinded her question. His pain, his fear of being trapped, it was all there in his eyes. She wished that she hadn't needed to ask the question.

Asher was looking down at his abandoned plate. He sat back against the booth up straighter and glanced out the windows into the night.

It wasn't until she seen two towers smoking in his mind that she realized what had happened. Everyone in America knew what those towers looked like, what had happened that day. But his angle of the smoking towers was off from what she remembered watching it on tv. He was looking straight up at them. Not from the side. Was it possible that he was there?

Panic, unlike anything she had felt in a hundred years filled her at this possibility.

Twenty Five

"I was there, in New York that day." Asher knew Emie was reading his mind now. Her eyes looked distant now. Emie let him know she knew what he talking about, but she didn't stop him, so he continued.

He rubbed his thighs and went on "I was mad at my dad, so I left here. He wanted me to go to college. Get my degree in fire fighting. Curtis didn't want to be the next chief, so I had to be. But I didn't want it either. We fought to the point of me leaving.

"So I took a vacation, I took some extra time off and drove to New York. I had only been there a few days, but I was in love the city. I was just starting to make plans to move there, figured I could go to college there, go home when I finished. I was desperate to get away from the Pier and my father, so I started talking to some of the department heads there in New York, the big wigs. They had an opening for me. I even had a place to stay."

He was resting his whole body up on his arms now; they were crossed in front of him leaning on the table. He shrugged and his muscles were bulging out of his shirt sleeves. He still wasn't looking at her. His mind was picturing the beauty of the busy city.

"That day, September 11th, I was sightseeing, headed out to Ellis Island, I wanted to see the statue of liberty, like every tourist visiting the city for the first time did. I had just reached the top of her. I was leaning out the ledge looking on the city, dreaming of what it would be like to live there. To work there.

"Then I saw the first plane."

Emie gasped at the sight. She too had watched the news. But seeing it from his eyes, seeing the beautiful shining city on a cloudless day with a plane flying straight into the tallest building, bursting the perfect picture and shattering it, seeing what his mind; a fireman saw, it was altogether different.

Emie covered her trembling lips with his t-shirt she was wearing so no one could see her reaction.

Asher seen people burning, not a building on fire. He seen families lives being destroyed, and he was too far to do anything about it. He didn't see the gossips of war, or hear the media's ideas of terrorism; he saw terror burning in front of him. He saw choking, black, billowing smoke, hot red man eating flames, he saw a building being ripped apart, the people inside it falling out. People he knew he couldn't fix even if he tried.

"They started evacuating the island when reports of terrorism were a threat to all the buildings in the area. I just remember looking at the tower, watching it burn, I remember feeling the second plane hit when we made it back to the island. The whole earth quaked under me.

"I remember driving my truck to the nearest fire station. People were just standing in the road. Looking at the towers. Watching. Wondering what in the hell just happened.

"One plane was understandable in that city. Forgivable even. But two? Not two. Two meant something worse then the first.

"I remember looking up and seeing the building as I wove in and out and around countless people just standing in the streets, wondering to myself what in the hell was I supposed to do? What could I do? I was from Michigan, not New York. There was a world of difference between the two. I'd only been there a few days.

"I made it to an empty station though. It was so eerie. Just days before it had been packed with trucks and firemen. Now it was empty. I grabbed someone else's gear, an ax, some hose lines, threw them in the back of my truck and drove like a bat out of hell."

Asher looked at Emie. If she had been any other women in the world, he would have sugar coated this for her. But this was Emie. She had risked her own life by giving it to him. He was sure he wasn't going to hold anything back from her. Not even his fears. She needed to see them, feel them, so she could understand them. Understand why he was who he was. And why he needed her so badly in his life.

He reached across the table and held her hand she had laying there. He grinned at the way she had her lips covered up under his t-shirt.

"I had parked blocks away. Behind many fire trucks. I was sitting inside my truck, baffled. Scared out of mind as I watched jumpers and papers, pieces of things I didn't want to know about, falling like rain around me. These building were hundreds of stories high. And I was about to get lost in one that was on fire and had a jet plane sticking out of it. I'd never even been in them, I knew nothing about them. People were jumping out of them, what in hell was I doing rushing into one of them?"

But he went in anyways, Emie thought.

"But I went into the second tower anyways. I was trained too." Asher rubbed his shoulder at that. "I knew how to search and rescue. None of the men standing in the roads looking at the buildings as scared as I was knew how to do what I was about to do.

"I had to go in. I had to." Asher sat back then, thinking about the decision he had made.

Emie watched as he looked down at the table remembering what the inside of the building looked like. The chaos around him.

"I stood there with mighty men. Who were just as scared as I was." Asher choked on his thoughts. "Chief's, Captains, the MFIC's!"

There was a joke there somewhere, but Emie couldn't see it. Just the faces of the mighty men he spoke of. All of whom had probably lost their lives that day.

"And then I watched as the first building fell around us outside. And when I say watched..."

She knew what he meant. He didn't just watch with his eyes. He watched with his whole body. His eyes, his mind, his heart, his feet, his hands; he watched and felt it fall. Watched and felt it rumble as it busted through the windows that surrounded him. Watched it through his own eyes as he fell down with it.

Watched as the mighty men around him that he relied on to lead him into danger, and walk him back out safely, disappeared into the cloud of smoke, and dust, and ash.

Emie had to look away from him. Had to reach out and touch him, her mind was still there in the darkness with him, and she needed to feel him. But the tears that threatened to fall uninhibited had to be held back. She couldn't cry for him now. Not here.

His mind was listening now. He could still hear the sounds of the bells and whistles from the fire mens suits going off. The radios were chaotic that day like they had been the other night at the station. Men and women were pleading for help, men and women who were there to help others couldn't even help themselves.

"In this world, there's real, and then there's make believe. I had seen enough in my life time to prepare me for what I couldn't believe was happening, but it wasn't real for me until the first tower fell.

"Everything went silent for a moment. The radio's, you couldn't hear anyone. I felt so alone in the darkness that ensued us. Trapped there in the smoke. But so many were dying around me. So many people up there still needed me. They all needed to be evacuated, quickly."

Emie felt her whole body jump when Asher remembered being struck by something. She almost lost the hold on his hand she had been holding to cover her mouth. It had hurt him so bad that the thought of it striking him still rattled him. Even now, years and hundred of miles away from it all.

"My shoulder had been struck. By what, till this day I don't know. I'll never know. But I heard survivors in the stairwell next to me.

"I ran up the stairs, pushing myself to go on, rushing people to get out as fast as they could. Begging them to hurry. I knew where they were going, what they were going to see when they walked out the stairwell doors, but still I had to get them out." Asher shook his head at the memories.

There was a crowd now around their table. No one had ever heard Asher speak of this. They knew he had been there, but no one dared to ask him what had really happened before. They all knew he was a hero, and that had been all that had mattered to them.

Emie was jealous of the waitress who was crying. She needed to cry too. For whatever reason, she had needed him to tell her this; she knew he too needed to tell her this. Was it really his first time speaking of 9/11 since it happened?

The mystery of his fears, of his scars, his heroic nature finally made since.

"I climbed those stairs as fast as I could. I'd finally made it to the other fireman, the ones who were still alive. There were too many people still around us to announce what had happened downstairs, what they hadn't seen yet, and what was likely to happen to them. So I helped them carry people down all the flights of stairs I had just come up. Praying we'd make it down just incase this building fell too."

For the first time Asher looked at Emie. Really looked at Emie. He hadn't had anything then to live for. He'd been reckless with his own life. He'd saved countless others, but what if he'd died that day? He shook his head at his carelessness and went back to his memories.

"We descended floor after floor, tending the wounded quickly. We did this for what felt like hours. Sending people down the stairs to safety. Carrying people from floor to floor. Knowing, waiting for the building to fall around us.

"When it did, I had been the last one in line with a group of men and women in the stairwell.

"We waited while it roared around us. I could feel it in my bones, in my ears. I prayed the prayer I had heard the Chaplin praying before he had perished downstairs. "Please God. Make it stop." Then I waited some more.

"When it stopped, there wasn't a sound other then the building breaking apart. We waited, knelt down, screaming for our lives. Not for the light of day light, it never came that day.". Asher looked out the window then. He needed to look at something other than what his mind feared. The darkness of that day he had been trapped in.

"Not even for our rescuers. For someone's hand to reach out to us and tell it was ok now. No. We were waiting for death to take us. It was all around us.

"We begged for it."

Emie knew where this story was leading. He was one of the survivors in the stairwell in the north tower. She couldn't believe she knew the story, but didn't know he had been there. Didn't know that day so long ago that this man she loved so deeply had been injured, left to die in a stairwell. If she had known then, she could have-

No. She knew history better than that. There was a reason he had to go through this.

"They found us the next morning. I was passed out from exhaustion on top of another fireman who I was trying to keep warm. He had died at some point in the night…

"I was sent to a nearby survivor hospital. They patched up my shoulder in surgery and I went home a month later, wishing I had never left this damned city."

Asher looked out the windows again. He looked out into the city he had left all those years ago.

He prayed what Joseph had talked to him about the day before would never happen to this city.

One man at the counter started to clap when Asher finished. And then everyone in the restaurant did.

Every one but Emie who had tucked her head inside her shirt to hide her tears…

Jordy was inside her head now. There was a storm coming. The reasons for Asher's fears she was still searching for reared its ugly head.

Asher had to stop by the fire hall before he could take Emie home. He needed to be in his world for just a moment longer. He needed a smoke.

He stood by the front red door with her. Wiped her face a little more where she had missed a tear or two. Puffed on his cigarette until it was gone and then lit another.

Blowing out his smoke in the wind he leaned up against the door, turned and looked at her. He knew his life had changed. Was changing with every second he was with her. He loved it. Loved the little moments he had with her.

Emie was looking away from him now. She still couldn't look at him. His scare would haunt her now. She could see him huddled in the rubble, waiting for death. She could see him in the elevator at the hospital, holding the rail for dear when he had first met her. She saw all the other times he had been so scared. Heard his heart now racing like before in fear of what was to come with her and who she was, but he always welcomed it.

She would never think him weak. She would never think of him as anything less then a hero.

Emie.

When she followed his voice and looked at him, he was grinning at her and winked. Emie had to bite her lip.

Asher threw his cigarette away and blew out his smoke. He reached over for Emie and held her. She looked like she needed it. He'd just told her his worst fears and why they had been brought to life. He'd shown her what no one else on the face of this earth would ever see. No book, no movie, would ever get it right. They'd never see what he saw. But she had. Like she had been there following him around floor by floor. She seen the terror he seen with his own eyes. Seen his fears, faced them with him. She felt more than any girlfriend ever should have to bare. She was stronger then she looked.

Joseph was going to torture him, slowly, for this, he laughed to himself.

Emie held back the tears, she wasn't going to cry again. She was done crying. What Jordy was trying to tell her would just have to wait till tomorrow. Asher was here with her now and that was all that mattered anymore. She inhaled him. She held him tighter. She spoke to his beating heart and whispered hope to him. Hope she believed would follow them forever.

Until she heard Cristina's dying screams.

Asher held her awkwardly. Emie had stopped moving, she was frozen in place. He knew this meant something was wrong. But couldn't understand for the life of him what was wrong with her.

When Asher tried to look at her face, she started screaming and Asher panicked.

Earlier that evening…

Joseph was sitting on top of the hospital. The evening breeze cooling his body to a chilling temperature through his soft, black, cotton shirt.

He'd listened in on Asher and Emie at Luna Cafe. Seen what Emie saw. Felt what Asher felt. Knew all of their lives had been changed by Asher. Asher was a welcome addition to the family, but he was going to have to learn some rules first.

Emie was his sister, and there would be no more treating her like she was unbreakable. She wasn't. She maybe the glue that holds his life and family together, he thought as he looked out over the lake, but she could be crushed by the weight of them all. Asher needed to learn this fast.

Two, Asher had another thing coming if he ever hurt Emie again. Asher had told him he understood the need for secrecy in their lives, but Joseph wanted to make sure he understood that better. He started making plans to show Asher what he'd learned from the government these last few months. They were learning they weren't alone in this world and they were planning an attack against the vampires. Experiments had already begun on those they had captured. Experiments Joseph never wanted his family to experience.

God help them all if Emie chose to turnAsher. Asher would be the best of them all. Joseph had been thinking about that a lot lately. Ever since Curtis's funeral, when Asher had spoken to everyone from the depths of his soul, Joseph couldn't believe one man could have such love and honor in him. He'd never met a man as passionate as Asher. A part of Joseph wanted to get to know Asher better. Asher was the kind of man Joseph had been looking for in a friend. Someone who was loyal and trustworthy, and at the same time fun and outgoing. Asher was someone Joseph could see him spending time with.

When Joseph heard the back doors open below him and not close, he wondered at it and took a peek over his legs. He was waiting for Cristina to get off work. They'd been talking to each other ever since Emie had left them. Every day he spent with her was like a day in paradise. She had given him back his reason for living after Emie had left. He sat up here tonight, hoping to surprise her but also worrying about Emie's reaction to what he had been doing with her friend.

He did this often, kept watch over the city from the rooftops. He felt like his favorite superhero comic sometimes and wondered why no one had thought to make a vampire a superhero in the movies.

Vampires really would be the best ones for the job, he thought off handedly as he took a leap off the roof from the top floor. If only the humans really knew who they were and what they were capable of, Joseph wished all the time this world was different and they would see this.

Joseph followed the men who had entered the door. He knew they were up to no good when they left a block to hold open the doors behind them, sneaking in like no one had saw them.

He picked up their scent as he followed them. They weren't just men, they were vampires.

He'd lost them for a moment, going around the different corridors, and then he followed them down the staircase to the basement. He was searching their minds and trying to find their motive, but came up empty. Their thoughts were silent.

Jordy had warned him of this. Probing vampires were searching the cities around the states, but it was still unknown what they were searching for. Joseph was hoping he could corner them if he ever caught up to them. If he could just trap one of them he and Jordy could question them later.

Just as Joseph was rounding another corridor by the surgical wing he heard Cristina screaming, he stopped dead in his tracks to listen again, then he flew and followed her screams until he reached her office.

The two men were on top of her already, biting her throat as they ripped her clothes off. One was biting into her wounded arm when

Joseph ripped his head off his shoulders. The other man hadn't even had time to react; Joseph grabbed his neck and twisted till it came off.

Joseph didn't think when he snapped their necks, he didn't care who or what they were anymore. These vamps were the worst kind of monsters. He was to busy hushing Cristina as he held her bleeding neck in his hands.

"I'm here Love. I'm here." He hushed her more, and tried to comfort her. He looked around wanting to scream for help, but there was no one close enough to hear him or her.

Hard as this was for him, this was Cristina; he reeled in his instincts and the smell of her blood trying to think of how he could save her. If he could save her.

Cristina had been his hero. She'd saved Emie from herself. Gave her a life worth living again; gave her hope, when Emie hadn't any.

Gave him hope again.

Cristina was beautiful. She was everything any man would want in a woman. Her body was something he had dreamed of more than once, from her tan body she worked so hard on to make look perfect, to her over sized breast that she always tried to cover up that Joseph could never stop looking at.

But this beautiful woman was dying in his arms and he hadn't even had the chance to tell her about their future together. Why hadn't he told her before? Why had he let his pride rule over what he was, destroy any chance with her? She was classy, she was gorgeous, she was outrageously funny when she wasn't so shy she was hiding in her shell, and she had the biggest heart of any other women he knew next to Emie.

It was Emie's voice that had pulled him out of his state of confusion. She was pleading with him now, but Joseph didn't know how to fix Cristina. Her and bites were too deep. The arteries had been severed. The young vampires hadn't injected enough venom to change her. They had been looking to kill her not to change her.

If he were in a surgical room, or even if he had an assistant to help him get the supplies he needed, maybe then he could save her.

Joseph had never felt so alone.

Cristina was looking at him, begging him with her gorgeous eyes to save her. Her mind was screaming from the pain. Her body was withering fast from the loss of blood. She had a death grip on his arm, her other hand was clutching at his hand that was holding pressure on her neck.

Joseph looked around desperately. Cristina was going into shock. He needed help, but there was still no one on this damn floor. No one worked down at this end anymore now that Emie wasn't working down here. The surgical wing was probably full of people, doctors, nurses, but he couldn't get to them, or very well tell them what had just happened to her and why the men that had attacked her no longer had heads on their shoulders.

Joseph looked back down at her again. Emie was begging him in his mind to save her. He couldn't let her die. He couldn't.

"Cristina, love, I'm sorry. This is going to hurt you, but you're going to be alright, ok?" Joseph had no idea if she knew what he was going to do, she was passing out and almost unconscious, but for some reason he thought he needed her permission before he did this to her, or to at least inform her... Something felt wrong about just taking her, but he didn't have a choice anymore.

So he did the only thing he knew would save her. He bit the other side of her neck and let a rush of his venom fill her veins. The healing she needed now would go faster for her with his venom. It would kill her, yes; but it would save her. The alternative was to let her die, and Joseph couldn't let that happen to her. Not Cristina, not the woman he wanted to love.

Joseph knew when he let go of her neck there was no turning back. She was bleeding out now and his hand was covered in her blood. Blood was pooling in her wound and bubbling down her neck, all in her long dark hair, running towards him on the floor. It would take only seconds for her blood to run out of her body. These guys had done a messy job on her neck.

He lifted her body up to his mouth and bit down again on her shoulder. Her neck had been sliced all the way around; he didn't want to open her wound more, so he bit just below her neck and on the top of her shoulder. He followed her blood veins dragging his fangs to the best spot and then stabbed them deep beneath her skin again and again.

He pushed his venom until he knew it had finally reached her heart.

Cristina had jumped back to life and was clinging to him, embracing him; the burning of the venom would burn and sting until it filled her entire body mixing with her blood, killing her. He held her to him pushing as much venom into her as he could. The pain would last until his venom reached her brain and then she would lose consciousness again. She would die. And then his venom would change her. She would come back to life reborn.

When her body went totally and utterly limb, like death had finally taken her, he savored her blood that had pooled in his mouth. He licked her wounds clean with more venom, and cleaned up as much of the mess as he could. If it had been any other women he probably wouldn't have been able to hold back, the way her body smelled and tasted, it was already driving him crazy. The monster in him wanted to morbidly drink every drop. Cristina's blood tasted rich, and sweet. Her skin held a salty taste of sweat. Licking his lips and fangs clean he smelled her neck to make sure she was changing and smelled his venom all throughout her body. Listened as her heart pumped her new mixed blood of vampire and human dna through her broken body, changing it forever. Her wounds were closing now from him cleaning them with his venom.

Cristina in so many ways was now his. He felt such empathic pride in that knowledge looking at her, wrapping her tighter in his arms he rocked her. He had never had visions until he had met Cristina. When she walked into a room, he could see himself wrapped in her arms, could see her life played out with him. In his bed, with his family, walking his land hand in hand with him. But she had always been a vampire in those dreams, and he had never gone through with the visions.

Now that his venom was inside of her, he could see clearly what was to come.

Asher was standing outside the doors of what looked like a dungeon in the lower gullies of the Whitby mansion. Well he would have sworn it was a dungeon anyways, not that he knew what one looked like. The dripping wet stone, cold rock walls that were at least twenty or so feet above him, the massive wood beams that held the floors he had walked on earlier upstairs. The fact that this place existed in Luna Pier frightened him more. He kept trying to tell himself that they didn't sleep in coffins, they didn't turn into bats, and they didn't play with their food down here. Getting used to living with vampires was scary, but interesting.

"Well, sometimes we do." This from Jordy who had set up post next to Asher along the wall.

Realizing Jordy was referring to them playing with their food down here made Asher cringe. Asher would have nudged him in the side like he did his own brothers, but Asher was sure it wouldn't have the effect he intended it to.

Jordy nudged Asher with enough force to send him toppling over, then Jeremy who was on the other side tipped him back up with a chuckle.

Jeremy told him when he righted himself "I only play with my food when no one is looking." Then he flashed him a smile. Fangs and all.

Asher looked straight ahead then, trying his best to think of how to get them back. He was going to have to talk to Izzy. She could help him with that. There must be a way to play with vampires.

He felt Jordy go still next to him and wondered what was the cause just as Emie came forward and threw herself through the doors in front of him still screaming at Joseph like she had been doing behind the doors.

Damn but she was beautiful when she was angry, Asher thought to himself thinking she looked better in his fire t-shirt then he did.

"I told you NO Joseph! NO! Not yes, or even maybe! I screamed NO loud and clear!"

Asher agreed with her. She really had. And wondered how Joseph was still standing there, like he wasn't listening to her with his head down and his hands in pockets. Asher's sisters could level a man with a glare like Emie's. He was glad Emie wasn't directing her anger towards him in that moment.

Both of the twins agreed with Asher in his mind. They didn't dare speak it aloud. It was a beautiful sight, yet the scariest thing he'd ever witnessed. She was shaking the whole house with her voice.

Emie turned to Asher at his latest thoughts. She was so angry at Joseph for doing this to Cristina. She'd forgotten Asher was still here. If he feared the towers falling earlier, shaking the house might not be a good idea. Even if it was working and Joseph was begging her stop.

"You didn't tell me no until afterwards." Joseph said shaking his finger at her. "You weren't there; you didn't see what they were doing to her. I didn't have a choice!"

"You didn't have a choice? What the hell were you doing there in the first place? You could have said something to me about all this, damn it! Before you did it!

"You didn't even tell me she was going to die." Emie was angry now. Her brothers had really messed up this time. Had Jordy known about this?

"You just fucking did it. You didn't even ask me Joseph! I found out from Jordy!" she turned and almost spat at Jordy. Emie shook, from the top of her head to ends of toes. She turned away from Jordy then, she couldn't look at him.

"She was my friend Joseph."

Asher perked up when he heard Emie curse. He had never heard her curse before.

Jeremy laughed in his mind at that. Only when she's really mad man. And watch out, she gets colorful with it.

Asher wasn't surprised by that all. Everything Emie did was colorful.

"You know Em," and this Joseph told her in a quieter voice. "If she meant that damn much to you, then why didn't you ask us a year ago to take care of her, you just bloody left. While you were out soul searching, I was here, protecting her."

Emie rounded on him then, anger flared inside of her.

Even Asher flinched when she spun around. If she hadn't slapped him for all he had said to her, surely she would slap Joseph for that.

"How dare you!" She couldn't believe him! He told her not only a day ago that he understood why she had left.

Joseph huffed at her. "No, you don't get to bloody say that to me! You don't know the hell I went through, or the hell all of us went through. You don't get to walk back in here now and tell us what to bloody do. She's mine now Emie!"

"Hell? You went through hell?"

Uh-oh. Asher knew that look, that tone. Joseph was about to lose.

"I'm sorry, I seem to remember all the times you and those two bloody idiots over there didn't give a flying fuck about me when it came to your own needs." She said crossing her arms in front of her not looking at the two men in question. "How many times have you three went gallivanting around this planet, doing God only knows what, while I sat here and fucking trusted you all?" She stepped closer to Joseph now, determined to make him pay for what all he had said and done tonight.

She lowered her voice now. "After all you've done, how dare you question me now. And after all I've done for you guys, you three can go fuck up your lives any fucking way you want! But when you start messing with me and the things that are mine! You better start kissing your own asses goodbye; I'm not going to bloody stand for it anymore."

Asher was thoroughly impressed now. He didn't like it, not one bit, and would be sure now never to raise her temper like Joseph had done. But damn, she was sexy as hell. And that British accent she had always got excited about sure as hell came rushing out of her when she was angry.

Joseph rubbed his head then. Emie was mad. She was really mad. And for the life of him he didn't know why. He'd saved Cristina's life, why was she so mad at him?

True, they had all done stuff like she was saying. But they had all kept in touch with her in some way or another.

"Tell me right now Em. I'm not going to do this anymore! Why are you so angry?"

Emie tried, she really did. But her brother was right. They needed to stop. She wanted to holler more, she wanted to scream at him more.

But she couldn't tell him all the reasons why he couldn't do this to Cristina, why they couldn't be together. She had to turn from her brother and try to hide it from.

"Will you tell me why already?"

Emie turned around again at his question.

Joseph had been asking this question over and over for the last hour. Emie would tirade on without answering him. Explaining how many different ways why this was bad, but not why she was so adamant against her best friend now being a vampire. She should be happy, Joseph thought, but Emie wasn't, she was visibly shaken and disturbed.

It didn't make sense to him. Cristina had been more then willing-

Emie stared Joseph down then. Reading his thoughts about how he'd liked Cristina all along was not helping the matter right now. He'd kept his feelings for her best friend hidden from her all this time. He still didn't get it.

"Who's going to take care of her right now Joseph? You?" Emie shook her head trying not to think about why he couldn't. She rubbed her head that started hurting again, and said "Damn it all!" out loud.

"Are you gonna train her, stay with her? What about all that talk about a storm coming?" Emie didn't have the time Cristina needed right now. She'd just gotten Asher back... She wanted to throw up her hands in the air, she was so frustrated.

Joseph looked at her then. He had rarely used his abilities on his family, but he had to now with her. He had to make her see. She had to stop fighting with him. "Tell me. Right now."

Emie tried to stand her ground. Joseph's powers, when they finally hit, could do damage. She was useless against him now. Her mind went blank and Joseph was there inside of her, making her see his will.

She'd been a miserable friend over the last year to Cristina. She'd left for a place to hide and had left Cristina to fend for herself here. Alone. She'd broken her promise to her... Emie could see all that Joseph was showing her now. All the days Cristina had spent alone here in this city where she knew no one but Emie's family. All the problems that had arose in her life that Joseph had neatly taken care of. She could see all the phone calls between them, all the text messages.

Emie turned around ashamed. She had to leave last year. She knew now it had been wrong, but none of them had been in her own skin then.

Why she hadn't thought about Cristina and all her needs, Emie didn't know. And she was ashamed of that now.

Joseph took Emie in his arms then. They had been fighting for too long. He'd broken through finally. She finally saw what he had been trying to tell her all along. Emie had been so busy loving Asher that she forgot to look around and see what else was going on. Life and death were happening. And they all needed her. Including Asher.

He tried one other thing while he still had her in his grasp. He showed her how much they all loved her. She always thought they didn't love her, that they didn't care about her. She'd even said as much. But they did. He showed her now how much they did. "Do you understand now, baby girl?"

Emie needed to turn and walk away from her family. She couldn't let them see what else she was worried about. But it was Joseph's arms around her who wouldn't let her go, the comfort she had only felt in Asher's arms that brought her to tears, and her mind finally gave up and showed Joseph what it was she was so afraid of. What he needed to know now. If he loved her as much as he said he did, he would understand this then.

"Oh God."

Joseph's arms fell away from Emie and she knew he understood now. He stood behind her stunned into silence.

Asher nudged Jeremy. "What did I miss?" he asked.

"Cristina has a little boy at home. She won't be able to be his mother now that she is a vampire. Cristina is going to be pissed. This is fate far worse for her then death."

Emie turned back to her brothers. She wrapped her arms around herself. She needed to think, but she was running out of time. She looked at the four of them. They were the most important men in her life. She needed them right now to help her figure out what she should do.

"Neely is four years old. His father left Cristina when she told him she was pregnant and her parents made her move out on her own when they found out. When the father found out she was going to go through with the pregnancy against his will, he tried to kill her. She has been alone, running, on her own for four years now. Working to support her and her son. He means the world to her." Emie raised her hands and lowered them in a defeated sigh.

Emie knew how Cristina felt about Neely, the strong bond between them. "When Cristina wakes up, she will not be able to be his mother anymore.

"What will happen to Neely now? She won't be able to see him again. She won't be able to make the necessary arrangements for him Joseph!"

Joseph cut Emie off by grabbing her arms and holding her steady. "Why don't you go get him?" Joseph asked honestly. "They can disappear together. No one would ever know. We can keep him here and raise him for her until she's ready." Joseph was willing her to make sense of it. He wanted this life, for both of them. Emie would have to understand that, he wasn't about to give them up now. "The boy already knows you, right?"

Emie was stunned by all that. Stunned just to look at Joseph. Did he want Cristina that bad that he would take on her son as well? He'd always been the best parent anyone could be to the three of them, she thought as she looked into his eyes. He'd raised them with greatness and honor and respect for life. Given them everything he could in this life. He would be good for both Cristina and Neely. "What about this storm you keep talking about?" she eyed him questioningly.

Joseph stood up straight then. He sighed a sigh of relief knowing Emie had accepted it. "All the more reason why he should be here, with us. Right?"

Joseph silently told Emie he would be there for them from now on. He would help this boy become a man like his father should have done; help Cristina find her way in her new life. He would be there for them, just like he had been there for his family.

Asher seen Emie one second, then she was gone the next. Joseph was the one to tell him where she had gone.

"She's going to the day care center for Neely. Let's go upstairs. I need a drink."

Joseph knew now why Emie had been so mad. She was mad because she had thought he had done this out of his own pleasure. She thought Joseph had a choice. But he hadn't.

It would have been better for Cristina to die then to have to live with the knowledge she couldn't be a mother to her child anymore. He understood that now. Neely was still small. Just a child. He would need his mother. He would need her to hold him, to talk to him, teach him.

Cristina was going to hate them all soon. She will want her son, she will want to see him and be with him. But she won't be able too for a long while. And she was going to kill anyone who tried to stop her.

~ Twenty Six ~

Emie was laying tangled up in Asher's arms in her bed. Asher couldn't sleep. So much had changed in their lives. So much more was about to change.

The sun had risen bright and early that morning, like all their lives hadn't changed a bit, and life still went on without them, all around them.

Asher was learning to love that.

Emie was thinking about Asher having to leave soon for work. She could hear him thinking about it. How was he going to return to reality like this? Knowing how much the world had changed for him, she wondered.

Everything Jordy was sharing with them was haunting both of their nights. Emie was so upset by the thought that these fallen vampires, or whomever they were, they were now so close to home. Attacking people's lives and homes. Wreaking havoc on this earth that no one had seen coming or could prepare for. What other damage had they caused, she wondered.

She hated them for it. She hated what they had done to her friend, what they were doing to her city. What they were about to do to her world around her.

Emie thought about Cristina. Her bright smile. Her laugh. Her scattered thoughts that all made sense, sometimes... She wondered if Cristina would carry all the same traits with her now into her new life. She hoped and prayed her friend would make it through this. Some vampires could never overcome the want and need for blood. Other vampires would have to take them out. Everyone's lives depended on the secrecy of the humans never discovering that vampires existed.

Emie wouldn't let that happen to Cristina. She wouldn't. She loved her too much. Cristina would overcome it. She was a good person at heart. She was goofy and funny and witty, everything Emie had craved and missed while she was gone this last year. She really couldn't wait to spend more time with her new and improved friend.

Joseph had taken her by surprise earlier. His desire for Cristina had been so strong. He had ignored it for years and Emie had never seen it. She couldn't help but wonder why though. Why had he hid his feelings from her of Cristina?

Had it been Emie's love for Asher that had changed his mind? Had their love for each other made him want the same thing in his own life? Why was he having thoughts of loving Cristina now? Joseph had so much on his mind lately; she wondered if this was his way of distracting himself from it all like Asher had with her. Or was it this damn war coming that had brought his true feelings for her to life.

Cristina had met Joseph once or twice, maybe more in the past, she wasn't sure anymore. Cristina too had taken Emie by surprise. Cristina had thought Joseph was handsome in the past. Emie had thought then that it had been all the stories the girl read about. Vampires were a common thought in Cristina's head as of late. She had seen right through Emie's lies when they had first met.

Emie smiled remembering Cristina's thoughts. Why didn't Emie eat or drink? Why had she never seen Emie in the sunlight? Why wouldn't Emie talk about her childhood?

Emie had been good at hiding all that. But one day Cristina had tricked her and told her she had blood dripping down her mouth. Emie had been so frightened she had flown from the room. Cristina had laughed and kept right on tapping away on her keyboard. Emie had read her thoughts and seen that she was just teasing Emie. Emie had wanted a friend for so long; she didn't even try to lie to her. Cristina's unspoken promise of silence had been enough for her. They had been best friends ever since.

Emie now just couldn't imagine what they were going to do with Neely. Not a clue.

She had told the day care worker she was taking Neely home for Cristina. When the authorities would find the dead men in Cristina's office they would just assume Cristina had run away with Neely in fear for her family.

The Luna Pier Police knew Cristina had been on the run from her family, and always watching out for Neely's father. They would just assume she had run off.

The world would have more things to worry about now once they discovered who those men really were. Cristina and Neely would never be seen or heard from again.

"There's just something about you Emie."

Asher had pulled Emie out of her thoughts completely then and neatly rolled her towards him. Emie let go of her worries then. Everything would work itself out. Somehow. For right now she had Asher all to herself.

"I remember everything about that first night. I remember what you wearing. What you smelled like. How you just took my breath away." Asher knew Emie was a million miles away from him in those quiet moments, but he had been thinking about her and needed her to see him. See his need for her.

"I didn't know how I was going to get you to talk me. How a girl like you could ever see a guy like me. I wanted you to see me so bad. I wanted you to want me." He told her this now because sometimes she didn't feel real. After everything that had happened the last few days, she still didn't. He was still waiting for someone to wake him up and it would all be some kind of cruel nightmare.

Stroking her face helped. Laying here in the early morning hours with her, naked under the covers, their bodies still heightened from their brief moments of love making that always seemed to pass too quickly for him; he felt like he was finally right where he was supposed to be. He'd never felt that way before. Telling her this just made it more real for him.

"Asher." She could see what he meant, but he was still so clueless to how she had felt about him, and that frustrated him. He had so much to learn about her, it almost wasn't fair.

Emie laid half across his chest staring up at him. "That night, I saw you first." When he questioned her she continued. "I watched you lay at the foot of Curtis's bed. I wanted to stroke your hair and comfort you. I saw you come in the elevator before you saw me. I knew who you were. I'd known who you were since the day you were born." She was close to his face now, stroking his cheek like he had hers. "I just had to wait for you to see me. I had to wait to love you, to be loved by you."

It took him by surprise, their feelings for each other. They had both always felt them for each other. Even when they hadn't known each other, they had felt it. Felt that there was someone out there, someone just for them. On that night when they finally saw each other for the first time, they knew. They knew who they were supposed to be. They knew who they had been meant for. Each other.

Love truly did exist at first sight.

Asher rolled onto Emie, no longer feeling quiet so lonely, no longer quiet so unsettled. She loved him, and he would love her for the rest of his life.

Asher took Emie's face in one hand as his body laid down between her legs. She had opened up the sheets for him to climb in and he rolled unto her, her hands had instantly ran down his back and hips as he kissed her and found their own way down the mounds of his butt. She squeezed gently on his right cheek. Gently while he made love to her mouth and slid himself inside her body, she softly dragged her nails up and down his butt with every thrust of his hips.

When she finally broke his kiss and pushed her head back into her pillow calling out to him moaning, he thrusted deeper, making her body quiver. She was wrapping her legs and arms tightly around him, begging him for more.

Asher stopped before he lost all control, holding Emie. He felt her perfect ability seep into his heart and bones. He loved it when she did this for him.

"Emie?" he questioned in her ear, letting her see what it was he was asking her to do.

Emie knew the stories of vampires seductively biting humans. She had seen the movies and had never wanted to do that to anyone. But what Asher was asking her now, she wanted to do it for him.

She giggled out loud at his thoughts while he kissed her neck.

Emie was hesitant at first. Could she do what he was asking for? Could she follow the scent of his veins, find that one spot that not only turned him on, but would allow her access to his blood without killing him?

Smelling in his neck while he was kissing her and continuing to thrust inside of her was throwing her over the edge. She found the spot she was looking for. His body responded as she drug her fangs against his shoulder and back to his neck. It was a spot just above his collar bone. Not too close to his jugular, but close enough that his blood would flow freely for her to sip on. His cock inside her twitched with anticipation. He wanted this just as much as she did.

Moaning his name and marking the spot with an indent of her teeth, she licked his neck and kissed it, running her hands all over his body driving him insane inside his mind for her. His blood was boiling inside of him making his body perspire and his temperature rise temptingly.

Asher knew it was coming. Knew the moment she would pierce his skin and welcomed it. The bite felt painful as he thrust once more inside of her. She cried out so loud against the thrust of his body she had to close her mouth over him just to silence her screams. His body responded to it like any other time she touched his body. He wanted to feel this like he had wanted to feel the inside of her body. She suckled from him slow enough that the pain faded and only the squeeze of her around him would drive him deeper inside her.

He kissed her, touched her everywhere. Died every time she moaned his name. Gave her ecstasy. Sent her body over the edge and back again. Until his body couldn't stand the intimate pleasures of her no longer, and gave himself the one pleasure every man searches his whole life for. Release inside of a beautiful goddess who holds the keys to his heart and soul. Who knows just when to open it for him so he can show her his ever present need for her in his life, in his heart, so he can mate his soul with hers.

Emie was his beautiful goddess. She was his whole world. And it felt so good to just let go of everything and fall into her. Melt into her body and lose himself in her. He became part of her that night, even though they were worlds apart from one another.

She was his vampire, and he was her hero.

Emie spent the day without Asher. He had went to work that morning, kissing her goodbye like they had been doing it for years instead of just the few days they had been back together. She watched out her bedroom windows as he pulled down the drive followed by Joseph who would let him out the back gates that would take him back into his world.

Luna Pier. The city he would fight for and defend till his dying days.

Emie headed down to the basement where Cristina was, she needed to check on her progress and see how she was doing. But Joseph was already there, so Emie spent the whole day with Neely, letting him ride a bike inside the house so he could learn his way around.

Joseph had been calling in orders for Neely's favorite foods to be delivered, and enough toys to open his own toy store. Joseph had said all day, "Only the best for this little guy." winning over Neely's heart. Joseph had even hired a crew to come in and install a bathroom on each floor for their new human guests. Asher included.

Finally that evening, when the rest of the house was busy, Emie went down to check on Cristina. Entering the doors of what Asher had called the 'dungeon' just the night before; Emie felt the chill in the air from the height, and damp coolness of the stone walls. Cristina was sitting at an old table, chained up to a chair.

Emie sighed at the top of the stairs. Cristina was a mess. Her head was in her hands, her damp long brown hair hanging down all around her. She hadn't even looked up to acknowledge that someone had walked into the room. She looked defeated, Emie thought.

Emie walked over to her and sat in the chair next to her. She waited for Cristina to lift her head and listened into her thoughts. Cristina was so distraught all she could think about was Neely.

"Where is he Emie?" Cristina said, finally lifting her head off the table, looking blankly at Emie.

"He's upstairs. Safe. I cleaned out your house and brought everything here for him."

Cristina sighed. Her body still thinking she needed the air. It would take time for the old habits of the body to stop. Relaxing on its own without the old habits took practice.

She looked up at Emie, tears of blood still dripping from her eyes had stained her face.

"I need to see him Emie. I need to know he's ok."

Emie loved Cristina so much she wanted to bend to her will, but looking at the monster she had become, she knew it wasn't what Cristina really wanted. Wasn't what Neely needed.

"You might want to look in the mirror first sweetie."

Cristina stared at her friend. "How do I do this Emie? I just want to die!" Cristina said on a cry that ripped through the walls and was sure to have been heard up stairs.

Emie reached for her hand, but Cristina pulled away. It hurt Emie, she needed Cristina just as much as she needed her.

"You will get through this. I promise. I'm going to help you. You will grow strong. You will overcome the powers. You're just gonna have to trust us."

"How long?" Cristina screamed. She looked wild, her thirst was making her sweat.

Emie walked over to the cellar walls. She took down a bottle of blood they kept stored down here, two wine glasses, and returned to her place next to Cristina.

She poured the two glasses full of blood, and watched as Cristina licked her lips in anticipation. Her disgust and revulsion she had been feeling this morning with Joseph long gone away.

Emie did this out of habit to remind herself, her own monster, that this was how she took the blood civilly. They didn't drink from humans or animals. This how they ate, this is how they drank. This, was how they survived. If anything it made her feel more like a human.

She pushed Cristina's glass closer to her. Cristina had never watched Emie do this before. But she watched Emie now, learned how it was done. It filled her with hope for the future. She slowly sipped from her glass and savored the drink.

"Oh, please. There's plenty. Drink up. You know you want too." Emie winked at her and encouraged her.

Cristina laughed and downed her glass. Emie poured them both another.

"I have a question for you sweetie."

Cristina looked at her questioningly.

"Have you noticed anything different about you? Besides the obvious?"

"Like reading minds, you mean?"

"Yeah." Emie was worried about the powers and abilities they all had. The boys could pass through walls, read minds, Joseph could even make you do things he wanted. What would be Cristina's gift, she wondered.

Cristina had been so quick witted and funny. She was flirtatious, beautiful and adorably shy when she was out of her element. But Cristina had charm, and Emie loved that about her.

"No. I can't hear you, or Joseph. I do feel very strong though."

Emie smiled at that. That came with the new body. Along with perfect sight and hearing, a very keen sense of everything around them.

"You're still new. It's only been twenty four hours." Emie shrugged.

"I was hoping for something cool, like being able to disappear into a ghost or even a bat." She smiled, downing another glass.

Emie chuckled at that. Cristina also loved to watch all the new superhero movies. Her favorite was the one about the bat. She even had the bat symbol tattooed on her foot.

"Never know." Emie winked.

They sat in silence for some time. Something they had always done. Cristina thought about everything, and Emie listened.

"So what's going on with Joseph, he seems very… tentative."

Emie choked on her drink. She didn't want to be the one to tell her that Joseph had feelings for her.

"Well, he was the one who had to do it to you. It was hard for him to make that decision without asking you first. And, there is a bond there, when we turn someone. You and Joseph will have a bond now like we all do towards each other."

Cristina nodded at that.

"When can I clean up? Get out of here? I don't know how much longer I can stay down here with that girl."

Emie's senses immediately went up. "What girl?"

"The one over there." Cristina turned her head and looked back at the cell behind them. "Who is she anyways? I thought you all didn't play with your food?" She smirked back at Emie.

Emie stood immediately. There shouldn't be anyone else down here. She walked over to an old abandon cell they used to store things in. Never to hide a body in.

 Inside she seen a young girl curled on the floor. Her long golden curls were laying all around her, her clothes were tattered and torn.

Who was she, Emie wondered worriedly? What was she doing down here alone?

The girl raised her head and looked up at Emie.

"Who are you?" Emie asked, in breathless voice, as she knelt down in front of the door to her cell.

The girl hissed, her golden curls falling around her face revealed a beautiful young women. Her eyes were as red as any vampire. Her fangs were bared to Emie now. Her face looked familiar, Emie couldn't quite put her finger on who she resembled.

"Izzy." Came a voice so steady and young from within.

Emie watched in horror as Izzy hung her head low and laid her head back on the stone cold floor. Her head snapped back up to the stairs when she heard Jordy enter through the double doors.

"Emie, listen." Jordy started.

"Listen?" Emie screamed in a monstrous voice, standing straight up. "No Jordy. No! I am beyond listening!" Emie looked back at Izzy. She had stood up to her full height now that Jordy was here.

Jordy rushed to Emie's side. He was holding onto the wall next to the cell with one hand, looking pleadingly at Emie. "You don't understand Emie. I had-"

"Had!" Emie bellowed. "You had to do this? Why does everyone keep saying that?

"How could you have possibly HAD no other choice then to turn Asher's SISTER into one of us?" Her hands were on her hips now, and her voice had risen to a degree she was sure it never had before. Anger, bright red venomous anger surged through her.

"I didn't do this Emie! I didn't turn her." Jordy now was angry too. He pointed his finger at Emie. "I have been trying to get your attention for over a year now! Trying to tell you I had seen things, horrible things. And now that it's happening all around you, you want answers and some one to blame. Well, I'm sorry sister, your not pinning the blame on me for her.

"Your best friend over there was attacked by two rouge vampires. Your lover's brother died because three other vampire's were burning this city down around us, and still are!

"While you were gone soul searching this last year, we have been cleaning up the mess and trying to warn you. And now, now his sister's life has been taken. How many others will have to pay before you realize that we can't just sit around and play house anymore?" Jordy stood tall next to his sister. His older sister who he loved and respected, who even scared him at times. But he had to get through to her. He had to make her understand. This was bigger now then all of them.

And understood she did.

Sickeningly, Emie looked back into the cell where Asher's little sister was standing. She had a pleading hungry look on her now.

Emie sighed greatly. She couldn't believe she had been so foolish. This was all her fault.

"How did this happen?"

"The night of the storm." Jordy relaxed a little, but he was dying to take Izzy out of the cell. He wanted to hold her. But Asher had been staying in the house, and now Neely was roaming around. He couldn't take the chance of her seeing or worse smelling them. Izzy was still hungry.

"She was out alone on the beach in that old tree of yours out next to the canal just before the storm hit."

Emie's head hung low as she too leaned onto the walls next to the cell for support. She had been so lost that night. If Jordy had tried to get her attention, would she have listened?

"There were maybe four or five vampires out hunting in the city that night. They drained their victims and left them for dead."

Emie for the first time ever since she had been turned felt dizzy. Asher had been out there that night during this frenzy. He could have easily been one of the victims.

"I found Izzy during an attack. Four of them had already bitten her countless times. I think they had been stalking her and choose her. She had been reading her books that night.

"Emie listen, they weren't trying to feed on her, they were changing her." Jordy said this last pleading with her to understand.

Emie sighed deeply. "How is she doing?"

"She has more venom in her veins then any of us do. She has an unknown amount of power in her. She's been struggling, but she's doing better now today though. But it's going to be a long time before she can even function without our help."

Izzy had been missing for four days already. Emie covered her mouth in terror. It hit her like a ton of bricks. Asher's family had to of known she was missing by now. They were probably out looking for her right now.

"When is the last time any of us has watched the news Jordy?"

"I don't, why?"

Emie looked up at Jordy and knew they were missing something. If that many vampires had hunted in the city that night, there was sure to be a lot of bodies lying around. And with three people missing, they were sure to have made the news and attracted attention. And if this had been going on in other cities too…

Emie suddenly remembered the night of the storms. Dundee had been hit harder than any other city around. Fire men had been calling out for help. What had happened there that night?

She was suddenly overcome with fear for Asher. He hadn't had his radio on him, or his phone since that night. If anyone had tried to get a hold of him, he wouldn't have known. He had been on their side of the city, and none of his friends or family knew where he had been.

He had already been away from her for twelve hours. What all had he encountered? Had his family informed him that Izzy was missing? Was he out looking for her alone?

"Stay here with them Jordy. Talk to them, teach them, and train them. Whatever you have to do. We must get them out of here as soon as we can."

Jordy watched as his sister ran up the stairs. She understood now. Good. He felt more relieved now then he had in a long time.

Emie was headed up to find Joseph now who would know what to do. Turning to the two women in the room with him he shuddered.

"You know she's going to kill you when she finds out you're in love with Asher's little sister, right?" Cristina said from her table, she looked like her old self again. Her legs were crossed and she was sipping from a glass like she had been drinking a fine wine. Swirling it around and around in the glass as she spoke to him.

Jordy looked at her in question. "How do you know?"

"Emie may be blind to all of you and what all you do around here, but I could see the way you were looking at Izzy. You've been looking at her like that every time you come down here." She told him as she took another sip and winked at him.

Jordy opened the cell door for Izzy who stepped out and rushed into Jordy's arms. "Bite me Cristina!"

What Emie doesn't know never hurt her before he thought to himself as he kissed the love of his life. His problem wasn't going to be Emie. He could handle this inevitable war that was coming. What he couldn't handle was when Asher finds out. When he finally would... that was something that had Jordy thinking about running. And Jordy never ran from anything.

Twenty Seven

The Luna Pier fire department sat right in the heart of the city. You couldn't miss it when you rolled down the main street at the 25 mile an hour speed. If you did, you were driving too fast and were in danger of being pulled over by the local police that guarded the city.

Luna Pier was a city where the 19,600 citizens could walk down the bike paths of Harold drive down to Water Tower Park with their kids and animals to enjoy all the park had to offer and where people drove their cars laden down with beach supplies for a day on the lake down to the sandy beach off the pier. Where the fishermen fished off the pier on sunny morning, and the moonlit evenings. Barbecues filled the air, late night bonfires and even fireworks were a nightly occurrence. Where boaters launched their boats for a day of sailing and boating. Canoes and kayaks could be seen in the canals and along the beachfront. Jet skis and rafting could be heard and seen all summer long. Sail boats colored the lake in the distance from the shore.

Two caf 's were on the beach within walking distance. A hot dog stand that sat under the beach lighthouse, where swimmers showered off so they wouldn't get sand in their dogs. Many would head over and get specialty drinks or ice cream at the Luna cafe to help cool off in the hot summer sun. A dance hall sat adjacent to the pier that served burgers and fries and pop. At night it was the place to be for young people.

Asher was sitting on a metal blue bench on the long cement pier that stretched a half a mile into Lake Erie. He had done this all his life when he was younger, with his brothers; fishing off the pier dreaming about his future, and when just a year ago he had been out here dreaming about his future with Emie.

Now all of those dreams, everything this city was, was going up in smoke. People weren't walking down the city streets or on the pier. There were no swimmers out in the lake in front of him. He had noticed on his drive out here that even the parks were empty where on a sunny day like today would have been filled with children playing on the playgrounds, some playing catch or tag in the grass. All he could see for miles around him was an empty city.

His fire radio on his side was calling out to surrounding departments. Many cities around them were fighting more fires than ever before. He cringed every time Monroe Dispatch called someone out for a medical call where a victim was found bleeding out of unknown wounds, or a deceased victim had been found.

Asher shook his head. There had been so many today. Knowing what he knew now of these rogue vampires, he couldn't help but worry about getting one of those calls here in town. He tried to think of how he would handle seeing a body sucked dry of all it's life. Seeing the fangs marks. He didn't know how to handle it.

What would he tell the family? What would he say to his men who looked up to him for direction?

For the moment, his city was safe. No one was hurt or dying. Houses weren't smoking or endanger of flaming over. Cars and semi's were moving smoothly on the expressway. Life was moving on, slower, and more cautiously.

All was well here… for the moment anyways.

It hadn't been like this in the last few days he had spent with Emie. Three more houses had burnt to the ground. While everyone was trying to recover from the storms and all the damage that was done, more problems were arising.

The atmosphere around the city had changed. The world was changing. People were afraid now. No one really knew what they were afraid of; the news reports were vague at best. People were going missing by the thousands. Bodies were being found with bite marks no one could explain. Homes, hell, whole cities where going up in flames.

Jerry was investigating the deaths of the three families that had perished in those homes, and also the deaths of two men and four women who had died the night of the storms. Jerry told him secretly earlier that he was calling in the FBI. These weren't normal deaths. Something, like everywhere else in the world, was amiss.

It was a sunny day at the end of June. Emie couldn't be out here with him now, but he knew she was in the back of his mind somewhere following him around throughout his day. He would give anything to see her right now. To be in her peaceful presence.

Asher had to shake his head at his playful thoughts.

After going home and changing, letting his dog out and smoking on the pier before going to work, Asher had started off his morning at the fire hall by sitting in the meeting room surrounded by his men in front of the HD television watching as the media reported all the latest breaking news. His men had been worried; they had voiced their concern with talk of leaving the city and bunking down with family or friends, riding this out. Asher's concern had been for his family and friends living here within the city. They all came to the same conclusion. Life still needed to go on. Work, which seemed never ending to him, needed to be done.

How was he supposed to keep everyone safe when he didn't have a clue how to keep them safe? From what he had learned of vampires, there was no protection from them. His own heart wasn't even safe from them.

Talking with Jerry hadn't helped. He was planning on bringing in more reinforcements. The FBI would be here snooping around. What Joseph had said about protecting Emie from people like them scared him now. What if they knew about vampires? What if they were actively hunting them? What if they found Emie? How would he protect her from them?

He had walked out to the pier to get away from it all for a moment. Hoping he could try to clear his mind and think. It wasn't working.

Thoughts of Emie filled his mind as he sat there on the bench cross legged. She was everything he had wanted in a woman. She was everything he needed.

A thought entered his mind about marriage. It was the next oblivious step in a normal relationship. He could see himself talking to his mother about it. Getting her approval would be easy, and then he would go shopping for the perfect ring for Emie. Then he would have to-

Asher's phone started to buzz in his pocket. He looked down and noticed it was Emie.

He was so excited to hear from her, but he had been thinking things he didn't want her to hear. He was glad to know she had just texted him and not entered his mind, or whatever it was she could do.

"Asher, Joseph is waiting for you at the fire hall." She said in a text message.

"I'd rather see you." he said to her.

"Soon my love, soon." She replied sweetly to him.

"What does the big bad vampire want now?" he asked patiently looking back down the road towards the fire hall.

"He won't tell me; just that he needs to talk to you."

Asher sighed. "Alrighty then. I love you Emie". He told her, looking one last time out over the water, meaning it with all his heart.

"Asher, I love you." Emie stated proudly.

Asher breathed in and breathed out. He would finish this day out like he had been doing and go home to her. Joseph and Emie would help him figure out what to do. How to protect this city and his family. Everything would work out. He may lose his heart to one vampire, but he'd be damned if he lost anything else to another.

Joseph was sitting in the little chief's room just off the meeting area waiting for Asher. Looking around the fire hall when he walked in Joseph was looking for small details that would help with his plan. But he couldn't get past the fact that this fire department needed so many

new updates. He'd failed to see it before, when Asher's father Frank had asked for more money all those years ago to remodel the old fire hall that was built in the 70's. Joseph had bigger plans then for the hospital and the city buildings all these years. He'd never given much thought to the fire hall.

He hadn't been in the fire hall in decades. It needed updates that would never come in time. These men, Asher included, had done without the basic necessities he head failed to give them.

Asher walked into the office just as Joseph was considering taking another look around since the firemen were out running errands and seeing to the fueling of the fire trucks.

Asher took a seat across from Joseph, taking his radio and cell phone off his belt, along with keys in his pocket that were too big for him to sit down with on the desk in front of him, wondering why in Hell Joseph hadn't warned him of the recent events going on around the city before he came to work this morning.

Joseph shook his head at Asher's thoughts. Asher didn't want the new responsibility of acting Chief. He never had. His shoulders slumped as he sat at the desk. The desk that was too small for a man of Asher's stature. He sank in a chair that was so old it creaked under his weight.

"So, how can I help you Joseph?" Asher asked, accidentally bumping his computer mouse that brought his PC to life. He noticed the number at the bottom of the screen as he scooted his chair closer to his desk, he had 13 new unread emails to go through today. Asher sighed and looked at over at Joseph waiting for his reply.

"I have some very important issues you and I need to discuss." Joseph could see no point in making small talk. Asking Asher how he was doing seemed irrelevant at the moment, there was much that needed to be discussed and very little time to do it in.

This Asher knew was somewhat late in the coming.

"First, we need to discuss Emie. There is something I think you should know. Something Jordy has been sharing with Jeremy and I, we need your help with." Joseph knew he had Asher complete attention now. It was a discussion that Asher had been looking forward too. He had a lot of questions that needed answers.

"Emie's abilities to be able to control the human mind is a valuable, vulnerable and somewhat dangerous ability. As far as I know there are no other vampires with these abilities like our families. One of the reasons we live in seclusion here. But what Emie is able to do is unlike anything we can do. To her it is useful when she helping someone or easing their pain, or like when she was first turned into a vampire, she was able to hide herself amongst a crowd until she learned how to be one of them again. Her ability in the wrong hands, Asher, well, it could be very dangerous."

As Joseph went on, Asher could see his meaning. If there was a rouge group of vampires out there who discovered what Emie could do, they could use her to accomplish whatever it was they were planning to do. He could just picture what her abilities could do now for the first time in the wrong hands.

"Jordy has seen something in the near future he can't explain. He has seen it since he was very young but none of us really understood it till now. He's been piecing together his visions and this is what he is afraid of."

Asher didn't like the sound of that. "Is she in any kind of danger I should know about?" Asher questioned out of fear.

Joseph promised Emie he wouldn't push this on Asher, but seeing his reaction to their fear and knowing he felt the same as they did, only made Joseph want to tell him more. "We believe there is a vampire rebellion going on. It is pretty obvious now. Either with or without the help of humans, they are moving fast, and taking over cities and countries. If they know of our family, we stand to lose everything."

"So what do you need me to do?" the question weighing on his mind.

"We need you to make a decision, quickly I might add, where you stand with us. This thing going on around the world is here. In the US, in Michigan, and as you've learned today, in this city."

Asher understood now why he hadn't told him this before. He needed to see it for himself.

"We need to go into deeper seclusion. But, with recent events between you and Emie, she has made you apart of this family, I'm sure you will need time to get your affairs and family in order."

Asher knew what he meant. If Emie needed to be in seclusion, he needed to go with her, but he couldn't leave his family and friends behind to fend for themselves right now.

Asher leaned back and folded his arms. He needed to think as he looked out the door of his office into the meeting room behind him. People started going through his mind one at a time, Ken and Miranda, their girls, his parents, his brothers and sisters. They needed him right now.

"Your father is going to be here soon, so I need to make this quick."

"My father?" Asher questioned, placing his head in his hand and squeezing his temples so hard his eyes shut. His father was the last person Asher wanted to see today. His lecture about what all Asher should and shouldn't be doing would end up coming to emotional blows that Asher didn't want to have with his father.

"You've been watching the news I take it?"

Asher shook his head in his hand in agreement. He wished Joseph would just get to his point; he had so many questions now that

Joseph was sitting here in front of him without Emie. He looked up to see Joseph studying him.

Joseph eyed Asher; the man should know better then to ask him anything he didn't want Emie to know. More than likely she already knew, he thought.

"I need to talk to you about your family. There's something you need to know." Joseph said in an authoritative voice. He placed his hands on his legs and straightened up in his chair. Asher needed to understand the importance of his visit. Joseph would have to lead Asher in the direction he wanted the conversation to go.

He had been thinking about doing this ever since it happened. He wanted to judge Asher's reaction for himself. He wanted to tell Asher about Curtis. He wanted to reunite them, but first he had to see how Asher handled the news about Izzy first.

Asher looked at him hopefully. He had prayed Joseph would be able to help him with his family. Maybe even help them escape if need be.

"Your sister, Izzy is missing Asher. She's been missing since the storms the other night. That's why your father is coming." He waited for that to set in. Asher was going to need a minute to grasp it.

Izzy was missing. Asher's arms were braced on the desk ready to stand up.

"No. Not really. But everyone thinks she is."

Asher's stared at Joseph, then angrily said "Don't play games with me Joseph." Asher knew he should be doing something. Calling his mom, calling Jerry the chief of police. Something. What did Joseph want from him right now that was more important than finding Izzy?

"I'm not Asher. You need to listen to me. Your sister is safe. She's at our house." Joseph waited for Asher to visibly relax, then he gave him the blow he knew was going to hurt him. "She's in the dungeon."

Asher stood then.

"Just wait Asher. Let me finish." Joseph reached up a calming steady hand, willing Asher to relax and sit back down. They needed to hurry.

Asher was fuming, but he sat back down reluctantly when Joseph didn't say anymore. What had happened to her, what had they done to her, he wondered. He knew now what the dungeon was for. Not the horrid things he had thought vampires did with their prey, but for other things. It was where they held newborn vampires to wait out their change. Had they changed Izzy? Why?

Joseph shook his head. Emie wasn't kidding when she said Asher's mind moved as fast as theirs. He wondered quickly, eyeing Asher sheepishly, what Asher would be like if he too were to change.

So help me Joseph! This from Emie who he knew had been listening in on their conversation. He promised her before he wouldn't change Asher, and almost laughed out loud at her reaction.

"During the storms, as I'm sure you've already learned, the cities around Monroe County were attacked by vampires. Izzy was out on the beach reading and got caught up that night during the storm and was attacked. Jordy had seen it and tried to stop it, but there were too many vampires for him to fight alone. He saved her from them, but she had already been changed. He's been holding her down there helping her."

"Why wasn't I informed of this earlier?" Asher growled.

"Jordy was just too afraid to tell anyone what had happened. And for that I am sorry. He, we should have told you."

Asher's thoughts betrayed him. He wondered if Emie knew about this, but he quickly fought them off. He pushed back in his chair and tried to stomp down his anger. He knew now if she had kept anything from him it was to protect him.

"She just found out Asher. I swear this to you. Emie worried about you Asher. Our world is very different from the world you know. She still battles with her decision to tell you things." This he hoped would ease Asher's mind. His love for Emie was growing stronger everyday. "Unlike any time before in the past, our secret needs to be kept."

Asher loved her. No matter what she was. End of story. "I need to know everything Joseph. And I mean everything. You can't hold back any more. Whether it will hurt me or not, it is my decision. I understand why she doesn't want me to know, but you have to understand, I need to know. I need to know everything. And I need to know what to do. Right now."

Joseph sighed and sat back in his chair. He needed to tell Asher so much more. About his brother, his sister's care, what was going to happen in the next few days; but his father was on his way here. He had a plan in mind and hoped Asher could follow through with it.

There's more Asher. "Are you feeling ok?" he asked him aloud.

"Yes, why?" Asher questioned him quietly.

"You don't look so good. You should go home, get some rest." Then Joseph told him why. Your father is here Asher. He's right outside the door next to me now. He knows what I am, he's had his suspicions for years. With everything that's been happening has only confirmed them for him. I don't know how much he overheard, but he's not going to let you out of here until he gets answers. Answers I can't give him. If we leave together he won't stop me. He won't make a scene in front of the men.

Men who had conveniently chosen the right time to come back into the fire hall when Frank had.

Asher grabbed his cell phone and radio and stood up. "Your right. I think I need to go home." He wasn't about to face his father alone with everything that had just been said and there was no way he was going to stay here and listen to him berate him in front of the men.

When they walked out of the office, sure enough his father was standing right outside the door. His look of disdain was written all over his face for Joseph. For his son, he was enraged.

"Asher, we need to talk." Frank walked past both men and tried to steer Asher back into the office.

"I'll be back dad." Asher walked past his dad with Joseph headed for the back door where he could sneak Joseph out the back doors.

"Asher! Where are you going? I need to talk to you." His father pointedly called his son out. Everyone in the meeting room visibly stopped what they were doing.

Asher turned around to face his father. A feeling that he remembered entered his body, like that night he had spent with Emie on the beach, a pain killing emotion that he welcomed. He loathed his father in ways he couldn't explain, calling Asher out in front of the men had been the last straw. His father had only done this to him once or twice, and at the time Asher had just been a black hat. Now he was acting Chief because his father had succumbed to a lung ailment since the fire that had taken his brothers life.

If Joseph hadn't filled him with this numbing emotion, Asher was sure he would have gotten in his father's face and done something he would have regretted.

Or gave him a heart attack. Joseph chuckled.

"I have everything here done dad. You are not needed here right now, go home and be with mom."

"Your sister is missing! You keep disappearing! Where is your head at boy? With that girl?"

Asher was only two steps away from cussing his father out if it hadn't been for Joseph's persuasive hold on him. Instead Asher towered over his father and pointed his finger at him. "I have it all under control dad. Go home!"

Asher turned his back then and walked out with Joseph. His father needed to know that he knew about everything with Izzy, now he knew. He could hear his father coughing and mumbling something under his cough. He knew his father was going to hate him for it, he knew his mom was going to call him later and try to smooth this over for him, she always did whenever his father and Asher got into a disagreement, and then she would ask him a hundred questions, including what they wanted him to do about Izzy, but right now, he needed to be with Emie and her family. This fire hall and his men were just going to have to work without him for awhile.

He also needed to call Ken. Out of all the men here in department, his loyalty was to Ken and his wife and girls. Those girls were like his own. They called him uncle and they depended on him. Asher needed to find Ken, but first he needed to ask Joseph.

With Izzy and Cristina now turned by vampires he just couldn't sit around and wait for another attack. Joseph felt the same as he did, he was sure of it.

What he hadn't expected, was to walk in the Whitby mansion and find his dead brother standing there in the midst of the great hall entrance.

Twenty Eight

"Curtis." Asher breathed in a whisper they all could hear.

"Asher." Curtis tried to console his little brother who looked like he was seeing a ghost after he had shut the main door behind him. He walked towards his brother closing the distance with his hand up reaching towards Asher.

Heat. Pure ruthless anger, mixed with hot flames that boiled in side of Asher's blood turned his skin a deep reddish color.

Joseph, Shelley, Jeremy and Jordy seen it and stood in complete silence and awe of Asher. They made a mental note to share their feelings later about this. In the meantime they needed to help him.

Emie noticed it too. She could smell the change in him and was surprised he wasn't smoking through his skin; the heat that radiated through him could be felt over by the stairs where she had been standing. Emie was at Asher's side in just one of his heart beats.

Emie had greeted Shelley and Curtis just moments ago unexpectedly in the main hall. One minute they are explaining to her why they were here, the next, Asher was walking in through the front doors. She had thought she was feeling overwhelmed until she seen Asher and realized it was his feelings. Glaring down at Joseph she let him see her anger. Was he betraying her again?

Seeing his own brother, standing in front of him, alive, his body the picture of perfection instead of burnt and scarred; Asher didn't know whether to fall down on his knees in joy or disbelief. "You're… You're… How?" He tried his damndest to understand.

He turned to Emie then. He felt so hot and mad and knew it was their fault. He tried to remember their words just a few days earlier but he couldn't recall them.

So fall he did. He had to look at Emie who had followed him down to his knees for support. He closed his eyes as the pain killing emotions numbed him. He held onto her shoulder with one hand and his head with his other hand as his brother tried to explain on his knees next to him that everything was going to be ok and as the woman he was with asked some else in the room if Asher was going to be ok.

Shelley. That's what Curtis had called her. Curtis had hissed at her in a set down tone that only Curtis could command. But the reasons why escaped Asher.

Asher was out of his head. He looked up at the woman who he had believed was just a nurse a year ago and tried to wrap his head around what had happened. She wasn't a nurse. She wasn't a woman …

Emie ordered everyone from the room. How much more did they expect him to take? He had enough.

She reached for him now, but he was already getting to his feet again.

Asher stood there, stuffing his hands deep in his pockets for comfort, staring at everyone. Disbelieving everything that was happening around him. Curtis was alive! Shelley had turned him instead of taking him to the morgue that night he had died. Emie hadn't told him any of this in hopes of trying to protect him, and Joseph had let him believe it.

He remembered then that Emie had been gone for a year. Had she been with Curtis? Had she known all along? He looked at her then, not knowing what to think of her. Had she went to his brothers funeral with him, watching him grieve, watching him cry over his brothers death. Had she known then his brother was alive and hadn't told him?

All of his pain from that day returned. He had to wipe the hatred dripping off his lips. How could she?

Emie stood next him, heart broken. She looked up at him unsure what to say, what to do. Anger flamed and fueled inside of her.

Trust me Emie. This from Joseph right behind her. Protecting her.

He had thought about telling Asher down at the fire hall, but his father had interrupted them. Plus, Joseph needed the help of everyone in the room. It was going to take all of them to help Asher now. He had to shake his head in amazement at Asher. He hated that he had to do it this way. But knew from what Jordy had told him, this would work out the best.

I promise Emie, this was the best way. He will be ok. This from Jordy who was still standing over by the stairs next to Izzy.

They were trying to calm her, soothing her. They knew she was going to hurt them anyways when she got a free chance, so they tried to ease her the best they could.

You'll be lucky to have your bloody heads if this doesn't. I swear it. She told them all.

Asher looked around the room more and spotted his sister Izzy next to Jordy.

Jordy backed up a step when Asher's eyes had seen them holding hands. Asher's eye's. Do you see this Joseph?

I do. Said Joseph.

Years of education, learning and planning, knowing what to do in any given situation or tragedy, couldn't have prepared Asher for any of this. His whole life, time had been his enemy, flying past him faster then he could keep up with. The moment he needed both of them to save him, they failed him.

It was Cristina, who appeared in front of him out of nowhere, like an angel who could save him, giving him the time he needed. Emie beside him who was numbing his pain, and Joseph who gave him direction, all of them consuming him with powers he never knew existed.

Now kneeling again, he sat there in the main hall, for what felt like hours, trying to let life fix what it had broken in him. Staggering and fainting had never happened to him before. For once in his life he let the feelings take him down to a place he hated. A place where he knew he wouldn't be strong enough to fight them off.

For once, he felt peace. A peace so wonderful it felt like it was taking years of pain and disappointment out of him, and replacing them with a perfect serenity so great it scared the hell out of him. For the first time in forever, he didn't have to do anything. Nothing but to just let go. Everything was going to be fine.

Asher woke up much later that evening, his head in Emie's lap who was stroking his hair. She was humming a song he didn't know, still numbing his pain.

His eyes opened slowly and he took in his surroundings. He was in her living room again. The one at the back of the house with all the windows.

He closed his eyes tight as the memories flooded his mind. His brother. His sister.

Emie's betrayal.

Or was it?

It wasn't betrayal, he told himself. They loved him. They were trying to protect him, not hurt him. The last few days with them all had proved that. He hadn't wanted to believe it before, but he did now.

Emie shook her head listening to his thoughts. Just when she had been about to tell him those things, he again surprised her and had found the truth out for himself.

"Tell me I was dreaming sweetheart?" He asked her squeezing her hand in his hair tight for comfort. They were sitting on the couch facing a dim lit fire. Thoughts of his brother, alive and well filled his mind.

But Curtis wasn't alive anymore.

Asher squeezed his eyes shut and rubbed his temple.

"I wish I could tell you yes, my love." Emie whispered to him softly. "Please know though, I didn't know of my brother's decisions to bring this all to the light the way they did. I was just as stunned as you in the hall."

Asher closed his eyes again and smiled. He loved her new nick name for him. He remembered a time when he would have given his left arm to have her call him that, or anything for that matter. Anything was better than nothing. He had spent too much time without her, and not enough time with her.

It was that knowledge that he had now, the wisdom to know what life was like without her, that made him realize he could forgive her for this. She had done all this, to protect him. She had forgiven him of his shame in all he had done to her and thought about her last year. Even though he would have to live with the shame of knowing what he had done to her for the rest of his life, he'd made her run so far away that no one could find her and lived with his words in her heart and mind, it broke him to think of it. That it was all his fault, he would use it to remind himself that he didn't deserve what she so freely had given him. Her love. He didn't deserve her love, but he needed her to love him.

He needed her trust. He needed her to know she could trust him. He didn't ever want to lose her again, and he was so grateful she had been here when he woke up. He was so ashamed of his thoughts earlier. He hoped she could forgive him for that as well.

He craved her. He wanted her. He needed her.

She had said her brothers hadn't told her of their plans. She had tried so hard to keep it a secret from him. To let things unfold naturally.

He wondered if there was something else going on here he couldn't see yet. He remembered the way Joseph had been talking to him at the fire hall. They must have distracted her well to play this out. He smiled at the thought of what she was going to do to them now for it.

"Don't worry. Karma is a bitch. I have plans to do bodily harm to all three of them now."

Asher grinned at her bending his head up to her. She would too.

Asher wondered what they had in store for him now. He held onto Emie's hand. He needed her touch right now.

He knew she was listening in his mind. He hoped she'd heard the way he loved her. He squeezed her hand a little tighter in reassurance. When she did the same he knew she'd heard him.

Asher wanted just a little more time to not think. He just wanted to sit here and feel Emie around him playing with his hair and listen to her voice. So much was waiting for him to decide. He didn't want to think about any of it.

If only for a few more minutes…

His brother's voice pulled him out of his reprieve. Curtis had cleared his throat from somewhere behind them. He knew it was Curtis even though he hadn't heard his voice in over a year. They were brothers, and now they would be brothers again.

"Asher?" He called to him.

Asher first took one last look up at Emie, then he sat up a little too quickly and had to sit with his head in his hands for a minute. He still felt dizzy.

Curtis rounded the couch and sat in the big overstuffed chair next to Emie.

"I'll leave you two alone Asher."

He looked over at Emie and smiled back at her. She was wonderful to give him this time he needed with his brother. He loved her all the more for understanding.

"I'll be right over there if you need me." She smiled back at him and kissed his cheek. She walked over at the piano and very quietly filled the large room with a soft melody.

Asher looked at his brother. He still couldn't believe it.

Can he hear inside of me Emie? He needed to know. For more reasons then just privacy. .

No, Asher. He's not like us.

"Asher, man, I had hoped I would never have to tell you any of this. There was a time I had hoped you would never find any of this out."

Asher took a moment and just looked at Curtis. He really was alive.

"Why? Why would you hide something like this from me? Why did you wait so long to tell me?" Asher had to know why. He and Curtis had a relationship unlike any other brothers he had ever known. He wanted to know why his brother hadn't trusted him. He couldn't blame Emie for this any more. Curtis was just as much to blame.

Asher heard the way Emie missed a note on the piano. He hoped it was because she felt relief from his forgiveness.

"Because man, I wasn't in a place where I could stand to be in the room with you." Curtis chuckled, and hoped Asher would understand the joke. "You gotta understand that. It is still hard for me right now. I don't know how Emie does it…" he grinned at his little brother then back at Emie.

Asher wondered the same things lately. Emie was so strong when it came to being with him. He had noticed more then once that her brothers had to gulp down hard and swallow when ever they were face to face with him. He had never doubted at all that she was having trouble with her need to feed on him.

Curtis took a second to look at Asher seriously. He needed him to understand this. "Asher, I'm not the same man you remember."

Asher understood what he meant. Curtis was no longer a man. Even now, Asher could see the perfection in his features that set him apart from all humanity.

"So where have you been all this time?" Asher asked him, honestly wanting to know.

Curtis hung his head and casually covered his nose and mouth trying not to breath in Asher's scent. "When Emie first met you, I was dying. Joseph knew I didn't want to let go, I didn't want to die. But my injuries were too severe. I wouldn't have had any quality of life had I survived. He and Shelley took me to Florida after they turned me. I've lived there with her for the last year.

"While you two love birds were falling in love, and then again," he added more pointedly at Asher, "Shelley and Joseph were making plans for this upcoming war. Shelley knew they were going to need my help." Curtis bowed his head and Asher watched as he struggled with his thoughts. "Me and you, Asher, we have certain gifts. They need our help. We have to help them."

Asher had to think about that one. How could they, how could he, a mere human, help them? Asher didn't understand though, he had thought he needed them more than they needed him.

"Each of us has our own powers from with in us. A God given gift if you will. Some humans are destined to become vampires. God allows us to live and walk amongst the humans to learn their ways, so we can relate to them. Emie has the ability to heal and blind the mind, Joseph can control the mind. Jordy can see the future. He and Jeremy can manipulate the earth's matter. Jeremy can do the same things with animals and humans that Emie can do only with humans. Cristina can play with time... somewhat now, she's still new but she can also disappear. She's been playing around with reappearing into a bat form. Which is really cool if you ask me." He winked. "It keeps us distracted from our thoughts. Bad thoughts." Curtis said more to himself then to Asher.

"And what can you do?" Asher asked, silently awaiting the next part of this conversation. He heard Curtis when he had said "we" and "us", meaning him and Asher together. Possibly even meaning Izzy. She too had been in the hall hours ago. Would they all ask him to become like him next? He had thought about this before, hell, he'd even dreamed about it.

Curtis's slumped a little at his question. "I can shift through time. I can't stop it, but I can move through from one place to another. I don't have the power over minds the way they do, but, I am strong. Very strong. Shelley has had a hard time with me this last year."

Curtis had Asher's undivided attention now.

"You're... a shifter? Like in the movies? That's cool man. Very cool." Asher reached his hand out for a fist bump that Curtis returned.

For the first time in a long time Curtis didn't feel like a freak. Having his brother's approval meant more to him then he knew it would.

"I haven't wanted to play with it much. It feels weird... I've been too busy trying to figure out how to survive on what little bit of blood I can get my hands on."

Asher sat back and gulped at that.

"Don't worry little brother; you're in no danger of me taking you down. Luckily, for Izzy now though, she won't have to be afraid me. But everyone else, dad, mom, the boys; you should do everything possible to keep them away from me."

That was a no brainer, Asher thought off handedly. No one could know Curtis was alive.

"Things are about to change Asher. Everything is going to change. You have to keep them all safe. We all depend on you now."

Asher's feelings of fear, and anger over all the responsibilities that were now on him, returned full force. "But how!" Asher stated.

He wanted to say more. He didn't know if he could do all this anymore. He wanted to beg his brother for help, but instead Curtis smiled. His fangs showing enough that Asher had to wonder if he should be bracing for an attack.

"That's why I came home, Asher." Curtis smiled. "Super man to the rescue." Curtis said, holding his arms in an superhero muscle arch.

They both chuckled at that. Super man had been their childhood hero growing up. Asher had always thought that his brother was invincible like super man until last year when he had seen him fall to his death. Now, sitting in front of him as perfect as a statue, Asher's fears that he had been feeling of impending doom, where finally starting to dwindle.

Asher had to wonder what that made him. If Curtis was super man, did that make him some kind of half cocked side kick?

Asher worried then. He worried over the future and what would come. He worried about death, and life. How could people live nowadays facing the unknown of what was to become of them. Even he didn't know what was to become of himself. How was he supposed to able to help and protect people if he couldn't even protect himself?

Emie choose that moment to walk back over to the men. Her eyes met with Asher's and she filled him with a numbing ease he had enjoyed many times before with her. Her worries for him eased as his pain eased. She listened deeper into his thoughts. What did he need, she wondered. Then she found it. It was the one thing he always wanted and needed when life straightened out for him.

"Asher, my love, getting hungry yet?" She cocked her eyebrow up at him in question and knew the moment his mind registered her questioned. He straightened up and smiled at her like a little boy.

Asher looked up at the woman he hadn't been able to stop thinking about since he'd met her. Once his eyes met hers, his hunger pain slowly dwindled away. The only thing he was hungry for right now was her. He stood then and leaned closer to her. She was grinning from ear to ear at his thoughts. He was sure she could feel his need too.

"What did you have in mind sweetheart." He smiled.

Curtis and Asher were sitting at a counter in the Whitby kitchen, Asher's hand was wrapped around a cold bottle of beer. He stared at it, watching drips of condensation make their way down to his fingers. He was trying to hold onto his sanity as he thought about his brother who was sitting next to him, Curtis was finishing his third bottle of what looked like beer, but Asher knew better.

Emie was making him some little southern dish, looking quiet cute in her tight jeans and black silky button up shirt. Asher couldn't take his eyes off her the whole time she walked around the kitchen. He felt passion surging through him like never before.

Curtis was telling him something about Florida, but Asher had stopped listening when Emie set a plate of food in front of him. He had never been more torn between food and desire before. If his brother hadn't been in the room with them, he would have taken Emie right there on the counter.

Instead he ate every last bite, knowing he was going to need all the energy he could get to face the next days.

When Asher had finished his plate he had almost gotten Emie wrapped in his arms while he set his plate on the counter next to the dishes she was doing, but Joseph choose that moment to make a grand entrance in the kitchen with them. Asher almost growled when he turned around, but he smiled at Joseph instead. Didn't anyone know he wanted nothing better to do than take Emie up stairs and lock her doors?

Now it was Joseph's turn to growl.

Asher shrugged his shoulders and went back to sit next to his brother. He opened another bottle of beer and drank from it thirstily. He needed a smoke.

"Think you can handle seeing everyone again, Ash? We have much to discuss." Joseph asked putting both hands on the counter in front of him. He wanted to give Asher more time, but they were going to need all the time they could get to plan things out. Izzy's disappearance was weighing heavily on his family and they needed to come up with a plan.

Asher smirked at his use of his nickname. "Yes. Are we having a family meeting or something?" It felt odd saying that. Family had always met his family. Now he belonged to Emie's family. Everything had changed so quickly for him. But he was welcoming the change. Sort of...

"Yes." Joseph said as he caught Emie and wrapped his arm around her neck as she walked by and kissed his sisters cheek. He flashed his fangs at Asher and chuckled as she swatted him away, then he walked out of the kitchen after Curtis.

Asher was tempted to take Emie right then and there on the counter when they left, he knew Joseph knew his desires for Emie, he wanted nothing more then to be alone with her in that moment; the big, bad, scary vampire be damned. He thought better of it though when Joseph scared him and growled at him in his mind.

Grrrr! Asher growled back

"Serves you right! You know how hard it is to keep a straight face in front of your brother when you are thinking of those things?" Emie giggled swatting at him with her dish towel as she entered the space between his knees, wrapping her arms around Asher's neck.

Asher looked down between them at his growing hardness then, looking sheepishly back up at her, proving her point by showing her how excited he was from his desire of her. All she had to do was look down to know exactly how hard things were for him.

"Oh, I guess you do." She grinned.

"Let's get this over with shall we?" Asher smiled up at Emie wrapping his arms around her waist. He kissed the top of her forehead and raised his hands to run down the back of Emie's hair. He cupped her curls in his palms and let them fall down the length of them. It tickled his palms and he loved the chills it gave him.

Emie closed her eyes when he did this. She leaned forward and rested her head on his chest. She sighed in a deep breath of him. His scent filled her lungs and made her dizzy with desire. A mixture of desire she could never quiet make out. His scent was filled with a ashy smell, mixed with the heat of his body, mixed with his blood. Her body heated at once and venom dripped from her fangs onto her tongue. She swallowed it and loved the taste of his scent mixed with her venom in her mouth. She loved even more the taste of his blood, but she couldn't have that right now.

When she looked up at him she seen in his eyes the same desire as hers.

She could read his mind then. Her eyes turned dark and red in his mind. She knew she was scaring him. He was already fearing them all knowing who and just what they were now.

Being this close to her, with her heated desire changing from sexual to real hunger, he knew what she wanted from him.

In a blink, Emie eased his mind, made him see her like he remembered. Her eyes were now deep brown in his mind. Her smile wouldn't reveal her fangs. She washed over him a relaxing emotion filled with her love.

Asher shook his head. He loved seeing Emie's desire for him, scary as it was. It was something he made a mental note to explore later. He inhaled her deeply and lifted her into a strong embrace, lifting her off her feet, making her squeal, and walked into the hallway carrying her. He needed to find their family and get this "matter of war" or whatever it was, figured out.

Twenty Nine

"Please, Asher and Emie, join us." Joseph motioned to the circle table everyone was sitting at, for them to sit at too.

Asher had never been in this room. It was some sort of out dated parlor room off of the dining room. It was dark, painted a dark green or black, with no windows that Asher could see. There was a bar that lined the back wall, with a mirror behind it and enough liquor to supply a chain store. In the center, was a table that looked like a blackjack table he had seen in the casino in Detroit with a bright light hanging over the table, lighting somewhat of the room; Joseph was standing on the other side of the table, he was wearing a crisp white shirt that he unbuttoned at the neck and his dress black jacket he had been wearing was hanging over the edge of a table.

As Asher and Emie joined them at the table, Asher leaned in close to Emie. She reached her hand under the table and patted his leg for comfort. She reminded him that Joseph liked to have everyone's attention.

"Well he sure has mine." Asher whispered aloud to no one.

Joseph addressed them all placing his hands on the table in front of them all. "We need to discuss first what to tell the Stone family about Izzy." He looked at Asher now. "She needs to go to Florida with Curtis and Shelley. She needs time to adapt to this new life and be trained. She can not risk being caught now. Not with all that's going on."

Asher nodded his head to Joseph in understanding. If the authorities caught her, there was no telling what they would do with her. The Whitby's needed to protect her, and she would be with Curtis.

Asher looked to Izzy and smiled at her. His little sister was going to have to grow up fast without any of her family. He wondered if she would be ok.

Looking at her now, how much she had changed since the last time he had seen her, how beautiful she was, he was proud of her. "Are you ok, Izzy?' he questioned her lovingly.

Izzy, who for the first time, got to speak freely, looked to her big brothers. The Whitby's who had been taking care of her, always seemed to be one step ahead of her. They knew everything she needed before she needed it. Jordy, who had been her comfort over the last few days, had been everything she had needed also.

She still couldn't believe she was sitting here, not only in a house full of vampires, which only excited and fascinated her, but she was sitting next to a man who was everything she had ever dreamed of and more.

"Better than ever Asher." She told at him, beaming at him with excitement.

Asher took a deep breath and looked back over to Joseph. "How do we tell our family?"

"She can either call them and make up some story about running away, or… she doesn't do anything at all."

Asher knew the later would be worse then the first for his mother. He rubbed his jaw and looked away. They would need to tell his mother something. If she could be lead to believe that Izzy had ran away with Emie's brother Jordy, his mom would have an easier time with it. Thinking that she had lost another child to death's door would be too much.

"What about your father though? He could make this bad for us."

"I'll handle my father." Asher stated simply.

"Alright then. Jordy and Izzy can come up with a story to tell them and initiate it. Asher, you and Emie can handle the rest of it as you need too with your family.

"Next we discuss the plan for protecting this city. We need to implement a plan that Asher can use. He has family and friends he needs to protect and we need to help him. But it has to be understood by you Asher, that no one, and I mean no one, can learn about this family."

Asher knew this, but there was one friend he needed to know about what was going on. "What about Ken?"

Everyone looked to Jordy then, who was still stunned by the fact Asher wasn't killing him. "Um… I need some time to see that one."

Emie sighed aloud. "Let me and Asher deal with all that. You all need to get the hell out of here."

She had surprised everyone with her comment. In her head she could hear all the arguments that had started inside of everyone's head. From Asher and Joseph who were adamantly swearing at her now, Jordy who refused to leave her alone, and Jeremy who looked like he had something entirely different in mind. Curtis even had something to say about it, but Emie understood it was his family and friends that he was thinking of. Surprisingly Shelley was the only one who agreed with her and was ready to go home.

They all started to speak at once beckoning and trying to will her to hear them.

"No. Stop. Everyone." Emie stood up then and looked at Jordy. "Jordy you need to get Izzy out of here for all the reasons Joseph just stated and you need to stay with her. Shelley and Curtis need to leave also, if the FBI shows up at our door for whatever reason the last thing they need to find here is Curtis. And I can't even begin to wonder what would happen if his family seen him." Emie looked at Asher with that, knowing he would understand this the most since he had just experienced that.

"As for Cristina and Nelly, they are safer in Florida then they are here. Joseph you know this better then any of us, you can't protect everyone at the same time. You have to be with all of the them and make everyone safe. They need you." This she knew he understood. The lives of everyone couldn't be sacrificed. The majority needed to be safe. "Jeremy can stay here with me. He can help me and Asher."

"Because Jeremy doesn't have anything to lose?" He questioned them all quietly into silence, turning his ball cap backwards.

Jeremy was tired of being the odd one out, he thought as he sat alone. He wanted to tell them he had found someone he couldn't afford to lose, someone who he had spent his days and nights talking too for over a year now. Email, text, phone calls. He had carried out a long distance relationship in private. His biggest mistake was doing what Emie had done. He hadn't told her the truth about who he was. And now, now when the world was falling apart around him, he didn't know how to save her when he had his family to worry about. But all of this he kept to himself. They couldn't know about Juliet...

"I have things that I need to take care of also. I'll help where I can, but when the shit hits the fan, I'm out."

Stunned, but not surprised, Emie looked at her brother. He was fooling everyone but her with his proud guy attitude. She dug deep inside his heart where she knew he was hiding something. She kept it from her other brothers and easily wound around inside of him. She seen these last months that she had been missing. Jeremy had been alone, but unlike he had ever been in the past, he had been happy. When Jeremy got lost in thought Emie seen the girl there in his mind he was with down in Kentucky. It was just a glimpse and she knew he had been hiding her there from everyone, but didn't know why. What was he up too she wondered.

"Fine." Joseph stated simply. He crossed his arms and stood up tall.

It would be enough. He hated to admit it, but Emie was right. They all needed to leave and let Emie and Asher handle things here.

"Shelley, take Curtis and Izzy, and Jordy with you. Tonight.

"Izzy, you need to call your family, they need to call off the search for you."

"We will take care of them, I promise Izzy." Emie looked in Izzy's direction at her thoughts. Izzy knew better than anyone here what all was happening around the world. She had been the brunt of the rogues aggression that night.

Just like what had happened to Emie so many years ago. Emie could see her fears and could see how she hated this.

Emie promised Izzy she would take care of her family just like she had taken care of her own, and was trying to now. She was giving them all the best chance she could now.

Joseph listened to his sister's word as she spoke them to Izzy. Emie was sure she could do this, and was taking the choice from him. She had everyone believing she could do it. But it was Jordy, who was sitting in silence that caught Joseph's attention. Jordy knew differently. But there was nothing he could do about it. She was making this sacrifice, and he had to let her. For the sake of everyone here, he had to help the majority. He looked to Asher then. Asher would have to be her saving grace.

"I will stay behind for a few days with Cristina and Neely. Asher? If I'm not mistaken, there is a fireman's banquet coming up next weekend?"

Asher nodded his head in agreement. He didn't know if anyone would attend now, but yes, they had their annual banquet every year.

"You and I will start the planning. When your father sees you and I together he will give up on trying to accuse us of Izzy's disappearance."

Asher doubted that, but for intense purposes he let Joseph believe it. He smiled down at Emie now. He'd never taken a date to the banquet, this year he would be able too. More than that, he would be able to spend time with her doing something other then planning for a war. It would be the distraction the whole department would need.

"That and we can try to distract the cities attention from everything and in the midst come up with a plan.

"Emie, when I was at the department today, I noticed a lot of things that need the city's attention. The building itself needs repairs. That and the kitchen needs a makeover. Since you do not have a job at the moment, think I can hire you to take over and see it through." Secretly he informed her so Asher wouldn't hear, that his main reason for this was so they could stock up the department with the supplies they would need for a shelter.

You and I need to discuss this more in depth when Asher isn't around. He's needs to be focused in what little time we can give him, not planning for the worst.

Emie tried not to lose the excitement in her smile as Joseph finished. Decorating and makeovers was something she would love to do. Helping people was what she knew how to do.

Think Miranda would like to help me? She asked Asher as Joseph turned back to everyone else discussing plans for them all to leave.

Asher, taken back by her need for privacy, tried to listen to Joseph talk about the funds they all had set aside for this. He looked at Emie. I think she would like that very much sweetheart.

Her and I got to talking at the fire hall the other night. I would really like to meet them and get to know them better.

Asher had to remember how to breathe. Miranda had been as close as a friend to him as Ken had been. Sitting here worrying about them and not knowing how to help them, Emie had neatly made all that worry go away. He used the arm he had resting on the back of her chair and leaned her on her side and pulled her into him and hugged her closer to him.

Joseph continued on making plans. Everyone was to leave tonight except for him, Cristina and Neely, and Jeremy. Asher and Emie would wait for Izzy to call the family before Asher would go home and smooth things over with them. When Joseph had the banquet up and running he too would leave with Cristina.

Looking over at Cristina, Joseph could feel the love that was growing in him for her. It excited him every time he looked at her. Possession was an obsession he was beginning to like indeed.

When Emie eyed him curiously at those thoughts he could have sworn he felt a blush creep up inside of him.

"Em, hold up." Joseph stopped her by grabbing her arm before she walked out with everyone else at the end of the meeting.

Emie turned, shocked that he had not only spoken aloud to her, something he usually did in private, but had also grabbed her arm.

"What is it?"

Asher nodded to the both of them, giving them the moment alone he knew they needed. He turned to his brother and sister and followed them out into the hall to talk with them.

"I have a few things we need to talk about, come back in here." Joseph was silently afraid now. Afraid of Emie who had found the courage to make these decisions and also Asher, for reasons he wasn't ready to talk about now.

"For the next week, we need to turn that department into what it should have been years ago. I don't know how you're going to do it, but spare no expense. Makeover and stock up the kitchen on supply's that could last for months in case things turn for the worse. Medical supplies, food, water, and new gear for all the men. The best you can find."

Emie looked at him in acknowledgment. But there was something else... "What is it Joseph."

He took her farther away from the door, not wanting anyone else to hear him. Asher needed to be able to think this next week that everything was going to be ok for as long as he could. "Under the fire department, in the truck bay, there is an old oil bay where they used to work on the trucks. It's huge Emie, it's as big as the bay under there. And it's under ground. If things turn for the worse, people can hide down there from whatever is coming. Even Frank doesn't know it exists.

"When the time comes, tell Asher, get everyone down there. But wait till it's time. I don't want anyone to know about it. Under the rack that holds their gear is a door. You will have to bust through the concrete we used to cover it up, but you can easily put the racks back over it to hide the door again."

Emie sighed. He and Jordy must know something she doesn't. Either this was about to get really bad, or he was just over planning.

"I don't know anymore Em. But you've made the decision to stay and help him. This is all I can do to help right now. This is the only place close enough in the city to keep everyone safe from the rouges. It's big enough they can survive in, but they will need supplies to make it work."

"I know Joseph. It's going to be alright. I promise." She reassured him.

Joseph hid his fears from his sister. She would need hope right now more then she would need fear.

Emie walked out into the main hall followed by Joseph who walked quickly over to Cristina. Neely, they all could see was peeking around one of the posts at the landing at the top of the stairs. He missed his mother.

Joseph came up next to Cristina and held her hand while she waved at Neely from where she was standing. Emie watched as Joseph struggled not to kiss Cristina in front of everyone. Emie had to turn away from looking at them. It was sweet and tender, and so much like what Joseph had always wanted in life.

Asher reached his arms around Emie as he came up behind her and held her against him. He whispered tenderly to her "Can I steal you for a moment also?"

Emie smiled and leaned into his whisper. "I'm all yours now, Asher."

Asher had been waiting to hear that for days now. He didn't mind it here in her home and he hoped one day she would give him a tour of the place, but he longed to get Emie away from her brothers and stay somewhere more private with him.

They said their goodbyes to everyone in the hall. Every one had packing to do, and preparations to make. Emie even stopped by her room and packed a few outfits. She wanted to stay with Asher for as long as she could. Joseph would have to shut down the house and prepare it for the worst. He would have to board up the windows and lock it up safe and sound. The wolves would protect it the best they could, but they were up against an army they wouldn't know how to defeat.

Asher was smoking waiting in his truck for Emie. He had been out here only a few minutes. He watched Jeremy sit on the ledge of the steps keeping an eye out for the wolves for him.

His mind wandered to thoughts of Ken and Miranda. He wanted to go to them and tell them everything that was happening. He knew Miranda already knew some of what was going on. She was always worried about something like this.

Miranda's family lived in different parts of the country. She had three sisters who lived in Arizona, Florida, and Indiana. Her parents lived in Florida also with one of her sisters. She was the youngest, and not having family close by only seemed to worry Miranda more.

Ken's family also lived out of state. Ken and Miranda would need help keeping their girls safe.

Asher didn't know why he felt the need to keep them safe in his protection, but he did. Everyone else on the department would have to weather this storm on their own. But Ken and Miranda were his best friends. He would have to make Emie understand this.

Emie climbed in his truck into the passenger seat.

"Did you buy a new truck?" she questioned him.

"No," Asher told her. "It's Curtis'." Asher smiled knowing he would have to give it back now.

Emie looked at Asher now. "I'm so sorry Asher. So sorry you had to go through all that." Emie looked away from Asher ashamed.

"No, honestly Emie." Asher took a deep breath and sighed. "I understand it now. I know now why things happened the way they did. I see things so differently now. I never understood why things happened like that. Why some would die when others lived. Being on the department, I seen so much of that. But now I understand it's just the way things are supposed to be. We have to be patient and learn that things will work out in the end even though they don't go the way we want them too.

"If you had tried to reveal all this to me last year, we wouldn't have what we have now. And I wouldn't trade any of this for anything. You are in my life now." He told her reaching for her hand and holding it in his. "Living without you for a year Emie, I don't ever want to live like that again. I don't ever want to lose you again."

Emie held tightly onto his hand. "As long as I live Asher, I will do everything in my power to make sure that doesn't happen."

Asher smiled at her and started his truck. "Me too, Emie. Me too."

Emie heard in his heart what he was longing to ask her. She didn't have an answer for him yet. She didn't know how to tell him what to tell Ken and Miranda.

While he drove away from her home and into the darkness of the shadowed woods, she told him, "Asher, let's go see them. I really want to meet them and get to know the people in your life."

Asher looked over at Emie. Bless her heart, that was one of the sweetest things she had ever done for him. She was so wonderful to be able to understand the needs of his life and want to give it to him. He reached over and placed a kiss on her hand. "I would like that very much Sweetheart." But first he wanted to take her home. His home. Where she belonged.

After Asher started his shower, he sat down in his bathroom and tried to think of all the things he needed to do. He needed to wait till Izzy called his parents before he could go over and talk to his mom. He needed to talk to Ken and Miranda and check on them. He needed to start the preparations for the banquet and help Emie with the fire hall. He had so many things to do at the department but wondered what it would matter any more. The city seemed eerily quiet as he had driven down Lakewood drive.

Would anybody be down there working when he showed up? Could he fault them for not being there? Was anyone going to work anymore now that the world was upside down?

He thought of an apocalypse and wondered if they were in one now.

Emie choose that moment to knock sweetly on the door. The room was starting to fill up with steam and he was only half undressed. He walked over to the door and let her in.

Emie was taken back by his appearance. Asher was standing there by the door holding it open for her. He was clearly miles away from her at the moment. But it was his body that had caught her off guard. He was standing there in nothing but his jeans hanging off his hips. It was rare that she got to see him without his shirt on in the light. Seeing his tan well muscled upper torso covered in tattoos made her shiver.

Knowing now, that nothing else mattered in the world to him except her, Asher hurriedly removed the rest of their clothes. He pulled Emie into the shower with him and made sweet love to her in his stand up shower.

Kissing Emie up against the grey, subway tile glass wall, pressing her body up against his, he was reveling in the feel of himself inside of her again. The world was going to hell in a basket around them, and they were hiding in his uppers floors making love like nothing in the world existed but the two of them. The irony of it all made it more magical for them.

Emie stood there leaning against the back wall of his shower watching as his back muscles moved and rippled as he washed. He had just made powerful love to her with a passion that out did her own. His scare cut through the flames like it was tattooed there with the rest of his designs. Nothing Asher did was without reason or purpose. She loved that about him. She loved being apart of that in his life.

Asher turned around about to ask Emie a question and was shocked to see her staring at him the way she was. She caught him looking at her and she shook off whatever it was she was thinking. "Oh no," he said turning around wiping the water off his face. "What was that all about?"

Emie had been caught off guard and wished she could blush just so he would know exactly what she had been doing. She was slightly embarrassed by her girlish behavior. "I was just admiring your body, that's all."

Asher, stunned by her revelation, asked her what she was talking about.

"Seriously?" she questioned him. "Have you not looked in the vanity mirror lately?"

Asher shut off the water and opened the curtain to look in his mirror curious now, joking around with her.

Emie shook her head at him and walked out of the shower.

Asher watched as she did. He watched and took in an eyeful of his naked, beautiful… Beautiful what?

Thoughts of marrying her again crossed his mind. He didn't just want a girlfriend, and Emie was more to him then just a girlfriend. He should be proposing to her, down on bended knee asking her to make him the happiest man alive.

Emie froze at his thoughts and Asher wanted to kick himself. That was supposed to be a secret.

When she didn't move Asher started to worry. "Emie?" he called out to her. He was standing there with his arms resting on the shower rod. But when she turned around, he could tell she was only in shock over his thoughts. The smile that she wore said it all. She was even tearing up.

"Why do I always cry around you?" She said turning back around and grabbing on his towels off of his shelves.

Asher knew why, but she wouldn't like his answer. He had three sisters, and no matter how brave they tried to be, they were still women.

Emie smirked at him then. But her irritation with his answer wore off quickly when he walked up to her and took her hand.

"Emie, in a perfect world, that is where my heart would be- Is! Definitely, is." He corrected himself. He shook his head and looked back up at her shyly. "I want to marry you Emie. Someday. I want to spend the rest of my life with you sweetheart." He wiped her tear for her then. "I don't have anything to offer you, hell! I don't even have a ring for you." He laughed a little too when she giggled. He put both of his hands on her face then. "I don't even know if I can buy one anymore. But I swear it to you right now. That's where my heart is. And I need you to know that."

Emie knew. She really knew. She wrapped her arms around his neck then. "I love you Asher."

When too much time had passed Emie looked out over the water through the doors in his upper rooms. She knew they needed to go and talk with his friends. She waited for her brothers to bud in and tell her no, or what to do. They didn't though. All was quiet tonight.

She looked out over the moon lit lake and remembered the night she and Asher had spent out there together. He had been so playful that night. Nothing weighed on his mind then. There was no threat to the city then. He was safe. Emie wondered how safe he was with her now. If the army Jordy kept talking about were looking to destroy vampires like her, what would they do if they found Asher with her?

"Emie." Asher said from behind her.

Emie closed her eyes then at his voice. They were so interconnected now that he could feel her needs and her moods. He wasn't even a vampire, she told herself. How could he do this already, she wondered.

In the dark room they were standing in on his upper floors was a room he had set up as an office of sorts. It led out to a porch that overlooked his yard below and the lake stretched out for miles in the distance.

Emie turned around at the sound of Asher. He was dressed again, the same as always. She reached her hands out for his chest and listened to his beating heart. She would die if anything ever happened to him. She needed to be with Asher every moment of the day. She never wanted to be without him again.

"Tell me what to say to them before we go Emie. I don't know what to say to them."

Emie breathed in. "Let's just go and visit and see how things go. Let's hold off on telling them who I am, and the plans we have set for them. When we need to tell them, we will know."

Asher held her face in his hands and placed a kiss on the top of her head. "Thank you." That was the exact answer he needed.

Ken and Miranda lived in a story and a half home on Twelfth Street off of Lake Wood drive. The girls were fast asleep and Ken and Miranda had been snuggled up on their couch when Asher and Emie came over to visit them.

Asher was glad the girls had been in bed. There were things that would be said tonight he didn't want them to hear. Even though Gabby was sixteen now and Asher knew she was old enough to handle what was going on in the world, he wanted her to hold on to her innocence as long as she could. Katie was five. She was still so young and would be frightened by the idea of vampires.

Ken greeted them at the door and went back over to the spot on the couch next to Miranda. Miranda greeted Emie with a knowing smile. She had been expecting them to come over and visit with them.

Asher noticed they were watching the news. He hated the time that he spent watching it in silence with them on the little couch next to Emie. There was breaking news of three small cities in the U.S. that were being rioted and looted while it burned to the ground.

"I just don't understand it Asher. People are so afraid and they think they can just ruin their cities and destroy the life we have worked generations to build."

"I know man." Asher said to him, not looking at him, but watching the tv.

Emie sat in silence also. She hadn't watched tv in almost a year. Seeing it live on tv now only confirmed what Jordy had been trying to tell her. Cities, lives, everything was being destroyed now. In the riots Emie could see the vampires running around on the streets. She could tell the difference between them and the humans.

How long would it be before they came here? She wondered. Why weren't they here already?

Miranda spoke up then. She had been wishing Ken would turn off the tv when Asher had come in, but they both seemed so engrossed in it. She had to divert their attention to something else. "So what have you two been up too lately?" She questioned at them, not caring who answered.

Asher looked over at her then, determined not to look back at the tv. He smiled over at Emie when he said "Reconnecting mostly. Trying to see where we left off."

Emie smiled proudly back up at him.

Miranda beamed from ear to ear. She loved the love match they had found in each other.

They spent time talking about the mundane. Asher asked about the girls. Ken told him how they were handling the news and glad both girls were off school for the summer. It made both of their lives easier knowing where both girls were at all times.

Miranda asked them if they were hungry and got up to get the pizza she had made earlier.

Asher explained to Emie how much Miranda liked to cook. "We call her Chef Miranda." He told her excitedly.

Emie had never watched the show on tv he was comparing Miranda too, but she was excited to know she could pick Miranda's brain on the foods Asher liked that she would need to fix for him. Anything to keep him away from Luna Cafe.

Miranda explained how much she cooked for both Ken and Asher, almost like she had been reading Emie's thought saying her exact thoughts. "They would eat out day and night if I didn't cook for them both."

Asher explained to Emie then that their specialty was fire fighting, not cooking.

Ken told Emie also how much they did for Miranda around the house, making Miranda blush, it was an even trade off and they all enjoyed doing things for each other.

Emie settled in closer to Asher. This was exactly what they needed tonight. Normalcy. The way life was supposed to be.

Asher watched as Emie ate the pizza. He looked at her knowingly. Emie knew how to pretend, but it was the way she was pretending that Asher loved. She was doing it for Miranda. She was trying to be the friend she really wanted to be to her. Like she had done with him a year ago. It took his breath away to finally see it. To finally see what she had been doing with him. She had wanted him so bad that she had done the same thing with him. When she looked at him at his thoughts, Asher bashfully looked away.

Asher walked outside to smoke and he asked Ken to join him.

"So, really, how are you both holding up?" He questioned Ken.

"Miranda is in survival mood." Ken jested to Asher. "She's been so worried about something happening here in the city. She's always been good at being prepared. She's been shopping and using all of our savings to stock up on medicine and water, juice for the girls and packaged foods. Tents even!"

Asher chuckled at that. Ken hated camping.

"I hate tents Asher. There's no way she's getting me one. I'd rather sleep in my truck."

Asher was glad to hear that. "You know, the fire department has a lot of them same supplies. Emie and I are making plans to do the same thing down there. There's a lot of more supplies we need to get for down there just in case though."

Ken listened to all Asher had to say about that. They made plans together also, ticking off a list of things they needed and didn't have. It put both their minds at ease planning.

Miranda was in kitchen now with Emie. They were discussing the girls. Emie had wanted to know their names and ages, what they liked to do in their spare time. Emie had found pictures all around their little home of the girls. Her favorite had been the black and white pictures of the girls wearing Ken's firemen gear. They each had their own picture, then there was one of them all together surrounding Ken dressed in his gear. It was the sweetest thing she had ever seen. The smiles and happiness on the girl's faces made Emie's heart melt. She couldn't wait to spend time with them.

When Emie asked about their summer vacation and what they planned to do, Miranda went silent.

"I don't know if they will have one. They keep asking if they can go over to a friends house but I'm just so afraid to let them go anywhere. You know what I mean?" She questioned Emie honestly. "It seems other mothers have the same fears also. None of their friends have asked to come over either. I keep the news on in the bedroom and go in there to listen to it. I don't want the girls to know too much." Miranda stopped to take a break from putting dishes away.

She looked so tired to Emie. "You all have been on Asher's mind a lot. Is there anything we can do?" Emie reached out to her in friendship.

Miranda looked at Emie and smiled. "No sweetie. You two have a lot to be working on. Don't worry about us. We will be ok here."

Asher and Ken walked in then. Ken told Miranda about the plans he and Asher had made for the next day. Telling the women they were all going shopping together seemed to excite them.

Asher was pleased. He had his own little family now all together.

Emie looked to Asher then as he sighed. She smiled to him and whispered words of love into his heart. When he felt them he looked to her and winked.

Outside in the driveway as they were saying their goodbyes, Asher took Ken over to his truck.

"I want you to have Emie's number, just in case you might need it."

Ken got out his phone and Asher could tell there was something on Ken's mind.

"Is there anything you guys need Ken?" Asher asked, hoping Ken would be honest.

"No, we're fine." But the look in his eyes said differently.

Asher looked more directly at Ken now. "Ken listen. You're like a brother to me man. Emie has one of the most powerful and wealthiest families I know of."

Ken put his hand up to stop Asher, but Asher insisted.

"Listen, if there is anything Miranda or the girls need, you make sure you ask me. Don't hesitate. Don't put pride before your families needs. There is a lot of things going on out there, and I don't know what's gonna happen. But I'm here for you Ken. You know that. You and Miranda aren't alone. I don't care what it is, or what time it is, you call me. And if you can't get a hold of me, you call Emie, she will know where I am."

That seemed to do it. Ken had put his head down, but he had agreed.

"I'll see you both in the morning. Don't forget what I said." He pointed at Ken playfully.

Ken thanked Asher and shook his hand. Asher looked over to Emie then. She was hugging Miranda and saying goodbye. They would meet up tomorrow and go shopping with the girls.

"Make love to your wife tonight Ken. Stay home and protect them. Call us in the morning early and we can stick together."

"I hate shopping." Ken said honestly.

The men chuckled knowingly. Neither one enjoyed shopping, but they knew being together as friends it would make it bearable.

Asher sighed as Emie walked over to him. He wondered how long it would take for him to stop feeling like he was dreaming or she wasn't real.

Emie hugged Ken goodbye also. She adored his friends and was looking forward to tomorrow.

Asher helped her get into the truck and closed the door behind her. He looked back at the porch where his friends stood holding hands.

Asher could remember a time he had longed for what they had. Having Emie in his truck, taking her home with him, it was everything he had wanted. He waved goodbye to them and prayed they'd be safe.

Thirty

"I like them." Emie stated simply when Asher climbed in.

Asher knew she meant it. Her and Miranda looked to be enjoying themselves tonight and he was glad for it. Ken and Asher spent a lot of time together when they weren't working. Miranda always did hate being the third wheel with them, now she would have someone to talk to other then the guys.

"You could read their minds Emie, tell me what you seen there?"

It was the first time Asher had asked her to use her abilities. It did something to her to know he was accepting her for who she was.

"They are scared Asher, like everyone else is. They don't know what to do, or how to plan. They are just worrying mostly about the girls.

"What you told Ken tonight was the same thing I told Miranda. If they need us, they should call." Emie tried to reassure him.

Asher was almost home now. "Will you know if they do, before they do?" he questioned awkwardly.

"Would you feel better if I had one of the guys watching over them when we can't?" Belatedly, Emie remembered she hadn't told Asher about the men who worked for her brothers.

"You mean one of your brothers?"

"No." Emie wondered if now was good time to be telling Asher this. She couldn't believe in all their talks Joseph had to have with Asher no one had mentioned the wolves. She waited until Asher turned down fourth street to explain.

"Remember the guy that met us at the fire hall the other day?" she waited for the memory to hit Asher. When it did she was surprised to know that Collin had taken off his sunglasses in front of Asher. She would have to talk to him about that some day. "Yes, his name is Collin." Emie said to his memory of him.

"I always wondered how you all took care of that place by yourselves." Asher thought aloud.

Emie waited now until Asher pulled in his drive and put the truck in park before she continued.

"Ok, out with it. I know you are holding back something Emie."

Emie smirked. He wasn't going to like it anyways, so she just started with, "How much do you know of about werewolves?"

Asher shook his head. "I knew those weren't dogs." He stated flatly.

"Yes, well, they work for Joseph. One of Joseph's projects many, many years ago was to help them. They too have a purpose in this life, I'll let Joseph explain that part to you." Emie took a deep breath hoping she never would have too. "During the day they are like normal men, they can walk around in the sunlight and what not. But they can turn into wolves. Dangerous wolves." She added with a sigh. "But like I said, they work for Joseph and I can have one of them watching out for Ken and Miranda if you'd like."

Asher was unsure about that whole dangerous part, but he trusted Emie. If she thought it was ok, then so did he. He watched Emie as she picked up her phone and called Joseph.

Joseph agreed and got to work on it for them. Ken and Miranda would be safe now.

Asher walked in to his house with Emie behind him. Cookie was excited to see them both and jumped up and down for Asher to pick her up. He reached for her leash and grabbed a drink before he headed outside.

Emie looked around the house while Asher was outside. His home was a typical single guy's home. His living room was decorated with scenes of baseball themed pictures and knick knacks. A big screen tv was set in the corner next to a set of sliding glass doors that overlooked his yard and the lake. He had four recliners set up facing the doors. The living room opened up into the dining room, which opened up to the kitchen. She loved the floor plan of his home.

What had surprised her the most about his home, was his decor in the dining room and kitchen. His pool table had lights hanging over it that were made of fire helmets. His mini bar that was set into the wall dividing the rooms was the back end of a fire engine with a mirror set in it to resemble that of an actual bar.. He had a fully stocked bar of alcohol, she noticed. His kitchen sink even had hose nozzles instead of a faucet.

His kitchen cabinets were a deep chocolate color with set in stainless steel appliances. Beyond the kitchen lied another bathroom, a laundry room and another room she had not seen yet. All were decorated with fire department things.

There was a closet inside the kitchen that Emie found curious. When she opened it, she saw it was a pantry. An empty pantry... She shook her head. Only a single guy like Asher who worked full time could have a kitchen like this and not have it stocked with food.

She turned her attention to the refrigerator just as he was walking in.

"Hungry?" Asher asked her as he set Cookie down and opened the sliding glass door. He needed a smoke so he left the door open while he blew his smoke outside. Cookie had finished her business quickly and had wanted to get back inside to Emie. Asher didn't blame her.

Once Asher realized what he had said though, his felt his heart skip a beat.

Emie froze when she opened the refrigerator door. She took in the fact that it was empty also, except for the beer bottles on the shelves. He had some leftover dinners from the restaurant but Emie would bet that they were all old.

No, what scared her was his question. She was hungry. She couldn't remember the last she had anything of substance. She had been so wrapped up in Asher, she had completely forgotten.

Emie turned around and smiled at him. She was going to have to leave him for a bit.

"Oh…" Asher said, seeing in her eyes that she was.

"Yeah…"

Asher threw out his smoke and walked slowly over to her then. Eyeing her closely. She was thinking. "Is there anything I can do?"

"No." she said looking up at him. "I just need to run home real quick. There is a few things I forgot to grab anyways." And with that, Emie placed a kiss on his lips and vanished, shutting the slider glass door shut in her wake.

Asher sighed to himself. He would have to fill the void with tv, but not the news. He turned on the sports channel instead and watched the highlights from the day's game he had missed.

Emie stood in the Whitby kitchen talking to Shelley and Cristina about the move to Florida, sipping on a bottle of fresh blood Joseph had stolen from the morgue. They discussed Neely and how he was doing with everything. Cristina told her how wonderful Joseph had been with him, and how excited Neely got whenever Joseph walked into the room.

"I guess he will have to be homeschooled now. I had been wishing and praying for him to be able to settle here in Luna Pier, but now seeing the world the way I see it, I don't want him out of my site. I couldn't stand sending him to school now."

Emie remembered the talk she had shared with Miranda and Ken. She would never be the mother these women were, but she would be the best Aunt to all of them and love them with everything she had to give.

Shelley spoke up then. "I think him and Curtis will get along in Florida. Curtis loves sports, all he does is watch tv and go outside at night to play basketball."

Emie smiled then. Shelley had been so adamant on saving Curtis. She could see in her mind how much she loved him. She wondered why they weren't together yet.

"So what going on with you two?" Emie questioned her.

"Seriously?" Shelley questioned Emie.

"Ok, for the sake of our company, who can't read your mind, and for that matter, for me, who you are clearly hiding something from, what's going on?"

Cristina was thankful for that. It irritated her and was so hard when they all spoke to each other in their heads. She missed out on so much and it drove her crazy.

"Well, if you must know, the man is stubborn. His mind runs in a hundred different directions. He's always wanting to talk to me..."

Cristina wondered why that was a bad thing.

"Because! It's been a year. I'm done talking; I'm done explaining the world to him. He has to have to it figured out by now, and he needs to realize I'm not getting any younger here! Hello! 3000 years is a long time to go being alone. And now that I have him, I want him!"

Emie chuckled at that. "You were never alone! Come on, you had me!"

Shelley drained her glass and winked at Emie. They had a go of it in the last hundred years.

"Have you noticed any more powers lately?" Emie questioned Cristina wonderingly. They would need to know if she had.

Cristina was still in awe over Shelley's age when she thought harder about Emie's question. "I noticed this the other day." Cristina said, lifting up her pant legs to show Emie her foot. "It's my tattoo. Look."

Emie looked down at Cristina's right foot. Cristina had gotten a tattoo of batman on her foot many years ago. Emie was surprised to see it had made the transition with her into her new life. She wondered if the same would happen to Asher when he turned.

That thought worried her. The when's and how's of Asher changing always seemed to do that to her.

Just as Emie was about to say more on the subject and ask Cristina what Joseph thought about that since he had this fascination about himself and batman, she heard the faint sound of the fire sirens in the distance. Bracing herself for the worst, Emie got to her feet and started packing her bags she had sitting at her feet with the blood packets Joseph had brought home for her.

Emie said goodbye so fast to them both that Cristina almost hadn't heard her. She had ran at a lightening speed out of the kitchen for her car.

Cristina downed the last of the contents in her wine glass and poured herself another before she turned to Shelley. They had a vampire to entice tonight and Cristina was more then ready to help her new friend.

Emie made it to the fire hall knowing Asher would be there before she would. She parked her car next to his truck and noticed their vehicles were the only ones parked in the driveway. The truck bay was open though and one of the trucks was missing. She was at first glad to see it wasn't a fire and he hadn't taken out one of the fire trucks, only the rescue unit was missing. Emie ran into the radio room and listened over the radio for the dispatcher.

She wished she had learned how to use the radio in this room so she could ask about the call. She threw her hands down on the table in anger. She had no way of finding out where he was.

Emie walked around the empty fire hall for almost an hour before she heard Asher's voice over the radio. She sighed as he told the dispatcher they were headed back to the station. She would have to relax and not bombard him when he walked in, but she was going to have to make him realize he needed to keep in contact with her. He couldn't go out by himself any more like this.

Emie had a list now of things they would have to buy for the department at the store.

First on the list would definitely be a new kitchen. The old kitchen needed to be updated. A new face on all the cupboards and new stainless steel countertops. A bigger refrigerator was top on that list. They needed a large double door industrial one in here. Not the small one they had in the corner next to the little dilapidated freezer. She would need to stock it also and jotted down the different stores she would need to go to accomplish that. Next was a new stove. It would need to be gas incase of an outage, and would need to be much bigger than the four burner one they had now. She didn't know how they got along with such a small one, and then she seen the microwave and shook her head.

Joseph should be ashamed she thought to herself, in hopes that he heard her.

Secondly, were tables and chairs. The tables and chairs here were so old they were coming apart at all the important places.

Third was a new laundry room. The big old washer and dryer they had took up too much space. She would need to find them a stackable one and install a wash tub/sink for the room. She couldn't believe they didn't have one, she thought shaking her head. They would need shelves also, a lot of shelves she thought as she looked at her list. They were so disorganized because they didn't have the things they needed.

Next was the meeting room. It needed to be gutted of the old retro wood paneling. The tv and the stereo system would need updated and she would add a projection screen and projector like the one she bought for the schools last year. They would need the new technology to teach the new recruits.

The trophy case they had on one wall would need to be better organized and displayed differently. She made a note to talk to Asher about it and get some ideas from him. The bar would need updated also, she told herself. And stocked. She added.

While the rescue unit was being pulled in the truck bay, Emie noticed the place where Joseph had told her the little hidden door could be found. She tried not to look at as Asher walked up to her.

"What are you doing here?" He asked her. He was glad that she was though.

"I heard the sirens from home and knew you'd be here." Emie looked as three men came out of the back of the truck. "What happened? Is everything ok?"

"Yeah, one of the guys at the apartments fell out of his wheelchair."

Emie looked oddly at him. She had worried for him for over an hour because some guy fell out of his wheelchair? "And... he called 911 why?"

Asher shook his head at her and smiled. She wasn't being heartless, he could see on her face the relief she felt at knowing he was ok, and he was kicking himself for letting her worry so long. He honestly hadn't even thought about it. He had just responded like he always had in the past.

"When someone needs help Emie, they call us. It's all apart of the job. Jack is an old drunk who falls asleep in his chair a lot. He has no family to help him, so when he falls out and can't get back in, he calls us. One time he laid on the floor for three days because he couldn't reach his telephone." Asher shook his head remembering. A neighbor had found Jack and called 911. It had broke Asher's heart.

"Me and the guys bought him a cell phone that he keeps on him all the time now." Asher sighed shaking his head thinking about old Jack Dugger. The guy was in eighties now; he wouldn't be around much longer. It was sad really to Asher. The old man always hated when the guys left. He enjoyed having company so much that they all wondered if he did it on purpose sometimes. "People that age are lonely Emie. They hate to have to call us for things so silly as falling, but we go nonetheless."

Asher reached up a hand into Emie's hair. He cupped his hand and let it fall softly down her curl that was hanging down her side.

"I'm sorry." Emie told him ashamed.

"No, I'm sorry, I should have said something to you before I left."

Emie felt ashamed at what she had said. He took his job so seriously. The idea he had left his home in the middle of the night, in the middle of an apocalypse at that, to go help a man get back in his wheelchair softened her heart. "So, all the stories of fireman climbing trees to rescue cats, are those true also?"

Asher tugged on her curl and smirked at her before he kissed her lips. "Nah, we spray them with the hoses and they figure out real quick how to climb back down."

Emie eyed him curiously as she pictured that happening.

"I've got to stay here tonight sweetheart. Bob and Derrick are going to stay too. They were just as upset as I was no one was here." Asher looked at her knowingly. He knew she wasn't going to leave here, but he also knew he couldn't sleep with her tonight here. He was so tired and torn; he didn't know what to do with her or where to put her.

"Oh… well, that is a problem isn't it?" She wondered aloud. She didn't need to sleep, but Asher did. "Why don't you go up stairs with the guys and sleep, and I'll hang out in your office. I've been working on a list we will need tomorrow to go shopping with." She showed him her list and he nodded comfortably to her.

"Alright sweetheart." Asher worriedly, sighed deeply and put his hands in his pockets. "Just promise you won't leave? You'll be here when I wake up?" He almost pleaded with her.

Emie almost melted in front of him. His honesty about his fears was there in his eyes, the way he put his hands in his pockets. He didn't even try to hide it. She reached up and touched his cheek with her hand in comfort. "I promise, my love. I won't go anywhere."

Asher bent forward to give her a kiss, but one turned into three and before he knew it he had her pressed up against the side of the rescue truck. His clipboard fell to the floor along with the reports he could care less about, not like anyone was going to read them anymore.

Pulling Emie closer to him Asher tucked his leg neatly between hers. He could feel the moment her desire turned into wanton passion. She craved this just as much as he did. These stolen private moments alone.

Emie pulled on the hair behind Asher's neck. She needed more of him. The feel of him pressed so neatly up against her was driving her mad with want.

Asher stopped her for just a moment and looked behind him in the meeting room. He walked over and closed the door that led out into the other bay where the stairs led up to the mens room upstairs. He walked back over to Emie and opened the rescue truck door.

Emie looked curiously into the rescue. There in the middle of the truck was a cot wrapped in a crisp white linen. She looked at Asher questioningly then. "Isn't that just for patients?"

"Not tonight." Asher said as he climbed in the back of rescue with Emie.

Thirty One

Asher was sitting out in the sunlight on the pier. He had a banquet to plan, people from all around the city to invite, and the love of his life to surprise. Saturday was just a few days away. He had everything ready for the annual fireman's banquet, just a few more important people to invite. And one very large, very scary vampire to ask a certain question to.

Asher pulled out the tiny box the jeweler had given him to place the most expensive thing he had ever bought into. The white velvet box held the prettiest ring he had ever seen.

A couple days ago, while walking in the mall with Emie, he'd seen it in a window as he passed by with her holding hands. She'd stopped to talk to a vendor that was selling butterfly clips for her hair. He'd walked away from her and knew she could hear his thoughts, see what he had seen. But he looked at the ring anyways. He gazed on the one thing he had to have. That ring belonged on Emie's finger, forever.

He'd bought it today; gotten up early with his mind made up. He really had no idea how to marry a vampire. He only knew he had to do it.

He was going to propose in front of his family and friends. They would all be at the banquet Saturday, and he couldn't wait. Right there on the dance floor, with a song in his heart and a mic in his hand, he was going to ask her on bended knee to make him the happiest man alive, even though he already was.

Asher knew the world around him was falling apart. He felt the fool for planning this banquet, but it had helped him focus on life rather than death. He didn't understand why it had been so quiet in Monroe County. Toledo had been hit by the riots and the whole city seemed to be losing the battle with the citizens. Detroit had been on the local news everyday for the past week. Detroit had been on fire for days. That wasn't unusual for Detroit, but it was nonetheless.

Luna Pier sat right dab in the middle of both big cities.

Asher opened the box again. The diamonds were sparkling in the sunlight blinding him. The long skinny marquee cut diamond reminded him of Emie's body. The gold circle band that held diamonds all around its length was a sign of his love that started and ended with her. It would go on forever. He had engraved on the inside "I Love You" so she would never forget that he loved her. All she ever wanted in this life was to be loved, and he loved her. He loved her so much, he thought as he put the box back in his pocket and leaned back on the old metal bench out on the Pier.

Asher, I'm here.

Asher shut his mind off of his thoughts. Asher had asked Joseph to meet him at the fire hall today. He couldn't help but hope that Joseph hadn't already heard all his thoughts and plans for the day. Some things they would just have to let him have! Like his own thoughts. Asher grumbled to himself and wondered when this family was ever going to learn how to use cell phones like normal people.

I hate cell phones Asher. They take too long. This is quicker. Joseph told him.

Asher got up and walked to the fire hall to meet the 'Big bad Vampire.'

I heard that! Joseph said to him.

Asher shook his head and jogged back to the fire hall. Joseph wouldn't wait long out of spite for his slow human legs.

Joseph was waiting for Asher in the meeting area. He didn't have time to dilly dally like this today. He hoped whatever it was Asher had to say, he would make it quick. He knew it was about the banquet and had argued with Emie a moment ago about why Asher had to drag him down here to invite him.

He had always been invited to this thing. Laughing and joking with humans wasn't his thing. He never got their jokes and they never got his. Well, he'd never told any of his. They'd probably expire at the thought of bleeding hearts and open windows. He didn't mingle well with humans.

Joseph was ready to get to Florida with Cristina and Neely. The FBI and Jerry Winkleman had stopped him on more then one occasion to ask him if he knew anything about the disappearances around town.

Joseph hated worrying, and he loathed the idea Jordy was trying to get him to see about Frank and Jerry. Frank may think he knows what they are, but he'd never be able to convince anyone else of that. Jordy's plan would have to wait.

Asher was not only a good guy; he was turning out to be a lot of fun around the house. He'd finally figured out that he could scare the boys with lighters and cigarettes. And they'd finally figured out how they could hang him from the rafters in his sleep without giving him a heart attack.

Joseph had to stop chuckling at the memory of Asher waking up in the rafters one morning, when Asher came through the door of the meeting room. Asher's body had woken from its slumber upside down slowly and he hadn't screamed like a little girl like the boys thought he would. Instead he had stayed there, waited patiently for Emie and threatened out loud for hours he was going to pay them back, and they were not going to like it one bit. The boys were still waiting for it and they were starting to worry about when and just what Asher was planning.

Asher's face was beat red when he entered the meeting room, and Joseph tried his best not to read his thoughts or lick his lips at the blood that was draining from Asher's cheeks.

"You know, if the boys were here-"

"I know, I know. Take a seat." Asher said hurriedly. When Joseph didn't, Asher reminded him that he needed one and it would be awkward if Joseph was to remain standing.

Joseph took the hint. He wasn't a sitter, but he did it for Asher. Asher looked serious, and that couldn't be good. They sat down together at the tables in the middle of the room.

Two men with missions on their minds. This was Joseph's favorite kind of conversations. Business. It took his mind off all the things he couldn't control, and gave him something he could.

Asher took a deep breath and steadied himself. He was ready for this.

"Ready for what?" Joseph questioned.

"Just wait, listen. I want to ask you something, and I don't want interruptions." Ok? Asher pushed him for patience

Joseph leaned back in the chair gently and agreed. Ok.

"Joseph you know I love Emie, and you know she loves me." Asher didn't wait for his acknowledgment. He didn't need it. This was just a formality for him. Permission he didn't need either, but he was going to get it anyways. He didn't know if vampires did this still, but they seemed old fashion enough, and he knew this was something he had always wanted... no, that wasn't right, this was just something men did. And they were both men. Kind of.

"I want to ask you if I can marry her Joseph. I want to marry Emie." Asher took his tiny white box out of his pocket and set it in front of Joseph and opened it.

Joseph took a minute to reply. He knew Asher had just begun to see what their worlds were like. He picked up the ring, impressed, glad Asher hadn't thought about money, but had thought about his sister when he had bought it. Emie wouldn't want anything expensive, she never had. She would love this. He handed it back to Asher.

He knew Asher hadn't a clue what he was asking. If he'd been asking this the right way, he'd be asking Joseph to turn him and make himself like her so he could be with her forever instead of this silly human need to tie each other to each other with a ring and vow. But Asher's mind wasn't thinking that far ahead yet. He was still in the heat of passion.

Joseph leaned forward. Set his arms on the table in front of them and folded his hands.

"Asher, I'm not going to tell you yes or no. It's not my place. I'm not her father. I didn't think any of this with you was good idea in the beginning. The only reason your still around is because she loves you. She deserves this. And you are a good man for the job.

"On the other hand, I would be proud to have you as a brother. But you need to ask yourself one thing before you do this. It's something we've all been wanting to ask you, but none of us know how to, or when the right time is to ask you.

"Are ready to become a vampire Asher? Are you ready to truly lay down your life for her, and give her the one thing she really needs?"

Asher was quiet for a minute. He had thought of this. He really had. He had just been hoping to put it off for awhile. Marry her, build a house together, live away from her brothers somewhere together... Those were the things he had been thinking of.

"You need to think of the bigger picture here. Emie needs a protector, not just a human promise of a future together."

Asher rubbed his legs. He hadn't meant to talk about this.

"Listen Asher, she needs you. She needs someone to protect her, guide her. She's a strong woman, but she's breakable. Her heart sometimes is in all the wrong places. Like loving a fireman."

Asher smirked at that. But he got Joseph's point. He could have hurt her. He did hurt her. Once; never again.

"She might not have come back Asher." Joseph was going off Asher's last thoughts. "She would have run to the ends of the earth to protect you. She did it for us once. What brought her back, I don't know. Maybe it was fate. Like she keeps saying." He sighed then and looked down at the table that Emie had replaced and shook his head.

"She made us for her, you know. She didn't want to be alone anymore. I love her for it, don't get me wrong. And I thank her all the time. I'm loving this life." He smiled widely, "But the question is, are you ready? Are you ready, for better or for worse," he jested, "to be the man, or vampire if you will, who loves, honors and protects her? Forever?"

When Asher took his time to respond, Joseph looked around. Giving the poor guy a moment to think about it. This hall really needed more than a makeover he thought to himself. It still had the same old trophy case he helped carry in sixty years ago. He shook his head remembering Emie showing him the dishes too. They were the same old ones they had bought in fifties.

This place smelled old, Joseph sniffed.

Asher wanted this. He did. He wanted Emie in every way possible. He didn't want to be her weak human who couldn't protect her.

She was his, and he loved her. Forever.

There wasn't anything vain about it. He wanted to love and protect the woman he loved. He just didn't know how. Or when.

Asher looked to Joseph for help.

Joseph smiled evilly in return. His fangs showed, and Asher smirked back.

"You'll have to wait of course. You can't go to the banquet as a vampire. You'd have fun, but that's not what you want."

Asher crossed his arms at the bad jest.

"See, this is why I hate joking with humans." Joseph sat back in his chair and relaxed a little. He was enjoying himself immensely though. "Trust me, one day you're going to find that funny." Joseph pointed out.

"Anyways, so you will be able to make your proposal you are planning like normal, but after the banquet, you need to decide what you are going to do."

Asher nodded his head at this. He completely agreed with Joseph now. He looked over and saw Joseph leaning back in a chair looking ever the virile vampire. He had to wonder what it would be like.

Asher wondered if the stories were true about mirrors and if they still had a reflection.

"Only if you move. Then you blur a little."

"What?" Asher asked, confused, trying to remember what he had thought about that Joseph had answered.

Joseph looked bored, he was cleaning his nails that looked sharper then Asher remembered, and his eyes were a deep red. No whites, just red. He thought it odd at first when the brothers started letting their guard down around him.

"Mirrors. Keep up kid. We can see our own reflection in them if we hold still. Humans can't see us in them if we move around." Joseph informed him.

"Guess I'll be the hot fire man in the calendar this year again." Asher jested. "How will I… eat?" Asher questioned.

Joseph handed him a flask out of his pocket then. Asher turned away disgusted.

"It's a flask Asher.

"It's easier if you just give in. The savage beast won't be so hard to handle if you keep something with you all the time." He hoped Asher would learn it fast. It was better to drink what Emie gave them then it was to walk among the living hungry.

The smell filled Asher's nostrils then as Joseph tipped it towards him. The smell of blood was so overpowering.

Joseph smiled a wide grin then. He sat back in his chair and downed the flask before anyone walked in and seen what he was drinking. He had started to think about how he would do this for Asher. He sat there and it planned out. He would take him home and take him to the den first. He would get Asher so drunk the boys would have to help him take him down to the dungeon. He would stalk him around a chair and distract him by talking to him, then he would strike Asher and Joseph could see the spot in Asher's neck he would put his dripping fangs into.

"So what's up with the dungeon then?" this Asher said bringing Joseph right out his daydream. "If you can bust through walls and leap tall buildings?"

Joseph wondered then if Asher would be able to read minds. He was already doing it sometimes. "Mainly because of the screams during the process."

Asher held very still. It sickened him to think of himself as weak, but he knew there were some things worse than death.

"Trust me, you won't regret it." Asher needed to be reminded of what and why he was doing this. The mind was an easy target to be taken over by evil. Joseph had a feeling that Asher didn't have an evil bone in his body, but just to be sure he was gonna take his time getting to know if this was for Asher.

Joseph leaned forward, all intent in his eyes. Asher leaned back slightly. "Two things vampires are afraid of. The sun, which is outside ready to claim the life if they disobey rule number one and try to escape the dungeon, and, another vampire. An older more wiser one anyways. Which I am, and can rip you to shreds if you disobey me."

Asher gulped down the saliva he had been savoring on his tongue. He still was new to all this and had a lot to learn. He scratched his head out of habit and wondered when he would be able to do this. His banquet was in two days. Emie had been helping him every day for over a week now. He had to finish this banquet and then pop the question to her about this. He wondered now if she had been listening in on their conversation.

"She's busy with Cristina. I told her before I came down here to check on you to check on Cristina and Neely."

Asher leaned forward and set his heavy arms down on the table that felt like dead weight. His shoulder hurt so bad and he wondered if changing would take that all away. He brushed his hair out of his face and closed his eyes trying to remember Emie. He hoped nothing with her would change. He couldn't imagine what it would be like, but he was sure he was ready to find out.

Joseph wondered at that too. Jordy had showed him a few things that scared the hell out of him. He just wished this stupid banquet he had made so public to everyone would hurry up and be done with.

"For the next few days we are going to be getting everything ready like normal for the banquet." Joseph willed him to understand as he spoke clearly to Asher. Asher was going to act and live like nothing had happened with him and the Whitby's. Like normal. They didn't have time for anything else.

Joseph remembered Jordy's warning and knew they didn't have much time. But they could make time for what Asher had planned with Emie.

Asher interrupted him, questioning him. "Like normal?"

"You have to act like you haven't met and fallen in love with the enemy Asher. If anyone finds out that we are vampires Asher, they can destroy us."

Asher instinctively reached for his cigarettes. He wasn't going to need them soon. Easiest way to quit, he laughed to himself. But the thought, the addiction of having something to do, to go outside and think like he needed to now, while smoking would probably still there.

"Normal. Got it." Asher was thankful he had a proposal to keep his mind off of the vampires that would be in the room that night.

But, he just couldn't shake the thought now. What would he be like as a vampire?

Joseph leaned back, crossed his arms and smiled. "Asher, I can feel you now. See deep into that soul of yours. You were raised to save lives, protect property. That power you feel inside you, it will be stronger when you turn. You're going to be just fine." Joseph was sure of it. So was Jordy, who had already confirmed it. But neither of them had expected what Joseph was looking at now. Asher looked, smelled and tasted like a raging fire. Joseph had never believed in fate until now.

Asher would be their saving grace after all.

Asher wanted to look into Joseph's mind. He wanted to see what he seen.

When Joseph showed him, Asher had a feeling Emie was going to kill him. Looking at himself in Joseph's mind, Asher could see the change he seen. He would look different, stronger, more powerful than even he thought possible.

"She probably will." Joseph grinned. "But I'll be there to put you back together."

Asher smiled back and stuck his fist out for a bump, realizing too late Joseph wouldn't know what that meant.

Joseph knew what it meant. He looked at Asher and held out his fist. It was what Asher did with his brother. Asher felt close enough to Joseph now, like brothers, and this pleased Joseph down deep to his core. He'd never had a friend before. One he could trust. One he liked.

Asher looked into the eyes of the man Emie thought the world of. He had to admit, Joseph was a good man. Ken and Jerry would think it odd that he couldn't spend time with them anymore. But he was doing this for them too. Even for their families. He had to do this so he could protect them all.

Asher took a deep breath, one he would never do again soon. He hit his fist with Joseph's. For the first time in a long time Asher was ready and willing for the next chapter in his life. He'd finally had two things worth living for.

"Think you're ready yet?"

Asher eyed him questioningly. "You really think I can? Do this I mean?" Asher wasn't looking at him when Joseph told him the truth.

"Asher, you won't hurt anyone. It's your family. Your friends." He showed him what his words couldn't. He showed him how he had reacted to his brothers when he had first turned. How he did it so long ago.

When Asher seen it, he believed it. He trusted Joseph. But he had so many question.

"Who are you Joseph? What are you? How did this all start?" Asher knew this question already. Joseph had told him before. But he needed to hear it again.

Joseph knew what he meant. Asher would now be one of them. He was surprised by it though. No one he knew had asked this question so quickly except for him, even he'd had to seek his answers. Everyone else craved desires and blood. Asher craved Emie, and answers.

"We have been here all along Asher. We were the protectors."

Angels. Asher thought aloud.

"I would be an ang..."

"Sort of..." Joseph interrupted showing him. "We walk, talk, and interact with the humans, unlike the angles. Help them, guide them, and protect the ones we can. They can see us, but they can't see what makes us heavenly. We are reborn and transformed into the image of the heavenly angels. But we are still the perfect image of God."

"So why the secrecy? What's up with the sun?" he questioned again.

"Somewhere around the tower of Babble, men have always wanted to be like us. Craved it even. So God separated us from them. Wouldn't let us out during the day so they couldn't see us anymore for what we are. Sometimes they find out and it's our job to fix it. Some men squander this gift. Want it for other reasons."

Asher had never been religious, but he had a hard time believing what he would become, was anything godly.

"Awe, come now. What do you see here that goes against God?" Joseph held his hands out in surrender.

Asher thought about that. Thought about Emie. They didn't kill; they didn't really go against anything God had set for rules. The boys had just been really bad pranksters.

"It wasn't until the humans killed his son that God closed the books so to speak. Gave us free rain. Save the ones that are His, the rest are ours to do what we will with them. Hell on earth so to speak. But there's a reason for everything. And we are never to mess with reason, or will. God's will is ever present. It's our job to respect it and protect it."

Asher rubbed his head again. So he was to lead the life of a saint now.

"You always were Asher, you just didn't know it."

Asher smiled at that. So God had heard his mom's prayers all them years ago. She had always told him God had plans for him.

"I might even let you tell her if you behave." Joseph loved mothers. He missed his and treated them all that deserved it like his own.

"What about bats? Were wolves? And silver bullets? Crosses and garlic?"

Asher's mind was moving faster now. Joseph would have to keep this in mind when he changed him. Curtis had been the same way with Shelley. "Cristina is the only one I know who can change into something other than a human. She has chosen bats, like her little tattoo on her foot." Joseph smiled at the thought of her. Before she had changed, she had loved to watch the movie. Joseph had instantly loved the thought of being her superhero.

"Although you might wanna stay away from the servants at night... But that's another story." He assured him, shaking off the memories. "Silver bullets were something an old man figured out he could use to slow us down when vampires turned on humans back in the 1500's. Any kind of steel works really, it's got something to with the fire it's made in. That's why we have steel cages in the dungeon, vampires can't escape them.

"Crosses won't burn your eyes and garlic just masks the smell of human blood. They are all just old wise tales meant to boast men's egos. Only thing that can kill you is fire. Hence the whole sun thing. That and another vampire."

For a brief moment Joseph remembered his father chasing Emie with a shotgun full of silver bullets, when Asher started looking around for trouble.

Joseph stayed him and had to smile at Asher's protective nature. He could read them already and they hadn't even changed him yet.

Asher smirked at him thinking of his next question.

"My scar? What about my scar? And the pain?" It was so intense sometimes; Asher couldn't imagine a life without it.

Gone.

Relief spread through Asher at Joseph's thoughts. There were some things he wasn't going to miss.

"What were you thinking about a second ago?" Asher questioned him. He was worried that Joseph had gotten silent when the talk had turned to things like killing vampires. Emie did that same thing when she was thinking of something she didn't want him to know.

"If you keep asking all these question we are never going to get out here." Joseph stood and had to smile at Asher. He would have two, Cristina and Asher. It pleased him thoroughly.

Asher knew he was right. He wanted out of this fire hall and wanted to see Emie again. Joseph played out quickly in his mind what Asher needed to know about Emie. Showed him her life whole in a blink of an eye as they walked out.

Asher understood now. Understood why he needed to be with Emie. Understood why Vampires existed. He hated himself for treating Emie like she had been the worst thing imaginable when she was the best thing that ever could have happened to him.

He understood now. Now he could live together with her. Now he could spend the rest of his life with her.

Now he had to just figure out when, and what to do with everyone else in his life.

"Are you coming?" Joseph was standing by the door already. Asher knew he was. He was ready for a new life.

~Thirty Two~

Saturday night. Luna Pier's 63rd Annual Firemen's Banquet.

Joseph and Emie had gone all out for the banquet this year. Joseph had ordered new white table cloths for the department and got rid of the old ones. He had shipped in white chairs to match. New china had been shipped in from Italy. Gold plated china with American flags painted in its depths. 'We will never forget!' memorandum engraved on the bottoms of each at Asher's request. Paper plates were brought in by the box load for every day dinners at Joseph's request, along with everything else their kitchen needed to feed these young heroes. A new, giant, double door, stainless steel refrigerator was placed in the kitchen. A large industrial gas stove with eight burners and a grill rack, and two ovens had been installed also with enough new pots and pans and baking items. A microwave, a double pot coffee maker, a new popcorn cart for parties and events, two pop machines, and enough food and drinks in the pantry to feed an army. Joseph had even made sure there was enough water in cases for the men for an entire year.

Every cupboard had been refinished and every closet had been restocked. Every wall had been painted and they had decorated each room according to its own unique style. There wasn't a room left untouched in two weeks.

Asher had gotten with one of the wives of the firemen and ordered her all the decorations she needed for a costume ball. The wives had loved the change of plans and sent out new invites. It was received by all as a welcome change as well.

The trucks had been moved out of the hall, the long dividers that separated the truck bay from the meeting room had been pulled open to make more space. The walls had been professionally cleaned and painted yesterday. Food had been catered in, a DJ from The Saloon was setting up in corner of the hall.

Asher was helping with a disco light ball hanging in the middle of the room when his father walked through the bay doors. He was looking around with his hands in his pockets. Asher couldn't tell if Frank had been pleased or not with the change in the department.

"So why the change son?" Frank asked up at Asher who now was standing next to him. Frank did a double take at his son then. Asher was happy, it was written all over his face.

"Well, what do you think dad?" Asher questioned him, unsure of how his father would respond. He sent up a prayer his father would be happy and not angry with him. He didn't want to fight with him, not tonight.

Frank turned around and looked around. "It's been a long time coming." Frank coughed then and turned away from Asher.

Asher would take what he could get. He was folding up the ladder he had been standing on to hang the disco ball and felt more accomplished then he had in years. He would never be able to thank the Whitby's enough for what they had done.

"Izzy called." Frank hissed.

"She did?" Asher questioned nonchalantly. He had been expecting this from his father. He had already talked to his mom about it.

Cyndy hated what Izzy had done, she had cried to Asher. How could she have up and left them in a time like this. She was still a child in all their eyes. Asher had tried to explain to his mother the story they had all come up with for his family. He told her of the secret relationship Izzy had been having with Jordy for some time now. They had been afraid of her father's wrath and could no longer stand to be without each other. It was only a matter of time before she made the decision she had.

"She's with that rich pompous-"

Asher noticed the moment Frank paused and stopped talking. He noticed his eyes and what his father seen. Asher had two fang marks on the side of his neck from Emie. No one else had noticed it before.

Frank hacked some more and had to bend over to finish coughing. He held on to Asher as he did.

Asher picked up the ladder and walked away from his dad. He couldn't stand to watch his father slowly die while not seeking treatment anymore let alone talk about Emie's brother. The Whitby family may be rich, but they were not pompous. They weren't vain or boisterous, or any of the other things his father had called them over the years.

"If you know where she is Asher-"

His father started to say as Asher was walking away, but Asher was done talking to him. He wouldn't tell him where she was even if he could.

Asher slammed the door to his office and slumped down in his chair. Dragging his hands down his face and back through his hair Asher looked at his watch. He still had a few more hours before he needed to go home and change. He refused to be moved by his father's hatred.

Asher's mother came through his door just as Asher was about to stand up and go back out in the meeting room. She knocked slowly on the door as she pushed it open.

"Well, look here now. You even got a new room." She told Asher proudly.

"Mom, come in. Have a seat." Asher greeted her by standing up and closing the door behind her. She sat in front of his desk in the little chair designated for guests in his office. She made herself comfortable and watched as Asher settled in the chair behind the desk.

Asher noticed there were tears in her eyes and asked what it was about.

"Oh, I'm fine. Just so much changing in the world around me. Your father and I are empty nesters now." She said as she pulled out one of her handkerchiefs and wiped her tears away. "I just wanted to see you and since I haven't been here with your father being sick and all... Seeing you behind that desk Asher..." She sighed aloud, and smiled over at him, trying not to cry again.

Asher knew exactly what she meant. He hadn't wanted this. This was supposed to be Curtis' office, not his. He longed to tell her. It ripped at him inside knowing he couldn't share that with her. His mother still grieved Curtis.

He wondered if a change in topic would help ease their pain now.

"I have something to show you mom."

Asher pulled the ring box out of his pocket and set it opened in front of her. She looked at the box and the ring within and tried to smile, but the tears ran anew anyways.

"Well it's about time." She smirked up at Asher. She picked up the tiny box and looked at the ring.

Asher grinned back. Leave it to his mom to cry at this. "I'm going to give it to her tonight during the banquet."

"Tonight?" she asked him, smiling brightly, tears running down her cheeks. Her hand covering her lips was shaking a bit. She was delighted for him. "Oh honey. Come here and give me hug."

Asher's own delight deepened as he rounded his desk and reached down to hug his mother. He would give anything to give his mother everything she wanted. He hoped this was worth something.

In the end now, he knew he would conquer being a vampire to be with his family. He would never let anything overpower him to the point he couldn't be with or protect his family.

Jerry busted in his office, and excused himself for barging in when he seen Asher's mother.

"No, no. It's fine. Come on in Jerry sweetheart, I was just leaving." Cyndy told Jerry as she hugged her son one last time. "I love you son." She told Asher as she patted his face looking at him. "You two boys have a lot to talk about tonight. I'll see myself out."

"Make sure you take dad with you." Asher jested as she closed the door knowingly.

"What's up Jerry?" Asher asked as he sat back down at his desk.

Jerry didn't even bother to sit down, he placed his hands on Asher's desk. "It's happening in Atlanta now."

"Atlanta's a long ways away from here Jerry."

Jerry had been watching too much news this last week. He'd been giving Asher up to date reports twice a day like clock work. Asher was tired of it. He had done everything he could around here to keep things light and keep things going. He had rallied the men and gave them something worth fighting for.

Living.

They would protect this city from whatever they could. They would hunker down and keep watch. Asher needed Jerry sane right now. And Jerry didn't seem sane right now.

"Damn it Asher! This plan of yours to have this banquet is suicide! It's like gathering pigs in a pen for the wolves to eat!"

Asher stood then, pointing his finger at Jerry. He wanted to tell him he didn't know what wolves were now that he had seen the real ones, but he couldn't say that to him.

He stepped back from Jerry and put his hands on his hips he hung his head now. He felt on fire with rage and Jerry didn't deserve it. But he wanted him to see it.

Asher glared back at Jerry. "Listen, I know what's going on around us."

Jerry didn't let him finish before he interrupted. "Do you? Do you Asher? Cause you sure as hell haven't been acting like it. You're so hell bent on having this thing and decorating the fire hall, do you really think anyone is coming?"

Asher stared Jerry down then. "I do Jerry. Cause while you've been sitting down at that station, bunkering down, pacing around like a war general, I've been out talking to people. Checking on people. Making sure everyone is ok, and seeing if they need anything. Joseph Whitby has been bringing in loads of needed supplies in trucks. While I've been 'shopping', as you put it yesterday, I've been checking out the local stores and seeing who has what, and who is still in this God forsaken city! So don't tell me I haven't been doing anything, cause so help me Jerry, if I hear it again, I'm going to walk you out here and lock the door."

He continued when he seen he was getting through to Jerry. Jerry was now holding his own hands on hips and looking down listening to Asher. "These men don't need to hear how bad it is out there. They know how bad it is! They're just as scared as you. But we can't stop living Jerry. That's what they want. That's what the media wants. They are instilling fear in all of us. And that's when we are our weakest Jerry. When we fear what's coming instead of preparing for it."

Jerry sighed deeply. He rubbed his head and started to pace. "I know. I know. I just can't stop watching it Asher. You've seen what's happened around here!"

"And we've faced it, together. And if you can hold yourself together we can keep on doing it."

Jerry stopped then and took a deep breath. He looked at Asher then. "You're really going to do this tonight?"

"Yes."

Jerry looked down at his police boot. "Fine, but I'm bringing in some of the guys from Erie to help me tonight. While all you firemen are getting your party on and drinking, we are going to keep watch."

"Isn't that what you always do?' He asked Jerry, trying to lighten the mood.

Jerry smiled then. "What's on the menu?" he asked, remembering the good food that had been brought in years past.

Asher nodded then. He had gotten through. "Steak."

Emie wanted to pace the floor in her bed room. But Cristina was trying her best to get Emie to hold still, she had one more diamond to put in her hair.

Emie hadn't seen Asher in four days. Four. It was driving her crazy. Asher had Emie texting now, a lot. Every time she turned around she was getting a picture of something he had bought or seen at the store. He had been on more calls then he could count, and had a lot of work to do around the fire hall. She'd never known this whole banquet thing was such a big deal over there.

"Emie, I swear, If you don't hold still I'm gonna break your foot off and hide it! You won't be able to dance tonight!"

"Someone is getting testy." Emie said to her jokingly.

"Well you have Joseph so busy I can't even talk to him let alone spend time with him. If you let me hurry, we'll get there faster."

Cristina looked down at her work on Emie's hair. Emie looked beautiful.

"Go look." She told her.

"Why, I can see it in your eyes." Emie hung her head. She didn't feel pretty enough even with all Cristina's work. Asher needed more than she could ever be in a woman. Tonight would prove it when she got there looking like this.

"GET UP!" Cristina told her angrily.

Emie stood unwillingly, and had to give Cristina credit for putting up with her these last few days. She couldn't shake the feeling that Asher didn't want her anymore.

What Emie saw in her reflection was like a blast from the past. She could remember a night. A ball she had been invited to. Her father had spent more money then he had on a dress that looked just like this one. He had wanted Emie to go to town and find herself a gentleman. He had wanted her to marry well.

Emie had felt so out of place that night. So much like the wallflowers who lined the wall at the ball. But her father, like Joseph, was known in town and respected. He had led Emie all around the ballroom showing off his only daughter to every eligible bachelor.

They were called home early by their servants that night. Emie's mother was sick. She had been visiting the sick at the hospital with Joseph all that week, and had developed a fever. A fever that would take her life years later.

None of those bachelors had ever called on Emie. They'd never sent flowers, never came to offer condolences on her mother's sickness. She never went back to another ball. Never felt pretty enough or adequate enough.

Looking in the mirror now, she could only wish she had looked like this all them years ago. Maybe she would have married well, maybe her life would have turned out differently.

Cristina was good at what she did.

"Only because I have the perfect canvas to work with." She leaned over her shoulders and placed Emie's gold chain around her neck. She tied it in back so the charm hung higher on her chest.

Emie had wanted to see it too tonight. It reminded her of so much in her life.

Emie held the charm of the broken wing of a little butterfly. She had it dipped in gold many years ago. She had broken his gentle wing the night she had been turned when her book had fallen to the ground while she was being attacked. Days later when Emie had been run off by her father she had picked up her book and seen the butterfly, still staggering under the weight of the book. Emie picked him up and held him in her hands until he died. She had carried him with her for years in her book. He was the only part of her old life she had left. Butterflies lived all over her land in Whitby. She loved to sit and read in their midst. When he died, it had broken Emie as well. She missed her old life everyday.

Until she met Asher.

Emie looked at Cristina. She had heard Cristina just as she finished the clasp. Emie was like this butterfly. She had been cocooned these last hundred years, now she was free to fly. Free to live a new life with Asher.

"You look stunning Emie." Joseph's voice had been a shock. Emie had been hoping for Asher, but it had been Joseph she'd seen in the mirror behind her. He blurred as he walked up behind her. Then with a gentle kiss on her shoulder, he shared her reflection in the mirror.

Emie's hair was sparkling in the mirror from all the diamonds Cristina had placed in her hair. Her long flowing dark blue dress was hinted with specks of diamonds too. They led a trail around her breasts and swirled around her in circles till they reached her hem. They reminded her of shooting star dust in a midnight sky. Her bare shoulders were dusted with just a hint of sparkles to add shine to her pale complexion. Her long hair was pinned up in long curly lengths that spilled around her shoulders and down her back. She'd never worn her hair this way before. Cristina had placed her curls just right. Her only jewelry was her necklace. It was the only thing she needed.

"You look the goddess Asher keeps dreaming of."

Emie would have blushed if she could have. No one had ever called her that. She felt the heat rise in her body at Asher's name spoken. She missed him.

"He misses you more little sister." Joseph winked. "Let's get you to him before you turn into a pumpkin." He jested. He lifted her dress a little to see if she was wearing glass slippers too.

He didn't get to see the shiny ones she was wearing. Cristina had drummed his head with her hand and sent him toppling. Just a little. He was laughing and grinning playfully at the both of them.

They all loaded up in his black SUV and headed into town.

Asher, dressed in a black tux, holding a bottle beer, looked just as impressive as the firemen surrounding him. The only thing making him stand out in the makeshift ball room was his height and his stature. He was too big for the tux, too big for the bottle he was holding.

Asher had been looking all around him for the last half hour looking for Emie. Leave it to Joseph to make Emie fashionably late. If they didn't hurry they were going to miss the awards.

Asher looked at the clock on the wall above the old/new trophy case Joseph had bought just today and began to worry. Looking out the bay doors he had the feeling like he needed a cigarette, and wondered if he still had time to smoke one, just as a blue shimmer caught his eye.

He followed the blue dress up the body of an amazing woman until his eyes found the sight he had been looking for.

Emie.

Emie found him immediately, at the sound of his voice in her mind saying her name. He was standing by the bar with a bottle of beer and looked more handsome than he ever had since she met him.

What was different tonight, she wondered. Had it been the absences of him that brought on the strong rush of emotions? He was grinning like a little boy at the bar waiting for her, watching intently her every move. When she got close enough to him, she almost lost her footing. She couldn't get to him fast enough.

"Emie." Asher was at her side now. He picked up her hand in greeting and kissed it. "You look amazing sweetheart."

Emie looked up at Asher. She had to gulp down the blood that was rising from her belly. She couldn't believe the sight that was Asher standing in front of her. His face, his eyes, his clothes. The man she loved. But there was something different about him tonight. He was hiding something.

He winked at her. And it took her by surprise.

Asher gave Joseph a freighting look then. Joseph had been just as excited about this as he had. He wondered if Joseph had told her. He hoped he hadn't spoiled the surprise about what would happen after the banquet. He had plans of telling Emie later.

Emie patted Asher's chest to calm him down, Joseph had kept whatever it was he was hiding so well, and then she let her fingers linger there as she took him all in. She inhaled his scent deeply. What was it tonight, she wondered. Why did he look and feel so different?

"You look incredibly handsome tonight Asher." She told him honestly.

Asher wrapped his arms around her then and held her closer. He knew they must look odd to everyone around them, standing in the middle of a crowd with no music, holding each other close and looking into each others eyes like they were dancing and never wanted it to end.

He couldn't help himself though. Emie was his beginning and his end. She was his life ever after, and he wasn't about to let her go. He reached down and placed a gentle kiss on her lips. Just enough to raise her passion. He watched as they moved in slow motion. Watched as he made her eyes close, and felt her body lean into his. Felt that same rush of feeling course through his body he always got when she was near.

He felt Emie's smile on his lips and heard Joseph's voice in the back of his mind.

Oh please you two. Get a room! This from Joseph and a look from Cristina.

The Luna Pier Firemen's banquet was a hit. Everyone around the city who had been invited, including the mayor had all enjoyed the d cor and food.

When it was time for the awards, Frank and Asher stood to pass out each trophy and shake the hands of each firemen awarded. They paused only long enough to have their pictures taken.

Asher this year got to pass out the officer's award and presented it to Ken Kruse, the Chaplin on the department, Asher's best friend. Asher had always wanted his friend to have the award, and was proud of his father for finally seeing Ken's progress on the department. Ken had finally made captain this year, and had worn the hat proudly. Proved himself on the department as a leader.

After the awards were over, dinner was severed. Prime Rib and potatoes with all the fixins. Asher was proud of the menu. He'd had it prepared by the chef's just a little rarer then normal for his special guests tonight.

When the plates were cleared, and tables pushed back for the dance floor, Asher walked up to the stage and asked for the mic. He'd never felt more nervous then he did now.

He looked out over the crowd who had all hushed. Emie was sitting with her brother and best friend Cristina. His mother was sitting at the head table beaming proudly at him. All of his siblings were here tonight except two. His friends on the department didn't know what he had planned, but somehow was expecting it.

Everyone knew Emie now. She had become apart of the department just by her presence. And most likely all the fresh pastries she kept bringing them from the local bakery in town.

"I wanted to thank everyone for coming tonight. This time of year is my personal favorite time." Asher smiled deeply at the knowing crowd. "It's like Christmas for a guy like me, passing out all these awards and such." When everyone chuckled he continued. "Every one of you who worked hard this last year deserves that award sitting in front of you" This he said more to Ken then any one else. "And tonight we're going to celebrate that hard work, with partying and dancing, like we do every year." When his men started a playful hooting and whistling, he calmed them down with a calm hand. "But first, I have a surprise for a certain lady." Asher looked at Emie then. He watched as she fidgeted in her seat. "As chief this year, I get to present the chiefs award. And this year it goes to a very special lady.

"She's done so much for me this year, and this city in the past. She's seen me through my highs and lows, she's made me stronger than I ever thought I could be. And if you look around you tonight, you can see her handy work all around. She's dedicated herself to this department without even being asked. She's here every day, working hard for the good of others. For the good of her community.

"She deserves not only this award from us, but she deserves better me."

This was it, he thought to himself. He turned to the Dj, and felt the first strings of his new song. He would sing it to Emie, who Joseph would send up to the stage, and she would make him happier then he was now.

He'd written it the morning he woke up and left her to go get her ring. He knew the words and fell in love with them all over again. He wanted her to hear them before he asked her.

He knew she'd hear the words in her heart. Understand them now that she'd seen him and how happy he was. He wanted to be apart of her world now and he wanted her to know it.

Emie was being bumped by Joseph. She had just wanted to sit there and listen to Asher. She'd loved hearing him sing in his truck, his showers, or just when they were walking on the beach. Now here he was singing a song she didn't know. In his sweet southern voice she loved. And every word was his, not someone else's.

It was that last morning she'd seen him. The same melody he had been humming.

When she stood, his words were bringing up the butterflies again. He would pick a love song like this to sing to her. She wasn't sure why she was walking up, but she just went to him anyways. He'd written this for her, and his words were ringing all throughout her broken heart.

Emie didn't like being the center of attention, but in that moment it was really just her and him. His eyes never left hers as he handed her his heart.

Asher walked off the stage mid song and met her on the dance floor. Her eyes were shining and she knew what was coming. Knew he'd get down on one knee when the song ended, because he couldn't stop thinking about. Knew she'd say yes, because really how could she not?

And he knew, this would always be their song. He reached inside her hair for the side of her face and ended his song on a high note.

Asher loved this woman more than anyone else in this world. He got down on one knee and made her his forever. The best way he knew how.

He pulled out her ring and held the box open.

"Emilie Whitby, you already made me the happiest man alive when you told me you loved me," he winked at her at his jest, then added "will you now, become my wife and spend the rest of your life with me?"

Emie looked at Asher, seen him on his knees in his gesture of love. She thought she had already given him everything he wanted. Apparently he wanted more. She fell down next to him and kissed him.

She couldn't speak, she'd cry. He'd loved her so much. He'd given her the best gift anyone could have given her. Love.

Asher picked Emie up and spun her around while the crowd cheered for them both. He almost dropped the ring. Almost.

Emie was lying in bed with Cristina looking up at her ring. Neely had fallen asleep early tonight, so Cristina had called her into his room so they could look at her ring again. They were still both dressed in their shimmering ball gowns and felt like princesses in a castle.

Neely's room had been decorated like a tree house. The floors and trim resembled the old wood, and his walls were painted with tree branches, his ceiling was the sky. Joseph had painted it just so that it looked like a sunny day. There was even bright glowing fireflies that would light up at night, with sparkling stars and a moon when the lights were off.

He had every teddy bear from the toy store in his room to add to the outdoor feeling. Even had a bike and pair of skates to roll around the house in.

"You looked so happy tonight Emie." Cristina whispered to her.

Emie rolled her head gently towards her, smiling. She felt happy. Emie looked at her ring again and wondered if Joseph would do the same for Cristina. One day make her just as happy. Emie sighed and looked back at Cristina. Theirs was another story altogether.

Asher peeked his head in the double doors of Neely's room then. He glanced up into the tree loft bed and seen the two beautiful heads of Emie and Cristina pop up. He put his finger to his lip and motioned Emie down. He watched as Emie climbed the ladder down and wanted to run under her dress and run his hands up her-

I can hear you, silly.

I know. He smiled down at her when she reached him and stood up on her tippy toes to kiss him. I love you Emie.

I love you more Asher. She told him, looking up at him, proud that she had finally beaten him. He always seemed to say it first, it was a fun game they played now.

"Oh go get a room!" Cristina told them as she shooed them out of her son's room, closing the door firmly behind them.

"I need to take you somewhere Emie." He let her see his cabin up north and begged her to help him pack now so they could leave together.

Emie was remembering back to the night of the funeral; let him see it too, and how she had wanted to go with him that night.

Asher shook his head at the memories. Looking at her now he wondered how he had missed all that that night. But it didn't matter anymore. Those were just the pages that made up their story in this life, and he really wouldn't trade not one of them.

"I didn't want you to know then because I was afraid of losing you. I selflessly wanted to keep it that way as long as I could." she was remembering again sweetly; "I wanted to be the woman with you so bad, I didn't want anything to ruin it."

Asher kissed her hand and looked at the ring. "You will always be the woman with me."

Asher and Emie headed for East Lake in Upper Michigan. Asher had told and showed Emie how breathtaking it was up there. His foggy memories had all been during the day time, their new memories would be made at night.

When he pulled into the dirt driveway, they made a mad dash, huddled under a blanket from the bright summer sun for the front doors. Emie tickled his butt while he fumbled for the right key to his cabin. Laughing out loud they stumbled into the old rustic smelling cabin.

Asher had told Emie the stories of this place on the eight hour drive up there. He couldn't wait to just be alone with Emie. With no interruptions. No menacing brothers. No news, or talk of a vampire uprising.

They rolled under the blankets till they found there way out, and came up passionately kissing. By the time they reached the bed room, their clothes had been scattered all around the hallway leading to his bed room.

Asher shut the door on the outside world. Four wheeling and midnight fishing would have to wait until the last rays of the sun were out of sight. He really couldn't wait to show Emie everything around here, and discover all the newness of the world around him.

It was in front of the fireplace, lying naked together wrapped in soft sheets, with a low fire in the hearth, that Asher finally started to wonder. The summer sun was almost out of sight. He was excited to go outside and explore with her, but had so many questions. There was an angel lying next to him, and he wanted to know more about her.

"We are not angels Asher." Emie whispered in his neck.

His hand wandered to her bare back. She knew what he was doing there. She let him see it in his mind. The way he followed her wings up and down and brushed her feathers with his finger tips. She let him feel their silkiness and the feelings of desire that were spreading through her like wildfire.

Asher had Emie in a tight embrace. This had all happened so fast. He couldn't believe they were finally here. Just like he had pictured.

He rolled on his back and started to play with Emie's curls absentmindedly.

"So what did you want to know about?" Emie laid half on his chest, laid half of her body alongside him. She was looking bright eyed at him.

He had gotten good at hiding his thoughts from her. Finally figuring out what had taken them years. He was learning so fast from them already, he wondered what it would be like soon when he became like her.

Asher looked at his angel and wondered why God had blessed him. Whatever he had done to deserve her, he would pay him ten fold. Emie met the world to him.

He held up her left hand in his that he had put her ring on. He tilted it this way and that in the light of the fire with his fingers. He brought it to his lips and kissed her fingers.

"I want to travel with you. I want to go everywhere, and anywhere. I know we can't right now, but I just want you know how I feel. I want to spend every waking moment of your life together."

Emie hid her smile in his side kissing him softly. She knew he was still hiding his thoughts. "If you're not going to tell me what is on your mind, we are going to sit here and plan out our wedding." She lifted her eyebrow and gave him that look. The one her brothers were afraid of.

Asher took her face in his hand. She was so beautiful to him in this moment. He hated spoiling it. "One is, I need a cigarette. You are going to have to let me in a little bit." When she started shaking her head no, he continued with: "And, two; I've decided."

"Decided what?" she asked him.

"Decided that I want to spend the rest of your life making love to you."

Emie giggled at his joke, but then she was taken back. "My life?" she whispered faintly.

"Yes. That's what I've been trying to tell you. I want to be there everyday of the rest of your life. Weren't you listening to my song at all?"

Emie had been made happy this evening by his proposal. But this made her happier still. "You are sure Asher?"

"Very sure. But, that's not why we are here. I'm up here with you because I want to spend these last few days with you as me. Before everything changes and I become a raving mad lunatic that wants to drink every one's blood." He said the last in his best Dracula voice he could manage. Then he became serious. "Emie, how long will we have together?"

Emie was actually surprised by that question. That's what he wanted to know? Emie gave him a dubious look.

Was there an end at some point in time for them? Like a dead end road. A sudden stop at the end? No turn arounds? That's what he wanted to know.

"Asher." Emie was on top of him now. Looking down at his lovely face, she told him what his heart couldn't see, everything he hadn't figured out and was still reaching for. "Destiny has no end, only a beginning. Fate has an end. But love, love has a beginning, a middle, twist and turns, up's and down's, highs and lows. But love never ends. What we have is destined, it's fate, and it's love. We are in the beginning of our happily ever after." She let each word show her meaning. She wanted him to feel it.

Asher ran his hands up into Emie's hair just under her ears. He listened again as she told him something he knew were words only the heart of an angel could speak, for the words she was speaking to his heart were the words that described heaven on earth. Being here with her, just like this, he could feel the love, the passion, the destiny she was speaking of. He never, ever wanted it to end.

He wondered if she would miss his heart beat, the heat he would feel in his cheeks when she made him blush. Then she remembered for him, brought back to her memory what all those wonderful things did to her, and he was sorry for them. Sorry for her pain she felt around him, but he was amazed at her will power. She was still able to love him. She was able to see through his flaws, his humanness, his weaknesses. And still she loved him.

This is when Asher kissed her. When he made love to her for hours.

Emie and Asher spent all night long together. They went walking in the woods, running through the grass barefoot, swimming in the lake. Emie let him smoke, but he was never alone.

Everything was playing out into a happily ever after, until James, Asher's brother, called.

"It's dad Asher. We took him to the hospital, he's in the ER now."

Asher was standing on his porch looking out over the lake. He and Emie had just ridden all around it on his four wheeler. He had been having the time of his life this night, just thinking it couldn't get any better than this. Then his phone had buzzed in his pocket.

Wanting another cigarette and needing an excuse to do so he climbed the porch and prayed the sun rise would wait just a little longer. Emie walked in the cabin and he could hear her bare footprints on the bathroom floor as she stepped into the shower. He answered his brother and lit his cigarette.

Blowing the hot smoke out he listened to his brother and almost dropped his phone. His father had a heart attack and they were trying to bring him out of it.

"How long was he down?" He knew with heart attacks, time was of the essences. If he had been alone and no one had been around to help him, he could have permanent brain damage. Asher was eight hours away. He hadn't a clue how to get there fast enough.

James told him all the details. Asher wished he could see in his mind through the phone like Emie could. The boy's emotions were clouding his voice and Asher wasn't getting the answers he needed.

Asher assured his brother everything was going to be ok. He told him what all he needed to be doing, like comforting their mom and listening quietly to the doctors, just like a big brother should, like Curtis would have done for him, then he ended the call with "I'll see ya soon." and headed straight for Emie. She would know what to do.

Emie didn't have a clue what to say to Asher on the road back home.

Emie tried to ease his mind, but there wasn't anything there to ease anymore. His heart wasn't racing, so the numbing effect was lost on him.

Everyone around him was eventually going to die and pass on. But why had he had to learn this lesson so quickly in life, she questioned.

This was exactly why Emie hated being a vampire. Exactly why she didn't want Asher and Cristina to become one. They would forever be empty, and cold. Dead. Life would just pass them by, go by way too slow.

Emie watched as the miles flew past them. They were almost to Detroit now. Asher hadn't heard from his family in some time. His mind was remembering so much of his past now. He didn't even know she was searching his mind, watching him. He was too busy concentrating on his family. Losing his brother had been so hard on him, losing his father now... She could only hope he would be ok.

Emie reached for Asher's hand and turned in her seat to face him.

Out of instinct he jumped at the cold feel of her hand. He looked at her not thinking and told her to buckle up.

Emie gave him a second to let his words register and watched as he laughed at himself and rubbed his chin.

"I need a smoke Emie."

Emie reached in her purse and handed him one. She watched as he breathed in the smoke and let it out in a way that was too much like a sigh. She noted it as he took a hit and went back to thinking about his brothers while holding it out the cracked window.

Asher didn't know how to play the role of dad and Chief. He didn't know if he could handle any of this. He needed his father. He missed the days when Curtis and his father ran things.

Asher just wanted to be him, the guy that lived and loved with no responsibilities. Not the guy who ran everything for everyone in a little city where people couldn't cook a grilled cheese sandwich without burning their house down. They lived in a city by a major expressway where accidents were an everyday event. Sometimes they were so bad he would have nightmares for days about them. Now his family was calling him looking for help. He didn't know how to be father, big brother, and fire chief, all wrapped up in one guy.

"Tell me to quite the department Emie. Tell me there are better things in this life I could be doing."

Emie closed her eyes. She didn't want to be the one that told him that.

"Tell me..." He started to say something, anything, but he didn't know what that was. This was all he knew. There was nothing else.

She could feel the heart ache. She could see the tears that should have been falling down his cheeks. She squeezed his hand and told him it was going to be alright.

"It's too early to tell about your father Asher. Just try to relax."

He looked over at Emie who had her feet up on the dash, and was resting her head against the window. The absence of heat on the windows where a steamy fog should have been, wasn't. No one would ever know just to look at her that she wasn't human. She looked like she was sleeping but she was following his thoughts again, he could tell. Listening to his every fear, his every tribulation. Why was he always bringing that into her life? He hated drama, and that was all there seemed to be around him lately.

If it wasn't his family, it was the department. When it wasn't that it was something else. Now it was this stupid war and he couldn't even let her leave to be safe, he'd had to keep here and get her mixed up in it. Maybe she would have been better off without him then with a man who can't even take care of himself.

"If you really think I would have been better off without you, then why did you follow me and beg me to stay?" This she said looking up into the night with a sigh, moving her hand into her hair and sighing like she already knew the answer.

It angered Asher. Joseph was right. She didn't know what was good for her. He certainly hadn't been, and the question still hung in the air over him like a chill that left goosebumps; would he ever be right for her?

"I shouldn't have." He told her, wishing to God he hadn't now.

But you did it because you loved me. And I stayed because I loved you, and couldn't live in this life anymore without you Asher. I don't want to be anywhere else, or with anyone else. Just with you.

She let that sit in for him before she added more. "In the past you questioned those things because you are human. Your duties and responsibilities to your family and friends and the department are the most important things in your life. You care about making the right decisions because of their importance to you. You worry about making the wrong decisions also because of those important to you would be affected by the wrong decisions. That's what makes you human. Sometimes worry and stress and fear are a God given gift to help us make the right decisions. And that's what makes us good people.

"You had a lot of responsibility put on you at a young age Asher. Learning how to save lives is a great and powerful responsibility. It can weigh on the strongest of men and women. What you did with it is heroic even. You are a great man Asher. You've done great things in your life.

"You're not weak Asher." She told him squeezing his hand in hers.

"When you're a vampire and have the ability to seek God's council, and the council of his mightiest men, you will be able to make those decisions with ease. Take on the world Asher with this God given gift, and be greater than you were before." She looked at him when she spoke next, and willed it to his heart and mind to hear her when she said it. "I fell in love with you Asher because I believed in the man you were. The man you strived to be. Now you have the chance to be greater. Be greater Asher, and believe in yourself. And trust those who will follow you to help you. Those who love you."

Asher took his eyes off the road for a second and turned to Emie. Damn, he loved this woman. She would walk to the ends of the earth and back for him.

I did that already. It's not as romantic as it sounds… This she told him with a wink. "Look to the future my love. A future with me."

Asher grinned. To be loved. To be loved by her. That's why he did it. That's why he loved her.

~Thirty Three~

Mercy Hospital

Frank was sitting alone in his hospital bed thinking about the Whitby family. He'd always thought he knew who they were, finally now, he knew he was right. At home he had sent himself into a panic attack about it all and was now paying for his hatred towards them.

Frank had seen them at the banquet with his son. Watching his oldest son Asher at the banquet, proved his worst fears. Asher had spent more time talking to Joseph then he had any one else.

Frank had seen the marks on Asher's neck.

Asher had changed, for what Frank had thought the better, but now he knew it was the worst. Asher was one them now. He was going to be one of them. He'd known they had taken his little sister and was ok with it. Frank tried to stop it with Asher, tried to keep him away from that family, but he couldn't because of Emie.

Frank needed to wait. He needed to stay alive until he could talk to Asher. Tell him the one thing that could save them all.

Asher walked to his father's bed side, happy to see him alive. The drive home had taken forever. Frank's machines were beeping and his tube down his throat was enough to make Asher turn away. His hatred for his father had been over powering sometimes. Seeing Frank now, lying in the same kind of bed he'd seen Curtis in was making him regret all those years. He didn't know why there was so much animosity between him and his father, but none of that mattered now.

He didn't know how to lose a father so soon after almost losing his brother.

Emie was by his side and holding his shoulder while he sat next to his dad, but it was Frank's thoughts that scared her.

He knew.

She worried what would happen to Asher, she wondered, when he found out what Frank was thinking? She knew it would tear him apart. Frank knew now beyond a shadow of a doubt what she was. What her family was.

But yet he didn't.

Frank was thinking of who and what she was; she had to leave before she responded to him.

"Asher, I'm going to step out. Ok?" Emie told him what his father had been thinking privately. He needed to know. He needed to make sure he hadn't told anyone else.

Asher heard her thoughts. His mind went into overdrive as he sat next to father. He clasped his hands between his legs and hung his head. He didn't know how to talk to his dad when his dad couldn't respond.

Asher hadn't spoken to anyone about Emie. No one knew what he knew now. He looked at his father in wonder.

Asher watched as his dad choked and coughed and the nurses came in to help him. He worried more when they started to take out his breathing tube.

I'm on my way Asher.

Joseph called to him while Asher watched the nurse's work on his father. How long would it take for Joseph to get there? Would his father announce it for everyone to hear that Emie was a vampire? That the women he loved, and her family was a threat to all humanity.

Asher's hatred for his father was returning…

Joseph walked in just as the nurse was unplugging the machines that were now flat lined. Asher's entire family was in the room with Asher, except two. Joseph looked to Asher for signs that he was needed in the room. When he saw none, he told Asher "I'll wait with Emie."

Asher just nodded. He didn't know what else to say to him. Asher held unto his weeping mothers hand and grieved with her.

The nurse had come into the room just after Emie had left. His father had reached for her hand and made her take out the tubes in his lungs. He didn't want them anymore.

The first words out his mouth was cancer. "I have cancer Asher."

Asher wasn't surprised by it. He'd known it was something like that wrong with his father.

"I'm dying, and I'm leaving everything behind that I love in your care. You have to protect them. You have to promise me Asher."

Asher had promised, even though he felt he wasn't included in his father's love. He'd never known why his father had felt that way towards him, so he asked. Just before his father breathed in his last breath, he'd ask him the question that had plagued his entire life, and would now haunt him for the rest of his life.

Asher walked out into the waiting room where Emie and Joseph had been waiting. He seen that Emie knew something was wrong. But he couldn't talk to her. He needed to talk to Joseph.

"When I told you I wanted to know everything, what part of that didn't you understand?"

Joseph, dumbfounded by Asher's anger, surprised by Asher's domineering attitude, looked at Asher. "What?" Then he read in Asher's mind what his father had told him. "Asher wait..."

"Me Wait? No. Why did YOU wait to tell me this? This is something you should have told me when we met. Hell, why didn't you tell me when I met her?" This he said holding his hand up in Emie's direction, but he dared not to look at her. He needed to finish this. "Jordy had to have seen this coming." Asher turned to Emie then. "Please tell me you didn't know this?"

Emie looked at Joseph then. She was clueless now to what was happening, only that Joseph had done something very, very wrong to Asher. Every ounce of blood inside of her flamed and burned up.

"What have you done?"

Joseph turned around then and shuffled on his feet away from the both of them. He hated Frank with a passion that would never die. Just like Asher was a curse to his father every time he looked at him, so would Asher be his curse now. With Frank's last dying breath he had thrust the thorn in Joseph's side a little harder.

"I did not kill him Asher."

Emie looked at both men shocked. Neither one would tell her what was going on.

"Why would he lie Joseph?" Asher spat each word at him.

Joseph had to look around, they were in a public place. This couldn't happen here. He led them to the elevator, not meaning for it to be the one they had met in, ironic as it was.

Asher went in anyways. He had to see this through from where it started. Once the elevator started moving, Joseph stopped it and started to tell Asher the truth.

"You are a twin, just like your father told you."

This news caught Emie off guard, but she stayed quiet and let them finish.

"They never told you, because they didn't want you to know. Your bother was the first born. Your father tried to sacrifice you to save him. He was ashamed of it all these years. He lived with that guilt everyday. A parent should never have to deal with that. It drove him insane." Joseph hung his head then. This really was Franks fault. This was also Joseph fault.

"I was driving down Summit Street one night the year you were born. The roads were icy and I wasn't paying attention to what I was doing. I was trying to open a bottle so I could drink and I couldn't get the damn thing open. Next thing I know I had T-boned a car, sent it spinning out of control across the road and into the Lake.

"It was your father Asher. You and your brother were asleep in the back seat when it happened. I got out and ran as fast as I could, and jumped in the lake. I pulled your mother out first, then your father started screaming and diving back under the water to the car that was sinking in the freezing water.

"I couldn't understand what he was doing, so I tried to drag him back to shore. When I realized what your father was doing, why he was fighting me, I tried to save you both but there wasn't enough time. Your father and I were under the water together, he could see I wasn't struggling like him to breathe and it just made him aware of what I was. Then your father pointed at your brother and told me to save him.

"He watched as I ripped the door off chewed through the seat belts and saved you. But it was you that I had to save. I had to save you."

Emie hated that Joseph looked at her then

"He hated me because of our money and the control we had on the city. After that night I wasn't only a rich man's son, I was some monster who had hit his car and killed his sons, and I could afford to buy my way out of it.

"I raced back up to the shore and worked hard on you till you came back around. I couldn't go back after your brother, it was too late, I had to save you." He said again. But making Asher understand it was like talking to a brick wall.

"Your father begged me to go back and save him. He had this idea that I could heal his son and bring him back because I was some kind of superhuman when I saved you, but that's not how this works. I couldn't just turn an infant. All your father's allusions about vampires weren't real. He spent the rest of his life hating me and trying to tell everyone what he thought I was.

"What I am." Joseph thought better of it. He wouldn't have to hide from Frank anymore though.

"Every time your father looked at you Asher, he saw me. Every time you messed up or failed at something, it was my fault. When you were little, he thought you were brain damaged because of me. But then you excelled at everything. You were stronger, brighter, better than the rest. And still, that was my fault. He thought I had poisoned you, or I was coming back for you. I don't know..." this Joseph said leaning back against the elevator.

"He was so hell bent on blaming me for every little thing with you instead of thanking me for saving you."

"You were the one who hit his car Joseph."

"No." And this time he pointed at Asher. "That's just it. It wasn't me. I was found not guilty. Not because I had used my abilities, or because I was rich, like your father believed. It was because your father pulled out in front of me off Sterns road that night. I didn't see him because I was distracted, yes. But your father took a chance on those icy roads and pulled out in front of me."

Asher almost had to agree with him on that. He knew the roads Joseph was talking about. It was a narrow road down an island patch out by a lake shore in Morin Pointe. His father had never told him any of this, and that was probably why. He had never wanted to admit he was the one in the wrong. He hated Joseph that much.

"Why didn't you tell me any of this?" Asher asked him.

"Why would I have told you? What right was it of mine to tell you? This is something your father should have told you." Joseph whispered.

"Why didn't you tell me?" Emie asked softly. Joseph should have told at least her she told herself.

Joseph looked at her and sighed, and then he hung his head. "Because it was Jordy who told me who to save. And he was afraid for you to know what he had done."

Asher hung his head then. They had both meddled in fate. He didn't know what that meant, but he knew for sure he didn't want to know what would have happened if they hadn't.

Asher pressed the button for the elevator to start descending again. He needed to get away from Joseph. When they reached the bottom Asher reached for Emie's hand and walked out of the elevator.

Joseph grabbed his arm just as Asher stepped off the elevator.

Asher looked down at his hand on his arm and glared down at Joseph.

Joseph saw it then. Saw all the reasons why he had saved Asher all those years ago. But it frightened him.

The Whitby's had sacrificed Asher's brother Axel because of the evil they knew was there in him. Asher was the soft hearted tender child.

Asher was the one.

Joseph showed Asher. He used all his powers to do it, but he showed him. He had to make Asher see it.

Asher had to kneel under the weight of it. He could hear Emie telling Joseph to stop. Asher wanted him to stop. He had lost his father. Not just tonight. He had lost him years ago. And it was Joseph's fault. Joseph hadn't done anything to stop it. He had done nothing to make it better. He had kept his secret so tight that he had ruined Asher's life. He had made a fool of his father everyday he had kept his secret. And Asher didn't know how to forgive Joseph for it.

Joseph let go then. His heart was retching now. How could Asher not see the truth? This was the first time he had used his abilities to such an amount, and it was the first time it hadn't worked.

Joseph stepped back then. He looked at Emie and willed her to understand.

"You ruined his life Joseph." Emie shook her head at him in disbelief.

Joseph looked back at Asher then. Asher was kneeling. "One day, I don't know when, but one day, you will understand this." Joseph told them both and walked away.

Thirty Four

The night of Frank's death was the night a vampire driven force stormed the streets of Monroe County. Every living soul, walking or hiding, was found and sucked dry of life. Buildings had been started on fire. Cars had been overturned. Utility poles and lines had been snapped in half. Transformers had been set ablaze. There was no way to stop them. There was no way to know where they would strike next.

Asher and his men had heard of the destruction via the Monroe County Dispatch. All channels were full of police and fire personnel trying to respond to a city in chaos. And then, it had all just stopped. Not since the day the system had been put into action had that happened. Never had the system failed, or stopped. 24-7 it had worked, and saved lives. On that night, no one was left to man the radios or control the city. They were all just gone.

It was Emie who had helped them. Emie who had taken them and their families to safety. She had worked quickly with them to break through the floor and brought down all the supplies they would need to hide and stay safe.

Emie stayed with them a few days, but with the setting sun of the second night, she told Asher she couldn't stay any longer.

Asher and a few men knew there were things that they needed to go in search of. One woman needed medicine, Ken's kids wanted their dog and Asher knew he needed to find Cookie. He prayed she was safe in his house.

Asher came back to Emie then. It was the first time he had really talked to her since that night his father had died. He needed her to know he didn't blame her.

Emie was bent down listening to Ken's mom as she told Emie where all her medicine was. He watched as Emie reassured her she would get everything she needed.

"Emie, I need to talk to you sweetheart." Asher said interrupting.

Emie looked up at him and nodded standing up. She had been waiting for this moment for what seemed like forever. She knew she just needed to be strong and be patient. Something he had taught her she thought as she followed him to a quiet little corner.

"I need to know you are going to be ok up there. Joseph had worried-"

Emie stopped him by placing her hand on his heart. "Asher, I'll be fine. Jeremy is at home, he's waiting for me. I'll get you to your house and be back to you before you are done. I promise." Emie said.

Asher looked down into her sweet eyes. He hoped she understood why he had been so withdrawn lately. He hoped she wouldn't leave him again over it. Not now.

"I need you to promise me Emie. Promise me you'll come back for me?"

"Forever, remember?" This she said holding up her left hand for him to see. She showed him her sparkly ring he had slipped on her tiny fingers. He was hers now.

Asher picked up her fingers and kissed them. He loved her so much he couldn't explain it.

Little Katie Kruse interrupted them then. She tugged on Asher's shirt to get his attention. "Uncle Asher?" she called out to him softly.

Asher turned to see little Katie. He picked her up in his arms to get her up to his height so he could talk to her better.

She giggled at him.

"What is it Katie Bear?" He asked.

"Dad wouldn't let me get Kitty and blanket off my bed the night we left." She looked back at her dad and turned Asher's face over towards him also with her fingers. "He hollered at me." She told him crossing her arms pouting.

"Well then, I guess I will have to go rescue her for you. You said she's on your bed?"

Emie was just staring at them. He was acting like the bravest man holding her in his arms the way he was. She admired him for it.

Katie shook her head yes. "Aren't you afraid of the zompires Uncle Asher? Please don't let them get you Uncle Asher. I need my Kitty."

"Zom-what?" he asked her trying not to laugh.

"Gabby said they were walking dead people, like zombies. But the news said they were vampires. So I call them ZOMPIERS!" She growled, nudging her little nose with Asher's.

Asher laughed right along with her. Setting her down, he looked up at Emie who was also covering up a hidden laugh. "I promise to bring back Kitty, Katie." He kneeled down then and winked up at Emie. "But you have to promise me something?" He questioned her. He wanted her to stay down here where it was safe with everyone else. Katie was known for wondering in places where she didn't belong. Like following her dad down the road when there was a fire close by. She would drag Gabby and her mother down the road following the smoke, wanting to make sure Ken was ok.

When she got all excited and promised him anything, he continued. "There is someone very important down here I need you to keep and eye on. She's our cook."

Katie laughed then. "You mean mommy?"

"Yes. I need you to keep an eye on her and make sure the big bad vam-"

Emie and Katie said in unison "Zompiers." Reminding him.

Asher looked to Emie then as he said "The big bad zompiers. Make sure they don't get your mommy. She is the only one who knows how to cook down here, and if we lose her we might starve." He tickled her belly for effect.

"Ok Uncle Asher. I'll protect her." She stated proudly.

Asher sent her back over to her parents who were in an unbreakable embrace. He looked at them and prayed.

Emie reached for his hand then. "I'll keep them safe. I promise."

Asher nodded his head and they headed over to the party that would go out and get the things they needed.

When Emie made it home, after leaving Asher safely at his house, she noticed the place was empty. It was just an hour before sun rise and Jeremy wasn't here anymore. She wouldn't have time to look for him.

She tried reaching for him in her mind but he wasn't there either. She left him a note in the kitchen and drank heavily from the bottles of wine he had left her. It had been hard for her stuck under the fire hall with all the beating hearts. She could hear them all around her in the confined space and it drove her insane some moments.

She couldn't take any of the bottles with her. She couldn't risk someone finding them in her bags. She would have to sneak out with Asher when she needed too.

Frightened and worried about how long they would all have to stay down there together, Emie slowly made her way back to Asher.

She couldn't stop thinking about little Katie and how cute she was. She couldn't wait to get back to her and see her face light up over them bringing her back her little Kitty teddy bear.

Asher had found Cookie hiding under his desk up stairs. He had tried and tried to coax her out, but she wouldn't budge. It wasn't until he heard footsteps coming up the stairs that he stiffened.

"Riddle me this, riddle me that. Who is this, and why is that. Oh yes, that's right, because you were fathers favorite."

Asher couldn't believe his eyes when he turned to the man's voice behind him. It was like looking in a mirror.

Another man, a tall slender man was behind Asher's brother. Asher had never said it about another man before, but this man was beautiful. There was no other way to describe him.

"Where is she?" The man questioned.

"She's not with him. He's alone." Asher's brother spoke again.

"Where is she? I don't want him, I want her!"

Just then one other man entered the room. Asher could tell just from the look in all their eyes that they were vampires. The blood red eyes, the fangs they didn't try to hide like Emie and her brothers did; it gave them all away. He had no idea what to do to protect himself.

He knew Emie would be here soon, and he worried. If she was the one they were looking for, he wouldn't be able to protect her. But he could feel her inside of him. She was coming.

Asher begged her not too. And hoped Jordy could see this. How couldn't he have seen this? Asher wondered. He had seen everything else!

"You're my brother Axel?" Asher questioned, trying to get their attention.

"So, our father did tell you after all." He said to Asher putting his hands on his hips. "And from the way you are looking at me I take it the stories about you and her are true. You seem to know what we are."

Axel looked to the other man, the one Asher could tell was in charge, and told him of what he had heard. "The group told me they had seen her with him the night of the banquet. Can't understand why, do tell us brother, why is it you find her so attractive? Are you drawn to them the way I was? Do you long for this life?" he kneeled down in front of Asher then. "Our father chooses you over me because you were the good one. Tell me why then do you want her?"

Asher felt sick. Joseph had tried to explain this to him but he wouldn't let him. How did Jordy not know his brother had lived?

The humanness in him wanted to know Axel better, but another side of him, the stronger side, didn't care and wanted to kill him. If his brother was with the rouges, then he was one of the thousands that had been killing people. Probably the ones who had been killing people here. The ones Asher couldn't save.

He was the evil one. That's what Joseph had said. Asher wished Joseph was here now.

Asher had found his way out of every fire he had went in to. He couldn't see a way out of this though.

Axel looked back at Asher then. "Just so you know, I have big plans for your girlfriend."

"She's my fianc ." Asher told him, growling. A heat was building inside of him. But he almost fainted under the powerlessness he felt. He couldn't save Emie from them.

"This, that, it makes no nevermind to me. She has an ability we need. But in order to keep her with me, she has to have a reason to stay. Which means you need to die."

Asher could see it then. The plan. Masterminds always had a plan. Axel could take his place as Asher and they could get Emie and use her.

"She will never stay with you." Asher spoke up then, trying to distract them again. A flash of something behind him caught his eye.

"Oh that's where you are wrong brother. See, I have an ability too. And a few others she is going to enjoy." He smirked at Asher.

It was then that Emie came flying through his screen door screaming. It wasn't until her feet hit the floor that she seen the man she had feared ever seeing again standing in the room with a man who looked just like Asher.

Because she stumbled, because she hesitated, Axel and the other man who had just come in the room grabbed her.

"Damn!" Victor, the leader said aloud. Emie wasn't supposed to see Asher and his brother together. They were supposed to kill him and make Emie think Axel was Asher.

Axel sniffed her hair. He turned to Asher and winked. "She smells good brother."

"Keep her still. Do not let her go." Victor told them. He walked over to her then, staring at her. "I have been looking everywhere for you my sweet. Where did you go that night so long ago?" He pulled her hair then and tipped her neck back sticking out his fangs. "I wasn't finished with you yet."

He walked over to Asher then, around behind him. Kneeling down he said to Asher, looking up at Emie. "She really is something isn't she? This ability you see, I saw it in her before I turned her. But her family got in the way. I lost her for sometime, but now, ah, now I have her. And it was so easy too." He told him laughing. "Her own brother told her everything I needed her to know. He listened to all my whispers of the future, and made sure you all did as I bided. All I had to do was wait for you to fall in love with her."

Emie struggled. She tried so hard to break free, but the vampires holding her were stronger then her.

"See, I can make people see what I want them to see too. I gave her this. But I could also make them do what I want, she took that from me when I changed her. She gave that to Joseph. And now, with her, once I get a hold of Joseph, I can have everything I need to take over this earth."

Asher did a twirl round about then and knocked the man off his feet. He wrapped his arm under his neck and held his lighter to the mans face. To his brother he said, "Let her go or I swear I will light him on fire." Scared out of his mind, Asher could only hope by taking the leader that they would listen. He could only hope the man felt the same thing her brothers did when he threatened them with a lighter.

In his ramblings, which Asher was trying really hard to listen to and not to listen too, he hadn't noticed that Asher had picked up a lighter that had fallen on the floor. Asher wanted to kill this man. He didn't want the man to live. He had caused so much death and destruction. Asher had never killed a man before, but he would make an exception for this man.

Asher felt him mouth something to the men and in a flash; Emie was standing on the outside of the porch glass doors.

"Asher, look, it's almost sunrise. You need to put that thing away, and we will bring her back in. Or don't, and she will die. I know where Joseph is now. He will do just as good."

Asher couldn't believe it. The sun was almost rising. He had no idea what to do next. He could feel the man under him pressuring him. He could feel his insistence the same as he had felt Emie's abilities in the past. He didn't give in to it like he had done with Joseph. He wouldn't let them win this.

Even if he killed this guy now, Asher knew they would overpower him and kill him out of spite, or worse. And Emie would not only have to watch but she would do everything in her power to save him.

He knew also, if they kept him alive, everyone under the fire hall was in danger. His family and friends; little Katie bear. This man could coax it out of Emie or him where they were.

Emie was begging him now. She could feel inside him what he was prepared to do. He refused to do it any other way.

Emie was banging on the glass, tears dripping from her eyes. She was screaming so loud he was sure they could hear her under the fire hall.

Asher let go of the man he had been holding onto with his arm, he reached for his steel blade he had tucked in his boot incase something happened tonight. Victor was laughing, paying Asher no attention thinking Asher wanted to use the blade on him.

Asher wasn't about to let these vampires take him. Especially his own brother. He would do the ultimate sacrifice Curtis had done for him. He would take his own life, and free Emie.

"I'll see ya soon sweetheart." He mouthed to her in a goodbye he hoped she would understand. And then he slashed his own throat.

Saving Emie...

~Thirty Five~

Two days before Christmas ...

Abandon. Luna Pier was abandon too.

Juliet drove over the overpass of I-75 and noticed the abandon city of Luna Pier was like every other city in Michigan. Like every other city in America now. It was over grown and unkept. The snow wasn't too deep for her truck to drive through, but she was aware of the massive, ice covered lake at the end of the road as she came into the city.

Looking down at her phone again she read her last email from Jeremy. It had been many months since she'd heard from him. The last time she had service on her phone. Before the beginning. Before the end.

Jeremy had told her if she ever needed him she could come to Luna Pier. It was supposed to be safe here. As she looked around the forgotten city she could only hope he was right.

Juliet had lost everyone in the end. A war of some sort had begun in the summer. It had taken the world by surprise. When communications had been cut off; the internet, the phones, TV and radio, she had to rely on the word of strangers to find out the worst. Living in New York City, a population of 8,175,133, everyone was a stranger.

She couldn't stay in New York. No matter which way things went, good or bad, New York was no place for a girl like her. She had wanted to go home and find her family. She wanted to find Jeremy.

She'd never found her family and had lost touch of all her friends when she had left New York in search of her family. By the time she had reached Michigan her family was gone. The farm, their lands, even the small city of Hanover where her parents lived had been abandoned. Only her mother's hound dog, Harley, a small beagle, had been left roaming the yard in front of the house when she'd arrived. Their horses, their small herd of farm animals, even the barn cats had all disappeared. Everywhere she had looked around the land looked like a tornado had blown through. The barn was barely standing, the fences and pastures were torn apart, the sheds and the garage were in shambles. Things were missing, like the cars, all her step father's equipment and four wheelers, his tools, there was nothing left.

Her house though had been boarded and locked up. It was stocked with enough supplies to last all winter and maybe longer. Her step father had hid enough guns around the house for an army. There were no notes left for her, no sign of where her parents had gone, and as far as she could see no reason for them to leave, other then the destruction outside.

Juliet had lived there as long as she could. Just her and Harley. When winter had come in like all other Michigan winters in the past, she'd stayed in hiding in the house; from what she still didn't quite understand.

In the beginning the reports on the news were brief. Thousands were found dead and left to rot. Bodies had been drained of all life and were found broken, torn apart. Cities were being burned to the ground. Some said there were monsters walking as men killing everyone, some whispered about vampires. She hadn't believed the stereotype Hollywood ideas then, but when the communication systems went down and the government had lost its power to control anything, panic had ensued. She was amazed at how such a great country could be overthrown by its own people in panic in a matter of days, and how no matter how long she waited, there never came a rescue. She hadn't seen a police car or even the National Guard since she'd left New York.

When she had left New York City, it was more out of her own will to survive. There was no law in the blacked out city. People walked aimlessly around the streets afraid of their own shadows and what they didn't know. There was no more law, no more reason for people to act civilized.

She had to drive back country roads, and steal food, fuel, whatever she could to make it home. Steering clear of anyone and everyone who looked suspicious to protect herself. She had to make it home.

She'd never run into any one other then humans. She'd never seen the zombies, or vampires the news had talked about. But there was clearly something or someone causing all the destruction she had witnessed.

But home had been a mere image of what she had known.

Her decision to leave home now was one of desperation. She had always hated living in the country growing up. She would go days then not seeing another living soul other then her parents. Now, seeing no one ever, was driving her crazy.

On the anniversary of her meeting Jeremy, she had to wonder if he was still alive. If anyone was still alive. There must be someone somewhere. A place where she could start over, again.

Driving down Lakewood drive, following Jeremy's directions to his home in Luna Pier, she could only hope he was still here and he hadn't moved on like everyone else. She had to find him, he was her last hope.

She glanced down the numbered streets and listened for sounds of life. Harley was whining in the seat next to her.

"It's ok boy. We're almost there." She consoled him, petting his head.

Juliet tried to remember the man she had met over a year ago. He had been a hero that night, saving her off the side of the road when she had ran out of gas in Kentucky. He'd taken her to a gas station, bought her gas and took her to a little roadside restaurant to eat dinner. It was like he knew she needed someone in her life to take care of her. Anything could have happened to her out there on that road at night alone. But he had came along and saved the day. They'd talked for hours over dinner, getting to know each other. They'd exchanged numbers and he had followed her back up the expressway into Michigan. Protecting her.

They had emailed each other over the last year. Texted each other and talked on the phone for hours on end. Shared memories and made new ones together. If she hadn't been trying to sell her new novels over the last year, she would have met up with him and possibly started a life with him. He had joked so many times about her moving to Luna Pier, and looking around now she could see why. This abandon lake side city had been everything he said it was.

Now, she prayed him and his family were safe and hadn't been killed. If he wasn't here, she had only two choices.

One: bunker down here somewhere till spring, until the roads were passable again and she could head south to a warmer climate. Start a new life some place else. Or two: leave this state as soon as possible and head into the unknown in the dead of winter. She preferred the first one, but she was scared enough to try the second.

Looking at the houses she was passing that were boarded up, she wondered if they were stocked like her parents house had been. Maybe if she could find Jeremy's house she could stay there and venture out during the day to find supplies she would need to last through the winter. She had packed her truck up with enough food and clothes to make it till spring before she left home. But it would be nice to find something other than canned food. Her health nut parents hadn't left her anything that was appetizing. There was only so much dried meat, nuts, canned fruit and veggies she could eat. She was dying to find some junk food, a cold soda, even some frozen food she could warm up over a fire would be nice. She missed fast food, pizza and Chinese take out. She was dying for a hot cup of coffee.

When she reached the end of Lakewood Drive, she noticed a bridge over a canal. Huge signs that read 'No trespassing' hung on either side. Giant, black, rod iron gates loomed in front of her.

She looked down at her email from Jeremy again.

"When you drive into Luna Pier, hang a right at the memorial park just before you reach the lighthouse by the water. The road is called Lakewood Drive." She understood why now. The road was lined on one side with tall trees, and the opposite side was the lake. "You'll pass numbered streets. When you get to the end, go over the bridge and wait at the gate. When you call, I'll drive down and let you in." She wondered now, looking at the impassable gates how she was going to get in. She couldn't call him.

She tapped her hands on her steering wheel and looked over at Harley with a funny face. He cocked his head and wagged his tail back at her.

"Well, we can go on foot from here I guess. What do you think?" She asked Harley, who was excited to get out of the truck after hours of driving. He stood in his seat, wagged his white tipped tail, and looked around outside.

Normally, a drive from Hanover to Luna Pier would only have taken her an hour and a half. But now, well it had taken her ten hours today. Driving back roads so not to be spotted by anyone, monster or not, dodging debris and abandon freeways that had snowed over, she'd had to drive at a slow pace and constantly be on guard.

Of all her step father's dogs that could have stayed behind, she was glad it had been Harley. He had been trained as a hunter to seek and find, watch and listen. If there was anything out here that she would need to be aware of, Harley would let her know. To him this was all a game he loved to play.

Juliet reached behind her seat for her step father's heavy winter jacket and shot gun. She had layered her clothes today just incase she had to walk in the snow. The three pairs of socks she was wearing helped fill out his boots too. Boots that where too big for her feet, but were sturdy enough for her to use in the Michigan snow. She put on a pair of gloves and put on the hood from her Michigan sweatshirt underneath that Jeremy had sent her for her birthday. He had hoped it would have encouraged her to move to Michigan, she wore it all the time now.

Harley already was sporting his jacket her mother had bought him the previous winter. At the time Juliet had thought it was ridiculous for a dog to wear a jacket, but now understanding how cold the winters here were, she was glad he had one.

"Ready boy?" she asked him hopefully. Harley barked too loudly in acceptance. She smiled wearily at him and got out of the truck unto the snowy graveled drive. She put her keys in her jean pocket and locked it up. It was all she had left now. What little bit of memories and pictures she could take with her from her mother's house was in her truck now. Food and supplies she couldn't afford to lose where safe as long as no one stole it.

Harley walked through the snow happily. He was looking over the edge of the canal into the frozen water under them like she was doing.

Juliet sighed out loud. "Well, let's get this over with." She looked down at him and watched as he huffed and wagged his tail. He looked as scared as she was.

They headed up to the gates and Juliet looked helplessly at them. They looked strong enough to hold against a semi barreling through them. She looked through them into the forest and overgrown paved road. The road curved east towards the lake hundreds of feet in front of them. She could almost make out a house, or was it a barn, she wondered.

Defeated she rested her head on the cold iron. She could see her breath now in the cold winter air. The crisp wind was rushing past her. Night was descending on them soon; she could already see the moon in the cold winter evening blue sky. Thoughts of not being able to get out of here or seeing another human being started to haunt her like they did in her nightmares. She willed them away.

She lifted her head up and grabbed a hold of the iron gates, gave them a push and was surprised to find they squeaked forward a little. Was it possible they weren't locked? She pushed harder and found that they opened all the way.

Opening them up enough for her to drive through, she raced back to the truck with Harley. She drove down the paved road and wound through a thick forest of trees that held back the snow. She drove right past a barn that looked like it had survived the worst of a fire. She willed herself not worry about it. Everywhere she had been since this had started, every city, every town, had traces of fire. Whether from arson or something worse, she didn't know, but she tried not to think about it. It had become the norm.

Abandon, forgotten, deserted or burnt. That was just the way of things now.

She followed the snowy drifted road till she came to another road that led to where she could only assume was the lake, and chose to drive straight instead, hoping she would find a house at the end of this road. Jeremy's house. She drove for a mile or so then broke into a clearing that held a massive mansion. She couldn't remember Jeremy telling her he lived in a mansion, but hoped against all odds this was his home.

Seeing the house now, she knew it too was abandoned. The hedges that lined the circle drive were well over grown, and the tall snowy grass looked just as unkempt as the city. She made her way up the drive to the front steps of the house and parked her truck as close as she could. She sat back in her seat and took a deep breath.

"Well boy, were here." She looked over at her only friend and wondered if she had officially gone crazy. Months ago she never would have dreamed she was the kind of girl who would wander out like this. But survival had done this. Had dared her to learn and do things she never thought were possible for her.

Looking at the place she could only hope was Jeremy's she wondered if she had the willpower to do this. She wondered also if she could stick it out here if she couldn't find Jeremy. She was worried about the size of the place, but surely this was better then her little farm in the middle of nowhere in Hanover.

"I wonder if there is a library?" She asked excitedly, looking over at Harley who cocked his head at her and wagged his tail.

Shaking her head, she turned off the engine and got out of her truck with Harley on her heels. She locked it out of habit, and stuffed her keys in her pocket. She turned against the wind and faced the cold stoned house. Sighing she started up the cracked stone steps towards the large double doors that were left ajar, swaying in the wind.

Behind her, she heard a howl of what sounded like a wolf. Not wanting to find out if it was one or not she hurried up the steps. Just as she reached the top, she heard a growl. Looking down at Harley, they both turned to find two overly grown dogs by her truck. Their mussels were dripping saliva and blood. Their hair was standing on end as they hunched down growling at her. They were dirty and covered in snow. They looked beautiful, but hungry.

She reached down and grabbed Harley before he could bark and went straight through the doors without looking back.

Dogs? Or Wolves? Juliet wasn't sure, but what she did know is they were very big and very angry at her.

Leaning up against the inside of the front double doors of the mansion, inside a front hall that looked abandoned and forgotten by workers, Juliet could hear her heart racing as the two giant ravenous wolves dug and smelled under the door she had manage to close behind her in her haste to escape their claws and blood thirsty teeth.

She stepped farther inside and farther away from the door when it jolted and threatened to come off its hinges. Looking around wildly she called out quietly for help.

"Hello? Is anyone here?" She beckoned into the room and beyond. But no one answered.

The dogs, as they ran away, left in a howling rush. Or worse, maybe they were headed around the house looking for another way in she thought. She worried they knew of one she didn't know of yet.

She continued to look around the front hall in amazement despite the terrorizing fear of the dogs that had chased her in here.

She wondered how she was going to get out of this place. Clearly plan one and two were both now questionable.

Worriedly, she looked back at the doors. On either side of the double doors were large stained glass windows that overlooked the western setting sun, letting in streaks of red and gold rays adding to the richness of the well cherry stained paneled oak walls around her. The rays bounced off the crystal chandelier that hung over the middle of the room that clung to the white washed high ceilings above her. The sun light was the only light that could be seen in the oversized front hall, dancing on the marble floors.

A large wooden encased marble staircase unfolded in the middle of the room, red Parisian carpet flowed down each step and widen at the bottom and led under her to the double doors behind her. Leaves and snow had been blown in from the open doors like they had been that way for months. Dust and webs danced around floating in a crystal haze of the sunlight.

On the left side of the room stood high two more double doors that were closed half way and hung off their hinges like someone had tried to tear them down.

Juliet looked more closely at both doors. Something wasn't right here. The grounds where she had left her truck parked at out front looked widely unkempt, if not recently then at least for years, it was hard to tell how long from the amount of leaves and tall grass that could be seen under the drifting snow. But inside, the way things looked in here, was like it had been being remodeled and then abandoned just recently.

Someone or something had come through those front doors, had torn through the double doors, leaving the doors wide open. Well, if they had left was still a question.

She ran her hand through her blonde hair and let her cold fingers linger on her forehead as she tried to decipher what she was seeing. She could only hope Jeremy or one of his family members would come walking through one of the doors she could see around the hall. She let her heart rate slow to an agreeable pace as she took in more of this house.

Ladders, scaffolding, paint and drape clothes were lying around like they had been abandoned by its workers also. Paint cans were still open with brushes in them, rollers were still lying in their pans. There was even a floor wax machine lying overturned on the right side of the room. Juliet noticed that its cords went behind the staircase where she saw a hallway that stretched east of the mansion. In its dark looming depths she could make out taller windows that looked like they took up the entire east wall overlooking the lake.

Juliet sighed deeply. What was she to do now? There was obviously no one within hearing. The truck that was probably being attacked by the dogs had little if not enough gas to get her out of here. She was kicking herself now for being in such a hurry to get here that she hadn't put herself at least a couple of gallons gas in. There was a gas station right by the expressway, she wonder if the dogs didn't follow her out of this place if she could steal some gas from its pumps to get her headed south. She had just wanted so badly to find Jeremy; she hadn't thought about escaping if she needed too. She never would have guessed this place had dogs in the size of wolves roaming around wildly. In Hanover, yes, she could understand that, but in this little city?

"So much for hunkering down Harley." She sighed as she looked down at him. He was scared and cowering at her feet. Scooting as close to her as he could.

"Think Juliet, think!" She knew she couldn't go back outside. Not with the dogs running around.

Your just going to have to search the house, she thought to herself. She lowered her arms and wondered which door she should try. The broken ones to her left? Or the red one on her right? Or the hall behind the stairs?

Juliet decided to try the red one on her right. She was closer to that one anyways. She quietly walked across the glass looking floors to the door. There was no knob on the door to turn, which she found odd and decided to knock on the red door instead, listening behind it for signs of life.

Nothing.

Great, she thought. Couldn't be that easy, could it.

She tried to the door open but it was locked tight.

Juliet jumped at the sound of the wind picking up outside, knocking something up against the doors. She leaned her head against the door quietly trying to listen for anything remotely human.

She took a deep breath and wondered how on earth she had gotten herself into this mess. She shouldn't have come here she told herself. She headed for the broken double doors on the other side of the hall. There was nothing else left to do other than to start crying, and she wasn't about to break down here.

At least not yet.

Juliet knew, on her way here, when she had crossed the canal and approached the gate that she was headed in the right direction. But how could this be, she wondered as she stepped over and in the broken double doors that lead her into a giant dining hall. The tap of Harley's nails behind her kept her sane knowing she wasn't alone. Jeremy had spoken of this place like most people speak of a well loved home. Not like he had been living in wealth and riches his whole life. This lovely mansion, if you could call it that now, had once been a well cared for, attractive home. Jeremy had never mentioned this.

The dining hall was laid out in a long narrow room. The floors in this room were glossy tan wood that shined in the light of what was left of the setting sun. The windows on her left were bay windows that jutted out. Hedges were scraping against them in the wind. The long table in the center was draped with a painter's cloth and more ladders and scaffolding littered the floor, along with what looked like pulled down wallpaper of some sort. They must have just finished that part of the project in here she told herself, just getting ready to paint over it all.

They must have been remodeling when all hell broke loose.

What had happened to them?

A huge stone fireplace was on her right. It was the only piece in the room that needed no work done to it. Its ancient finery had held throughout the centuries. Paintings hung on the walls draped with more cloths. Juliet was tempted to remove them to see what was behind them, but knew she was running out of time. She looked around more carefully now, she needed to find a candle, or a flashlight.

There was a door at the back of the room in the corner next to an old grandfather clock and a long buffet table. The clock, as old as it seemed, still ticked away and filled the room with the only sound she could hear besides the wind blowing outside the windows.

China was stacked in stacks on the center room table she noticed as she walked passed them. Boxes of silverware were overturned on the table; some had fallen on the floor. Juliet began to wonder if the place had been robbed or worse ransacked as she fingered the expensive silver. So why hadn't they taken the silver, she wondered.

She tried the back door. To her surprise it opened and led into a long dark hallway.

Juliet sighed, she needed to get out of here she told herself as she looked back and forth down the hall. To her left she saw another hall that led in opposite directions and looked like she could see light on either ends. To her right, were more doors, but she lost sight of most of them in the darkness. She left the door ajar to the dining room and headed to her left.

From the outside, she wouldn't have guessed this place was this overly large with this amount of rooms, but then again Juliet had never been in a mansion before.

She decided to head for the lighted rooms and prayed she could at least find a candle. Or humans.

Once she reached the end of the hall she turned to her right and saw another larger dining room, with large garden windows that held an enclosed garden porch with more tables and chairs that overlooked the lake below. This room was decorated in old oil wallpaper with a French or English ancient scenery. People were walking around ponds in a pleasant atmosphere surrounded by a summer scene. Hot air balloons floated up near the ceiling where another large chandelier hung.

Juliet turned back around and headed into what looked like a hall that led to a kitchen. Old wood cupboards and drawers filled the hall. This must be where the staff kept the china and waited on the patrons within.

She found her way into the old kitchen, where a horrific bloody scene unfolded before her. The steel counter was littered with bags of what looked like blood packets, broken open and bleeding on the counter. Bottles, wine bottles were broken on the floor. Had they been filled with blood, or wine? She was sure it was blood by the look of it.

Juliet plugged her nose at the stench that filled her nostrils. Blood...

The double doors to the fridge were open, no power to it. More blood spilled out from its floor. Food had been lying in it and had spoiled. Juliet looked around the kitchen in horror. There were knives and cleavers, bloody corkscrews stern about the surfaces. Cupboards were opened everywhere, dishes and china littered the floors and counters. The open windows were above the cupboards letting little light in and a cold breeze. Juliet knew she couldn't stay in here any longer. She ran back through the halls back to the door she had left ajar. She ran along the dining room table and back out the double doors to the front hall with Harley hot on her trail.

What had she done? What place was this? Where was Jeremy? Was this even his house? She questioned.

Had the news and all them crazy people she had ran into in New York been right? Was it possible vampires, or monsters had done all this? Taken over the world... How many other survivors, if any were there?

Was someone else besides Jeremy's family residing here?

Juliet grabbed the beautiful carved wood post of the stairs in the hall and tried to hold on to her composer. She closed her mind to all the blood she had seen and tried to think. Looking back at the main doors where she knew held no escape for her, she began to panic. What else would she find if she searched the rest of the house? She could only hope if there was anyone or anything here, Harley would at least alert her to them.

She knew she was running out of time. The sun had completely set now. She was looking frantically around the front hall, her eyes well adjusting to the darkness.

Should she go upstairs, or should she try the back of the house? She was barely breathing now as she looked up into the darkness of the second floor.

Try the back of the house.

Holding unto to herself, she braced herself to walk to the back of the house behind the stairs, praying she would find something. But what something was she looking for now?

She ticked off a mental list as she walked slowly to the back room, as she had done so many times in her past. One: she would need a flashlight or a candle. Two: batteries, or a lighter, or both. Three: food...

Juliet never thought she would be in this place, she thought as she looked out the large looming back windows into the night, the sandy shores of Lake Erie were in the midst.

She took a deep breath and looked around the makeshift gathering room again. Furniture was scattered all around in seating areas. There a was long grand piano in the midst of the windows turned completely over on itself. Juliet tried not to shiver at that.

As she looked around a seating areas she found pictures frames. One she noticed as she picked it up, held a photo of a family. Juliet sighed as she recognized one of the guys in the photo standing next to woman. It was Jeremy. She smiled greedily at his picture standing with his family. She was thankful more than she could describe that she had found his home. She was in the right place.

The long glass windows stretched the length and breadth of the north and east side of the mansion. Another hallway led south and Juliet wondered where it led too. She looked at the picture one last time and returned it back on the table and walked away.

More doors, more winding hallways were all Juliet could find. Some locked, some already broken open, but they were dark and she was afraid to search them. Juliet leaned against a locked door on the inner wall across from another door at the end of the south hall by a long broken window. Mentally she was keeping track of her directions so she could find her way back out.

"Jeremy, where are you?" It had been forever since she had heard a sound besides her beating heart and Harley's tapping nails, her own voice sounded strange to her and Harley both.

One more door, this door, she told herself as she stepped forward. She braced herself for whatever she would find as it creaked open.

It was the door that led back out into the main hallway. Juliet sighed with relief as she stepped onto the marble floors. She left the door ajar, as it had no handle on this side, just in case she needed to go back in there.

She looked across the hall at another set of doors along the same wall as the dining room doors. She walked across the hall and slowly opened the door.

Juliet stood in amazement again at the inside of her chosen room. It was a library of some sort. Book shelves lined the walls. Maybe it was a den, she wondered more as she walked inside farther.

There was a long desk that looked more like a tree cut open and laid flat to create a work surface, all said work scattered along the floor. The desk was set in the middle of long windows, the drapes were pulled back letting in a little of the moon light from the lake outside. A stone hearth, that would look inviting if it held a fire in its depths sat against the north wall. Expensive wingback chairs encircled a glass table. There were glasses setting on it like they had been abandon also, half full of some sort of dark liquid. Juliet was determined not to see what liquid was in them after the scene in the kitchen.

It was definitely a gentleman's room. A room her step father would have enjoyed if he were visiting here. There was a pool table, and a long shuffleboard along one wall, even a dart board hung above it.

She wondered if it was a room Jeremy had been in. She looked around in wonder then.

Juliet found herself running back to the desk. She was still hoping to find candles or a flashlight, but all she found were papers littered and scattered on the floor. A laptop was sitting half closed, but when she opened it there was no power to it. She searched the drawers for anything useful, but came up empty.

Juliet fell into the chair behind the desk. What was she to do now?

Juliet mentally looked back where she had been and remembered the upstairs. It was the one place she hadn't been to yet. Surely if this were Jeremy's house his room would be up there. Something was drawing her to that decision. She needed to search the upstairs.

Someone could still be here, out of ear shot. They might still be hiding up stairs some where. If anything she could get a good look around outside from the upper floors.

Juliet stood and made her way back to the front hall. This time almost running through the hall with Harley as she went, still afraid, still listening, always listening for sounds of life. She headed for the front of the stairs, trying not to pay attention to the wide doors she had seen that led out towards the lake. She couldn't chance going back outside. She had seen enough scary movies of people being attacked by dogs, and she wasn't about to be one of them.

Once she reached the stairs, she took them slowly one at a time. It wasn't until her hands touched something wet on the railing that smelled of blood that she felt her legs go weak. She looked down at Harley who groaned and huffed and wagged his tail at her.

Just keep going. She felt her mind say it, but she was going numb inside. She didn't know if she could keep going as she wiped her hand off on her jeans. She had reached a landing that branched off in two directions. One led up to the south side of the mansion and the other led to the north.

Which way? She stood there debating again.

South.

Juliet bit her lip, why did her own thoughts remind her of Jeremy's words?

South, that's where she had met Jeremy. She took a chance and ran up the long stairs to what looked like a south wing.

Another hall, Juliet thought as she slumped her shoulders.

At the top of the stairs she found herself in another dark hall. Large pillars loomed beside her, ancient broken molding etched the ceilings and walls around her. They were so white that the hall was moonlit brighter than the rest of the house.

There were doors on the left side of the hall, moon light was coming through the windows on her right as she walked farther down, and there was another set of double door at the end of the hall. Juliet kept walking towards the double doors; something was pulling her towards it as she reached for the handles. But there wasn't any.

Juliet felt frantically around for the handle. How could doors not have handles?

She turned around at the sound coming from down stairs.

Someone had opened the front doors. Juliet slumped down on the floor next to Harley and grasped his muzzle before he could bark. She told him "No." quietly.

When she heard footsteps in the hall Juliet ran quietly back down the hall, belatedly noticing that none of the doors in the hall had handles and questioning quietly to herself again why.

"Where do you think she is?"

Juliet had made it back to the landing on the stairs just in time to hear the voice of a man in the front hall.

"She will follow the scent of blood."

That stopped her dead in her tracks where she was at the top of the landing. She sat down and quieted Harley. He was about to bark, she was sure of it.

"Let's try the kitchen, and then down into the basement. If she's found Jeremy we need to trap her there. He will tell us everything if we use her against him."

Basement? Jeremy? Juliet clamped a hand over her mouth.

Her heart was thudding so loudly in her ears she couldn't hear the men's footsteps in the hall anymore. She tried to compose herself but failed.

Someone was trying to hurt this family. That's what had happened here. It was happening like that everywhere. The wrong people were hurting all the right people. And she was being trapped.

Ok, before she panicked she thought to herself, what do you know? Juliet hated not knowing what was going on. She absolutely hated it.

One: You shouldn't be here. That was a given, she told herself.

Two: You should have brought in your gun. That again, was a given.

Three: Jeremy and possibly his family were in the basement. But where was the basement?

And Four: There were men looking for her. You need to hide.

She thought about that more as she held onto Harley. She needed to find out who those men were. She needed to follow them, but Harley wasn't good at sneaking; he would bark and give her away. She'd need to hide him somewhere before she could go sneaking around to find them.

Juliet closed her mind and remembered the hallway just off the dining room. It must lead to the basement. She hadn't gone down there because it was too dark, but it made sense to her now, in all her writing years she had spent writing about servants, and all the research she had done, there would be a door off the main kitchen that the servants would use to go down stairs into the basement. There must be storage sheds down there.

She took a deep breath and tried to hold back the tears. She didn't want to do this. But Jeremy, if he was alive, and apparently he was, he needed her. His whole family could be in trouble. And she needed people. People she knew and could trust. Sure, she'd only met him once, but right now he was the only one she wanted. There was just something about him she trusted. In all the time she had talked to him, she remembered over these last few months, he was strong, and sure of himself. Out of all the people who she believed could survive the way the world was now, it was Jeremy.

His family had grown up in England and had moved here to Luna Pier when they were younger. They lived off this land for years and knew all the things she didn't know to survive right now. She needed them, his brothers and sister he had talked so lovingly about.

Juliet stood and walked softly down the carpeted steps holding unto Harley.

Hurry Juliet. She knew she needed to hurry and snuck down to the hall. She needed to hide Harley before he started barking and gave her away.

This is crazy, she told herself. If she snuck down to the basement, they would just capture her too. They knew where they were going. She didn't. She couldn't go down there.

The den. Juliet suddenly remembered the den. Like a vision stopping her in her tracks, she realized what she needed and where she could find it. There had been a bear skin rug, and deer heads on the walls. Well, shadows of them anyways. Had there been any gun cases? She had left her shot gun in her truck, she needed a gun.

She had to find something. Or she would have to hide well until these men left. She knew she could escape out the windows from the den if they did decided to come in the den. It was her only choice.

Just hang on Jeremy, just a little longer...

"Where is she?" Jesse asked James as they entered the dungeon.

"I don't know. But if we don't find her down here, we are going to have to find another way out, cause I'm not walking through that mansion in the dark while she tries to kill us. Or sets it ablaze with us in it." James was tired of all these vampires. This new one they had followed into the city knew right where the Whitby's lived. She had drove right through the gates and headed up to the house.

They had to wait for her to enter the house, and had to wait until the dogs got tired of pacing around her truck before they could sneak in here after her. They had thought she was a friend of one of the brothers at first and then remembered that Jeremy had been the only one without a mate. He must have been contacting her in some way. Leading her here so they could escape.

Jesse nodded in agreement as they walked up to Jeremy.

James had constructed a steel iron cage that would penetrate through Jeremy's body while pinning him to the ground. Surprisingly, it had worked. James had gotten the idea from Frank's notes they had found in his desk at home. Steel iron was the only thing that could hold onto or penetrate vampires.

Seeing Jeremy again, alive, face down on the wet, blood stained, stone floor of the mansions main dungeon, was enough to send a shiver through both men. James was still in awe of what they were doing. He had half expected Jeremy to have died in the three weeks they had been holding him down here. But James had been wrong. The iron stakes piercing Jeremy's back and arms and legs were holding him down, but it was the stake they had thrown in the back of his head that was keeping his abilities at bay. For now.

His father had told them about the powers some vampires held, and how Jeremy and Jordan could get inside the minds of humans to trap them. Like this family had done to Asher. No one had any idea what had happened to Asher after he had left with Emie, but the scene they had found in his kitchen was enough to confirm their worst fears. Like their father had said before he had died, the Whitby's were vampires.

They'd been held up in the fire hall of all places since the first waves of attacks on the city had happened back in the summer. Hardly anyone had time to prepare for it. The phones and TV and radios had went out the night before, and no one knew of the attacks that would follow.

James hadn't believed it until he and Jesse had stalked Jeremy here in the abandoned mansion after the attacks had stopped; they were trying to find their brother Asher. They watched as a preoccupied Jeremy walked all around his house just by passing through walls.

James and Jesse were committed to finding out where their brother was. Their father had told them about this house. And that if Asher ever disappeared like Izzy had, then they were probably here with them.

But Jeremy wasn't talking. Nothing they said to him, or did to him had worked. They had all but given up, and were going to leave him here to rot, until this woman had showed up.

She was beautiful, and pale like Emie. It was enough for James. They had to find an end to this. He needed answers to his questions. And Jeremy was going to answer them.

They needed to know if they were safe. How to be safer. They wanted to know most of all, the truth about their brother.

James knelt down next to Jeremy. "Are you going to talk now?"

Jeremy tried to lift his head off the floor. He had been drifting in and out of consciousness for hours, days. But he couldn't. Something was holding him down. He looked up at his captures, still wanting to know how they were doing it. He couldn't read them. Jeremy groaned at James and rolled his eyes.

James looked up at the wood beamed ceilings and sighed. "Well, maybe she can tell us what we want to know."

James looked over at Jesse and pointed at the doors. They waited with their steel bullet, loaded guns drawn and at the ready, then they walked out.

Jeremy looked, pushed his future ahead as far as he could. He could see her walking down the stairs, see her face and wanted so badly to run to her. He could see as both men would fire at her and she would fall tumbling down in front of him.

He couldn't let her fall; he had promised her he never would. He couldn't let these two men's prejudice and stupidity destroy the one thing in this life he couldn't live without, the one person he wanted to spend the rest of existence with. He entered her mind one last time and showed her the only thing that would stop her from coming down here until it was safe.

Thirty Six

Juliet had found what she needed in the den. A case under the desk that held two large, loaded pistols. She ran back to the hall, but when she reached the back of the staircase, she could hear both men coming out of the dining room, so she crouched behind the stairs.

"She must be upstairs." One man said to the other.

Both men were tall and broad. She was no match for either of them. Her hands shook as she held the guns to her side. She had never shot anyone before, let alone two men. She waited as they disappeared up the stairs.

Juliet silently took off through the doors to the dining hall and headed down to the basement. If Jeremy was down there he could help her escape and explain what was going on.

Out of the dining room and in the dark hall she found a door open with a set of dark stairs that led into flickering light.

When she finally reached the bottom of the stairs she found a massive room lit by torches. The only light she had seen in what felt like hours. The large room branched off into another lighted hall that she followed. She came up to another set of double doors and wondered if they had Jeremy kept behind them. The rest of the hall loomed in front of her, darker and she lost sight of where it went in its depths.

Juliet turned now to the doors and opened them quietly despite there creaking sounds.

The room laid out before her reminded her of a dungeon she had written about before. Large blocked stones lined the walls. She hadn't realized how far down the stairs had taken her until she had seen the depth of this room. Cold and wet dripping sounds filled her ears, torches dimly light the room in front of her, and the sound of something thrashing around brought her attention to a gate on the floor on top of something, or someone she noticed as she walked closer to it.

Fingers, a hand was jutted out from under the gate. Juliet wasn't sure in the light who it was, but when the fingers started to move, Juliet ran closer and knelt down, lying the guns on either side of her.

Tears, her tears were dripping down her cheeks, clouding her vision. It was Jeremy's hand.

How he was alive Juliet didn't know. Large stakes where piercing through his back and arms, his legs. One large one was going through the back of his head. He was lying in a puddle of his own blood.

"Oh, Jeremy." Juliet whispered amidst her tears. She had finally found him, but she had no idea how to save him now. Who were those men, and what had they done to him?

Juliet.

Someone called to her in the darkness beyond what she could see behind her.

"Who's there?" Juliet questioned, wiping her tears and reaching for the guns she had set down.

More thrashing and the sound of hissing filled her ears.

Juliet looked closer into the darkness as she stood and spun around. There was no one in the room with her, but she could clearly hear someone… she had heard a man's voice, not her own.

"Juliet, my name is Jordy. I am Jeremy's twin brother."

She had wondered often if she would go crazy being alone like this. Had it finally happened?

"I need you to listen to me, we need your help Juliet."

Juliet was sure she had heard someone then. She looked around again, but some of the room was cast in darkness and she couldn't be sure. She rubbed her head worriedly.

I need you to listen to me. You can't see me, but I'm here with you.

Juliet looked back at Jeremy, the man's voice sounded so much like Jeremy's. Her tears ran down her face more. "I don't-"

"Just listen to the sound of my voice."

"I don't understand." She could hear him so clearly now, but she was sure he wasn't in the room with her.

You have to trust me, Juliet.

Juliet relented then at the sound of his voice in her mind and knelt down by Jeremy. "Just tell me how to save him."

He's a vampire. Jordy stated simply. And so am I.

"No, that's not possible!" Juliet almost shouted. She had questioned many things in her life, this was going to top them all. She knew Jeremy. He wasn't one of them.

But. Then. How could Jordy be reading her mind and talking to her? And how had Jeremy survived these stakes in his body, she wondered as she reached out to touch him.

There was no such thing as vampires. There was no such thing as vampires! She kept telling herself this, everyday it seemed. But here she was, knelt down beside one, and listening to another.

Listen, Jordy interrupted her. We are, and I am. That's how I am able to speak with you now. And so is Jeremy. That is why he is still alive in that cage.

When Juliet registered his meaning, her head fell into her hands out of fear. She was doomed.

Jordy continued. I don't have time to explain much more to you, those men are going to come back here looking for you. I need to help you escape, and there's only one way to do that.

"But I, I don't understand." Juliet said through her hands looking at Jeremy with tears in her eyes. She felt trapped. She felt so alone in this world she didn't know how to escape from. She didn't want to believe Jordy, but with Jeremy lying on the floor in front of her bleeding and broken, it was making that hard to do.

The man lying before her was the man she had longed to see again. The strong man who had saved her that night and protected her. The man who had talked so sweetly to her over the last year. The man she had longed to find here and wished she hadn't waited till now to find.

Juliet, you have to listen to me now. I know you're scared love, but I need you to help us.

We are not like the vampires that have done this to the world. We have been here for centuries. Jeremy was a vampire when you first met him. And he didn't let any harm come to you then. He won't let any harm come to you now.

Juliet wondered how his brother knew her name and her nickname Jeremy had given her. But he used it just like Jeremy had, and oddly he sounded just like Jeremy then.

She hated that he sounded just like Jeremy. And she wondered if she could trust him, vampire that he said he was. How long had they been vampires? Had Jeremy really been one all along?

"What can I do?" She questioned and couldn't help that she was scared out of her mind.

You must do exactly as I say. Jeremy has been under that gate for many weeks now. He is weak, but he is very strong. And he needs to feed Juliet.

Juliet visibly shook again and wept, biting her lips. She had never been more afraid then she was right now.

I need you to lift that gate off of Jeremy. It is heavy, but I know you can do it.

"I, I can't-" Juliet feared she couldn't.

You can, and you will. Once you have the gate off of him, I need you to leave this room. Go back to Harley and wait in the den.

"How did you know-" Juliet couldn't understand how he knew the things he knew. "I can't! Those men are out there, and the dogs won't let me outside, I can't leave. I can't."

I can read your mind Juliet. It's an ability that I have. I can see your future. I can see you. Please listen to me.

I'm not going to lead you into danger. I'll show you where to go.

I'm the one who led you here. You are all Jeremy has thought about since this happened. I've been watching you and leading you here ever since you first got to Michigan.

But why, she wondered.

I need your help. I need you to free Jeremy. He's been trapped down here for months.

He's been watching you too and he's longing to help you, but as you can see, he's been a little busy.

Juliet waited for that to sink in. She remembered all her feelings the days leading up to this journey she had taken out here. She had been led here. Led here to help Jeremy. His brother couldn't be lying. She could remember all the times she had feared doing this, coming here to this place, and the strength she had found that had astounded even herself at times.

Will you help him? Jordy questioned her. There's not much time? They are looking for you.

A flood of memories assaulted her then. Jeremy's voice as he talked to her that first night. His easy smile. The way he had helped her into his truck. The comfort she had felt being near him. The way he had talked to her while they ate dinner together. The stolen kiss they had shared before they said goodbye at the last stop on 75 before they went their separate ways.

Everything she had ever felt for Jeremy was there in her heart. She could feel it in her soul. She didn't know how, but she knew it was real.

Juliet looked back at Jeremy and wondered how she was supposed to lift the gate. She had to help him.

You can!

Juliet jumped at the sound of Jordy's voice in her head. "What will happen to him if I lift the gate? Those stakes are buried deep inside him."

He will be fine. He can heal himself. But you must leave him alone as soon as you get it off of him. He will start to move, but Juliet, he hasn't fed in awhile. Do you understand? He must not see you when he wakes up. Those stakes are all that are holding him down.

Juliet didn't know much about vampires. Why would she, they were only fictional characters. Until now. She rubbed her head again, cold sweat now dripping down her forehead and the back of her neck. She knew what they fed on. Blood. The blood she had seen in the kitchen. The blood of others.

There is so much you don't understand right now. I know you are scared. We can help you. We can protect you from what is out there. You won't have to be alone anymore.

Jeremy has been waiting for you and hoping you would come here. You are our last hope. But Juliet, there is no time. You must do this. Once he is out, you can not be here.

"How do I know you all won't come after me?" Juliet asked in fear

Suddenly Juliet's mind was filled with images of Jeremy again. All her memories of last December. All her hopes and dreams of him helping her through this hell she was in. Jordy could not only read her mind, but also enter it. As much as she hated it, she wanted the memories to be real. The alternative was a life of loneliness, or worse, death.

Juliet, he is and always has been the man you have been dreaming of. What he is, won't hinder what you're looking for in a life together with him.

Juliet closed her mind when she seen Jeremy in her mind kissing her like he had done the night he had rescued her. She missed Jeremy, she still wanted Jeremy. She needed this man she had been talking too. He was all she had left of her previous life.

Juliet took Jeremy's hand that was lying outside the gate. She crept closer to it and took it in her hand and held it. She felt as he squeezed it gently, just once, and she knew he was in there. Her good ol boy, roughneck with the crooked smile. Her handsome cowboy that smelled of fresh air and leather.

Her mouth fell open as she whispered his name and fresh tears dripped inside her lips. She needed him to say something.

Juliet.

This time it was Jeremy's voice she heard inside her mind, pleading. She could feel his pain also.

It had been him all along also. He had been leading her here with the help of his brother. Guiding her mind to him since she left home. He was guiding her now. He needed her help.

Juliet sat one more moment longer. Salty tears dripping down her cheeks and lips, slipping inside her mouth she couldn't quite close anymore. Some things a heart just wouldn't listen too. She should be running far away from here. But even when blood thirsty vampires could be threatening to take her life, her heart and soul still wanted him. She didn't want to leave him like his brother had told her too, she didn't want to go back up into the mansion alone, but she knew she had to.

She looked up at the gate and prayed she could lift it off him. Prayed it wouldn't hurt him like she knew it was going to hurt her. Pulling up and listening for sounds of Jeremy, Juliet managed to get it off of him.

Now run Juliet. Those men won't see you. Just run.

Jordy's words followed her out the door as Juliet ran. Her feet didn't stop until she got behind of the den door and sank to the floor.

"Jeremy?" Jordy's voice questioned him through the darkness. He didn't know the extent of Jeremy's damage yet. They had never been injured since their new birth. But the steel stakes that had penetrated Jeremy had been in him for a long time.

Jordy was locked inside a cage by Jeremy. He hadn't wanted Juliet to know he was there. The temptation had been so great to call her to him, coax her to open the gate and let him out, and drink from her blood.

Juliet belonged to Jeremy though now. Jordy could see it now. The life they would have together.

"I'm here." Jeremy told him as he crawled up to a kneeling position. He had to keep his eyes closed against the light as his body healed itself. "Just give me a minute."

Jeremy knew what was going on. But his mind was still hurting from the pain of the steel stakes that had prodded his body for so long. The wounds would heal quickly of course, but the pain would linger.

Jordy dimmed the fire lights of the torches for him. "They're coming Jeremy. I need you to hurry."

"Where is everyone?" Jeremy questioned him looking over into Jordy's cell.

"It's just me here."

Jeremy and Jordy had been left at the hands of Asher's brothers while everyone else had been out looking for Emie. His brothers had taken Jeremy and Jordy hostage. They wanted to know where Asher was.

"We need to hurry Jeremy. She needs our protection from them." Jordy didn't trust Jeremy right now around Juliet. Or Asher's brothers. He needed to drink.

"Jeremy, you have to let me out. You're not strong enough to take them both."

Jeremy knew Asher's brothers were coming, and knew that even though he wanted nothing more then to drink them dry with his hatred for them, he couldn't. He leashed in the monster inside him as Jordy let him see his plan as he opened the steel doors of his cell. The steel burned his hands but he was able to get it open enough for Jordy to help him after he busted the steel lock with his foot.

Jeremy and Jordy could pass through walls and doors, but steel was their enemy. So were the steel bullets both James and Jesse had loaded in their guns. Jeremy and Jordy had to take them at the doors and put them in the cell Jordy had been caged in, bending the steel so they couldn't escape.

Jordy, looking inside the cell he had been caged in, at Asher's brothers. Soon Jordy would have to tell them as much as he could to get them through what was about to be the most trying time of their lives.

"You can't keep trying to kill us. You won't win." This last, Jordy told them slowly. Each word dripping out of his mouth. He needed to fed as soon as possible.

Both men argued pointlessly with him. Jordy knew there was nothing left he could say to them. They wanted answers he couldn't give them. He too was just as hungry as Jeremy.

They needed to get out of here. He looked at Jeremy who was now on the floor trying to finish healing.

"I'll be right back, I swear it." He told his brother honestly.

Jeremy willed him to resist the temptation to go to Juliet, even though he loved his brother and knew in his heart he wouldn't take her life. His mind was just so clouded still from the stake.

Jordy understood. He felt the same way about Izzy as Jeremy did about about Juliet. He needed to find blood for them.

Jeremy stayed on the floor. His body healing as he cried out in the pain he now felt.

Both caged men were lucky they were Asher's brothers.

Juliet had been pacing the floor of the den for what felt like hours. She had no idea how long she had been in this God forsaken mansion. How long had she been waiting in this room? What was she waiting for? Her demise?

Or for love?

Jeremy was a vampire! How could she love a vampire? How would she live the rest of her life knowing what and who Jeremy was? After everything she had seen and heard, how was she supposed to trust him?

She walked over to the windows where she looked out into the real world around her. There was no sign of the dogs anywhere. Could she make it to her truck before they reached her? Could Harley keep up with her, she wondered as she looked down at his shaking body.

His ears where down now like he knew they were in danger. He no longer wanted to play this game.

She could see the wind in the cold snow falling in blankets on the ground. Swirling around the grass and floating back up against the house and the large oak trees that surrounded the mansion.

But an honesty washed over her she couldn't explain, if she tried to run where was she going to run away too.

Juliet heard Jeremy's soft, gentle voice by the door.

"Juliet."

Jeremy was standing inside the room by the door, she noticed when she spun around at his voice. How did he get in here, Juliet wondered. It was still closed and she hadn't heard it open.

Harley was barking now, growling deeply at Jeremy. But he oddly walked over towards Jeremy, who knelt down and reached out for him. Once Harley smelled Jeremy he wagged his tail and walked back over to Juliet, panting and wagging his tail like everything was ok now that Jeremy was here.

Her hands that were wrapped around her felt colder then before and she started shaking. He looked like the same old Jeremy, dressed in dark jeans and a black shirt, but he wasn't the same Jeremy she remembered.

Her mind couldn't grasp the concept that he was a vampire and that he was safe.

"Juliet, listen. There is so much I have to tell you, that I never wanted to have to tell you. I sure didn't want to tell you like this." He said edging closer to her.

She willed him not to walk any closer by putting up her hand. She was still afraid of him. And with every word he spoke to her, gentle as it was, he was getting too close.

"I won't. I'll stay right here." Jeremy told her with his arms wide open to her.

"How… can hear me too?" She questioned shakily.

"Yes. I can." Jeremy hated this. He had no idea how to proceed. He didn't know what to say to keep from losing her. He couldn't let her run away though. "I've always been able to hear you love."

Juliet was losing feelings in her legs. Her whole being felt numb. What would happen next? Would he hunt her? Would he change her like him?

"No, Juliet, please. Please don't be scared. You have to let me explain this." Jeremy edge slower to her. She was behind the desk now, and that was fine. But he knew she couldn't see him clearly in the dark, and he needed to be close to her.

"I don't know if I can Jeremy. I don't… I don't know what to do anymore." Juliet almost cried out to him as tears dripped down her face. She was so scared of him. Scared of the world around her. Her fingers were trying to hold on to the desk under her, she found herself tapping her hands in fear to her words.

But she had this feeling inside of her. She wanted him to hold her like he had so long ago and make all of this go away.

"I will love, if you'll just let me." He pleaded with her.

Juliet feared the worst at his words. She couldn't let him near her. What would he do, she couldn't help but wonder. "No. Please, don't-"

She had misunderstood him, and Jeremy almost ran to her then. He finally understood why Emie had left Asher so long ago. It was killing him now the way Juliet was feeling.

"I'm not going to hurt you. I'm not like what you're thinking love. Just let me explain." He told her as he edged closer to the desk she was now holding onto.

There was a knock at the door. Juliet's eyes grew wider. She didn't know who was at the door, or who would come through it. All the possibilities ran through her head.

Jeremy needed help and knew Jordy was just outside the door. He begged him to come in. He needed him right now if he was going to save Juliet from herself.

Jordy opened the door and walked in. Jeremy smirked when he did so. It had been many years since he had seen his brother open a door. Not since Asher had first started coming around.

"Juliet, this is my brother, Jordy." He proceeded to introduce them slowly, watching as Juliet gulped her fear down; he tried to give Juliet a human moment to meet Jordy. Her heart rate he noticed had slowed with the introduction. She was even trying to brave a smile as she looked at him and wiped away her tears. He took a chance and edged again closer to her on the same side of the desk.

His heart flipped around when he watched Harley look at both men awkwardly and walk over to greet Jordy the same as he had done to Jeremy. Harley walked over to Juliet then and Jeremy couldn't help but smile at the little dog he didn't know and thank him for showing Juliet what she needed to see.

Jordy was the first to speak. He took a few steps away from the door and walked slowly to the edge of the desk. Juliet noticed his attire was much like Jeremy's. Jeans, a simple black shirt. His hair was exactly the same as Jeremy's. Blonde, spiky.

He was absolutely breathtaking. Just like Jeremy. It was their eyes that held Juliet's attention though. They were a deep, dark red that she could see in the darkness. Just like vamp-.

"I know right now this is all a lot to take in. But if you just let me explain, all this will make sense for you." Jordy interrupted Juliet. He couldn't let her finish her thoughts.

Juliet looked at Jeremy. She wanted so badly for this night to be over. Jeremy was looking at her now in the moonlight. She did the only thing she knew how. She nodded at him in acceptance. "Ok. I'll listen."

Jeremy took a deep breath then. He loved this woman so much. He took the few steps closer to her and reached out for her hand. The feeling of her hand so sweet and tender again in his did things to him he couldn't explain.

"I'm so sorry Juliet. So sorry. For all of this."

Jordy took that moment to step closer also in her direction. "Juliet, I can help you understand this better and it'll be faster for you. If you will take my hand, in a moment, all of your questions and the answers you've been searching for will make perfect sense to you."

Jeremy looked at Jordy when Juliet flinched at his now outreached hand. He wasn't sure she could handle this. He looked to Jordy for guidance.

She'll be ok Jeremy. Jordy reassured him. This was the best way for her to understand.

Jeremy knew then, with the way Jordy could see in the future that he was right. This was the easiest way. Joseph had a way of showing people things. It was his ability. How had Jordy found this ability? He wondered.

In a moment, a blink of an eye, only a few heart beats for Juliet, she would know everything she needed to know about them, and him. She would fully understand it all and accept it. They could show what all had transpired in the months she had been hiding in fear for her life.

Juliet looked up at Jeremy now. He was her only saving grace now.

"I promise, with all that I am love, no one here will hurt you. I will be right here beside you."

Juliet had no idea what he was talking about, or what was about to happen. She only heard his words of love. She believed him in her heart that it would be ok. Juliet reached up for his arm, but he took her in his arms instead, holding her against him hugging her.

"Oh, Jeremy." She cried into his shoulder, holding him too. She had longed for this moment for so long. He smelled of the dungeon, and irony blood that he must have drunk before he came in here to her. When he nuzzled her neck she tried not to flinch, but she couldn't help it, her body responded unwillingly.

Jeremy felt her flinch. He hadn't meant to add to her fear. "Juliet, I swear it to you. I won't hurt you love." He whispered into her ear. He wished he could take all this away from her.

"I know. I know." Juliet buried her face deeper into Jeremy's shoulder and chest. She just wanted to hide herself in his arms. Months of fear and worry were built up inside of her. She hadn't slept or ate. She had been on constant guard since she couldn't remember when. She needed the warmth and security of his arms. She needed the promises he and Jordy had shown her.

Jordy took his chance. He eyed Jeremy over her head and reached out his hand to Juliet's shoulder. Once he touched her, he showed his visions.

In a flash, Juliet's mind was filled with heavenly hosts. Angels and demons. A war that no human had ever known was waged. Jeremy held her through it all, protecting her.

Demons had run ramped on the earth. Invading humans and taking over their minds. Angels were turned into vampires to walk among the earth and destroy the damned before they could destroy God's people. She saw the Flood and the tower of Babble, bible stories she remembered from her youth. She watched as the vampires walked amongst men and lived with them. She saw through time as the humans became so overpopulated that the vampires increased their numbers and joined forces with the humans, giving them the abilities to do as they did. Protect the innocent. Destroy the damned.

To her surprise, she saw her own savior as he walked upon the earth and explained in parables to the elders, but no one had listened or understood him.

Juliet then watched painfully as Emie had been changed, and as all her parents and friends, except for her brothers, rejected her.

She watched as the Whitby family lived together and strived to protect themselves, all while doing the will of God. They started their lives here in Michigan, in Luna Pier, generation after generation, becoming all the city would need to survive in this ever changing economic world. They were not at all what legends had foretold them to be.

Jordy then showed her how Asher had come into their lives, how the war had begun and why. How vampires had overtaken the governments and kingdoms of this world. How they were carelessly feeding on those that remained. And how Jeremy had ended up trapped here by Asher's brothers. How if she hadn't come here to save them, they wouldn't have made it much longer. James and Jesse were going to kill Jeremy and Jordy. They were young and didn't understand who the Whitby's were.

Juliet, now knowing everything she needed, looked up at Jeremy.

Jeremy looked down at her. He stroked her hair and held her in his hands. He felt so much for her and he was dying to share it with her, but Juliet's mind was overtaken again by Jordy. He was now showing Juliet everything of their first encounter. How Jeremy had come to her rescue, sent by Jordy just in time before this war had come. He showed her how, if it wasn't for Jeremy, how her life would have been affected. How she wouldn't have made it alone out there by herself. He then showed her the love that Jeremy felt for her. And how even after they had left each other, the love that had grown in Jeremy for her, how he had still longed for her.

Then, a Jeremy, broken and beaten by James and Jesse, laying on the cold floor of the dungeon had called out to her mind, hoping and pleading with his heavenly maker that she would come to all of their rescue. She was the only one who could. Juliet was the only other one who knew of Jeremy that could help him.

The rest of the family had to stay away. Jesse and James could have killed them, or worse, they would have killed them. And no one else but a human could remove the steel from Jeremy.

"You see Juliet, it was your love for Jeremy that saved us all, and we will forever be indebted to you." Jordy left her with those thoughts in Jeremy's arms.

Juliet now clung to Jeremy, crying anew in his chest, holding unto him for dear life. No woman could have ever been given more reassurance in knowing the man that she loved, loved her the same.

Jeremy looked at Jordy in a silent thank you. Jordy nodded and walked over to the fireplace to start a raging fire that would warm them all.

"So what now then?" Juliet asked, pulling away from Jeremy's chest, but not out of his arms. She had to know what to do now. "What about your sister, Emie?"

Jeremy looked down at Juliet. She never ceased to amaze him. Her world had just been flipped upside down. She was hungry and thirsty like he was, but first she wanted to make sure he was ok. She humbled Jeremy.

Jordy walked up to Juliet, handing her a glass of something that would ease her mind before he left them both alone. He told Jeremy he would be waiting for him in dining hall later should he choose to meet up with him. There was much to discuss and Juliet's future was on the top of that list.

Jordy wanted to leave and go to Izzy. He had been away from her long enough. And there was still the matter of finding Emie.

Jeremy nodded at Jordy, and then encouraged Juliet to drink. "Its ok, It's just brandy."

Juliet watched as Jordy walked through the doors without opening it. She drank the warm brandy then and was thankful for its warm heat that filled her down to her toes.

"That is scary." Juliet said aloud, looking at Jeremy sideways to try to lighten the mood. She was finally alone with Jeremy and still wasn't sure how to act. Thoughts of all that had happened down in the basement and up here entered her mind.

"He's a dramatic kind of guy." Jeremy hoped now was a good time as any to start joking around with her.

Juliet set down her empty glass on the desk.

Juliet noticed his smile then. It was exactly like she had remembered; it was crooked and took up his whole face, genuine.

Tears, but new joy filled tears instead of fearful ones, ran down one of Juliet's cheeks. Jeremy brushed it away with one of his thumbs, tenderly.

"What it is?" He wondered aloud.

"I must have pictured the day we would meet again a hundred different times, a hundred different ways. I never thought it would be so dramatic." Juliet wrinkled her nose at him in a jest.

"Cause the way we met was so less dramatic, right?" Jeremy laughed back at her.

Juliet nodded her head back at him laughing with him. She picked up her glass and looked back at him more seriously. "You might wanna keep a lot of this on hand for me."

Jeremy agreed with her.

Juliet sighed into him and snuggled back in his chest. She didn't know what to do now, and for the first time in along time, she didn't care. She was safe now, from the outside world that had threatened to take her away from this life. She was safe from the demons she had thought them all to be just moments ago.

Jeremy sighed too at her thoughts. If his family thought they had seen love, they hadn't seen anything yet. He would die for this woman.

Jeremy could hear Juliet's subconscious. She was hungry, and needed a few moments alone. "Juliet, is there anything I can do for you?"

"Is there a bathroom in this house of vampires?" She questioned him.

Jeremy smiled. It had been many years since he had need of one, but yes there was finally a washroom here. When Asher had lived here months ago, Joseph had turned a room upstairs off of Emie's rooms into one just for him. There was another one closer to them now. It had belonged to Cristina's son Neely.

"Yeah, just follow me." Jeremy said to her as he led her out of the den.

Thirty Seven

Juliet had taken a few moments alone in the wash room to herself. The days events had unfolded for her in her silence. The endless days alone, the long grueling trip here, blood thirsty wolves, men who wanted her and Jeremy and his family dead or worse. Finding out the man she loved was a vampire, and had a family who were vampires also. But weren't...

His family was like angels of some sort.

Juliet looked in the mirror at herself then. She was worn and tired, and the night wasn't over yet.

She steadied her composure and made herself look presentable. Walking out into the hall she found Jeremy crouched down petting Harley. She watched as he slowly stood up and grinned at her.

Juliet smiled shyly back over at him and walked up to him. Still taken back by his appearance and handsomeness she tried her hardest to keep her gaze off his strong body. Never before had Juliet ever thought she would find herself with a guy as perfect as Jeremy. She tried to shake off her awkwardness around him.

She leaned against the same wall he was and took a deep breath. "So what's next?"

Jeremy shook his head at her. She was stronger then she gave herself credit for. "Well, we have to get in touch with our family in Florida somehow. We need to find our sister."

Juliet thought of her family then. "Jordy wouldn't happen to know what happened to my family would he?"

Jeremy had been dreading this question from her. "We know." He hung his head then and placed a booted foot against the wall behind him. He knew exactly what had happened to her family. It had happened to them the same day it had happened to Emie and Asher. "Just please, don't ask me to tell you how it happened. I think it's better if you don't know."

Jeremy watched as a tear fell down her cheek. She hadn't expected that answer. He put his arms around her, pulled her into his embrace and warmth and kissed the top of her head. He showed her mind how hard he had tried. How he couldn't be everywhere at the same time and how torn he had been between his sister, her family and trying to save her at the same time. In the end he had been almost useless.

He couldn't make it to New York in time, and even if he had, he wouldn't have been able to find her in the midst of such a big city. He had been not even half way there when Emie had been captured, and on his way home he had learned from Jordy that her family had all died a terrible tragic death.

"I can keep you safe here with me love. But it's your choice what you want to do next." He gave her the choice. He didn't want to take it from her.

Juliet looked up at Jeremy then. A little shocked, but then she realized what he was saying. He wasn't trying to make her do anything she didn't want to do. "Even if I did have somewhere else to be Jeremy, I would still want to be here with you."

Jeremy tipped up her chin then, grateful for her feelings towards him, and was about to kiss her, but they were interrupted by a very large, very dirty, very angry, Asher. He had stormed through the front doors dragging two bodies with him.

Jeremy took Juliet's face in his hands after she had caught sight of what had come through the doors. "Don't look. Please don't look." He gave her a wink and assured her she was safe, then directed his attention to Asher. "Where not alone here anymore Asher, just so you know." Jeremy told him nodding towards Juliet. "Your brothers are down stairs."

Asher huffed out his displeasure, smoke coming out his nostrils, and continued dragging his dinner through the broken dining room doors to the basement.

Jeremy looked back down at Juliet. "Are you ok?" her eyes were shut tightly now, she was counting in her head.

"I take it that was Asher?" she questioned quietly.

"Yeah. He's, a little dramatic also in his new life. He wants answers to questions no one has."

"He looks angry."

Asher was angry. With every right, Jeremy thought. Asher had spent more time without Emie then he had ever spent with her. Life kept getting in the way.

"It's the writer in me, I apologize. I get curious and want to know every detail. But I'm learning there are something's I don't need to know." This last she said winking up at him.

Jeremy looked at her then. Really looked at her. She had been through so much these last few months. All he had been able to think of was her. Now she was here, holding onto his shirt for dear life. He smiled down at her and kissed her forehead. He was happier then he had ever been in his whole life. Aside from the world falling apart around him, vampires destroying anyone and everything, families destroyed and cut down; he'd never been happier. Irony, he was learning, was a cruel joke.

Jeremy put his arm around Juliet and started walking her towards the doors Asher had just walked into. "Well then, you are going to love my family!" he jested down at her.

Jordy had been waiting patiently for Jeremy and Juliet, lighting the candles he had placed on the table for Juliet. They had a lot to discuss. Now that they were free of Asher's brothers and Asher could take care of them on his own, they needed to find the rest of the family, get them back here into the city and try to put things back together. Asher didn't want any help finding Emie, but what he had forgotten was she wasn't just his, she was their sister. And no matter what, they would find her.

Speaking of the devil, Jordy turned as he watched Asher come into the dining room dragging two dead bodies in his wake. Jordy shook his head. Asher's new life had changed him, in some ways that were totally humorous. What no one had expected were the abilities he had now. Jordy had a feeling back when he had met Asher, but it was nothing like what Asher had become.

"Seriously?" Jordy questioned him honestly looking at the two dead men.

"What? I wasn't finished when you summoned me." Asher told Jordy this wishing he could be rid of their abilities inside of his head.

Jordy shook his own head again and pointed Asher towards the kitchen. Every time Asher brought home food to share, they would split it amongst themselves and the wolves. It was a bloody scene in the kitchen he was sure Joseph and Emie would have a panic attack over.

When Jeremy and Juliet walked in and sat down at the table with him, he and Jeremy exchanged knowing looks about Asher.

Jordy sighed greatly and took his place feeling awkwardly like Joseph. "I am going to leave before sun rise and head down to Florida. I think the two of you should stay here and help Asher. He has plans…"

Jordy let that last linger for Jeremy more then for Juliet's sake.

"Now what?" Jeremy questioned Jordy exhausted.

"I'll let him explain." Jordy told him, not wanting to be the brunt of Asher's anger again. Asher couldn't read minds, or see the future like Jordy could and it frustrated him. Asher now was not a man any of them wanted to cross. Watching him go through what he had after losing Emie was enough to scare them all.

Sounds from the kitchen of Asher working on his next meal could be heard. Jeremy hung his head and shook it. "I apologize Juliet. He's new to this life, and hasn't learned decorum when it comes to feeding."

Juliet looked moved by it, but was accepting it.

"He's gone now. He's in search for something for you." Jordy motioned to Juliet then. "Asher doesn't like to eat alone." He told her.

They both looked to Juliet then in apologetic unease.

Juliet wasn't sure if she could stomach anything at the moment and swallowed down her hunger.

"When I get back with everyone we can continue the search for Emie. In the meantime, I'd stay clear of him if I were you." Jordy said to Jeremy.

"Is there anything I can do?" Juliet questioned, unsure of what to do.

Jordy smiled at her. Jeremy was going to be happy, finally.

"I'm sure Asher will have a lot for you to do when his family gets here."

Juliet wondered if his family was like them.

"Asher has human friends and family down at the fire department. He was a fireman before this all happened." Jordy explained. "They need a safe place to stay now, and there is more people in the city that will need protection. That's why I am bringing home our family. If things play out the way Asher wants it too, we can try and rebuild this city, or least get things cleaned up."

Asher came walking in the dining room doors to them. He was carrying a case of water he landed on the table in front of them and a box of groceries he had found in Juliet's car. He disappeared in the kitchen and came back out with a arm full of beer bottles.

Juliet eyed her box with somewhat of disgust. She had been eating cans of fruit and dried meat for months now. She eyed Asher in somewhat of a thank you, and noticed his dirty shirt he was wearing. It had rips and tears in it, but there was clearly a maltese cross patch on his left shoulder that branded him as a fireman.

Jordy and Jeremy shared a look at each other. They would have to get her some real food soon.

Asher sat across from Juliet and Jeremy now. He was drinking heavily from his bottles. Trying to be civil and not bring in his cut up meat and suck it dry, he drained what he could into the bottles like they had showed him.

Jeremy cut into the water case and grabbed some water for Juliet. She thanked him and he turned to the two six packs Asher had brought in for Jordy and him. He scooted Jordy's over to him and sat back down next to Juliet.

Asher started the conversation they were all dreading to hear. "Once I talk to my brothers and change-"

"You can't just change them because you want to Asher." Jordy stated spinning his bottle in between his fingers.

"I can do whatever the hell I want Jordy, and I need your help!"

Jordy's anger was peaked now. "You can't change their will Asher, it's not allowed. They will not want to be like us. Right now they are scared and don't know what's going on. And when they do see things the way they are, they still will not want this life."

Angrily Asher stared him down. "I need them, and you to help me find her! I don't care what they want!"

Jordy looked at Asher with disdain clearly written on his face. He wanted so badly to blame Asher for Emie's disappearance. "Deal with them however you choose Asher. They are your brothers. But, this isn't the first time I've lost my sister Asher." He said pointedly to Asher. Wanting him to see his point. "She can take care of herself, if you remember correctly."

Juliet was lost and wondering what they were talking about. She looked to Jeremy for help, but he was looking at Asher like something was about to happen.

Asher stood then. Scooting back his chair across the floor to the wall behind him not caring if he scared Juliet or not. He placed his big hands on the table in front of them all. He looked deeply at Jordy and forced his point. Smoke was dangerously coming out of his mouth and nose as he breathed in and out. "There is nothing in this world that I understand better than that, Jordy. You'll take care not to forget that again."

Jordy looked carelessly at Asher. He wanted to stand, he wanted to force his issue and remind Asher who he was and what Emie meant to him. But he understood what Asher was going through. He just wanted Asher to see he too loved Emie. And he knew her better, well, almost better then Asher. She would be ok. She just needed a reason to live now. She didn't know Asher was still alive. He could only hope his sister had enough faith in all of them to know they had taken care of Asher when she needed them too.

"I want to bring every one of my family and friends down there, here. First I have to deal with my brothers, then we are going down there to help them."

"How do you plan on getting a group of that size down here without a fight? You know they are out there watching us Asher." Jordy asked, knowing Jeremy would prove his point.

"They are just waiting for a chance to strike at them and us." This from Jeremy, who knew it to be true.

Asher smiled then and drug his chair back to the table. "I'm going to use the fire truck."

Both men looked at Asher then.

"The hull of tanker is a steel container. If I bust through the bottom and open a hole in it, they all can safely sit inside of it undetected."

Jordy thought about that. It was brilliant plan. "Alright."

Jeremy eyed them both questionably. Asher had many plans these last few months. All of them were valid. He had to admit the man was sometimes a renegade when it came to things that mattered, but like Jordy had thought, this was brilliant. He looked down at Juliet then. He wanted her to look at him and prayed she understood what she was getting into, but her mind was still working out Asher's plan.

When Juliet figured it out while they were discussing it more, Jeremy fell harder for her as he seen her plans. She heard there were children in the group Asher was bringing over and he saw in her mind her excitement.

Juliet had wanted to be an English teacher before she had written her first novel. She was schooled and educated for early education in the lives of young people. Jeremy could see the longing in her eyes to be busy doing something useful. Something more normal. She would make a good teacher if she ever got the chance.

"What have you uncovered about your brother?" Jordy asked.

Asher knew which brother he was talking about and growled a deep low growl into his last beer bottle. "He's not my brother."

Jordy watched as smoke ringed out of Asher's nose while he drank heavily.

"They were headed to Washington through New York before I lost track of them. They have control of the new government there. Emie wasn't with them that I could see. She would have heard me." Asher looked down at the table then, slouching in his seat and looking more human than he had in months. He slipped his hand deep in his right jean pocket and downed the last few drops he had left in his bottle. "When I find her, he will pay for this."

Juliet looked to Jeremy then, she needed answers to understand what they were talking about.

I promise, I'll tell you later.

Juliet nodded at him. She knew this must be important. Asher, as frightening as he had been was sitting in front of her now looking defeated.

Jordy was nodding his head now, not looking at Asher. They too would want their turn making Axel pay for what he had done.

"So Jeremy, are you going to introduce us?" Asher asked.

Later that night....

Jeremy was walking Juliet up the grand staircase. He made a last second change as he reached the landing. He had been about to take her to his rooms, then thought better of it. He remembered that first night he had met her how his truck had been in such a disarray and her reaction to it. He thought maybe she would be more comfortable in Emie's room.

"We do not have guest rooms in the house anymore. We all have our own apartments. Think you will be ok alone in my sister's room tonight?" Jeremy asked her as Harley padded along beside them.

Juliet wasn't sure where she would be comfortable, if at all. But a safe room with a bed was better then where she had been staying.

"Normally, the servants would have aired out the rooms and cleaned them up, I would have sent them to your room and had them see to your needs, but as you can tell, we haven't any at the moment."

Juliet smiled sweetly up to him in understanding as they walked up another flight of stairs.

She was nervous, Jeremy could tell. But she was handling everything better then he had thought she would.

When they reached Emie's apartments, Jeremy opened the door and showed her in. Emie's rooms had been left abandoned. Her closet doors were left open, her bed was made and set right, but the empty bottles left sitting out on her night stand made Juliet look away. She knew now what they were.

Jeremy picked them up and threw them in a trash can over by Emie's desk. He looked back at the bed where Juliet was now standing by. She was looking around the open room in awe.

Emie's design of her rooms were more elegant than the rest of the house. Black and red silk hung around the bed in the center of the room inclosing it in an atmosphere of privacy. Her deep red wine walls darkening the room, but gave it an air of richness. The mahogany trim on the walls and connecting doors added a warm feel to the room.

Juliet noticed right away the drapes on the windows had been pulled tightly shut to the outside world.

Jeremy noticed her direction of thought and wondered how to explain it best to her. "It is supposed to rain and be cloudy all day tomorrow, so we should be able to leave these open for you."

When he started over to them, Juliet stayed him. "It's fine. I understand. No sunlight." She said nodding her head in acknowledgment towards him.

Jeremy grinned at her sheepishly. "You are taken this better than you need to for someone who has so many questions." He stepped closer to her and rubbed her temple. "Whatever it is, now is a good time to ask me."

Juliet tried her hardest not to giggle. "Where do I begin?"

"Make me a list." He told her. Remembering the many list of questions she had emailed him in the past. She knew everything about him from his favorite color to his favorite horse, but there were many things she wanted to know now.

"Ok." She said thinking out loud. "Let's start with the sun." this she told him taking his hand and walking over to the bed. She sat down and curled one leg under her looking up at him.

Jeremy took a stance in front of her. He tried his best to reign in his desire for her and think about her question. "It's big, round, hot!" He jested.

Juliet giggled then. How could she not. "No. Seriously, tell me."

Jeremy sighed aloud then looking up into Emie's ceiling. He closed his eyes as he told her, "It's a curse if you will. God wanted to protect humans from us. We have free roam in the night, or when it's overcast like it will be tomorrow. If we go out in the sun, it kills us. Burns us up."

Juliet thought more about that. She decided to wait to ask him more on the subject. She already knew what he ate. "Do you sleep?" Coffins entered her mind then.

Jeremy laughed a little at her thoughts. "Well, as you can see, we don't sleep in coffins." He sat down next to her in ease. Conversations with Juliet never started off easy, but he always ended up enjoying himself. "But to answer your question, no, we don't sleep."

Juliet nodded her head again.

Jeremy moved her long hair off her shoulder. He was glad she had relaxed enough to take off her big coat and jacket. She was left now with the hoodie he had bought her earlier this year. In a twisted sort of way, his plan had worked.

"But you, love, need to get your rest if you want to keep up with me tomorrow."

Juliet leaned in to him then as she watched Harley circling on the fur rug in front of the bed. He plopped himself down and sighed deeply. He would sleep soundly tonight. He wouldn't have to worry about her anymore.

"Tell me a story then. Tell me more about Asher and Emie."

Jeremy sighed at that. It was a story filled with heartbreak and longing. It was sure to fill her with nightmares. He decided to tell the end of the story and catch her up to speed. But he would leave out gruesome parts.

As he started his story of how they had met, and fell in love he noticed she was yawning. He picked her up and carried her to the side of the bed, never stopping in the telling of his story. He placed her under the covers and took of her shoes for her, then he slide the covers up over her.

Juliet listened to every word. She dreamt mostly, but she did her best to listen to closely. She fell asleep and lost her battle near the end. Asher had sacrificed his life for Emie. It was so endearing and wonderful she fell asleep with a little smile on her face.

Jeremy stood and walked to the hearth in Emie's room. He lit a fire there for Juliet and watched as Harley lumbered closer to it and fell asleep on the rug nearby. He patted his head softly and told him good boy. Jeremy sat there on the floor next to Harley for a few hours watching over her sleeping.

It wasn't until he was summoned by Jordy that he left her.

Juliet rolled over in her bed sweating and ashamed of the drool that had formed on her pillow. She wiped at it and opened her eyes. There was a fire in the hearth close to her bed keeping her warm.

Stunned by the sights around her she took in what she could remember. The night before had been the worst kind of night mare. Jeremy was a vampire. His entire family, including Asher who had been the scariest of them all, were vampires. They drank blood, and hunted humans, just like the stories had told.

She rolled over in Emie's bed and wondered where he was. She laughed to herself then. One second she was afraid of him and the next she missed him.

A smell in the room caught her attention and she lifted up off the bed following her nose. At the end of the bed she seen a tray with a dome shaped lid.

Breakfast! She hoped...

There was a single rose and a glass of cold juice sitting next to it. Juliet crawled over to it. She sat Indian style in front of it and smiled. While drinking her juice she lifted the dome lid and laughed, spitting her juice. There was one piece of bacon next to a lil note that read: Hungry? Let's play a game of hide and seek. I'm hiding, come seek me out for your prize. Jeremy.

Juliet shook her head and closed her eyes laughing. Only Jeremy, she told herself, setting the lid back on the tray. He loved to play games, she remembered.

She took a minute to look around before she left, and noticed there was a light on in a room off the bed room. She jumped off the bed and headed for the room. She found another wash room as she peeked inside.

Of sorts...

There was a fully lit chandelier hanging over a gigantic tub in the middle of the room. The room was tiled from top to bottom with tan tile stones with a roman design. In the ceiling was a plaster display of heavenly hosts in the billowy clouds.

Juliet stood in awe and walked inside the room. Over by the sink and vanities were her boxes of clothes and things she could use to freshen up. A note stood on top of the box.

"Incase you were hoping for a warm bath, we turned on the generators so you could freshen up. Turn on the water and enjoy. Jeremy."

Juliet looked in the mirrors in front her and raised her eyebrow in excitement. A nice warm bath sounded just like what she need. She hadn't had one in months.

Jeremy had spent the night cleaning the kitchen and putting Asher to some useful tasks. They had found some food for Juliet, and for Harley who had stayed by Jeremy's side every where he went. Jeremy smiled knowingly when Asher and Jordy sat on the kitchen counters and finally asked about how he and Juliet met.

Jeremy talked about that first night like it had happened yesterday. He told them of the months they spent together talking over the phone and internet. Remembering how it all had happened had been freeing for Jeremy in the telling. He had kept her a secret for so long. It felt good to finally tell someone how happy he was now.

"You know how I was Jordy." Jeremy told him. "I never wanted a woman in my life. Hell, I was too busy for that stuff."

Jordy remembered all to well. He knew Juliet was going to happen to his brother one day, but he never expected Jeremy to be this happy about it.

Jeremy was sitting in one of the stools as he talked to them. "I always thought a woman would just complicate things for me. Get in the way of all the things I had going on. Or all she would want was my money and spend her days selfishly indulging in all I had worked so hard to accomplish." Not like anything in his bank accounts mattered now. They were useless, just numbers on paper now he told himself. He had lost all of it a few months ago.

"Juliet was different though. She had her own career, she had made a name for herself in New York as an author.

"No matter how much I begged though, pleaded with her, she wouldn't move here." Jeremy remembered how hard he tried.

"She is different then any girl I have ever met."

"How come you never told us?" This Asher asked.

"You know better then anyone why."

Asher looked at him confused.

"Emie. She would have dragged me out to the pastures and beat me." Jeremy told them holding his head down. He would give his right arm to see Emie now and let her do it to him.

Asher thought about that. Emie had a temper when it came to her brothers not listening to her. But she would have been happy for Jeremy. "Hell, Jeremy, she probably would have helped you." He told him hopping off the counter.

Jeremy thought about that. He wondered if she would have. He laughed when he thought about it. "You might be right. But I wasn't taking a chance. Plus, it kept things interesting not letting you all in on it."

Jordy knew what that felt like. The thrill of the danger he had felt those first few days with Izzy had been interesting to say the least.

"Speaking of interesting..." Asher pointed towards the door where Harley was looking out wagging his tail in excitement.

Jeremy looked and felt excitement as he waited for Juliet to walk through the door. He had just finished making her breakfast moments ago, and couldn't wait to watch her eat. Well, he couldn't wait to watch her do just about anything. He had waited long enough to see her again.

Juliet walked into the room Harley and three large men were waiting in for her. She had been surprised walking out into the hall and it had been all cleaned up. The floors even shined like glass. The dining room wasn't a scattered mess with the doors hanging off the hinges. And the kitchen, to her surprise, didn't look like a murder scene anymore.

Looking at the two twin brothers at first was hard on her. One was sitting on the counter drinking, and the other was seated in front of her. They looked so much alike. But easily, as she got closer, she noticed Jeremy's crooked smile as he looked over his shoulder at her. She looked at the differences she could now make out. Jordy was neater and stood broader, where Jeremy was bent slouching on his stool. Nothing was out of place with Jordy. Jeremy, well, she smiled to herself. Jeremy had a look like he had just crawled out of bed. His hair looked like his hands had messed it up, his clothes were a little wrinkled and untucked, and his boots, she noticed, were muddy.

Delighted that Jeremy had stood and smiled at her, she walked up next to him, touched him and said "Tag. You're it." As she placed a kiss on his cheek.

Jeremy chuckled at Jordy and Asher's looks of confusion. Juliet and him had a bantered back and forth many times just like this. He knew exactly what she meant.

"Are the servants back?" She asked sweetly winking at him as she took her seat he was holding for her.

"The haunted house look was growing old." He said winking back at her as he pushed in the stool she sat in. "Hungry?"

"You have no idea." She said in her best whiny voice.

"Good." Jeremy said as he rounded the counter looking at her. He lifted the lid on another dome and set the plate full of food on her placemat.

Asher set down another rose in a vase next to her plate. He hopped up on the counter next to Jeremy.

Jordy disappeared through the wall and returned with a tall, chilled glass of milk. "We kept it outside to keep it cold for you."

Juliet took in her meal in front of her. They had prepared her favorite. She looked knowingly at Jeremy. He was very good at listening to her ramble on about all her favorite things in her emails they had shared. Pancakes with sweet maple syrup and bacon. She didn't care how he had found it or where he had gotten it from. She was just so hungry.

Looking for Harley she found him under Jeremy's legs, who was leaning up against the counter behind him in front of her, sleeping peacefully.

"He ate already this morning." Jeremy told her.

Juliet nodded her head thankfully. She sighed and dug into her food.

Jeremy watched in amazement at how she devoured her food. He was glad he had Asher to remind him of her needs and had set his watch for every few hours to remind him she needed to eat something. Asher had found all the things on Jeremy's list around the city and had stocked the cupboards full with all her favorite things and enough food for Harley to last them all winter. The roses had been cloth roses Jordy had found at the gas station. There wasn't much left there and the roses were a nice touch Jeremy had appreciated. He knew Juliet would get a kick out of it too.

Juliet sat back when she was too full to eat another bite. She was glad Jeremy had remembered she needed milk.

Jordy took note of that reading Jeremy's thoughts. They nodded at each other as Jordy made his exit.

"It was nice to meet you Juliet. I hate to leave you two so soon, I have some things I need to see to."

"Oh. It was nice meeting you too." She told him honestly.

"I should go too. The boys have been down stairs long enough." Asher told them all nodding at Jeremy and Juliet.

Juliet smiled at him too, and thanked them for her breakfast.

Jeremy stood across from her with his arms crossed on his chest. He waited till the guys were out of ear shot and asked, "So you think I'm sloppy?"

"Not sloppy!" She grinned wide.

"Well what then?" He asked playfully coming up to the counter she was sitting at and placed his hands in front of her.

"I don't know... hillbillyish?" she toyed with him.

Jeremy turned his head sideways and laughed out loud. He looked down at his booted feet, afraid to look back up at her. He knew without a doubt now that she found his looks sexy indeed, and it drove him insane. He had always wanted Juliet, and last night had been tempting, if not murderous to say the least.

He shook his head and looked back up at her smile.

Juliet grabbed her plate and walked over to the sink and shyly told him, "I'm just a fool for falling in love with a tornado."

Jeremy was behind her the second she set down her plate in the sink. His arms wrapped around her waist and his lips landed on her bare neck. He felt her jump, but held her still. He softly placed a kiss there on her neck. She relaxed when he lingered. She straightened up tall against him and her hand found the back of his head and she ran her fingers through his hair there.

Juliet looked in the reflection of the shinny steel backsplash in front of her. She could see the silhouette they made there and it reminded her of all the lonely days she had spent without him. She sighed into his kiss.

"Jeremy?"

"Yes?"

"Promise me something?"

He placed his nose against her neck resting there. "Anything."

Juliet turned in his arms and looked up into his eyes. "I don't have anyone left. No one." she said as tears threatened to spill over her eyes. "I don't want to be alone anymore. Promise me you won't forget that?"

Jeremy looked down into her eyes. He bore his promise down into her soul. "As long as I live love, I'll never forget that. I'll even do one better then that." He told her, kissing off the tears that fell on her cheeks. He picked her up and set her on the counter. "I promise to be everything you will ever need. You'll never want or need for anything again."

Juliet felt ashamed of her tears. Of her weakness. If this all hadn't happened she would still be in New York. In her little cute apartment. Just her.

Ironically she was glad it had happened. But she still hated that it had to happen before she realized where she really wanted to be.

Jeremy bent down and sealed his promise with a kiss he had been wanting for a long time. They had only shared one. And with this one, he wanted it to be what they had both been dreaming it would be.

Juliet had always called him her tornado. It was her nickname of sorts for him. He was the perfect storm. He was wild, and unkept, and a million things all at once. Always too busy, but never to busy for her.

She had always wondered what it would be like to be in his arms, but she had never imagined the whirlwind she was feeling now. He was raging and warm but cold as ice. He was lightning and thunder, shocking and vibrating inside her. In his arms he bent her and molded her to his body. She felt him inside of her body in places it was impossible for him to be stroking. She could feel how his touch had dampened her and was leaving her wet like rain pooling inside of her.

With on quick move he had cleared the counter top of everything and had her under him there. He had found her core as he kissed her neck and was stoking it sending up bursts of sparks out her body like a fire was a blazed and melting her. She wrapped her leg around his and begged for more.

She cried out his name when he stopped kissing her and drug his nose down her neck. He did it again inside her and smiled at her when she opened her eyes.

"How?" was all she could manage to say.

Jeremy placed his hands on either side of her and cocked his head. "Promise me something?"

Juliet looked up at him seriously then.

"Promise me you'll never forget what that felt like? And keep coming back for more."

Juliet smiled wider then she ever had before. She closed her eyes and thought about it. When she opened them again he was there waiting for her answer. "If that's all you got, I might have to rethink this whole vampire thing." She jested, truly worried about his response.

Jeremy, loving her breathlessly for who she was and how much fun they always had together, was now speechless. He had given her a kiss better then any women in the world had probably ever experienced, and she had said that!

Instantly he remembered a promise he had made to her one night in an email. She had just won a bet after one of their favorite shows had ended. Because he lost, he had to write her short stories about the two of them for a month. In his first story he promised her then that when he saw her next he was going to tickle her till she stopped teasing him so much. Even though secretly, he loved her teasing.

So he tickled her till she not only remembered his promise, but until she promised him she would "Never ever forget! Jeremy! I promise!" She said breathless when he finally stopped.

"I promise. I'll never forget." She promised.

Jeremy reached down and placed a kiss on her nose. "Good." He told her, thoroughly impressed with himself. "Now, we have to go help Asher."

Jeremy regretted having to leave. Having Juliet under him was like saddling up his favorite horse. He couldn't wait to do much more with her. She melted just like a candle under his flame. Like a glass of whiskey she was going to be easy to make love to.

Juliet eyed him curiously.

Jeremy shook the thoughts from his head and got back to their conversation. "He has his brothers in the hall now. He wants us to go down to the fire hall with him." He jumped off the counter and helped her down then. "There is a lot of people there who have been hiding out. We need to help Asher get them back here where we can help them better."

"You mean Asher's fire truck plan?"

Jeremy laughed as he led her out. "Yeah. That one."

Thirty Eight

Later that night...

Asher's plan had worked. He had finally done something right, he thought as he stared off on the moon lit lake. What was left of his family and friends were now safe at the Whitby's.

He had Juliet to thank for helping with the children. He hadn't expected lil Katie to be so hurt. She had ran away from him screaming. It had taken hours before her tears could be kept at bay. Hours again before she could even look at him. It had ripped at him to see her like that.

He could see the light house off in the distance. The beacon on the lake had been there ever since he could remember. Looking at it now, dark and deserted, it looked like it was falling apart like the rocks falling into the lake around it.

Asher was sitting on the highest point of the Whitby house alone. Every thought of Emie he tried to chase from his mind. It was the first time since he'd met her that he didn't want to think about her. It was like losing her all over again and he hated the feelings he had been having lately.

He wanted to be strong like her family was; he thought as he planted his feet harder on the roof and looked down at his knees. He wanted to think she had escaped and was on her way back to him right now. But it was hard. He wasn't strong enough. He knew how she felt about losing him. The last sight of him she had taken, was the sight of him dying in front of her.

Asher had tried to see God like the others did. He had tried to seek his counsel over the last few months. But he couldn't get over the brokenness he felt when ever he thought of God. Why did God want to separate them so much? Why couldn't he just let them live happily ever after?

He could see her face again even now. She couldn't save him and it was all over her face that it was the end of everything for them. How could God just let that happen to an angel like Emie? Someone so perfect as her deserved more than this.

She wouldn't know that Curtis had flown through time like a bat out of hell to save him. She wouldn't know now the months her brothers had spent helping him. Adjusting to this life had been hard for him, but it paled in comparison to losing her.

He wanted to share with her his new abilities that had shocked everyone. He wanted her to see the faces of her brothers as they learned just how powerfully he had become.

Asher took a breath full of the cold night air and sighed. Where was she? Could she feel he was still alive? Why hadn't Jordy seen this? Why couldn't she communicate with her brothers anymore? He had so many questions, and no hope to look forward too.

Joseph's haunting words from a year ago filled his soul and scared the hell of him.

"She's just gone." He heard him say. Just like that night out by the barns. Asher's disappointing thoughts had driven her so far away from all of them, no one could find her.

Off in the distance, a figure appeared out of nowhere.

It was Curtis. He moved with a grace and ease Asher had never seen. Once up on the rooftop with Asher, he sat next to him.

"She's fine Asher. You have to trust us on this."

Asher continued to stare out on the lake like he wasn't moved by what Curtis had said. Asher was tired of all their optimism. It wasn't helping.

"You weren't there, Curtis. You didn't see what these men looked like or were capable of." If they harmed Emie in any way, Asher was going to sentence them to life under his punishments. Death would be to forgiving. He would set them on fire forever.

Curtis chuckled when he seen the smoke coming out of Asher's nose.

"I know you don't want anyone's help in finding her, but I have a plan you might want to hear."

Asher put his face in his hands and rubbed his face. He was tired of hearing their ideas also. "Go ahead."

"One of the downfalls of my abilities is that I can't transport you unless I know where I'm going. If you can give me an exact location, I can get you there."

Asher knew this already. "I know."

"One good thing about Jordy is he can get us through walls."

This too Asher already knew. "Tell me something I don't know."

"You seem to have forgotten that Cristina can stop time. With the three of us, we should be able to get her out of where ever she is."

Asher had thought of that also. He had planned it all out. His problem was, he didn't know where she was, and all his planning was pointless.

Curtis sighed loudly for effect. His brother was a mess and trying at times. "You need to think Asher. Think like a vampire. Where would they be hiding her?"

Asher tried. He really did. What he had learned from the humans in New York was that a bigger army had moved in a month ago. They had enlisted the help of humans in exchange for their lives. The description he had learned from them of the leader seemed like it could have been Victor. Asher had bribed a guy to talk about him. The guy had told him he looked like an angel. The most beautiful man he had ever seen. Just like Emie had described of Victor when she had talked about him, and just like Asher could remember. But the guy didn't know the location of the army. Asher had pushed the guy for information until he had all but squeezed the life out of him. Asher had spared his life in the end though. The man's life wasn't required, and Asher couldn't take it.

"If I knew Curtis, we would already be there."

"Think Asher, you've been there before. Where would they set up a one world center to take down the world?"

Asher, stunned into silence, knew with just Curtis' words, where they were. He breathed it out loud and Curtis heard him. "The world trade center. World. Trade. Center." Asher had just been there recently. It had been rebuilt, stronger than ever. By new men then, strong enough to withstand the mightiest of forces. But not strong enough to withstand him.

It all made since now. Asher had been there before. He wondered now if Victor had a hand in it all. Had it all been to kill him before? Had they destroyed it all just for him? Had his strength been enough to save himself?

Destiny. Emie had always talked about destiny. It had to have been destined. It had to have been some ones master plan that he would survive it all. That he had went there, and could now go back and destroy the one thing that was bringing the world to an end.

Asher looked up to the heavens now. He could have sworn he heard the angels singing.

God had given him Emie once, no twice, he corrected. He would give her back again if Asher just believed.

Curtis was still sitting in silence. He knew what had happened to his brother there in New York. It all made sense to him also. "Joseph once said you would be our saving grace."

Asher nodded. "Let's roll." Asher quoted the famous saying that had come out of all that destruction. He used it now not as a metaphor, but as the undying truth of what was about to happen.

Vengeance.

Jeremy was watching Juliet sleep again for the second night. He was nervous and found himself pacing the floor of Emie's room. Juliet was under the covers wrapped up in only a blanket, a t-shirt, and a pair of skimpy undergarments.

The suspense was killing him. He was so tempted by her presence all day. Being a gentleman around her was hard work. It had been years since he had been with a woman. Seeing Juliet now, he knew it would be impossible to be with any other woman but her ever again.

The kiss they had shared had sealed it for him. He wanted to feel her under him again. He wanted to make love to her. Now.

With an exhausted sigh, in a flash he removed all his clothes, slid with ease under the covers with her and kissed her neck.

Excitement rose in his body as she stirred.

"Jeremy." She moaned, backing up against him.

"Yes love." He cooed.

Juliet rubbed her eyes and squinted at him in the dark room. "What time is it?" she questioned him.

"Only a few hours since you fell asleep."

Juliet smiled against his lips as he placed a slow, tender kiss on her lips. "You couldn't wait a few more hours?"

Jeremy growled at her in response.

Knowingly, she turned towards him and he enveloped her in his arms, kissing her sweetly everywhere. "You are naked already?" she asked in surprise.

"Mm hm." He breathed, kissing her lower down her neck, he reached down and pulled her top up over her shoulders. He went mad with need seeing her naked under her shirt. He lifted it up over her head. "You haven't forgotten the kiss earlier, have you?"

Juliet was sure she could never forget. "Never." Jeremy had found his way down her chest and was licking her skin now. She was coming unglued. He was awakening her inch by sensual inch.

His leg was neatly placed between hers. She found herself lifting up into him, trying to find the source of her pleasure. His lips found her nipple and she rose up to his waiting mouth. She sighed and breathed his name as he sucked her in and repeated sucking her till she grabbed his head and begged for more.

Jeremy switched then and tortured her other breast with his mouth. He wanted to bury himself deep inside her right then, but the slow ecstasy of her passion was rising and he planned to wait until she exploded in it before he gave her more. He stirred her emotions, but left her core untouched this time. He would wait till the perfect moment where he would stoke her flames and send her over the edge.

When he finished with her breast he crawled up her body and laid his length between her legs she had spread for him.

Juliet looked between them. Her brows rose as she eyed him. "Impressive." She told him sweetly.

Jeremy wanted nothing more then to please her for hours with himself. But there was a question running wild in his mind he needed an answer to. He moved himself up and down on her. When she threw her head back into the pillows under her, he asked. Whispering to her.

"You know what I am now. I have to go slow and easy with you." His mouth was open and the venom was filling his mouth. He had to swallow the monster inside him and concentrate on her pleasure. "Is there anything I should know before I take you, Juliet? Once I start I won't be able to stop." He started kissing her again. His hand lifted her off the bed under her hip and moved her towards him. She was ready for him.

Juliet didn't want to answer his question. She hated that at her age, unlike all the girls she knew, she was still untouched by a man. But she hadn't wanted any man to touch her like Jeremy had. She wanted to beg him for this. Plead with him to take her.

Jeremy, dizzy now with need, was lost in the moment. Lost in her taste and smell. He could hear her thoughts and wanted to kick himself for not knowing this about her. For all her teasing in her emails he wouldn't have guessed she was untouched.

He went back to kissing her neck. He lifted her more up to him. He stirred with in her a pleasure so great, and let it kindle until she was begging him with her own need for release. He had to make her more then ready for him.

He made a promise then. A promise to himself he knew he could keep. Juliet would be his now and forever. He would take her virtue; he would make love to her more often than not. He would be her pleasure till her dying day.

He kissed his way down her body then, letting go only to move lower on her. He not only wanted to feel her steady wanting, he wanted to taste it. He wanted to give her in this first moment something to remember that every woman deserved their first time.

Once he was between her lying nestled in her legs, he kissed and opened her up to his waiting tongue. Placing one hand under her, and the other one on her belly, he licked and tasted and stirred her from the inside out. Her moans mixed with her racing heart was like the sweetest of melodies.

When her pleasure was stoked to its fullest, he flew up her body and her cup ran over as he entered her body. He wouldn't have to go slow now. He wouldn't have to stop at his evasion of her sweet tight body. She accepted him, gathered him in her loving arms and wrapped herself around him. He would no longer have to toy with her emotions, her pleasure was there for him to take and ride to his own oblivion.

Juliet cried. Never had she ever felt so loved. Jeremy wasn't just taking his own pleasure. He was giving her more pleasure then she had ever thought possible.

Juliet was at a loss for words. She would never be able to describe what he was doing to her. She found herself reaching higher for something she knew would undo her in ways she could never recover from.

Jeremy whispered to her, repeated over and over again for her as he stroked inside of her, beaconing her to let it go. "Feel me, love. Feel me inside of you Juliet, all around you. Cum love. Just cum."

Juliet couldn't reach any higher. It was there waiting for her. She accepted it like the gift he was giving her. It entered her soul and let her go. She cried out his name then and finally let go.

Jeremy held her through it, he lifted her hips into him and pushed into her higher cradling her head in his hand he kissed her neck and whispered it to her again. "Just let it go love."

He felt the moment she did and reveled in it. Juliet collapsed under him and he rolled her over on top of him and held her there on him, releasing his own pleasure, pushing up into her and filling her as he held her close and felt the tremors of her ecstasy fade into shivers.

Jeremy placed a hand on her head and pulled her in closer to his chest. He waited for gravity to bring her back down. Her soul was still floating inside of her. He smiled as he felt inside of her body. She was thoroughly, and breathlessly pleasured.

Juliet kept her eyes closed as she felt his embrace. She still had no words for what had just happened inside of her. She just wanted to feel his love.

She was glad she had waited for this. She was glad no one had ever touched her or robbed her of this moment. Jeremy had perfectly and without a flaw made all her dreams come true.

She smiled when she realized that this was only the beginning.

Hours had passed. Jeremy was cradling Juliet in his arms where he had neatly tucked her into his side. Her limbs had pulled him tightly into her and she refused to let him go even in her sleep.

He felt the night slip away in to day. He thought about the next few days and with excitement he hoped for Asher that his plan would work in bringing Emie back home.

He would have to clean her sheets, he thought recklessly, and move Juliet into his room now. He had kept her here out of his reach, but he had failed at that miserably. Not she was complaining, he told himself looking at her face while she slept. He listened in to her peaceful dreams and led her into a dream of them horseback riding in Paris and Rome. Pink flowers were floating in the air. At night there were fireworks. She was happy there.

Jeremy nuzzled his nose in her chest and breathed her scent in. He would let her sleep for a few more hours before they returned to reality.

Joseph was waiting in the dining room for Jeremy and Juliet. Cristina and Curtis and Shelley had come back with him from Florida. Izzy and Jordy were now seated with them all after just arriving. Their conversations were distant to him now. He was looking at Asher now who was sitting solemn and worried by himself.

Asher knew his plan would work. But he feared the cost of those involved. Joseph's family had become his now. He would worry about them now like he had worried about his family at the department.

Joseph in that moment forgave Asher. He couldn't hold it against him any more that Emie had been taken. Seeing the way Asher was paying for everything now, Joseph knew it hadn't been his fault.

Joseph had been mad at Asher since the attack on Luna Pier, since Asher had chosen to believe Frank's mad ravings of insanity on his deathbed. He had hated Asher for not seeing things Joseph's way.

If Joseph was completely honest with himself, he hated Asher more for losing Emie. But Emie's words had filled his soul when he had walked back into this house. There was a reason for everything. He just had to trust Asher. He had to trust his sister more. Trust that there was reason for all this. She had believed it all her life, and the more Joseph looked at their life, he was starting to believe.

Asher would be their saving grace.

Joseph looked over at Cristina. He read her mind and knew what she was dying to tell Asher. It was a gift she had for him that would make all the difference in his plan.

Jeremy walked in then holding the door for Juliet who entered under his arm. He nodded to Joseph when he caught sight of him and led Juliet to the seats Joseph held for them.

Joseph walked back to his place at the front of the table. As much as he loved his family, he hated these kinds of meetings. He tapped his hand on the table getting everyone's attention, ready to begin.

Or so he thought he was going to begin…

Shelley spoke up before him. "You're going to need a plane."

Joseph looked at her confused.

"It's a good thing I'm a pilot" She beamed at him.

"Well, now that the transportation is in order," Joseph winked at her and continued. "Curtis, Shelley, Cristina and Jordy will accompany Asher to New York. Jeremy, Juliet, myself," he said smiling over at her reassuringly. This was first time he had seen her and Jeremy together. "and Izzy will stay behind here and hold down the fort till you return.

"You will all be leaving immediately. Gather some weapons and load Shelley's plane. Oh. One more thing." This he said to Shelley and

Cristina who were sipping on wine bottles. "No one eats or drinks till afterwards. I want you all blood thirsty when you get there."

Shelley looked at him in disgust.

Cristina took one quick last sip.

Asher shook his head. "What if they have radar set up Joseph. They will see us coming."

Shelley looked at him and laughed. "I know how to fly under radar Asher."

Joseph looked over at Cristina then. "Cristina has something to share with you about that."

Cristina took a moment then. She looked over at the love of her best friend's life. She wanted to do this for Emie and for Asher. "Asher, I've been playing with my ability as a bat," She felt ridiculous saying it now, but she believed in what she had been doing, and knew she could help, so she continued. "and I've seemed to master it very well. We don't have to land close by. I can fly there and check things out before we go in. I'm hoping to be able to fly around the city and find her myself before they even know we are there."

Asher looked at her in wonder. In all his planning he had never thought he would have this advantage. He looked to Joseph then, venom dripping from his fangs and pooling in his mouth. He was ready to leave right now.

Joseph eyed Asher curiously. Smoke was rising out of his mouth he had open.

"You alright man?" This from Jordy, who was bracing himself.

"I feel..." Asher started to say he felt good. He felt like his anger was reigned in and felt... ready. Ready for a fight. He couldn't wait for it.

He stood then and put his hands on the table in front of him. Smoke was rising all around him.

"Extinguish your feelings in the house Asher. Now!" Joseph laughed as he crossed his arms. The last thing he wanted was Asher trying out something new again. His rage was real, but his anger was nothing to be tempered with.

Asher shivered back his feeling. "I'm ready. Let's roll."

Joseph had a few more words for everyone before he would let them leave. He wanted to discuss in length the protection that Cristina would need.

They were interrupted by Ken Kruse, who tapped quietly at the door and let himself in.

Asher went to his side immediately and walked out into the hall with him.

"What's wrong?"

Ken took a deep breath and stood as tall as he could next to Asher. His friend had become a sight indeed. "Your brothers and I couldn't help but notice that something is about to happen. Is there anything we can do?"

Asher relaxed a little then.

"We just wanted to see if there was anything we could do."

"No," Asher told him. "It's Emie."

Ken nodded in agreement. He had noticed she wasn't with him when he had come and rescued them all from the fire hall.

"She was kidnapped some time ago. We think we've found her and we are going to get her." Asher stuffed his hands in his pocket. There was no one on the face of this earth he trusted more than Ken. Ken had always had his back in every situation. He wished now he could take his friend with him.

"I need you guys to stay here. Everyone still in danger here, and you need to protect your family Ken. Joseph and Jeremy will be here also." He stopped when he seen the hesitation in Ken's eyes and the way Ken started shaking his head at Asher. It was valid after everything they had been through down at the department but Asher needed Ken to trust them.

Asher placed both his hands on Kens shoulders. "You are my best friend Ken. I would never put you or your family in harm's way. I trust these men with my own life, and the lives of my family. You have my word as a brother that these men will not harm you. Because of Emie, these men are our brothers now. Trust them, ok?"

Ken swallowed deeply. When Asher put it like that, he trusted him. He nodded his agreement to Asher. "Alright. You just get yourself back here in one piece ok?" Ken eyed him sideways and laughed. "The girls are getting restless man. I'm not as cool anymore next to you."

Asher laughed out loud. "Like you ever were." He told him, pushing on his arm.

"Nah, you always were the man. So what are you now? Like some kind of creepy superhero?"

Asher thought about a conversation he and Curtis had about that. "Minus the tights." He leaned in and chuckled with Ken.

Joseph and everyone choose that moment to come walking out of the dining room and into the hall. Ken watched as all the vampires in the house had gathered together. He remembered a bible verse then he had read some time ago. "There shall the eagles be gathered."

Ken shook his head and walked away as Asher joined them.

Days later…..

Juliet had been sitting in the den reading to Katie, and two other children. She would look over often at the older Gabby and noticed her listening in on the stories she was reading to them. Gabby had been having a hard time without her cell phone. She looked lost sometimes in her thoughts staring at her phone. Like she didn't know what to do with herself sometimes without the internet. Hers would be one of the lost generations who would had never learned to play or read a book.

Looking over at Jeremy sitting slouched in a wingback chair, Juliet watched him think. She knew his thoughts were with his family. He worried about them silently and wondered how they had progressed.

There was a question in her mind now. She had been thinking about it for the last few hours. Gabby had played a song on her phone that had reflected her own decision to ask Jeremy her question.

Would he still love her when she was no longer young?

She couldn't bare the answer. She couldn't bare to look at his beauty and not long for her own. She didn't want to know what life for him would be like without her once she passed away.

It was vain, she knew it was. But she knew in her heart it was the right decision. She hated being weak. She hated not being useful to the people who might need her. She had no plans for her future now except for being with Jeremy. How was she supposed to be with him as a mere human? It couldn't be the way things were supposed to be.

Juliet sat up and handed the book over to Gabby who had looked forlorn that she had stopped reading. "Will you read to them for a minute?" She asked.

Gabby tried not to look excited as she grabbed the book, but continued the story right where Juliet had left off. Juliet smiled as she walked away. If it was the only good thing that would come out of the story that one life could learn the mystery of a good book, Juliet could be happy with that.

She walked over to Jeremy and sat in one of the wingback chairs next to him.

When his attention turned to her, she asked, "I have a question for you that has been plaguing me."

She noticed the moment when he read her mind and sat up a little straighter turning towards her. "Forever is a long time Jeremy." She told him as she looked down at her hands. "I can't leave this world without you."

Jeremy smiled at her. "When this is all over, then you can make that decision. I won't have you making a rash-"

"Because you know my mind better than I do?" she interrupted him.

It stung, and she knew it did. But she wouldn't have him telling her what she could do in the matters of life and death. Only she could do that.

Jeremy sighed greatly. He was that guy who never thought he would ever tell a woman what to do. His sister had taught him that. Juliet needed a reality check before she stomped off and found the first vampire she could and make them change her. She was angry enough at the moment to try something stupid like that. But she was cute enough that Jeremy wouldn't let anyone but him touch her ever again.

Jeremy rubbed his chin. "Look back over at the girls."

When Juliet did, Jeremy watched as her mind figured out what she needed to know.

"If I change you now, right now, as tempting as that is for me," he swallowed his venom as he thought about all the possibilities of doing just that. "And believe me, it is tempting."

"They would know…"

Jeremy looked at her as she turned her head and looked back at her hands in her lap. "They need you to be you right now. I know you want to help. I can feel what your feeling."

All the feelings of insecurity that had plagued her mind, the what if's and how she could be more helpful, even her vain wanting of what all this life had to offer her; they weren't valid enough to give him reason to do it. "This decision needs to be made under different circumstances. And believe me love, I will be the first to tell you when that time is." He grinned at her.

Juliet eyed him sideways. "Could you be anymore adorable?"

Jeremy stood then and took her hand in his. It had been forever since he had made love to her. He wondered if that was what she needed right now.

Juliet took his offered hand. She was worried about the children though, and the time of day, when a noise from up stairs startled them all. Little Katie came running across the floor to Juliet then, who scooped the little girl up in her arms.

Juliet looked to Jeremy and the look on his face told her everything she needed to know.

Jeremy walked over to the fire place then. He moved a rock which opened a secret door in the wall.

"Take the girls down stairs and tell Ken to lock the doors."

When he leaned in to kiss her, Juliet pulled his head down to her neck. She whispered to him, "Don't leave me alone. You promised me Jeremy."

Jeremy took her face in his and kissed her. He patted lil Katie's head so she wouldn't be scared even though he could feel her shaking in Juliet's arms. He looked Juliet in the eyes and promised her he would come back. "Then stay safe for me."

Jeremy walked out into the hall. Sounds of destruction filled his ears. A fight had ensued with men he didn't know. He watched as Ken, and Asher's men who were supposed to be down in the dungeons where he had sent Juliet and the children, were now up here fighting with his family to save them from the unwanted men that had invaded his home.

He could see the doors left open by them in their haste down stairs to find out what was happening now. He could see his worst nightmares of Juliet being torn apart by these men who cared nothing for her soul or the children's.

Watching as his brother and Izzy fought to save themselves from the men who were ganged up against them; Jeremy felt torn. Like a moth drawn to a flame, he wasn't strong enough to make a decision. He was torn between running to save Juliet and running to help his family.

He felt shame and confusion, he could hear bones breaking and nails scraping. He could hear the screams of everyone involved. But if he stayed and fought and they lost, Juliet and the children would die a worse death than any of them.

Time was running out and he was starting to lose his faith. He knelt down and prayed. Prayed to the only one who could save them all. He had never done it before in either lives, but he did it now. He didn't know how God was going to save him from it all, but for once in his life he trusted him to do it.

When he closed his eyes he seen the face of the angel he had seen the day he was born. Emie. The young woman she had been then who had cradled him in her arms and held him, promising him a life full of adventure and mystery. She was a lot like Juliet. Driven by the powerful essences she had found in her books.

She had given him the full life she had dreamed of for them. It was full of adventure and mystery, and love and so much more.

He needed Emie then. He needed his sister to come and save them all.

Had Asher made it in time to save her? Where they headed back? Would they make it in time for him to save Juliet?

Thirty Nine

Emie had been tossing in her make sift bed for days. She had been counting the days since she had last seen Asher alive. Day one she had been transported in a steel cage by Victor and his army. By day ten they were in New York. By day thirty she had been left underground to pay for her sins of not complying with Victors demands.

Emie refused to vainly give in and live the life he had tempted her with. There was no life for her outside of Asher. And Axel was a sad excuse of a man that Victor tried to tempt her with.

Victor would pace in front of her cage and demand she bend to his will. He needed her abilities to finish the work they had begun here. The take over of this world, killing pointless humans and reducing their numbers had been his job since the beginning. Finding those who he could change and use to help wage the war was now Axel's job, and Axel needed Emie. Needed her to bend their will and bring those chosen ones to them. But Emie wouldn't follow Axel. She wouldn't even try.

Frustrated, Victor had to know why. He wanted to know what he could do for her to change her mind.

"If not Axel, then who?"

Emie would cry and scream holy unrighteousness at him. Victor had taken her life when Asher had ended his. He would never understand the love Asher had given her, and there was nothing no one could ever give her to replace that love. She wanted nothing to do with this life anymore.

She would beg God for days; plead with Him to just kill her. She only wanted to be with Asher. She didn't care anymore about why she had been created or what else she needed to do here on earth. She was ready to leave this earth and be done with all its unrighteousness.

But softly, ever so sweetly, she would hear Him whisper to her that it was He who knew everything. And He alone would take care of her. She just needed to trust Him.

By day sixty, high above the New York skyline, encased in a steel building Victor had built just for this war, she had no hope of ever escaping; she could only watch the destruction of the once great city fall under her. She gave up longing for a rescue. She could no longer wish for her brothers to save her against Victor's vicious army. She prayed they would hear her cry for them to stay away.

On day eighty, it dawned on her where she was. Like a blow to her gut she listened to Axel as he told her where she was when he dropped in to bring her something to drink. The ironic state of it all made him laugh.

"You realize Victor built this tower with you in mind? When he destroyed the first ones trying to get rid of Asher, he built this one planning on destroying everything in Asher's life, but the fool born idiot finished the job for us."

Emie sat in wonder, not over what Axel had said about Asher, she could care less what he thought of Asher. Or the real fool, Victor, who thought he could use her. It was the thought of where she was, and where Asher had been; what had happened to him here so many years ago.

It was on day ninety nine that Emie laid still trying to forget the life she had lived. Tried to forget all the wonderful things in her life she had been given.

She wondered how differently her life would have been if she would have listened to Jordy.

She wouldn't get back up to her feet till the day after Christmas. She had spent the week weeping over the past. Over her family she would give anything to see again and spend one last Christmas with.

She wept over Asher. All the last moments they would never have. She couldn't even remember the last time he had kissed her. So she tried harder. She tried hard to remember everything about him, from his smile, to his shyness, to the smell of his body. All of her favorite things about Asher she finally let them play over and over again in her head.

The feel of his body inside of hers brought her up to her feet. She had to stop thinking about him. She couldn't face the memories anymore. The sweetness of them were slowly killing her inside.

She found herself looking out her steel barred windows of the observation deck, wishing she could see his face, just one more time.

Emie closed her eyes and prayed. She could see those last moments in his life. She could see his decisions torn between losing her and protecting her. He chose to save her life instead of his, and took it in his own hands.

His death was not only honorable, it was heroic.

She had listened to Victor as had explained to Axel many times what they had planned to do with Asher. They wanted to use him and hurt him to bend her will and make her do what they wanted. If Asher hadn't done what he had, the world would be lost. She wasn't strong enough to watch them hurt him. She would have done whatever they wanted her to do.

Somehow Asher was able to see that before he died. He knew they would have done all those things. He knew also she would have broke under their spell.

She prayed harder, and answers started to form in her mind.

What if her brothers had come to save Asher? What if he was still alive?

Emie closed her eyes tighter. She was afraid of the hope she could feel inside of her.

She prayed her brothers hadn't. They wouldn't be able to fight against this army. They couldn't win. She'd seen Victors army for herself. It was unlike anything any of them could ever have imagined.

But what if....

It was the kind of tragic ending, like a horrible movie that was too scary to watch. She had to close her mind from those thoughts. She didn't want to know the ending other story.

When Emie opened her eyes that day, she looked for some sort of sign. She didn't see a dove or a rainbow as a sign that all would be well.

She saw a Bat.

Emie looked harder in the distance as it flew past her and stretched its arms to turn back around and face her. With knee weakening astonishment, Emie could see the bat more clearly. It rounded the building and came to land on the landing of her window. In a blink of an eye, Cristina appeared on the ledge. She was smiling and placed her hand on the glass.

Emie was overpowered by the emotions she felt. She placed her hand on the window where Cristina's was. Tears in both their eyes blurred their vision.

"Cristina." Emie whispered aloud. She turned then and made sure no one was around. If her captures seen Cristina, there would be no stopping them from killing her.

Cristina tapped on the glass and got Emie's attention then. Emie turned around and face her. Cristina started pointing to Emie's heart.

Confused, Emie whispered aloud, "My heart?" She knew immediately then, as Cristina nodded her head through the window what she had meant.

"Asher." Emie breathed aloud.

Cristina nodded her head again and pointed somewhere off in the distance.

Emie squinted then and followed her direction. There in the midst of the ocean stood Lady Liberty. Emie had never seen her before. Never even cared to look. But she was unmistakable and breathtaking in the distance. Emie looked at her hand then. It was hard not to in the night around them.

In the hand of Lady Liberty was a torch. A torch that had never been lit before. Until tonight. Asher had lit it for her knowing she would know his signal of love.

Fire.

Asher, her heart, her love, her reason for living, was alive!

Emie stood there holding her breath with her hand. Tears streaming down her face, she feared for them all. She looked at Cristina and shook her head no. She looked in the room around her. She had to tell them somehow they had to leave her here and forget about her.

Cristina tapped on the window again. She looked at Emie and placed her hand on the window again. There under her hand, on her wrist was a tattoo that she was pointing at.

The Celtic heart. It was a symbol of the interconnectedness of all things. A symbol of hope. The eternal web represented the continuous cycle of existence.

Emie looked back up at Cristina with hope in her eyes. She nodded her head at her. Cristina had gotten that tattoo with Emie. It was a symbol of their friendship. Emie was never supposed to forget it. Every time she had ever looked at Cristina's wrist she remembered the bond between them.

She would wait. She told Cristina as much. As she watched her friend leap over the edge, she lost sight of her. When she reappeared, she seen the bat that Cristina had become. She watched as she flew down the building out of sight.

Emie's heart leapt at seeing her disappear. She could only hope Cristina would make it back safely to her family where they could protect her.

She put her hand back on the glass where she could see the Statue of Liberty. She looked at the flame burning her hand. Asher was alive. He was close. He was here. And he was coming for her.

They were coming for her, she told herself. She wanted them too, so badly it hurt inside of her heart. But yet she didn't. Cristina had told her something she had forgotten all this time; they were all bonded and connected together, all of them.

Emie slumped down to her feet then. She would wait. She would wait forever for them.

Asher sat in the midst of the midnight waves trying to think. Trying to plan his next move. He had made it back to the island where he knew he would be able to see the new tower.

The icy waves were raging around him. He was holding out his hands just letting the freezing waves and the wind roll under them. He hadn't felt this close to Emie in a long time.

Asher rubbed his face with the water from the waves. Moon light danced around him. He remembered the night out on the lake he had spent with Emie. She had laughed freely with him. She had willingly given him her desire and wanted Asher with powerful emotions he still didn't understand. How would she love him now for the monster he had become?

He missed Emie with a need so great it was hurting him. She was so close, but yet so far away. He needed to hear her voice, see her lovely face.

He had watched as Cristina flew from the tower and dove straight back to Liberty Island. He knew what she had found up there in the Tower. He was jealous of her at that moment. He could hear the cheers coming from within the Statue as she told every one of where Emie was located.

Asher stayed in the waves longer. He looked at the tower and listened for Emie. He still couldn't hear her.

The tower was designed from top to bottom of American steel. The windows were reinforced with it. She was encased in the one thing that could separate him from her.

Asher looked down at the waves again. They were his only comfort just then. For the first time he thought he could hear Emie. He could almost hear her voice as she told him all the reasons why she loved him. She had called him her hero. Asher hung his head in shame. He didn't feel heroic now.

It was that small tiny voice of hers that flooded his mind. It reassured him now of what he had to do. What he was supposed to do. But he was falling to pieces, choking up under the weight of his decision.

He knew in his heart it was the right decision, but he didn't want to do it. He didn't want to leave this spot he was in. He wanted to stay as close to her as he could get. Right here, in the midst of the midnight, standing in the rolling waves and wind around him, he felt her peace. He could feel her love.

He closed his eyes at the memories of that day so long ago, when he watched the towers fall in front of his eyes. He had watched those planes flown by evil men fly right into those buildings knowing damn well what they were doing. The damage, the destruction, all the lives that had fallen because of all that happened to those buildings. What had happened to him as he stood in there inside of the buildings; at that time he couldn't think of anything worse than that day. Until now.

The work of evil doers had caused it all. And those same evil men were up to no good again.

He knew his plan would work. Slip Curtis inside the building and he would bring Emie back here in the blink of an eye. She would be back in his arms forever. It was simple and quick. No one know what happened to her.

But Asher knew Emie wouldn't want him to just rescue her. She would want him to defeat the evil that was now going on. He wasn't sure he was strong enough to leave her, but there was only one way to find out.

"We have to go, now." Jordy said pleading with Asher when he rejoined them in the statue.

Asher held up his hand. He looked at Jordy and willed him to understand. "I know what she wants. She doesn't want this."

"What!" everyone exclaimed at the same time.

Their whole reason for being here was to do just that.

"Listen to me. If we just take her, they will hunt us down, and destroy everything we have left behind us in Michigan before we can even get back there to save them all." Asher knew what he was saying. He had no idea how to change his plans now, but he had too. He had no idea how to defeat an entire army without the help of more people, and he knew it meant leaving Emie where she was longer then he wanted too.

Silently they all acknowledged him. They knew he was right.

Asher looked out the windows back to where Emie's tower stood and placed his hands on the railings. He needed more time to think. He needed to be alone. Planning was what he had spent his whole adult life doing.

"We are going to need a bigger plane." This from Shelley, who Asher turned around on.

"Well, they came down once with a plane." She gulped down her next words. She was no longer glad she was a pilot.

Jordy was standing stiff and still as Asher looked to him for direction. This is where he would chime in and tell them if this plan would work. But he was just standing there.

"What is wrong with him?" Shelley asked, clearly not understanding what was going on.

Asher had a bad feeling about it, but he hated not knowing what was going on in his head. It figured that he was stuck without being able to be a mind reader.

"Jordy, snap out of it man!"

Jordy looked at Curtis then and grabbed his arm. "Don't question me. Just do it. Grab Asher and go home. Now!"

One second Asher was in New York, the next he was in Luna Pier. They were standing in front of the Whitby house. He looked at Curtis then. He was ready to cuss him out like never before for taking him away from the island. He couldn't have been farther away from Emie now.

Curtis got his attention then. "Asher, look!"

Asher looked then at the mansion. There were wolves, not Joseph's wolves, but someone else's attacking some of his friends on the steps. The doors were both wide open; he could hear the fight and gunshots coming from with in. There was smoke coming out of the upper floor windows. There was no way out for anyone within.

He ran at a speed faster then he knew possible and tore through the open front doors.

Curtis started grabbing people. He started with Ken and the other firefighters and took them back to the safety of the fire department, telling them all to stay put, Asher had this. They listened like they all once had to him and he was grateful for their trust he thought he would never have again with them.

He came back just as Asher was lighting vampires on fire and was killing all the vampires in the house he could reach. He grabbed Joseph and Izzy then and took them outside to fight the wolves. The last people he grabbed was Jeremy and Juliet and all the children who were in the dungeon hiding, just before they were attacked by vampires.

Asher stood outside of Emie's home with his hands in his pockets after the fight was over and watched as it burned to the ground. There was no stopping it now. He listened to the screams of the vampires with in. They had taken over the entire house. He had never seen so many other vampires in one place before. All he could do was start a raging fire within it once everyone was safely out to destroy them all.

It was the first time he had ever been able to use his powers like that.

Joseph was next to him then. "You couldn't think of any other way? You had to use fire."

"It was already burning. They had lit the upper floors on fire before they broke in."

Joseph looked at Asher then. He knew without Asher in his life now he would be useless to his family. Asher had been everything Joseph had needed and more. He would give anything to give Asher the one and only thing he wanted in return, but he couldn't.

He looked back to the house, his home, his families home, and watched it burn down with all his hopes and dreams in it.

"What now?" Asher sounded as defeated as Joseph felt.

"There were some who ran away. I can only hope they will spread the word about a big bad vampire who just whooped all their asses. They just might not come back."

Asher hung his head then and laughed. His hands were still in his jean pockets and he kicked up a little dirt with his booted foot. When he looked back he watched as the last of the house fell down. As a firefighter Asher knew it would continue to burn and smolder now. Everything in it would melt and turn to ash.

"Amen." He said turning to Joseph. He stuck out his fist for a fist bump from Joseph. Joseph grabbed his hand instead and hugged Asher. It was what Emie would have done. And Joseph owed him at least that much gratitude.

When both men straightened back up and looked back to the house, they were joined by the rest of their family, minus one. They all stood there looking at each other and back at the house.

Jeremy was the first to speak. "Everyone is safe back at the fire hall Asher. You didn't lose anyone."

At the end of every call, they were to report back to Monroe county Dispatch over the radio and to use a special call sign to signal that everyone was back home safely. He said it now, and Curtis was the only who understood it. "All the horses are back in the barn."

Asher turned then. He had an idea and need to talk to Ken. He started walking and was surprised when they all followed him. He turned around and looked at them all.

Joseph spoke then. "We have nowhere else to go Asher."

Asher nodded to them all. "Let's go home then."

Forty

Asher was hammering away at a new sign on the fire department he and Ken had designed. It had only taken them a month to build a new steel building over the existing one. He and his new family had to destroy all the other buildings around it to accomplish it, but they used the extra supplies to help in the building of the new department.

There was a yard in the center for the children to play outside in. There were suites in it for families to live together in. Enough gathering rooms for everyone to share to be together in and become as one.

With the knowledge they all had gained from studying the new tower in New York, with the help of the children who loved being busy doing something useful with the adults, they used it now to help them build a safe place for everyone. It was made of steel, reinforced with it so it couldn't be penetrated from any angle. And woe unto the person who tried to gain entry. They would be met with a very powerful force indeed.

"Luna Pier Fire House. I like it." Ken said, leaning back in the ladder he was standing on.

Asher hit the last nail in the sign and leaned back like Ken. "It's a house now. Not just a building or a department." He knew if Emie were here, she would be in love with it. He took a deep breath and held back his feelings. Soon he would be back to her saving her. Now that her family was safe, he could go back to her.

But even after he saved her, they would still have a long haul ahead of them. There were vampires scattered all over the world now, trying to take over and rule. But for some time, they could live here in peace.

But first, he needed to talk to Ken.

As the men crossed the street and looked at their handy work from the church parking lot across the street, Asher folded his arms into his chest.

"Tell me something Ken, how do I talk to God?"

Ken turned his entire body to Asher. He was almost speechless by Asher's question. Out of respect for Asher, Ken had never talked to Asher about religion. Sometimes Ken felt ashamed of it. He always worried about dying one day and not seeing Asher there in Heaven with him. But now, well now Asher was… whatever it was he was, Ken thought to himself. Surely as an angel of some kind he would be able to speak to God in ways he never could. But to look at Asher now, Ken was rethinking that theory.

Ken knew how salvation worked with humans. Believe and repent. Ask God for forgiveness they didn't deserve and accept the sacrificial gift He gave them all in His son Jesus. It was easy. But not everyone who said the words were saved. It had to be a heart thing. The truth was only meaningful when it was felt. Forgiveness belonged to everyone, but they had to want it.

God wouldn't make any one do what they didn't want to. That's what free will was all about. If they didn't want God, then He wouldn't make them. That's what everyone wanted. Their own will and freedom to make their own decisions. So that's what God gave them.

It must be true for vampires as well, Ken thought to himself. Just because they were turned into Angels, didn't make them one if they didn't believe. They could be corrupted by evil just like humans could.

Asher hadn't found God yet.

It all made sense then, and Ken looked heavenward in thanksgiving for the answers. But he asked for help in talking to his friend. He had Asher's back in every situation that ever counted in life and on the department. He wouldn't let Asher down now.

"If you had asked me six months ago if vampires, werewolves, unicorns…" Ken thought remembering Jeremy's "horses" he had seen walking in the pastures on the Whitby land. "Were real, I would have told you no. There was no such thing. In fact, I think I had that same conversation with Katie Bear once." He told Asher chuckling. "But now, I'm learning there are mysteries in this world God doesn't reveal to us for a reason. Everything happens for reason Asher."

This Asher knew. Emie had told him that once and he still believed it.

"God is real, Asher.   You know that now better than any of us humans." Ken looked at Asher now and was impressed with what God had done with his friend.

"God isn't just sitting up in some throne room, directing the rotation of this earth like a movie being brought to life. He walks amongst us, and lives everyday beside us.

"Imagine that Asher, if you will. Creating a world and space in between. Giving men breath and life, only wanting to be accepted by them and returned to Him the love He gave them, to walk amongst them day after day, blessing them in ways no one else could. And never to hear a word from them in thanks. Just rejection everyday.

"The only time people call on God is when they needed Him, and even then if they don't get the answers when and how they want them, they curse him. Never understanding why God isn't taking control of this situation, or that one, when they didn't want him there to begin with. Only to think of God as useless, or unloving. Never seeing all the things God did do."

Asher looked down at the ground then. He had done this many times.

"He created you, and beautifully made you, crafted you and molded you into who you are today. God doesn't make mistakes Asher. He's just waiting for you to talk to Him like you do me Asher. He longs to be your friend. Be the God you need him to be. But the choice is yours Asher. He won't interfere with your life, or be something you don't want him to be." Ken knew that feeling better then anyone. Many people had turned their backs on him because he was a religious guy and held the rank Chaplin. They never gave him a chance to be their friend like Asher had done.

"You're my best friend Asher. And believe me, God is a jealous God. And I know he is jealous of that. He wants to be your friend Asher, your counselor, your comforter. He wants to give you the answers you're seeking. Not me."

Asher listened with his entire being. Every word Ken said to him made so much sense. He dug his booted foot against the ground and said, "I knew you were good at preaching man, but wow. That was deep." Then he lifted his head sideways and gave Ken a cheeky smile.

Ken looked back at the firehouse then. "Well, what did you expect?"

Asher looked at the firehouse too and sighed, doing his best impersonation of Ken, he said, "Bow your head Asher, say this, this and that. Amen." Asher waved his hand around him in a cross.

Ken laughed then and did his best imitation of Asher and said, "Bow your head Asher, say this, this and that. Amen."

Asher laughed out loud and grabbed his friend around his neck and walked back to their new home.

Emie had spent New Year's day in the basement of her tower. Victor had seen hope in her eyes and wanted to know how it had found her. Emie wouldn't tell him even to save her own life. Even when he threatened he would destroy her family.

Her thoughts had been consumed with Asher. Her hero. He would take care of them for her. He, and only he could save her.

She didn't know how he planned to do it, but Asher never did anything without planning it out just right. He would have every detail well thought out.

Emie knew in her heart her family would be right there along beside him. She thought about that more then. She wondered how well they were doing with Asher. He was stubborn, and cranky sometimes. He wanted everything to go the way he wanted it to and when it didn't, he could get whiny and unreasonable. She laughed to herself and remembered how he was.

She wondered if he was a vampire now. What would he look like now, she wondered. What would his abilities be? She had worried in the past if he had changed that he wouldn't be the man she loved anymore. There was always a chance once they changed someone that they would fall to evil and be so bloodthirsty they wouldn't be able to be anything other than a monster.

Emie spent days after that praying, hoping, wishing with all her might that everything would go as planned for him. She had to see him again. She needed him.

Victor tried to change her mind. He filled her with terrible thoughts. Told her his own plans he had for her saviors. But Victor didn't know Asher was alive. He didn't know the heroic might Asher had in him. He didn't know the honor Asher knew as a firemen. Asher would protect and serve with his life.

Some days she felt sorry for Victor. Even for Axel. The innocent boy who had become a man in this terrible world. Without Asher's mother to raise him like she had Asher, Axel would never know what love was. Or how to overcome evil. He was surrounded by evil night and day.

Emie had never seen evil like she had in these men. Their thoughts were worse then most evil men. More vile then the wretched imaginings of most humans. Only demons could have those thoughts.

Emie shook her head in her bonds. Steel was wrapped around her arms, legs, and neck. She was trapped in them. She knew these men all needed to be destroyed, but she didn't know how it was possible.

Only a hell fire hotter than the sun could wipe them off this island. It would take God himself raining down fire from heaven to kill them all. And she would be trapped here with them in their Sodom and Gomorrah.

When Victor finally returned her to her perch above the city, he worried of an attack on the ground level. He knew he could only win if Emie was out of site. So he put her back there and sentenced her to isolation.

Emie raced to her windows where she looked for her beacon of hope. It was still burning, and she wondered if Victor had seen it.

She stayed there for hours and worried over her family. She had so much more to lose now. But she held her head high. She was waiting for Asher.

Axel visited her in the days that followed. He brought her bodies to feast on, but Emie wouldn't budge from her perch. She listened as he taunted and tried not to look at him, even though her eyes were longing to feast on him if for only a moment to see Asher again.

When finally they all left her alone, Emie began to worry. She stayed by the windows and waited and watched.

It wasn't until she saw a plane out in the distance that she really worried.

"He wouldn't..."

No, but I would!

Emie heard the unmistakable laugh of Shelley and couldn't believe her eyes. She watched as Shelley smiled at her crashing into the building under her from the window seat of a big Air Force plane.

Emie closed her eyes under the weight of the crash that rocked the building. Sirens and alarms were deafening even to her ears. She waited as the sprinklers turned on and drenched her in water. She didn't know what their plan was, but she was ready for anything.

Jordy appeared then through the doors of the stairwell. He thanked heaven that the stairwell withstood the blast of the plane and the fire below and was able to take him to the floor he needed. If not he would have to squeeze through walls and be burnt by the steel.

Emie reached for Jordy then and met him halfway in the middle of her room. Her bonds, now attached to the floor stopped her in her tracks, but didn't stop Jordy from wrapping her in his arms so tight.

Emie held him for a moment longer and sighed into him. She smirked at him when he cussed at her bonds.

"That might be a problem." He told her looking at her chains.

It wasn't until the elevator next to them beeped that she lost all hold on reality. She didn't know who was going to come threw the doors of the elevator. If it was Axel, she was sure they were in trouble.

When the doors opened she saw who was in there. It was Asher. He was leaning up against the back wall as the doors opened with his hands tucked in his pockets.

But he wasn't Asher any more, it was true, but he was something more than she had dreamed he could be. His hair was wild and a mess, she seen as he tried to run his hands through it to scatter the dust off him. He was dressed like he always had, in ripped up dirty jeans and fire fighter t-shirt.

Were his muscles bigger? She thought, not able to believe her eyes. He was a hot mess for sure.

He walked up to her, the flattered fool she knew him to be, and looked at her with eyes full of redemption and saving grace. His smile was encugh to weaken and unsteady her.

Jordy had to catch her when her legs gave out under her. She was crying and he didn't know how to help her.

Asher shoved Jordy out of his way and took Emie's hands in his. He tried not to get angry over her bonds and what they were doing to her skin. He looked back to her sweet face and held it in his hands. Trying to be reassuring he said, "Hey there sweetheart. I'm here." He whispered to her. "Don't cry."

When he reached down to take off her bonds, Emie tried to stop him. "No Asher! You can't touch them." She begged.

"Watch this." He winked up at her.

Asher lit both his hands on fire with his breath and melted the chains that were holding her to the floor. He grabbed her then and held her in his arms after he freed her and almost danced around with her. "I got you Sweetheart. I got you."

Emie held Asher so tight in her arms. She was gulping down all her pain she felt inside of her as it fled from her. Asher was here. He was in her arms. She could feel him. He was hers. He was alive!

When she took his face in her hands he could see her excitement and the fire in her eyes that he had missed. She was about to unleash on him a holy wrath that only she could deliver, when an army emptied out of the stairwell next to them and stood ready to take them all down.

Asher heated in his surroundings. Smoke, astonishing smoke rose around his entire body. Jordy reached for Emie then and hid under a window with her, protecting her from what Asher was about to unleash.

Emie watched through Jordy's arms as Asher set the entire room on fire. All the men in the room turned to ash. Pillars of their former self. Asher stood there, trying to breathe , coughing on the smoke and ash.

"Jordy?" She questioned.

"Yeah, yeah. Amazing, I know."

She turned his face towards her then. "Is he ok?"

Jordy really looked at her then. She had missed so much. "He's fine. I promise. He's been waiting to do that for long time." He told her brushing her hair out of her eyes.

Emie looked back at Asher who was heading over to them.

Jordy let her run to him, not like he could stop her. Or Asher for that matter.

Curtis appeared then in their midst with Shelley in his arms. One look at Asher and where he was going, Curtis took a step back. He was still breathing smoke and Curtis knew better then to mess with him when he was mad.

Asher took Emie in his arms and whispered so only she could hear. "I love you Emie."

Curtis coughed aloud then. Asher knew he only had seconds left. Victor couldn't get to Asher at this level, but Asher had to get to Victor before he could escape.

"Emie. I need you to go with Curtis now. He is going to take you home."

"NO!" Emie shouted up at him.

Asher laughed a little. There was a time she would have scared him with that. But even as she looked at him shocked that she had no effect on him, he placed a kiss on her hand and handed her over to Curtis. "I'm right behind you sweetheart."

Emie tried to resist, and Asher had to turn away from her. It hurt him more than he could tell her to let her go.

In a blink of an eye, Emie and Curtis and Shelley were gone. Before he could say a word to Jordy who was waving goodbye, he was gone too. He nodded at where they had been and stuffed his hands in his pockets. He would thank Curtis later. He had saved them all and would see them safely home before Victor even knew they were gone.

Asher had a war to wage with Victor, and thanks to Cristina, time would stand still until he had finished with every last one of them.

Victor was waiting on the main level, directing everyone within earshot to obey him. He was going to rip limb from limb who ever had flown into his building. He hoped the steel in the building would keep them trapped on whatever level they were in and the fire would incinerate them.

Axel stood next to him awaiting his orders. Victor looked at him and tried to bark an order at him, but the man couldn't move. He was frozen.

Victor waved his hand in front of Axel's face.

Victor turned in circles then. He noticed that everyone on the floor with him were standing in the same way.

"What the hell!" Victor said aloud, apparently to no one.

He looked out the windows then, there was a brightness outside he couldn't understand. Baffled he walked towards the windows. Fire was lighting up the night sky.

Victor looked back at the elevator that had just beeped next to him. He watched as the elevator doors opened and in the midst of it stood Asher. But it wasn't the Asher he remembered.

Shocked and stunned into silence Victor watched Asher lift himself off the back wall he had been leaning on, watched as he took his hands out of his pockets, watched as the man he thought was dead walked up to him.

Victor backed up into a the main hall desk behind him. Smoke was coming out of every door and window. He was trapped by steel and fire all around him. There was no escape.

Asher had been waiting for this moment for what felt like forever. He had dreamed of it. Willed it into existence. He watched outside as rain of fire fell from the heavens above. It wasn't him. And because he was who and what he was now, he was the only person on the face of the earth who could stand in the midst of the hell fires God was now raining on all the demons on this God forsaken island. It made him smile at God's plan.

Victor fell on his knees. "I don't believe it." Everything he had built, all his plans were being ruined by the one person he had spent a lifetime trying to destroy.

Asher shook his head at the man so weak at his feet. "It's too late for that now." He wanted to kick the man while he was down, but he had promised himself if Emie hadn't been harmed he would make Victor's death quick. Not painless, but quick. Asher had somewhere else he wanted to be.

Asher pointed his finger at Victor as he lit it like a cigarette. "I want to thank you for all this."

Victor still speechless looked up into Asher's eyes then.

"If it wasn't for you, I still wouldn't believe either. And there's something sweet about it all. Knowing God's will is done and I was able to help him." Asher knelt down on one of his knees and faced the man he hated with a vengeance that had almost destroyed him.

"There's a special place in hell for guys like you. I plan on spending every day you are there forgetting about you, and enjoying the little piece of heaven God gave me. He will make up for every single day you took her from me. He will bless me with everything you tried to destroy. And he will give her back the life you so foolishly stole from her. All while you watch, and burn."

Asher had met God one day out on the pier alone. He had spoke with him and learned all of his plans for Asher's life. Asher wouldn't trade that day for anything in heaven or hell.

Victor bowed his head then. He waited for the death he knew was about to come. The wrath that Asher had in his eyes was enough to bore into his soul that he was damned for all eternity.

Shocked when it didn't happen, he looked up, only to find smoke and dust filling the room around him. It enveloped him as he watched blindly and waited.

Asher sat on top of the tallest building in the world. He watched as Angels like him destroyed the city that was now damned. He would give anything for a shot of whiskey to toast God with.

Asher watched as a bat flew out of the smoke under him. He saluted her and watched as she flew west. The sun would catch up with him if he didn't hurry also. Asher stood, took a bow to the eastern sky and said so long to New York. He would never return, he thought as he felt the building he had lit on fire from the inside crumbled under his feet and fell to the ground below him as the arms of his brother Curtis wrapped around him.

Forty One

Emie stood in a bed room looking around. It looked like her room... but it wasn't. When she turned around to ask Curtis where she was, he had vanished.

Emie started counting the seconds he was gone, fidgeting with her fingers. Asher had said he was right behind her. Curtis should return in seconds with him. But she was distracted by the room around her.

Everything from the color of the rich red walls, the mahogany trim, to the bed in the center of the room was the same as her room, but wasn't...

Something was off she thought as she counted to ten. She walked deeper in the room and noticed the shelves, like in her room, were empty. Her piano was missing, along with long drapes that should be lining the windows. She looked at the lake off in the distance outside the windows and noticed the position of the room facing the lake wasn't just right either.

By the time she counted to fourteen, she started to ramble off and lose tract.

Where was she?

Emie wandered to her closet and opened up the long double door. Standing there dumbfounded by the contents that were no longer in her closet she stomped her foot in irritation. What had her brothers done with all her clothes? She walked in her closet angered by the emptiness she found on the missing shelves.

Clothes, shoes, everything she owned was gone!

Curtis and Asher stood in the mist of Emie's new room seeing where she was now standing in her closet.

"Good luck with that, man" Curtis said to Asher.

Asher smiled a knowing smile. Emie would forget about all that in seconds he knew. When he turned around to say just that to Curtis, he had disappeared. Asher just shook his head and rested up against the bed frame of Emie's bed. He waited for her to notice him and she took his breath away when she turned around.

Emie was counting all the things that were now missing in her room when she turned and seen the man standing in the midst of her room.

"Asher." she breathed aloud.

It took her only seconds to make her way over to his arms. She watched as he leaned into her and caught her up in his arms, twirling her around in the middle of her room.

Asher leaned in and held unto to Emie for dear life. He reveled in the way she held him. He would never get enough of the way Emie held him. "I got you sweetheart."

For Emie it had only been seconds since she had last seen Asher. For Asher it had been an entire night of hell on earth. He had accomplished everything he had been longing to that night. All of her demons were destroyed. They could now live in their happily ever after God had promised him.

"Asher." Emie breathed again.

Emie's nose found his bare skin and she drank in the scent of Asher. He still smelled of fire and smoke, and she now understood why. Asher was born to be what he had become.

"I'll never let you go again Emie." Asher breathed. He could feel her essence all around him. Everything he missed about her was now in his arms. He would never, ever let go of her. He would move heaven, hell, and earth to make sure he kept his promise to her if he had too.

"Where are we, Asher." She asked as they swayed together in each others arms.

"We lost the mansion in a fire." He told her, holding her tighter when he felt her slump in his arms. "I saved what I could… This room is just one of many we have rebuilt. We are above the old fire hall now."

Feelings of dread and fear started to fill her. Asher could sense it rolling of her and squeezed her tighter. He took a deep breath and whispered to her, "They are gone, Emie. You have nothing to worry about anymore."

Emie stood on her toes and looked into Asher's eyes surprised. "Can you-"

"Read your thoughts?" he said looking down at her. "No."

When she had a look on her face of relief, Asher felt his anger rising. "But that doesn't mean you can hide anything from me!"

Emie smiled up at him and patted his chest. "I know, I know." She stopped just long enough to see a hint of smoke leave his lips.

Asher shook his head. "It makes me crazy when I see you all talking to each other like that. I feel left of out, or like you all are hiding something from me."

Emie eyed him at that. "It's a family thing. Something we've been doing all our lives."

"It's a bad habit, damn it!"

Emie reached up smiling and placed her hands on his face. She stood up on her toes then and slowly, very sensually, reached up to kiss his lips. She watched as Asher lost all track of his thoughts and followed her kiss. Her lips touched his and the heat of it ignited his soul. She felt as his hands fall lose around her, but he held her hips in his hands. He bent down and dragged his lips over hers; kissing her like he always had before. She felt as his desire built and his arms wrapped tightly around her. She drug her fingers through his hair and pulled him down closer to her.

Asher growled in Emie's kiss. She drove him crazy when she did that too, and he loved it. It made him so hard he thought he would bust. It had been forever since he had made love to her, and he needed to right then and there.

He thought about the bed, but they never really made love there. Thoughts of the tub he had moved up here into her new room crossed his mind then. When he felt Emie smile at his thoughts he picked her up and walked her into her wash room never breaking his lips from hers.

It was dark in her wash room. The moon light from the sky light in her room was letting in just enough light to help them see around the room. Asher crushed her up against the door ravishing her neck and chest with kisses.

Emie started moaning as Asher tore at her clothes. He left her standing breathless as he quickly filled her tub and kicked off his boots and ripped off his shirt. She watched as his arms and chest bulged out as he removed his shirt. She couldn't believe his tattoos were still there on his arms and chest. She bit her lip at the thought of them.

Asher stood there in the middle of the room. He had discarded his shirt and was just looking at Emie. He had taken off everything on her body but her shirt. He looked at her, leaning up against the door with one leg propped up on the door, breathing breathlessly, biting her lip with one of her fangs. He shook his head then and raised a hand on his hip. "I just can't believe you're here." He looked around the room and remembered the days he spent in this room rebuilding it. He had worried over her never coming home. But he had built it anyways, hoping one day, any day, she would be here like she was now.

Emie took a step away from the door and walked over to Asher. She had heard every thought he had had. She never wanted him to feel like that and hated that it had happened to him again. She wanted to wash away every thought from his memory.

She raised her shirt up over her head and unclothed herself in front of him. Eyeing him closely she finished walking up to him. She watched as he cocked his head to the side and he leaned forward into her when she reached him.

Emie looked down and pulled at the buttons on his jeans until they were all undone. His hard on was full and ready to be freed. She looked back up at him and winked as she walked over to the tub, throwing off her shirt and followed the steps down into the tub that took up half the room.

Asher ripped off his jeans, kicked off his socks and ran up behind Emie just before she sat down in the tub. She laid back against him then and sat in his lap.

Emie leaned back and let the water engulf her body as she laid back in the arms of Asher. He found the swell of her breast in his hands and let her nipples fall in between his fingers as he squeezed them, pulling her down hard on him. He found her neck and kissed until she moaned and reached her hands back in his hair.

When Emie cried out his name at his ministrations on her breast, he let one hand fall underneath the water down her body. He pulled her belly into him more and watched as she let his cock side up into the folds between her lips. His own head fell back at the feel of being there. He let the fingers of his hand find their way there also and rubbed the bud he found there stirring her core until she cried out.

Asher stepped off the ledge they were seated on into the water deeper and turned her around unto him. He found her mouth and used his hands to guide himself into her body. He let her slide him deeper into her body as he grabbed her face and held it as he deepened his kiss. He had to bite her lips at the feel of the inside of her body. It felt more amazing to him then he had remembered and wondered if that was possible.

"Emie!" he cried to her.

Emie giggled as he put his forehead on hers and couldn't kiss her anymore. He drove in and out of her body holding onto her. When his rhythm picked up all she could do was shutter and let herself go in the dizzying feelings that were overwhelming her. Holding onto reality was too much. She kissed it goodbye into his neck and held onto the man who had become not only her hero, he was her heart and soul and everything that made her who she was. He was hers. And she was his.

Asher lost himself in Emie. Something about being in these moments with her, where she let him love her and came unglued by it all like he was doing, made him feel like forever wouldn't be enough time to love her. He couldn't stop himself, and liked very quickly his new body he had now.

Emie giggled then and found herself laughing so hard she had broken the spell they were under. "Men, I swear."

Asher spun her around under the water and leaned against the opposite edge of the tub. "You wouldn't understand." He smiled up at her moving her hair with his hand behind her ears and letting it trail down it's length.

Emie sighed into Asher's arms just looking at him. She cocked her head to one side and said, "So what have you been doing these last few months."

Asher grinned at her then. "Oh, this and that. A little of this girl, and a little of- Ouch!" He squealed.

Emie had twisted his nipple and pulled almost pulling it off, grinning back at his cheekiness.

"And what have you been doing? Huh?" He asked playing with her more.

Emie went still for a moment. She knew Asher hadn't meant it when he had asked her. But his mind had went there anyways.

Asher reached for her face then. She quickly looked down and he felt like the biggest ass on the earth. "Emie, sweet heart. I didn't mean it."

"He never touched me Asher, I swear." She couldn't look up at him then. She didn't want him to see how close it had been for her.

"Emie, look at me." Asher pleaded. When she reluctantly did, he tried to finish. He seen so much pain there, that he wished he hadn't caused.

"No." Emie said as she pushed off of Asher and swam just a little distance from him. She wrapped her arms around her and realized it hadn't even been an hour yet since she had been in that hell hold. "I need you to know, that I was strong enough. That I fought them with everything-"

Asher walked up behind her. He didn't know how to touch her again. He interrupted her then, not caring if she had failed, but knowing if she had, he would go to hell and kill them both again. "Emie, I can't imagine what you went through sweetheart, and I beg of you not to tell me." Asher said to her shaking off the heat that was building inside of him. "You have to know though, that I-"

Emie turned then. She placed her hand on his chest and one on his lip. "I know. I know that." She reassured him she knew he didn't care. She looked down like he was and he rested his forehead on hers placing his hands around her hips he drug her back over to him.

Asher kissed her forehead then. "You know me inside and out sweetheart. You have to tell me what's going on inside of you." He wanted to kick fate in the ass for not letting him be able to read minds. It frustrated him.

Emie wrapped her arms around Asher's neck then. "Have you ever gotten drunk Asher?"

Asher thought about that answer. "Yeah..." he questioned her.

"That's what it was like all those months for me. I was so gone from my soul like that. I thought I had lost you that day. I thought you were dead Asher."

Asher planted his feet then. He had wondered if she had thought that about him.

Emie willed him to understand. "It wasn't until Cristina came to my window. She told me then that you were alive. I almost didn't believe her." Emie choked on the tears that filled her eyes and were swelling in her mouth.

"I thought you were gone." She wept.

Asher held her then. He hadn't known. He had thought she would have figured it all out. Had she spent all that time thinking he was dead? He could remember his own pain then when his brother had died. It had been enough to rip his heart in tatters if it hadn't been for Emie. She had saved him then, and this was the first time he had ever realized it.

He sat lower in the water then and held her as she wept and clung to him. He let his hands stroke her hair and kept telling her it was all alright now.

Emie let it all out then. The months she had spent thinking he was gone. Wondering what life would have in store for her then, and not letting it take her down any further. She had waited for answers. She had pleaded with God to kill her. It was now that she understood it all. There in Asher's arms she found the will to resurface and live again.

She sighed and squeezed him closer. With her hands she found him again and pleaded with him to make love to her.

Asher understood and knew this time, he wasn't going to stop. He made love to her there until the water went cold, then he found warmth with her in her bed and made love to her there until the break of day light. Until her family and his were knocking on their doors. And then he made love to her some more.

~Epilogue~

Jeremy, Juliet, Jordy and Izzy were sitting out on the moon lit beach in Luna Pier just a few days before summer began. Night time had engulfed the city and they were free to roam the beach were the humans had vacated for them just hours before. Luna Pier was a fast growing city now. Humans from all around the Monroe County area had been led to the safety the city had built here by the Luna Pier Fire Fighters. The Whitby's lived with them now in peace, but would soon leave and turn it back over to them. Always staying close enough by to help and protect, to serve them.

Juliet let everything Jordy had just said enter her heart like the turning of the pages in her most beloved books. Jeremy had been filling in the holes where Jordy had left out moments he had thought were important and together they had finished the love story of Emie's life.

Izzy held unto her legs and sighed. "Wow, Jordy.'

Jordy was lying back on his arms that were stretched behind him. He looked over the moon light dancing on the water like diamonds and remembered the night he had found Izzy out here. He nodded his head in answer to them. It was a beautiful story.

Jeremy whispered to Juliet, "You should write about it."

Juliet looked at him surprised. She wondered if it was possible. She had written stories like this in the past. She looked at him then and smiled. "What would I call it?"

He tucked a strand of hair behind her ear that the wind had blown loose. "All they ever wanted was to be loved."

Juliet looked off into the moon. She tried it out loud. "To be loved."

All four of them looked out to the rushing waves. It was all they had ever wanted.

This isn't the end… It was just the beginning. Of destiny, of fate, of love, and their own happily ever after.

Made in the USA
Monee, IL
16 February 2020